THE
RING OF
FIVE DRAGONS

Volume One of The Pearl

ERIC VAN LUSTBADER

TOR®
fantasy

A TOM DOHERTY ASSOCIATES BOOK
NEW YORK

For Victoria,
always and forever

This is a work of fiction. All the characters and events portrayed in this book are either products of the author's imagination or are used fictitiously.

THE RING OF FIVE DRAGONS

Copyright © 2001 by Eric Van Lustbader

All rights reserved, including the right to reproduce this book, or portions thereof, in any from.

Edited by David G. Hartwell
Map by Ellisa Mitchell

A Tor Book
Published by Tom Doherty Associates, LLC
175 Fifth Avenue
New York, NY 10010

www.tor.com

Tor® is a registered trademark of Tom Doherty Associates, LLC.

ISBN: 0-812-57233-5
Library of Congress Catalog Card Number: 2001021943

First edition: May 2001
First mass market edition: July 2002

Printed in the United States of America

0 9 8 7 6 5 4 3 2 1

The Kundalan people have suffered for a century under the viciously oppressive technologically-superior V'ornn invaders. In the resulting crisis of faith—why hasn't their goddess Miina saved them?—Kundalan religion has fallen under the control of evil forces from within who forbid the teaching of traditional sorcery, pretending to have no magic of their own. The V'ornn's mysterious leaders, the Gyrgon, know better, and search for the lost Ring of Five Dragons, the key to the door of the fabled Kundalan Storehouse, and perhaps to Kundalan sorcery as well.

But misused, the Ring is the trigger of seemingly inexorable annihilation for V'ornn and Kundalan alike. Now from among the oppressed must arise the hero of prophecy, the Dar Sala-at, who alone can wield the sorcerous power to save the world.

Praise for *The Ring of Five Dragons*

"An imaginative, otherworldly culture clash between technology and spirituality fires this ambitious first novel in a projected multi-volume epic fantasy from bestseller Lustbader . . . a huge cast . . . parades against the backdrop of Lustbader's richly detailed tapestry, with its complex plotting, fluid action writing and vivid descriptive passages . . . both newcomers to Lustbader and his ardent admirers will champion this novel as a potent portal to fabulous mythic realms."—*Publishers Weekly*

"Lustbader is in good form. . . . Enthralling and exciting reading, full of unexpected twists and surprises."—*Booklist*

"There's much to like about *The Ring of Five Dragons*, including an exceptionally strong female cast, and hero Annon Ashera, a V'ornn who plays an important role in Kundalan prophecy."—*Starlog.com*

*Part of this book was written at
Radius Restaurant in Boston, MA.
My grateful thanks to Michael, Chris, Este
and everyone else who made my stay memorable.*

Ice Caves

Little
Rushing

Three Fish

Heavenly
Rushing

Dern Marre
Mts.

Stone
Border

Borobodur
Forest

Exchange
Pledges

Outer
Market

Land of
Sudden
Lakes

Marre
Pine Forest

Joining
The Valleys

Eleana's
Cottage

Silk
Bamboo
Spring

Three Fish

Blue Bone
Lake

Middle Seat

Chuun

Great
Phosphorus
Marsh

Axis Tyr

Legend

Abbeys		Steppes	
Forest		Marsh	
Foothills		Desert	
Mountains		Waterfalls	

Sea of
Blood

Illuminated
Sea

Unknown Territories

Great Rift

Djenn Marre Mts

North

Site of Za Hare-at

The Korrush

Okkamchire

The Great Voorg

Kundala
The Northern Continent

Alis Mitchell 2001

PROLOG:

The Lorg

When they were fifteen years old, Giyan and Bartta found a lorg. It was hiding, as lorgs are wont to do, beneath a large flat rock of a golden hue lying like a wart on the belly of a bone-dry gully. Konara Mossa, their Ramahan guardian and teacher, had told them to keep a sharp eye out for lorgs, for lorgs preferred the thin, kuello-fir-scented air that drifted along the shoulders of the Djenn Marre. *Beware the lorg,* she warned them with a frightening sweep of a gnarled forefinger, *for lorgs are evil creatures, ensnaring the souls of dying infants, hoarding them like grains of milled oat grass.* Superstitious nonsense, Giyan thought privately. The lorgs might be ugly to look at, but they seemed harmless enough; in fact, they were beneficial inasmuch as they ate stydil larvae, and everyone knew how destructive those insects could be to the oat grass and glennan crops.

It was Lonon, the Fifth Season—that eerie time between High Summer and Autumn when the gimnopedes swarmed; when, on clear nights, all five moons, pale green as a dove's belly, could be seen in the vast black bowl of the sky; when The Pearl had been misused; when the V'ornn had come to Kundala.

Giyan and Bartta, both Ramahan novices, had had the enormous misfortune of being born twins, an evil omen among the mountain Kundalan, a certain sign of bad luck that their mother tried to rectify by winding their own umbilicals around their soft pink necks. Their father, entering the birthing chamber, had cut the cords with his own hunting knife. While they squalled their first breath of new life, he had had to slit the throat of the scheming midwife, who had whispered goading superstitions in their mother's ear, egging her on to commit infanticide.

They had learned all this years later from their father, just before he left home for good. Their father and mother never should have married, that was the truth of it. Their father was a no-nonsense trader who saw the world in a straightforward manner, while their mother was entangled in the dark skein of magic, superstition, anxiety. They had no basis to form a connection, let alone to fall in love or even to discover a comfortable tolerance.

Cheated out of her attempt to mend her ill fortune, their mother brought the twins to the Abbey of Floating White as soon as they were old enough. In a most unseemly manner, she begged Konara Mossa to train the twins to be Ramahan, praying that their wholesale devotion to the Great Goddess would spare them the usual fate of twins.

And so they were made fluent in the Old Tongue, they were taught from the scraps of *Utmost Source, The Five Sacred Books of Miina,* memorized and set down over the decades by successive konara after it was lost. They were taught the creation myths, the legends of The Pearl, the seventy-seven festivals of Miina, the importance of Lonon, the Fifth Season, Miina's time, the season of change. They learned the ways of phytochemistry, of healing with herbs and mushrooms, of divining portents, of seeking with opals, and, most importantly, they were taught the Prophesy of the coming of the Dar Sala-at, the Chosen One of Miina, who would find The Pearl and use it to free the Kundalan from their bondage to the V'ornn.

It was curious how two sisters—twins at that—could absorb the same lessons and arrive at different conclusions. One saw the vessel half-full, the other saw it half-empty. For Giyan, life at the abbey had brought alive the rich history of her people, where sorcerous beings like Dragons and narbuck and Rappa and perwillon mingled freely with the Kundalan, males and females sharing equally in every facet of life, where those with the Gift were trained to use Osoru sorcery well and wisely, where each festival was an excuse for music, dancing, singing, the fervent excitement of being alive. Now, it was said, only the fearful perwillon remained, slumbering deep in their caves. For Bartta, the history lessons told another story—of what had been taken from them by the V'ornn, of the diminishing of Ramahan power and influence, of the rise of the new Goddess-less religion, Kara, of the violence of the male Ramahan and the betrayal of the Rappa, of a need to break with the old sorcerous ways—known only to those born with the Gift—that had come back to haunt the Ramahan, of the Kundalan being abandoned by their Great Goddess, who had quailed at the coming of the V'ornn, had been rendered irrelevant by the aliens' superior technomancy. Of the failure of the past, of Osoru, of those with the Gift, of Miina's teachings as they had been originally set forth to protect Kundala against invasion.

The twins were hiking north of their home in Stone Border, on the steep and narrow path that led to the Ice Caves. On either side, the brittle sepia-colored land fell away from them, pitching downward to the green-and-blue fields that carpeted the broad, fertile valley far below. Brown kuello-fir needles crunched beneath their cor-hide sandals. Forever after, this soft, dry, intimate sound, so like the rustling of wicked blackcrows' wings, would send a tiny thrill through them, for it was forbidden for anyone but Ramahan priestesses, like themselves, who dwelled in the nearby Abbey of Floating White, to tread this dangerous path.

Giyan paused on the path to stare upward at the immense, jagged, ice-crusted pinnacles of the Djenn Marre. And as she paused, so did Bartta. Giyan was the twin blessed with height, beauty, a slender figure. Even worse, from Bartta's point of view, she had the Gift and could be trained in Osoru sorcery. What did Bartta have save her fierce desire to lead the Ramahan?

"To think," Giyan said, "that no one knows what lies beyond those mountains."

"Just like you," Bartta said sourly, "to be thinking of questions that cannot be answered. Your foolish diversions are

why I will be promoted to shima, to priestess, next year while
you will no doubt stay a leyna, a novice."

"I am Miina's servant just as you are," Giyan said softly.
"We each serve the Great Goddess in our own way."

Bartta grunted. "Well, I'll tell you something. It has become embarrassing to be your sister. Your . . . perverse views
are the talk of the abbey."

"Perverse, sister?" Giyan's whistleflower-blue eyes reflected the sting of the rebuke.

Bartta nodded emphatically, happy to have scored a point.
"Our world is a simple one. We are good, the V'ornn are
evil. How you can distort such an obvious black-and-white
truth is beyond me."

"You misunderstand me," Giyan said. "I do not question
the evil of the V'ornn's deeds; I merely question this so-
called truth of Good and Evil. Nothing in this life is so black-
and-white. When it comes to the V'ornn we know them not
at all. I sense there is a mystery there we cannot yet fathom."

"Oh, yes. You *sense.* Your accursed Gift has spoken to
you, I suppose."

Giyan turned away, her gaze lost in the snowcapped
mountain peaks. She was remembering the hideous vision
she had had three years ago. It had coincided with the onset
of puberty, on a brilliant summer afternoon in a courtyard of
the abbey. One moment, she had been planting herbs and the
next the world around her had disappeared. At first, she
thought she had gone blind. She found herself enclosed in
darkness—not the darkness of night or even a cave, but utter
blackness. Voices rustled like the wings of birds, but she
could not make out what they were saying. She was terrified;
even more so as the vision took shape. With breathtaking
clarity, she saw herself from above. She was dressed oddly,
in the pure white of mourning. She was standing on the wishbone of a narbuck, the two prongs in front of her. At the end
of the right prong stood a Ramahan in the persimmon-
colored robes of a member of the Dea Cretan. At the end
of the left prong was a fierce-looking V'ornn in battle armor.
She saw herself walking to the base of the prongs, knew

there was a dreadful choice to be made, a fork in the path of her life. The V'ornn raised his arms and in them she saw a shining star, which she knew was the Dar Sala-at, the prophesied savior of her people. In her vision, she watched herself walk to the left, toward the Dar Sala-at, toward the V'ornn. . . . What did it mean? She could not know, and yet she could not forget the power, the sheer force of the vision. She had never dared share it with anyone, not even Bartta. But it had haunted her ever since, and was surely at the core of her unique, conflicted feelings about the aliens she knew she should loathe.

"The V'ornn have enslaved us, maimed us, tortured us," Bartta was saying now. "They kill us at their whim in games of sport. Though the resistance exists and continues to fight back, it is no match for the V'ornn. The aliens have driven us from our cities, forced us to find shelter in the hillsides and mountains until we have become strangers in our own land. They have slaughtered thousands of Ramahan. Our own abbey is the only one left intact. You know this as well as I do."

Giyan turned back from the peaks of the Djenn Marre, from the latent image of her vision. Her thick copper-colored hair flew in the wind. She put her hand tenderly on her sister's shoulder. "I hear the pain and fear in your voice. We have prayed to Miina for eighty-five long, terrible years without hearing a response."

Bartta shook herself away. "I feel no pain or fear."

"But you do," Giyan said even more softly. "It is your deep and abiding fear that in Her wrath Miina has left us in the hands of the V'ornn forever. You told me so yourself."

"A moment of weakness, of illness, of disorientation," Bartta said curtly. "I am surprised you even remember."

"Why wouldn't I remember, sister? I love you deeply."

Bartta, trembling a little, whispered. "If only it were so."

Giyan took her in her arms. "Have you any real doubts?"

Bartta allowed her head to briefly rest on her sister's shoulder. She sighed. "This is what I do not understand," she said.

"Even the konara, our elders, have no answer for Miina's strange silence."

Giyan took Bartta's head in her hands, looked her in the eye. "The answer is clear, sister. It lies in our recent history. The Goddess is silent because we ignored Her warnings and misused The Pearl."

"Then it's true. Miina has abandoned us," Bartta whispered. There were sudden, stinging tears in her eyes.

"No, sister, She is merely waiting."

Bartta wiped her eyes, deeply ashamed that she had showed such weakness. "Waiting for what?"

"For the Dar Sala-at. The One who will find The Pearl and end our bondage to the V'ornn."

Bartta's expression changed, hardening slightly. "Is this true faith, or is it your Gift talking?"

"I have been taught by Konara Mossa to turn away from the Gift, just as we have been taught to shun the Rappa because they were responsible for Mother's death the day The Pearl was lost, the day we were invaded by the V'ornn."

"The Rappa had the Gift, and it led to our downfall." Having spotted a chink in her sister's armor, Bartta's eyes were alight. Spite, the twin of her envy, overrode her inner terror. "And yet, you *defy* Konara Mossa, you *use* the Gift."

"Sometimes I cannot help it," Giyan said softly, sadly, "the Gift is too strong."

"Sometimes you *deliberately* use it," Bartta hissed. "You are being trained in secret, aren't you?"

"What if I am?" Giyan looked down at her feet. "Sometimes I question whether this thing inside me—this Gift—is evil." Her voice dropped to a whisper borne by the wind. "Sometimes, late at night, when I lie awake, I feel the breadth and scope of the Cosmos breathing all around me, and I know—I *know*, sister, in my heart, in my very soul—that what we see and hear and smell and taste—the world we touch is but a fraction of the Whole that exists elsewhere. A beauty beyond comprehension. And with every fiber of my being I long to reach out and *know* that vast place. And it is then that I think, How could such a feeling be evil?"

Bartta was looking at her sister with profound jealousy. *What you know, what you long for,* she thought. *As if I do not long for the same thing, and know it will never be mine.* She was about to say something clever and cutting, but the sight of the tail stayed her tongue. The lorg's tail flicked once then, illusory as the whiff of water in the Great Voorg, disappeared beneath a long, flat rock of a golden hue.

"Look there!" she said as she clambered down into the shallow gully. Beyond, a steep and treacherous falloff mined with loose shale and broken twigs. "Oh, sister, look!" And planting her sturdy legs wide, she bent and flipped over the rock.

"A lorg!" Giyan cried.

"Yes. A lorg!" Bartta backed away, fascinated and appalled, as her twin clambered down to stand beside her. The lorg was indeed a hideous beast. Its hide was thick and warty, its watery grey eyes bulging, turning this way and that as if able to see in all directions at once. It appeared all belly; its head and legs were puny and insignificant. It seemed boneless, like the double stomach of a gutted lemur, and this somehow made it all the more hideous.

Bartta hefted a stone in her hand. "And now we must kill it."

"Kill it? But why?"

"You know why," Bartta said icily. "Lorgs are evil."

"Leave it. You do not need to take its life."

With an expert swing, Bartta skimmed the stone through the air. It made a peculiar humming sound, like an angry blackcrow. She had that, at least over her twin, her outsize physical strength. The stone, loosed from that powerful slingshot, struck the lorg with a sickening *thunk!* The lorg's disgusting pop eyes swiveled in their direction, perhaps sadly, but it did not move. This seeming indifference enraged Bartta all the more. She grabbed another stone, a larger one this time, cocking her arm to throw it. But Giyan caught her upraised wrist in her hand.

"Why, Bartta? Why do you *really* want to kill it?"

The wind rattled the kuello-firs, whistled through devious

clefts in the rocks. A hawk floated on the thermals high overhead, vivid with intent. Bartta's gaze did not stray from Giyan's face. The twin who was tall, beautiful, clever of tongue
and hand. An inchoate rage curdled the contents of Bartta's
stomach, gripped her throat like a giant's hand. With a violent twist, she jerked herself free, and before Giyan could
utter another word, she hurled the stone with tremendous
force. It struck the lorg's head, causing a gout of blood so
pale and thin it might have been water. Grunting like an
animal, Bartta gathered a handful of stones and, as she advanced upon the lorg, peppered it until it sank into the
ground, split open like a side of meat.

"There. *There*." Bartta, standing over it, light-headed,
trembled slightly.

Crouching beside the dead creature, Giyan passed a hand
over it. "Great Goddess, tell me if you can," she whispered,
"where is the evil here?"

Looking down at her, Bartta said, "That's right, sister.
Shed a tear for so ugly a beast that would not move even to
save itself. If its death hurts you so, use your infernal Gift.
Return it to life."

"The Gift does not work in that way," Giyan said without
looking up. "It cannot bring life from death."

"*Try,* sorceress."

Giyan took the ragged lorg in her hands and buried it in
the shale. Dust and blood coated her hands, remaining darkened in the creases even after she wiped them down. At last,
she looked up at Bartta, beads of perspiration standing out
on her forehead. "What have you really accomplished?"

"We will be late for afternoon devotions," Bartta said. As
she set off for the high, glistening walls of the Abbey of
Floating White she saw the owl circling the treetops, as if
watching her.

Book One:
SPIRIT GATE

"Inside us are fifteen Spirit Gates.
They are meant to be open.
If even one is not, a blockage oc-
curs;
a sickness of spirit that, left un-
treated,
can and will rot the soul from
within."

—Utmost Source,
The Five Sacred Books of Miina

1

Owl

Sixteen years—a lifetime—later, Bartta, now a small, dark, hunched figure not unlike a lorg, found herself on the same path. The sky was cloudless, of a blue so achingly rich it bore the appearance of fresh lacquer. The sun was in its waning hours, magnified by the atmosphere, so that its curious purple spot seemed like the pupil of an eye. Miina's Eye, the Ramahan believed, that saw and recorded everything.

Borne upon the air was the scent of the kuello-firs, and when Bartta's sandals crunched the brown needles she felt again that tiny shiver of recognition of things apart. In an instant the afternoon she had killed the lorg came rushing back to her. She paused, looking for the dry gully and the large flat rock of a golden hue under which, years ago, she had found the lorg.

Bartta wore the long, persimmon-colored robes of raw silk reserved for the konara, senior priestesses of the Dea Cretan, the Ramahan High Council. In the old days, before the coming of the V'ornn, the Ramahan were ruled by one woman: Mother. That was her title, which she inherited as a child, when her name was taken from her forever. At that time, the Ramahan had been made up of equal numbers of women and men—if such a thing could be imagined! The men had been purged after their innate greed led to the loss of The Pearl, the sorcerous Rappa had been destroyed, and the Dea Cretan was formed to ensure that the violence that had engulfed the Order would never again occur, that the sorcery that had been inextricably bound into Ramahan society was carefully weeded out, strand by strand.

As Bartta moved along the path she was immersed in a halo of myrrh, oils of clove, and clary-sage, the incense she burned when she prayed. These spices gave her strength of conviction and clarity of thought. She tapped her forefinger against her thin, unpainted lips. Where was that rock? She was close to it, she knew that much.

The passage of time and the vagaries of her memory caused her to walk past it twice. Each time, however, her Ramahan training compelled her to turn around, and at last she recognized the rock, whose golden color flashed only here and there beneath a dull layer of shale dust and kuello-fir needles. Lifting the hem of her robes, she half slid down the slope into the gully, picked her way carefully across the loose shale and the odd tufts of yellow wrygrass that had sprung up. Over the years, a geological eruption had warped and scarred the depression. The rock now lay like a kind of bridge across what appeared to be a fissure in the gully bed.

She bent to touch the cool, rough, golden skin of that rock, stirring even after all this time with images of the lorg. She cursed heartily. That lorg had certainly been an evil omen. Three days after its death Giyan had been captured in a raid, taken to Axis Tyr to be the slave of the V'ornn. That was sixteen years ago, and never a word from her since. She had heard stories, many times, about the regent's Kundalan mistress. Giyan was sharing her bed with a V'ornn! How could she? It was unimaginable! Thinking of the dreaded V'ornn, Bartta shuddered. That is when she heard the sound—tiny, indistinct, echoey. She turned back, looked around the perimeter of the gully. Nothing stirred save the shivering tops of the graceful kuello-firs.

The sound came again, trickling down her spine like a rivulet of ice water. On her knees, she peered into the fissure. Darkness greeted her beyond the sliver of opening between rock and shale bed.

"Hello?" she called in a voice as quavery as if it were underwater. "Hello?"

A sound, neither human nor animal but somewhere in between, came to her. It made her jerk erect, her scalp prickling eerily. She backed up, stumbling a little, righted herself, then turned to flee across the gully. Failing to lift the hem of her robe, she tripped and fell, ripping the robe and skinning a knee. She gave a little cry, regained her footing, and ran on. As she reached the slope at the edge of the gully, she paused to catch her breath, squinting upward into the luminous ultramarine sky. Her pulse hammered, and her mouth was dry.

The soft, eerie moaning of the wind made the boulders and gullies seem alive even as it concealed that other hideous sound. She turned her gaze toward the stands of kuello-firs and breathed deeply to rid herself of the last splinter of fear. She started as the great horned owl emerged from shadowed, needled branches, swooped low on enormous, soundless wings. She called Miina's name, for the owl was the sacred messenger of the Goddess. It seemed to be heading straight for her. She pressed herself against the slope. Too late to run. She was murmuring a prayer when it passed close enough for her to feel the backwash of its mighty grey-blue wings. Then it swooped even lower, and she whirled to follow its flight. The owl passed over the long, flat rock, then again, and a third time, before lifting on powerful pinions, and wheeling away into the dark kuello-fir forest.

A peculiar terror gripped her. The owl was an omen, of course. An extraordinary omen, because an owl in daylight signified imminent death. Her sense of dread escalated, but she knew that she could not ignore an omen from Miina. But that could not be; Miina had passed beyond the rim, or so she had convinced herself. Then what was Miina's messenger doing here? She had to find out.

Reluctantly, she retraced her steps. She fell to her knees beside the stone, grimacing with pain. The sun sat atop the collar of the forest; the shadows in the gully were long, blue, dense.

Bartta grunted. The rock moved with the reluctance of an invalid, its protest in the form of a miniavalanche of shale. The chilling sound came again, and on her belly she stuck her head into the fissure. In the last of the light she could just make out a small figure curled in a corner. It was Kundalan, not animal—and small, certainly not an adult.

Once again, she almost turned away. She had no desire to descend into that dangerous darkness. But her training held her. Miina had spoken; now she must act. How long had it been since Miina had given the Ramahan a sign? Bartta did not know. A long time, anyway. A *very* long time.

"Hold on!" she called, clambering down. "I'm coming for you!"

Nearly choking in a cloud of dust, she descended, cursing mightily, using her thick, work-hardened hands to grasp small outcroppings to keep her from pitching headlong into the fissure. She needed to be especially careful because the friable shale was all too apt to shear off or crumble beneath her weight. The preponderance of sedimentary rock in this area, she knew, was due to the Chuun River, which flowed from here all the way down to Axis Tyr, the Kundalan city the V'ornn had chosen as their capital. Bartta had heard many stories of Axis Tyr as it had been before the V'ornn invasion, a beautiful city of blue-and-rose stone sitting astride the Chuun River. Now, from all she could glean, the only Kundalan inside the city were miserable prisoners or slaves. Like Giyan.

Bartta's hard heart was wrung out with the terrible sacrifices she had made. It had become a poor shrunken organ no more useful than a stone. Yet she could still hate. Her blood ran cold when she thought of the V'ornn. Such monsters! So nasty to look at; hairless as a rotten clemett and twice as smelly. You could never be certain what the hairless beasts were thinking, though members of the Kundalan resistance had come to know how they would react in certain situations. But the resistance was largely impotent. Of what use was their deaths? One hundred and one years after the occupation and nothing had changed. There was no help for it. One had to learn how to live with the yoke around one's neck.

Miina be praised that Giyan had been taken by the V'ornn and not her. Bartta knew that she would surely have hung herself rather than be made to serve them or touch their rancid flesh. Anyway, she thought sourly, her twin had shown a perverse curiosity about the V'ornn. Now she had her wish.

Bartta had begun to sweat. It was unnaturally hot inside the fissure, and she made her stumbling way around the perimeter to avoid the worst of the heat, which seemed to be rising in sickening waves from the jagged rock floor. A copse of pink calcite stalagmites rose from the periphery of the fissure floor like grasping fingers. The heated air shimmered and burned her lungs so that she hastened to the spot where the figure lay. A girl of perhaps fifteen years, Bartta saw, who was shaking as if with the ague. A cloyingly sweet-smelling sweat rimed her forehead, matted her long, tangled, blond hair. Her beautiful features were clouded, darkened, ravaged. When Bartta scooped her up in her arms, the girl felt as if she were on fire.

The girl cried out as Bartta carried her back to the opening she had made by moving the rock above.

"Stop your sniveling," she snapped. "I will have you out of here in a moment. You're safe now." But judging by the girl's flushed and dry skin, Bartta did not believe that. The Ramahan were great healers as well as mystics. Bartta could well read the signs of duur fever, and she liked not the advanced stage the virus was in. This fever, which came in five-year cycles, had ravaged the Kundalan for a century now. The Ramahan believed that the V'ornn had brought the virus to Kundala; the resistance was certain that the Gyrgon, the mysterious V'ornn caste of technomages, had manufactured it as another weapon in their overwhelming arsenal to bring the Kundalan race to its knees. In any case, the Ramahan had had only limited success in saving the victims of duur fever. If it was caught within forty-eight hours of the onset of symptoms, a poultice of a mixture of the rendered seeds of black loosestrife and the thistle heart of coltsfoot digitalis had proved effective. Otherwise, once the virus reached the lungs it replicated so rapidly that within days the victim drowned as if lost at sea.

With the girl in her arms, Bartta stopped and looked up at the wedge of darkening sky. It looked a long way off, farther by far than the floor of the fissure had looked before she had scrambled down here. The girl was dying, no doubt about it. Of what possible use was she then? Perhaps, if she, Bartta, was able to get her out of here and back to the village she could prolong her life a week, two at the outside. But to what purpose? Already the girl's face was distorted by pain, and her suffering would only grow. Better to leave her here; a quick death would be merciful, a blessing even.

But as Bartta was setting her down, a small earth tremor sent shale scaling down on them. Bartta braced herself against the trembling side of the fissure as the girl cried out. Her eyes focused and she moaned pitifully, clinging to Bartta. Waiting for the tremor to abate, Bartta had cause to recall Miina's sacred owl. Now that the Goddess had at last spoken, She had chosen Bartta! The owl had passed three times over this fissure. Why? Certainly not so that Bartta should leave this girl here to expire. But what then the meaning of Miina's messages? Perhaps the Goddess meant for this girl to become her property. But, again, why? Was she in some way special?

Bartta peered down at the face so ethereally beautiful, so ashen she could plainly see the play of blue veins beneath skin unnaturally taut and shiny with fever. Brushing lank hair back from the girl's forehead, she said: "What is your name?"

"Riane." Her heart was beating as fast as an ice-hare's.

"Hmm. I do not recognize that name. Where are you from?"

The girl's face wrinkled up. "I do not . . . I can't remember. Except . . ."

"Except what, my dear?"

"I remember skelling."

"Skelling?" Bartta frowned. "I do not believe I know that word. What does it mean?"

"Skelling. You know, climbing up and down sheer rock faces."

"Don't be foolish," Bartta scoffed. "No one I know does that."

"I do," Riane said boldly. "I mean, I did. I distinctly remember coming down Four Whites."

"But that is impossible," Bartta said. Four Whites was the name of a sheer mountain cliff that rose a kilometer above the abbey. It was too steep, rugged, and ice-strewn even for the surefooted mountain goats.

"Not really. I've done it many times."

Bartta's frown deepened. "All right, let's say you did this skelling thing. What happened next?"

"A handhold I had been using sheared off. Maybe the rock had fractured when the earth tremored. Anyway, I fell."

"All right, dear, but how did you wind up *here*, beneath the gold rock?"

"I . . . don't know."

Bartta sighed. "What *do* you remember? What about your mother? Your father?"

Riane shook her head.

"Think, girl. Think!"

Riane shied away from her, curling up into a ball. With an effort, Bartta softened her voice. "Please try," she said. "It is important."

"Everything else is a blank."

Amnesia, Bartta thought. *She must be injured as well as sick.*

As if to underscore this, the girl whimpered, "I don't feel good."

"You are going to be all right," Bartta said automatically, though she doubted that very much.

"Don't leave me," the girl blurted suddenly.

Bartta felt as if she had a millstone around her neck. Forcing herself to smile, she said, "We will leave together. Very soon you will see the—"

The girl's startling blue eyes bobbled this way and that as another tremor possessed the fissure. With a hiss and clatter, more shale shook loose, scattering itself across the rock floor. "Will we die here?" the girl asked. She was obviously unaware of her condition.

"We will not die here." Bartta arranged her features in

what she hoped was a reassuring smile. "I am Bartta of Stone—"

Riane screamed as the third and most violent of the tremors shook the fissure. "No sense in crying," Bartta said sternly over Riane's moaning. "We will be out of here soon enough." Over the girl's head she could see layers of shale sluicing toward the center of the fissure floor, where they vanished into an opening the tremors had pried open in the bedrock. *I must get out of here,* Bartta thought, *or I will die.* Again, she considered leaving the girl behind, but the image of Miina's owl remained in her mind's eye, bending her to its imperative.

She stood and, bracing herself against the side of the fissure, hoisted Riane until she was draped over her left shoulder. "All right," she said. "Hold on tight now."

Thus burdened, she began to climb. It was slow going. She was savvy enough to know that a goodly number of the hand- and toeholds she had used on her way down had been compromised by the quakes. The ones she found she tested twice before moving cautiously upward. All the while, Riane's weight bore down on her, bowing her back, spreading an ache through her shoulders and hips that quite soon bloomed into outright pain. Still, she continued her climb, willing herself not to hurry, to test each makeshift rung lest it crumble beneath her, sending her and the girl back to the fissure floor. But always in the back of her mind lurked the spectre of another tremor, which would surely dislodge her. She felt more vulnerable than she had since entering the Ramahan sinecure of Floating White but, most curiously, she also felt a kind of exhilaration as she connected with her body again, using it as she had when she was a little girl. It felt fine to have dirt beneath her nails again, to feel the flex and draw of muscle and sinew as they worked. She was aware of Riane whimpering behind her, and she prayed that in her weakened state she would be able to hold on.

Two-thirds of the way up, Bartta ran out of handholds. Three separate possibilities crumbled under her grip, the third breaking apart only as she put all their combined weight on it. She fell back to her former perch with a jolt that caused a painful percussion up her spine. Riane passed out. *Just as well*, Bartta thought. *The girl is terrified enough for the both of us.*

Despite instinct urging her nerve endings to move, Bartta took time to breathe deeply. For the moment, the earth had grown still, but cocking an ear she heard not a single birdsong, and this she interpreted as warning that there was more seismic activity to come. Living all her life in the embrace of the Djenn Marre, she was no stranger to quakes. They were lightest in the lower foothills, increasing in intensity the farther one penetrated the high crags. Once, when she was on her way to deliver the monthly ration of supplies to the Ice Caves, she had been unlucky enough to be caught in a quake that had sheared off a section of cliff face not seven meters from where she had crouched in terror. The Ice Caves were infrequently visited and only by Ramahan acolytes. They were carved out of the granite Djenn Marre like the eyrie of a fantastic mythic raptor five kilometers from the abbey and a kilometer above the waterfalls of Heavenly Rushing, at the headwaters of the Chuun. How the Tchakira lived up there was anyone's guess. But what more did they deserve, these dregs and outcasts—criminals, misfits, madmen who had been expunged from society? Still, they were Kundalan. The Ramahan felt it the sacred duty of Miina to ensure that these poor wretches would not perish in the wind- and ice-swept peaks of the Djenn Marre. Not that any civilized Kundalan had ever seen a Tchakira. But they existed, all right, for when the Ramahan acolyte arrived at the Ice Caves, as Bartta had, the previous month's rations were gone. She, like all the acolytes before her, had paused only long enough to lay down the small, dense packages of food and herb concentrates, consume a gulp or two of cloudy rakkis, and head back down the ice-encrusted, nearly vertical trail.

Now another nearly vertical trail loomed above her. Despite her elevation, the evening sky seemed farther away than ever, a mocking shell, blackened like a burnt offering. A star emerged from the enveloping darkness, crackling blue-white fire, and just to its right one moon, then another poured their reflected light into the fissure. Bartta felt it first in the soles of her feet, and she braced herself, praying furiously for Miina to extend Her protective hand. A clap like thunder broke the low rumbling, echoed painfully in her ears. As the earth lurched, she slipped, desperately hanging on. The fissure all around her seemed to be breaking apart, and she was certain that she was about to breathe her last.

Stillness so absolute it was unnerving enveloped everything. Looking up, she saw that the wall itself had split so that the upper tier now stepped back in a kind of ragged staircase. Instinct drove her upward. In an instant, she had reached the natural steps and, scrambling as quickly as she was able under the circumstances, made her way out of the fissure.

Gaining the floor of the gully, she did not pause even to catch her breath, but half ran with the insensate girl still over her shoulder. Not until she found herself safely on the path that wound through the kuello-firs down to Stone Border did she even dare look back over her shoulder. What she expected to see she could not say, but in the wan moonlight spilling down like milk from a she-goat's udders she saw nothing out of the ordinary. With a grunt, she shifted her burden to a less painful position, then hurried down the path toward home.

2

The Vine

A heartbeat after Annon loosed his arrow and Kurgan fired his bolt, the gimnopede dropped from its descending flight path over the thorny crown of the sysal tree. The bolt pierced its plump blue-and-yellow breast; the arrow had missed it by a hairbreadth.

Annon pumped a triumphant fist over his head. But Kurgan, hurling a rude gesture in his friend's direction, lunged forward, running headlong through the copse of sysal trees they had made their early-morning lair, for it was well-known among the V'ornn that the luscious gimnopedes made their nests in the highest branches of the great, gnarled, ancient trees.

"Ah, yes, the kill is mine!" Kurgan breathed. He plucked the bloody, encoded metal-alloy bolt from the dead bird's breast, pressed it back into the tertium link on the outside of his left forearm. "You see the superiority of V'ornn technology?" He shook the ash longbow Annon carried. "Why you insist on fooling around with these pathetic, backward Kundalan weapons is a mystery."

"It was an experiment," Annon said.

"A failed experiment, I warrant. You've only to use your eyes to see it."

Kurgan skewered the dead gimnopede with the slender triangular blade of the knife he always kept with him. It was his most treasured possession, the one weapon of his he allowed no one to touch, not even Annon. Not that Annon cared overmuch; he had no great love for V'ornn weaponry.

Kurgan grunted. "But the Ashera are known for their love of the Kundalan, eh?"

"Why do you keep bringing that up?" Annon said stiffly.

"You are being raised by a Kundalan. It is not natural. Whatever she teaches you is as defective as that bow she gave you. At the very least, it will come back to bite you on your tender parts."

Annon chose not to keep this topic alive, touched his own link, instead. "You rely too much on the okummmon."

"And why should I not? It sighted for me, calculated the vector of the bird's flight, the wind speed, the time of flight to a nanosecond. It loosed the bolt at just the right moment. What did this Kundalan joke do for you? The okummmon gave the kill to me, not to you."

"Without effort. The very same way it teaches us when we are Summoned to plug in."

"Just so, empty-head." Kurgan grinned as he rubbed the bolt's stubby shaft. The okummmon had already "metabo-lized" the gimnopede's blood, breaking it down into nutrients easily absorbed by his bloodstream. He clapped his friend on the back. "The okummmon is a privilege not to be under-estimated. We Bashkir are the only Great Caste to be linked. Be proud of it, and pity the Genomatekks, a Great Caste in name only. Pity the Khagggun, the warriors; the Mesagggun, the engineers; the Tuskugggun, the females—the Lesser Castes. They are all soto—those who cannot be Summoned. It is proof that we are superior."

"To me the Summoning feels like a tether."

Kurgan nodded. "To bind us most closely to the Gyrgon."

"I want to be bound to no one."

"You are Ashera—the dynasty ordained and anointed by the Gyrgon—Those That Summon. Your father is the second of the Ashera Dynasty and you will succeed him and your son will succeed you and on and on."

Annon thought of the three sisters he hadn't seen since their births. They lived in a different hingatta of their mother's affiliation—his mother, too, whom he had not seen since just before her death seven years ago. At that time, she had been unable to speak. In her final delirium, she had not recognized him. "I don't want that."

Kurgan laughed. "Then give it to me!"

"If I could, I would."

Kurgan's expression changed to that of someone who is deeply concerned. "You have such strange notions, Annon Ashera! I warrant they come from that Kundalan sorceress who takes care of you. Why, she's even taught you to speak and read Kundalan."

"That's a secret between you and me, Kurgan."

Kurgan snorted. "If your father knew what nonsense she was feeding you, he would throw her out on her tenderest part!"

"My father seems content with the manner in which she

is raising me." He grinned. "But she *has* shown me some of the secret Kundalan passageways that honeycomb the palace and has told me of her village of Stone Border high up in the Djenn Marre."

"Ah, yes, the Kundalan. Keeping secrets seems to be among their most annoying traits. But who cares if they have secrets, I say? What have we to learn from inferior cultures?" He put his hand on his friend's shoulder. "I know it's hard for you. A slave rearing you! What *is* the regent thinking? He is besotted with her, say the people who wag their lips and cluck their tongues. Behind your back, of course."

Annon's face grew dark with blood. "I have dealt with those skcetttas."

"And made a potful of enemies along the way. Just like your father."

"My father is afraid of no enemy."

"True enough. But the way he flies in the face of tradition . . . That Kundalan female of his is but one example."

"If my mother hadn't Broken Faith—"

"If your mother hadn't Broken Faith you would never have come to hingatta liiina do mori. You would have been raised by her, like your sisters, in hingatta falla do mori." Hingatta were communes of eight V'ornn females of childbearing age. These communes were where children of the Great Castes were born and raised until one year after the Channeling, when they were permanently joined to the Modality via their okummmon. "We would never have met, never have become friends. And I never would have had the opportunity to beat your oh so tender parts at hunting!"

"My father disapproves of our friendship."

"It drives mine mad!"

"He thinks your father put you up to trying to find out the secret to salamuuun."

"Our fathers hate one another, and that drug is the root of it, that is true enough," Kurgan said. "But to think that I would ever take orders from him!" He laughed. "Wennn Stogggul can rot in N'Luuura for all I care of him!"

He strung up the gimnopede by its neck, hoisting the bird

where it joined the others. "Regard, my friend!" His grin was wide and mocking. "Four gimnopedes and not a single, solitary, stinking one for you!"

Annon indicated two small quadrupeds hanging from a branch. "A brace of ice-hares is good enough for me."

"Ice-hares, hah! Precious little flesh on those long bones, and what there is of it tastes like a mouth full of silicon."

"And you would know well the bitter taste of silicon, wouldn't you, my friend?"

"I? Let us wager on who has tasted more silicon!"

"We've only to set the stakes." Annon laughed.

"Three rounds of fire-grade numaaadis."

"Make it cloudy rakkis."

"That Kundalan swill? It smells like rotten clemetts."

"Too strong for the likes of you, eh?"

"Never!"

Doubtless, the banter would have continued in this vein had not something odd appeared in Annon's peripheral vision.

"Kurgan!" he whispered as he crouched. "Kurgan, look! Over there!"

Kurgan sighted along the line indicated by his friend's extended arm. A brilliant triangle of sunlight oozed through a gap in the trees. Within that triangle, a flicker of movement. Kurgan, shifting to get a better angle, snapped a dried twig beneath his boot sole. Immediately, Annon clapped a hand over his mouth to stifle his foul exclamation. The two boys froze.

V'ornn were hairless with long, smooth-skinned tapering skulls and a pale yellow cast to their flesh. Annon's virtually colorless eyes and solemn mouth instantly set him apart from Kurgan, whose thin, angular face was made all the more so by contrast to his night-black eyes. Both of them could see the continued flicker of movement within the triangle of white light. By an unspoken agreement born of being raised together in liiina do mori, the two friends made their cautious, silent way to the far side of the sysal copse. At the very edge of the triangle of light their mouths grew dry.

"I don't believe it!" Kurgan whispered.

"What a find!" Annon responded in the same low tone.

"Magnificent!"

"Just what I was thinking!"

"But I said it first, so it's mine!"

"Over my tender parts!"

As they peered out into the dazzling sunshine, the cool sound of the creek—one of the many offshoots of the mighty Chuun, which fed the Great Phosphorus Marsh twenty leagues to the west—rippled into the copse. With it came the soft tinkle of delighted laughter, for the object of their attention was no bright-feathered gimnopede, no six-legged marsh lizard. Not even the sight of a narbuck with its precious spiral horn—gone from Kundala with the coming of the V'ornn—could have moved these teenage boys the way the sight of the young Kundalan female did.

With the hem of her robe piled high on her creamy white thighs, she had ventured into the shallows of the creek. She wriggled her toes, stirring up sediment and tadpoles. It was the sight of these tadpoles scattering, the boys surmised, that had set off her tinkling laughter. Not that they paid much mind to the sounds she was making. No, no, they were staring with rapt attention at her *hair*. It was thick and brown as leeesta fried in a pan. It was piled on top of her head, set with a pair of long filigreed shell pins typical of the race. As they watched, she ventured another step into the creek. Now her feet were covered. Abruptly, she raised her head and took a look around her. Both boys froze, holding their breath lest she discover them spying on her and run away. They were not afraid of her, of course. They were V'ornn; they were unafraid of any Kundalan. Rather, they found themselves drawn to her, each in his own way. And then there was the matter of her *hair*.

Doubtless, because the V'ornn were an utterly hairless race, their reaction to Kundalan hair ran the gamut from revulsion to erotic preoccupation. It was rumored, in fact, that the Gyrgon were frequent visitors to the Kundalan kashiggen, where they paid for the services of the mysterious Imari, who wore their hair so long it was said an attendant was required to hold it as they walked. Since the Gyrgon were fond of planting rumors and myths concerning themselves, on this matter no one could properly separate truth from fiction.

The boys watched, stupefied, as the young Kundalan female reached up and pulled the filigreed pins. Her hair cascaded like Heavenly Rushing, tumbling between her shoulder blades. Then she began to undress. First, the vest, then the blouse, then the long, layered skirt. With an uninhibited cry of delight, she plunged naked into the water. As the water purled around her thighs, they saw all her hair.

Kurgan had dropped his double brace of gimnopedes. They lay at his feet, broken-necked prey, forgotten now, in the heat of the newest hunt.

"There's a choice clemett ripe for the picking," he said thickly. "I must have her."

Without another word, he broke cover. Annon, dropping his longbow, was right beside him as they both raced toward her. Annon was the fleeter of the two. Kurgan, seeing he would lose this race, stuck out his leg. Annon tripped and went sprawling head over tender parts onto the greensward.

Kurgan, making the most of his sudden advantage, reached the edge of the bank in no time and leapt into the water just as the young Kundalan female became aware of him. She gave a shriek, trying to get away from him as he took hold of her. She struggled as he forced her down, plunging her head beneath the water repeatedly until she was sufficiently winded that he could drag her without further resistance into the shallows. There he fell heavily upon her, covering her mouth with his own.

Annon, lying amid sprays of wrygrass and whistleflowers, witnessed this assault with a divided nature. He, too, felt the quick heaviness in his loins at the sight of the girl; he, too, felt the urge to fall on her and sate his lust. Intrinsically, there was nothing wrong with this. The Kundalan were inferior—one more slave race the V'ornn had conquered. And yet . . . And yet something—some dimly heard voice—restrained him, whispering in his ear: *This is wrong.* He trembled. Of course, it was Giyan's voice inside his head. Giyan being Kundalan was a matter of no small import to Annon, since she was the one who had raised him. Of course, if she had not been the regent's mistress she would never have been given such an important job, would never have been allowed to join hingatta liiina do mori nor any other hingatta, for that matter. But Eleusis *had* been chosen as regent by the Gyrgon, and while they might not allow him to make laws on his own, his word among all the castes was Law. His word was Law because it rang with the weight of the Gyrgon. Others might gripe and grouse about the regent, as Stogggul did, but that was all it amounted to: whispers of dissatisfaction like the chafing of skin under ill-fitting clothes.

Of course, Giyan raised him. She was his father's mistress; she did his bidding. Like a good slave. A slave whose whisper somehow had the power to penetrate his skull even when she was not present. Perhaps Kurgan was right about her; perhaps she *was* a sorceress.

In any event, he could no longer bear to listen to that voice. He ran into the brilliant glare of sunshine, shot down the steep bank like an arrow, and fell upon the struggling pair. He could see Kurgan's bare buttocks, the intent, almost half-mad look of bloodlust in his friend's eyes. Curiously, these observations served only to spur his determination. To do what? To scratch his itch, to lighten the curious heaviness in his loins, to fight for his own fill of this nubile young Kundalan female. *To negate that maddening whisper filling the corridors of his brain.*

He dug his fingers into the bunched muscles of Kurgan's shoulders. Kurgan reared up, swung his upper body toward Annon, and swatted him with the back of his hand. Annon, unprepared for the blow, staggered a little. He came on again, right into a short, powerful jab. He knelt in the water, seeing stars. But as his vision cleared, he saw the look on the girl's face and his blood ran cold. She was no longer resisting. Instead, her eyes had a glazed look, as if she were peering into the very far distance, to a place where no V'ornn could venture. It was a look he had seen many times on the faces of the Kundalan slaves in Axis Tyr. It was a look that enraged him, made him feel his mother's abandonment of him as if it were a knife wound in his belly. And somehow that feeling of rage led his mind back to when he was a child, crying in the night. He had wanted his mother but what had he gotten instead? A Kundalan slave! He would call his mother's name in fear, but also to vex Giyan, to punish her for being where his mother ought to be.

If it was a night when she was not pleasuring his father, Giyan would answer his call. Without his asking, she would rock him even though he could barely abide her touch—the touch of a Kundalan his father inexplicably adored! She would recite strange, disquieting legends of the Goddess Miina and the Five Sacred Dragons that had created Kundala or sing him to sleep with lyrics borne on eerie melodies that wormed their way into his brain. She possessed a beautiful voice, he had to give her that.

But there was something about her, a profound sadness perhaps that informed many of her expressions, that bled the pleasure from her smiles. Once, he awoke in her arms to find her weeping in her sleep. Tears rolled down her cheeks in unending streams as she dreamed her terrible dream, and even though it caused a catch of revulsion in his throat, he slipped his hand into hers and held her alien fingers tightly.

He was half-blinded by the sunlight reflected in dazzling scimitars across the creek. His rage overpowered his inertia. Growling like a caged beast, he punched Kurgan in the jaw, struck him a ragged but powerful blow on the point of his chin, and was thus able to pry him loose from his prey. The girl lay, half-dazed, until Annon reached down. She flinched as he hauled her up by her arm. She shrank away from him when he released her.

For a moment, they formed a peculiar tableau—the male conqueror and the female slave, their alien eyes locked, their alien hearts beating with unknown intent. This was the moment to take her, Annon knew, the moment to strike back at the Kundalan sorceress who had suckled him as a babe and at his father, who needed her more than Annon did. The moment to claim, as a V'ornn, what was rightfully his. But he did nothing. Behind him, Kurgan groaned, a sound not unlike the breaking of a bottle's seal.

"Get out of here!" Annon growled into the Kundalan's bewildered face. Then, more forcefully: "Do as I say, female, and do it quickly before I change my mind!"

Kurgan, on his knees, groaned again and coughed up pale blue phlegm. As the Kundalan waded hastily toward shore, he lunged after her. She screamed. Annon dragged him back into the creek. Kurgan kicked him in the shin.

"I want what I want, my friend," he panted as they grappled. "Stay out of my way, I warn you."

"I have given her safe passage," Annon said.

This made Kurgan laugh. "Are you mad? Who are you to grant her such a thing?"

"I am the regent's son." Why was he doing this? Annon asked himself. What was this alien female to him? His mind's eye was filled with the sight of Giyan writhing in bed with his father while he called his mother's name. The night, he had come to learn, is the time to give voice to one's own pain.

"Oh, yes. Eleusis the Great, Eleusis the Powerful," Kurgan sneered. He was angry and frustrated. "The man whose father was anointed by the Gyrgon, held on close leash by the Gyrgon, a regent like all others, without power. Power which resides solely with the Gyrgon."

"And yet, your own father lusted after the regent's crown and moved heaven and earth to claim the Gyrgon vote," Annon countered.

"My father is a fool, obsessed with his enmity against your family. Had I been him, I would have found a way to become regent."

"And then what? The regent serves at the pleasure of the Gyrgon. The power resides with them. This is the way it has always been."

"But not the way it must be forever!"

Then they were at it again with tooth and nail, muscle and sinew, brute strength and guile—drawing on every asset available to their powerful, youthful minds and bodies.

Eleana, the Kundalan girl, watched with a certain fascinated terror as these two alien beasts fought in the shallows just below her. She gathered her clothes, not with the due haste Annon had ordered, but with a languor born of this battle. Now to have two V'ornn fighting over her, it was, well, overwhelming. True, they were beasts, cruel and hairless and stinking and unknowable. And yet, the one with the colorless eyes had come to her defense not, as she had assumed, to take her himself, but to save her. She felt a curious linkage, a warmth for him, small as a stydil larva, yes, but one that could not be gainsaid.

And so, counter to all logic, she lingered, listening to the drumbeat of her heart. It was she who saw the sacred gyreagle first—The Goddess Miina's right hand—plummeting down from a sky white and flat with noontime sunlight. She lifted one arm to shield her eyes against the glare and saw the enormous bird heading for the two V'ornn. It was golden, with a pure white crest and a terrible reddish beak used for rending its prey's flesh from bone. By this time, it seemed as if the V'ornn with the colorless eyes had the upper hand. Now she could hear the rapid beat of the gyreagle's wings, see the spread of its curved yellow talons.

The gyreagle struck the V'ornn with the colorless eyes, scoring bloody lines along the right side of his rib cage. He screamed. In what special way had he angered the Goddess? Eleana asked herself. A question without an answer. Both boys scrambled away, their own pitched battle forgotten. The wounded V'ornn writhed in the shallows, while the other— his friend?—scrambled to his knees, raised his left arm straight as a javelin and, as the gyreagle was gaining the sky, shot it through the heart with one of those hateful metal bolts. Eleana cried out. The majestic bird spiraled to the ground, panting out its last breaths. Another mortal sin among many perpetrated by the V'ornn against Miina.

In five huge strides the V'ornn had caught up with her. She was paralyzed by the attacks and by the sudden death of the bird. He threw her to the rocky ground and, before she knew what was happening, took her with the deep grunts and loud groans befitting a victorious V'ornn.

I don't want you telling anyone about this," Kurgan warned.
  "You're thinking of my father's recent prohibition against raping Kundalan females." Annon was bathing the four diagonal gouges the gyreagle's talons had made in his flesh.

Kurgan nursed his swollen side. "Stupid though it is, it's still the law."

The shallows of the creek where they squatted were filled with the shadows of grey rock, the brief swirl of turquoise V'ornn blood in the eddies. Of the tadpoles and the young Kundalan female there was no sign.

"I mean, the Khagggun do whatever they wish in the countryside far from the regent's prying eyes. Or so I have heard it softly spoken."

Annon had heard this as well, but he said nothing. Both boys inspected Annon's wound with growing curiosity.

"I like it not. This is terribly swollen." Kurgan pressed the reddened skin between the gouges. "By Enlil, I think he's left a bit of his claw inside you."

"I guess we had better try to get it out."

Kurgan nodded, removed a thin-bladed skinning knife from his belt, held it tip up. "Ready?"

Annon nodded, gritting his teeth. He averted his head as the tip slipped into the wound. He cried out, and again until Kurgan gave him a length of rawhide he used for stringing up his catch. Annon gratefully put it in his mouth and clamped down hard. Three minutes later, he had passed out.

Kurgan splashing water on his face brought him around.

"It's no use," his friend said. "I can gut a gimnopede, but I am no surgeon. The damned thing kept going deeper the more I pried. I cannot go on."

Annon felt wrapped in pain. "Thank Enlil, God of War!"

"I doubt there will be an infection," Kurgan observed. "We've cleaned the wounds thoroughly." He tore the sleeve from his blouse.

"Oww!" Annon cried. "Careful how tight you tie that!"

"Has to be tight. We don't want you bleeding as soon as we start to walk, do we?"

Annon took a couple of tentative breaths.

"How does it feel?"

"I won't die."

Kurgan chuckled. "Spoken like a true V'ornn."

Annon nodded, accepting the compliment. "We had better get going if we want to make it back home before supper."

"I was serious about what I said before." Kurgan put his hand on his friend's shoulder. "Before we leave let's make a pact. Let's swear the seigggon: we will never speak of this afternoon to anyone. Agreed?"

"Agreed," Annon said. They gripped each other's wrist in the seigggon, then allowed their okummmon to touch. A spark arced briefly between them.

Kurgan rose and helped Annon to his feet.

"What do you make of that bird?" Annon winced as they waded to shore. "I've never heard of one attacking a person."

Kurgan jerked his head in the direction of the avian corpse. "Well, one thing's for certain: it won't be attacking anything else."

Annon picked his way along the shoreline until he was standing over the gyreagle. With some difficulty he squatted down. "You're right," he said. "Look here, it's lost one of its talons. And there's fresh blood at the stump."

"To the victor go the spoils," Kurgan said. "Part of that damned bird is inside you now."

Annon stood. He was silent a long time. "To N'Luuura with it!" he growled. Then he turned and retraced his steps back to where his friend waited for him.

"That's right!" Kurgan threw his head back and laughed. "To N'Luuura with it!"

Together, they went slowly up the creek bank. The sun looked compressed in the thicker atmosphere closer to the horizon. After the cool water, the afternoon seemed hot and sticky and still. Gimnopedes twittered and flitted as they neared the first stand of sysal, but both boys had had their fill of the hunt for one day.

"So you think my father's law against raping Kundalan females is stupid, eh?" Annon said.

"Of course it's stupid. They're nothing more than soulless animals, right? Why shouldn't we take our pleasure from them when and where we please?"

"As stupid as his plans to build Za Hara-at, I suppose."

Kurgan turned his head and spat. "I have heard many V'ornn say that the idea is an abomination." He possessed the watchful eyes of a snow-lynx. Annon knew that he could be every inch the bully that his father was, but he also had the ingenuity of a chii-fox, the small mammal that haunted the middle reaches of the Djenn Marre. "Imagine! V'ornn and Kundalan working side by side! Idiotic! It would give the Kundalan the false impression that they are our equals."

"And yet, against all odds, the building is scheduled to begin within weeks." This wasn't the first time Annon had been required to defend the regent's policies, and he knew it would not be the last. But this was Kurgan, his hingatta-mate, his best friend. "You know what I think? I think my father is right. There is more to the Kundalan than we suspect."

"That will be the season!" Kurgan guffawed.

They had reached the trees now, and Annon was obliged to pause. He could not seem to catch a breath without pain flaming through him.

"Shall we take a break?" Kurgan asked.

They sat in silence for a time. Annon was thinking about the Kundalan female. He felt sick at heart. Her beautiful face, that haunted look in her eyes, the expression that had fleetingly passed between them all unspooled in his mind's eye, replaying over and over. He wondered where she had come from, where she was now. He hoped she had not run into a Khagggun pack.

He looked over at Kurgan, who was sharpening one of his bolt points. "You know, if I was Gyrgon, I probably

wouldn't need this bandage. I'd already have found a way
to heal the wound."

"The Gyrgon are technomages," Kurgan said, "not sorcerers."

"But aren't they always trying to beat death? I mean,
there's that saying of theirs: 'The mystery of death can only
be solved by the mastery of life.' "

"And you think you know what that means?"

"The Gyrgon are Great Caste just like us, only they have
been genetically altered before birth, their genes realigned,
their flesh and blood and bone embedded with tertium and
germanium circuits. They're all hooked into one gigantic
biomatrix, that's why they call themselves the Comradeship."

Kurgan laughed. "Stories, lies, half-truths. Don't kid yourself, my friend, *no one* knows a thing about the Gyrgon. Not
that I wouldn't give a couple of fingers to find out what
they're up to. They're far too secretive. I bet they're a complete mystery even to your father, and he's the only one I
know of who actually has any direct contact with them. All
they do is experiment in their laboratories all day. And what
if you're right?" He shuddered. "Do you really want to share
your thoughts with every other member of your caste? Ugh!"

Together, they rose and headed off. As they reached the
first straggle of sysal trees, Kurgan picked up the pace. "What
are they working on, that's what I want to know? Some
grand plan, but it's all a big mystery. If I were regent, I'd
find some way to make the Gyrgon tell me their secrets."

"You know," Annon said, "if there were no castes, the
Gyrgon wouldn't have the power, and we could all share
their secrets."

Kurgan grunted. "More Kundalan subversion from your
nanny." He picked up his two-brace of gimnopedes, waited
while Annon retrieved his longbow and yanked his string of
ice-hares off a tree branch. "Castes are synonymous with
civilization. They create order out of chaos. Just imagine if
the Khagggun could become Bashkir. What would military
men know of the fine art of being a merchant-banker? Or if
the Mesagggun wanted to become Khagggun. What do en-

gineers know of waging war? Or if Genomatekks, our physicians, wanted to be Bashkir? It's ridiculous! And, to take the most extreme example of all, what if the Tuskugggun wanted to become Gyrgon? I mean, *women* making the laws for all V'ornn? It's unthinkable! What do women know of laws, governing—or of business, for that matter? They bear children, they rear them, help educate them. This is what they were made for."

"They also compose our music, create our artwork, our books. They make the clothes—even forge the armor the Khagggun wear."

"I'll grant you all that, Annon. But so what? When was the last time you listened to music or looked at a piece of art?" *Two nights ago,* Annon thought, *when Giyan took me to her workroom when I could not fall asleep. I saw the sculptures she creates when she is not tending to me or to my father.* "Can you picture a woman *wearing* the armor she made?" Kurgan continued. "I, myself, would laugh myself into a stupor at such a ridiculous sight!"

"But see, here's the thing," he continued, as they made their way through the thick copse of sysal trees. "You're looking at the problem from the wrong end of the telescope. Being *realistic*, the only way to find out their secrets is to gain control of the Gyrgon themselves."

"Oh, really? And how would you go about doing that?"

"I have no idea. But there's got to be a way."

When Annon laughed his rib cage ached, but that scarcely stopped him. "That so? Send me a message in about three hundred years when you've figured it out."

Laughing together, the two friends disappeared into the dense western quadrant of the forest, heading back to Axis Tyr.

The city, white-pepper residences, cinnamon palaces, cinnabar warehouses, shops and ateliers of brilliantly colored floating cloth canopies, was laid out in both a logical and an artistic fashion fanning northward from the Sea of Blood. Gripped now in a mighty mailed fist crackling with ion energy. Music stilled, theaters dark and empty, festivals banned—a culture snuffed out like a flame. Walled, densely populated, churning, chained, and bound. The erosion from Kundalan to V'ornn wearing down Axis Tyr like a magnificent edifice half-buried in a hail of sand.

"Annon, your father wants you to spend the evening with him at the palace," Giyan said, as soon as the boys came through the door. It was as if she had been waiting anxiously for his return. Not that he noticed.

"Regard!" He held up his game. "I killed two ice-hares."

"With my longbow?" Giyan said as she took the weapon from him. "You never accessed your okummmon? Not once?"

Kurgan snorted as he dangled his two-brace of gimnopedes in their faces. "If he had, he would not have had to rely on luck."

"Luck has nothing to do with using the longbow," Giyan said. "It's a matter of skill."

Kurgan laughed scornfully. "As if I should listen to *you*!"

"It would not harm you to do so," Giyan said calmly.

Kurgan cocked his head. His face wore a smug grin. "Following that logic, I should listen also to the nattering of the three-fingered sloth as it swings from the trees."

"The three-fingered sloth holds secrets in her head you could not imagine."

"Oh, yes!" Kurgan was laughing outright. It was clear that he could not help himself. "Like how sore her tender parts are from defecating!"

Annon searched her face as Kurgan turned and went toward the scullery, there to throw his catch upon the thick wooden chopping block. Perhaps he was fearful of recognizing the same expression that he had seen on the girl's face in the creek.

But Giyan held her ground with the courage of a V'ornn. She wore the floor-length garment of deepest maroon—the regent's color—that all the women of the hingatta liiina do mori were required to wear. Color marked the uniform of the Tuskugggun. Around her hips wound a sash of night-black woven silk, another swath of the same silk held her thick copper-colored hair back from her face, binding it so that it hung in a heavy oval, the tip of which brushed her between her shoulder blades. She kept her head uncovered, unlike V'ornn women, who were required to wear the traditional sifeyn, a kind of heavy cowl. This was widely seen as an uncivilized act of defiance on her part. Decent Tuskugggun simply did not parade around in public with their heads bared. That kind of erotic provocation was best left for the bedroom—or for the Looorm—Tuskugggun whose business was bartering their bodies to V'ornn males of all castes. Just as shocking, the sleeveless dress also exposed the fine down on her arms. In short, to say that even after all these years she remained the object of intense curiosity was perhaps something of an understatement. Even here in hingatta liiina do mori, the Tuskugggun watched her covertly with a curious mixture of contempt and envy.

"Would you continue to laugh were I to best you with the longbow?" she said to Kurgan's back.

At this, the Tuskugggun looked up from their painting, designing, composing, forging, or the chores they were performing for their children. As with all Kundalan-built structures in Axis Tyr, the V'ornn had transformed the beautiful asymmetrical space with its central atrium open to the elements into utilitarian cubicles—in this case, to allow the eight women who made up the hingatta to work and live with their children. Where gardens had once grown more cubicles had been built, the myriad altars to Miina had been ripped out, and the maddening labyrinthine layout had been replaced by a mathematically precise pattern. As in every aspect of V'ornn society the sizes of the cubicles were dictated by a strict hierarchical pattern relating to a complex formula that measured skill, seniority, and kinship.

Giyan, being the caretaker of the regent's only son, was in possession of the largest suite of cubicles. This would have rankled the Tuskugggun even if she had not been Kundalan. The irony of this state of affairs was that Giyan had no great desire for the larger space, would have gladly exchanged it for another had such a thing been allowed in V'ornn society.

Now the Tuskugggun rose as one and entered the central atrium where she stood with the two boys. If Giyan was aware of their scrutiny, she did not reveal as much. Instead, she kept her gaze fixed upon the open doorway to the scullery.

Soon enough, Kurgan sauntered back with a nonchalance that only Annon identified as false. It was Kurgan who took especial note of the complete attention that had come to him like a high-profit deal. The power waxed inside of him like the sun at midday. "And how would you offer such implausible proof to V'ornn satisfaction?"

"I would propose a contest of arrows."

"A contest, eh?" There was that cunning glint of the snow-lynx in Kurgan's night-black eyes. "I thirst for contests."

"That is unsurprising," Giyan said neutrally. "No V'ornn can resist one."

"You being the expert." He went to where she had set the longbow against the limestone wall and hefted it. He grinned, sure of himself now. "On behalf of the V'ornn, I accept." He walked over to where Annon stood and held out the Kundalan longbow. "I will use my okummmon and your master-child will use this inferior—"

The words died in his throat as Giyan plucked the longbow out of his grasp. "Your contest is with me."

"With *you*? You cannot be serious."

"I am perfectly serious. You will use your aberrant V'ornn link and I will use *this*!" She lifted the longbow over her head.

"You mock me, slave! I reject this farce!"

"But no, you cannot." Giyan made a sweeping gesture. "In front of the entire hingatta you accepted."

"But I—"

"She is right, Kurgan," Annon said. "You accepted."

Kurgan felt betrayed. Why had Annon taken the Kundalan slave's side? Could he actually feel something for this inferior creature simply because she had suckled him, nursed him, tended to his needs? That is what Tuskugggun did with their lives. One did not take the side of the help. Perhaps Annon spoke so as a bit of mischief to humiliate him. In any event, Kurgan could see that he wasn't going to get any help from Annon. He looked around from face to face. It was clear to him that none of the Tuskugggun would raise a voice in protest, not even his mother. Well, what could you expect from *females*, he thought bitterly. They would not contradict Giyan directly; but behind her back they were oh so adept at tearing her to ribbons. And then another thought came to him: what if they were as afraid of the Kundalan sorceress as he was? This caused a sharp stab of anger to impale him. Afraid? Of a Kundalan? It was shameful! He was eldest son of Wennn Stogggul, Prime Factor of the Bashkir! He would take on any alien sorcery and crush it beneath his boot soles! He had the okummmon; he was linked with the Gyrgon!

"I accepted, it is truth," Kurgan said, glaring at Giyan. "The contest is sealed."

"Sealed, then," murmured the Tuskugggun and their offspring as one. "For good or for ill."

Idiots! Kurgan thought as he grabbed a handful of bolts. "Outside," he said, hoping it sounded like a command.

"Wherever you prefer," Giyan told him. She was about to strap a square quiver full of arrows across her back, when Kurgan stayed her hand.

"A moment," he said. He pulled the arrows out and inspected them, an offense that would have spawned a decades-long blood feud had she been a V'ornn. Though she was the regent's mistress and had been granted certain rights above other Kundalan, she was what she was, doubtless too backward to have the V'ornn's keenly civilized sense of honor and disgrace. Did an animal care where it shat? Of course not. And no civilized person expected it to.

Outside, the architectural order of the city was striking. Beneath a cloudless cerulean sky neat rows of two-story buildings of rose-and-blue limestone with kiln-fired green-glazed tile roofs lined cobbled streets that radiated from a central plaza like the spokes of a wheel or the rays of the sun. At the heart of this open space stood the regent's palace, a structure of bronze-and-gold spires, red-enameled minarets, carved cinnamon-colored walls whose overall appearance was altogether too ethereal for V'ornn tastes. A wide avenue, neatly bisecting the octagonal plaza, ran due south to Harborside with its kilometers-long Promenade where the Chuun River, which skirted the city to the west, spilled its seed into the Sea of Blood. Merchants and traders of every description filled Harborside, a rough-and-tumble neighborhood where could be found the only enclave of Sarakkon on the northern continent. The Sarakkon were a wild, piratical race inhabiting Kundala's southern continent. The V'ornn had long ago judged them insignificant, their land so devoid of decent natural resources it was not worth occupying. Besides, it contained pockets of radiation, making it unfit for even the hardiest of Khagggun. The V'ornn appeared to tolerate Sarakkonian presence, even occasionally trading with them, for the Gyrgon were possessed of an interest in materials of their manufacture.

One hundred and one years ago, when the V'ornn had come, no walls encircled Axis Tyr, there were no ramparts from which sentries might espy an oncoming enemy. You could see, depending on which section of the city you were in, the sysal forest to the east, the Great Phosphorus Marsh to the west, to the north the Chuun River flowing down from the foothills of the Djenn Marre, and to the south the Sea of Blood.

"So open!" the V'ornn shuddered when they first occupied the city. "So vulnerable to attack!" It was unthinkable for them to inhabit a place thus unfortified. In consequence, thousands of Kundalan had labored for a full year to construct a V'ornn wall around the city. The wall was hewn from massive blocks of the same black basalt the Kundalan has used to build the Promenade. The V'ornn, obsessed with their safety and security, drove the workers to their tolerance level and beyond. Hundreds of Kundalan perished, an unseemly and grisly foundation, but one which the V'ornn found to be another appropriate deterrent to insurrection.

The V'ornn wall was fully thirteen meters thick at its base, tapering to just over eight meters at its apex. It rose twenty meters above street level, making of the city a prison. The whereabouts of Kundalan, including their passage in and out of the three gates at the western, northern and eastern boundaries of the wall, was monitored through the use of an okuuut, a subcutaneous identity implant embedded in the flesh of the left palm. Each okuuut was synchronized to the individual beat-rate and harmonics of the Kundalan who wore it, making identification virtually instantaneous.

Now, all the members of hingatta liiina do mori were in the courtyard that fronted a wide avenue that ran straight to the regent's palace, a thousand meters to the north. Kurgan and Giyan stood facing one another while the others spread out in a semicircle around them. Almost immediately, as if to preempt her opponent, Giyan strode off fifty paces. With the point of one of her arrows she scored a thin vertical line in the rough bark of a sysal tree. "There," she said, loud enough for everyone to hear. "The target." As she watched Kurgan fitting a bolt to his okummmon she could see that her voice had drawn the attention of those nearby. By the time she returned to stand beside the V'ornn a sizable crowd had formed. And why not? It wasn't any day that a Kundalan—and the regent's mistress, at that!—challenged a V'ornn.

Giyan lifted an arm in Kurgan's direction. "You have the honor."

With an almost contemptuous sneer on his face, Kurgan lifted his arm to the horizontal. It was a casual motion, no more, surely, than if he were giving directions to a traveler who had lost his way. He barely seemed to look at the tree and the bolt was loosed in a whir and a blur. In an instant, it had sunk home right in the center of the line Giyan had scored in the bark.

"Perfect!" he cried in a tone of voice that brought instant applause from every V'ornn watching. Now he turned to Giyan and, in a coarse parody of a courtly manner, said: "The honor is now yours."

As Giyan took up her bow, he said: "It would give me pleasure to sight for you."

"I am certain it would," she answered amid a chorus of V'ornn laughter, a rough, raucous, beastly noise that grated on sensitive Kundalan ears. "But I do not intend to lose." This last brought a low, melodious soughing from the sprinkling of Kundalan in the crowd. Giyan took a moment to regard them out of the corner of her eye. She did not mistake their positive reaction for love of her. She was the regent's mistress. Perhaps they despised her an iota less than their V'ornn masters. But it was also entirely possible that they hated her even more, for surely they had marked her as a collaborator.

These were her people, and yet, when she looked at them, bedraggled and forlorn, she felt nothing—or next to nothing. Perhaps they were right about her, for the truth was that she seemed at home with the V'ornn—or at least with Eleusis and Annon. She did not long for her village of Stone Border, the chaotic furor of the packed-dirt streets, the constant tension from V'ornn raids, the terror of their random and capricious murders and beatings of innocent Kundalan.

Truth to tell, Giyan's Gift had made her feel like an outsider at the Abbey of Floating White where she and Bartta had been trained as Ramahan priestesses. Kundalan life had begun to break down, and the sporadic raids perpetrated by Khagggun packs terrorized the countryside into a state of semiparalysis. Here in Axis Tyr there was, at least, order and an overarching sense of purpose. Of course, it was V'ornn order and V'ornn purpose. But the regent, Eleusis Ashera, was unlike the majority of V'ornn, on that fact she would stake her life. He did not view Kundalan as inferior, as slaves disposable as food, animals without souls (this was the V'ornn view of the universe, not the Kundalan, who knew that every animal possessed unique knowledge as well as a unique soul). This was why he had treated her as his love, not as his property as the other V'ornn supposed. In the utter privacy of the palace, he allowed her to worship Miina, to mix the potions and poultices that healed and mended him and Annon, to practice the element-magic that was her birthright. Above all, he did not question her Kundalan heart, but rather sought to understand it. These were, among others, their secrets, each one of which, should it fall on an unfriendly or jealous ear, would doom him even—he felt—with the Gyrgon who held him in such great esteem.

And this was why he had been intent on creating the great experiment of Za Hara-at—had risked the enmity of Wennn Stogggul along with many other V'ornn of both Great and Lesser Castes—so that he could fashion the first city in which V'ornn and Kundalan traded freely, exchanged information, learned from one another.

Giyan's reverie was abruptly terminated as she became aware that every eye in the crowd was focused on her. And what a throng it had become! She drew an arrow from her quiver, stroked her fingertips along its smooth, straight length, notched it to her bow.

"I don't know why you bother," Kurgan said. "You will have to split my bolt to win. Your arrow cannot scratch V'ornn alloy. Concede defeat now and avoid unnecessary humiliation."

Giyan smiled sweetly, aimed at the tree and pulled back the bowstring to its very limit. A hush fell over the crowd. Then she raised the bow until the arrow was pointing just shy of vertical and let fly.

"Are you insane?" Kurgan said as the arrow arced into the sky. He turned to the expectant crowd. "She is insane, my friends. You can see with your own eyes. Utterly and completely insane."

The arrow, having reached the apogee of its arc, now headed back downward. It struck her as odd—almost comical—the V'ornn's long, shining, hairless skulls moving in concert as they monitored its descent. With a soft, musical *thwang!* the arrow buried itself at the foot of the tree bole.

"Aha! Not much more could be expected from a feeble Kundalan attempt," Kurgan cried, already beginning his victory march to the sysal tree. He was brought up short by Giyan's voice. "Do not touch the arrow," she warned. But

Kurgan, emboldened by the crowd and his triumph, ignored her. Reaching the foot of the tree, he grabbed the arrow to pull it from the ground, but immediately let out with such a cry that the spectators expelled a collective gasp.

"Yow! It's hot!" Kurgan waved his reddened hand aloft. "The thing is burning up!"

Indeed, there appeared to be movement at the arrow's feathered end. A haze had appeared—the kind that made the air dense and crazed with heat ripples. Were the feathers melting away? No, as they craned their necks the spellbound spectators saw that the feathers had been transformed into a vine of a green so deep it bordered on black. This vine very rapidly grew runners that sought out the bole of the sysal tree and wrapped around it. As they climbed, they grew notched leaves of a shape no one—neither Kundalan nor V'ornn—had ever seen before. In no time at all, the runners reached the cut Giyan had made in the bark. As if with a mind of their own, they twined around the V'ornn bolt. In a trice, it was completely engulfed.

"What is this?" Kurgan stood with hands on hips. "What is going on here?"

Giyan, enwreathed in a small smile, pulled at the runners. Even as they wrapped themselves around her slender wrist they began to crumble to a silvery powder until, quite as rapidly as they had appeared, they had vanished. The stunned throng crept forward, the murmuring among them rising to an incredulous babble. For there was no sign of the bolt Kurgan had shot into the tree.

Giyan plucked the arrow from the ground, but before she could replace it in her quiver Kurgan had snatched it from her. His fingers traced the arc of the feathers, the long, straight wooden shaft, the metal point which, now that he looked at it closely, had the exact shape of the vine leaves.

"What manner of magic is this?" he muttered.

"Sorcery, yes." Giyan took possession of the arrow. "Kundalan sorcery." Her piercing blue eyes were firmly fixed on Kurgan. "Dark sorcery . . . Powerful sorcery. The contest is over. I have won."

"Won? Won?" Kurgan howled. "How could you win? My bolt struck the tree at its heart. Your arrow never—"

"Here is my arrow." Giyan raised it over her head for all to see. "Where is your bolt, Kurgan?"

"You *know* where my bolt is!" He leapt to the tree. "If you require proof, I will show you! Here is where the bolt I shot—" He was brought up short as he ran his hands down the bark in an increasing frenzy. "Where is it?" he cried. "Where is the cut?"

"What cut?" Giyan asked in a silky voice, for there was no sign of the bite the bolt had made in the tree. Save for the vertical line Giyan had scored in the bark, the tree appeared exactly as it had before the contest was called.

3

Portents, Secrets, and Lies

Enter, Morcha," the regent Eleusis Ashera said effusively. "Today we have much to celebrate!"

"Regent?" Kinnnus Morcha was a huge, hulking V'ornn with a deep scarred crease along the left side of his shining skull. The four gold suns on his purple silicon polymer uniform marked him as the commandant of the Haaarkyut, Khagggun handpicked by Eleusis and trained by Morcha himself, loyal and answerable only to the regent.

The day's business at an end, the two V'ornn found themselves alone in the Great Listening Hall of the regent's palace. It was an asymmetrical space—roughly oval in shape—that the V'ornn found unsettling. A gallery ran around the perimeter one story up. This gallery was capped by a plaster ceiling held aloft by alabaster columns set on black-granite plinths. However, the entire center of the hall was open to the elements. Now, late-afternoon lights bathed the three highly polished heartwood posts set in a perfect equilateral triangle that spanned three meters on a side.

Eleusis roamed within the precincts of this imaginary triangle as his Haaar-kyut commander watched silently. He often did this, in a vain attempt to fathom its meaning. Was it religious, spiritual, practical? Even the Ramahan he had consulted, even the ones who had been interrogated by Kinnnus Morcha in the bowels of the palace, had no explanation. How old were these posts? Could they have predated even the palace?

"Line-General, do you have any idea what the Kundalan used these posts for?"

Kinnnus Morcha shrugged. "My suspicion is that they were part of a weapon."

"Spoken like a true Khaggun." Eleusis pursed his lips. "If so, then why was it never used against us?" He shook his head. "No, the Gyrgon assure me that the posts were never used as a weapon. What, then? Are they decoration? Part of a temple to Miina? We have been on Kundala one hundred and one years and we still do not know." He cocked his head to one side. "Does that not strike you as odd?"

"To be honest, regent, I give the Kundalan thought only when I have to kill one."

Eleusis nodded, as if he fully expected that answer. "Still, it makes its point."

The Line-General waited several moments before he said: "What point, regent?"

"That no matter how much we know, there is always more to learn." Eleusis strode swiftly out of the triangle, raising an arm for Morcha to follow him. They passed through an open doorway into the regent's private anteroom.

Eleusis could no longer keep the smile of satisfaction off his face. "Today's case in point. I have just received a communique from the site of Za Hara-at. They have signed the last contract!"

"Contracts," Kinnnus Morcha scoffed. "You should have let me take my wing of Khaggun and dealt with the Korrush tribes the way we have dealt with the local Kundalan." The

Korrush was the local name of the Great Northern Plains, 250 kilometers northeast of Axis Tyr. To its north was the Great Rift in the Djenn Marre, to its east was the beginning of the Great Voorg, the vast, trackless desert.

"And have the added expense of stationing a permanent pack of Khagggun at the site to ensure against vandalism and random attacks?" The regent shook his head. "Dealing with them this way makes far more sense, Line-General. Now they will join our work crews. At Za Hara-at goodwill is everything."

"Pardon my bluntness, regent, but what is goodwill to a Khagggun?"

Eleusis laughed good-naturedly as he slapped the Line-General on his broad back. "Imagine it. V'ornn and Kundalan working side by side to create what is sure to become the greatest trading city on the planet. So much for Prime Factor Stogggul and his reactionary cabal." He was grinning from ear to ear. "It seems as if allowing Kundalan businesses to flourish in the same garden as V'ornn trading houses will be a most lucrative endeavor."

Eleusis, tall and slender as a milkweed, filled two shanstone goblets made at liiina do mori, thrust one at the Line-General. "Join me, Kinnnus!" He laughed. "What makes you so glum?"

"I am not—pardon me for saying this, regent. But I am unused to hearing myself called by my given name alone. It is not the V'ornn way."

"No. It is a Kundalan custom, Kinnnus, and a fine one at that. It tends to engender a feeling of trust."

"Trust never comes easily to a Khagggun, regent."

"Neither does change, Kinnnus."

The two men were standing in the center of the alien octagonal room, an antechamber off the Great Listening Hall of the regent's palace—what the Kundalan had called Middle Palace. The floor was pure white marble over which smooth rugs of V'ornn manufacture had been set in a precise mathematical pattern that complemented the geometric pattern in the rugs themselves. Light came not from the traditional

Kundalan filigreed lanterns, but from eye-shaped fusion lamps manufactured in V'ornn power plants established decades ago. This cold, revealing light illuminated the vaulted ceiling in a manner inconceivable to the Kundalan. It was dark blue, decorated with gold stars and streaking comets. At its zenith, intricately carved, were the five moons of Kundala, each with the face of a beautiful woman—all aspects of the Goddess Miina. Trios of white-marble pilasters, delicately veined with vitreous obsidian, rose up each wall like vines in a garden, their apexes carved into the shape of stylized fronds. The tall triple-arched Kundalan windows had been something of a problem. The commandant had suggested mortaring them up for security reasons, but Eleusis had come up with a more elegant solution. He had had tapestries woven by the finest Tuskugggun artisans hung over the windows, thereby placating Kinnnus Morcha and pleasing himself, for it was told and retold by the Khagggun of the Haaar-kyut that the regent could be seen from time to time peeling back the tapestries to peer out the windows. What he was observing was a source of constant comment.

In any event, these remarkable tapestries depicted, in one manner or another, the endless saga of V'ornn wandering. For the V'ornn were a nomadic people, their homeworld an uninhabitable blackened cinder ever since the binary star that had been their sun, their light, their warmth had gone nova. That was many eons past. Now they wandered the stars to conquer, to live for as long a time as the Gyrgon required to ask their mysterious questions of whatever alien place they were in, and then they were gone, never to return. For the V'ornn there was no possibility of going back; they pressed forward into uncharted space. When a group of them found a world rich in natural resources like Kundala, members of the leading Bashkir Consortia were dispatched from the main fleet moving in eternal convoy on the ion currents of deep space to stake their claim, to reap the rewards of costly space travel.

Such was the artistry of these tapestries that all the pathos and yearning and mystery inherent in V'ornn culture were interwoven into the scenes as carefully as were the jewel-tone fabrics. Utilitarian V'ornn furnishings made of metal alloys—lightweight but strong—had replaced the ornate, curlicued wooden pieces of the Kundalan. As Kinnnus Morcha had said when he had first seen the lounges and chairs, they looked as if they would splinter the moment a V'ornn sat in them. But then Kinnnus Morcha, like most V'ornn, found nothing esthetically pleasing in the alien architecture. Why, even here in the central palace of the city, none of the rooms seemed large enough for a V'ornn's sensibility. And there was so much wasted space! Colonnaded terraces, sweeping agate staircases, filigreed cornices, plinths and friezes, ornate statues and strange carvings, lush gardens that mirrored the mazelike interior—and everywhere shrines and symbols to the accursed Goddess, Miina.

Unusually, the thick heartwood doors to the regent's private quarters stood slightly ajar. Kinnnus Morcha took a discreet look at an area of the palace that even he, as commandant of the Haaar-kyut, had never seen. Some privileges were forever beyond almost all of the Lesser Castes.

Eleusis turned and shut the doors firmly. The regent was dressed formally in white and gold: low boots, tight trousers, metallic-mesh blouse beneath his waist-length, braided, high-collared jacket, the sleeves cut short enough to expose his okummmon. He glanced at Kinnnus Morcha's goblet. "Come, come. You haven't touched your drink. We must remedy that." He lifted his goblet high. "To Za Hara-at! My noble experiment!"

"To our enemies!" Kinnnus Morcha said in the traditional Khagggun salute as his free hand cupped the pommel of the double-bladed shock-sword that hung through a titanium clip at his left hip. Though the Khagggun used many highly sophisticated instruments of attack, the shock-sword remained their weapon of choice when it came to hand-to-hand combat. "May destruction possess their houses!" His wide face, the color of curdled cream, contracted as he quaffed his drink. "Ah! A Kundalan cloudy rakkis! No V'ornn fire-grade numaaadis for the regent!"

Eleusis laughed. "You know me too well, I'm afraid."

"Ah, no chance of that, regent. What Khagggun knows the mind of a member of the Great Castes?"

Eleusis nodded as he refilled their goblets. "I grant you there is a cultural gulf between us, but I value you nonetheless for your keen insight."

Kinnnus Morcha fairly bowed. "The regent is generous with his praise."

The regent, eyeing him judiciously, returned the goblet to him. "You have served me well, Kinnnus. I know that your personal feelings for the Za Hara-at experiment are mixed."

"I am Khagggun, regent. I have no use for inferior life-forms."

"Nevertheless you carried out my orders to be even-handed with the Kundalan, to keep the Khagggun raids to a minimum, and ban altogether the hunting parties that killed Kundalan for the sheer sport of it."

"I live to serve my regent."

There was a small pause while the regent led Kinnnus Morcha to the far side of the antechamber, where they arranged themselves before the Kundalan shrine to the Goddess Miina. It was composed of a plinth ornately carved out of a block of solid carnelian heavily striated with gold ore. Above it, on the wall were high-relief carvings of the Five Sacred Dragons of Miina. Nowadays, the plinth served as base for a selection of Eleusis' favorite objects: a copy of *The Book of Mnemonics* bound between incised copper covers; a thorn-gem he had secured from the perilous underworlds of Corpius Segundus; the preserved birth-caul of his son; the skeleton of his original okummmon, which had been replaced by the singular purple germanium one, which was his right as regent; a white rose, caught at the peak moment of its life and kept in that state of perfection by the enigmas of Gyrgon science. This last was a gift from the technomages on the day of his Ascension.

In being brought before the plinth, Kinnnus Morcha knew he was being given a signal. This was the place where the regent conducted his most private interviews.

Eleusis cleared his throat. "Kinnnus, let me be frank. I know what a difficult assignment I gave you. Prime Factor Stogggul is a most difficult personage to deal with in the best of circumstances. Keeping an eye on him could not have been fun."

"I will match the regent's frankness," Kinnnus Morcha replied. "Being a spy comes naturally to me. The helm of battle, the mask of a spy, they are interchangeable to me. It is well you had me keep an eye on Wennn Stogggul. He still chafes under your kindness toward the conquered."

"But you do not."

"As I say, the regent chose wisely."

"I am gratified." Eleusis sighed. "I don't mind telling you that Wennn Stogggul concerns me."

Kinnnus Morcha sat forward. "In what way, regent?"

"Ah, ever the loyal hunting dog!" Eleusis laughed at the Line-General's dark expression and shrugged. "Well, one hears things. One employs people to watch and to listen and to report." The regent paused for a moment, staring into the darkness of the smoke-blackened fireplace. "So, then, it has come to me that Stogggul is gathering support to petition the Gyrgon for my ouster."

Kinnnus Morcha frowned. "I have heard nothing of this, regent, and I believe I would have. Are you certain of this?"

"My source is."

The Line-General shook his head. "But that is monstrous, regent! It is unprecedented! He must be stopped before—"

"Which is why we are having this conversation."

"We must never forget that it was Wennn Stogggul who was your competitor for the regent's mantle. By all he says and does it seems clear that he will never forget nor forgive the sting of his defeat. His animosity—"

"Is of a somewhat more *personal* nature than that."

"Well, yes, of course, regent. Who does not know of the intense rivalry between your Consortium and his? On Nieobus Three, the planet we conquered before we arrived here, our fathers were always at each other's throats, always seeking ways in which to take business out of the other's pockets.

The Prime Factor's father finally prevailed, driving your father's Consortium to the brink of bankruptcy. Until you stepped in, regent, and made the deal for sole mining and export rights to salamuuun, the so-called plant of the tomb."

"Tell me, Kinnnus, have you ever tried salamuuun?"

"Once." Despite himself, the Line-General shuddered. "I felt as if this life I was living was but an illusion, and the Truth was . . ."

"Was what, my friend?" There was an odd intensity in Eleusis' eyes that the Line-General did not catch.

"I don't know." Kinnnus Morcha's huge head swiveled, he looked away for a moment as he struggled with disturbing thoughts. "It made me think that the Truth was something I could not fathom."

"Or did not want to see?"

Kinnnus Morcha nodded. "Perhaps."

"Something terrible, then."

The Line-General shook his head. "Something *different*." His huge shoulders shrugged. "In any event, it was an experience I have no wish to repeat."

"It is fortunate for my Consortium that you are in the minority, Kinnnus."

Kinnnus Morcha looked up. "Ah, yes. The Ashera fortune lies in salamuuun."

"And, ultimately, its power." The regent's eyes swept around the room. "That is what Wennn Stogggul truly desires: the secret to salamuuun—where it is mined, who I forged my deal with, how he can wrest it from my Consortium." He paused. "But there is something more."

Kinnnus Morcha sat ramrod-straight. In the light falling from the fusion lamps the scars on his skull appeared deeper, more grievous. Despite being all ears now he had the good sense not to prompt the regent. The Line-General was a patient V'ornn—a patience born and bred in the intense cauldron of interplanetary warfare. He was a V'ornn who could sense victory when those around him were stumbling in starless night.

"We were friends, once, Prime Factor Stogggul and I. Did you know that?"

"I did not, regent."

"Well, it's true." The regent rose and stood before the mantle. He picked up *The Book of Mnemonics,* turned it over and back again. "He gave me this, a long time ago, when we were still striplings on Kraelia. Had it made for me. For the day of my Channeling." He was speaking of the rite whereby every V'ornn male becomes an adult. "Yes, we were good friends—until we locked skulls over salamuuun." He put the book back. "Then a bitter rivalry that had lain unacknowledged between us rose up and raged out of control. His father died attempting to find the source of salamuuun."

"His spacecraft was sabotaged, so the story goes."

"Well, that is the Prime Factor's version, anyway." The regent's gaze locked on to the Line-General's. "Another is that the elder Stogggul's greed made him imprudent. His craft got caught in a gravity well and imploded."

"Do you know the truth, regent?"

"It is my experience that people define their own truths. Which, I surmise, is behind the overwhelming popularity of salamuuun. However, I will tell you this: there was no need to sabotage the craft because the old man was on a fool's errand."

Though he longed to ask the regent what he meant, Kinnnus Morcha held his tongue, knowing that Eleusis would answer no questions on that subject. As a high-ranking Khaggun, he well knew the power of knowledge. In battle against any enemy, knowledge was everything.

Eleusis turned his back to the plinth, broke into the other's thoughts. "I have told you this history for a reason. I want you to understand that while Wennn Stogggul and I are business rivals, I am certain that his bitter and unrelenting vocal opposition to my policies is personal in nature."

"I understand completely, regent."

"I doubt that you do." Eleusis smiled wanly, reached up, and touched one of the sculpted Five Dragons on the wall.

"You see the niche here in this dragon's mouth? When Annon was young I would find him here, teetering on the top
rung of a ladder with his hand in the dragon's mouth. What
did he find so fascinating, I asked myself. What did he expect
to find?" The regent looked at Kinnnus Morcha for a long
time; then he looked past him. "I have ordered Giyan to bring
my son here tonight."

"Do you fear for him?"

The regent's gaze locked with the Khagggun's. "I fear
nothing, Kinnnus. Our fate is our fate; it is already written.
If you had tried salamuuun again, you would know that. No,
I am merely being prudent. For the time being, at least, I
want my entire family under the protection of the Haaar-
kyut."

"Absolutely, regent."

"You will see to my family personally. My wife, though
she shamed herself, is dead, but I still care about the children."

"It will be done."

Eleusis nodded. "I know it will." He downed the last of
his drink. He guided the commandant through a discreetly
narrow-arched doorway. They emerged onto a wide veranda
banded in gold marble, which overlooked the regent's star-
rose garden. The cerulean sky had taken on a golden hue
down near the horizon and just a hint of fair-weather cloud
rode overhead. For some time, Eleusis stood against the fret-
worked balustrade, gazing downward, breathing deeply. His
hands were clasped loosely behind his back, but he stood
ramrod-straight as if he were more Khagggun than Bashkir.
His cool, appraising eyes swept over every corner of his garden: the varieties of climbing star-rose with their luscious
blooms, glossy leaves, and woody, thornless vines.

"How peaceful it is here, Kinnnus. How deeply satisfying
that peacefulness is."

Kinnnus Morcha, standing beside him, had nothing useful
to say, so he said nothing.

The regent went on: "It used to be that our only danger
came from other races, unknown encounters. Now I see that

unless we are very careful, our own history may very well take a chunk out of our tender parts. Times are changing. I feel it in my bones. There are stirrings and portents—"

"Portents!" Kinnnus Morcha fairly spat. "That is Kundalan talk. I do not believe in *portents*. I believe in war, in statistics. Since you have succeeded your father, resistance activity within Axis Tyr has dropped eighty percent."

Eleusis Ashera smiled. "Like the threat of your strong arm, Kinnnus, portents do exist. Giyan has shown me this. And these portents speak of great changes."

Kinnnus Morcha grunted. The regent seemed to the Line-General to be almost eerily calm. He felt, unexpectedly, a welling up of affection. "You will forgive an old Khagggun his grumblings, regent. I meant no offense."

"I took no offense, my friend. But I fear that unless we are extremely vigilant, we are doomed to repeat our most grievous mistakes."

There was a small, uncomfortable silence.

"I mention the portents because I want you to be on your guard to—"

Eleusis broke off, his body suddenly tense. His okummmon had begun to hum with a sound beyond description— a song/no-song that lapped at the very edge of audibility like the ocean at the foundation of a seawall. The atmosphere grew preternaturally still and preternaturally hot. A bead of sweat bloomed like a nocturnal flower on Kinnnus Morcha's skull, ran down the deep crease.

Eleusis turned abruptly. "Kinnnus, you will have to excuse me."

"N'Luuura, it is the Summoning." Kinnnus Morcha gulped the last of the cloudy rakkis and with a *clink!* that rang through the garden set his goblet atop the balustrade. "I will escort you myself to the Temple of Mnemonics, regent."

Eleusis gave a curt, almost absentminded nod.

The two men returned silently through the doorway to the antechamber, past guards of the Haaar-kyut, past handmaidens and servants, past members of the regent's staff. All inclined their heads to the left in deference to him. Their footfalls echoed on the marble; their shadows chased themselves along the corridors, into chambers large and small, through pools of mellowing sunlight, patches of shade made pale by veinless white marble, at length out through the high, magnificent sea-green-shanstone and gold-jade gates.

Kinnnus Morcha was relieved to be out of that alien place that so profoundly disturbed him. Not that he would admit this to anyone, but he felt the silence there—what the regent spoke of as peacefulness—like a weight upon his shoulders, like sets of alien eyes watching him, judging his moves, weighing his fate in some unseen court of alien law he could not begin to fathom. A late-afternoon breeze broke like surf against his hairless skull. They mounted single-seat hover-pods, punched in their destination, and sped across the city at a height of twenty-three meters.

When the V'ornn had first taken Axis Tyr, the Gyrgon had installed themselves in a complex of buildings that had housed the Abbey of Listening Bone, the Ramahan's main religious sanctuary. Its occupation was a stunning and dispiriting blow to the Kundalan—one that, in Eleusis' opinion, at least, had been calculated down to the last decimal point. But then the Gyrgon were masters at inflicting humiliation and pain both physical and psychological.

"I do not know how you do it," Kinnnus Morcha said when they had set down in front of the Temple. "Were it I— were I Summoned before the Gyrgon—my tender parts would be shrunken like an old V'ornn's."

The regent had to smile. "This from the valorous Khaggun who fought in the First Wave at Argggedus 3, who slew nineteen Krael at the battle of Yesssus, who defended for twenty-four sidereal cycles the Gyrgon enclave on Phareseius Prime, who has, it is rumored, come face-to-face with the Centophennni?"

"It is instinctive, regent. Every time the Gyrgon speak my blood freezes."

"I always said you had good instincts, Kinnnus." With that, the regent Eleusis swept through the arched portals of the former Abbey of Listening Bone.

* * *

The V'ornn Temple of Mnemonics sat atop the only hill within the precincts of the city. It was in the Western Quarter. Up until the coming of the V'ornn it had been an area housing the most influential Kundalan families. Strangely, however, the V'ornn found these houses no larger than those in other parts of the city. This perfect symmetry went against V'ornn notions of hierarchy and status. After the Kundalan were killed or displaced, the most wealthy of the Bashkir moved in, enlarging and renovating the houses as befit their status in V'ornn society.

This essential change in the fascinating, alien structure of the city did not please Eleusis, for he had come to see the Kundalan in an altogether different light than did his fellow V'ornn. But then in so many ways he seemed not to fit into the rather monolithic V'ornn mold. It was a constant source of wonder to him that the Gyrgon had chosen him to be regent. Stogggul would have been the obvious, the expected choice. But then, he reminded himself, the Gyrgon rarely did the expected. Not that he, Eleusis Ashera, was ill suited to be regent. Quite the opposite, in fact. But that the Gyrgon tolerated—even at times condoned—his unconventional ideas was a mystery he doubted he would ever solve.

As soon as he stepped through the gates, he was inside the Portal. A misty greyness, luminous as the shell of a sea-snail, engulfed him. He had been here often enough that he knew what to do. Even so, a part of his mind still quailed, wanted to run screaming back out into the last of the sun-shine, where Kinnnus Morcha was patiently waiting. Eleusis forced his legs to move, walking forward, looking neither to the left nor to the right. A great moaning arose, as of a violent tempest, gaining in volume. Still, he moved forward, not only because it was his duty as regent but also because he knew it was a test. The Portal never looked or felt the same as it had on previous visits. Each time he was Summoned, there was a different sort of fright awaiting him. *The Gyrgon enjoy observing you,* he told himself. *The Gyrgon distill my fears, brew them up like vintage numaaadis. It is*

*some form of twisted game they enjoy playing, perhaps to
engrave their superiority upon me, so that I will never forget
my place, never overstep the boundaries they have set up.*

Darkness, and an intense sense of vertigo. Eleusis was
deathly afraid of falling. As a child of four, he had fallen
from a window ledge while his mother had been painting.
His father had been so furious that he had banished her from
every hingatta on the planet. Eleusis had never seen her
again; he had been raised by his father's lover, a Tuskuggun
who had kept him on a short tether and never let him climb
upon a windowsill.

Wind howled and when he made the mistake of looking
down, he saw the floor far below him. At once, he broke out
into a cold sweat. *It is only a dream*, he told himself sternly.
Only a vision from your own nightmare. But he could not
stop sweating. His hearts hammered in his chest, he felt the
urge to spit, and his pulse rate was erratic. He paused on his
path, took three deep breaths. The urge to turn and run was
a terrible weight upon him. *I am that I am*, he said silently.
*I am on Kundala, in the Western District of Axis Tyr, in the
Portal of the Temple of Mnemonics. The Gyrgon may have
control of my senses but they do not have control of my mind.*

He wiped his wet palms down his trousers and moved on.
His mind screamed in protest, certain that he was going to
fall to the floor below. He walked stiffly, carefully, deviating
neither to the left nor to the right. And with each step, his
fears lessened. He did not fall. Thank Enlil, he did not fall!

Stars came out, and a cold blue moon the size of Kundala's spotted sun appeared high in the sky. Eleusis, traversing quartz-flecked sand dunes, recognized that moon. It was
the moon hanging in the night sky of Corpius Segundus.
Ahead of him loomed the gargantuan sloping gates to the
underworlds.

Enter, a voice commanded in his skull. At least, it seemed
to be in his skull even though he knew that it actually emanated from his okummmon. *The time of Summoning is at
hand.*

If this were, indeed, Corpius Segundus he knew what

would be waiting for him. There was a scar on his left shoulder—a deep, livid indentation scooped out of his flesh. The underworlds were habited by thirteen species of raptor—at least, that was the number the V'ornn had cataloged—each more deadly than the previous one. It had been no mean feat to bring back a thorn-gem, and he had paid the price. The eight-legged razor-raptor had taken its pound of flesh even through his battle armor.

The sloping Portal blotted out the stars, then the moon. A remembered stink assaulted his nostrils, making his stomachs grind and heave. It was an evil place, the underworlds.

"Why did the V'ornn come here, regent?"

He stopped, peered through the dim light, ruddy with the fine, choking dust of the caverns.

"What was your purpose?"

An ill-defined shape loomed before him.

"You could not defeat the denizens of these underworlds; the thorn-gems herein were of no practical use to you."

An evil-smelling razor-raptor lounged against an outcropping of rock. It leered at him with a smile bristling with triangular teeth made expressly for ripping and tearing flesh from bone.

"And yet you came. Why was that, Ashera Eleusis?"

This was no Corpius Segundus razor-raptor, Eleusis knew. Indeed, it was no raptor of any kind. Only the Gyrgon used the ancient form of address that put the family name first. "Because it was there," he said.

The creature before him repeated his answer, drawing out each word as if to savor its meaning. "Yes. Very good. I believe you are correct." And immediately thereafter, the razor-raptor dissolved like smoke. In its place stood a Gyrgon.

"Summoned, I am come to you, to hear and to serve," Eleusis said in the ritual greeting.

Instead of completing the ritual, the Gyrgon detached himself from the cavern wall. "Do you know me, regent?"

Eleusis peered through the artificially manufactured haze.

"I believe you are Nith Sahor. I was before you at the previous Summoning."

"That is correct."

"I have never been Summoned by the same Gyrgon twice."

"Do you know that for a fact, regent? We can change our shapes, you know."

Eleusis licked his lips. "I had heard something to that effect."

Nith Sahor stood unnervingly still. He was perhaps a full meter taller than Eleusis. He was clad all in black, wrapped in a tasseled greatcoat. His eyes had pupils like star sapphires; they seemed to follow you without him having to turn his head. And what a head he had! His skull was the color of pale amber. From the edge of the occipital ridge to the base of his massive neck a visible latticework of tertium and germanium circuits was embedded in the skin. No one knew whether the Gyrgon were born this way or whether they came by it in some horrific postnatal operation.

"Tell me something, regent, do you serve the Gyrgon?"

"Yes, Nith Sahor. In everything, I serve their wants and needs."

"Indeed."

"Do you disbelieve me?"

"Yes, regent, I do. You have taken a Kundalan female to your bed. You allow her to worship this Goddess of theirs, to make her potions and her poultices, to whisper in your ear when darkness is absolute and the formal business of state is at an end." Nith Sahor's expression was entirely unreadable. "In addition, you conspire secretly with the Pack-Commander Rekkk Hacilar to keep the Kundalan resistance warned of our hunting parties." He crossed his massive arms across his equally massive chest. "Do you deny any of this, regent?"

"Who speaks against me? Prime Factor Stogggul?"

"You will answer my question, regent!"

Nith Sahor did not raise his voice, did not move a muscle. Nevertheless, Eleusis jumped as the bite of hyperexcited electrons was transmitted through his okummmon into the nerves in his arm.

"I deny nothing," he said calmly. This was yet another test; it must be. "What you say is truth."

"And in these matters do you discern the will of the Gyrgon?"

"You have not stopped me from being with Giyan. Or from my friendships with Rekkk Hacilar and Hadinnn SaTrryn."

"Again, I suggest that you answer my question."

Eleusis made a point of not looking at his okummmon. He felt a certain tension in the backs of his legs and willed his body to relax. "It pleases me to be with her. It pleases her to do these things, and thus I am doubly pleased."

"And as for the Pack-Commander?"

"Does the entire Comradeship know?"

"You would not be here; you would not be regent if it did."

Eleusis let go a breath he had been holding. "Rekkk Hacilar, Hadinnn SaTrryn, and I are of a like mind when it comes to the Kundalan."

"So, then, when you claim that in all things you serve our wants and needs you are a liar."

"I am so only if you believe it, Nith Sahor."

There was a long silence. The artificial wind howled through the caverns, the artificial stirrings of the artificial raptors echoed off the artificial stone walls. Nith Sahor raised his arms and the underworlds of Corpius Segundus vanished.

"I do *not* believe it, regent. That is why you are Summoned before me."

Eleusis found that they were in a chamber of the Temple of Mnemonics. It was circular, high up. Through the delicately triple-arched window he could see dusk approaching, smell the familiar scents of Kundala. The walls indicated that this room had been a sanctuary, for each section of wall held a carving of one of the Five Sacred Dragons of Kundalan culture. Significantly, Nith Sahor had not covered them with V'ornn artwork. Just as significantly, the Gyrgon had kept all the original Kundalan furniture. The single V'ornn feature was a white oval cage within which sat a beautiful multi-colored teyj, preening its fours wings one by one. As he moved, the bird paused in its fluffing to fix Eleusis in its golden eye.

"It is good to be back on Kundala," Eleusis said.

"Curious," Nith Sahor said. "I entertained the selfsame thought." The Gyrgon raised a hand clad in an odd metallic mesh about which many terrible myths had formed. Eleusis tried not to look at the finely worked chain mail. "Be at ease, regent. You are my guest."

Eleusis did not know whether he was more surprised to see Kundalan furniture here or by what Nith Sahor said. "Forgive me, I am at a bit of a loss. I have never been a guest of the Gyrgon before."

"Perhaps it is simply that we never told you before."

Eleusis looked up. "Is that a joke?"

"Do Gyrgon make jokes?"

"I have no idea," Eleusis admitted.

As Eleusis observed the Gyrgon, he had the distinct impression that this Summoning was going to be unique. Before, they had consisted of giving a report on current affairs, being peppered with blunt, difficult questions, being given orders to carry out, and being summarily dismissed. Bantering with a Gyrgon was distinctly new to him.

As if to give added credence to this train of thought, Nith Sahor said: "Regent, I want you to tell me about desire."

"Desire?"

"Precisely that."

Eleusis was struggling hard to keep up with the strange twists and turns of this Summoning. "I am hardly qualified to tell a Gyrgon—"

"Oh, but you are, regent. *Eminently* qualified." Nith Sahor fingered the wide cuff on his right wrist. "But perhaps you suspect me of being disingenuous." He raised a mailed hand to forestall Eleusis' response. "Did you know, regent, that the Gyrgon are neither male nor female?"

"Neither . . ." Eleusis felt as if his mouth was full of silicon.

"We are both."

"I . . . I did not know, Nith Sahor."

"Of course you didn't. It is a secret we Gyrgon keep to ourselves. As such, desire is . . . alien to all of us—at least, to *almost* all of us. Occasionally—very rarely—there is an unexpected and unexplained genetic mutation." Nith Sahor sat and waited for his quid pro quo. He had created a simple barter—something a Bashkir could sink his teeth into.

Eleusis was desperately trying to figure out whether the Gyrgon was telling the truth or simply prevaricating in order to get the regent to lower his guard. He realized, however, that there were many paths Nith Sahor could have taken to elicit the information he desired. The one he chose was doubtless the most astonishing. Why would a Gyrgon confess to anything so intimate? Why would a Gyrgon willingly let go of a secret? Secrets were in large part what gave the Gyrgon their mystique, their power over the other castes, great and lesser alike. Did Nith Sahor trust him that much? How was he to know?

"I assume by desire you mean my desire for Giyan."

"In a way. I meant for the Kundalan, yes."

Eleusis' keen mind realized that the Gyrgon had left out the word *female*. At last, a clue. He chose a beautifully fluted Kundalan ammonwood chair and sat down.

"Are you comfortable?" Nith Sahor sat in the matching chair.

"Quite comfortable."

"As am I."

And there you had it, Eleusis realized. The reason for this Summoning. For whatever reason, the Gyrgon wished to talk candidly about the Kundalan. "Sometimes," he said, "I wish I wasn't locked up tight in Axis Tyr."

"Why is that?"

Eleusis gazed into the terrifying, enigmatic face and said to himself. *To N'Luuura with it.* "Too many V'ornn. Quite honestly, part of me longs to be in the Djenn Marre, to walk among the Kundalan, to learn their ways."

"Their secrets," Nith Sahor said. "We Gyrgon trade in secrets."

"Isn't that why we wander the reaches of interstellar space instead of finding a new homeworld, why we hunt down other races—so that you can absorb their secrets, in the hope that the secret to life may one day be revealed to you?"

"Your bitterness is showing like a mesh singlet on a Looorm, regent." Nith Sahor sat forward, elbows on knees, laced his fingers. "Life and death—the eternal twins. We are bound to them. You know that, don't you?"

Eleusis was forced to look away from those terrifying starsapphire eyes. "Yes." He nearly choked on the word.

"Then you know just how important our search for freedom is, to find our way out of the labyrinth that is the universe as we know it. You see, regent, we Gyrgon can *feel* that the universe is not all there is. It is not enough for us. We yearn to travel beyond . . . well, we do not yet know beyond what. But the barriers that keep us *here* in the known Cosmos must fall. Do you understand our pain of confinement?"

Eleusis was in control of himself again, and he swung his gaze back. "I think I do, Nith Sahor."

"Then tell me that which I need to know."

"I am not . . . I'm not certain that I have answers for you. At least, none that will make sense."

"Please leave that determination to me. Speak of what is in your hearts."

"All right." Eleusis sat up straight. He had the feeling that he was on the edge of a precipice, and he fought off the knife edge of panic. "I have come to have a special feeling for the Kundalan. Undoubtedly, it stems in part from my relationship with Giyan, but as you yourself noted, that is not the end of it. Sixteen years ago, I brought her back as a trophy from a Khagggun hunting party I accompanied in the foothills of the Djenn Marre. She was nothing to me then, but quite quickly that changed."

"How did it change?"

"I . . . I don't know."

"Yes, you do, regent. Think."

"Well, I . . . I think what happened was that being in such close proximity to her I stopped thinking of her as the defeated enemy."

"And how exactly did that come about?"

Eleusis thought a moment. "I remember. It was almost a sidereal year after I had brought Giyan back to Axis Tyr. I started awake in the middle of the night and went to slake my thirst. Down the hallway I saw her. She was standing by an open window. She was staring out at the Djenn Marre. I remember it was the night of full moons; the snow and ice on the mountains peaks shone as blue as Corpius Segundo's moon. She was weeping, the tears sliding down her cheeks, and I thought, *She misses her home, just as we miss our home.* And from that moment, defeated alien or no, there was no difference between us."

"But there *is* a difference."

"Yes, Nith Sahor."

"In fact, *many* differences."

"This is truth."

Light glinted off the metallic mesh as the Gyrgon rear-ranged his hands. "It may be anathema to say this, but that is no bad thing. I believe that it would benefit us greatly to acquaint ourselves with their differences."

Eleusis stiffened. "She trusts me, Nith Sahor."

"*I* trust you, Eleusis. That is why you were made regent."

"*You* were responsible for making me regent?"

"Your father. Others wanted Wennn Stogggul's father to assume the role."

Eleusis thought about this for a moment. "I will not betray her."

"We are your masters, regent. Do you think it wise to speak to a Gyrgon in this manner?"

"I am speaking to you, Nith Sahor."

"I am Gyrgon."

"I am speaking to *you*," Eleusis repeated.

The Gyrgon nodded and light played off the latticework in his skull. "Your perception is noted with especial interest."

"I believe, Nith Sahor, that there is a great deal we do not yet know about the Kundalan—that we never will know under the present situation. The establishment of Za Hara-at is the first step in a transformation I foresee."

"Do not be presumptuous, regent. It is not for you to foresee transformation."

"You do not understand, Nith Sahor. The creation of the city came to me in a dream—an astonishingly vivid dream that showed me precisely where Za Hara-at should rise, in the center of the Korrush. Subsequently, I traveled across the Korrush in the company of Hadinnn SaTrryn, who does business with the Korrush tribes, and much to my surprise we found a small, unprepossessing village in its center. The site is an ancient one, according to Kundalan lore, and when we began to dig we discovered foundations the tribesmen dated from many centuries ago."

"Za Hara-at is a word from the Kundalan Old Tongue. It means Earth Five Meetings."

"That's right. I believe this is the original site of Za Hara-at. I believe it to be a sacred place."

"Our near-defunct religion speaks of a City of One Million Jewels. Perhaps your mother was a secret worshiper of Enlil, the dead god. Perhaps she told you stories of this city when you were young; perhaps this is where your dream came from. In any event, the Gyrgon decree the V'ornn way, regent. Never forget that."

"Or perhaps Za Hara-at and the City of One Million Jewels are somehow linked."

"That would take a leap of faith precious few V'ornn could make." Green fire sparked at the tip of Nith Sahor's forefinger. "But you would be such a one, wouldn't you, regent?"

"Yes. I would be that one." Eleusis' hearts beat heavily in his chest. Was there still a trace of anger in the Gyrgon's eyes? *So difficult to tell,* Eleusis thought. On the verge of a headache, he thumbed his eye sockets. So much tension, so much at stake here. "We have remained on Kundala longer than on any other planet in recent memory. Why is that?"

"This is Gyrgon business."

"But it is my business as well, Nith Sahor. The accretion of Kundalan pain has become an unbearable anguish. It is a potent goad to action."

"Ah, you should know that such goads are dangerous, regent. And impatience tends to upset the delicate Balance."

He gazed directly into those star-sapphire eyes. "But that is my point, Nith Sahor. That very delicate Balance *must* be upset. For the good of V'ornn and Kundalan alike."

"You fool, the Balance is all!" Nith Sahor thundered. He rose to a transfiguring height. "Without the Balance nothing works: ions flare, neutrons die, electrons go berserk, the very fabric of the universe is threatened!"

The bright-plumaged teyj screamed. Nith Sahor's mailed right hand clamped into a fist, a corona of orange fire irised outward. An instant later, something cold, something invisible struck Eleusis in the chest. He was hurled violently backward, head over tender parts, until he fetched up painfully against the far wall. The bird fluttered around the top of its cage, clearly agitated.

"Oh, is this foolish work I attempt here?" The Gyrgon shook his mailed fist. "Are the others quite correct? Are you as dangerous as they say? Will my own hubris be my downfall?"

Eleusis stared at him, terrified. Bright ribbons of pain throbbed through him. He slowly picked himself up, massaging his chest with the heel of his hand as he righted the chair Nith Sahor had overturned. Screwing up his courage, he said: "It would be a mistake to annihilate the Kundalan as we have done to so many other races—or to leave them here, drained of all natural resources." Those eerie starsapphire eyes pounced on him, heavy as a storm-swept sky, then slid away as if he were of no import. "It is time for the paradigm that we have erected between ourselves and the socalled slave races to end here and now. The building of Za Hara-at will be proof of a new, better paradigm."

"Do not speak to me of Za Hara-at," Nith Sahor boomed. "There is no consensus among the Comradeship on this experiment of yours. And believe me when I tell you that debate is vociferous."

"The Comradeship do not yet understand about the Kundalan. If they could see how V'ornn and Kundalan architects worked together to design the city—"

"That is just the point. The repugnance they feel is in dealing with an inferior race as if they were our equals."

"But, Nith Sahor, the Kundalan—"

The Gyrgon's raised hand brought silence. "You are correct about one thing, regent. Za Hara-at has already become a symbol to the Kundalan, and therein lies our dilemma."

Nith Sahor went to the window, where he stood looking outside for a very long time. The silence built like a structure spun out of the supercharged atmosphere. Eleusis was now very frightened of Nith Sahor, but he found to his surprise that he was even more frightened of the immediate future. If the Gyrgon withdrew their support for Za Hara-at, Prime Factor Stogggul and his cabal would get their wish: whatever progress he was engineering between the races would die. No matter what, Eleusis knew that he could not allow that to happen. He could feel in his bones what he was doing here on Kundala was right.

Swallowing his intense fear, Eleusis said, "Nith Sahor, hear me. I understand how deeply ingrained is our xenophobia—"

"You are correct, regent. Even Gyrgon are subject to hubris," Nith Sahor said. "Hubris blinds us to the truth, isn't that so?"

"I believe it is, especially in this instance, because beyond anything there is one, single compelling reason why we *must* allow Za Hara-at its existence."

He waited, staring at the Gyrgon's back, but only silence ensued. Was that tacit approval for him to continue? Eleusis took a deep breath, all too aware that the fate of Za Hara-at and everyone involved in its planning and construction hung in the balance. He went to the section of wall decorated with the sea-green Dragon riding a stylized wave. "This is Seelin, the Sacred Dragon of Transformation. The Kundalan have a fundamental belief that social history does not evolve slowly, but rather leaps ahead during short, violent periods of transformation."

"Chaos," Nith Sahor breathed.

Eleusis' hearts leapt. "Chaos, yes, save for the fact that the Kundalan have no word in their language for Chaos." He could scarcely breathe. "Is this belief of theirs not, essentially, K'yonnno?"

"Would you now presume to vomit back to me the basic Gyrgon Theory of Chaos and Order?"

"I am simply pointing out that there may be more to the Kundalan than we believe or are currently willing to accept. I believe that this blindness may be *our* hubris as a race."

Silence, for a long time. Even though every muscle in his body ached, Eleusis dared not move. He tried to read the Gyrgon's response by how he held himself, but it was a fool's mission, and he began to weep silent tears for Za Hara-at, whose fate had now apparently slipped through his fingers. *Did I make a mistake?* he asked himself. *What else could I have done?* Wearying of enigmas he would never solve, he turned and stared at the Five Sacred Dragons of Miina, whose power and stern visages curiously never failed to calm him.

At length, Nith Sahor stirred. "You are correct in another matter, regent. We have been in occupation here for one hundred and one years, and still the Gyrgon have not solved the mystery of the planet or the Kundalan."

Hope surged through Eleusis. Some crisis point had been reached and turned so that he came out of his paralysis and risked taking a position just behind Nith Sahor. It was a good view out over the city, north to the ragged high peaks of the Djenn Marre.

"All we have are more mysteries," Nith Sahor continued. "This planet is a complete enigma to us. What power principles underlie Kundalan sorcery? What exists beyond the treacherous Djenn Marre? It is a question even Gyrgon cannot answer. All our superior science, our sophisticated telemetry mean nothing here. The perpetual snow and ice storms make an area three hundred thousand square kilometers impenetrable. Over the years we have sent a dozen experienced Khagggun teams into the Unknown Territories. As you know, none ever returned. What happened to them? Were they killed by the extreme weather, by beasts unknown, the resistance? We have no idea.

"As for the Kundalan, who are they? Where did they come from? Where are they going? Even the nature of the barbaric Sarakkon is an enigma to us. These are the basic questions of life—the ones we Gyrgon seek out wherever we go in the universe. Without those answers, we are diminished."

The level of Nith Sahor's frustration was clearly communicated to Eleusis. Perhaps that was what led him to strike out as he had. Unconsciously, Eleusis massaged his chest again.

"I am convinced that the answer to all our questions about Kundala and its people resides in The Pearl."

"The Pearl—if it ever existed—was lost forever on the day we invaded Kundala," Eleusis said carefully.

Nith Sahor's face arranged itself into an enigmatic smile. "Oh, it exists, regent. I think you know that as well as I do. And if it was lost, it can be found. We are always looking for a new avenue for our search." Abruptly, the Gyrgon turned, and the regent felt the full weight of his unsettling gaze. Eleusis began to get a bad feeling in the pit of his stomachs.

"To find The Pearl, we must first open the Storehouse Door in the caverns under the regent's palace. Tell me, Eleusis, have you heard of the Ring of Five Dragons?"

"I have not."

"Perhaps, then, I should have a talk with Giyan."

Eleusis went cold with dread. "She knows nothing."

"She is Ramahan. She is a sorceress. She is steeped in the lore of their Goddess Miina. She will know of the Ring."

"So presumably did the ten thousand other Ramahan you rounded up over the last century."

"They told us nothing. They knew nothing."

"By all means, bring her in," Eleusis said. The taste of fear was in his mouth. "Torture the information out of her."

"Ah, ah, ah, I was under the impression that you and I were beyond such rebukes."

Eleusis passed his hand over his eyes. "Sometimes I feel like a very old V'ornn. I have seen too much bloodsport, Nith Sahor. I have participated in more than my share. These days I see only conspiracies, hidden agendas, bargaining chips placed upon the table and withdrawn. I fear that I am part of a plan with which I no longer care to be involved."

The Gyrgon made an unexpected gesture. "Regent, give me your hand."

Eleusis stood deathly still. "It is said that the Gyrgon's touch kills."

Nith Sahor held out his mailed fist. "And do you believe it, regent?"

"I . . . I don't know," Eleusis admitted.

"I promulgated that bit of legend," Nith Sahor said. "It's an amusing one, I admit."

Eleusis gazed deep into Nith Sahor's eyes. "It is also said that the Gyrgon possess the power to hypnotize. Another legend you promulgated?"

"No. That one is true enough."

Eleusis felt another shiver of fear run down his spine.

"You see, what we have here, regent, is a test—a test of your ability—or perhaps your desire—to trust. I want the Ring of Five Dragons, and you must trust that I will use it wisely."

Eleusis licked his lips. His mouth felt as dry as the Great Voorg yet he was drenched in sweat. "We V'ornn are not given to trust, are we?"

Nith Sahor's extraordinary eyes continued to draw him in. "But in so many ways, regent, you do not conform to the Modality."

"Perhaps this is a test for both of us."

Nith Sahor laughed, a nasty sound. "Gyrgon are beyond tests, regent."

"In this you are wrong, Nith Sahor. You have attacked me in anger. That, in time, I could forgive. But you have threatened the person I love most in life. When you ask for my trust, you ask for the impossible."

"I would not harm Giyan. I meant to frighten you. It is possible that I miscalculated."

An apology from a Gyrgon? Now Eleusis had heard everything. What would make Nith Sahor act in this extraordinary way, he wondered, but fear? Some terrible imperative he could not yet see but could feel all around him like a dank prison cell. Curiosity overcame resentment. After a further moment's hesitation, he placed his hand on Nith Sahor's fist. No ball of fire smote him; no surge of hyperexcited ions attacked his neurons; he did not turn to stone. Everything was as it had been before. No, not quite. Slowly, the fearsome fist opened like a flower to sunlight and the Gyrgon's palm pressed against the regent's. The grip solidified and Eleusis felt himself being drawn toward the Gyrgon.

"Regent, there is a task I require of you," Nith Sahor said very softly. "Something of the utmost importance."

Eleusis' throat closed up. *Now the hammer comes down,* he thought.

"Only The Pearl has the potential to give us the answers the Gyrgon need. And to possess The Pearl I must first have the Ring of Five Dragons. You must find it for me."

Eleusis shook his head. "The Pearl is the most sacred artifact of the Kundalan—a gift from the Great Goddess Miina. If it exists, if it were to be found, it belongs to them."

"I must have the Ring and The Pearl! I strongly urge you to rethink your response."

Eleusis felt chilled to his marrow. "I will not betray the Kundalan."

"You are V'ornn, regent," Nith Sahor said with ire. "I should not have to remind you of that."

"I will not betray Giyan."

"That is your final answer?"

"It is my *only* answer."

He choked as the fearsome Gyrgon drew him so close that

they were against one another. Nith Sahor smelled of clove oil and burnt musk. He put his mouth beside Eleusis' ear and whispered fiercely, "You have shown me what is most precious to you. You have made your decision. Honorable or foolhardy, which is it?"

Eleusis found that he was trembling. He stood mutely before the Gyrgon, as if on trial. In the next beat of his hearts, he found himself back outside the front gate to the Temple of Mnemonics. Nith Sahor's words continued to reverberate inside him. He looked up at the swirling turrets and giddy parapets of the Temple. Was anything the Gyrgon said the truth? Or were they clever lies to trap a suspect regent? Why would a Gyrgon entrust secrets to someone outside his caste? He wouldn't. Perhaps he had been hypnotized after all. *What we have here, regent, is a test—a test of your ability—or perhaps your desire—to trust.* What was the game and how was it being played? How was he to know?

"Regent?"

He looked over, saw Kinnnus Morcha's concerned expression.

"Regent, is anything amiss? How went the Summoning?"

You have shown me what is most precious to you. . . .

"Routine, Kinnnus," he said, mounting his hoverpod. "I can't imagine why I was Summoned."

Kinnnus Morcha grunted. "Typical." He started up his vehicle. "What's that saying about Gyrgon logic? It takes three lifetimes to discover there isn't any!"

4

Oculus

hy did you do it?" Annon asked. "This display of your sorcery could get you into trouble with my father's enemies."

"I care not for myself. I did it to protect Eleusis," she said. "So his enemies would think twice about moving against him."

"Can you see what they are up to?" he said eagerly.

"Not unless they use Kundalan sorcery against him." She laughed. "Don't you want to know *how* I did it?"

"Oh, I think I can guess that part."

Giyan seemed pleased. "Can you now?"

It was just past dusk. They were walking through streets packed with V'ornn and Kundalan on their way from hingatta liiina do mori to the regent's palace. It was a short walk, but the scrutiny they were given by passersby made it seem longer than it was. Tuskugggun shopkeepers suspended their haggling, customers ceased their bargain-hunting. Burly Mesagggun, their sweat-streaked, muscled arms still smeared with grease and lubricating oil, coming off shift from tending the huge, complex V'ornn generators, poked each other and leered. Bashkir hurrying to or from business appointments, slowed and stared. Kundalan drovers, leading small herds of cthauros, the handsome, six-legged animals the V'ornn—especially the Khagggun—loved to ride, rose in their saddles, pausing long enough to comment to each other on the regent's mistress and son.

"You see?" Annon said under his breath. "Word has already spread about how you bested Kurgan in the contest."

"Word could not have spread about *how* I won," she said with the faint smile he had come to know better even than his father's perpetually furrowed brow. She threw a slim arm across his shoulders. "Only you and I know that secret, eh?"

Annon, imagining all those tiny, pale cilia brushing his hairless skin, shuddered beneath the slight weight. He looked away, to keep his mind occupied. Of course, there were those who paid them no mind: lines of Kundalan slaves, grimy, backs bent from their long stint working the mines in the foothills of the Djenn Marre. Periodically, the V'ornn paraded them through the streets of the city both to reinforce their superiority and to further demoralize the Kundalan. It was a dirty job extracting minerals from rock, so he had heard. These rail-thin Kundalan were aware of nothing save their own exhaustion. They deserved their fate: most of them had been in the Kundalan resistance, had been captured attempting acts of murder, arson, sabotage. And yet, oddly, when he saw them, saw the expression of pain on Giyan's face, he understood, and felt something, too, stir inside him. The same sense of shame he had experienced when Kurgan had grabbed the Kundalan girl.

"But *why* did you challenge Kurgan to the contest?" he said suddenly, wanting to tear his mind away from such thoughts. "And outside, as well, where so many people could see?"

"Was that wrong? Will your father punish me?"

"Of course it was wrong! Of course he will punish you!" Annon hissed. "Isn't it bad enough that you won't wear the sifeyn? Now you insist on displaying Kundalan sorcery in public! You could have caused a riot! You could have been hurt!"

"I'm touched by your concern," she said, as they continued along the street. "Perhaps I allowed my emotions to get the better of me."

"Kurgan won't forget it, that I can tell you. He ran out of the hingatta as if he had a N'Luuura-hound nipping at his tender parts."

They were about to turn a corner when Giyan put an arm out, held Annon back. A caravan of crimson-and-black Genomatekk hoverpods. The were heading south, flying very low to the ground. Khagggun hoverpods bracketed the caravan in front and behind.

"What's going on?" Annon asked her. He saw that her face had gone pale.

She had pulled him back into the shadows of a silk merchant's doorway. Lengths of finely spun colored cloth fluttered like flags in the skylit interior. Pedestrians, V'ornn and Kundalan alike, had moved to the side to make way for the caravan.

"The babies have been rounded up again." A terrible sadness tinged Giyan's voice.

"What babies?" Annon watched the sleek vehicles moving away, the surf of the crowd closing in around its wake, going about its business.

Giyan signed to him, and they continued on their way toward the regent's palace.

"The babies of violence," she said when he prompted her again. "The consequence of the Kundalan females who have been raped by Khagggun." They went past a Kundalan female, spinning wrygrass into baskets. They smelled sweet and fermented. There were only a few coins in her pay cup. "Some get pregnant. Each Khagggun pack keeps track of their conquests; it seems to be a matter of no little pride. But there is another reason for the strict accounting. Periodically, they return, make note of the females on their lists who are pregnant. They return again at the proper time to take their babies. The Khagggun ship them back here, where they are held in the Gyrgon Temple of Mnemonics until they are six months old. Then the Genomatekks are summoned and the children are taken to Receiving Spirit, the hospice near Harborside."

"What happens to them there?"

"No one knows," she said softly, sorrowfully. "Not even the resistance."

"Why do you care about them? They are freaks."

"I care about all life, Annon."

But he could tell that she had not told him what was in her heart.

He was about to order her to tell him when his attention was abruptly diverted.

"There is a shadow about you, young sir," a thin, reedy voice cried.

An old Kundalan seer had set himself up on the next corner. Across the top of his makeshift stall was a colorful banner that read: THE THIRD EYE SEES ALL. These self-proclaimed seers lately flourished inside the city's walls. Their so-called abilities came from their affinity with the potent and mysterious psychotropic drug, salamuuun. Though he was with a customer, the seer's head turned at the couple's approach. His night-black eyes had homed in on Annon.

He called out the same phrase again, and Giyan answered back sharply, "Keep your tongue in your head if you know what is good for you, old one. This is the regent's firstborn."

"I have seen you," the seer said. It appeared as if he had slipped into a trance. "You have been marked by the Ancient One. The scar runs right through you."

"I told you to keep still!" Giyan's fingers gripped Annon's shoulders, propelling him around the seer, toward the slender towers of the palace, their tops caught in the lingering rays of the dying sun.

"I see death, death and more death!" the seer cried after them. "Only the equilateral of truth can save you!"

"Ignore him," Giyan said.

"But what did he mean?" Annon asked.

"It is nonsense." Giyan picked up the pace in order to put as much space as possible between them and the old Kundalan. "Only fools concern themselves with nonsense."

They reached the regent's palace, at last. Just within the cyclopean jasper-and-bronze outer gates, they were halted by the outer ring of Haaar-kyut. They wore purple uniforms made of a nonreflective silicon polymer, a typical V'ornn material that was as practical as it was esthetically dead. Platinum markings of rank were affixed to sleeve and collar. In a society where caste was worshiped, the prominent display of rank among the Khaggun was everything, a sure sign that Order was being maintained.

Security was so tight Giyan had to submit her okuuut, even though she was in and out of the palace several times a day and was with the regent's son and heir. An oblong screen glowed pale blue as a Haaar-kyut named Frawn pressed the palm of Giyan's left hand to a tertium-copper alloy plate. She could feel a slight tingling. A row of red characters—a mathematical formula unique to her and unduplicatable, she had learned—appeared on the screen, running in a spiral inside out. Another Gyrgon attempt at reducing life into an understandable, and therefore easily manipulated, pattern.

"Cleared," Frawn said, freeing her.

"Tell me something," Giyan said. "What do you expect to see when I am screened?"

"I am trained not to expect anything, to anticipate everything."

"How horrid!" she cried.

Annon grinned behind the back of his hand.

"Do you not know me by now?" she pressed.

"You are Kundalan," he said in all seriousness. "How could I be expected to know you?" His gaze slid away from her, and he nodded formally to Annon. "You may continue."

"Thank Miina!" Giyan said sardonically, though only she saw Frawn wink at her.

They went down a hallway the V'ornn had deliberately narrowed and made dim so that anyone passing through was observed from unseen windows clad in V'ornn crystal recessed into the stone walls. Light was such that you could only see what was directly in front of you.

"Kurgan needed a lesson in humility," Giyan said as if there had been no pause in their conversation. "He thinks altogether too much of himself."

"He's very smart."

"Of that I have no doubt."

They came to a thick-paneled door girdled by riveted metal strips. It was guarded by Haaar-kyut of the inner ring. Again, Giyan was obliged to be officially identified by her okuuut. Annon wondered how much she minded being tagged like an animal in a long-term experiment. While he waited, he studied with fascination the Kundalan designs and sigils carved into the face of the door. Once, he had asked Giyan why none of the Kundalan artwork was signed. She had told him that artists and artisans both worked in the service of the Great Goddess Miina and for their own satisfaction.

"Tell me how I destroyed his bolt," she said, switching to Kundalan. They had entered a small three-walled antechamber that gave out onto an octagonal courtyard. This exceptionally peaceful and pleasant space was surrounded by a loggia, its sea-green tile roof supported by carved shanstone pillars, five to a side. Above the courtyard, the indigo sky seemed to underscore Miina's diminished presence. A soft breeze stirred the fragrant olive and rosemary trees that dotted the courtyard, lending punctuation to the vivid colors of the rows of star-roses that were Eleusis' passion. He had planted them himself on the day of his coronation.

Annon was grinning. "You *didn't* destroy it."

"I didn't. But everyone saw—"

"Everyone saw what you wanted them to see." Quick as an ice-hare he hooked a finger inside her sash, found the knot, and undid it. As he whirled it off her Kurgan's bolt clattered to the cold stone floor. "I knew it!" He picked it up, let out a long whistling breath, twirled it around like a prize. "You palmed it while everyone's attention was on the illusion of the vine."

"Well done!" Giyan was cloaked in her smile. "But what about the tree? What happened to the wound the bolt made in it?"

When Annon frowned he looked very like his father. "Well, to be honest, that part has me stumped."

She laughed and ran her fingers over his long, tapering, yellowish skull. "I am gratified I can still hold *some* secrets from you."

He handed her the bolt. "Would you teach me how to heal wounds?"

"It is Osoru, Kundalan sorcery, Annon," she said in her most serious tone. "For a V'ornn, dangerous knowledge."

"But I'd be careful! I swear I would!"

"And what would you do with this knowledge, I wonder?" Giyan asked, as they strode along the loggia.

Upon the inner walls were wondrously delicate Kundalan frescoes depicting the origins of Kundala. Here was Miina, floating alone in the Cosmos; here was the Great Goddess, gathering the cosmic material from which She birthed the Five Sacred Dragons; there they formed the endless Mandela, tip of fiery crescent tongue to tip of scaly tail, caught up in the Dance of Creation, the planet Kundala forming to

Miina's specifications; and there, when they were finished
with the world, they obeyed her final command and, exhaling
all at once, fabricated the most holy and sacred object in the
Kundalan universe: The Pearl. The sole oddity was a panel
in the lower right-hand corner. Either it had been damaged
or defaced during the first days of V'ornn occupation. In any
event, the images on it were unrecognizable. He traced faint
lines on the wall, added his own, drawing out of his imagination great beasts that seemed so ferocious but were tame
to his touch and voice.

Annon pointed to the panel. "Do you have any idea what
was meant to be shown here?" he asked.

Giyan barely glanced it. "We are late," she said curtly.

"But surely you must know."

"We have no time for idle speculation. Your father will
be cross with me if I do not bring you directly to him, Annon."

"When I was younger I was sure it showed beasts that
frightened everyone but protected me."

She looked at him curiously for a moment. "There used
to be a depiction of the Rappa, sorcerous creatures, always
at Miina's right hand."

"Why weren't they restored like the rest of the fresco? Did
the artists forget to put them back in?"

Giyan sighed. "Legend has it that the Rappa were responsible for Mother's death here in this very palace, on the day
the V'ornn arrived. Among the Ramahan, they are despised
now, expunged from our lore and our teachings. But, then,
from what I gather there have been many changes in the
Sacred Scripture since Mother's death."

He cocked his head, suddenly attuned to her voice and
expression. "You do not believe the Rappa are evil?"

"No, I don't. But, then, I have many strange notions, Annon." She smiled. "No doubt because I have lived so long
among you V'ornn."

He put his hand on the blank space as if he were able to
feel something no one else could. "I don't think they're evil,
either."

Once again, she gave him that familiar look of curiosity. He never knew quite what to make of it, or how to respond. It was as if she were looking at another person altogether. "Would you like to see what a Rappa looks like?"

"Would I?" he said excitedly.

Giyan took his hand from the blank space and replaced it with hers. When she took it away, the fresco had been completed. There were two small furry creatures with six legs, long bushy tails, intelligent eyes, and tapering snouts.

"How did you do that?" he asked.

Giyan laughed softly.

They turned a corner, continued to circumnavigate the garden. This was something Giyan always did with him when she brought him to the palace. Mostly, they spoke not a word during this walk; sometimes he was bored, impatient to see his father. Always, it appeared to him as if Giyan was deep in alien meditation or prayer, which engendered in him a dizzying sense of dislocation, as if for a moment he was somewhere else. It heightened his awareness, as if he could sense a rustling of unseen things, whispers of ancient days, perhaps, the ghosts of Kundalan past. Being here was, for him, like being lost in a dream—the strange and familiar blending into something new.

Abruptly, she turned to him. "You have not answered me. What would you do with your sorcerous knowledge?"

"I would become invincible," he said. "Why, there would be no fight I couldn't win."

"An excellent reason to withhold such knowledge from you! Have you no——" She paused and, gripping his arm, turned him to face her. "What is it?" she asked.

"Nothing," he lied. That damned wound he had received from the gyreagle was like a live flame beneath his skin. When he had bent down to pick up Kurgan's bolt he had felt a surge of pain, and now it would not let up.

"Do not lie to me, Annon," she said sternly. "You are hurt."

"I am not hurt," he cried. He had switched to V'ornn, which he always did when he was cross at her. He could not allow her to discover what had happened down by the creek. He and Kurgan had sworn the seigggon—

She pulled aside his jacket, saw the turquoise blood seeping through his silk blouse. "Ah, Miina! How long were you planning to hide this from me?"

"Till N'Luuura is consumed in flames!" he blurted, disgusted to be caught in the lie.

She slapped him across the face. "Don't you know how precious you are to your father? To me? If something should happen to you—"

"What?" he cried. "What would happen? Would my father grieve? Would you cry? Oh, yes. Because it would be the end of the Ashera Dynasty. As long as a son is born to a sitting regent, the power is passed from father to son. But if I were to die, who would succeed my father? The Gyrgon would choose another house, another dynasty to rule for them. So, yes, my father would grieve for the end of his dynasty, and you would cry because my father would turn his wrath on you. He would kill you in a flash for failing him, for letting me die!"

Something strange and, perhaps, forbidden flickered behind Giyan's whistleflower-blue eyes, and she pulled him close. "Oh, my dear, how very wrong you are in what you say. You must understand that—"

She stopped at the quick tramp of boot soles against the quartzite floor and Annon could feel the infinitesimal tremor run through her as if he were inside her.

"Little regent, your father sent me to fetch you as soon as you arrived." The rich resounding basso of Line-General Kinnnus Morcha echoed along the loggia like thunder down a gorge. As he came up, his wide intelligent eyes drank Annon in, analyzed his position and posited a theory. "Is anything amiss? Has the regent's heir taken ill?"

"No, Line-General," Giyan said in her meekest voice. "But he is tired. He and his friend, Kurgan, were out all day hunting."

"Aha, hunting!" Kinnnus Morcha boomed, not once looking at her or addressing her. "Were I so fortunate as you,

Annon. But, alas, I am stuck here inside this miserable fairyland of a building with so much light and air and open space I find that I must work harder to deliver the level of security required." Out of the corner of his eye, he watched for telltale signs in Giyan that his ill-disguised barbs had hit home. Annon knew that she would not give him the satisfaction, and he felt a curious pride in her.

"I long for the hunt!" Kinnnus Morcha boomed. "You can understand that, eh?" He clapped Annon on the back, making him wince against Giyan's breast. Kinnnus Morcha was a monstrously large man, even by V'ornn standards. Giyan was not a short woman, and yet the top of her head barely came up to Kinnnus Morcha's breastbone. Not that you could see his breastbone. It and everything surrounding it was sheathed in an alloy armor finely worked with aspects of the forbidding countenance of Enlil. "One day I myself will take you hunting, high up in the Djenn Marre, and if luck is with us we will bring back a perwillon!"

"Thank you, Line-General."

"Ah-ha, think nothing of it, little regent!" He clapped his huge hand around Annon's shoulder with such force that the boy bit his lip in order not to cry out. "And now I think you two had better be off. The regent awaits you in his chambers."

"Would you really go with the Line-General on his hunt?" Giyan asked, as they ascended the Great Staircase up to the second story.

Annon winced a little and tried to hide it from her. "To hunt perwillon? Of course!"

"Perwillon are nasty, unpredictable creatures." Giyan shook her head. "I do not think your father would permit you to hunt such a dangerous animal."

"I have had my Channeling," he said shortly. "I am not a child, you know."

She smiled and, with her warm hand on his back, whisked him down the balcony, through a secret aperture in the wall that led to the living quarters without having to go through the Great Listening Hall. They emerged onto another balcony, narrower but no less filled with light. Huge skylights opened the area to the heavens, washing the walls in vivid late-afternoon light. It was only after they had passed the door to his father's quarters that he asked her where they were going.

"Did you imagine that I would bring you to Eleusis with blood all over you?"

"Don't exaggerate. I told you it was nothing."

"And did you really expect me to believe you?" But she seemed gratified that he had switched back to Kundalan.

She took him through a door half-hidden in the shadows near the far end of the balcony and into the suite of rooms Eleusis had given her. Here, all was as it had been before the V'ornn occupation. He could smell the faint olfactory aftershocks of her incense: orangesweet and mugwort. She lit some now, then she carefully peeled off his jacket and blouse, parts of which were stuck to his rent skin. She grew these odoriferous herbs and strange, ugly mushrooms, he knew, in the secret garden she had somehow cajoled his father into setting aside for her. He grew angry with her over this intimate privilege no Kundalan should ever have been allowed, in part to inure himself from the fright in her eyes as she took in the mass of dried indigo blood surrounding the wounds, the slow turquoise ooze of fresh blood from the center.

"This is what you call nothing?"

Without another word, she guided him onto an oddly designed bentwood chair that put him in a reclining position. He was about to protest when he yelped in pain.

Giyan's face blanched as she gently spun off the blood-soaked tourniquet Kurgan had fashioned from his blouse. "Goddess in Heaven, what have you done to yourself?" Her delicate fingertips gently explored the wounds. Annon bit his lip. "Were you in a fight?" Giyan asked. "Was Kurgan hurt as well?"

Annon turned his head away and made no comment.

She moved closer. "There is something stuck in the

wound, deep down. Your side is purple and puffy. I believe it is infected."

"Fix it, then, with your sorcery," he ordered, angry at her for finding out about his wound.

She stood for a moment, hands on hips, regarding him. Then she went to a huge heartwood armoire worked with complex Kundalan patterns. She rummaged around inside until she found what she wanted. Pulling out a leather bag, she plopped it onto the floor beside him.

"Goddess knows what would have happened had I not suspected something was amiss."

"Oh, yes," he said, staring at the filigreed ceiling, "you are all-knowing and all-wise."

She knew better than to argue with him when he got into one of his moods. She took out mortar and pestle, bags of roots and vines, dried flowers and fruit unfamiliar to him. Despite his resentment he found himself captivated by the sure and deft manner in which she broke, shredded, poured, sifted, measured ingredients into the mortar. He wanted to ask her what each ingredient was and why she was using it, but a sheet of anger had formed like ice over his hearts. It was so familiar and comforting that he would not break it even to make himself feel better.

She began to grind the contents of the mortar with the pestle, then stopped. "I need fresh datura inoxia for Annon's wound," she muttered to herself, and rose. "I must run down to the garden. I will not be long." She summoned a spell of healing. "Stay still, breathe deeply and slowly until I return."

Alone, he continued to stare at the ceiling, wondering why he should be angry at her. Perhaps she was overprotective of him, but that was clearly the mission his father had given her. And as for his wound, well, it did pain him more than slightly. He would be glad to have it healed. Resolving to be kinder to her when she returned, he moved stiffly and expelled a tiny groan.

All at once, he stiffened and his eyes refocused on the room. That smell . . . what was it? He sniffed—bitterroot, that was it! Pungent bitterroot! Where was it coming from?

Was Giyan brewing up yet another concoction in the other room? No, it was coming from out on the balcony.

Slowly, stiffly, painfully he got out of the bentwood chair. Bare-chested, he padded silently across the room and out the door. On the narrow balcony, he looked this way and that. It was deserted. On the other hand, the odor of bitterroot was stronger.

He looked around. The setting sun caused shafts of light the color of pomegranates to penetrate the lower quarter of the skylights. They hung in the air like tapestries, burnishing the fluted ammonwood handrails, staining the swath of carpet that ran the length of the balcony, firing a thin sliver of the wall.

Curious, Annon padded down to the very end of the balcony. Sunlight dazzled a small strip of metal he had never noticed before. Here, the wall was not flat; the reflective metal jutted out perhaps a millimeter or two. He grasped it and pulled, almost ripping a nail clean off as his fingers slid off the slick surface. He got a better hold of the metal strip, applied a steady pressure, and felt it move. A wedge of the wall swiveled silently out. A hidden doorway opened up, like the one Giyan and he had used to get to the living wing of the palace. Except this one was unknown to him. Sucking on his torn nail, he poked his head into the aperture. Velvet darkness engulfed the interior, but the odor of bitterroot was almost nauseating in its intensity. He took a deep breath of the fresher air on the balcony and stepped through into the darkness.

He stretched out his arms and encountered solid objects: walls. From this evidence, he deduced that he was in a narrow corridor. He moved forward cautiously, but still he tripped down the first three steps and only a desperate grasp at the thin, cold metal handrail saved him from plunging headfirst into the abyss. The staircase spiraled down like the inside of a muodd shell. The pitch-black air was chill, acrid as silicon, laced as it was by the bitterroot smell.

He continued his descent until he came to a minuscule triangular landing. From here, the staircase branched off in three directions. He squatted down, felt around. The treads were of equal width; there was nothing to distinguish one from the other. Lacking a definitive clue as to which way to head, he chose the right branch. He could scent the bitterroot and was congratulating himself on his luck when something made him stop dead in his tracks.

He felt something, though he could not say what. The skin of his tender parts prickled in warning.

A strange pulse had been set off inside him. Somewhere, not far below him, something waited, something dark, vast, rippling. Terrifying. He stood very still, his hearts hammering in his chest.

He could not say why, but he knew he could not continue. The sense of danger was overwhelming. He began to back up, almost cried out as the back of his ankle struck the tread just above. He bit his lip. That strange pulse returned, stronger than ever. It was localized now beneath his ribs— from the very spot where the gyreagle had embedded its talon in his flesh. It felt as if the talon were on fire, pulsing to a rhythm far faster than his own double pulse.

He moved back up the stairs, careful to lift his feet high enough to reach the succession of ascending treads. All the while, his eyes frantically tried to part the heavy curtain of darkness.

Then he had regained the small landing. He was panting, sweat poured off him, but oddly his wound—or, more accurately, the embedded gyreagle talon—had ceased its frantic pulsing. Without thought, he plunged down the central staircase as fast as his legs would pump. A faint patch of dark grey seemed to wash the outer wall of the staircase, one moment real, the next seeming illusory.

Perhaps it was his haste that caused him to miss the last tread. He went over the edge, his hands grasped for the handrail that was not there, and he found himself hurtling down a spiral chute. He tried to scream, but the sound stuck in his throat like a milk-nettle. The grey patch of light grew in volume and intensity until it filled the chute with a blinding glare. Then, all at once, Annon was spat from the chute. He fell through the air for a space of perhaps three meters, only to land on a dank and musty stone floor.

As he rubbed his aches and bruises, he sat up and took a look around. He was in what appeared to be one of several interlinked caverns hewn out of the bedrock below the palace. At regular intervals around the rough rock walls, he saw beautifully fluted metal holders for pitch torches. A few held the remnants of such torches, but none was lit. Nevertheless, light fell upon him from high above. He craned his neck and saw an enormous oculus—a thick-paned window of an odd crystal in the shape of an eye which, Giyan had told him, had been made eons ago in a sorcerous fashion.

He scrambled up. Dead ahead of him was a cyclopean door, but one unlike any he had ever seen before. For one thing, it appeared to be made of solid rock. For another, it was perfectly round. In its center was a circular medallion with a wave motif into which was carved the mysterious figure of a dragon, just like the one upstairs he used to play with. He remembered putting his hand into its carven mouth. This one was curled into a circle, its head facing outward, its jaws hinged open. He stared at this terrifying and beautiful creature, powerfully drawn to it in some way he could not understand. He put his hands out, feeling its surfaces, tracing the intricate patterns of runes that covered it. He wished Giyan was there to translate for him. But perhaps she wouldn't. These looked like sorcerous symbols, similar to the ones in her cor-hide book, the one he had glanced through from time to time. Not that it had done him any good, he had no idea of the meaning of even a single rune since they were not Kundalan. And yet he kept coming back to the book, sneaking peeks at it whenever he was certain that he would not get caught. His fingers kept following the engraved lines like a blind person learning to read.

All at once, the round door rolled back into a previously hidden niche. It happened so swiftly, so silently he had no time to react. The light the oculus let in did not extend beyond the door. It was as if the darkness beyond was aqueous, the air swirling with thick eddies that smelled of the sea. A stirring from within, something huge, grotesque, monstrous. He felt a pulsing beneath his ribs at the point where the talon was lodged, but it was of a wholly different nature than when he had felt it on the stairs above. The moment the pulsing began, the angle of the light penetrating the oculus seemed to shift, sending a shaft of pearly light through the doorway. Annon felt it strike the back of his head with a kind of heat. Then it had shot beyond him, illuminating the thing that stood just inside the open door.

Annon had a quick glimpse of a floor littered with bones, skulls, tatters of Kundalan clothing. Then his gaze was riveted on the creature. It was so alien, his brain could scarcely take it in: it appeared to be six-legged, with a long, tapering, reptilian skull, horns that whirled like waterspouts, huge, sinuous sea-green body, long coral talons, gleaming teeth of pearl that protruded out beyond the silhouette of its head. Its powerful uppermost appendages were attached along their upper surfaces to a thin-veined membrane, triangular as a sail, moving like spindrift, gleaming prismatically. A long tail whipped back and forth like surf against a rocky shore.

These were brief but vivid impressions, taken in during the instant before one of the uppermost appendages reached out, grabbed him around the waist, and drew him quickly over the threshold into the inner cavern. In the wink of an eye, the door rolled shut, they were engulfed in the darkness, and Annon lost consciousness.

5

Starlight, Starbright

The only good Kundalan is a dead Kundalan." Having thus delivered this précis defining his core philosophy, Prime Factor Stogggul beckoned the Khagggun into his office suite. Though it was housed in a building of Kundalan manufacture, the interior space was wholly V'ornn. There were few windows, and those that did exist were fitted with a dark brown composite of silicon crystal with fiber-optic cables running through the panes.

The space was lighted at regular intervals by the cool bluish glow of teardrop fusion-lamps that illuminated not only the contents of the rooms but also a side to the Prime Factor's personality. Every geometric chair, desk, carpet, silicon case was arranged at right angles to one another. There was a severe and uncompromising symmetry: two of everything so that one-half of each room was the mirror image of the opposite half. The spines of each silicon wafer that contained books, charts, account ledgers, as well as plays, historical and philosophical texts were aligned just so. And there was another revelation illuminated: none of the rooms contained a knickknack, curio, memento, holoimage, or the like, nothing insofar as any visitor could see of his private life. It was as if his rank was on display as the sum and substance of Wennn Stogggul.

The Khagggun stood still as a sentry in a pool of shadow between fusion lamps.

Stogggul looked up from the holomap of Kundala that hung in the air above his massive copper-and-chronosteel desk. Blue, green, amber, black geometric shapes delineated continents, oceans, mountains, rivers, forests, swamps, deserts, cities. "Lead-Major"—he snapped his fingers in an irritated fashion—"what is your name again?"

"Frawn, Prime Factor," said the Haaar-kyut who had screened Giyan just hours ago.

"Ah, yes, Frawn," Stogggul said in a tone of voice that conferred his distaste for the name. "Have you a fear of being close to me?"

"No, Prime Factor."

"Then approach." Stogggul curled a forefinger. "Despite rumors to the contrary, I won't bite. Much." He laughed.

Frawn licked his lips and entered the room. As he did so,

Stogggul passed a hand across the holomap, simultaneously dissolving it and building another.

"Do you know what this is, Frawn?"

"Yes, Prime Factor. It is an architectural schemata of the regent's palace."

The sleeve of Stogggul's ceremonial black and crimson-trimmed robes rode back, revealing his platinum okum-mmon. "Very good." He was a heavyset V'ornn, with a massive frontal ridge to his skull that gave him a brooding, forbidding air even when he was laughing, which, admittedly, was not often. His son had inherited his dark eyes and almost obsessive intensity, but Stogggul radiated power as fearfully as a Khaggun Star-Admiral. He had a way of fixing you with his gaze, as if you were under surveillance. In this way, he intuited those he could intimidate and those with whom he needed to curry favor. Lead-Major Frawn was most definitely in the former category.

Stogggul looked from the hologram to the Lead-Major. "Tell me, Frawn, is there anything about the palace defenses you have failed to pass on to me?"

Frawn walked slowly around the schemata so that he could view it from all sides, but he seemed preoccupied. Finally, he ventured: "I do not believe I can add anything further—"

Stogggul held up a square-cut hand. "Take your time, Lead-Major. There is no penalty for forgetfulness, only for willful disobedience."

Frawn swallowed hard. "Well, there is one thing, though it would not be visible in this schemata. I heard a story, told to me moments before I left the palace. It concerns the regent's mistress."

"The Kundalan skcettta." The Prime Factor's hand cut through the air as if it were a shock-sword. "I am uninterested in animal behavior."

Frawn was silent for a moment. "From what I heard, this is most extraordinary." He hesitated, and Stogggul nodded.

"I suppose on this night of all nights I should hear *everything*. Proceed."

"The mistress was in a contest with your son."

"Which one?"

"Kurgan, Prime Factor." Frawn licked his lips again. "Kurgan shot a bolt from his okummmon which hit a qwawd's-eye. The mistress then used a Kundalan bow to fire an arrow up into the air."

Stogggul could not help grunting in derision.

"The arrow embedded itself in the ground in front of the tree," Frawn continued. "It magically grew a vine, which climbed the tree and ate the V'ornn bolt completely."

The Prime Factor's face grew blue with blood. "Lead-Major, why are you wasting my time with this nonsense?"

"Perhaps the Kundalan protects the regent with this self-same sorcery," he said. "At least that is what I have heard."

Stogggul gave a dismissive gesture. "Tuskugggun-speak! In a very short time, the Kundalan skcettta and her putative sorcery will be of no import." He ran his hands lovingly over the holoimage. "Because we move tonight."

Frawn's eyes flicked up. "Tonight, Prime Factor?"

"Now. As we speak. My pack of Khagggun is on its way."

"But I am unprepared."

Stogggul frowned. "One should never be unprepared, Frawn."

"I had no warning."

"Warning? Should I warn you every time I wipe my tender parts?" Stogggul tossed his head. "Go with all due haste to the main barracks and requisition an ion cannon, then return to the palace and see to your final preparations."

Frawn came to attention. "Yes, Prime Factor! At once!" He hurried out beneath the gargoylelike glare of the powerful Bashkir.

Stogggul peered at the schemata, cleared his throat. In a moment, another figure emerged through an open doorway to a room in which all the fusion lamps had been shut down.

"Nervous as a Looorm with her first customer." Stogggul did not take his eyes off the hologram. "Do you still trust him?"

Line-General Kinnnus Morcha strode across the room.

"That 'warning' concerning the Kundalan skcettta." He gave a curt nod. "He is the regent's eyes, all right." He headed for the door through which Frawn had come and gone. His hand closed into a fist. "I will take care of him myself before he leaves your residence."

"I would prefer that you didn't."

The Line-General paused and turned back. "I beg your pardon?"

"Blood in my house?" Stogggul shook his head. "No, that will not do." He came around, viewed the schemata from the opposite side. "Besides, I believe there is a better way to handle the Lead-Major, a way that will be more to our benefit."

"In my caste we execute traitors."

"This is the cusp of a new age." Stogggul's eyes rose slowly to take in the Khaggun. "I told you when we first agreed to join forces that nothing short of annihilating the entire Ashera family would do. Once we commence, we are committed. If we fail, if we are caught, we are the ones who will surely be executed. It is all or nothing with us, yes? Here is the nexus of our alliance: I become regent, establish my dynasty, and you and all Khagggun are elevated to Great Caste status."

"What about the Gyrgon? You never explained how you will ensure that they will choose you."

"Line-General, you of all Khagggun should appreciate the value of knowing only as much as you need to know."

"The Bashkir have a saying, do they not? 'Knowledge is power.' Between us, it is a matter of . . . well, I would say *faith*, but that word has not been in fashion for many sidereal cycles. So I suppose I must substitute the word *trust*."

The Prime Factor nodded. "We are in accord. If we cannot trust each other, then, sadly, we are nothing."

"Trust does not come easy to a Khagggun," Kinnnus Morcha said, thinking suddenly of his last conversation with Eleusis Ashera.

"To a Bashkir, either. Remember now, Eleusis Ashera must not be killed, not right away. I must get control of the salamuuun trade. That secret is locked away inside his head. By dawn you will unearth it for me, even if he is driven mad in the process."

Kinnnus Morcha showed long, yellowed teeth. "As the sysal boweth before the snow, so the old order boweth before the new." He gave a peremptory jerk of his head. "I had better return to the palace before my absence is noticed."

"Starlight, starbright . . ." Stogggul said.

The Line-General cocked his head. "Prime Factor?"

"Oh, it is the beginning of a song my mother sang to me when I was a child. It is not known to you?"

"It is not."

"Ah, perhaps it was only for the Great Castes, then." Stogggul was silent a long time. When he spoke again, it was in an odd, lilting tenor wholly unlike his normal voice: "Starlight, starbright, in your light I sleep tonight/Guide our way, build our might/Between the gulfs of airless night."

Stogggul made a scooping gesture with his hand and the schemata of the regent's palace disappeared into his fist. He strode to where Kinnnus Morcha stood and grasped his wrist as an equal. "About the Lead-Major . . ." He leaned in, put his lips against the other's ear, whispered to him. Then he pulled back and in his deep voice, he said: "May the starlight fall on both of us this night, Line-General, as we take our great leap into a new and glorious future!"

It was not until he was safely back inside the regent's palace that Lead-Major Frawn suspected that he was being followed. Of all the Haaar-kyut, he had been chosen by the Kundalan mistress to be the regent's eyes and ears among the traitors who had gathered around Prime Factor Stogggul's black-and-crimson skirts. Giyan had chosen well, for she had seen in Frawn that which his superiors had not: a V'ornn with keen intellect and fierce hearts, who nonetheless was born to the wrong caste. To protect himself, he had formed this decidedly dull exterior so that none of his superior officers would ever ask too much of him. He had invoked the reputation of being straightforward and utterly reliable. He was also as nondescript as a V'ornn could get, which is why Prime Factor Stogggul had singled him out to turn traitor. He was, however, ignorant of Kinnnus Morcha's treachery, and this lack would, finally, be his undoing.

This suspicion of being followed was the first inkling he had that things were amiss. Now he wondered whether he had been followed from the time he left the Prime Factor's residence. He had been so anxious to deliver his news to the Kundalan mistress who was his contact that he had not been as careful as he should have been. Cursing himself, he strode down the hallway toward the great staircase to the second story.

Instead of mounting the staircase, as he had planned, he went around it. He held the ion cannon close to his side, comforted by its weight. Night had gripped Kundala in its winged embrace. Moonrise had yet to commence, but the spray of stars seen through the openings delivered an icy, glittering light that mingled uneasily with that thrown off by the fusion lamps. Giving the impression that he was making his way to the Haaar-kyut auxiliary barracks, he turned abruptly down a shadow-filled passageway, went up two short flights of stairs to the gallery that overlooked the regent's Great Listening Hall. He went swiftly and silently along the rear of the gallery, keeping to the shadows as best he could. He stopped often to listen for the muffled footfalls he was certain he heard behind him.

Midway along the gallery, he paused long enough to thumb a hidden latch the Kundalan mistress had described to him. A slender section of the wall swiveled inward. The moment he stepped through, he put his back against the door and shut it.

Safe, he thought. He paused a moment to collect his thoughts. He needed to make his rendezvous with the Kundalan mistress, and he did not have much time. As she had directed, he went three paces forward and two to the right. Putting his hand out, he found the latch set flush in the wall and pushed with his thumb. He stepped out into a hallway on the second story

"You must tell me how you achieved that trick," Line-General Kinnnus Morcha said.

Frawn sucked in air as his hearts trip-hammered in his chest. "Oh, you startled me, commandant."

"What are you doing in the residence ring, Lead-Major? And armed with an ion cannon, no less. Are you planning to mount a coup?"

"Of course not, sir!" Frawn flushed. "The Kundalan mistress sent me to fetch—"

"To fetch what?" Kinnnus Morcha stepped closer. "*Information?*"

Frawn was wide-eyed with terror. "Information, commandant? I don't understand—Eh!"

The Line-General had slapped the ion cannon out of his hands and was dragging him back into the hidden room. "Now you listen to me, you slimy patch of filth, I'm onto what you have been doing—shuttling back and forth between the palace and Stogggul's residence. Do not insult me with denials. I myself have seen you." He shook Frawn until his tender parts rattled painfully. "What traitorous activities have you been brewing with the Prime Factor?"

"I . . . I have only been pretending to go along with him. He plans a coup. This very night his men will steal into the palace, kill the regent and his entire family. I am to man the west-ring guard station so that I can let his cadre in. But I was on my way to tell—"

"The regent?" Kinnnus Morcha's grip tightened.

"The regent's mistress."

"The Kundalan Looorm?"

"Yes. She is my contact. I am late for our rendezvous."

"Ah. Then by all means let us go to her with all due haste." The Line-General released his grip. "I myself will escort you to her so that no traitor may interfere." He grinned as they emerged back onto the residence-ring balcony. "Who knows how many Wennn Stogggul has enlisted from the Haaar-kyut."

Flooded with relief, Frawn nodded and led the way down the corridor. He passed the door to the regent's quarters. Behind him, Kinnnus Morcha's strong right arm twitched. They soon came to shadowed doorways. At the second one, Frawn stopped. His knuckles rapped out a soft set of taps. After an unaccountably long time, the door opened a crack.

With a roar, Kinnnus Morcha drew his double-bladed shock-sword and ran it though Frawn's back. With a sharp crack like a bolt of thunder, the ion-charged blades shattered his spinal column. Morcha used his bulk like a battering ram, staving in the door as he strode into the chamber. Instead of the Kundalan skcettta, he found himself face-to-face with the regent.

"Kinnnus—" he began, just as the Line-General thrust his sword points into his neck. Blood gouted over the carpet.

"A quick death is my gift, regent. For all we meant to each other. You were misguided, but you were fair in your dealings with me and my Khagggun." Kinnnus Morcha stood over Eleusis' body. "Your heirs will thank me. Wennn Stogggul would have you tortured until you vomited up all your secrets. I have spared you that indignity, at least, and hopefully kept a rein on his power."

Giyan, returning to her chambers after fetching the datura inoxia, heard the commotion. Being in the garden at the time of the attack had saved her. She screamed as Kinnnus Morcha swiped sideways with his sword, severing Eleusis' head from the twitching shoulders.

The Line-General ran after her, stalking through the rooms, his sword above his head, ready to deliver the death blow, but she had vanished. With Eleusis' dripping head held before him like a gruesome lantern, he went swiftly through each room of the apartment without discovering where she had gone.

"N'Luuura take her!" he cried in rage and frustration. He stared into the regent's bloody face. Was it his imagination or did it hold an expression of surprise and sadness? *N'Luuura take him, why had he fallen under the spell of that bloody sorceress?*

Just then, he heard the sounds of armed combat, knew that Wennn Stogggul's pack had made its way through the west-ring door, whose guards he had killed upon returning to the palace.

He ran back through the rooms and out onto the balcony. It was imperative that he show himself, show those still loyal to the regent that they were fighting for a ghost. It was over, he knew—or would be as soon as they hoisted Annon's head alongside that of his father. Nothing less would satisfy Prime Factor Stogggul, for as long as Annon lived the Ashera Dynasty would remain alive, and Stogggul's dream of ascending to the regent's chair would be just that: a dream. As for his overweening desire for the salamuuun trade, that would have to wait for another day. He rushed down the balcony, joined members of Stogggul's Khagggun pack as they were battering down the door to the regent's suite.

"The regent is dead!" he cried, holding high the bloody head of Eleusis. "Now for the son! Fetch him so that I may slay him with the same sword that felled his father!"

6

Spook!

When he awoke, Annon had a headache the approximate size and weight of a bull hindemuth. He lay in the underground cavern, staring straight up at the oculus. For a moment, his mind was blank, in self-defense perhaps, the way the body will go numb to protect itself from the onset of pain. Then it all came flooding back to him: the smell of bitterroot, the flight down the spiral staircase, the near encounter with the unknown terror, then the chute to the subterranean caverns, the round door opening and his confrontation with—well, Enlil only knew what that thing was.

And that was the last he remembered until awakening

here, drenched in the cool blue-green light from the fusion lamps in the palace above, flowing through the oculus. All at once, he became aware of a change in the light and, shielding his eyes, he rose up on one elbow and stared upward. Through the translucent lens of the oculus, he could make out the shadows of people, running this way and that. As he watched, one of them fell, spread-eagled across one section of the oculus. What was going on in the palace above?

He rolled over, groaned as his pounding head threatened to blind him. He closed his eyes for a moment, but the vertigo made him gag. He opened his eyes, drew his legs beneath him, and tried to stand. He keeled over, put the heel of his hand down to cushion his fall, discovered a book lying on the stone floor. It was small, bound in stained leather that looked very old. Surely, it had not been there before. He picked it up and opened it. It was filled with Kundalan writing—runes and symbols, lines of complex text he could not read. He stashed the book in the waistband of his trousers and slowly got to his feet, reeling a little.

Gasping, he put his back against the round Storehouse Door. The Kundalan runes seemed to sear his flesh. At length, it dawned on him that he was outside the door and that it was closed. Meters of solid rock now lay between him and the *thing* that had grabbed him. What had it done to him? What had it wanted? Why was he here now on the other side of the door? All these questions merely exacerbated his headache. He bent over, holding his forehead in his hands while his entire body throbbed.

Through the pain he heard his name being called. His head snapped up, and he groaned in agony. Giyan's voice, shrill with a hearts-wrenching edge of panic, came from what seemed a long way off. The instant he answered her, he found her inside his head. She began to guide him to her. He asked her what was wrong, but she only urged him to hurry, hurry or it would be too late. *Too late for what?* he asked her silently. *Please, please, please hurry!* The words swam in his head like frenzied fish, goading him on.

He had expected her to direct him to a stairway up to the

main floor of the palace, but instead she directed him deeper into the caverns. The farther he got from the oculus, the less light there was. In darkness, he was obliged to rely entirely on her directions. He did not hesitate. It was a matter of faith—a word she had taught him, one which he never had cause to test until tonight. It was an odd thing, he thought as he stumbled onward, to have such blind faith in someone—especially when that someone was a Kundalan! For some reason, he remembered the Kundalan female he and Kurgan had stumbled upon this afternoon down by the stream. His mind's eye opened like a whistleflower to the sun, and it was as if he were staring into her face again. He tried to discover what it was that had passed between them, felt it, grabbed at it, found it just out of reach. Then, as abruptly as it had appeared, the image vanished, and he was engulfed in darkness again.

Reach out your hand, Giyan's voice said in his head.

He did as she directed, felt her hand grasp his. Then she had pulled him into a fierce embrace.

"Thank Miina you are safe!" she whispered.

"Safe from what?" he asked.

She admonished him to lower his voice as she led the way. "Not what—who. Prime Factor Stogggul. He has moved against your father."

Annon's hearts contracted and he pulled up short. "Then I must go to him. He will need my help."

"That is impossible—"

"No!" he jerked away from her, turned in the blackness and started back the way they had come. "I will not listen to you! What do you know, anyway? You are Kundalan!"

"Annon!" she cried, her voice full of terrible anguish. "Your father is beyond your help. He is dead—"

"That's a lie!" Annon cried. "Kinnnus Morcha would never allow—"

"It was Morcha who slew him—Morcha the traitor, seduced by a deal with Wennn Stogggul."

"No, it can't be!" But he paused, thinking of the commotion he had seen through the lens of the oculus, someone falling, spread-eagled, possibly—no, probably—dead. "Ah, N'Luuura take the enemies of the Ashera!"

"Yes," she said with surprising venom. "N'Luuura take them all!"

He dug his knuckles into the ridges of his hairless skull. "My father is . . . dead?"

She came to him then and laid his head against her breast, but he jerked away.

"No! I'm not a little boy anymore. I am the eldest Ashera. By the Law of Succession I am the regent now. I must go back and command—"

"You will not go back," Giyan said firmly. "Stogggul's pack of Khaggun has joined with those Haaar-kyut who follow Morcha. They control the palace now. Everyone loyal to your father lies in a pool of blood—except you and me."

"But I have a duty—"

"Listen to me, Annon, at this very moment they are scouring the palace for us. The Prime Factor is desperate to destroy you because you are the only person standing in his way."

"My sisters?"

"Dead. As well as their children. All dead." Her eyes leveled on him, and he could feel that intensity she brought to his lessons. "Your duty now is to stay alive."

"All of them dead?" He turned this way and that. Tears stood quivering in the corners of his eyes, and he was shamed. He turned to her. "Remember the seer?" He saw her look. "The old V'ornn on the street corner. He said I that I should beware. That I was marked by the Ancient One."

"Nonsense. I told you."

"Maybe he saw all this." His eyes were open wide in shock and fear. "What am I to do? This is all happening too fast."

"Shock tactics. A key part of Stogggul's plan," Giyan whispered.

"What about the Gyrgon?" Annon said. "They must be my allies. By law I replace my father as regent when he dies."

Giyan put her hand over his okummmon. "Do not be so

certain. Have you been Summoned? Have the Gyrgon contacted you as they should have?" His silence goaded her on. "The only way to defeat Stogggul is to escape the palace and the city. To gain time to consider your options, to discover who may still be loyal to the Ashera, to discover from which quarters help may come. You cannot do this yourself. Please, Annon, you must believe me."

Believe a Kundalan, he thought. *Everyone is mad, including me.*

"All right," he said at last. "Lead the way."

Sudden light flared and Annon shaded his eyes, squinting, his hearts racing. Had they been discovered so soon? But no, he saw as his eyes adjusted, Giyan had lighted the remnant of an old pitch torch with a firestick. The thing coughed and sputtered and threatened to extinguish itself, but Giyan cupped her hands, shielding it from a draft and it regained life. She stood before him, dressed oddly for her in Tuskugggun robes complete with the traditional sifeyn, the cowl that covered her head.

He looked around, saw how V'ornn technology had carved out a series of saclike cells in this section of the bedrock. He peered inside, already knowing what he would find.

"How long did Kundalan prisoners last in there?" Giyan stared at the strange and eerie scalpels, clamps, wires, spadelike blades and pincers that protruded from the curved walls and ceiling like pustules on someone dying of duur fever. "Typically."

Annon poked his head into the second cell. It smelled very bad. "It depended on how willing the prisoner was to speak."

"What you really mean is that it depended on the form of torture the interrogators used."

Annon turned to her, but ignored her accusation. "Why are we lingering here?" He stamped first one foot, then another. "You said yourself—"

Giyan shoved her left palm toward him. "We will not get far no matter where we go or how cleverly we hide, when I have *this*."

"The okuuut!"

She nodded. "My identity implant. With this, they can track me anywhere we go." Her eyes were large, catching the bright yellow spark of the pitch torch. "We must be rid of it."

"But how?"

She produced Kurgan's bolt, held it out to him haft first.

"No," he said, his stomachs lurching. "You cannot mean—!"

"Annon, it must be done." When she saw him backing away, she said: "Listen to me, it is your duty—your *first* duty as the new regent. You *must* protect yourself. At all costs."

"But it will hurt so much!"

She smiled. "Not so much as you fear. I will guide you every step of the . . ."

Her words trailed off. Annon saw her staring at him. "What is it?"

"Annon, in Miina's name!" She pointed at his bare torso.

He looked down at his chest, his ribs—his ribs! There were no wounds, just a small discoloration. He pressed his fingers to his rib cage. No pain, so soreness, not even the hint of an ache. And the peculiar throbbing of the gyreagle talon was gone.

He looked back at her in wonder and started to tell her what had happened, but stopped as she thrust the haft of the bolt into his hand.

"There's no time," she whispered. "Tell me as you work. It will serve to distract me."

The best place for her to sit was inside one of the cells. He chose the least foul-smelling one and, taking the lighted torch, squatted beside her. But when he examined the four-tined point of the bolt he shook his head.

"What's the matter?" she asked.

"This will never work."

"But you've got to—"

He held up a hand as he rose. He went over to the wall full of interrogation implements, chose the sickle-bladed scalpel, and returned with it. He thrust the blade into the flame, cleansing it. Giyan watched the thing as if it were a poison-adder.

He held the glowing edge of the curved scalpel over the okuuut, waiting only for it to cool sufficiently.

"This is ironic, don't you think?" She looked straight into his eyes, would not look at the V'ornn-made horrors of their surroundings.

"I don't know where to begin," Annon said.

"Begin at the moment you left my chambers."

He knew that she had deliberately misunderstood him, and he was curiously grateful for that. He spoke at the same moment the scalpel penetrated her skin. She sucked in her breath, the blood commenced to flow.

"Deeper," she said, gritting her teeth. "You must get underneath it."

She put her back against the wall, spread her legs and braced herself, but as Annon held her left hand in his, as he continued to carve into her while he told her everything that had occurred since he had left her, he felt a kind of lassitude flow through her like a current of syrup, slowing her pulse, her heartbeat, even, if he could believe his senses, the very flow of her blood.

When he came to the part about the feeling that had come over him on the spiral stairwell, her glassy-eyed stare fixed on him, and she said in a strangely deep voice: "How are you doing?"

"Okay, I think."

"Are you underneath the okuuut?"

"Yes." Her blood dripped slowly between her spread fingers, ran down the side of his hand, dripped off his wrist.

"You will feel three threads, like wires," she said after a moment. "You must find the *thinnest* one and sever it. *You* must sever it *first*." Her voice seemed weird, slurred, but he dared not look up, break his concentration. He felt divided. He wanted to work as fast as he could to spare her more pain but he was afraid he would make a mistake, cut a nerve or artery, damage her permanently. For an instant, he was as aware as she was of every clever instrument of torture that surrounded them. Then, he set his fear aside and concentrated on recounting his story.

"The gyreagle talon pulsed inside you?" she said.

"Yes. It was as if it was drawing me down here to the caverns."

"And then the Door to the Storehouse opened?"

"Yes. And I saw the creature."

"Tell me. What did it look like?"

When he told her, she began to shake. "Do you remember its color?"

"It was the purest sea-green."

"The Dragon Seelin." Her voice was a hushed whisper. "No one living has seen a Sacred Dragon—"

"I *did* see it."

"I might have thought you were hallucinating," she breathed, "but only a Sacred Dragon could have removed the gyreagle talon and healed you like that."

"And when I woke up I found a book beside me."

"What kind of book?"

"An old book with worn leather covers. It is Kundalan, I think. I will show you when I am finished."

He could feel the three snakelike threads. It was difficult with all the blood and her own ganglia nearby to tell one from the other. The thinnest, she had said. Sever the thinnest first. Suddenly chilled, he hesitated.

"Go on," she said softly. "You can do it, Annon. I know it."

He licked his lips, looking very much like his father. "Giyan, tell me about the Dragons."

Giyan closed her eyes, whether out of pain or concentration he could not say. "The Five Sacred Dragons created Kundala and all the heavens around it. The Ramahan claim they are Miina's children, just like the Hagoshrin, guardians of The Pearl. What is the reality of it? I simply do not know. I doubt that even the konara, the senior priestesses who make up the Dea Cretan, the Ramahan High Council, could tell us."

One-two-three. He thought he had found the right thread. At least, it *seemed* the thinnest.

"I have found it."

"What are you waiting for, then? Cut it."

He moved the blade a millimeter.

Her breathing slowed. "Don't . . . Try not to damage the okuuut," she said. "With luck, it will continue to transmit for a time after you have severed it and we can mislead Stogggul's cadre as to our whereabouts."

He nodded and began. With her free hand, she wiped away the sweat running down his face. He could feel the hardness of the Gyrgon-made thread against the edge of the blade and he summoned his courage and strength, all at once shoving it forward, severing it.

Giyan gave a little gasp. Her head came down onto her chest, her sifeyn hiding her expression. "Thank you," she whispered.

He worked quickly now, moving the tip in a semicircle, lifting the thing out of her. While she dug out her herbs, he peered at the okuuut. It was filmed in blood, and he used his thumb to clean it off. He turned it over, saw the raw roots of the severed wires.

"It's dead," he said. "The moment I cut the ganglia it shut down."

"Bad luck," she said as she packed the wound with the herbs, wrapped it in part of the bandage she was going to use to bind his wounds. "There are times when misdirection has its merits."

"How are you?" he asked.

She looked at him. Her eyes were losing their glassy appearance. "I will be fine, Annon."

He stood, handed her the bolt, wiped the scalpel on his trouser leg. He almost let go of it, then thought better of it.

"Now, show me the book," she said.

Was it his imagination, or was she looking at him with an odd expression? He pulled out the small book from inside the waistband of his trousers and handed it to her. Her hands were shaking as she opened it.

"It is Kundalan, isn't it?" he said. "But the writing—You taught me to read Kundalan, but I can't read this."

"It is written in the Old Tongue." She was flushed and breathless. She held it out, but he shook his head.

"It is Kundalan. You should have it."

Her eyes were shining as she pressed the book into his hands. "It was given to you for a reason, Annon. Hide it, keep it safe, and under no circumstances are you to tell anyone about it. Understand?"

He nodded, wondering what had just happened. She was looking at him as if she had never seen him before.

He cleared his throat. "We had better be on our way," he said.

Kurgan Stogggul stood on the inner balcony of the regent's suite. The doors had been thrown open, and the curtains blew and billowed like clouds in the still night air. One of Kundala's moons had recently risen. Half its pocked face was visible, like the bones of a very old woman. It hung above the regent's chamber like a lamp about to be extinguished, striking with its cool reflected light the familiar features of Eleusis Ashera. His eyes, already filmed over, were wide and staring as if to make an eternal comment on his untimely death. Kurgan watched sourly as his father held aloft the trophy Kinnnus Morcha had secured for him.

The two of them had been fighting like children. From what he could gather, his father had instructed the Line-General to keep Eleusis Ashera alive long enough to torture him for the secret to the salamuuun trade, but events had gotten out of hand, according to Morcha, and he had had no choice but to kill the regent. Well, at least his father had a trophy for his bedside, Kurgan thought. In any case, it was his opinion that Eleusis Ashera would never have revealed his secrets in the limited amount of time the Line-General had to work on him. In order for the coup to succeed, his father had to announce by morning that all the Ashera were dead. Not that anyone was interested in his opinion, Kurgan knew. *To N'Luuura with them all!*

"The palace is secure. Victory is ours!" Kinnnus Morcha proclaimed.

"How long have I waited for this moment!" The Prime Factor's voice was hoarse from shouting. "Ever since the Gyrgon unjustly ruled against my father, ever since they installed the Ashera as regents? Oh no, longer than that! All my life, it seems I stood in Eleusis Ashera's shadow, all my accomplishments hollow next to the accursed Ashera." He held high the prize of Eleusis Ashera's severed head. "And now at the brink of my finest moment, I must content myself with this." He tapped the temple of his nemesis. "Everything that was in there—all the precious secrets—gone with one thrust of an ion sword."

"Be jubilant!" Kinnnus Morcha cried. "Do not allow anything to deny you this moment for, at last, your time is finally come!"

"You are right, my friend!" Wennn Stogggul spat into Eleusis Ashera's face. "This night I have almost everything I desire."

"And I have no doubt that soon you will have it all!"

The two of them toasted each other with fire-grade numaaadis from the regent's cellar.

"No more of that vile cloudy rakkis!" Kinnnus Morcha shouted, wiping his lips, only to down another glass of the strong V'ornn liquor.

Victory, yes, Kurgan thought. *For them. But what about me?*

"Line-General," the giddy Stogggul said, "when will your Khagggun bring me the head of Annon Ashera?" He lifted his bloody trophy high. "If heads are to be my prizes this night, I would have a matched set!"

"That depends," Kinnnus Morcha said. "If you contact the Gyrgon, they can track him instantly by his okummmon."

"*You* are my tracker, Line-General." Stogggul bit down hard on his contempt. The Lesser Castes knew so little about the Gyrgon. If he contacted them now, they would find Annon Ashera, all right. And doubtless place him on the regent's throne by right of succession. This was an outcome to be avoided at all costs. No, no. He had planned it well. He would go to the Gyrgon in a position of strength, not as a petitioner on his knees.

"And find him I will, make no mistake," Kinnnus Morcha said. "He is still within the palace walls. I myself saw him enter with the Kundalan skcettta. Trust me, he will not escape us. There is no one to give him aid; by night's end we will have executed them all!" The two men laughed like chii-foxes at the rising of the moons.

Annon came in with Giyan, Kurgan thought, observing them, cloaked by night and shadows. *If he escapes, it will be with her connivance. She knows every secret nook and cranny of this accursed place.*

He looked over the side of the balcony, grabbed hold of a sturdy vine from one of the oldest of the star-rose plants, shinnied down into the garden. He went swiftly along the loggia to where one of his father's Khagggun was manning the west-ring guard post.

He planted himself in front of the Khagggun, and in his most authoritative voice said: "My father needs a Tracker. Now."

The Khagggun looked at him, nodded distractedly, and handed over a metallic oval. "Mind it's returned to me. Those things are expensive." He raised his voice as Kurgan took off at a trot. "It will be my salary docked if you lose it!"

Kurgan thumbed on the Tracker as he went, dialed up the directory. This showed him the names of all Kundalan with okuuut registered within the palace's purview. It took him but a moment to scroll through the list. He highlighted Giyan's name, pressed a red button. The Tracker beeped three times as the screen cleared. He saw the word: TRACKING and then: FOUND. He watched, while the letters and symbols scrolled in a spiral over the screen.

They're in the subterranean caverns, he said to himself. *Very close to the northern perimeter. What can they be up to? What does the Kundalan female know that I don't? In this case, plenty,* he told himself.

Neither his father nor the Line-General would consider that the Kundalan skcettta might harbor maternal instincts toward her charge. An animal feeling protective toward a V'ornn? Unthinkable! *Adults*, he thought. *Slow as a hindemuth and twice as stupid.*

He raced through the labyrinthine corridors and chambers. He was almost at the north end of the ring when the signal blipped off. He paused, as much to catch his breath as to see what had happened. The diagnostic tab showed him the Tracker was working perfectly. Something had terminated the signal. That could only happen if Giyan was dead. He could only deduce that Annon was alone and doubtless frightened out of his wits. Kurgan imagined what he would feel like if his father was dead, if he saw his bloody head being held aloft.

He saw the north-ring guard post up ahead and slowed down before he was spotted by the Haaar-kyut manning it. He took deep breaths to get his wind back and passed by the idiot Khaggun in his father's pay. They weren't any brighter than Morcha's unit. He was smarter than all of them put together.

Laughing to himself, he sauntered out of the north gates. He paused to look around. More Khaggun were arrayed around the palace as if awaiting a major revolt—by what, he snickered, a herd of maddened cthauros? He threaded his way through the Khaggun. All of them knew Kurgan Stoggul, the Prime Factor's son. Prime Factor, soon to be regent.

Beyond the military perimeter, Axis Tyr lay in unnatural, enforced darkness. There was an air about the place of a military campaign, the acrid edge of brawny muscle, leveled weapons, and ominous threat. Here and there, tucked into far-distant corners of the city, fusion lamps still burned. But here, shadows bundled in the street, piled themselves in doorways, stretched forth their elastic fingers to embrace walls, windows, shopfronts, cthauros pens, and those few passersby drawn by the Khaggun's inevitable clamor.

Kurgan stopped to visually reconnoiter. This was a trick

the Old V'ornn had taught him when he had taken him hunting. *Don't look and walk,* he had said. *Stand still and let your eyes pick out the likely spots for game.*

Now Kurgan looked from sector to sector in an arc radiating out from the looming north face of the regent's palace. *Where would I put an exit,* he asked himself, *if I had built that subterranean cavern?*

Running from right to left, he saw a row of artisan's ateliers—Bashkir-run businesses where Tuskugggun past childbearing age plied their trades. He took them in quickly and superficially and went on. He recognized one of the city's four cthauros pens, from which V'ornn could ride into the countryside; a marble fountain, one of hundreds throughout Axis Tyr; more shopfronts—the northern edge of the market district, to be exact. Nothing out of the ordinary, little that seemed suitable, unless . . .

His eyes swung back to the row of ateliers. Many of the Tuskugggun needed kilns, deep pools of running water and the like, so they had appropriated these buildings from displaced Kundalan artisans because in most instances what they needed was already in place Their equipment required basements, foundations, water pipes, filtration systems—in short, extensive subterranean work spaces that might easily have been joined up in the past to secret passageways and hidden doors.

Having made his decision, Kurgan trotted off toward the ateliers. Every so often, he checked the Tracker, but it showed nothing. On Grey Weave Street, he clung to the shadows of the buildings, trying each door in turn. All were locked. Turning the corner onto Blank Lane, he discovered a narrow alleyway the Tuskugggun used to lay in supplies and set out huge barrels of castoffs and remnants. The alley was deserted and ill lighted. Kurgan walked its length, now and again peering in back windows, seeing little but his own ghostly reflection. When he reached the south end of the alley, he chose a spot behind a barrel reeking of dye-lot salts and hunkered down.

As it happened, he did not have long to wait. He heard a

noise first, and peered around the side of the barrel. He saw
Annon emerging from an underground cistern. Kurgan was
about to call out to him when he saw him turn, bend, and
extend his arm. He hauled upward, and out of the cistern
popped a Tuskugggun. Kurgan held his breath. What was
this? He wondered. Then the Tuskugggun turned so that her
face was briefly toward him. He sucked in his breath. The
Kundalan skcettta! Kurgan was stunned. With her okuuut
inoperative, she should have been dead. Then he saw why
Annon had been helping her: a bandage was wound tightly
around her left palm. She had surgically removed the okuuut!
Kurgan had never heard of such a thing happening; up until
that moment he had not known it was possible. But he was
someone who rejoiced in the new and unexpected, and now
he held his position, stilled his voice. He watched and waited.

When Giyan pointed north, he followed them to the cthauros pens. He watched, wide-eyed, as the Kundalan skcettta
went over the fence and walked into a knot of the animals.
He himself put no faith in the consistency of behavior of any
Kindalini animal and now he was astonished to see how
these sestapeds stamped the ground, bent their long necks so
that she could scratch their heads. She beckoned to Annon,
who nimbly vaulted over the fence. When she had put him
on a cthauros she had chosen, she grabbed another by its
thick neck hair and swung herself astride its broad back. It
lifted its head and rose on its four hind legs. Then she
slapped Annon's mount, dug her heels into her own, and the
two cthauros charged the north fence of the pen, soared over
the highest rail, landed on the street, and, with sparks flying,
took off in the direction of the North Gate.

When Kurgan returned to the regent's suite in the palace
he found his father sitting in a chair with his booted
feet propped up on a desk. Eleusis Ashera's personal silicon
wafers were strewn across the floor, caught in the edges of
carpets, flapping like the wings of wounded birds from the
louvers in the fusion lamps. Wennn Stogggul held an empty
bottle of fire-grade numaaadis in one hand and Annon's

birth-caul in the other. They swung in time to his singing, and what he was singing was something about starlight. He was singing this idiotic little ditty to a ragged line of dis-embodied heads which sat atop the desk, while periodically flinging wet kisses at them. Kurgan recognized them all: the heads of the former regent, his three daughters, their two small sons and one daughter.

"Ah, there you are," Wennn Stogggul said, barely missing a refrain. "Hiding in the shadows, eh?"

"No, I—"

"Well, who can blame you?" Wennn Stogggul's face grew violet with the gathering of blood. "I should murder you along with all your friends in the Ashera Dynasty."

"That is an unfair accusat—"

"Who said life is fair? Has it been fair to me? The differ-ence is, I don't whine about it." Stogggul's eyes were half-glazed, and there was a nasty expression on his face. "I don't suck up to the Ashera the way you have with Annon just to be in his reflected glory. Disgusting behavior. Now see where it has gotten you." He laughed drunkenly. "Fool that you are, you chose the wrong side!" His laughter rose to an earsplit-ting level. "Perhaps I should punish you! Yes, that is what I shall do!"

"You are always punishing me."

"And why should I not? My father did the same to me. Punishment is the quickest way to learn."

Kurgan bit his lip until he tasted a fine thread of blood.

Wennn Stogggul rubbed his nose. "Speaking of your grandfather, do you know what Kinnnus Morcha told me? Eleusis claimed the Ashera did not sabotage his spacecraft. Outlandish, what?" He threw Annon's birth-caul at the re-gent's head, toppling it off its perch. "And to compound his calumny he said that your grandfather was on a fool's errand! Can you imagine? Your grandfather a fool?"

Rage welled up in Kurgan, and he could no longer keep silent. "Eleusis was right. Grandfather *was* a fool to think he could directly challenge the Ashera claim on salamuuun."

Wennn Stogggul's face turned purple. "Don't say a word!"

he shouted. "Not one more word against your grandfather! He was a great V'ornn! A *successful* V'ornn, which is more than I can say for you! You aren't worth a grain-weight against him."

Something shut down inside Kurgan. He felt like an island in the middle of a raging sea. He knew he must do whatever it took to keep himself from being inundated by the rising water. "You are drunk on your victory, father. But it will be short-lived unless—"

"There you go whining again." Wennn Stogggul spat at his son's feet. "Unless what?" he roared. "Will you look into your magic crystal ball and show me the future?" He laughed harshly, contemptuously. "On to something of *real* importance! I am in need of more of this fine numaaadis."

"I think you have had enough."

"Who asked you to think? Fetch me another bottle, you little swine!" the Prime Factor shrieked, hurling the bottle at the boy.

Easily ducking the makeshift ordnance, Kurgan retreated to the hallway, where he ran into Line-General Kinnnus Morcha.

The huge Khagggun's booming laugh echoed down the otherwise eerily quiet halls. "Running your father's errands again?"

"I guess we have that in common," Kurgan said.

Kinnnus Morcha frowned. Unlike Wennn Stogggul, he was not too drunk to know what was being said. "You have an uncommonly acid tongue for one so young."

"I am not as young as all that. How about a drink?"

"A drink?" The Line-General's laughter boomed out again. "I warrant you *are* one of a kind. Why, the fire-grade numaaadis your father and I have been drinking would shrivel the markings on your tender parts. That is, if your tender parts *had* any markings!" He roared again as his jest.

"One drink," Kurgan pressed. "That is all I ask. It *is* a special night, after all."

Kinnnus Morcha regarded him with a remarkably sober expression. "Aye, there is no disputing that."

"Well, then. Where is the harm?" He grinned. "I won't tell my father if you won't."

The Line-General nodded. "All right. As you say, where is the harm?"

He led Kurgan into a midsize chamber that had been converted from a sanctuary into a library. Where images of the Goddess Miina had hung, now stood cases filled with silicon wafers and data-gems that held the entire cultural libraries of the races the V'ornn had conquered. Of their own past, however, there was precious little.

Kurgan waited until the other poured the liquor into Kundalan-made goblets and handed one to him.

"To our enemies!" Kinnnus Morcha cried. "May destruction possess their houses!"

They downed their numaaadis, and Kurgan had to control his throat from closing up. As the intolerable fire spread into the first of his three stomachs, he said: "Speaking of enemies, how goes the search for the new regent?"

Kinnnus Morcha's head swiveled like a predator's. "Foolish child! If you have even half a brain, you will not call Annon Ashera that in front of your father."

"But that's what Annon is, right? The new regent. Heir to the Ashera Dynasty."

"Only until we catch him and carry his head on a pike through the streets of Axis Tyr."

Kurgan went and refilled his goblet, spread himself comfortably into a gigantic V'ornn chair.

"One drink and no more," the Line-General stated. "I have to see to the search."

"The search, the search." Kurgan put his feet up, crossed one black boot over another. "The search, Line-General, is not going well."

Kinnnus Morcha slammed the goblet down with such force it shattered. "That is none of your affair."

"Possibly not," Kurgan said, taking a sip of the numaaadis. "But it ought to be."

"Arrogant pup!"

"Arrogance? Is it arrogance that I can tell you how to find the new regent?"

Kinnnus Morcha snorted. "I was a fool to let you have even a sip of numaaadis. It has gone straight to your head." He strode to the doorway. "I have no more time to waste with—"

"But I *do* know where he is."

The Khagggun looked down at him derisively. "Why should I believe you?"

Kurgan shrugged. "Because I have seen him."

"You what!"

"And he is not alone." Kurgan grinned again. "Contrary to your boast to my father, not all of Annon's friends are lying in a pool of blood."

"If this is truth, I demand that you—!"

"Line-General, you will pardon me for saying this, but you are in no position to demand anything of me." He got up, poured numaaadis into another goblet, handed it to Kinnnus Morcha. He gestured languidly. "Have a seat, and we will talk."

The Line-General looked as if both his hearts were going to explode at once. "Are you insane?"

"You should consider being more polite, Line-General." Kurgan sat down opposite the other. "As you Khagggun would say, I've just risen in the ranks."

"What is this—extortion?"

"Nothing of the kind, Line-General. I have something you need, and you have something I want." Kurgan shrugged. "It's a deal, pure and simple."

Kinnnus Morcha eyed him suspiciously. "Has your father put you up to this? Is this some sort of test?"

"My father is blissfully, drunkenly ignorant of this meeting. And I intend to keep it that way." All at once, Kurgan leaned forward. "You see, he may think of you as his errand boy, but I see your true worth."

"You do? You are only—what—fifteen sidereal cycles old."

"My chronological age is irrelevant. I have gone through

the Channeling. I know things. I can sense them when others beat about the bushes in the darkness." His eyes sparked. "What I am proposing, Line-General, is an alliance. I want to be your adjutant."

Kinnnus Morcha's mouth nearly dropped open. "Quite apart from the absurdity of the notion, I already have an adjutant."

"I know. His name is—what?" Kurgan snapped his fingers.

"Pack-Commander Rekkk Hacilar."

Kurgan nodded. "Ah yes, the renowned hero Rekkk Hacilar—intelligent, resourceful, ruthless, and—"

"And what?" Kinnnus Morcha's eyes narrowed.

"Well . . ." Kurgan looked down at his curled fingers. "There is a rumor . . . a disturbing rumor that Rekkk Hacilar was in league with Eleusis Ashera: that, like regent, the Pack-Commander has a soft spot in his heart for the Kundalan."

Kinnnus Morcha's canny eyes locked on Kurgan. "Information of this nature is rarely available to one so young. How come you by it?"

"I am like a Khaggggun in this, Line-General. I do not reveal my sources."

Kinnnus Morcha sat back and steepled his fingers. "What to make of you, Kurgan Stogggul? Are you clever or simply arrogant?"

Kurgan remained silent. He knew when to keep his mouth shut.

"The truth is . . ." Kinnnus Morcha paused, threw his arms wide. "The truth that will not leave this room is that I have had Pack-Commander Hacilar under surveillance for some time. Transferring First-Captain Olnnn Rydddlin to the pack was on my command, though I took pains that it should not appear so. Olnnn Rydddlin is my Khaggggun, hearts and soul. His assignment is to observe—"

"To spy, you mean."

Kinnnus Morcha shrugged. "To a Khaggggun, the two words are interchangeable. I have also kept Rekkk Hacilar's pack raiding in the west, where we have a less complete picture of the resistance cells, where he might feel more free to express his alleged predilections concerning the Kundalan."

"Has he betrayed himself?"

"Not yet. Olnnn Rydddlin says that he is exceedingly careful." Kinnnus Morcha turned his hands over as if emptying them of sand. "Perhaps, after all, the rumor is false. We all have enemies. Advancement breeds jealousy in those passed over."

Kurgan held the Line-General's gaze as carefully as he would hold a female's hand. "I say get rid of him before he does something traitorous."

Kinnnus Morcha's head shot forward, and his yellow teeth glistened in the fusion-lamp light. "You are a trollish little thing, aren't you?"

Kurgan let his breath out slowly in order to keep himself from choking on his fear of Morcha. "Do not make the mistake of underestimating me, Line-General. I may be young, but I know who I am."

Kinnnus Morcha, still on point, surveyed the other. "I know what you are—you are Bashkir. You could not be my adjutant even if I desired it."

"Please understand, Line-General, I also know what I want."

Those teeth glistened. "Tell me why I should care."

"You yourself have made a deal with my father to bring Great Caste status to the Khagggun. It is my belief that in the coming years the Khagggun will play a larger role in V'ornn governance. *That* is what I want."

"No, I think what you want is what *you* want."

Kurgan smiled a secret smile. "As do we all, Line-General. However, what I just said is not a lie."

At last, Kinnnus Morcha sat back. He looked into his goblet and downed its contents in one swallow. His head came up, and he pointed a murderous stare at Kurgan. The boy drained his portion of numaaadis in one swallow and with a fierce will held his stomachs still when they threatened to rebel.

"You swear you have seen Annon Ashera?"

"Yes."

"On which floor is he hiding?"

"He has already escaped the palace grounds."

The Line-General slammed his fist onto the tabletop. "This is bad news, indeed."

"Only if you do not know where he is headed."

Kinnnus Morcha cocked his head. "And you do, I gather."

"I can make an educated guess. And that, Line-General, is far more than anyone else can do."

Kinnnus Morcha's eyes were slits as a plan took shape in his mind. "I could send Rekkk Hacilar on this mission," he mused. "It would be a test, yes. If he has been allied, as I have heard, with Eleusis Ashera, he will show his traitorous colors in going after the son. And, after all, I have Olnnn Rydddlin to ensure nothing goes wrong." All at once, he sat forward on the chair so that their knees were almost touching. He extended his arm, and Kurgan took it. Kurgan felt a thrill shoot through him.

The Line-General held Kurgan's arm in a painful grip. "Kurgan Stogggul, if you are correct, if we find Annon Ashera, then you have my word. Everything you desire shall be yours."

7

Eleana

Came the deluge. Annon, who had been keeping an eye on the thick strata of cloud that had obscured the moon, felt the sudden sharp bite of the west wind, saw the brushy tops of the blesson firs whip this way and that, then bow before the downpour. The bleak sky opened up, and rain cascaded down with uncommon fury.

Within seconds they were soaked. Fifteen kilometers north of Axis Tyr, bent low over the sweat-slick backs of their galloping cthauros, they felt the rain as if it were a weight upon them. The world closed in until they could see no farther than several meters in any given direction.

By this time, they had joined with the river, which at this point ran almost due north into the heart of the Djenn Marre. But they could no more see the mountain range ahead of them than they could the silhouette of Axis Tyr behind them. They had come through the low plains, which, to the west below the point where the Chuun River turned, became marshland, dangerous and difficult to traverse not only for its uncertain footing but also for the creatures inhabiting it. Though they had intended to put as much distance between them and the city, wherever possible they had tried to keep clear of the small clots of the outlying villages that had sprung up like satellites to Axis Tyr's sun. The fewer people who saw them, the better. Even if it was mainly Kundalan who lived here, you never knew who might be in the pay of the V'ornn, for it was a well-known fact among the underground that the V'ornn were experts in co-opting Kundalan, preying upon their dissatisfaction, their petty rivalries, jealousies, and their level of poverty. It was said that the V'ornn paid well for their prying eyes and ears.

The banks along the Chuun now began to rise as they made their way out of the lowlands upon which Axis Tyr had been built. On either side of the river, what had once been oat grass and ammonwood fields had been supplanted by vast orchards of genetically engineered laaaddis trees, from whose fruit the potent V'ornn drink numaaadis was made. Hordes of Kundalan farmers had had their lands usurped by the mammoth V'ornn earthmovers, their crops plowed under to make room for the Gyrgon-created mutations. These same farmers were then indoctrinated in the care of the laaaddis orchards, reduced to serfs under the yoke of the invaders. Once, fifty years ago, the underground had set fire to some of these orchards. The V'ornn response had been swift and murderous. Kundalan children had been killed in front of their parents, then husbands killed before the horrified eyes of their wives. Only the women were left with the backbreaking burden of replanting the vat-grown young laaaddis, restoring the orchards to their former growth levels. To this day, no Kundalan could pass by these lands without an anguished heart.

For an hour or more, they plodded past these neatly turned rows of alien trees. The serrated leaves rustled like armor in the night wind, the corkscrewlike limbs growing heavy with the blackish fruit whose musty odor was so offensive to the Kundalan.

At long last, they reached the northern edge of the orchards. All at once, scruffy stands of evergreens—feathery blesson firs, grey-blue Marre pines, along with scrub-wood and curly-bark river lingots—overtook the almost obsessively geometrical patterns of the laaaddis, and gradually the small villages were reduced to a scattering of farmhouses. The well-trammeled earthen path they followed wound in and out of these forests, taking them first away from the churning Chuun, then back again. In the pounding rain, no creature stirred or hunted. In any event, the drumming sound of the rain mingling with their cthauros' hoofbeats drowned out everything but the rapid firing of their hearts.

Annon's mind was still abuzz with the horror of recent events. He wished that he had been able to see his father one last time, but perhaps it was better that he hadn't. From what he had managed to pry out of Giyan, his family's deaths had been horrific. Still, his mind's eye opened like an iris, his imagination providing the images his eyes had not seen. He wept to think of his father so ignominiously beheaded—and by the commandant of the Haaar-kyut, the very Khagggun sworn to protect him with his life! His fists tightened in the cthauros' thick mane, his teeth ground together. If it was the last thing he did, he swore to himself, he would avenge his father's death and the deaths of all the Ashera. Rage boiled up in him, almost unseating him in its intensity. He threw his head back and wailed into the howling of the storm. His mouth filled with rainwater and he spat it out, imagining that it struck Kinnnus Morcha's and Wennn Stogggul's decapitated heads. He would live to see that sight, he vowed. If it took the rest of his life, he would make it happen.

He missed Kurgan, missed his hard practicality, the razor-sharp clarity of his thoughts. Kurgan might be impulsive, but he was a genius at long-range planning. Annon could use those abilities now. Kurgan despised his father, but Annon had little idea of his loyalty to his family. Annon resolved to contact his best friend when the time was right. But not now. In the meantime, though, what was he to do? Even if they successfully fled to the mountains, then what? To whom could he turn? Who would help him?

More questions continued to plague him. He had no idea how they had gotten past the Khaggun manning the North Gate to the city. Astonishingly, they had had no trouble at all. It was as if all the guards had seen was a V'ornn Tuskugggun with her son. They had pulled up in front of the guard post and the markings on his tender parts had begun to itch as the Khaggun had emerged to confront them. Then something he still could not explain had happened. Giyan began to speak but in a language he had never heard before. Instantly, his eyelids had become heavy and he had observed the rapt faces of the Khaggun through the slitted lids of someone so exhausted he was asleep on his feet. Nevertheless, he was certain that the Khaggun had listened to Giyan's alien words as if they understood her perfectly. Then they had nodded, opened the gates, and waved them through. There had been no time to ask her what had happened, no time since then, either, since they had mercilessly spurred their mounts on without surcease from that moment on.

Now the land began to rise in earnest. It became rockier and rougher. Quite soon, the lowland forests gave way to stands of ammonwood, heartwood, and stone-oak—hardwoods that thrived in a climate farther away from the sea, in land where the water table was higher. Great swaths had been cut in these beautiful forests, as the V'ornn's ravenous thirst for raw materials increased the logging industry out of all proportion. Annon knew that there were many V'ornnmandated strip mines in the foothills of the Djenn Marre, extracting from Kundala every carbon-based and silicon-based ore they could find, plus some substances pulled from deep within the magma of the planet unknown even to the Kundalan. It was hinted that the Gyrgon studied them in their secret laboratories.

Annon felt more comfortable in these hardwood forests not only because it meant that they were farther from Axis Tyr and therefore farther from detection, but also because the huge, majestic trees served as the best natural screening for their headlong flight.

Sorcery. Of course Giyan had used her Kundalan sorcery to somehow convince the Khagggun guards that she was Annon's mother. In her Tuskugggun robes and sifeyn she had only to conjure a V'ornn face for them to become convinced. But if that was what happened, why hadn't he been affected? True, he had felt a deep lassitude come over him, but for him her appearance had never altered. He saw her face during the exchange and it was the one he had always known. He shook his head. Even when one mystery was solved, it spawned another, more vexing than the first.

Annon judged it to be three sidereal hours before dawn when Giyan slowed their pace to a trot, then a walk, and finally halted beneath the thick canopy of a heartwood. By this time, the river was some few kilometers to the east, as the path there had widened to a road along which there was sure to be traffic, even at this late hour. The V'ornn had dictated that their rape of the planet continue night and day without letup. Logging wagons used that road; it would be far too risky to be spotted as lone travelers heading north. The forest trail Giyan had found slowed them, but afforded far more security.

The sweet smell of damp decay mingled with the storm's ozone-edged frenzy as they dismounted.

"What is it?" he asked, coming around as she knelt at the side of her cthauros.

Giyan touched the beast so that he raised one of the hind legs. She inspected the sole of the hoof. "He picked up a stone," she said, using the head of Kurgan's bolt to pry it out. "He is so valiant that he didn't let me know until it pained him overmuch. Only then did I feel the change in his gait." She dug in her bag, massaged something into the cthauros' hoof. "It is quite sore and will take some hours to heal." She looked up at him as she dropped the hoof. "If I continue to run him, he will surely pull up lame and be of no further use to us."

Annon nodded. "I could use some rest." He put his hands on his own cthauros. He thought of what Giyan said about her mount, that he was valiant. Curious. He had seen these beasts many times, had even on occasion been near them. And yet he had never thought of them as being valiant creatures. Until now. Giyan was right. He stroked the heaving, steaming flanks, wiping down the sweat as he had seen the Kundalan drovers do. The cthauros turned its head, nuzzled the crook of his arm.

"My father used to ride cthauros, remember?" He turned to her, saw that she was weeping.

"Oh, Miina, they slaughtered him as if he were a beast, as if his life meant nothing, as if he were not beloved."

He moved nearer but did not touch her. The world outside the heartwood canopy was grey, shapeless, steaming with rain. He stood over her while she buried her face in her hands, while her shoulders shook and she sobbed.

What am I to do? he wondered. He felt the loss of his family but, curiously, it was at a remove. It was as if he and the memory of them were separated by a sheet of V'ornn crystal. Truth to tell, it was Giyan with whom he had grown up—Giyan, Kurgan, and all the others from hingatta liiina do mori. It was not that he hadn't loved his father—of course he had! It was more that he had had precious little experience with that love. He could count on the fingers of his hands the times he had seen his father in the last six months. And as far as his sisters were concerned, he had seen them only on occasions of state when custom demanded all the children be present at the palace. Meanwhile, his life had gone on; so had Eleusis', but they had been in separate orbits, coming in contact infrequently and for short periods of time. In consequence, Annon found that though there was a hole inside him, he did not know who it was that he was missing.

At last, he bent and took Giyan by the arm.

"Let's move out of the rain."

She rose, allowed him to guide her deep into the dense tangle of the heartwood branches. Owing to its thick root system, the ground beneath the massive tree was raised, making it drier than the ground around it.

"There," he said, sitting down beside her. "There."

And she looked at him, wiped her eyes, and said: "I'm sorry."

"For what?"

"For not being strong enough."

"I don't understand."

"To protect your father." She looked at him with sorrowful eyes. "You were right to question my motives for publicly challenging Kurgan." She gave him a wan smile. "Sometimes, I used to think that you were too smart for your own good, but now I'm glad of it." The smile, what there was of it, faded. "The contest was a public warning to those who wished your father ill, to show that my sorcery would protect him." She shook her head, dark, shadowed inside the sifeyn. "I failed. I swear I will not let that happen with you."

He stared out at the rain. He heard it drumming against the ground, watched it form rivulets and run off to low spots it began to fill. It pattered down upon the leaves of the heartwood, dripping here and there where there were gaps in the structure. It began to grow colder, and he shivered a little, despite the Khagggun cloak Giyan had procured for him from one of the stupefied guards at North Gate.

"You must be hungry," she said, and rose to her feet. "I will fetch us something."

"There was no time to bring anything with us. Where will you find—"

"I can always find food," she said.

She turned to go, but he reached up, held her wrist so that she turned back, stared down at him.

"Don't go," he said softly.

"Why?" She gave him a gently mocking smile. "This far from Axis Tyr and V'ornn control do you think I will flee?"

"Don't go," he said again.

Her expression changed, softened. Something familiar lit her eyes. She took his fingers from her, but not immediately. "It will only be for a little while. I promise."

With that, she left the sanctuary of the tree, pulling her Tuskugggun robes more tightly around her. It seemed to him as if she passed through a veil of tears, from their small, safe world to a larger universe where everything now seemed fraught with peril.

He turned his head away, not wanting to see her vanish altogether. The cthauros stamped and snorted, as if they longed to be with her, but they did not move, save to crop another patch of wrygrass. Annon wriggled to get more comfortable, putting the small of his back against the bole of the heartwood. Something pressed against him, and he reached around, pulled the small leather-bound book he had found in the caverns from his waistband.

He opened it but in the dense gloom it was impossible to see anything useful. He rubbed the palm of his hand over the supple worn leather. Judging by its cover, it had been read many times. *How old is it*? he wondered. Maybe he was the first V'ornn ever to see it. He looked at the text. Though he knew how to read Kundalan, these runes appeared to have no relation to the modern-day language. What root language had spawned them and why was it completely different? He stared at the runes, as if willing them to speak to him. He liked their curved and filigreed shapes. They looked like rain pouring off the marginless pages. Closing it at last, he pressed the book into the small of his back, pushing it down into his waistband so that he would not lose it. He drew his knees up, wrapped his arms around his shins, and stared out the curtain of rain. How far would Giyan have to go to get food? Would it put her at risk if she was seen? His head ached from questions that could not be answered.

He had every intention of remaining vigilant, but the long

day had taken its inevitable toll. Soon his eyes grew weary, his lids closed, and his head lowered onto his knees. He dreamed that he was a disembodied head roving the countryside, searching for his body. He knew he had left it someplace, if only he could remember where. He had just glanced down to see blood dripping from the raw and ragged stump of his neck when he awoke with a start.

His head shot up. The doleful dripping of the rain had synchronized itself to the rhythm of his dripping blood. But that had been a dream, right? He was laughing grimly to himself at his foolishness when he saw Giyan approaching through the veil of rain. She burst into the heartwood canopy, ran full tilt at him. She was only a meter or so from him when he saw the upraised knife blade and he rolled away from the tree bole, tangling his legs with hers and bringing her down. He clawed his way over her thrashing form, just missed a vicious knife thrust, and grabbed her wrist. He jammed his forearm against her throat, bent over her.

Peering into her face, he saw that though she was a Kundalan, she was not Giyan. For one thing, she was much younger, for another—wait a minute! He recognized this female! She was the girl he and Kurgan had encountered at the creek.

Recognition flooded her face at almost the same instant.

"Great Goddess Miina!" she whispered. "I almost slit your throat."

"As if I would have let you!"

Again, there was a moment when their silence, their very inaction spoke volumes.

"Animal!" he snarled.

"V'ornn monster!" she shot back.

He took the Kundalan knife from her, sat back on his haunches. Freed, she gathered her legs beneath her. He remembered with piercing clarity how shapely they were. While they were wrestling, her hair had come undone from its pins, and now cascaded over her shoulders and down her back.

"What are you looking at, *monster*?" she said. Her deep, beautiful eyes glinted defiantly.

"Nothing." He got up and went around to the other side of the tree. The sight of her was doing strange things to him, things he didn't like. He felt as if his hearts were in his throat, as if his tri-lobed lung could scarcely take in enough air. He heard her soft approach but did not turn.

She reached out to touch him where the Khagggun cloak had come undone from their tussle, then thought better of it. "Your wounds—I saw the gyreagle attack you, but now there's no trace."

"I am a quick healer," he snapped, drawing the cloak back over his chest.

She seemed to ignore his implausible answer. "I never got a chance to thank you," she said.

"For what?"

"You know for what," she said sharply. "Will you force me say it?"

Something in her voice made him look at her at last, and he felt weak, drawn in by the sight of her, as if his insides had liquefied. Her eyes spoke to him as if she had somehow slipped inside his brain, lodged there like an exquisitely painful splinter. "Forget it! Don't say . . . anything." He felt a delicious, painful drawing in his tender parts. "Here!"

She jumped back, her eyes wide. He had thrust the knife at her blade first. He turned it so that he held it by the blade, then offered it to her again. She hesitated but a moment, then snatched it from him as if expecting him to change his mind. A certain tension returned between them, centered on the knife. Understanding this, she quickly put it away.

"My name is Eleana."

He said nothing, concentrating on his breathing as if it were a complex operation he hadn't quite mastered.

"Won't you tell me your name?" she asked.

"It's . . . It's not important."

She seemed to think about this for some time. At length, she said: "Is it true what they say about male V'ornn?" She stroked her hair, made of it long, shining swaths. It billowed through her fingers as she spread them wider and wider. His jaw clenched.

"You needn't say anything." She was smiling. "I can see the answer in your face. Your V'ornn face." Was she mocking him ever so gently? She dropped her hands to her sides. "I like what I see in that face."

"Why is that?" He spoke despite his vow not to engage with her. It felt somehow dangerous, but not in any normal way.

"Because I see gentleness and compassion and honor, three things I never believed I would see in a V'ornn face."

"Perhaps I am tricking you."

"Then I will ask you outright. Are you tricking me?"

"Yes."

She laughed. It was a soft, gentle laugh that transformed her face. "I do not believe you."

He wanted to get angry—N'Luuura, he *should* have gotten angry! But to his surprise and consternation, he didn't. *I am enchanted*, he thought. *It is more Kundalan sorcery.* But he wasn't altogether certain he believed that. Surely not all Kundalan females were sorcerers.

"You have no evil in your face—Please, won't you tell me your name? It is hard enough speaking this way to a V'ornn without knowing his name."

"What way?" he breathed.

"Saying . . ." She turned abruptly away. "I cannot. Few Kundalan would have the courage to do for me what you did yesterday."

He felt himself take a quick intake of breath. He was unaccountably afraid to let it go. "I will tell you . . ." He had to begin all over again. "My mother had a name for me. Only she used it."

She turned back to him and his breath left him in a sigh. "When you were little?"

"She is dead now." Involuntarily, he sucked in his breath. They were all dead now, his family. In the heat of the moment, he had forgotten, but now the horror came flooding back anew.

She saw the pain in is eyes. "What is it? Are you ill?"

He shook his head, angry at appearing weak before her. "No. . . . But I am lying. It wasn't my mother who called me this name. I never knew my mother. It's . . . I was brought up by a Kundalan female."

She lowered her eyes. "I am sorry about your mother."

He searched her face, as if memorizing each feature. "This Kundalan, when I was very young she called me Teyjattt."

"Teyjattt." She tasted the alien word, getting the last syllable wrong. When he corrected her, she said it again. "What an odd sound it has."

"It is a nestling, a baby teyj—a beautiful four-winged bird from our home planet."

"What is the name of your planet?" she asked.

"I don't know," he said truthfully. "No V'ornn knows for certain. It burned to a cinder eons ago."

"But surely you have histories."

"We do not," he said.

"I do not understand. How can you know the name of this four-winged bird and not the name of your homeworld?"

"We brought teyj with us eons ago. All of us have grown up with them. On Kundala, the Gyrgon keep them, train them. They are exceedingly intelligent."

"It is odd that a Kundalan would call you by the name of a V'ornn creature."

"She is an . . . unusual female."

"Are you in love with her?"

"What? No!" He burst out laughing. "Are you crazy?"

His laughter vanished like smoke, he stood very near her. Her eyes watched him carefully as his forefinger lightly traced the fine down of hair on her arm. She saw a tiny tremor run through him and wondered whether he was attracted to her or repulsed. His hairlessness fascinated her. So many questions swirled through her mind. This moment felt more intimate than any she had experienced before.

"I would like to see a Teyjattt one of these days," she whispered. His image filled her eyes.

He smiled—his first smile since early yesterday afternoon. "So would I."

It was growing lighter, and the steady, drumming rain had diminished to little more than a heavy mist. In the nacre-grey of the early morning, the nearby trees were beginning to appear like ghostly Khagggun. With the storm's passing, the wind had died to fitful gusts, and the gentle racket of the morning birds had begun.

She indicated the two cthauros. "I see that you are not alone."

"I am traveling with someone—a female." He went to Giyan's cthauros, stroked its back, as if by touching it he could feel close to her. "She went off to find us some food, but that was some time ago. We've got to find her."

"My cottage is only a league from here," Eleana said, pointing off to the northwest. "I saw her go in that general direction."

"Do you know how to ride?" he asked her.

"My parents used to raise cthauros," she said and he pointed to his mount, which was closest to her. "Take that one," he said. He swung atop Giyan's cthauros, saw Eleana deftly follow suit. He grabbed the mount's mane and dug his heels into its flanks. "Let's be off then, and all good speed. She has been gone long enough for me to worry."

They cantered through the woods, Eleana leading the way through dense underbrush and thickets of mountain-nettle that sprouted up like tufts of whiskers from the thickly needled bed of the forest floor. As they went, Annon automatically listened for birdcalls, trying to identify them, as any hunter would, in order to single out those he might wish to bring down. He had identified half a dozen when the forest fell deathly still. Not a bird sang, not an insect hummed, whirred, buzzed, or droned. For a moment, not even a breeze stirred the highest branches. Then he heard a disturbingly familiar sound.

He stopped his cthauros, and Eleana did the same. The sound came clearer now, threading a certain dread through his bones.

"What is it?" she asked.

"Khagggun hoverpods. They use them off-world in search-and-annihilate missions. Here on Kundala they usually prefer to ride cthauros." He swallowed, his stomachs in turmoil. "They are equipped with instrumentation that can pinpoint body heat or the sound of a pulse, but they have to be in a direct line to detect us."

Eleana seemed breathless. "How close are they?"

He cocked an ear. "By the sound, I would estimate that they will be here within minutes."

They galloped the rest of the way. The air behind them began to sizzle and a sharp smell of burning pricked their nostrils, as the ion-induction thrusters of the hoverpods literally gobbled up the air around them, metabolizing it, digesting what was needed, spewing out the rest.

Leaves and twigs whipped by them, scoring welts on their cheeks and arms. The cthauros' thundering hooves threw up clods of damp black earth, fallen pine needles, and emerald-green moss in their wake. They jumped over fallen logs, crawling with powdery white insects; through puddles of rainwater, dark and reflectionless as an abyss. As if sensing the danger behind them, the animals lowered their heads, pumping their powerful legs all the faster, and it seemed to Annon as if they fairly flew over the narrow, twisting path that his companion could see but he could not.

As they broke out of a particularly dense section of the wood, he abruptly stopped his mount, waved Eleana back. They retreated into the forest just as two hoverpods, filled with Khagggun, bristling with weaponry, came into view. He groaned inwardly. Too late. They would never find Giyan now.

"They always hunt in pairs," he said to Eleana. "The Khagggun are methodical and merciless in their work." Then his blood ran cold, for he saw the insignia on the side of the leading hoverpod: three crossed fists looking like a horrid mailed flower. "N'Luuura take it!" he breathed.

"What is it?" she asked, guiding her cthauros close beside him.

"Pack-Commander Rekkk Hacilar." Annon did not take his eyes off the hoverpods as they slowly approached. They were coming in over the tops of the trees, their view hampered by the foliage. "He is one of the bravest Khaggun. Also, one of the most ruthless. He has killed many hundreds of enemies. I have heard that his battle helm is carved out of a Krael skull."

"Is that one of your animals?"

He laughed without humor. "Oh, no. The Krael are one of the many races we conquered."

He looked into her eyes for a moment. But only for a moment. The hoverpods were close enough so that they could make out the heavily armored uniforms of the men—articulated purple-blue titanium slabs topped by high helms sporting Hacilar's crest. These helmets, Annon knew, were filled with sophisticated systems that enhanced the Khagggun's senses and also linked them into a single pack entity so that the individual soldier was lost within the matrix of the hunting whole. This was a palpable example of the V'ornn Modality: one multiheaded creature bent on his destruction.

As they watched, mesmerized in terror, a thin spear of blue energy sliced down from the lead hoverpod, incinerating a swath of trees. There was an odd, clicking sound. The Khagggun were laughing.

"I have never heard of him," she said. "His pack does not hunt anywhere near here. Why is he here now?"

"There is only one reason I can think of." Annon pulled her back from the edge of the woods. "How in N'Luuura did they find me?"

She gave him a sharp, startled look. "Are you a criminal?"

"That depends on whom you ask."

She briefly squeezed his hand. "I've never met a V'ornn criminal before."

He smiled grimly. "To be honest, neither have I."

"What are we going to do?" she asked.

"The only thing I know how to do," he told her. "Keep

out of their direct line of sight. Otherwise, they'll find us and use that ion cannon on us."

Feeling helpless, he watched the cold blue light dance blindingly as it lanced downward into another section of the forest. Pines and ammonwood exploded, hissing like snakes as they hit the waterlogged ground. He could sense Eleana flinch beside him.

"Hunters, you said. They're trying to flush us out." She dug her heels into her mount's flanks. "Come on! I have an idea!"

He took off after her. For the first few hundred meters they more or less paralleled the hoverpods, until Eleana abruptly turned them away. An enormous felled tree lay in their path. They bent low over the cthauros' backs and urged them upward. Eleana's cthauros leapt over the trunk, coming down within millimeters of its blackened, peeling bark. But Annon was riding Giyan's mount, and its lame hoof was enough to prevent it from getting the lift it needed. It came down with its hindquarters squarely across the tree. It screamed as its hind legs fractured. The stub of a broken branch pierced its belly. It thrashed and screamed again, turning on its side to free itself, pinning Annon beneath as he tried to scramble away. His eyes bulged in pain, and he arched back as Eleana wheeled her cthauros around and galloped back.

"I can't get free!" he panted. The cthauros continued to scream, but more weakly.

He could see that if the beast rolled any farther, it would crush his chest. He was terribly afraid.

"Hold on!" She dismounted, ran toward him. She pulled out her knife, slit the dying cthauros' throat, jumped back in time to avoid the huge gout of blood. The beast looked at her for an instant as if in relief, then its eyes rolled up and filmed over.

She tried to pull Annon free, and he almost passed out with the pain.

"It's no use," he said. "You can't free me that way."

"I won't leave you," she said.

He pulled out the curved scalpel he had kept with him from the interrogation room in the caverns beneath the regent's palace and held it out to her. "Use this. It has a longer blade."

"What do you want me to do with that?"

"My only chance is if you cut me out," he said.

She looked dubious. "I don't know."

"Eleana," he whispered, wide-eyed. "I cannot feel my legs."

She took the scalpel from him.

"Do you know what to do?" he asked.

She was concentrating on the animal. "Keep very still."

She could see that one leg was pinned between the side of the cthauros and the fallen tree. Thank Miina he had missed the broken branch. Using the curved blade, she cut into the soft belly of the beast, gave a stifled cry at the stench of released gases, the quick ooze of intestines that came slithering forth. She rubbed under her nose, continued her incision all the way up the side, praying she could free him before she encountered the first of the beast's thirty-seven ribs. If the densely boned rib cage was on the V'ornn, she would never be able to free him.

Blood was everywhere, but Eleana did not cry out or weep. She kept her eyes firmly on her task while he concentrated on breathing deeply. At last, she threw aside the scalpel, grabbed his shoulders. He used the heels of his hands against the rough tree bark to help her as best he could, and slowly she slid him out from under the dead cthauros.

She held him awkwardly up. They were both covered in blood and pale green, ribboned tissue. "Can you stand?" she asked him.

She shrieked as a focused beam of dazzling blue light sliced through leaves, branches, tree trunks to slit open the forest floor not three meters from where they stood. Half of the cthauros corpse was incinerated before they had a chance to react.

"The pack!" Annon hissed. "It's tracked our body heat!"

"Miina protect us!" she whispered, as she backed them

away, his leg dragging uselessly through the muck of the forest floor.

"Your Great Goddess can't help us now," he said with a groan of pain. "Not against their weaponry."

As if to underscore his words, the forest exploded again in light and agitated energy. The fallen tree disintegrated, along with the rest of the dead cthauros. Annon reached up, dragging his cthauros back by its mane. It stamped and snorted, but as if aware of the danger, was otherwise silent.

"We've got to get out of here before they home in on us." Eleana swung up onto the cthauros.

Annon looked up at her with pain-racked eyes. He held himself on his good leg only by grabbing handfuls of the beast's mane. "I'll never make it."

"Sure you will," she said, bending down. Ignoring the bit of bone she saw protruding from his torn pant leg, she gathered him around his waist and launched him up behind her. All the breath went out of him as pain exploded, and for an instant he swung dizzily, about to pass out. Then she brought his arms around her slender waist, locked his fingers together over her sternum. "Here we go," she whispered back at him. "Hold on tight."

She felt the press of his chest against her back, the weight of his head on her shoulder as she urged the cthauros away from the next burst of ion-cannon fire.

"Where can we go?" he said to her. His voice was slurry, and she prayed to Miina that he would not lose consciousness.

"There is a place I know, a hidden place. But you must tell no one about it."

She did not wait for his reply, but galloped down the incline and into the long gully hidden by a dense stand of ancient, towering Marre pines. Above them, the cathedral of the forest hid the gathering morning sunlight, immersing them in deep emerald light. Behind them, another explosion detonated as Eleana guided the cthauros on down the gully. Standing water from last night's storm hampered them, as the cthauros had to pick its way blindly down the spine of the gully.

The ground began to rise, the ammonwood and feathery white mountain pines giving way entirely to the huge Marre pines. The air smelled sweetly of pine and pitch until another blast of the ion cannon sent acrid fumes whirling at them. A Marre pine fell on the spot they had been in a moment before. Annon felt the brush of one long branch across his back.

"It is no use," he whispered. "They have our scent; we cannot outrun them."

"Have faith," she replied, as she navigated the cthauros through the deeper water.

"Faith," he whispered. "What is faith?"

The water here was dark, tea-colored, without reflection. Snakes wriggled out of their way, but she kept an eye out for the large predators she knew to inhabit the depths of the Marre pine forest. Huge boulders added to the gloom, but for once she felt comforted by the hulking presence.

"How are you?" she whispered. She had become afraid of speaking in a normal tone.

"Fine," he replied, but she felt the convulsive shiver run through him.

She wondered how badly his leg was mangled. The image of his protruding bone haunted her. His leg was fractured or worse, if the bone had been irreparably crushed. With an effort, she turned her mind away from those gruesome possibilities and continued giving gentle but firm guidance to the cthauros.

They had entered the upper reaches of the Marre pine forest, the part she knew best. The cthauros was laboring a bit as it struggled up the increasingly steep incline. Stones and bits of shale flew from beneath its pounding hooves. She was worried about one short stretch they needed to cover to get to her hiding place. It was a ridge of blue-green rock where even the hardy Marre pines could not put down roots. They would be exposed for at least a couple of minutes. Desperately, she thought of alternative routes, but there were none. They had to cross the ridge.

She pulled the cthauros up just at the edge of the trees. Before her loomed the ridge. The open space between where they were and the straggling line of Marre pines on the upper side of the ridge could not have been more than three or four hundred meters, but to her it looked like a couple of kilometers.

Annon's clasped hands were white, rigid, and cold. She whispered to him. When he did not respond, she put her warm hand over his and squeezed. "Hold on, Teyjattt," she whispered. "Just a little longer. We're almost there."

With her free hand, she stroked the cthauros' neck. Its sides rose and fell like a bellows pulling air, and its nostrils flared. She steadied it, calmed it, kept it quiet while her ears pricked up for the slightest aural sign of the hovercraft. She heard no hum, but there were no bird sounds, either. Sweat stood out on her forehead as she concentrated. Should she go or stay? She did not know what to do. Neither seemed the right decision. She remembered all the times she had sneaked away here on foot, delighting in the beauty and the solitude. Now this secret place might be the only thing standing between them and incineration. They could not remain here at the verge of the forest, she knew, but she panicked at the thought of crossing the bald expanse of rock.

As if to make up her mind, a swath of Marre pines disintegrated into cinders, riding a column of blue flame that scythed through the wood. She bit her lip to keep from screaming, dug her heels into the cthauros' flanks, almost stood up in her effort to urge the beast forward. They burst out of the sanctuary of the Marre pine forest, and the glare of brilliant sunlight made Eleana's eyes water. She dared not look to her left, where the ridge abruptly fell off into an almost sheer drop of five hundred meters or more. Cooler air swirled up from the chasm, eddying like the dangerous currents of a whirlpool. The cthauros' hooves sparked and clattered over the blue-green stone. She winced with every sound they made. She could feel herself panting with each labored breath of her mount.

Up ahead, she could see the line of Marre pines where the

densest part of the forest began. Beyond them was a series of caves impossible to detect unless you were specifically looking for them. She herself had passed them by many times when she had come this way, until late one afternoon she had slid on a dry patch of loose shale, lost her balance, and slid into them. But right now they seemed like an eternity away.

The ridge continued to rise to the crest. She was bent low, her cheek against the whipping mane of her mount. She kept squeezing Annon's clasped hands, hoping to keep him conscious. Then the air just above her right shoulder sizzled, and something exploded so near them she gave a little yelp. The cthauros ducked its head and whinnied. Eleana dug her heels into its flanks to keep it going, but another blast struck it dead on and it went down beneath them.

Eleana deftly rolled them out of the way of the cthauros' still-twitching legs. There was an awful stench coming from the smoking hole in its side. She turned to look behind them, saw an armored Khaggun scrambling methodically over the rocks toward them. He held a portable ion cannon. Fear seized her in its mailed fist. She thought about running, but remembered that Annon was crippled. Besides, the V'ornn was too close. The ion cannon was at the ready; he would not miss if they turned to flee.

Eleana pulled her knife, but it was a useless gesture—foolish, even. The Khaggun would never give her an opportunity to use it. And even, if by some chance, she got close enough to him, she knew her blade would shatter against the armor.

"Teyjattt," she whispered.

"I am here," Annon answered. "I'm sorry I brought you into this."

She squeezed his hand by way of reply.

His head felt light, his body weighed down with waves of pain and numbness. Even so, seeing the Khaggun come on, he could not believe that it would end like this, all his dreams of avenging his family's slaughter dying so quickly, so finally. Stogggul had won, and the worst of it was he hadn't even put up a fight.

The Khagggun strode quickly to within two paces of them. The ion cannon was pointed directly at them. This was it, he thought, awaiting death.

But, inexplicably, the Khagggun's gaze swept past them without recognition.

"What is—"

The Khagggun's head swiveled in the direction of Eleana's voice and Annon clamped a hand over her mouth, shook his head when she looked at him, letting her know that she shouldn't make a sound.

The Khagggun stood as still as a statue. It appeared as if he were scarcely breathing. Annon looked around, and there she was: Giyan. Still cloaked in her Tuskugggun robes, her sifeyn concealing the upper part of her face, she came from behind the immobile Khagggun, moving across the rocky ridge as if it were the palace floor.

She placed a forefinger across her grimly set lips. She turned her gaze toward the fallen cthauros. For a moment, nothing happened. Then Annon felt a wave of energy brush by him and the corpse slid toward the edge of the ridge. It dangled at the precipice for an instant, then vanished over the side.

While Annon's and Eleana's mouths were still agape, Giyan went to where they lay, stooped, grabbing Annon under his arms. He could see that Eleana was stunned. Nevertheless, she rose, took up position on his other side, and put her arm around him.

They began to make their painstaking way across the rocky scree. Once, Eleana turned her head, worried that the Khagggun had come out of his eerie trance.

"Don't look back!" Giyan said softly but sharply. "Keep going!"

Eleana turned back, swallowed hard, and nodded. "I know where we can hide," she whispered, looking furtively at the robed woman. Her eyes opened wide when she saw that Giyan was Kundalan.

Giyan nodded, and they moved on. The simple act of walking exhausted Annon. Once or twice, his mangled leg dragged on the ground, and it was all he could do not to cry out. The pain was almost overwhelming; all he wanted to do was lie down and rest, but the two women on either side of him would not allow that. They crossed the remaining expanse of the ridge. Just as they passed within the deep shadows of the Marre pines on the north side, the air began to hum, crackling and sparking behind them. Hidden, they turned, watched a brace of hoverpods appearing over the tops of the Marre pines south of the ridge. They were startlingly, frighteningly close. So close, in fact, that they could see the imposing figure of Pack-Commander Hacilar, his head covered by the pale grey ridged skull of a male Krael. A slender man with the insignia of First-Captain on his armor stood at Hacilar's shoulder, relaying his commands to the pack.

"That is Olnnn Rydddlin," Annon whispered. "He is Hacilar's second-in-command."

Rekkk Hacilar was directing Olnnn Rydddlin's gaze to the sentrylike figure of the lone Khaggun Giyan had immobilized. He barked an order.

"We've got to get to the caves," Eleana whispered urgently.

"In a moment." Giyan was staring fixedly at the Khaggun. "Hacilar is trying to access his Khaggun's telemetry." She was vibrating as if she were a tuning fork. Annon became aware of a kind of resistance, as if he were in the ocean, swimming against the tide. It was as if concentric circles of energy pulsed out from her. They did not hurt him, but they made him even more tired than he had been. Colors sparked and twinkled all around him, the blues and greens and browns of the world seeming more vivid than he had ever remembered them. Then something went through him, like an eel through deep water, and he shivered.

As the hoverpods came abreast of him, the Khaggun who had killed their cthauros lurched into movement. They could see Rekkk Hacilar shouting orders that the Khaggun apparently could not hear. Instead, he walked, stiff-legged to the edge of the precipice. He stood there for a moment before losing his balance and tumbling over the edge.

Giyan turned back to them. "That will keep them occupied." She turned her most charming smile on Eleana. "Now. How do we get to these caves of yours?"

You have drawn blood against your own."

"You have violated the Law of the Summoning."

"You have acted without supervision. You must be punished."

Three Gyrgon circled Wennn Stogggul as he stood in the rain-slicked center of the regent's garden. Behind him, Mesagggun were busy ripping out Eleusis' star-roses by the roots. It was one of the first orders he had given on gaining complete control of the palace.

Even Wennn Stogggul had to admit that the Gyrgon were an awesome sight. Clad in their shimmering alloy armor, they looked like gigantic insects, wings folded, thoraxes puffed, their faces shielded by high helms-crowned ion spiral horns. In any event, it was an extraordinary sight to see them outside the Temple of Mnemonics, their terrible carapaces glistening and glinting as they moved in concert in the pale predawn light. But then these were extraordinary times.

"Would you punish me," Stogggul said, "for carrying out your wishes?"

"We did not—"

"How dare you intimate—"

"What would you know of our wishes?"

For an instant, Wennn Stogggul's anger got the better of him. "You think of me as some Bashkir half-wit whose petition to be regent you dismissed out of hand."

The three Gyrgon were still. There was something eerie, disconcerting about their perfectly synchronized movements, as if they were not really V'ornn at all, but something else, something truly unknown and unknowable. Be it truth or illusion, Stogggul knew, it was effective.

"Are you gainsaying our decision?" the first Gyrgon demanded.

Wennn Stogggul licked his lips as his tender parts began to shrivel. Then he berated himself; to show fear to Gyrgon was tantamount to fueling their derision. "What I am saying is that was then. This is now."

The three continued their circling. "Amplify," the second Gyrgon said.

Wennn Stogggul smiled to himself. They had given him his opening. "We have been on this planet too long. Eleusis Ashera was stalling, fighting the inevitable moment we all know will come, when we leave this world a spinning ash heap. The evidence of overstaying is all around us." He lowered his voice so it would not carry back to the workers. "The Mesagggun grow restive, the Khagggun grow soft in their enforced idleness. By building an alliance between the Bashkir and the Khagggun, I have begun a new era in V'ornn history. I am revitalizing it."

Behind him, the Mesagggun made ragged piles of the star-roses. He had his own plans for the space, and they did not include flowers. Though the inscrutable silence threatened to devour him, he screwed up his courage, forging ahead. "As long as Eleusis Ashera remained as regent the Kundalan culture continued. Am I wrong in this?"

"There are many paths to an end," the first Gyrgon said sharply.

What are they not telling me? Wennn Stogggul asked himself. He knew that he had taken an enormous risk in moving unilaterally against the Ashera. He knew there would be the inevitable fallout among the Gyrgon. In fact, he never would have made his move if the Ring of Five Dragons hadn't come into his possession. What a coup that had been! He had been all set to name Bronnn Pallln, a long-time ally, as his new Prime Factor, when he had been asked to dinner by Sornnn SaTrryn.

He had almost said no. After all, Sornnn SaTrryn was only a year or two older than Kurgan. On the other hand, the SaTrryn were a Bashkir Consortium of the first rank, though Stogggul had known the patriarch, Hadinnn SaTrryn, only in passing, and then only when he dealt in the spice trade that was the SaTrryn's prime territory. When Hadinnn SaTrryn had died suddenly and unexpectedly last month, Sornnn SaTrryn, as the eldest son, had taken over. As a consequence, Stogggul had automatically dismissed the Consortium.

Over a very fine dinner, Sornnn SaTrryn had impressed Stogggul with his clever mind and sharp business acumen, no more so than when, over dessert and drinks, he had offered him the Ring of Five Dragons. At first, Stogggul was disbelieving. After all, the Ring of Five Dragons was the stuff of legends. No V'ornn had ever seen it; it had been lost on the same day 101 years ago when the The Pearl had vanished, when the V'ornn had landed on Kundala.

"And, lo and behold, here you are, presenting it to me." Stogggul had shaken his head, but his hand was shaking when he held the Ring, for his trained Bashkir eye knew it was made neither by V'ornn nor by present-day Kundalan.

Then Sornnn SaTrryn had told him the story of how he had come by this miraculous artifact. He was but a day returned from one of his regular trips into the Korrush where, like his father before him, he spent time with the local tribal leaders who supplied his Consortium with its spices. The day before he was scheduled to depart, his business being finished, he was presented with a gift of enormous prestige. He was taken to an archaeological dig many kilometers north of Okkamchire, one of the spice centers of the area. It was a barren, utterly deserted section of the unbearably stark Korrush. Crude wooden ladders led down into the dig, which was already some nine or ten meters belowground. Through cramped and airless tunnels Sornnn SaTrryn was led until he found himself longing for the harsh tang of the gusty Korrush wind. The thick, hot air was gritty, lifeless. Up ahead he saw torchlight. A moment later, he and his guide emerged into a chamber. The walls were covered with colored glass tiles depicting beasts with gleaming eyes and sharp fangs. There, Sornnn SaTrryn was introduced to the head of the dig, a large male with curling black hair and beard, pale ice-blue eyes. They sat cross-legged, ate a meal of flat bread, dried fruits, and cold gimnopede pie. During the meal, they spoke only of inconsequential matters. This was the Korrush way. When they were done, the archaeologist took Sornnn SaTrryn on a tour of the chamber, pointing out the beasts of legend that ringed the chamber.

On the way out, a member of the dig surreptitiously approached Sornnn SaTrryn's guide. They spoke in low tones for a moment before the guide beckoned Sornnn SaTrryn over. And there, lying in the digger's leathery outstretched palm, dusty and age-encrusted, was the Ring of Five Dragons. It had been found at the dig just that morning. It was supposed to have been tagged and cataloged by the digger, but he had not done that, intuiting perhaps its value. Whether he knew what it was, Sornnn SaTrryn neither knew nor cared. The digger knew who Sornnn SaTrryn was, and he wanted an enormous sum of coins for his find. After the requisite rounds of bargaining, Sornnn SaTrryn bought it. He would have paid any amount for it.

Now, at dinner with Stogggul, he exacted his price. He wanted to be named Prime Factor. Stogggul, ever the pragmatist, had readily agreed.

The Ring had given Stogggul the power he needed to stand his ground with the Gyrgon. Or so he believed. In actuality, when it came to the Gyrgon one never knew what ground one was standing on. He had been required to trust his instincts. And now here he was, at the crowning moment of his life. He knew better than most V'ornn that now that he was in their presence the Gyrgon could kill him on a whim— they merely had to send a charge of hyperexcited ions through his okummmon and his hearts would be fried. Or they could spend many sidereal cycles causing him such excruciating pain that he would beg for the release of death long before they would grant it to him. Still, he pressed on, concentrating on what he must do now to garner their support.

"Well?" the third Gyrgon barked. "You will speak now, or you will regret your actions."

"I have no doubt." Wennn Stogggul held up his hands. He saw that they were unmoved. "Hear me, Gyrgon. In moving against the Ashera I have saved your caste much time and vexatious effort. Time and effort better spent in your laboratories. Am I wrong in this?" Belatedly heeding their warning, he hurried on. "I know full well that unlocking the secrets of the Kundalan has been a long and exceedingly frustrating process. We have killed them in great numbers, tortured them individually. We have subjected them to a decades-long campaign of terror both with sporadic Khagggun packs and with methods of infiltration and misinformation. To date, nothing has worked. In fact, I have in my possession reliable reports that over the past sidereal decade the strength of their underground has increased fivefold. Short of finding some technology that will dissect the Kundalan mind and thus reveal all its secrets, continuing in this vein will prove fruitless. I think we are in agreement about this assessment."

He looked at all three Gyrgon in turn, hoping to be able to glean something of their thinking by reading their expressions. Instead, he felt like an illiterate. Their faces were as blank as a Nieobian wall. He strangled his frustration and plowed on. "Therefore, I propose an alternative—a way to break the Kundalan once and for all, destroy their will *and* their underground all in one stroke."

The Gyrgon were silent, but they kept circling like predatory birds that had scented fresh blood. *They are trying to unnerve me,* he thought. *They are taking the measure of my mettle. If I displease them, they will roast my tender parts over an ion spit, oh yes they will. But I won't make that mistake.* He took their silence as tacit approval. "Here is what we will do: we will use their own secrets against them."

The Gyrgon ceased their movement.

"Impossible!"

"The jabber of idiots!"

"You spew meaningless riddles!"

"No! I speak the truth!" It was an effort keeping his enormous need out of his voice. "Would you cast out my petition to be regent a second time?"

The Gyrgon stood quite still.

"It is possible—"

"We would consider—"

"The truth is where we live."

The Gyrgon exposed their mailed hands, an implied threat. The preliminaries were over.

"Make your stand, Stogggul Wennn," the third Gyrgon demanded. "Tell us the truth."

At the back wall of the garden, the Mesagggun had lighted a fire under the star-roses. Wennn Stogggul sucked the strong, bitter scent deep into his tri-lobed lung. He had never noticed it before but burning star-roses smelled of victory. He held up the Kundalan artifact. "Here is my truth," he said. "Let it speak eloquently to you."

As one, the Gyrgon peered at what he held between his fingers.

"It is the Ring!" the first Gyrgon said.

"The Ring of Five Dragons!" the second Gyrgon said.

"The Kundalan artifact said to open the Storehouse where The Pearl lies in wait!" the third Gyrgon said.

Triumph surged in Stogggul's chest as he absorbed their excitement. "How many years have you been trying to get through the Door to the Storehouse?"

"One hundred and one," said the second Gyrgon.

Stogggul went down on one knee, his hearts hammering in his chest. "I offer this Ring to the Gyrgon, to break the Kundalan once and for all, to gain all the secrets it has been the Gyrgon desire to obtain. And all I ask in return is that you grant me the regent's mantle and break the Ashera Consortium's stranglehold on the salamuuun trade."

In one terrifying stride, the third Gyrgon closed the space between them. He plucked the Ring from between Stogggul's fingers.

"The Gyrgon accept your offering."

The Prime Factor rose, his pulse pounding. He was on the brink of his heart's desire. "Then you will name me new regent?"

"No," the first Gyrgon said.

"What?" Wennn Stogggul fairly howled. His fingers

curled into fists, his eyes turned bloody and murderous. "We had a deal! How can you—"

"Deal? What deal? We accepted a gift from you, nothing more," the third Gyrgon said. "Ashera Annon lives. So long as this is fact, the Ashera Dynasty continues."

"This is Law," the first Gyrgon said. "It cannot be otherwise."

"Ashera Annon is the new regent," the second Gyrgon said, "Until the moment of his death."

"Then, N'Luuura take it, kill him!" the Prime Factor cried. "Fry the skcettta!"

"We reject your sentence," the third Gyrgon said.

"Gyrgon do not murder regents," the first Gyrgon said.

"It is for you to succeed or fail," the third Gyrgon said. "Bring us the head of Ashera Annon, and we will proclaim you regent of Kundala."

"And what of the salamuuun trade? It should be mine."

Silence.

"It should be mine!"

This is Eleana," Annon whispered, introducing the girl to Giyan. "Giyan is the female who raised me." He made no mention of his first encounter with Eleana.

"Thank you for helping Annon," Giyan said. "I owe you a debt I can never repay."

"You owe me nothing," Eleana said.

"I thought you were lost," Annon whispered.

"I am never lost," Giyan told him, and smiled. "I found food and shelter. I was coming back for you when I heard them."

"How did they find us so quickly?"

"I do not know." Her whistleflower-blue eyes held his for a moment. "But it is troubling." She peeled back his bloody pant leg. "How did this happen?"

"The hoverpods came, and we went looking for you. I was riding your cthauros—the one with the lame hoof."

"I remember."

"It didn't make it over a tree trunk."

Inside the caves, she had shed her Tuskugggun robes to form a makeshift pallet for him. Her thick copper-colored hair was unbound, and she looked every inch a Kundalan female. She also looked pale and drained, but she nevertheless examined his leg with the care of a physician.

He licked his lips. "How bad is it?"

"Do not fret, Teyjattt. It can be healed."

The multicolored walls arched over their head, extending far back into absolute darkness. Here and there, red and orange lichen sprouted in furry patches, clinging at impossible angles. Heavily filtered light from the Marre pine forest bathed the mouth of the cave, extending to where the trio had made temporary camp.

Annon's head tossed back and forth on the pallet, and he groaned.

"What is it?" Giyan asked as she stroked his head.

"Nothing. Just a bout of dizziness. It will pass." But his voice was so weak he could barely hear himself. "I am thirsty."

"There is a small spring farther inside the cave," Eleana said.

Giyan handed over her sifeyn and the girl went off to fill it. She watched until Eleana was out of sight, then she put a hand on Annon's forehead. Immediately, he felt a warmth suffusing him, relaxing him. In a moment, he was deep in sleep.

Giyan unwound the filthy bandage from around her left hand. The wound was entirely healed. She smiled to herself, placed one hand on each side of Annon's broken leg. She began to chant in the Old Tongue of the Ramahan as she unwound the bandage. She could feel the air around her stir, come alive. Ripples purled the atmosphere, which grew thick as water. At the same time, a certain light emerged from the palms of her hand, bathing the places she held. Still chanting, she pulled on the leg below the knee. At once, the bones popped back into place. Her fingers now worked the torn and ragged flesh, and where she touched them they mended.

Giyan watched his face. In repose, he most resembled the

small child she had held to her breast, had sung to, who dwelled in her heart. She felt that she had never been closer to him. It was odd what surprises adversity could bring.

It was time to wake him. Again, her hand passed across his forehead. He stirred and opened his eyes.

"Did I fall asleep?" he asked in a furry voice. "I feel so much better."

She knelt over him, took his hand in hers. "Your leg is going to be fine, Annon."

"You know that?"

"Yes." Her smile deepened. "I do."

"It feels better."

"Tomorrow you will be able to walk on it, but only for a little while."

She could see the emotions playing across his face, and her heart broke as it had so many times since she had first held him; he did not yet know who he was, and she could not help him. She struggled once again to escape the trapped feeling. So many secrets bound her, kept so much of her inside. How many times had she cried herself to sleep in the crook of Eleusis' strong arm? No more. Even that small measure of solace was gone.

"Why are you crying?" Annon asked.

She was spared lying to him by Eleana's scream. She jumped up, peering into the darkness of the cave. With an effort, Annon maneuvered himself around until he was facing the heart of the cave.

They could see dim movement now, and then the girl appeared, running directly toward them. A look of blind terror was on her face. Instantly, they saw that something was pursuing her. It was still a smudge in the darkness, but it was large, and it was moving fast.

"Get out!" Eleana screamed. "I cannot believe it, but I stumbled upon a perwillon!"

"Miina protect us!" Giyan breathed. "We have no weapons, and the perwillon is impervious to sorcerous spells."

"Give me the bolt!" Annon shouted at her.

"What?"

Eleana was spun around by a massive paw, the outline of the perwillon just behind her came clear.

"Kurgan's bolt! Quickly!"

They saw a thick, furred body twelve meters in length, four powerful forepaws, a long, black-muzzled face with triple rows of teeth. The girl grunted, desperately tried to spin away.

Giyan handed him the bolt and he fitted it into his okummmon.

Eleana stumbled backward, jerking free of the beast. She slammed into the wall of the cave, righted herself, raced toward them. Having gotten their scent, the perwillon reacted predictably to three strangers encroaching on its territory. Its massive jaws opened wide, its crimson teeth dripping a thick nasty-looking liquid. It rose up on its hind legs and, its long, curved orange claws raking the air, charged the interlopers. It struck Annon a blow across his chest that knocked all the air out of him.

Eleana screamed as he fetched up against the rock wall. The perwillon, scenting blood, charged again.

Annon's arm came up. He did not think or aim; the okummmon scanned its target even as it locked on. The bolt launched, passing through the oncoming perwillon's left eye, embedding itself in the beast's heart. It roared and clawed the air, mortally struck. Still, its forward momentum carried it toward the trio. Eleana stepped in front of Annon and Giyan stepped in front of the two of them.

The perwillon stumbled, went to its knees, then collapsed over onto its side not a meter from where Giyan stood guard. The stench of the beast filled the cave.

Eleana ran to where Annon lay, stanching the fresh blood with strips of her own clothes. "That was close." She turned to Giyan, ducked her head. "I believe we have need of your healing powers."

Giyan knelt beside Annon and looked closely at the new wounds. She reached into her pouch. "We will have to use ground herbs and roots," she said with a worried look. "My sorcery will not heal a wound from a perwillon. It is a creature from another age, impervious to sorcery of any kind."

Eleana stared at Giyan for a long time. "I had heard tales of sorcery such as yours, but I did not imagine that it actually existed."

"The young have stopped believing," Giyan said. "That is a sadness almost too great to bear."

"I believe now, and I will tell others."

"Not yet." Giyan was packing the bloody wound with the dried mash. "When the time is right."

Eleana rose and approached the perwillon. She unsheathed her knife and hacked expertly through the thick fur. "At least it died for a good cause. We will have fresh meat to eat."

Annon, Eleana, and Giyan ate their fill of the perwillon's liver and heart, the most nutritious parts of its innards. As for its brain, it was a small thing, located just under its thick shoulder muscles, not worth the digging. They ate these Kundalan delicacies raw, for they dared not risk building a fire, lest its smoke be observed by their enemies. Then Giyan left the cave.

Afterward, Giyan left them for some hours as she searched the hills and glens for herbs to help heal Annon's wounds. When she returned, she immediately set about her preparations. Annon and Eleana broke off their quiet conversation to watch her.

"Judging from the single roots, you were not able to find much," Eleana said.

Giyan nodded. "But what I did find is very potent, indeed." She held up the twisted, dark red root. "This is mesembrythem. It is one of the most powerful herbs in the pantheon of sorcerous remedies." She continued her work, shredding the root with her nails. "In all but the most practiced hands, it is very dangerous and highly addictive. Its regenerative powers can instantly morph into the deadliest poison, either through overdose or the introduction of oil of heartwood."

She took the shreds into a corner of the cavern, put them in a pile on the ground, and squatted over them. Annon and

Eleana turned away, heard her urinating on the root shreds. "They need a weak acidic solution to activate properly," she said, rearranging her robes. "This will have to do."

Within fifteen minutes they had swelled up, the dark red color fading into the faintest of pinks. Giyan gathered them up. She looked down at Annon and smiled. "The mesembrythem will, first of all, stanch the blood. Then it will give you strength."

Annon nodded. She placed the shreds in a complex pattern over his wounds. Her concentration was so absolute that neither of the others said a word.

When she was done, she expelled a small sigh, and said to Eleana. "I fear I must rely once again on your goodwill." Annon closed his eyes, growing drowsy with exhaustion and the effects of the herbal remedy. "We must continue our flight."

"Is it wise to move him? He has lost a great deal of blood."

"I fear we have no other choice. Our enemies are too close on our heels. Besides, the mesembrythem will heal him in a few days, I hope."

"You have a safe harbor?"

"I believe so, yes."

"I have friends along the way who will be able to help."

"My thanks, Eleana, but you saw what happened here. I do not want to put anyone else in danger. We will purchase two of your best cthauros."

"Your coins are no good here," Eleana said. "The cthauros are yours."

"Thank you for your generosity."

"It is the least I can do." Her eyes flicked toward Annon, then returned to meet Giyan's level gaze.

They regarded once another silently for some time before Giyan rose. "I will reconnoiter to make certain the hoverpods have moved on."

"You are as generous as you are courageous, Giyan." Though she was very grateful for this time alone with Teyjattt, no matter how short, Eleana did not dare meet the other woman's eyes. When Giyan had disappeared out of the mouth of the cave. Eleana bent over Annon.

"You will be leaving soon. It is time to say good-bye."

"Good-bye?" His voice was thick. He had eaten little, having had no appetite for the strange, gamey organ meat. Now he felt both nauseated and light-headed. "No, no. You must come with us."

"Alas, it is impossible. I have obligations here. I know you understand about obligations."

"Yes. I do."

She stroked his forehead, smiled down at him. "Teyjattt. Would Giyan be jealous if she heard me call you that?"

"I do not think so, no. She likes you."

"And you?"

He lifted a hand and she took it in hers, squeezed it tight. She bent even lower over him. "Ah, that face," she whispered. "I will know it anywhere."

"I wish you were coming with us."

"As do I."

His hearts constricted. "Eleana . . ."

Tears came to her eyes. "I am pleased Giyan likes me."

He looked at her, searching for answers, found only her enigmatic smile. For the time being at least, it was enough. A shadow from the cave entrance came toward them and automatically their hands unwound.

"It is time," Giyan said.

"I must go," Eleana whispered, "to fetch the cthauros." She reached down, unwrapped something from her waist. "I leave this token with you, Teyjattt." She laid her knife in its polished ammonwood scabbard on his chest. "Until we meet again."

8

Vessel Half-Empty

"It is an evil omen, you bringing the boy here," Bartta said ungraciously.

"I am happy to see you, too, sister."

"You live with the ruler of our conquerors. I do not see you for sixteen years, and now here you are on my doorstep, asking for succor for a V'ornn, no less!"

"Try to see him as a boy under threat of death from his father's enemies," Giyan said.

"His father was my enemy also."

"So are the V'ornn who seek him."

Bartta stood back, allowing Giyan to half carry the still-weak Annon inside. But she did not lift a hand while her twin transported him to the room where Giyan herself had slept when she was a child. The cottage, on the next to highest of the village's thirty-seven tiers, had three bedrooms. Bartta now slept in the room that had belonged to their parents. She had put Riane, the girl she had found beneath the flat stone, in her old bedroom.

"How did you know to look for me here," Bartta said, "and not at the abbey?"

"I remember everything, sister," Giyan said. "Including your penchant for retreats here, to try to fathom the pattern of the powerful bourns—those mystical power paths that crisscross Kundala Miina laid down at the world's creation." Giyan cocked her head. "We Ramahan have been trying to make sense of the pattern for close to a century. Are you any closer to solving the mystery?"

Bartta made a sour face. "You mock me now."

"Not at all. On the contrary, I admire your persistence."

Bartta followed Giyan, watched with avid eyes as her sister set Annon down. "Have you used your Gift on him?"

"He was mauled by a perwillon."

"Miina protect us! Those beasts are daemon-spawn! What ill luck that you happened upon one."

Giyan busied herself making Annon comfortable.

Bartta came cautiously into the room. "He is not unpleasant-looking, for a V'ornn." She moved closer, bending over Annon. Her forefinger jabbed out. "What made this discoloration?"

"He was attacked by a gyreagle. It left its talon in him."

"He's lucky it did not pierce his lung. V'ornn have only one, I am told." She sucked at her lower lip. "It happened when he was a small child, yes? The wound is long healed."

"No," Giyan said, standing up. "It was a recent attack. Less than a week."

Bartta's eyes opened wide. "Sorcerous work."

Giyan turned to her. She took her twin by the arm, led her back into the great room.

"Osoru—the Five Moon sorcery—has been banished from the abbey ever since Mother's death," Bartta hissed.

"Do not admonish me, sister. The sorcery worked on Annon is not of my doing."

Bartta frowned, sat down beside her exhausted twin. "Whose, then?"

"I haven't eaten in a day and a night."

Bartta nodded, put a big iron stewpot on the fire. Giyan looked around. The whitewashed walls were, here and there, streaked with soot, but otherwise the cottage seemed much the same as it had when they were growing up. A fire winked and crackled in the old stone hearth, the black, potbellied kettle stood on a wooden shelf with all the other cooking paraphernalia, the same dark-hued hangings sagged on their pins, the ammonwood furniture was worn to a glossy sheen. There and there, were oddities that made Giyan understand that this was no longer her home. Like the ornately carved heartwood chest in the great room and their mother's lovely perennial garden. Once, it had been filled with swirls of delicate pink thistlewort, yellow mountain laurel, white snow-lily, and aromatic rosemary. Bartta had transformed it into a botanical laboratory of sorts. There was shanin, Pandanus, latua, datura inoxia, plus at least a dozen varieties of exotic mushrooms, all of which and more Eleusis had allowed her to grow in the secret garden inside the palace. They were mostly subtropical plants, but her sister had apparently found a method to adapt them to the harsh mountain climate. This high in the mountains of the Djenn Marre, mornings and late afternoons were almost always chilly, even in High Summer. Nights were either cold or frigid, depending upon the season.

It had taken them four days and four nights of almost constant riding to get here. Along the way, Giyan had twice spotted Khagggun hoverpods at a far remove. They were still sectoring the Marre pine forest; because they were awkward to maneuver over the foothills' steep gradients, they no longer appeared to be a threat.

She had allowed them to stop only to relieve themselves, which was still an awkward and time-consuming procedure for Annon. They ate the foodstuff Eleana had given them while riding. They had ascended through the land of sudden lakes, through increasingly rocky scree and acutely pitched ridges, along winding paths of well-trammeled Marre pine needles, past swiftly flowing streams and small waterfalls. Above them rose the majestic, snowcapped peaks of the Djenn Marre, becoming ever more awesome the closer they came. Giyan pushed the cthauros to their limit. By the second day, Annon had slept off and on while she guided both animals on the path she had chosen into the upcountry where her home village of Stone Border lay nestled. Once, sliding into an exhausted sleep, she had dreamed her terrifying dream of bloody hands, and a fire crackling, consuming her. She had awoken sobbing at the cold, glittering stars. A soft wind stirred the treetops. The moons were gone, as if unable to bear any longer her inner torment.

"They did not harm you, the V'ornn?" Bartta, stirring the stewpot, broke the awkward silence.

"No harm came to me, sister," Giyan said wearily. "Quite the opposite."

"That is difficult to believe." Bartta was piling dried fruit and crusty bread onto a plate. "I had given up hope."

"In Axis Tyr I fell in love." Giyan was staring at her hands. "I do not expect you to understand."

Bartta ladled stew into a bowl, brought it and the plate to the table. She poured Giyan some sweet, dark mead.

Giyan was famished, but she hardly tasted the food. Her thoughts were with Annon. Her heart ached for him. She tried to banish the fear that had grown in her ever since they had left Eleana. She had important things to tell Bartta, but she was suddenly afraid. "Tell me about life here," she said.

"It has been hard," Bartta said. "Harder by far than when you were here, because now we are losing our folk to the V'ornn *and* to Kara." She gestured. "Once these Kundalan were followers of Miina. But Miina has forsaken them, they claim, and so they give themselves over to this soulless, Goddess-less religion that threatens the very fabric of our spirituality."

"For once we agree on something." Giyan put food into her mouth, chewed slowly, tasting nothing but the mounting fear inside her. "Kara brings no good to either its followers or to us. It is a dead end."

"It is worse. Each Kundalan who converts to Kara is another wound inflicted on the Ramahan corpus. As the Ramahan go, so goes the Kundalan, eh, sister? Though its practitioners claim Kara gives them hope, at the heart of Kara is a certain nihilism that seeks to obliterate our history, our lore, the very essence of who we are. No, truly we have no need of such a latter-day religion."

"And yet each month it grows stronger."

"Yes, fed by the anger of Miina forsaking her children."

"And every day the Holy Scripture slips farther away from us, isn't that so?"

Bartta's voice was fueled by equal parts envy and contempt. "I am surprised you remember Scripture. You have the Gift."

"Like water, we always return to the source," Giyan said softly.

"Does it seem strange to return, sister, after all your time among the conquerors?"

Giyan pushed aside her plate. "To be honest, I feel somewhat . . . displaced."

"I will take you to our mother's grave," Bartta said shortly as she cleared the table. "If you stay long enough, that is."

"And what of Father?"

"Kara took him. He could not resist the new religion's practical message of the here and now."

And there lay their personal history, trammeled in the dust. Giyan felt oddly defeated. Not for them the cries of delight, the tears, the deep love that twins so long separated should feel. From the first, a wary cynicism had established itself, as if they were two enemies meeting to hammer out a truce after a long, drawn-out war.

"You are a very different person than the one who went with the V'ornn sixteen years ago," Bartta said. There was a certain bitterness in her voice that scored Giyan's heart like the talons of an all-too-familiar creature. She had returned to the doorway to what had once been her bedroom. Inside, Annon lay sleeping.

"But what can one expect?" Bartta continued. "By the look of you, dressed in alien finery, you are now more V'ornn than Kundalan!"

Giyan turned to face her sister. She pushed back the sifeyn. "You know better than that."

Bartta turned her closed face away. "Forgive me. I am distracted this morning. I have been for a week. I found a girl, the same age as your V'ornn charge. She is in the acute stage of duur fever. Despite all my efforts on her behalf, she will die within the hour." She looked to her twin. "Unless with your Gift—"

"I cannot bring life to the dying. You know that better than anyone."

"You must try. I beg of you. Perhaps your coming here is another omen."

"*Another* omen?" Giyan stiffened. "Speak plainly, sister, for I, too, must tell of omens."

Bartta folded her arms across her birdlike chest, gave her sister a curious look. "Seven days ago, I saw an owl before sunset." She scowled. "The night messenger of Miina never shows itself during daylight hours unless it brings unexpected death in its talons."

"The owl is a harbinger of change," Giyan replied. "There is always fear in change."

"Not for the Ramahan," Bartta declared.

"I think, these days, *especially* for the Ramahan."

Bartta shook off her sister's words. "The owl—Miina's messenger—led me to this girl, Riane. It came out of the forest and circled the spot three times. I was *meant* to find her, don't you see? Why? She is dying, and I cannot save her. It makes no sense. And yet there can be no doubt of Miina's hand in this."

"Have you notified her family?"

"There is no family—at least none that she can remember. She has no memory."

"Poor thing."

The sounds of people screaming stilled Bartta's response. The sisters rushed to the window. Beyond the herb garden, past the unpainted cedar gates, steeply stepped streets descended to the village plaza. It was filled to bursting now with townsfolk, Khagggun, mostly on foot, a few riding cthauros.

"Miina protect us!" Bartta cried. "Another cursed Khagggun raiding party!" She ran to the door. "We thought our cliffs would stop them, but it only stopped their hoverpods. They steal cthauros from the villages below and march on." As she opened the door, Giyan held her back.

"Don't go out there, sister." She peered down to the square, could see the dreaded insignia on the Khagggun's helms. "This raiding party has more on its mind than random terror."

Bartta's eyes became slits. "What do you mean?"

"Someone betrayed us, saw us steal out of the palace. But I cannot imagine who."

Bartta tore away from her sister's grasp. "Stay here," she ordered. "If you are right, the Khagggun will doubtless begin a house-to-house search. I must find a away to keep them away from here."

"What can you do?"

Bartta went out the door without another word.

Giyan turned away from the window. Annon was still asleep. To distract herself, she went into Bartta's bedroom, saw the girl Riane lying deathly pale. Despite her lack of color, her lank, greasy hair, her emaciated body she was a strikingly beautiful girl. Giyan stood over her for a moment, said a prayer to Miina. She put a hand on the girl's cheek. She was burning up with fever. Giyan let out a long breath, allowed her mind to clear of all thought, all imagery, all emotion. Riane was so near death it took some time and effort to gather in enough of her faint aura.

She summoned Osoru.

She tried to direct the spell toward the girl, but something was blocking it. She was of no more use to Riane than Bartta had been. She tried again. Nothing. She did not understand. The power always came when she summoned it; it always obeyed her wishes. Why had it failed her now?

She turned as she heard the front door burst open, and rushed out to see Bartta. Her face was pinched and drawn.

"You were right. The Khagggun are looking for the boy." She ran a hand through her hair. "But, in true V'ornn fashion, they have decided not to waste their time searching the village themselves. The First-Captain has ordered the Khagggun to begin *interrogating* the townsfolk."

"The First-Captain? What about the commander?"

"I know him not. He sits upon a cthauros, hidden inside the skull of a Krael, silent as a grave marker."

"Odd that the Pack-Commander should let his First-Captain do his work."

"Work? Is that what you call this . . . abomination?" Bartta said. "Living among the aliens has addled your brain. The

interrogations are but prelude. The Khagggun promise to
slaughter us one by one until the boy is delivered to them."

"But the villagers know nothing."

"They know that you are my twin sister," Bartta said.
"Where else would you be hiding but at my cottage?" She
waved a hand. "Not to worry. No one has said a word, and
no one will. We would rather die than give up a secret to
those monsters. But I cannot allow my people to be sense-
lessly murdered." She bulled past Giyan. "We will give the
Khagggun what they want."

"What?" Giyan clawed her sister back. "Are you insane?
We cannot—"

"No, sister, *you* are insane if you think I will harbor a
V'ornn while my own people are being tortured and killed."

"You don't understand."

"Oh, I understand well enough." Bartta's entire body was
shaking with rage. "You have brought this evil down on us."

"Sister, the Khagggun will kill Annon. They will have his
head on a pike, just as they did with his father."

Shrieks coming from the square rose up through the
streets.

"It has begun," Bartta said ominously. "The Khagggun are
slaughtering our innocents."

"Annon is innocent, too!" Giyan cried.

"But he is a *V'ornn!*" Bartta screamed. "Miina damn you,
why are you protecting him?"

"Because he is my son."

"What?"

Giyan was weeping. Her heart was breaking. She had
sworn to tell no one. "I fell in love with Eleusis Ashera. I
mated with him."

Bartta made the sign of the Great Goddess. "Miina save
us all!" she breathed. "What have you done to us?"

"I have done only what was in my heart!"

"Then I curse your heart!"

"Think what my life has been like since I bore him. No
one save Eleusis could know he was my child. You know

that the V'ornn systematically collect the children of mixed race."

"And why not? Most don't want them, anyway."

"Ripped from their mother's milky bosom to what cruel fate?" Giyan shuddered. "What the Genomatekks do with them inside Receiving Spirit is anyone's guess."

"What they do with them is the V'ornn's foul business." Bartta trembled as more cries came to them through the open door. "Ah, Miina, his fate will be no better than theirs!"

"Sister, listen to me," Giyan said with matching passion. "We cannot sacrifice him. Annon has seen Seelin."

"One of the Five Sacred Dragons of Miina?" Bartta took a step toward her. Her upper lip curled, spittle flew from her mouth. "Do you even know what you are saying? He is V'ornn!"

"Of course I know. I am Ramahan."

Bartta shook her head. "After all these years with a V'ornn in your bed you are apostate."

"I keep the Goddess faith as you do, sister," Giyan bridled. "I revere Miina every moment of my life." She took Bartta's hand in hers. "Sister, listen closely to me. Miina's gyreagle marked him, left its talon inside him. You know the Prophesy as well as I do. The talon serves as a kind of lodestone; it guided him to the caverns beneath the palace, to the Storehouse. The Storehouse Door opened for him; he saw Seelin. The Dragon touched him, took back the talon, healed his wound."

Bartta snatched her hand away. "Heresy!" she hissed. "You are speaking heresy!"

"Am I? Think of the Prophesy. It is written that the Dar Sala-at can summon the Dragons and command them."

"Yes, but—"

"It is written that the Dar Sala-at will be born at both ends of the Cosmos." Giyan's whistleflower-blue eyes searched her sister's face. "You see it, don't you? The omens, the Prophesy—they are all coming true, just as Miina said they would. Think, sister! Half-Kundalan, half-V'ornn—the two ends of the Cosmos. The Prophesy finally makes sense!"

Abruptly, Bartta switched tactics. Her face smoothed, her voice dropped to an even, honeyed cadence. "Ah, Giyan. I understand now. He is your son. You will do anything, believe anything in order to save him. I do not blame you; I would do the same. But while we stand here arguing, innocent people are going to their deaths. Let his death have some meaning, at least. He will be saving hundreds of Kundalan lives. A noble fate for a V'ornn, eh? More by far than any V'ornn deserves."

Giyan shook off her sister's words. "I myself saw the wound the gyreagle had inflicted. Its talon was embedded in his flesh. Not an hour later, the wound was as you see it now. Only a Dragon's touch could have healed him."

"I do not believe it."

"There is no other explanation, you know it as well as I do. Annon is the Dar Sala-at, the One destined to free us from our servitude. We must protect him by *whatever means necessary*. Miina has shown Her face to us, sister. She has shown us the path we must take. We must bow to Her wisdom and Her will."

"But even if what you say—even if this fantastic story is true—how are we to save him and our townsfolk?"

Giyan's eyes were lambent. "Together we will conjure the Nanthera."

"The Abyss of Spirits?" Bartta was aghast. "You cannot be serious."

"We must! It is the only way out of this terrible dilemma!"

Bartta shook her head. "Listen to yourself, sister. Since the time we transgressed against the Goddess, since the time The Pearl was lost, we have been enjoined from conjuring the Nanthera. Without Miina's intervention, it is too dangerous, too difficult to control the Portal to the Great Abyss. When it is opened there is the danger that all those abominations Miina has banished to that Goddess-forsaken pit will escape."

"Miina will protect us. She is here with us. Because of who Annon is. Because of your Riane."

"What do you mean?"

"I went to her while you were gone," Giyan said. "I tried to use my power. I could not. As you said, she will die within the hour. Could that be Miina's will? You yourself said that it is not. Miina means for her to live. You begged me to save her from death. This is how."

"It is said of the Nanthera that the two essences must battle for supremacy in the one mind. Do we dare place the Dar Sala-at—if, indeed, Annon is the Dar Sala-at—in such peril?"

"It is true that we know nothing about the aftereffects of the Nanthera, but what choice do we have?" Giyan said. "Besides, Annon is strong and Riane is weak. You said yourself that her loss of memory had placed a veil over her life."

They both started as Annon called out in an agonized voice. Giyan rushed to his side, her twin following behind. Annon was awake. Giyan knelt beside him. "What is it? Why have you cried out so? Is your pain worse?"

"No." He looked up at her. "I have heard the sounds from outside. I know Khagggun have come to take me back to Wennn Stogggul."

"Hush, now," she said, cradling his head. "Go back to sleep."

"No!" He struggled to lever himself into a sitting position. "I know the cruelty Khagggun are capable of. Even though they are Kundalan, I don't want these people to be slaughtered because of me."

Giyan would not let him go. "I made your father a promise. I will keep you safe as long as there is a breath of life left in me."

"It is my life. One life against many. I will not live with their blood on my hands."

As he struggled to rise, compensating for his weakened leg, Giyan turned her beseeching face to her sister. "You see his heart now, sister. I beg of you, heed Miina's message. It is no coincidence that the owl came to you, that we were driven here in our hour of utmost need. Annon needs to be trained in the ways of the Ramahan. He needs to be taught the Holy Scriptures. Who better than you to do this holy

work? The Great Goddess commands us. We can do ought
but serve Her."

For a long moment, Bartta said nothing. She looked at
Annon, valiantly trying to march out to his fate, to save the
Kundalan of Stone Border from certain death. She recalled
the great owl swooping down at her, circling three times the
spot where Riane lay, deathly ill. *What does this mean?* she
has asked herself over and over during this long and arduous
lunar week. *Why would Miina have me save her only to see
her die days later?* It was a conundrum that had consumed
her, robbed her of sleep. It had not made sense. But what if
Giyan was right? What if this half-V'ornn had been touched
by one of Miina's Sacred Dragons? Improbable as it might
seem, what if he *was* the Dar Sala-at? Then her fate was
clear: she was the one destined to train him, to control him,
to bathe in his power and be exalted by it.

"Forgive me for doubting you. Your logic is faultless, sister," Bartta said, kissing Giyan on both cheeks. "Let us make
all haste to carry out the Great Goddess's commands." She
smiled into Giyan's face, found the place inside herself
where her love for her twin dwelled, chained in perpetual
darkness. "Carry him into the great room, and I will bring
Riane. If we are to succeed, we have very little time." She
fought to keep her apprehension in check. The Nanthera had
not been conjured in more than a lunar century. The implications of what they were about to do made her skin prickle
and her stomach contract painfully.

Giyan was crouched beside her son when Bartta returned
to the great room. She carefully laid Riane down next to
Annon, then went to the carved heartwood cabinet. Unlocking it, she swung wide the door, revealing row upon row of
stoppered glass jars, vials, bottles filled with all manner of
powders and liquids. She took down several of these as Giyan began the chanting in the Old Tongue. As Bartta mixed
her powders, she joined in the liturgy and the Singing of the
Bourns began in earnest.

In a circle around Riane and Annon, Bartta placed nine
hawk feathers. In the spaces between them she daubed ani-

mal blood onto the floor. Onto these she sprinkled an earthy powder she had ground from uva camarona, tupa, To-shka, and Goddess's-Flesh mushroom. The blood daubs spontaneously ignited into deep blue heatless flames. Giyan gripped her son's hand tightly as the bourns were set in motion.

Annon twitched in Giyan's embrace. "I feel an itching all down my skin." He was clearly frightened. "What is going on?"

Giyan forced herself to smile reassuringly. "Your protection arrives on brave wings, Annon."

"It is time," Bartta intoned.

"Time for what?" He looked up at Giyan with an expression that made her heart constrict.

Kneeling beside him, Giyan bared one breast. She cradled the back of his skull in one hand, lifted her breast with the other.

"What . . . what are you doing?"

"Look at me," she said softly, gently. "Only at me, Te-yjattt."

He gazed deep into her eyes and his lids grew heavy. His mouth closed over her nipple and he began to suckle as he had when we was a babe. Almost immediately, his eyes closed, his breathing became deep and regular. "That's right," Giyan crooned, rocking him. "Sleep now." She lovingly stroked the back of his skull. "Sleep now, beloved, in the safety of my arms."

"He does not know that he is your son, does he?" Bartta said.

Giyan shook her head, too full of emotion to speak.

"That must have been painful for you." She said this with a curious glint in her eye. "He felt the power of the bourns forming. I should have said that was impossible."

"Not for the Dar Sala-at." Giyan caressed his face. "From the moment of his conception there was nothing usual about him. He spoke to me while I carried him in my womb. We had conversations. I sang to him, wove him the tales of Miina, of the Five Dragons, of *Utmost Source*."

"What would you know of the *Five Sacred Books of*

Miina? It was lost in the time before either of us was born."

Giyan, keeping her thoughts to herself, said, "I know no more than you, only what we were taught at the Abbey of Floating White."

"We have no more time." Bartta held out her hand. "Come!" she commanded. "Hurry now, sister! The Nanthera has been conjured. The bourns have found their tempo. They cannot be stopped."

Giyan did not move. She looked with horrified eyes at Annon.

"Sister, you must step out now!" The circle of flames grew in intensity. The feathers fluttered even though no breeze wafted through the cottage. "Riane is dying. If she does so before the Nanthera is completed, Annon will be doomed to wander the nonworld forever."

Giyan seemed paralyzed. "Look at him, Bartta. So help-less, so innocent. It is hard, so very hard to say good-bye to my son."

"Forget him now, sister. Soon he will be Annon no more. He will have been to a place no Kundalan was ever meant to walk. He will have seen things no Kundalan was ever meant to see. If he is the Dar Sala-at, he will walk alone. So it is written, so it will be."

Giyan sprang up. "I don't want to lose him!" She came to the edge of the circle of eerie, heatless fire.

"Sister, come to me now! Step out of the circle before you are caught up in—"

They both heard it at the same instant: a bone-chilling howling. At first, it seemed as if it was coming from a long way off. Nevertheless, the howling echoed in their skulls, setting their teeth on edge, making their hearts hammer in their breasts.

"What is that?" Giyan whispered.

"The cries of the abominated. They sense the Portal open-ing. They clamor to be released."

Giyan was wide-eyed with terror as the howling grew nearer. "Miina preserve us!"

"Riane is slipping away," Bartta told her urgently. "I can

feel her leaving us. There is no time. Come here. Please. The Nanthera was conjured for Annon. Only for him. Sister, you must be outside the circle when the Portal opens completely or risk being infected by the filth that abides in the dark pit."

"Miina will protect him," Bartta said as she drew her twin out of the circle, holding her tight. "Have faith."

The entire aspect of the room has altered. Nothing can be clearly seen. The two women do not draw breath, their hearts have ceased their steady beating, the pulses in their wrists are as silent as a gravesite. It is as if they have been transported beyond the structural limitations of time and space. Before them, within the circle of heatless fire, the Abyss of Spirits is open. Even healers such as they must shiver with the portent of this dark sorcery, for they find themselves suspended Outside, peering down into what appears to be an unending spiral. They grow cold as something rises from the unimaginable depths.

"What is that—*thing*?" Giyan says hoarsely.

"I know not," her twin says.

"Miina, what have we done?"

"We are saving them both."

"For what? So this *abomination* can have them?"

Whatever it is, it comes for Annon, and it is a fearsome thing—indefinable, unknowable, utterly dreadful. The entire room cants over at an angle, darkness is made visible, manifest, light reduced to shadow. The thing is about to engulf Annon—her son. Giyan feels as if her heart is being torn from her breast. A deep rumble like thunder rattles the room in its fist. Giyan takes a step toward the sorcerous circle.

Bartta moans. "Oh, Giyan, come away! You invite disaster by interfering with the circle of the Nanthera."

"Leave me be! He is my son. I am afraid for him." Giyan stretches her arms out, breaking the circle. She cries out as darkness, thick and sinewy as a liana, lances up her arms, twining itself about her. Instantly, her hands go numb and she feels a pain unlike anything she has ever felt before, as if her bones are disintegrating from the marrow outward.

She cries out again, her anguish palpable. Her voice sounds odd, distorted, turned in on itself. She is paralyzed by the pain in her hands where they have entered the Nanthera. She wants to thrust herself whole into the circle, but she cannot. She wants to reach her son, but she is fighting a fierce and evil whirlwind of unknown origin. Her bloodstained robes swirl and flutter out behind her.

"It is too late! He belongs to the Nanthera now. You cannot have him back." Bartta turns her head. "Ah, Miina, Riane slips away. We have left it too late."

"Don't take him from me! I want him back!" Giyan's voice seems to be falling away from her, falling into the darkness of the Abyss.

Just as Bartta grabs hold of Giyan around the waist, she sees Giyan's hands caught in the penumbra of the hideous thing that has come for her son. Bartta shudders, clamps down on the urge to vomit, as a triangle of the V'ornn robe flutters into her hands. Sobbing, she hauls with all her might. Giyan stumbles backward. The vortex tries to suck her into itself, the hideous thing crouches, preparing to spring at her. It seems to be grinning, licking its lips. Bartta wraps the fabric around her forearm and jerks mightily, pulling Giyan back through the border. As Giyan comes free of the circle, the thing turns away. It crouches over Annon. His form begins to shimmer and lose substance, becoming like a lacewing butterfly, nothing more than transparent gossamer.

"Too late for fear." Bartta clutches her twin to her.

Annon loses definition.

"Too late for remorse." Bartta feels her twin shuddering and shaking.

His human outline is transmuting.

"Too late even for love." Bartta places her hand over her twin's eyes, averting her own gaze from that which no Kundalan was meant to witness.

An unnatural darkness engulfs them as the two sisters rock together. It is so palpable it beats against their eyelids, scours their skin like a sandstorm in the Great Voorg. Giyan is sobbing with no thought for her own pain. "My son," she wails. "My son!"

"We tried to protect them," Bartta says, "but we may have killed them instead."

As the abomination inside the sorcerous circle completes its fearful task, the darkness emanating from it seems to want to eat them alive. It overlaps the circle, the heatless flames flicker and start to gutter, and now they see long, slithery things emerging from the vortex of the Abyss. In horror, the sisters glimpse the first wave of a frightful host. Impatient, the thing advances to the edge of the circle.

"Miina protect us! Sister, your rash intervention has broken the circle. It comes." Bartta makes the sign of the Great Goddess, commences another chant in the Old Tongue.

"No, I will not allow it!" Giyan throws her arms heavenward as she slips to her knees. "Hear me, Great Goddess. I have never asked you for anything, but now I beseech you! Help us! I will do anything you require of me, make any sacrifice you ask! My life, my very soul are yours! Just give me back my son!"

With a deafening silence peculiar to sorcery, the preternatural darkness begins to lighten. There comes a howling as the slithery things are hurled backward into the Abyss. The thing, knowing that it is next, struggles, but to no avail, In a moment, it, too, vanishes downward whence it sprang. The last notes of the power bourns sing their song, and then it is over. The Abyss of Spirits is sealed once more. The Nanthera is done.

Giyan, her gaze fixed on the body of Annon, remained on her knees. The flames were gone, the hawk feathers bits of ash. Bartta cautiously knelt beside Annon, put her ear to his chest. "Sister, he does not draw breath. Your son is dead."

A wailing came from deep inside Giyan's body, rose up through her as if she were some great instrument of the Goddess, filling the cottage with heartache and lamentation.

Bartta moved to where Riane lay pale and inert, repeated the procedure.

"Dead, too," she whispered to herself. "Poor orphaned thing. Not knowing where she came from, not understanding her end. What short life did she have? Less than most. Far less." And at last the peculiar kinship she felt for this girl overwhelmed her, and she laid her, head on the girl's breast. While Giyan's wails swirled around her, she allowed herself a small allotment of tears. But, then, something happened. The rib cage beneath her stirred, rose as it filled with air and then subsided again. This wavelike motion occurred three more times before her stunned brain made sense of it.

She lifted her head, felt the girl's warm breath on her cheek. "Miina save us, she breathes!" She put her hand across Riane's forehead. It was damp with sweat, but it no longer burned.

"Sister, sister, come see! Riane is alive! She has survived the Nanthera! And her fever has broken!"

Giyan joined her sister, saw that she was right. Already the color was returning to Riane's cheeks. Her breathing was deep and even.

"Annon, my most beloved son, what kind of life will you have now?" Giyan whispered.

"You must call her Riane now." Bartta put a hand on Giyan's shoulder. "Let her sleep now. The Nanthera was interrupted. No one can say what the outcome will be, and it is unwise even to consider the question."

Giyan nodded, but could not stop herself from caressing Riane's cheek. Outside, in the streets, the shrieking resumed.

"Come." Bartta urged. "It is time for the final act."

Standing beside the corpse of her son, Giyan wept silently. Though she continued to grieve, the wailing had left her spent. "Good-bye, my beloved."

"Quickly, sister." Bartta pushed her forward. "Every minute you delay another Kundalan dies."

As if she had been transmuted into a sleepwalker, Giyan bent down and picked up the body of her son. She turned toward the open door and heard her sister's indrawn gasp.

"Miina, look at you!"

Distractedly, she glanced down at her hands. They were black, hard as crystal, numb as lead weights from her fingertips to just above her wrists.

"What does this mean?" Bartta was clearly horrified.

"It is my penance, I suppose. My sacrifice to Miina for my transgression." She looked at Riane sleeping peacefully. "Small price to pay. . . . for life."

"How can you say that?" Bartta hissed. "You have no idea of what the darkness of the abyss has done to you."

"It does not matter now. My son is safe from the enemies of the Ashera." Tears streaming down her face, she kissed her sister on both cheeks. "Teach him well, Bartta. Teach him what he needs to know to rule us wisely."

"You will be back, sister."

"No, I do not think so," Giyan said with a wan smile. "I was Eleusis Ashera's mistress. Doubtless, Wennn Stogggul will find a suitably vile way to punish me."

She walked out the door, down the stone pathway through the garden, out into the street. She passed gaping townsfolk, who took one look at her, started jabbering and ran before her down the steps to spread the news. The taverns were empty, storefronts closed and locked, windows shuttered. The air buzzed with the martial beat of the Khagggun's ion-powered weapons. Below, in the central plaza, the shrieking had come to a halt. Blood filled the gutters and corpses lay at First-Captain Olnnn Rydddlin's feet. A thousand or more Kundalan stood stiff and silent. Rekkk Hacilar sat some distance away, looking not at the bodies, his helm faced the Abbey of Floating White which, mercifully, had been spared the despoiler's shock-sword. But he turned back as the Kundalan female with the blackened hands approached the plaza with her offering. Without being ordered to do so, the Khagggun parted for her. Their eyes were wide and staring. A hush stilled even the wailing prayers for the dead.

Giyan said nothing. There was no need. Rekkk Hacilar knew her on sight, knew Annon as well. She stopped only when she stood before him. His cthauros stamped and snorted uneasily at the scent of fresh blood. First-Captain Olnnn Rydddlin urged his own mount slowly toward them.

As if he were the V'ornn god Enlil himself, she offered up the corpse of her son to him. For what seemed an eternity of agony, he did nothing.

First-Captain Olnnn Rydddlin smirked. "At last, the son of privilege returns," he said in his silky voice.

Rekkk Hacilar ignored him. Slowly, he removed his helm. His long, handsome face was stoic as he stared silently into Giyan's eyes. He seemed attuned to her anguish. Inclining his head slightly, he spoke softly, almost sorrowfully. "Please lay him on the ground."

Steeling herself for the expected outrage to come, she complied, lowering him at the Pack-Commander's feet. What choice did she have? Besides, she was committed to this path now, no matter the cost to her.

Annon's face was covered in dust and blood. Rekkk Hacilar's dark eyes did not leave hers.

"First-Captain, have the body bound across the back of a spare cthauros."

Olnnn Rydddlin frowned, sidled his mount closer to Rekkk Hacilar's. "Pack-Commander, are you forgetting protocol? Annon Ashera must be dragged around the plaza seven times. His skin must be flayed from his body to set an example."

"We have what we came for," Rekkk Hacilar said curtly. "Our work here is done."

"Pack-Commander, I must lodge a protest—"

"Do whatever you have to do, but do it at another time."

"You cannot do this, Pack-Commander," Olnnn Rydddlin hissed. "It will set a bad example."

Rekkk Hacilar's voice was steel-edged as he wheeled in his saddle. "I gave you a direct order, First-Captain." His gauntleted hand closed around the hilt of his shock-sword. "If you fail to carry it out immediately, I will cut you down where you sit."

Olnnn Rydddlin said nothing. His fury abruptly vanished. In its place, a small smile played across his lips. "I have done my duty, Pack-Commander." He nodded curtly. "It will be as you wish."

Rekkk Hacilar was paying scant attention. His gaze was fixed on Giyan, who stood with her back straight, her eyes focused on the horizon. As Khagggun roughly took up Annon's corpse and wrapped it in sheets of plain muslin, tears rolled down her cheeks, dripped onto the muddy ground.

"Treat the body with care," Rekkk Hacilar ordered. "Our esteemed new regent requires his proof of his death. No mark must mar the face or head."

Through her tears, Giyan felt a wave of gratitude. If her years among the V'ornn, her time with Eleusis had taught her anything, it was that these aliens were far from the monolithic evil menace most supposed them to be. Beneath their fierce warrior exterior beat hearts that were capable of compassion and love, souls that could feel remorse and, perhaps, even shame at what they had wrought on Kundala.

She turned her head, watched the Pack-Commander with intense curiosity as he dug his heels into the cthauros's flanks, urging it gently forward.

"I am prepared to die now," she told him with her head held high.

He bent toward her, scooped a powerful arm around her waist, drew her up, and swung her onto the cthauros' back behind him. Extending a mailed fist over his head, a sign for his pack to begin their bloodcurdling ululation, he cried in a voice that carried over the increasing din: "To the victor the spoils!"

As Pack-Commander Rekkk Hacilar and his Khagggun pack withdrew from Stone Border, Bartta hurried back to her cottage. She had seen enough—more than enough, if truth be told. It seemed to her now as if her twin was fated to live her life in the arms of the enemy. First Eleusis Ashera and now this murderous Pack-Commander. She shook her head. She had seen how he had looked at Giyan. He had been ready to take her the moment she dropped Annon's corpse at his feet. Bartta thought it a wonder he hadn't. That would have been the V'ornn way, to heap humiliation upon humiliation. But perhaps he had thought it sufficiently soul-destroying for her to watch Annon's corpse being trussed like a cor for the slaughter. She had to remind herself that only three people knew that Giyan was the boy's mother—and one of those, Eleusis, was dead. What had the Pack-Commander been thinking while his eyes were on her? she wondered. She shuddered. What matter? Now that the V'ornn had taken her again, Giyan was doomed.

Bartta shrugged her shoulders in resignation. *We all have our fates*, she told herself. But she did not envy Giyan hers: forced to endure the humiliation of returning to Axis Tyr with her dead son in tow, there to receive whatever punishment the regent could devise, while she, Bartta, was left alone here to raise the Dar Sala-at as she saw fit. There was a certain irony in the twist fate had brought the two sisters. The golden girl—beautiful, Gifted—with her face in the offal of the V'ornn's making; she—homely, bent-backed—rearing the Kundalan savior. She must tell no one about the Dar Sala-at until it was time, until everything was in readiness and she could ensure that all the power would flow to her.

Behind her, the townsfolk were wailing, preparing to bury their dead. Bartta closed her ears to the sound. She had already been witness to enough grief in her lifetime.

The aurora of darkness that gripped Stone Border, the bitter smells of wet limestone and fear, sickly sweet stench of blood and death, put her in mind of the first—and only—time the V'ornn had entered the walls of the abbey. Five years ago, the night after Konara Mossa had been buried. Konara Mossa, who had led the Dea Cretan, who had taken Bartta under her wing. The entire abbey had been in mourning, the Ramahan in their cells, praying. A dreaded Gyrgon in its hideous insectoid biosuit, attended by two heavily armed Khaggggun of high rank, stalked the stone corridors. The Gyrgon had singled her out, speaking to her alone, in private. A small chamber, nondescript, almost devoid of furniture. The grace of Miina only shining inside the bronze oil lamp. She remembered the repeating song of a mockingbird coming from a tree outside the open window. She remembered the exact color of the moonslight illuminating the mosaic tile floor. She recalled with absolute clarity the cloying scent of clove oil and burnt musk as it wafted from the alien. She could even recall the tonality of the Gyrgon's voice. But nothing of what was said. Her conscious mind cringed from the details, having long ago buried them away in some dark, deserted corner of her mind. All she knew was from that moment on she had the Gyrgon's assurance that the abbey would remain inviolate, the Ramahan inside free and safe, if she continued to do what Konara Mossa had done since Giyan had been taken by the V'ornn sixteen years ago. Giyan was the last of the Ramahan from the Abbey of Floating White to be seized, setting in motion Konara Mossa's desperate scheme.

Thereafter, twice a month—sometimes more often, depending on the circumstances—Bartta made a half hour pilgrimage down the winding, rocky path to a small, abandoned hunter's hut, and there secreted the information she had scribbled by hand, information concerning resistance plans, movements, personnel she had gleaned from Konara Mossa's contacts in the village. All to keep her Ramahan safe from harm. The V'ornn had not invaded the Abbey of Floating White as they had the other abbeys, had not taken her Ramahan to be interrogated, tortured, and killed. No, she had spared all Kundala the horror of seeing the Ramahan wiped out. It served no useful purpose to consider the price she had had to pay. No price was too high for the survival of spirituality.

She trudged up the stepped streets, the grief of her village falling upon her like her mother's casket, which she had borne into the ground on her own. Her father was dead to her, caught up in Kara, that horrid new Goddess-less religion, Giyan had been taken by the V'ornn. She alone had had to say the ritual prayers over her mother's corpse. She alone had had to burn her mother's clothes. She alone had had to bury her. Because no one cared. But she was dutiful, always,

because duty defined her life. Without it, she was lost in all
the sickening moments of her childhood that began with
strangulation and ended at the moment her mother took her
last, sour breath.

And so could she really be faulted for rewriting Scripture
of a Goddess who obviously no longer cared about her people or, worse, no longer existed? From the time she had been
made konara, she had made a strategic decision. Following
a dead Goddess would only lead the Ramahan down the path
to irrelevance. The horrifyingly rapid growth of Kara and all
it implied for the future of the Ramahan was a clear enough
rationale for what was required of her. She had told herself
that she was doing Miina's work so many times she now
firmly believed it.

She looked up at her cottage, which she could barely
make out through the gloom, where Riane lay. And now,
after so many years toiling in Miina's fields, the Great Goddess had seen fit to reward her by giving her the Dar Sala-
at to raise and to mentor. And how right was her decision to
keep the abbey safe and secure. Now the Dar Sala-at would
have the home she needed.

Inside the cottage, she closed the door firmly, went immediately to the hearth, where she put on a thick stew to
simmer. Riane was still sleeping. She took her up and went
into the bedroom Annon had been in, figuring that when she
woke it would be to more familiar surroundings. Setting her
down and covering her with a quilt, she said a prayer to
Miina. When she was through, she dragged a chair over to
Riane's side, sat down wearily and fell instantly into a deep
but restless sleep, where she dreamed she was running, running, running in a great circle. It was dark where she ran,
and cool, so it must have been a woods, though she saw no
trees, smelled no forest scents. At some point, she became
aware that she was being pursued. She glanced over her
shoulder, saw an enormous owl swooping down for her. She
tried to cry out but discovered that the owl had already
yanked out her vocal cords. They dangled like vitals from

the predator-bird's beak. Its beaconlike eyes raked hers as if trying to tell her something.

She awoke with a start, put a hand to her neck, cleared her throat as if to reassure herself that her vocal cords were still intact. It was past moonrise. She rubbed her eyes, padded out to the hearth, tended the fire, and stirred the stew, which was thickening nicely.

She started, certain she heard stirring from the other room, but when she went to look, Riane was still deeply asleep. Looking at her pale flesh in the flickering lamplight, Bartta felt a tiny shiver run through her, as of an eel slithering into a crevice between coral-encrusted rocks. All her life, the envy she had felt at her twin's Gift had eaten away at her like acid. Now she would have her revenge, for the Dar Sala-at was Gifted in special ways. If she could manipulate the Dar Sala-at, then she could control her Gift. What a glorious moment that would be!

Unaccountably, guilt pricked her. She grabbed her traveling cloak from the peg on the wall, wrapped herself in it. What was it Giyan had said? *The owl is the harbinger of change.*

She went out into the blustery night. The funereal wailing wafted up from the central square. The bodies of the dead had been laid out, cleaned of blood, dressed in their best clothes. They lay in a line upon a bed of dried oat-grass chaff. All around them ranged the villagers of Stone Border. So she was not too late.

Hurriedly, she joined her sister Ramahan. They stood before the bodies in a shallow semicircle. The chanting began, the syllables of the Old Tongue swelling until it swallowed the wailing whole, enclosing it in the love of Miina. A designated member of each family that had suffered a loss this day made a fire. When all were lighted, Bartta blessed them one by one. She was handed a torch, which she blessed with her hands and with a prayer. She held it above each fire in turn until, like a living thing, the flame leapt to the torch. The crowd gasped as one as the torch sprang to life.

The prayers of the Ramahan filled the plaza until it and

everything in its seemed to vibrate in a harmonic to the tones of the Old Tongue. At the climactic moment, Bartta dropped the torch onto the bed of chaff, and fire sprang up, spreading quickly, rapaciously, until the entire bed and those that lay upon it in their final repose were engulfed, eaten, consumed along with everything but the village's grief.

Nothing felt right.

Annon, sitting up in bed, was staring down at his delicate hands. He turned them this way and that. Not his hands; someone else's hands. Icy fear clutched at him. These hands, so small. . . . And there was *hair* on his arms. And, speaking of his arms, his muscles seemed to have dissolved. Frantically, he pushed the quilt off his body.

"N'Luuura take me!" His breath was an indrawn gasp. "Where are my tender parts?"

At once, he put his hand to his throat. What had happened to his voice? It was more than an octave too high.

He scrambled off the bed and almost fell to the floor. Nothing worked right. His arms and legs were too short, colors seemed strange. He remembered this cottage from before he went to sleep—Bartta's cottage, Giyan's twin sister. But everything looked slightly different, as if he was seeing it in a mirror.

A mirror! That's what he needed.

He crawled along the floor, pulled himself to his feet by leaning against an old and ornately carved chest of drawers. He steadied himself as a wave of dizziness overtook him. He swallowed hard, hoping he would not throw up. When he began to feel better he went frantically through the drawers, pushing aside clothes and personal items until he located a small, oval hand mirror. Whipping it out, he held it up in front of his face.

"N'Luuura take it!"

He was a she! There was thick golden hair sprouting all over the top and back of his head! He was a Kundalan!

This was a nightmare. It could not be happening. He slammed the mirror into his face again and again, but the reflection did not change. Where was his own body? Where was *he*?

"Giyan!" he screamed in the high female voice as he stumbled through the cottage. "Giyan, where are you? What has happened to me?"

He dropped the mirror. He heard it shatter only dimly; he was retching too hard. Gasping and groaning, he dragged his lithe alien body back to the bed, pushed aside the bedcovers that had fallen to the floor. Digging with alien nails, scrabbling with alien hands, he pried up the floorboards he had discovered were loose just after Giyan had brought him in here. The old leather-bound book Giyan had cautioned him to keep safe was still there, as was the knife Eleana had given him. He pulled them out, ran his hands over them. They were real. He wasn't insane. His past was his past. Safe. It was his present that was uncertain and unknown.

He would have to keep his thoughts to himself until he could find Giyan and—

He stiffened at the noise. Someone was coming into the cottage. Quickly, he stuffed his precious possessions back into the hole, placed the floorboards over them. Then he scrambled back into bed and closed his eyes, not a moment too soon.

Returning to her cottage, Bartta went directly into Riane's room. Seeing that the girl was still asleep, she returned to the great room, hung up her cloak, and took up the long wooden spoon on the stones by the hearth. She hefted a thick, shallow bowl of green ceramic and ladled some stew into it. She had meant to eat it, but she found that she had no appetite, so she took it into the girl's bedroom.

Riane was sitting up, staring at her.

Bartta froze as if there was a spice-adder curled up on her bedsheets. She could feel her heart hammering in her breast, and for a long moment it felt as though she had forgotten how to breathe. *Now there is no help for it*, she thought, the future staring her in the face.

"How do you feel?" Bartta said when she at last found her voice.

Riane said nothing, and Bartta smiled, stepping over the shards of mirror, cautiously offering the bowl. "You must be hungry. You haven't eaten in days."

Riane grabbed it from her, ate with ravenous speed while keeping a wary eye on her like a creature from the wilderness. Bartta was required to fill the bowl twice more before the girl was sated.

Bartta sat beside her. "Can you talk to me, Riane?"

"Where is Giyan? I need to talk to her."

"It's all right."

"Now!" Riane screamed, throwing the empty bowl against the wall.

Bartta slapped him, hard then, as he began to fight back, pressed him back into the bed.

"You are safe now," she said, her face close to his. "But you must come to terms with the changes." She glanced again at the broken mirror. "You are no longer Annon. You are Riane, a Kundalan female. For your own good and the good of those around you, you put aside your male V'ornn personality." Annon, inside the body of Riane, struggled against her, unused to this body's lack of bulk and strength in comparison with his own. "Annon's enemies are everywhere. If you do not adjust, if you allow Annon to leak out, they will surely get wind of it, and they will destroy you. I am Ramahan. I have few ways to fight back against the V'ornn." She shook Riane violently. "Are you listening to me?" she roared.

The girl stared up into her face, an expression of rigid denial on her beautiful face.

"What was done," Bartta said more calmly, "had to be done to save you."

The girl continued to watch her, but at least she was for the moment quiescent.

"I know you saw yourself in the mirror before you broke it," Bartta continued. "You are beautiful."

"Let me up," Riane said.

"Have you calmed down?"

Silence.

Bartta let go, backed off the bed.

"Riane—"

The girl scrambled off the bed and backed up until she was crouched in the far corner of the room. "Don't call me that!"

"What else shall I call you?"

"You will call me by my real name."

"Riane is who you are now. Please try to understand. Your—that is, Giyan and I transferred your essence into the body of Riane. It was the only way to protect you. Your enemies believe you are dead."

"If that is true, then let Giyan tell me herself. I will believe her."

Bartta sighed. "Giyan is gone. She took . . ." She wet her lips. "In order to prove to your enemies that Annon was dead, she took the body down to them. So the Khagggun would stop killing the townsfolk. You remember that, don't you?"

Riane stared at her.

"You remember that you were going to sacrifice yourself to save them. Well, in a very real sense you did. They have your body, and they have Giyan, as well. She was taken by the Pack-Commander."

"Rekkk Hacilar."

"Yes, well, I doubt she's coming back, so you will just have to—"

"I will go find her," Riane said, rushing past her.

Bartta grabbed her around the arm, swung her around, hit her again, harder this time, so that the girl fell back against the bed. Giyan, Giyan, it was *always* Giyan.

"That is Annon talking," she said. "I told you we'll have none of that." Seeing the girl ball her hand into fists, she said hurriedly: "And what a foolish notion it would be to go after her. You are alone, in an alien body. You are one of the conquered now, and a female to boot. You would not last a week on your own."

"Then take me yourself."

"It was Giyan's express wish that you remain here with me, that you become an acolyte of the Ramahan at the Abbey of Floating White, where she and I learned Scripture."

"I do not believe you."

Bartta hit her again. "Then *learn* to believe me, Riane. The quicker you do, the better it will be for you. You already have quite enough to get used to without my having to hit you. I don't want to hit you, I get no pleasure from it, but you have to learn. You have your whole life ahead of you."

Riane uttered an incomprehensible V'ornn curse. "I am V'ornn! I live now only to revenge myself against Wennn Stogggul and Kinnnus Morcha!" She uncoiled herself, snatched up a shard of broken mirror, and lunged forward. Bartta jumped back but not before the razor-sharp edge ripped her robe and scored her skin. Blood flowed from her shoulder. Rage spurted through her, and she smacked Riane so hard, the bloody shard of mirror went flying across the room.

Bartta hit her again and again. "Forget revenge, forget Giyan, forget your life of leisure and privilege in Axis Tyr. It no longer exists. *Annon Ashera* no longer exists." Panting and grunting, she continued with the thrashing until Riane lay unconscious.

"There," she said, panting still. "There." For some reason, she was put in mind of the lorg she had killed so many years ago. That cursed memory! Was she fated to carry it around with her forever? Why? It was just an animal, and an evil one at that, Giyan's protestations notwithstanding.

Spent, Bartta sat on the blood-spattered bed, slid her robes off her shoulder in order to tend her wound. "Miina protect us," she whispered as she stanched the blood. "I own you now. I will never let you go. The Great Goddess Herself has seen fit to grant you life. But it is a life no one would envy! You will experience firsthand the murderous, hateful, hopeless life under V'ornn rule. You will see for yourself how they have systematically stripped us of everything that was once ours. Perhaps, given time, you will even mourn for us, for there is scarcely a Kundalan alive who remembers what

Kundala was like before the V'ornn invasion. A time when narbucks roamed the plateaus, when Osoru had not yet been corrupted by the Ramahan males and by the accursed Rappa, when lightning rimmed the sky, presaging the appearance of Miina's glorious Sacred Dragons. Where are they now, eh? Where?" Bartta's hands were squeezed into white fists that pounded against her thighs. "Ah, that time is long gone; I fear it will never be again! And now we are left without our Goddess, without the magical narbucks, without even the lightning to bring us sorcerous energy. We are left with our dead and our pain and the terrible compromises we have had to make.

"But, for better or worse, it would seem you are the Dar Sala-at." She put her hand out, stroked Riane's hair back from her forehead. The girl's face was just beginning to darken and swell. "Riane, Chosen of Miina and of Seelin. My holy secret. So life you shall have, just as Miina has decreed. But you are in my hands now. Whatever mysteries you hold will one day be mine. Of that you can be assured!"

Book Two:
GATE OF LIFE

"The Kundalan spirit is composed of five elements: earth, air, fire, water, wood.

The interaction of these elements— whether harmonious or acrimonious, sweet or bitter, curved or straight, flowing or rigid, determines the personality—and therefore the Path—of each individual. With such a volatile mix, it would be dangerous to believe that Equilibrium can be achieved. Indeed, it may not even be advisable."

—Utmost Source,
The Five Sacred Books of Miina

9

Vessel Half-Full

The Abbey of Floating White was aptly named. Built on a rocky bluff overlooking Stone Border, it was a long, rambling structure of bone-white stone that sparkled in sunlight, shone silvery in rain. On moonless nights it glowed with an ethereal light marked by everyone in Stone Border. Nine slender minarets rose from sacred shrines within its high walls. These were crowned by domes pulled upward like taffy, coated with silver leaf. They were so tall they became lost when the ridge was shrouded in fog or low clouds.

No Ramahan now living could remember a time when the abbey did not exist. Indeed, legend had it that the structure was conceived and constructed by the Goddess Miina Herself. There were hints and clues to the veracity of this notion, the most compelling of which was the makeup of the stone itself. It bore no resemblance to that of the Djenn Marre mountain chain. It was dense and so hard the huge blocks showed no wear. Indeed, save for the former Abbey of Listening Bone in Axis Tyr (now the V'ornn Temple of Mnemonics) it was unique in all of known Kundala.

Riane could see the abbey quite clearly at the southern edge of the kuello-fir forest as she worked daily in Bartta's sorcerous garden. Below, along the steep, stepped streets, she saw townsfolk moving in short, quick bursts, a stillness in between, a lassitude born of the absence of happiness of any kind. Wrapped in their dark cloaks, they hurried about their business, stood solitary, deep in contemplation in their shadowed doorsteps or at half-shuttered windows. Waiting, their shoulders perpetually hunched against an unseen storm.

Where was the bustle and clamor of voices raised in argument, in haggling over prices, in minor disagreements? Where were the shouts of recognition from across crowded markets, the squeals of children at play? Where, most of all, were the numerous Kundalan celebrations to commemorate the change of seasons, the harvests, special days on the calendar Giyan had so lovingly described to him? The quiet unnerved Riane. Annon and Kurgan had often spent time in the countryside surrounding Axis Tyr when they had gone hunting, but always they had returned to the heat and frenetic beat of the city.

Surrounded by strange scents that made her light-headed and slightly nauseous, Riane toiled away under Bartta's keen eye. Her face, neck, and shoulders were still bruised and swollen from the beating she had received. At night, the pain kept her awake. She did not swallow the sleeping draught Bartta concocted for her, spewing it out the window the moment Bartta left her alone.

She thought she was being clever but, as it turned out, she wasn't so clever after all. One night, three days after her thrashing, she tried to sneak out of the house. She waited until the reading lamp went out in Bartta's bedroom, until the entire cottage was dark. She rose from her bed and stood at the open windows, staring out at the night. Low clouds scudded across the sky, obscuring the mountaintops and the minarets of the abbey, and the air felt dank and chill. Pulling on a cloak, she climbed through the window and came face-to-face with Bartta.

Bartta hit her, sending her to her knees. Then Bartta gripped the hair at the back of her head so hard it made her eyes water, but she was determined not to cry out. Her teeth ground together in fury. Bartta opened her palm, a ball of light in a miniature lantern hovered there, illuminating their surroundings.

"Look!" Bartta commanded, jerking hard on Riane's hair.

Riane had no choice but to look at the flower bed just outside her bedroom where, for the last three nights, she had been spitting out the sleeping draught. The flowers were wilted, the petals shriveled.

Bartta bent down. "Stupid, stupid Annon," she hissed. "Did you think I wouldn't be able to fathom your tricks?" She took her fist from Riane's hair, pulled her up. Her voice changed, softening. "Riane would never think about leaving, why should she? Somewhere in these mountains is her home, she is among her own kind, she is about to be inducted into the elite society of her people, to learn all the secrets Miina has to offer."

She stood her up, brushed her down, caressed her cheek. She took Riane to another part of the garden, and said kindly, "Here, see this plant with the trumpet-shaped flowers and the teardrop-shaped nuts?" She knelt, and Riane knelt beside her. "This is Brugmansia sanguinea, the blood brush." She plucked off a nut, peeled back the green skin to reveal a reddish nut, which she placed in Riane's palm. "I will teach you how to make a paste with this that, when ingested in just the right amount, will keep you warm even in subfreezing weather." She looked at Riane. "This is a secret no acolyte knows, Riane. It is not widely known even among the novices." She put a hand gently against the nape of Riane's neck. "But I will teach it to you. Would you like that?"

Riane, bewildered by this abrupt change in attitude, nodded, though she could not see how she could make use of the knowledge.

Two days later, Riane was awakened by the vibration of the power bourns. Bartta had told her that they crisscrossed all of Kundala. It happened that this cottage was built upon a bournline, but then so was the Abbey of Floating White—in fact, according to Bartta, all the Ramahan abbeys were sited on major bournlines. This otherworldly power grid was of no little interest to Bartta; she asked Riane all the time if she felt them. Riane always said no, but she also said that she would try because she wanted to keep Bartta talking about them. Riane gathered that among many other things lost to the Ramahan over time was a detailed map of the bourngrid. Without it, it was impossible to make sense of the lines; without knowing where they linked up, it was impossible to understand the nature of the grid and what it had once been used for. Apparently, nowadays very few Ramahan could even feel the bourns, let alone attempt remapping them.

Riane arose, feeling the humming in her bones, as if her body had been turned into an instrument whose strings were being plucked by an unseen virtuoso. The sensation was not unpleasant, but it was certainly eerie.

It was just past daybreak, but with the low sky full of black-and-blue clouds, the morning promised to be only slightly less dark than the night. She stood in the center of her bedroom and closed her eyes. Silence enveloped her. Birds twittered fitfully outside; rain pattered gently against the windowsill, fell silkily onto the sorcerous garden. There was no wind at all.

The wretched primitiveness of the place had begun to prey on her. There were no fusion lamps, no ion accelerators, no tertium matrices, no equation-building fields, no neural-net generators. Heat from fires, light from oil lamps, and nothing to give you a sense of what was happening in the outside world. The village was, in effect, deaf, dumb, and blind. No wonder the Kundalan had been so easy to conquer.

A sudden creak, as of someone moving across the floorboards, caused her to freeze. Now she could hear Bartta moving about, and then she heard Riane's name being called. She drew on the Kundalan robes Bartta had given her and went into the great room.

Bartta was sitting at the wooden table. There were two bowls filled with vile Kundalan grain. Riane had no taste for it. She wondered if Bartta would mention the singing of the bourns, and was somewhat surprised when Bartta said instead, "Come and eat your breakfast. There is much work to do today."

Riane sat without a word, but she did not pick up her wooden spoon. What she wouldn't have given for some roast corribs right now. She tried to concentrate on the eerie singing.

"The salve I made for you is working. Your face is looking much better," Bartta said, just as if the swelling had come from an accident. "Very soon now I will be able to take you to the abbey to live."

Riane stared sullenly at her unappetizing breakfast. Her stomach rumbled emptily. She had not had much dinner. The root stew Bartta had served her had smelled and tasted bitter as dirt. What little she had eaten had erupted back out of her mouth an hour or so after she had gone to bed.

"Eat," Bartta said, more sternly. "As a Kundalan—"

"Giyan wouldn't eat this."

Bartta paused with her spoon halfway to her mouth. "Giyan was taken by the V'ornn, made to live with V'ornn, forced into a V'ornn bed. She was required to adapt in order to survive, just as you must adapt."

Riane thought about this for a moment. Bartta knew how to get to Annon; she simply used Giyan as a goad. Riane grabbed the spoon. Pretending it was roasted cor meat, she shoveled the cooked grain into her mouth, swallowing as fast as she could.

In the blink of an eye, Bartta was up. She swiped the spoon out of Riane's hand, took her by the shoulders, shook her madly. "You eat like an animal!" she screamed in Riane's face. "Is that what you are, an animal? Kundalan do not eat like animals! Kundalan are civilized!" With a shove that rocked the chair, she released Riane. "Go on, pick up your spoon. Now wash it off and come back here so I can teach you how to eat properly."

When Riane was again seated, Bartta standing right over her, Bartta said, "Now take a spoonful of the glennan and put it into your mouth. While you are chewing it put your spoon down so that you can savor the taste. Swallow. Now pick up the spoon again. . . ."

And so it went. Halfway through her breakfast, Riane realized with an unpleasant lurch that Bartta was right. It would be far better for her if she simply did as Bartta asked. If she was stuck in this accursed body, the least she would have to do was adapt to it. And learning Kundalan customs wasn't all bad. Take this breakfast, for instance. It might not taste great, but at least her stomach wasn't rebelling as it had last night from gobbling down her food.

No sooner had she thought this, however, than the V'ornn warrior rebelled again. *I am not Riane*, she shouted doggedly in her mind, her heart pounding. But she was. Looking into Bartta's face she knew what would happen to her every time Annon reasserted himself. N'Luuura, she wished Giyan was here. But she wasn't; she was with Pack-Commander Rekkk Hacilar. He—she—Annon—Riane—might very well never see her again. Something caught in her throat, and she almost choked. She swallowed the last of the glennan and took a deep breath. Rage and despair were vying for control inside her. Resignation had never been a dominant male V'ornn trait; it was difficult even to comprehend. She set her mind on a goal: survival. *To survive*, she told herself, *I have to adapt.*

Obediently, she ate every last spoonful of glennan, then took her bowl and spoon to the sink for washing. Beneath her, the bourns hummed a song only she could hear.

A week later, Bartta told her to pack her things. They were moving to the Abbey of Floating White.

On the way, Riane got her first comprehensive look at the village. Stone Border was built like a bowl scooped out of the mountainside just below the abbey. In all ways, it was reminiscent of an amphitheater, the steeply inclined streets leading dizzily downward toward the "stage," the central plaza.

As she walked beside Bartta, she observed the way in which the townsfolk bowed to her, murmuring prayers to Miina for her blessing and her continued good health. They cut through a lovely park, ringed with tall pines, meticulously groomed, but they were alone in it. Young men, their faces grimy with sweat, clustered in taverns for the noonday meal, eating standing up, while they drank out of tankards and talked softly among themselves. She could feel their haunted eyes following her down the near-deserted street like a hand gripping the back of her neck. She heard no music, just the wail of an infant and the whisper of the wind through the pines in the park behind them. And, then, another sound arose. They were obliged to take a detour when the street Bartta wanted was clogged with mourners walking behind a white coffin. Riane caught a glimpse of tear-streaked faces, of veils and long cloaks. The sound of massed weeping was like rain in the gutters. Sadness dripped out of every doorway, lay along the shadowed streets like panting, half-dead animals. The power bourns were graveyard silent.

At last, they turned onto the narrow, cobbled path that wound steeply upward for some six hundred meters to the towering entrance to the Abbey of Floating White.

As was emblematic of Classic Kundalan architecture the interior of the abbey was a veritable labyrinth of rooms, shrines, corridors, gardens, loggias, balconies, sweeping stairways, courtyards, and atria. The young acolytes and many of the leyna, the novices, were forever getting lost, and even the shima, the full priestesses, occasionally found themselves in sections of the abbey unknown to them. Only the konara, the senior priestesses of the ruling Dea Cretan, always seemed sure of their whereabouts.

Nine times during each lunar cycle—that is a day and a night—crystal chimes sounded a pentagon of tones that magically built one upon the other, creating the wholeness of the Great Chord—symbolic of Miina's love and presence. At those times, all activities in the abbey ceased and for as long as the Chord resounded, the daily devotions were chanted in lovely call and response. Because the gardens of the abbey were filled with orangesweet trees, the delicate scent was inextricably bound up with the Sacred Songs, giving them a dimension beyond mere words, a sign, as the Ramahan said, that the Holy Word of Miina was borne aloft to the four corners of the world.

That first morning at the abbey, Riane came up against another kind of trial. Bathrooms were communal affairs within the levels of Ramahan society. That is to say, the acolytes all shared facilities, as did the leyna and the shima. The konara all had their own private bathrooms.

As she entered the showers, Riane was paralyzed with panic, seeing all the naked Kundalan girls. She had to remind herself all over again that she herself was a Kundalan female. And where had she developed this sudden aversion to crowds? She heard the acolytes talking about their bodies—who was too fat, too thin, whose legs were too short, too thick, not shapely enough. He heard them gossiping about their faces—whose nose was too long, too pug, whose eyes were too close together, too small, were crossed, who had pimples, who was just plain ugly. He heard false laughter, brittle as silicon, saw groups of girls ganging up on others, cruel jests perpetrated on the weak, on the shy, on anyone who was "different," heard whispered conversations about who was the worst teacher, the nastiest teacher, the strictest teacher, the ugliest teacher, about lessons missed, tests copied, about touching oneself, about nighttime escapes, about assignations with boys waiting in the nighttime shadows just outside the abbey's walls, parties where drugs made in secret from the produce of the herb and mushroom gardens were ingested, where laaga, smuggled in from outside, was smoked. Annon knew something about laaga. It was made from the dried, ground leaf of a tropical plant which, when smoked or chewed, produced a pronounced narcotic effect that was highly addictive. It was a crude and dangerous drug, especially when compared to salamuuun, which, unlike laaga, was not addictive. The Ashera Consortium kept tight control on salamuuun, allowing it to be sold only in licensed kashiggen.

Riane continued to listen to the hushed, excited burble of conversations. There was no talk whatsoever of Miina, of sacred texts, of devotions, of the mission of the Ramahan that Giyan had spoken of so often, to return the Kundalan to the state of grace they had enjoyed centuries ago.

While Riane was trying to absorb all this, a couple of acolytes spotted her and, taunting her, dragged her into the shower while she was still in her robes. Her robes clung to her body, making them laugh all the harder. They stripped her, pushed her under the hot sprays in the long, soapstone shower chamber, made fun of her modesty, called her names. Meanwhile, Riane was, of course, having a decidedly odd reaction to being in such close proximity to naked females. Every time Annon felt the tidal pull of sexual arousal, a wave of revulsion would sweep over Riane, bringing up feelings of shame and confusion.

Confusion was not a safe emotion for Riane. It caused the Annon personality to emerge. Riane lost the fragile facade of femaleness, of where she was, of *who* she was. She reverted and, in reverting, lashed out at the girls. Not surprisingly, her sudden aggression stunned and frightened them. They began to scream, to run from the shower like so many raindrops flung this way and that by storm winds.

The screaming attracted the attention of the novice on duty, Leyna Astar. She was a handsome woman, not too old, not too young. Her hair was a lustrous chestnut color, save for a streak of silver that ran through it. She wore the pale yellow robes of raw silk and muslin of a novice.

"What is going on here?" she asked, in a melodious voice.

"There's something queer about the new girl," one acolyte said.

"Yes. She's weird," said another.

"She tried to hurt us," chimed in a third.

"We don't want her around *at all*," said a fourth.

"Now, now, girls." Leyna Astar was smiling a smile that somehow short-circuited the acolytes' fear and animosity. "Riane is new to our abbey—*and* she has lost her memory." Her smile deepened as she looked around at the acolytes, one by one enfolding them in her gaze. "You all remember how difficult it was in the beginning. Think how much harder it is for her. Riane has much to learn. We must help her adjust as we ourselves want to be helped—as we were helped. That is our way, isn't it?" As they nodded, she bade them run along and dress, as they were already late for morning devotions.

Alone with Riane in the shower chamber, Leyna Astar turned to her. "Are you all right?" she said softly.

For a long time Riane said nothing. "How do you know about me?" she said at last.

"I was briefed," Leyna Astar said simply. She held out a towel. "Would you like to come out now?"

Riane took the towel from her, wrapped it around and around the body she could not get used to. She peered into Leyna Astar's face, which was open, friendly, and blessedly without guile.

"Why did you hit them, Riane?" Leyna Astar asked this in a thoroughly nonthreatening way. She seemed genuinely curious.

"I feel things," Riane said hesitantly. "In my body, I mean. I don't know what they are." She could not tell Leyna Astar that what she felt was the rage of revenge against the murderers of Annon Ashera's family.

"You are a healthy teenage female," Leyna Astar was saying. "Those are hormones doing their work, building muscle and bone so you can grow. The feelings are nothing to worry about; they're perfectly normal."

"Not for me," Riane muttered.

Leyna Astar was still smiling at her, as if she had not heard.

"Why don't I escort you back to your quarters," she said.

"I don't think Konara Bartta would like that. I'd be missing devotions."

"There is always time for devotions." Leyna Astar said breezily. "At the moment, getting oriented to your new surroundings is far more important, don't you think?"

Riane was so grateful she merely nodded.

Riane's day ran like this: she rose before dawn for the first devotion, then ate a spare meal in the refectory with the other acolytes before heading for lessons with a series of Ramahan teachers, broken only by another devotion. The midday meal was the largest of the day, followed by another devotion, then work details most of the afternoon until the evening devotion, after which, she returned to her quarters to receive private tutoring from Bartta herself. She would have preferred to spend evenings with Leyna Astar, but that was out of the question. Bartta was jealous of her time alone with Riane, and made no bones about it.

In the showers, the acolytes no longer taunted her, they did something far worse: they ignored her. She listened to their conversations over the hissing of the water, feeling like the alien she was, still uncomfortable and awkward in her skin, the eternal outsider. There were times when it became too much, when she laid her head against the wall and cried bitterly for the life Annon had once had, the life of wealth and privilege, now swept away as if it had never existed. Annon never had to throw out garbage, scrub vegetables, dig tubers out of the ground with his bare hands. He had never had to work twenty sidereal hours a day, sleep four. He had been free to eat when he wanted, play when he wanted, hunt when he wanted, go where he wanted. None of those things was available to Riane. She was, in actuality if not in name, a prisoner.

You had better get used to your present life, Bartta never tired of telling her. *It is the only one you have.*

It was all so unfair!

The water sluicing down blessedly hid her tears, but what did it matter? The acolytes brushed rudely by her, or turned their backs to her as they clustered at their daily gossip, oblivious to her pain and suffering.

Every detail of her life was a struggle—from the conversion of the V'ornn measurement of time in sidereal hours to the Kundalan equivalent in lunar hours, from the food she was forced to eat to the cot she slept in. Each time she exercised, showered, dressed, or eliminated, she was overwhelmed by the alienness of her new body. What could she make of her breasts or the place where once Annon's tender parts had dangled? And as for what she did have between her legs, it was completely devoid of spots, making her feel as if she had regressed back to childhood. She tried to avoid mirrors, for the face she saw reflected back at her so unnerved her that she would begin to shake uncontrollably. There was an essential disconnect between the person she saw in the mirror and who she was inside. She could not seem to bridge the gap, and it was impossible to say whether she even tried because she could not bear to lose who she had been. She was terrorized by the thought that if she accepted who she had become, all that was left of Annon would, in fact, die.

She had good reason to fear this. Every quotidian aspect of life as Annon had known it was being systematically obliterated. There were times when this knowledge was almost too monumental to bear. It was like watching yourself die, slowly, inexorably, precious pieces torn from you like pages from a book. There were times when she was certain that she would lose her mind, because what is sanity but a rational sense of self? If there is no self—or if that self is rapidly deliquescing—how can sanity exist? In what can it make a home—to use a psychological metaphor—if there is no home?

Terrified, she would pry up the tile beneath her cot that she had painstakingly loosened, and extract the two worldly possessions she had smuggled into the abbey: the knife Eleana had given her and the ancient Kundalan book she had found in the caverns beneath the palace in Axis Tyr.

Riane could not help but weep each time she ran her hands over the knife. It brought up so many emotions inside her that she did not know how to handle. When she thought of Eleana, an ache filled her breast to bursting. In retrospect, she could see that she had begun to fall in love with Eleana, although the V'ornn she once had been never would have admitted such a thing. But what to do with that love now, that beat in her breast as firmly as the spotted sun beat in the cloudless Kundala sky? She was female. The reality was so strange she could not get her mind around it. Perhaps it was within Annon to accept being in a Kundalan body—but a *female* Kundalan, that was simply too much.

If only I had not fled the palace, she thought. *If only I had followed my first instinct to return upstairs and slit Wennn*

Stogggul's throat. If only I had not come here with Giyan. If only I had stayed with Eleana. But who was this "I," anyway? *You had better get used to your present life. It is the only one you have.*

Occasionally, despite the harsh punishments that ensued, her black despair made her lash out—as Annon the V'ornn would have—bloodying the nose of a bully here, blackening the eye of a tormentor there. She found that this body, despite its relative weakness, was possessed of extraordinary reflexes, great stamina, and a dogged heart. Oddly, these heroics did nothing to endear her to the bullies' other victims, who perversely cleaved closer to the cliques they longed to be a part of. And so, she remained friendless, an outcast even among those whose cause she tried to champion.

And there were other times, more frightening and bewildering by far, when, in her anguished longing for her old life, she remembered frozen steppes, ice-encrusted scarps, snow-bejeweled cliffs with such vivid detail she knew she must have lived there. And yet Annon had never seen holos of these places, let alone been to them. She moaned softly, holding her head as if otherwise her brain would fly apart, great drifts of snow obscuring the corridors of power within the regent's palace in Axis Tyr, all of Annon's life which, in those moments, she struggled desperately to bring into focus.

Without question, these bouts were the worst. They invariably left her sweating and shaken. But she told no one of them, not even Bartta, who had known Annon, if ever so briefly. And that was another thing. Annon had always had Kurgan to confide in; Riane had no one. She dared trust no one—not even Leyna Astar—with the truth. Even so, Leyna Astar managed to bring a measure of solace to Riane. Astar regularly sent her to the Library, the vast two-story repository of all Ramahan knowledge, where for hours on end she read swiftly, almost needfully, losing herself in volume after volume of reading that she absorbed wholesale. Often, Leyna Astar met her in the Library, and they read side by side in a kind of silent companionship.

She did not tell Bartta about her new friend, even though Leyna Astar began to tutor her in how to act, what to say and, perhaps most importantly, what not to say. Even Bartta began to notice the change. Astar made of her lessons a clever and increasingly challenging game, piquing Riane's innate desire to win, while at the same time channeling the aggression raging inside her. In this way, Riane came to think of Leyna Astar as a kind of guardian angel, a shining oasis in the hideous place into which she had been thrust. And yet, even though she was slowly and painfully learning what it meant to be Kundalan, to be female, to be Ramahan, she remained isolated even from Astar by the terrible secret she carried inside her.

Riane gradually learned to do what Bartta told her to do, no matter how menial or unpleasant the task—or how many of those tasks were loaded onto her shoulders each day, more by far than any other acolyte was given, more by far than she could ever accomplish. Thus, no matter how hard she toiled she was doomed to failure, to displease the very person whom she needed to please.

One day, six weeks after she had been installed at the abbey, Bartta came to her during Third Chime and bade her follow. Silently, they wended their way through the labyrinthine corridors, atria, and gardens until they came to a square chamber filled with three acolytes kneeling in a precise row. Garbed in the same blue raw muslin robes she wore, they all faced one way, watching expectantly as a konara in persimmon-colored robes of raw silk stood with her hands clasped in front of her. Riane recognized two of them as girls who were regularly tormented in the shower.

Sunlight streamed in through the intricate patterns of incised wooden shutters, throwing arabesques of brilliant light and deep shadow across the tiled floor. Upon the whitewashed walls were hung rectangles of cor parchment covered with the same strange form of Kundalan writing she had seen in her leather-bound book.

"Konara Laudenum, this is Riane," Bartta said in her clear,

strong voice. "She is an acolyte of only six weeks in need of your . . . special instruction."

The priestess smiled and spread her hands, but Riane did not like her face. It was shut tight as a prison door. "It will be my pleasure to instruct her, Konara Bartta."

Doubtless sensing the girl's reluctance, Bartta put her hands on Riane's shoulders. In response, Riane dug in her heels.

Bartta bent down. "Do what you are told," she hissed in Riane ear. "If you embarrass me, it will go ill with you this evening."

Riane balled her hands into fists, the rage burning in her. She tried to think of what Leyna Astar would counsel in this situation. She tried to think like a Kundalan, like a female, like a Ramahan. Instantly, she knew she could; the trouble was, she did not want to.

"I do not care," she said loudly enough for everyone to hear. "There is something evil here."

"Evil?" Konara Laudenum laughed. "Nothing evil can enter the abbey. Miina would not allow it."

"There, you see," Bartta said. "Nothing to worry about." She whispered again so only Riane could hear. "All part of the training I promised Giyan you would have."

Riane noticed that the other three acolytes stared straight ahead as if they had not heard a thing. In fact, they seemed to be in some kind of trance. She could feel the power bourns; they had been distorted somehow, interrupted. The intermittent pulse gave her the willies.

"Riane, I know how intimidating new situations can seem at first. But I assure you that feeling will pass." Shima Laudenum was smiling. "Why don't you come and sit beside me?"

And then Riane felt Bartta's powerful fingers digging painfully into the muscles of her shoulders.

"Do as she says, Riane." With a vigorous shove, Bartta propelled her forward.

Riane walked on stiff legs to the spot the priestess indicated, and sat cross-legged on the floor rather than kneel as the other acolytes were doing. When she looked back, Bartta had vanished.

"Now, then," Konara Laudenum said with that awful fake smile plastered on her face, "we can get right down to business." She spoke directly to Riane, as if the other students did not exist. Riane felt an eerie shiver run through her.

The chamber fell into darkness, and Riane looked around to see who had pulled the shutters. She discovered that she was alone in the darkened chamber with Konara Laudenum.

"Where are the others?" she asked.

"What others, Riane?" Konara Laudenum's hands wove a complex pattern in front of her. There appeared between them a translucent cube. As the priestess set it down on the floor, black flames flickered up from inside it. Riane held her hand out, but felt no heat emanating from the fire.

"That's right, Riane." Konara Laudenum's eyes were gleaming oddly as she observed with an avid gaze. "Put your hand into the fire."

Because she could feel no heat, Riane moved her hand forward. The moment her fingers touched the flames, their blackness disappeared. A fire like any other she had seen flickered and sparked. She snatched her hand away from the sudden, blistering heat.

"How did you do that, Riane?" Konara Laudenum asked.

"I. . . . I don't know."

The priestess pointed. "This is the Cube of Tutelage. It exists, but only in a way."

"The way the other acolytes existed?"

Konara Laudenum's smile was back in place, impregnable as the abbey's walls. "Yes, Riane. Just that way." She lifted her left hand, and the fire disappeared from the cube.

"This is sorcery," Riane said. "Bartta says that Osoru has been banned from the abbey."

"It has, and quite rightly so." Konara Laudenum did something to make the Cube of Tutelage spin. "But this is sorcery of another kind altogether."

As Riane watched, the cube, which had been spinning slowly in a counterclockwise direction, began to pick up speed. As it did, it grew in size. From something that was no more than two handspans in each direction, it blossomed out so rapidly that Riane had to scramble back. When it had reached three meters on a side it slowed, and came to a stop.

"Get in," Konara Laudenum commanded.

"What?" Riane jumped up. "You can't be serious."

"Get in," the priestess repeated. Her smile had become a rictus. "Do it now."

"And if I refuse?"

Konara Laudenum raised her arm, her forefinger beckoning, and Riane felt all the warmth drain out of her. A dread chill flooded her, making her shiver, her teeth chatter uncontrollably. She wrapped her arms around herself without effect.

"Stop it," she whispered hoarsely.

"Only you can stop it, Riane."

Throwing Konara Laudenum a murderous look, Riane stepped into the cube.

"You see, Riane," Konara Laudenum said from just outside the cube, "the Ramahan cannot exist without sorcery. But with Osoru only those with the Gift were able to practice. This created an artificial caste system that we discovered was intolerable. It led to the most flagrant misuse of power; it led to the loss of The Pearl, to Mother's death. Nowadays, Kyofu has replaced Osoru. Everyone can learn Kyofu, given the right frame of mind." She raised a finger. "But the right frame of mind is *essential*." That repugnant smile was back. "The Cube of Tutelage is conjured for just this purpose."

Riane put her palms against the slick sorcerous surface. "Can't you just teach me Kyofu?"

"I'm afraid not." Konara Laudenum did not look the least bit apologetic. She watched with a kind of maddeningly detached interest as Riane tried to find a way out of the cube. "I could tell you that resistance is quite useless, I suppose," she said. "But from what I have been told, you need to find this out for yourself."

The harder Riane beat against the translucent walls of the cube, the weaker she became. She broke off suddenly, stood panting, staring at Konara Laudenum's malevolent smile. *What am I to do?* she thought.

"By the look of things," Konara Laudenum said, "I do believe we are ready to begin."

The atmosphere inside the cube began to grow thin. Blood pounded in Riane's temples, a headache commenced behind her eyes, and she stumbled, growing dizzy.

"Excellent." Konara Laudenum had taken a step closer to the cube. "Now we are getting somewhere."

A curious image popped into Riane's whirling mind. She saw herself hiking along an icy ridge. Plumes of permafrost whirled up into the deep blue bowl of the sky. She reached the base of an enormous icefall, and began to climb. The thin air tumbled out of her nose and mouth and, instinctively, it seemed, she breathed in, all the way to the bottom of her lungs, and held the air there. She continued upward, breathing in this odd fashion, and, even as the air grew thinner, she was never out of breath.

Without even thinking about it, Riane inhaled to the bottom of her lungs. She did not exhale. Watching Konara Laudenum, she made herself stumble again, this time falling onto her backside. She lolled her head, she closed her eyes to slits as if she were on the verge of unconsciousness.

She saw Konara Laudenum extend her hand through the barrier of the cube, pull it apart. The cube disappeared, and Riane made herself flop over on her side. Her heart beat fast as she saw the priestess draw three concentric black circles in the air. The circles moved until they were stacked directly above her head. Then they began to descend.

Riane exhaled slowly and, with great care, inhaled again, and held the air in her lungs. She felt the dread cold of the black circles as they approached her, then settled around her like a web. Her last thought was of Giyan before she was hurled into unconsciousness.

W hat had been done to her? Riane had no way of knowing. She sat on her narrow bed in her cell, her knees drawn up to her chest. She knew that Bartta was a sorceress just like Konara Laudenum, and she was terrified that Bartta would conjure up some way to crawl inside her head. Her stomach threatened to regurgitate its contents at the thought of Bartta being privy to all her most intimate thoughts, that she might find out about the knife and the book and take away her last physical links to Annon's life.

She felt a sudden compulsion, running through her like wildfire, to open the book. It was crazy, she couldn't read a word of it. She shivered, drew her legs up, jammed her back against the whitewashed wall, unadorned save for the image of Miina's sacred butterfly. "It's finally happened," she whispered to herself. "I've gone mad."

Silence. The beating of her heart, the rush of blood through her veins. But the quietude of the abbey failed to alleviate her terror. On the contrary, it multiplied her isolation, the panicky feeling that madness had at last claimed her.

Something was crawling around in her skull, she could feel it, like blood slowly seeping between her fingers. Again, alien thoughts rose, unbidden—images of mountain peaks, ice storms, cold clear nights bundled against the bitter wind, memories of running through thigh-deep snow, dropping by rope down sheer cliff faces, of burying two adults—Mother? Father?—while tears froze in her lashes, on her cheeks. In her mind, she screamed, searching for one—just one—memory from Axis Tyr, but they seemed remote, alien, as if she had read about them in a book, as if they had been lived by someone else.

This must somehow be part of the Kyofu conditioning, part of what the three black circles had done to her. She would not allow it.

She gasped and slammed her head against the wall until blood was seeping from it, matting down her hair, dripping into her eyes, pooling in her ear. Still she kept banging herself against the wall until Bartta, made suspicious by the noise, ran in and stopped her. She cried out, not really knowing who was restraining her or why. With a frantic twist, she broke free, flinging herself across the tiny cell, stumbling over a three-legged stool, passing out as she hit the blood-spattered stone-tile floor.

"That's all right, Shima Argolas, I will take over now."

The tall, thin Ramahan priestess clasped her hands in front of her and bowed deeply to Bartta. "Yes, Konara. Please do not tire her; she has been through a difficult time."

"How are you feeling, dear? Better, I trust," Bartta said, smiling benignly down at Riane. But as soon as Shima Argolas left the infirmary, she sat down at Riane's bedside. Her smile died. Her cold eyes stared hard at Riane. "What on Kundala do you think you are doing, damaging yourself like that?" she said, crossly. "Do you want to be put in restraints at night, because I can accomplish that with a snap of my fingers."

Riane said nothing. She was wondering if the violence she had done to herself had managed to get those three black rings out of her head.

Bartta sighed. "And how are we getting on with Konara Laudenum? She is a bit much, don't you think? She has the most unpleasant socialistic air about her, longs for all konara to be created equal, don't you know. Well, that is only because she hasn't been elected to the Dea Cretan. Doubtless this eats at her, just as it eats at her that I have gained control of the Dea Cretan. 'Why does Konara Bartta have all the power?' " she whined in a passable imitation of Konara Laudenum's voice. "Foolish Ramahan!" She snickered behind her hand. "Knowledge is Power and Power is All!" she sang softly to herself. It was a melody that had become familiar to Riane in the last several days as she had drifted in and out of consciousness. But, until that moment, she had never heard the words.

Bartta leaned over her, sucked in her lower lip, her teeth shining yellowly. "What am I to do with you?" she whispered. "How am I to train you properly when you continue to act so rebelliously?"

She gently stroked the girl's bruised forehead. "Any more of this violence, and you will disfigure yourself permanently.

We can't have that." She smiled that same benign smile she had offered up to Shima Argolas. "A modicum of trust, Riane. That's what I thought we had. Well, you surely made a muodd out of me." She rearranged the girl's hair. "You won't get a second chance, this certainly is true."

Bartta dug in a cor-hide bag which hung at her waist and withdrew a tiny copper sphere. This she placed in the center of Riane's forehead. "The Third Eye sees, and with that, Sight comes Knowledge." Her forefinger circled the sphere seven times, touched it once, and it sprang open, making a star-shaped indentation in Riane's forehead. "But if your Third Eye is blinded." With the pad of her forefinger, she pressed down until Riane's eyes crossed, and she groaned in pain.

"The Sphere of Binding."

The infirmary seemed to have lost the sharpness of its dimensions. The walls began to bleed, the ceiling melting away, until the square space had become a sphere that pulsed and glimmered with a dark energy. It held them in its slowly beating heart. A murmuring arose, no more than the rustle of a breeze through tall grass. Nevertheless, it caused the hair at the nape of Riane's neck to stir. If only she had Annon's bow and arrow—or a Khagggun's shock-sword. But she was weaponless. Worse, she was gripped by an odd and disquieting lassitude. The sphere around them flashed colors and patterns that were making her dizzy. She tried to look away but they were everywhere. The lassitude stole through her, robbing her of energy, mental stamina, determination.

"The Sphere of Binding, yes," Bartta said. "A most potent spell, one not often used. That idiot Konara Laudenum tells me your mind has shown remarkable resistance to the Rings of Concordance, so now I am forced to take drastic safety measures." Humming happily to herself, Bartta took up the open sphere. Touching it again caused it to retract, and she put it away. In the center of Riane's forehead, a red star-shaped mark was slowly fading, but the spell had reopened Riane's wound. "The Sphere binds you to another until the death of one. And death *will* come, make no mistake. It always does with this particular spell. As the mark fades, so will your memory of this," she said to Riane. "I was never here. You never woke up." She recited a short incantation in the Old Tongue. "The spell I used cannot be seen, smelled, heard, tasted, or felt, even by another sorceress." She was busy wiping off the fresh blood when Shima Argolas reappeared.

"Dear Miina, what happened?" she cried as she ran to Riane's side.

"Alas, she became violent again." Bartta shook her head as if she were pained to her very soul. "I could do nothing to calm her save give her a sleeping draught." She sighed. "Whatever shall I do with her?"

"Miina knows." Shima Argolas nodded in sympathy.

Bartta rose. "My time is not my own, unfortunately. I must attend to the sacred affairs of the Great Goddess. I will leave the girl in your capable hands for the time being."

Sometime later, when Shima Argolas sat dozing on cushions she had set up beside Riane's bed, Leyna Astar entered. She stood in the doorway some time, listening for something only she could hear. Perhaps she was making certain that Shima Argolas was indeed asleep before venturing inside. She made not a sound as she glided across the cool stone floor. She knelt on the other side of Riane. Her slightly cupped palm moved in the air just above Riane's form. Wherever the hand went a kind of glow appeared for just an instant. Depending on where the hand was over Riane's head or body the color of the glow changed, now blue, now green, now purple, now orange or red. Leyna Astar's hand paused over several places, most notably the spots where Riane had been injured. When she removed her hand, all traces of blood had vanished; only a few small and insignificant scars remained. She spent a moment, head bowed as if in prayer, her body so still that had an observer been present she would not have seen Leyna Astar breathe. Then she rose and quickly retraced her steps, vanishing into the labyrinth of the abbey.

10

Rings

D alma, look what I bought you."

The Tuskuggggun in the gimnopede's-blood robes and woven-gold sifeyn smiled. "A ring."

"Not just a ring," Wennn Stogggul said, grinning. "It is the Ring you have coveted for—"

"It is the Ring!" Dalma cried. "The one I have wanted for months!" She plucked the ring from his fingers, and he swung her around. "But how did you get it, Wennn? It was already sold—to a very wealthy Bashkir. The maker told me herself that she would not make another, and that even if she did, I could not afford it. But now it's mine!" She was laughing. "How, how, how?"

"I am that I am!" Stogggul's voice roared through the regent's palace, making guards come to attention, assistants cock their ears, attendants cringe. He ran his hands down to her wasp waist, over the flare of her hips. His tender parts began to swell at the look in her eyes. "Power breeds more power. I am regent now; I get what I want, when I want it. I can do anything. I have rewarded Kinnnus Morcha by promoting him to Star-Admiral. I have brought what they wanted most, the Ring of Five Dragons, to the Gyrgon. I have given them the head of Annon Ashera. What more do they want of me?"

Dalma licked the back of his neck, in just the spot he loved. "Patience, my love. The Gyrgon are tricksters. They will not be prone to give you what you want when you want it."

"This alliance between Bashkir and Khagggun is a new paradigm for our people. It will bring renewed stability.

Surely the Gyrgon see this. Surely they will take the sala-muuun trade away from the Ashera Consortium and give it to me. I asked them, but they have not answered."

"Give them time to appreciate your gifts, darling. In the meantime, I advise you to turn your attention elsewhere. I have heard that the new Star-Admiral has petitioned you to make your firstborn his new adjutant. You must be very proud."

"Proud." Wennn Stogggul shook his head. "That weasel should be applying himself at the bottom rung of my Consortium, preparing himself to one day take over from me. I will turn down the petition."

Dalma, who knew more than a thing or two about V'ornn males, continued with her ministrations. "Of course you're right, Wennn. It is what everyone would expect you to do since the Star-Admiral seeks to pluck a stone from the ranks of another caste."

Stogggul frowned. "But I mean to move the Khagggun up to Great Caste status."

"But how?" Dalma asked. "By turning down the Star-Admiral's petition you are setting precedent for the status quo."

"Yes, of course. It will be most difficult to change course later on," Stogggul mused.

"Kurgan is young yet. This detour could work out for the best."

"Really?" Stogggul said skeptically. "Pray enlighten me."

"Kurgan is not born Khagggun, but now he must serve within their ranks. It is a hard life, from what I have gleaned. You have called him irresponsible and wild. Serving under the Star-Admiral, he will learn the meaning of discipline, his wildness will be tamed."

Stogggul considered her words, as he always did. There was something different about her, something he had marked the moment he had first seen her at a party given by Bach Ourrros, one of his Bashkir rivals. It had pleased him, of course, to appropriate his rival's possession, especially since Ourrros was one of those revisionist Bashkir living in Za

Hara-at and one of the city's chief proponents. Astute V'ornn that Stogggul was, however, he had quite quickly come to appreciate her for all her many assets, and he congratulated himself all the more that he had stolen her away from Bach Ourrros.

Dalma slipped the ring over her finger. "A perfect fit!" She kissed him. "Now all that remains is for me to move in." She picked up on Stogggul's hesitation and gave him a smile. "I will show you a secret if you say yes."

He made a show of deliberating, but in truth he had already made up his mind. Eleusis had had a Mistress here—a Kundalan female, at that. Why should he not have his Looorm with him now that he was regent? Jeufffry would be angry, to be sure. But who was she save the mother of his children? Kurgan had grown beyond her control, but there were three others: the boy Terrettt, the females Oratttony and Marethyn. All required Jeufffry's guidance. Besides, she had her own artistic life in hingatta liiina do mori. She made hideous pottery that she nevertheless managed to sell.

"What kind of secret?" Stogggul betrayed none of his curiosity. It was a game between them, one they both savored.

Dalma stroked the back of his skull. "The kind you like best."

"Done!" he cried. "But only if I deem the secret fit!"

"Come, then." She took his hand, led him down shadowed corridors, through sun-strewn atria, past the torn-apart regent's garden, along loggias striped in sunlight and shadow. Once, he caught a whiff of a peculiar smell.

"What is that?" he asked.

Dalma tossed her head. "Bitterroot, perhaps?"

"Smells like decay," Stogggul rumbled. "I shall have it eradicated."

At last, they came to a set of private rooms Stogggul had not been in before. Dalma touched a spot on a plaster panel, and it swiveled inward. She took them through a short, musty passageway.

"Where are we?" he asked.

Dalma giggled. "Don't be so impatient. You'll see."

He took her wrist in the darkness, swung her around, pressed himself against her. She went slack in his arms and uttered the delicious sigh that caused his tender parts to swell.

"Would you take me here," she breathed, "against the wall?"

He could hear a rustling, knew that she was parting her robes. He could feel her heat and her dampness, and he could no longer control himself. Her slender fingers expertly unfastened his clothes, and with a grunt he slammed into her.

When he was finished she clung to him, climbing upon his sweaty body. "You have a plan, Wennn. I know it."

"What do you mean?"

"You gave the Gyrgon the Ring of Five Dragons. Is it not the key to finding The Pearl?"

"The Pearl!" he scoffed. "What need of I for an object revered by animals? And yet, unless I miss my guess, the Gyrgon have a keen interest in it." His tender parts swelled again. "*My* interest is in how to gain control of the flow of salamuuun. If I can help them find The Pearl—and it seems that the Ring of Five Dragons is the first step—they must give me what I desire most, what justice demands." His hand closed into a fist. "I will accomplish what my father could not. The Ashera killed him to keep the secret of salamuuun. It is not enough that I have killed them in kind. I mean to take more than half my revenge. I swear before long I will have every Ashera secret for my own!"

"Oh, yes! I was right about you . . ." Her words trailed off into a groan as he pierced her to her core.

Sometime later, they emerged into a tiny atrium, in the center of which was a garden planted with flora unfamiliar to him. Blank walls rose on all sides. This was a blind spot in the palace.

"What is this place?" he asked.

"It is Giyan's garden," she said. "Doubtless the source of the Kundalan sorceress's potions."

He began trampling the plants underfoot. Pungent smells

arose, tickling his nostrils. He sneezed mightily. Dalma took the opportunity to gently draw him out of the damp earth. "Why destroy this?" she asked.

"Because it belonged to the Kundalan skcettta and, by extension, to Eleusis."

"But these plants can be of use to us."

"How? They are Kundalan." He wrinkled his nose and sneezed again. "They smell like death."

She took his arm and led him to the secret doorway through which they had come. "I have a friend—a Kundalan female I have spent considerable time and effort cultivating. It was she who told me about this garden. With her help I believe I can unlock the secrets buried here."

Stogggul waved a hand dismissively. "I despise all things Kundalan. They are abominations."

She squeezed him tighter, licked his ear with the very tip of her tongue. "You are always saying that power begets more power, Wennn. Imagine the power you would have if in addition to the enormous authority you now wield you could command Kundalan sorcery."

T he Ring of Five Dragons represents the heart of Kundalan lore," the first Gyrgon said.

"It holds a secret we have been unable to obtain on our own," the second Gyrgon said.

"At last we will discover the truth," the third Gyrgon said.

The Gyrgon, in their insectoid alloy suits, stood in a precisely aligned semicircle facing the huge round Kundalan-made Door in the subterranean caverns below the regent's palace. Fusion lamps brought pools of shimmering light into a sea of twilit shadows. Echoes rose and fell on the tide of this sea.

Three Gyrgon, the one in the center holding the red-jade Ring. This Gyrgon turned suddenly and addressed a fourth, who stood, hooded by shadows, apart from them, observing.

"Perhaps, because this is a Kundalan artifact, and because of the months of arduous testing and authentication, our resident expert on all things Kundalan should have the honor of using it to open the Door to the Storehouse."

"I think not," Nith Sahor said. "This Door has resisted all our efforts. Science—not even our magelike version—can affect it. Therefore, I have concluded that it is not Kundalan in origin. Rather, it was created by their Goddess, Miina."

"What nonsense is this?" the second Gyrgon said.

"Miina does not exist," the third Gyrgon snapped.

"Hold," the first Gyrgon said. "Perhaps our comrade is correct. That would explain our one hundred and one years of frustration." He held up the Ring of Five Dragons. "If so, then here we have the answer. According to legend, this Ring was also created by Miina." He cocked his head so that his helm flashed in the cold, fractured light of the fusion lamps. "Is this not so?"

Nith Sahor inclined his head. "It is."

"Then whether the Storehouse Door was made by Kundalan or their Goddess is immaterial. We are now in possession of the key to open it."

Silence thundered in the wake of the first Gyrgon's echoing voice. The first Gyrgon moved to within a handwidth of the circular Door before turning back to Nith Sahor. "Of all of us, you alone, comrade, did not partake in the cranium of Ashera Annon. Have you qualms?"

"Qualms, misgivings, forebodings," Nith Sahor said.

Almost before he was finished, the first Gyrgon had turned away. He laughed, seeming to give a silent message to the two Gyrgon who flanked him. Facing the Door, he pushed the Ring of Five Dragons onto his gloved forefinger.

"This is a great moment in the history of the V'ornn," the first Gyrgon intoned. His finger curled, he presented the Ring to the circular medallion in the center. As he hesitated, Nith Sahor said, "Legend has it that the Ring fits into the Sacred Dragon's mouth."

"Legends!" the first Gyrgon snorted. "Are we scientists or dirt-eating savages?"

"That has yet to be determined," Nith Sahor said so softly no one heard him. But even if they had, they would not have understood, since he had spoken in the Old Tongue of the Ramahan.

The first Gyrgon placed the head of the Ring against the strange sculpted creature. Like the last piece of a puzzle sliding home, it fitted perfectly into the open mouth. For a moment, nothing happened. A click sounded and the medallion began to turn clockwise.

"Ah, yes," the first Gyrgon said.

"It is opening," the second Gyrgon said.

"At long last we will have what we want," the third Gyrgon said.

The medallion continued to turn clockwise, and the first Gyrgon moved to disengage the Ring from the carved Dragon's mouth. As this proved impossible, the first Gyrgon tried to remove the Ring from his finger. He failed. His hand twisted in concert with the medallion's turning. He attempted to compensate, but he had reached his limit of flexibility. Had he more time, he might have conjured a flow of ions of sufficient force to counteract the trap he was in. Then again, perhaps not. In any event, he had no time. His finger cracked, then his wrist fractured, his elbow joint broke, his shoulder tried to dislocate, shattered instead. The first Gyrgon collapsed to his knees, his good hand clutching his ruined one.

The second Gyrgon hurried toward him, stopped a pace away as the first Gyrgon threw his head back. Something was happening, a soft humming filled the cavern, echoing off the stone walls.

"This unacceptable attack on the V'ornn Modality must cease," the third Gyrgon said, raising his arm. Green fire rippled from his fingertips, interlacing with the alloy mesh of his glove. Gaining strength, it spat a tongue of cold flame on a direct line to the center of the medallion. It reached its target with the sound of thunder booming, but it was all echo. The third Gyrgon went rigid, a gurgling cry caught in his throat as he was impaled upon the recoil of his own ion spike.

The first Gyrgon was shaking now, as if in the grip of an enormous invisible beast.

"Come, comrade," the second Gyrgon said, "we must help Nith Kijllln."

Nith Sahor did not move. He watched as the second Gyrgon was caught full blast when Nith Kijllln's helm exploded. He did not flinch when fiery shards of alloy and bone clattered against his finely tooled exoskeleton or the fusion lamps nearest him blew out.

Three of his comrades were dead, but he did nothing. Nothing but wait.

In time, the great circular basalt Door rolled open halfway. Inside, was, he knew, everything he had ever dreamed of— his heart's desire and his mind's desire all wrapped in one. And yet, an instinct more ancient even than he made him hold his ground. In fact, he barely breathed, for soon enough he sensed the presence that stood just inside the shadowed doorway. He could feel its power in ways his comrade Gyrgon could not. That was to be expected, considering the nature of his studies. Still, he found himself unprepared. He thought he saw eyes staring balefully at him, dissecting him, feeding greedily on his thoughts, laughing at his impotency. Eyes in the dark, jade-green slitted pupils, preternaturally intelligent. Sensory organs that could be called eyes only because Nith Sahor lacked the experiential vocabulary to name them properly.

Nith Sahor felt a peculiar and thoroughly unpleasant tingling up and down his spine. The tingling made him jumpy, interfered with his thought processes. Nith Sahor had never before felt fear, but he had heard it described in a hundred languages, seen it defined in a thousand texts. Intellectually if not instinctually he knew that this was what he was now experiencing.

As he watched, something whipped out from behind the Door. In the eerie twilight, he could not tell what it was but he could see it making its way to the central medallion and thence to the carved mouth of the Hagoshrin. The end of it curled around the base of Nith Kijllin's broken forefinger. With a hollow snap, the finger was detached from the hand, then extracted from the Ring of Five Dragons. It landed on the stone floor beside Nith Kijllin's smoking corpse. Then the thing—whatever it was—whipped back into the shadows of the Storehouse, the Door rolled shut, slamming to with a bone-jarring sound. Deep in the bowels of the bedrock below the palace an ominous rumbling could be heard.

At long last, Nith Sahor stepped out of the shadows. He stared intently at—but did not approach—the medallion. There was the curled Dragon—Seelin, the Sacred Dragon of Transformation—its mouth now filled with the Sacred red-jade Ring of the Kundalan Goddess Miina.

So the legends are true, Nith Sahor thought. *The Hagoshrin guard the Storehouse of The Pearl. The Ring of Five Dragons opens the Door, but only if it is worn by the Dar Sala-at, the anointed of Miina. All others—Kundalan and V'ornn alike—die a terrible death.*

The rumbling came again, a deep and frightening sound like the tolling of a funeral bell.

He shuddered, despite himself. *Which means it's all true,* he thought. *Everything I unearthed in my research into Kundalan myth. The same research that has been ridiculed by my colleagues, three of whom now lie dead.*

Those who would seek to violate the Sacred Storehouse have tried to use the Ring of Five Dragons. They have failed. A fail-safe mechanism has been activated. The Ring has become a kind of detonator in a seismic bomb. The Ides of Lonon is less than four months away. If the Dar Sala-at does not take possession of it by then the crust of the planet will crack asunder, the seas will inundate the land, all life will be swept away, annihilated so that Kundala can begin again. So it is written, so it will be.

11

Ya-Unn

Imagine yourself dropped down a dry well at night. Now imagine what it must be like in that first moment when your rescuer shines her searchlight down the well's shaft.

For Riane, who had been dreaming of an endless night, the dawn came. She found herself on a plain—in all directions desolate, barren, bereft of color or signature. Another stood before her, a stranger who was nevertheless familiar. She stared into the eyes of this stranger and was afraid. She was afraid because she felt herself falling, falling into darkness without end. There was nothing to cling to, nothing to catch her fall, nothing to save her. So she fell, and in falling felt another with her—the stranger. And then the shift came; light flooded the darkness, and Riane saw that she was falling toward the familiar stranger. She tried to cry out, for in another instant they would collide. Then the light shifted again and she saw why the stranger was so familiar, saw that she was falling into a mirror. . . .

Crash!

Riane, alone in her own cell, opened her eyes. A wind was rising, an inner wind that resolved itself into the alien images she had seen before of snow- and ice-bejeweled landscapes high up in the Djenn Marre.

"What the N'Luuura are you?" she whispered.

The images were now accompanied by a song—a Kundalan song that Giyan had sung to Annon when he had been very young. Riane felt a sudden rage sweep through her.

Once again, she was assaulted by images: of herself dying. She had been meant to die, but at the last instant something happened. Two forces pulling at her, pain that could not even be imagined. And in that terrible moment, she had glimpsed the Abyss. . . . And every creature within it, saw them fleeting as a dream.

Riane, terrified to her core, shook her head violently. "Get out of my head, whatever you are!"

Instead, she saw the thing with five faces. In the Abyss. Pyphoros. Giyan had told Annon about Pyphoros, the daemon of daemons, who was cast down—

"Stop it!" Riane cried. "Stop it!" She was trembling violently, thinking of the five-headed creature that had grinned at her in her dreams.

But it was too late. She had seen everything. It was too much.

Riane squeezed her eyes shut. She saw Pyphoros. No one was meant to see him but Miina; no one but the dead he claimed. But she had seen him. Worse, he had seen her, and now he rode herd on her dreams.

Riane, her head pounding, found herself listening to the echoes of despair. She was drowning in this world and in the alienness of herself. There was no escape. No—

Open the book.

She froze, her heart hammering in her breast.

Open the book.

She worked the flat of her hand across the raw, undyed muslin of the bed sheet, as if to reassure herself of what was real and what imagined because the borders she had known and had taken for granted had begun to blur. But even this purely physical act was not enough now; she had begun to doubt everything. With a whimper, she reached beneath the floor tile and extracted the book. She opened it to the first page, staring at the incomprehensible Kundalan runes.

She blinked.

Panic flooded her again, squirting through her veins like fire. *What am I doing?* she wondered. *I can't read this form of Kundalan.* But somehow the strange, incomprehensible runes had the power to calm her wildly beating heart.

She stared at the incomprehensible pages, thinking of Giyan. Her lips moved, as if in prayer. But they could not have been a V'ornn prayer because Annon did not know the decaying prayers of Enlil.

All at once, Riane gasped. The runes were resolving themselves into letters, letters into words, words into phrases:

"*UTMOST SOURCE*," she read in wonder. "*THE FIVE SACRED BOOKS OF MIINA*."

Suddenly breathless, she turned the page.

> "*BOOK ONE: SPIRIT GATE*
> *Inside us are Fifteen Spirit Gates. They are meant to be open.*
> *If even one is not, a blockage occurs. . . .*"

And the thought came to her unbidden: *A blockage has occurred.*

Riane had gradually come to hate her female body less. The mysteries of her femaleness—sexual attraction, how this new body functioned, the sudden shifts of her raging hormones—still baffled her, but now that the body had fully recovered from the siege of duur fever she found cause to appreciate even more its stamina and strength. She had taken to rising an hour earlier than the other Ramahan so she could work her body so strenuously her arms and legs trembled and sweat poured off her in salty rivulets. She began to study her new self in the mirror, concentrating on observing how her shape was changing, her shoulders widening, her arm muscles becoming more defined, her legs even more powerful, and that pleased her insofar as she was able at the moment to feel pleasure.

One morning, promptly at the fourth hour, which was her appointed time. Riane presented herself in the doorway to Shima Laudenum's classroom.

The day had begun. The rich, amber sunlight of High Summer filtered through the arabesques of the wooden shutters, most of which were open. This gave the chamber an air of mystery, the ribbons, curlicues, and serifs of light seeming to create their own runic language, far more ancient than either Kundalan or V'ornn.

"Good morning, Riane," said Leyna Astar's soft, melodious voice. "It is safe for you to come in."

"Where is Shima Laudenum?" Riane asked.

Leyna Astar smiled. "She has offended Konara Bartta once too often. She has been reassigned."

Riane's heart leapt. "Does that mean you will be teaching me now?"

Leyna Astar's laugh was infectious. "It is good to see you in a lighter mood," Leyna Astar said as she led the girl to a low table by the wooden shutters. Arabesques of light seemed to float across the shiny lacquer surface as if in a dream. They sat cross-legged, across from each other on thin cushions. "Konara Bartta has assigned me to your formal instruction."

Riane cocked her head. "But you are a novice."

"I should have been made shima three years ago, but . . ." Astar leaned forward and said in a stage whisper, "I will tell you a secret: I am a bit of a rebel."

"So am I," Riane blurted out before she could stop herself.

"Well, I won't tell if you won't."

"It's a deal," Riane said, relaxing a bit.

"So." Leyna Astar put her hands together. "What has Konara Laudenum been teaching you?"

Riane told her about Kyofu, the Cube of Tutelage, and the three concentric black rings.

"First, let me explain the essentials of the Ramahan sorcery, something I am certain Konara Laudenum failed to tell you," Leyna Astar said. "There are two schools of sorcery—Osoru or Five Moons, and Kyofu or Black Dreaming. Only those born with the Gift can learn Osoru. Once, the two were a whole, but at some point those who had mastered both disciplines found that while the *principles* of both could co-exist in one mind, the *philosophies* could not. Perhaps because it can be learned by anyone with intelligence and determination, Kyofu was prone to corruption. It seemed to weaken White Bone Gate, the place inside ourselves most susceptible to the influence of evil. So, at some point, the two disciplines were separated, and each had its own faction within the Ramahan. Gradually, the Kyofu faction won out. Nowadays, primarily because of Konara Bartta's incessant lobbying, Osoru is no longer taught at the abbey. Doubtless because Konara Bartta was born without the Gift, those with it are shunned. As a consequence, only Kyofu is taught, but not as a regular part of the curriculum."

Leyna Astar looked deep into Riane's eyes. "Despite what Konara Laudenum might have led you to believe, few leyna are chosen for Kyofu training. Konara Bartta is far too covetous of her power. And as for acolytes, well, you are the first, Riane."

"What is so special about me?"

"For one thing you were able to return Kyofu's sorcerous black fire to its natural state." Leyna Astar reached out, plucked out of the air above Riane's head the three black rings. "For another . . ." She stacked them in the air. "You see, you did not absorb them. No one I know can resist the Rings of Concordance, but you did, Riane." She made a circular motion, and the rings dissolved with a small *pop!*

"I do not see how," Riane said. "I did nothing consciously."

"Let's find out." Leyna Astar put her delicate hands upon the table, the arabesques of light giving them an otherworldly dimension. "Shall we begin?"

"I did not bring my tablet or stylus," Riane said. Kundalan did not use data-storage devices as the V'ornn did.

"You do not require them," Astar said. "You need only your mind." Her hands rested on the tabletop, palms up. "As you know we have five seasons. Can you tell me which one the Ramahan honor above all others?"

Into Riane's head popped a legend of the queen of the gimnopedes. Where had it come from? It was not one Giyan had told Annon. "Lonon, the Fifth Season, is when the gimnopedes swarm," she said. "They mate during Lonon and give birth before Low Winter arrives, when they head south across the Sea of Blood to alight Miina knows where. Lonon is their time. It is Miina's time, as well."

"Excellent, Riane. Miina is the Goddess of, among other things, the harvest. The harvest time has many meanings for us here at the abbey. As it is for all Kundalan, it is a time of gathering food for the long winter, but for us it is also a time for cleansing our spirits. In the same manner in which the leaves fall in Lonon, clogging the gutters of houses and the storm drains in the streets, so too do our spirits become clogged during the long year. And so, in Lonon we hold special ceremonies to empty ourselves of the unneeded and unwanted, to scrub our insides clean of whatever impure or improper thoughts have accumulated. For us, then, Lonon is a sacred time, the Goddess's time, when spirituality reigns supreme."

The expressive hands wove gestures. "It is also the time of the Spirit House. Miina speaks of this aspect of Lonon in the fragments of *Utmost Source* that have survived. The Spirit House, where our ancestors temporarily reside, exists alongside our world." She curled both hands into fists, moved them in circles over the light-flecked tabletop. "These two worlds have their own orbits." She demonstrated with her fists. "In Low Winter they are the farthest from each other, during Lonon they actually touch. Then it is possible to call upon the Spirit House for strength and support."

She stood up, pointed to three places on her body—two above each breast, one at her lower belly. "Here are the places where we need to be restored—the spirit storehouses. We learn to gain our strength from the collected wisdom of the Spirit House."

"Can I ask a question?"

"Of course, Riane." Leyna Astar sat back down. "Here, with me, you have permission to ask anything."

"You said that the Spirit House is where our ancestors live, but you also said they stay there temporarily. Where do the spirits go when they leave the Spirit House?"

A warm smile spread across Leyna Astar's face. From inside her robes she took out a small beautifully embroidered velvet bag. She opened it, searching inside. "To answer your insightful question, the Spirit House is not a place—like Kundala is a place, a planet spinning in orbit around a sun. Think of it as a kind of way station, a nexus point that holds the insubstantial from wandering off into uncharted reaches. From this way station spirits wait for their time to return to the mortal sphere to be born again, to continue their own personal quest for enlightenment, the truth about themselves."

"Like luewondren," Riane said too quickly and, she worried, unwisely.

"I have heard of that alien word. It is the Gyrgon concept of reincarnation. Perhaps there are some theoretical similarities, but there is no proof that, for the V'ornn at least, reincarnation actually exists."

Riane wondered again how a novice came by such knowledge. Annon had believed, as all V'ornn did, in luewondren.

Leyna Astar's smile returned. "Now give me your hands." She placed Riane's hands palms up on the tabletop. "You must promise to keep still and try to relax. There will be no pain involved."

"What are you going to do?"

"Don't worry. We are merely going to replenish your spirit storehouse."

"But how? It is still High Summer. Lonon is weeks away."

"Yes, I know. But when the need is great enough, there are alternative paths. This is an important lesson to learn, Riane. No matter how things may appear, there are always alternative paths. You simply have to find them."

"But how? I wouldn't know—"

"Just relax now." Astar had taken a slender enameled case out of her bag. The case was covered with incised runes. From it, she slid out a pair of needles. They were odd, giving off no glitter where the arabesques of sunlight struck them. Rather, the light seemed to move through them as if they only faintly existed. Smiling still, Astar held one needle by an end. "I am going to pass this through the center of your palm."

Riane snatched her hands away.

"I told you it would not hurt. Do you think I am lying?" Riane said nothing.

"All right. This cannot be done against your will." Astar began to put the needles away.

"Wait!" Riane swallowed. "What . . . What will happen to me when you put the needle in?"

"I do not know. It is different for each of us," Astar said. "What I can say for a certainty is that you will be filled with a feeling of well-being."

Slowly, without taking her eyes from the novice's, Riane returned her hands to the tabletop.

Astar waited a moment, perhaps to be certain that the girl had made up her mind. Then she took one needle by its end and, placing it perpendicular to the tabletop, inserted it into the exact center of Riane's left palm. Riane felt a momentary flicker, something akin to a buzz of electricity, then nothing save a slow pulsing of warmth in her lower belly. Shima Astar had not lied, there was no pain. The novice repeated the procedure with the second needle, inserting it into Riane's right palm. The momentary flicker was different, heavier, deeper, ricocheting inside her, making her fingers spasm.

The pulsing took shape, passing from one hand to another as if across an invisible wire. From there it moved to her lower belly, up to her chest and back down again, as if completing an energy loop.

"I feel like I'm hooked up to some kind of machine," Riane said.

"An excellent analogy." Astar seemed impressed again. "The machine, Riane, is your own body. The needles—the qi as the konara call them—have opened up the chord of your inner energy; they have become the Channel through which your spirit storehouse is being replenished." She waited a moment. "One is forbidden to know this, but it is said that in the old days Mother was able to replenish her spirit storehouse at will without the aid of the qi."

"I know very little about Mother."

"Ah, Mother." Astar closed her eyes for a moment. "In

the time before the V'ornn, when The Pearl lay safely in the
Storehouse below Middle Palace, the Ramahan were led, not
by the Dea Cretan, but by a hereditary leader whose spirituality was all-encompassing."

"She was murdered on the day w—On the day the V'ornn
invaded Kundala, wasn't she?"

"It is said that she was murdered by the Rappa while a
cabal of male priests staged a coup. In those days, here as
in every aspect of Kundalan life, female and male had shared
roles. That ended when certain male priests took The Pearl
out of the Storehouse and misused it. Because they tried to
use The Pearl for their own ends, it told them only what they
wanted to hear."

"It lied to them?"

"Yes, Riane, The Pearl lied to them, as it was meant to
do. Only the pure in heart and spirit may gaze into The Pearl
and see the Truth." Astar turned each qi a quarter turn to the
right. The effect was like stirring a pot of bubbling stew:
new sensations came to the surface. "In Her wrath," she went
on, "the Great Goddess cast down the Kundalan, ensured that
they would be enslaved by the V'ornn until the time of Am-
bat, when the Dar Sala-at is born."

"Who is the Dar Sala-at?"

"The Dar Sala-at is the One who is pure in spirit and
heart—the One who will find The Pearl, who will use it as
it was meant to be used, who will free the Kundalan from
the yoke of V'ornn enslavement. It is also Prophesied that
the Dar Sala-at will be the one to reclaim both schools of
sorcery, heal what was mistakenly rent asunder, and bind
them into the whole that was originally meant to be."

Riane, who was feeling better than she had ever felt before, thought about this for a long time. She saw that Astar's
eyes were upon her with a grave intensity.

"I want you to do something for me, Riane."

She waited, barely breathing. An ethereal glow filled her
with warmth and light.

"I am going to ask you a question," Astar went on. "Just

one. And when I ask it of you I want you to answer quick as you can, without thinking about it."

"Is this some kind of a test?"

Leyna Astar gave her a shrewd look. "Yes," she said. "One that has never been administered before."

"Why?"

"The test is called the Ya-unn—the Meeting of Ways."

"Is it important?"

"*Most* important."

"But I am unprepared."

"In that you are mistaken." Leyna Astar twirled the qi a quarter turn to the left. "You already passed one test: you reverted the black fire." Leyna Astar made a final adjustment to the qi. "Tell me the first word that comes to your mind at this precise moment."

"Djenn."

Astar sat absolutely still. Her beautiful lips were slightly parted; her cheeks were blushed with pink. "Yes," she whispered, and smiled. "You see, Riane, you did not fail."

"I didn't?"

"You have proved what has already been suspected. You are special. *Very* special. We believe that is why Konara Bartta took you to be trained in Kyofu. For a certainty, it is why you were able to resist the Rings."

"We? Is there someone else involved?"

"There is, but—it is a secret." Leyna Astar lowered her voice. "I do not have to tell you that evil lurks around, do I?"

"No, but this is a bit confusing," Riane said thoughtfully. "Konara Laudenum claimed no evil was allowed inside the abbey."

"That was true enough, in the old days. But since The Pearl was lost, since Mother was deposed, since the Ramahan have lost their way many things have changed. For over a century, Miina has turned Her face away from us." Leyna Astar's eyes were shining. "Now you have come; the hand of the Great Goddess has reappeared."

Riane shook her head. "I do not understand."

"It is too dangerous now for you to know more," Leyna Astar said. "But, believe me when I tell you that at the proper time you will understand everything." She cocked her head. "Curious. You haven't asked the meaning of Djenn."

"But I already know," Riane said. "In the Old Tongue it means Dragon."

This seemed to give Leyna Astar pause. "How did you know that, Riane? You have only just begun to study the Old Tongue."

"I don't know," Riane said truthfully. She was about to tell Leyna Astar how she had opened *Utmost Source* one night and just like that had begun to read it, but she remembered Giyan's warning to tell no one of it. "I . . . I just do, that's all." She thought a moment. "I wondered whether it could have been from the Rings of Concordance."

"As I said, you are immune to the Rings' effects. In any event, they cannot impart that kind of knowledge wholesale."

"Another thing puzzles me. When you spoke of these qi, you said that the konara named them. The konara use them, then?"

"Only konara may use the qi."

"But you are a novice."

"Just so." Astar hummed a little as she removed the qi from Riane's palms, wiping them down with alcohol, replacing them in their runic case. "That is quite a conundrum, isn't it?"

12

Damage

In the privacy of his residence in Axis Tyr, Pack-Commander Rekkk Hacilar put his head in his hands and wept for his friend and his regent, Eleusis Ashera. Eleusis had been more—mentor and father figure. He had helped Rekkk escape the stigma his own father had left.

Rekkk's father had been one of the most notorious Rhynnnon in recent memory. Rhynnnon were rogue Khagggun, who rebelled against their command and their caste. Rekkk's father, like other Rhynnnon before him, had died in a bloody battle where the odds were overwhelmingly against him. Rhynnnon held a unique place in Khagggun lore because they were both despised and admired. Khagggun simply did not renounce their command. On the rare occasions when they did, they lived a life apart from the V'ornn Modality. They might make their living hiring themselves out to individuals with difficult and dangerous grudges to settle. But just as likely, they had an agenda of their own that involved a simple but compelling moral imperative—an injustice, some might say, that required action on their part that could not be taken as a Khagggun. That is what made for the dichotomy in how they were viewed by their former compatriots. In Rekkk's father's case, he had rebelled against the excessively cruel tyranny of the Star-Admiral whom Kinnnus Morcha had replaced. In fact, he had fulfilled his avowed purpose for becoming Rhynnnon; he had slain the Star-Admiral before being killed on the field of battle.

It had been Eleusis Ashera who had allowed Rekkk to overcome the strictures of his training and, for the first time, see his father for who he really was—a hero.

There was other news, unhappy as well. He had just received word that the new regent had approved Kinnnus Morcha's insane petition to have Kurgan Stogggul named his new adjutant. N'Luuura take it, the V'ornn was hardly more than a child—and a Bashkir to boot! On the other hand, perhaps it was not so insane once you considered it a form of "business marriage." The transfer linked the two V'ornn— Wennn Stogggul and Kinnnus Morcha—in a tangible way, signaling that their alliance ran deeper than anyone had suspected. It seemed an odd pairing—Great Caste with Lesser Caste. The pragmatic part of Rekkk was hardly surprised. When he had flagrantly broken protocol in Stone Border, he had not only borne Olnnn Rydddlin's wrath, but had risked everything—his status as adjutant, his rank as Pack-Commander. Everything. And for what?

He heard her moving around in another part of his residence. Giyan. He had loved her the moment he had first seen her in Eleusis Ashera's private quarters. It had been but a glimpse, really. More than enough to set his hearts afire with passion and guilt. And each time he had seen her (to his knowledge, she had never seen him) his desire for her had grown. To covet the lover of his friend was shameful—and a Kundalan at that! And yet, inexplicably, it was partly because she was Kundalan that he felt so powerfully drawn to her. He had carefully and painfully locked away that part of him. Until news of the coup had reached him.

It had not escaped his notice that Kinnnus Morcha had excluded him from the planning. Just as it had become painfully clear that Olnnn Rydddlin had been assigned to him as a shadow, rather than as a simple First-Captain. He had been careful not to give Rydddlin any cause for suspicion. Until the moment in Stone Border when he had refused to allow Annon Ashera's corpse to be dragged through the plaza. Looking into Giyan's brave eyes, he had felt his hearts melt. He could no more have submitted her to such humiliation and anguish than he could cease breathing. He had not stopped to think it out; he had acted.

Now the ramifications had begun. He was no longer adjutant to Kinnnus Morcha, and the newly appointed Star-Admiral had not summoned him. Bad sign. *Very* bad sign.

On the other hand, he should have seen this coming long ago. What had Kinnnus Morcha ever done to elicit his trust? Nothing. On the contrary, he had affixed Olnnn Rydddlin as his shadow. The future looked like this: Eleusis Ashera was no longer in power, and his former commanding officer, the single most powerful Khaggun on Kundala, had written him off. All that he might have been able to live with. If Giyan loved him. But the reality was quite the opposite. Despite the fact that he had told her that he and Eleusis had been friends, that she had nothing to fear from him, she had done nothing but treat him with cold disdain. What should he expect? Her lover had been slain most foully, betrayed by the very Khaggun who should have safeguarded his life. His son, the boy she had raised from infancy, was also dead. Besides, to look at her, he doubted whether she believed a word he had said. Why should she, when he had been chosen to hunt Annon down, when Annon's head had been delivered to Kinnnus Morcha like a hunting trophy?

He might as well turn his shock-sword on himself. It would be the honorable thing to do.

He strode through his residence to his weapons room and drew one of his shock-swords off the wall. He activated it, felt the small jolt as the hyperexcited ions arced between the surfaces of the double blades. He trembled a little as he contemplated his own death. He had killed many people, had seen the faraway look come into their eyes just before they glazed over, but never before had he asked himself what it is they saw at the moment of their passing. Why should he have? The bloodlust was running wildly through him, focusing all his resources on what must be done in battle. Now the memories surfaced like strange fish from the ocean's depths. Life to death. One small step. But he knew that it would take all his energies to plunge the shock-sword into his belly. Brushing aside these morbid thoughts, he prepared himself.

"Planning to kill yourself?" her harsh, mocking tone made him wince.

He turned at the sound of her voice, saw her clear, whistleflower-blue eyes open wide. "Here," he said, thrusting the hilt of the shock-sword toward her. "You have been wanting to kill me ever since I brought you back here. Now is your chance."

Giyan held up her bandaged hands.

"Ah," he said, defeated, "I forgot. How do they feel?"

"As if all the skin had been flayed off them."

They regarded each other silently.

At last he said, "I have told you this before, I think, but I know just what Eleusis Ashera saw in you."

"You are self-deluded."

"It gives you some form of solace to believe that, doesn't it?"

"I do not know," she said. "I am incapable of feeling solace."

"You treat me with contempt. Have I raped you, spoken to you harshly, touched you in any inappropriate manner?"

Her silence mocked him.

"Have I not treated you fairly?" he cried.

She laughed in his face. "You hunted down my—you hunted down Annon and trussed him like an animal in the streets of my village!"

"He was already dead."

"What you did turned my heart to ash."

He could not bear that cold, biting stare. "Peculiar in the extreme for a female to have a deep attachment for the one she has raised."

"Idiot! I am not V'ornn!"

"Of course, but you harbor this attachment for a V'ornn."

"How little you know of us." Her voice was withering. "There isn't an instant that goes by when I don't miss him, when I don't wish I could hold him in my arms again, to protect him, to rock him to sleep, to tell him that everything will be all right." Her voice caught like a fishhook in her throat. "But it isn't all right, and it never will be. I failed Eleusis, and I failed him; don't you understand? When he died a part of me went with him."

Rekkk took a moment to collect himself. "I cannot tell you how sorry—"

Her eyes blazed. "Save your hollow words for others. I do not believe you."

He shook his head. "No matter what you may think of me, Giyan, I mean what I say. I have not had you fitted for the okuuut as I was ordered."

"Please don't bother." She raised her black hands. "How would it be implanted?"

He stood stiffly, uncomfortably. The shock-sword still in his hand.

"You do not need to commit suicide," she spat. "You're already dead. You just don't know it yet."

She was right, and Rekkk knew it. How he burned to touch her, to hold her in his arms, to soothe away her pain and anguish. How odd to feel this for an alien! And yet, because of his friendship with Eleusis, not odd at all. From Eleusis, he had learned to accept his affinity for the Kundalan, the magnetic force that drew him inexorably toward them, away from his own kind. If he was no closer to understanding the nature of this force, Eleusis had taught him, at least, to accept it. But he and Giyan were separated by a gulf far wider. Her enmity flared out, coldly pushing him away. Her contempt was quickly crushing his hearts.

She turned partially away from him. "I would gladly give my own life to have Annon back. As for taking your life, I am afraid you must summon the courage for that yourself."

His voice lowered to a hoarse whisper. "Giyan, what happened to Annon . . . Had I found him alive, I would not have killed him. His father was my friend, my mentor. I would have died to protect his son."

"Words."

"Not just words. I would not allow him to be dragged through Stone Border."

"For that, I am grateful." She turned on him, her beautiful eyes blazing. "But ever since that moment I have asked myself why. Why would you do that? You yourself provided the answer." She crossed her arms over her breasts. "I see how you look at me. I recognize the naked lust in your eyes."

"No, you're wrong." But, of course, his voice lacked conviction.

"Eleusis is newly dead, and you have already scooped up the spoils. You claim to have been his friend? What an ugly and despicable jest! You are no better than his murderers, Stogggul and Morcha!"

His hearts withered some more. All the lights in the world seemed to go out at once. "The trouble with life is that everyone believes what they want to believe. It is so much easier and less complicated than the truth."

"More words."

With a shrug of resignation, he closed off the encoded ion stream, put the shock-sword back on the wall.

"Coward!"

He tried to seal himself off from her. The pain it caused him was exquisite. "It's time to change your bandages." He led her out of the weapons room and down a skylit corridor. In the bathroom, he sat her down, slit the knot he had made, and began to unwind the muslin strips on her right hand. He was aware of her gaze, as if it had as much weight as his shock-sword.

Supporting her hand from underneath, he continued to unwind the strips. Her fingers were red, raw, and shiny, having been smeared with a potent V'ornn antiburn unguent.

He carefully wiped them off with fresh squares of un-bleached muslin while Giyan moaned softly in agony. The wounds looked as angry and swollen as they had when he had first begun treating her. This was the fourth treatment he had used, a combination of V'ornn and Kundalan medicines. Why wouldn't any of them work? His face did not betray his mounting alarm.

"The burns are extremely severe," he told her as he applied more unguent. "They need more time to heal." He looked up. "I've seen you using your sorcery on them. Hasn't that helped?"

"You spy on my privacy?"

As far as she was concerned, nothing he said or did would be right, he thought in despair. "I simply wanted to know, that's all."

She turned her head away, walling him off again.

He paused in the application of the medication. "If you could tell me what happened to you, I would have a better idea of how to treat this."

"I told you I don't know. It happened when Annon was killed by the perwillon. There was some kind of glowing lichen in the cave—a species I had never seen before. Annon landed in a bed of it. When I dragged him out, it was torn up, and the liquid got all over my hands."

She was staring at the thing that covered her hands and so missed the anguished look he gave her. Missed, too, his attempt to say something he bit back into his throat.

Love curdled in his hearts, turning to rage. At his core he was still Khaggqun, quicksilver emotions rising like storms through him. And so he did exactly the wrong thing. His hand curled into a fist. "You will never leave here, you understand that, don't you?" She said nothing, and her silence provoked him further. "You are mine now, whether or not it suits you. You may as well forget your memories of Eleusis Ashera or anyone else in your past. Your life is in the here and now—at my side."

She was silent, and this galled him all the more. "You will answer when you are spoken to."

"Ah, yes, the master race threatens." She lapsed into a short silence. "If that is your wish, I shall obey it," she said quietly. "You are V'ornn and I am Kundalan. Of course, I will act as you order." Her head came up and her eyes flashed. "But don't think for a moment that you can change me. I will not—"

She cried out as he backhanded her across her face. She tumbled onto the floor, and he was upon her, pushing aside her robes, baring her lovely body. He reared above her.

"Go on. This is what V'ornn do best." She was like a starfish, splayed out on the stone floor. Her utter contempt was like a mirror, holding up to him his abominable behavior. He would have died to feel even one moment of her love.

Tears stood like diamonds in the corners of her eyes. She would not look at him. She lay as she had been, her body revealed to him, but otherwise utterly closed off.

"I am sorry," he whispered, pulling her robe around her. "So sorry . . ."

"You see how it is." Her beautiful eyes stared at nothing. "Your power is a pitiful thing."

He thrust himself away from her, ran from the room, but her mocking words pursued him: "You think you can have what Eleusis had." Her voice was a cold, dead thing. "But you can't. You never will. *Never*."

Filled with rage and humiliation, he slammed out of his residence, hurled himself mindlessly into the seething heart of the city as if in that way he could become as invisible to himself as he was to her.

If he had not been so profoundly distraught, he would have noticed that he was being followed. Not that he would have cared overmuch. In his current state, he would surely have welcomed the quick stab of an assassin's blade.

In due course, he found himself in the far northern end of the city, Mesagggun territory, a rough quarter even by Khagggun standards. The packed streets stank of low-grade numaaadis, lubricating fluid, and garbage. Since it was just past shift change, several fights had broken out among the half-drunk denizens. The combatants were being heartily egged on by those on the innermost fringes of the shifting crowds, all save the ineffectual priests, the last remnants of those who kept what was left of V'ornn religion alive. The war god, Enlil, had long since served his purpose. When the Gyrgon had risen to power millennia ago, they tore through the ranks of Enlil's Children, breaking the hold the Church had had on the Lesser Castes. Only a faction of the Mesagggun still worshiped at the shabby, makeshift temples in the Northern Quarter. These Traditionalists were persecuted mercilessly by the Forwards, the Mesagggun who believed the Gyrgon view of life was the only path to bettering themselves.

The Mesagggun who managed the Modality's machinery were an unhappy and unlucky lot. They lived in squalor with no hope of advancement, no respite from their lives of constant drudgery. Though they were the grease that kept the Modality running smoothly, they received no thanks, no hope, save the pathetic pap doled out by the priests. The other castes, Khagggun included, walked upon their strong, bowed backs without a second thought. In fact, when they weren't fighting among themselves, the Mesagggun got into brief but violent turf wars with the Khagggun. Like Khagggun, the Mesagggun possessed an exaggerated sense of honor, perhaps because they had nothing else to call their own. Blood feuds were numerous and vicious. Rekkk knew chances were good that he would not be welcome here. Doubtless that was why he had come.

Sure enough, he was spotted, and a couple of brawny lubricant-smeared Mesagggun broke off their wagering on the nearest fight to give him a closer look. The sight of his uniform was like a goad to them, and the fact that he was without a shock-sword warmed their calcified hearts. One of them swung a brindle-stick—a thick base-metal lever used in maintenance. Rekkk wasted no time in determining that this Mesagggun was the leader. He needed no taunts to further enrage him, but immediately waded in, slamming his fist into the armed Mesagggun's gut. The Mesagggun doubled over and Rekkk snatched his brindle-stick, beat him twice over the head with it before slicing it behind him, catching the second Mesagggun flush on the ear. The thick haft of the brindle-stick made blood spurt, and the big Mesagggun went down. By that time, the third Mesagggun was inside the perimeter of Rekkk's defenses. He got off a trio of punishing jabs that half dazed Rekkk and made him grit his teeth against the pain. But somehow the pain felt good and he dropped the brindle-stick. More Mesagggun joined the fray, punching, kicking, head-butting, and he was plowed under by their enmity. He laughed when his skin swelled and burst open, which made them redouble their efforts to beat him senseless. For a time, he gave as good as he got, but eventually their sheer number overwhelmed even his heightened state of fury. He took his beating like a V'ornn, never protesting, never crying out, his mind filled with what he had done to Giyan.

Wennn, you have disappointed me—again."

The regent Stogggul, having been Summoned by the Gyrgon, found himself in the dark, crowded house of his childhood. He faced his father, even though his father was dead, even though he knew he was, in actuality, somewhere deep inside the Temple of Mnemonics. The power of what he was seeing was inescapable. Quite against his wishes, he found himself feeling the old, familiar dread creep over him.

"When will you learn?" his father said sternly. "You will never be like me, you will never measure up no matter how hard you try." His father's head moved from side to side in his disapproving manner. "You are inadequate, a sore disappointment. I wish you had never been born."

The regent Stogggul found to his horror that he was trembling just as he had always trembled when he had faced his father. Even after all this time, even though the gulf of death separated them, nothing had changed because the truth of those admonitions had been ingrained in him, until his father's acute disappointment had become his own. He clenched his fists, trying to fight the feelings.

"You are a pathetic creature, Wennn, playing at power games far beyond your feeble grasp. I could always see clear through you, and I still can. You think I am dead, but I live on. I will be here every time you return. You are still my child; you always will be."

The regent bit his lip, vowing to say nothing. But something deep inside him had started to wail.

"Look at you." His father approached him, the ion whip he always carried snapping against his thigh. "Trembling like a leaf in a storm." He circled the regent, the sound of the ion whip a well-remembered jolt, a sensation like the taste of rancid meat, or poison on the tongue. "I did the best I could, but look at the raw material I had to work with." *Swapp!* The ion whip struck the regent's shoulders and Stogggul gave a little cry, of recognition as well as of pain. "You disgust me, Wennn." *Swapp!* "I am ashamed to call you my son." *Swapp!* "Get down on your knees, like the worm that you are."

"Stop it, stop it, stop it!" The regent Stogggul's voice rose from a husky whisper to a desperate shout. He closed his eyes against a brief wave of vertigo. When he opened them, he found that his father had morphed into a Gyrgon peering down at him with ruby-red pupils.

"Stogggul Wennn, we will see you dead."

The regent could see that he was kneeling on the floor of a tiered, open-air amphitheater that completely encircled him. All the seats, save one, were filled with Gyrgon. *There must be a thousand of them,* he thought. All were staring fixedly at him. He could feel their animus grinding him into the ground. His hearts pounded painfully in his chest. Gyrgon did not make idle threats, nor did they bluff.

"The sight of you offends us," said the Gyrgon with ruby-red pupils as he took his seat. "We do not know whether we feel more pity or contempt for you."

Numb with shock, weakened by evil memories, all he could manage to mumble was, "Tell me how I have offended you that I may make atonement."

The Gyrgon stood, his neural nets ablaze with his rage. "Your atonement, regent, will take this form: you will embrace our wrath and make it your own. You will galvanize the Khaggun. You and Star-Admiral Morcha Kinnnus will launch a campaign to root out and destroy all enemies, all traitorous elements. The gutters of Axis Tyr will overflow with blood, the valleys beyond will be filled with it. We wish to hear the wails of the mourners; we wish to see them turning in greater numbers to Kara, the religion that embraces V'ornn and Kundalan alike."

"And when I have accomplished what you ask, what then?" the regent ventured. "Will you give me the salamuuun trade? The Ashera murdered my father for it! It is only just that you—"

"You are not here to ask questions, regent, or to make demands!" the Gyrgon thundered. "You are here to listen and to obey!"

With a wave of his gloved hand, he caused the regent Stogggul to vanish, sending him back to his quarters across the city.

Rekkk Hacilar awoke in a filthy back alley, where someone had dragged him. His head lolled against a pile of trash bins. Rats startled away as he began to stiffly move.

He ached all over; it was only what he deserved. For a moment his mind was blessedly blank. Then, like a poisonous blossom, he saw again the image of Giyan crumpled on the floor, heard her words traveling through space and time to cause him misery once more.

He did not know where he was, nor did he care. The alley was narrow, blank-walled, featureless. In the distance he could hear the myriad sounds of the city. Bones crunched and someone groaned; somewhere close by another fight was under way. He staggered to his knees, vomited freely. He held his head as if that would stop the dizziness. Gradually, he was able to drag himself to his feet. He leaned against a stained and rotting wall, gaining strength with every wheezing breath. He used garbage to wipe the vomit off his boots.

When he felt able, he took a quick inventory of all his bones. None appeared broken, which was something of a miracle, but he could not take even a shallow breath without intense waves of pain shooting through him.

It began to rain, the drops feeling like tears on his cheeks. He gritted his teeth and staggered down the alley. He had not gone more than a score of paces when he came upon a doorway he had not noticed before. Immediately to the right of the doorway was a small, discreet alloy plaque that read: NIMBUS and just below, the phrase REFERRALS ONLY. What was a luxe kashiggen doing in this working-class district of the city? Kashiggen were once peaceful inns devoted to entertaining the Ramahan. The V'ornn, knowing a good thing when they saw it, turned the Kundalan kashiggen into salamuuun palaces.

Ignoring the warning, he stumbled into an interior plush with velvets and satin, hazy with the unmistakable sweet, spicy scent of salamuuun. Rekkk licked his dry, cracked lips as he tried to focus. He saw an octagon-shaped room filled with Kundalan-style furniture. The walls were padded with richly brocaded fabrics; across the vaulted ceiling was a spray of enameled stars. In one corner, sat an old V'ornn seer, her features sunken into her skull. She watched him like an owl with greedy eyes. Two exquisite imari did their best to ignore him.

"A mistake, surely." The dzuoko, a beautiful Tuskugggun in a pale lavender robe, confronted him. Clearly, the mistress of this kashiggen, her cloth-of-silver sifeyn was pushed back on her skull. She was eyeing him up and down with a distasteful expression. "None of my imari would come within an arm's length of you." By her side was a burly Mesagggun. His arms, thick as tree trunks, were crossed over his massive chest. Say this about him, he was clean and sober. He glowered at Rekkk from beneath formidable brows, pointedly ignoring his bloodied insignia. "Not that it matters. No one I know could possibly have referred *you*." She snapped her fingers, and the oversize Mesagggun took a menacing step toward Rekkk.

"On the contrary, Mittelwin."

Rekkk looked to his left. A young, striking Tuskugggun stood eyeing him. She wore a midnight-blue robe and sifeyn shot with glittering gold thread. She was very tall and slender, and she moved with an astonishing grace. Another of NIMBUS' imari? Impossible. No imari would dare speak to her dzuoko in such a direct and crude fashion. From what he knew, the imari tradition was an ancient one, even for the Kundalan. Decades of training were required, and relatively few made it all the way through.

"This is the Khaggun I have been expecting," this vision said sweetly. "A little worse for wear, I admit."

"A *little!*" Mittelwin guffawed. "Look at the poor thing; I'd say some of our fine locals have had their way with him!"

The Mesagggun stifled a giggle.

"What are you laughing at?" Mittelwin said. "Clean him up, feed him some leeesta—from the warm pan, not the three-day-old stuff. Then take him to chamber seven for Mastress Kannna's pleasure."

For Rekkk, the shower was both pleasure and pain. The needles of water stung him in every bruised and swollen spot on his body, but the heat sank into him, easing the deeper pain. He had four soaps to choose from, all with distinctive masculine scents. He stayed under the spray a very long time. Khagggun did not often have the luxury of bathing in this manner.

Afterward, he was given a robe the color of cor blood. It filled him perfectly. When he asked the Mesagggun about his uniform the V'ornn told him that it was being cleaned and pressed. As he ate the delicious warm leeesta, he wondered whether the Mesagggun was his servant or his jailor. The Mesagggun gave him water when he said that he was thirsty. No numaaadis or spirits of any kind were offered. Nor were any of his questions answered. Who was this Mastress Kannna, and how could she possibly have been waiting for him when he himself had had no inkling he would stumble into the kashiggen until the moment he had spied the door? *Patience,* he told himself.

When he had eaten and drunk his fill, the Mesagggun led him down a corridor dimly lighted by old-fashioned Kundalan oil lamps. The flickering flames held behind crystal stacks had a soothing effect on the psyche. Even the mountainous Mesagggun was polite as he opened the door to chamber seven. Rekkk watched him retreat down the corridor before he went in.

Mastress Kannna was waiting for him in a small circular room with a conical ceiling. She sat in a deep chair. Beside her was a Kundalan-style sofa, looking as inviting as it was comfortable. In his current state, Rekkk was grateful for the comfort. V'ornn furniture was strictly utilitarian; the esthetics of comfort and style had been edited out.

"You look tired, Pack-Commander," Mastress Kannna said. "Won't you sit down?"

From somewhere in the room came the scents of clove oil and burnt musk. "I am afraid you have me at a disadvantage. You apparently know me, but I am sure that we have not met."

"Not directly, no." She lifted a hand. "Are you perhaps incapable of sitting?"

He grinned despite himself, sat gingerly on the edge of the sofa.

"Please. Relax, Pack-Commander, rest assured I will not attack you."

He did not return her smile. "It is my training. If there is a certain lack of trust on my part, it is simply because—"

"Tell me, Pack-Commander, do you indulge?" She held before him a slim crystal canister containing a cinnamon-colored powder.

"I have been known to blow a few meters of salamuuun."

"Excellent." She popped the top of the canister. "This is prime-grade. The only kind Mittelwin purveys."

"I don't think so," he said. "Not this time."

"Ah, I understand." Mastress Kannna nodded. "It is a matter of trust again." She stared deep into his eyes. "Tell me something, Pack-Commander."

"Only if you answer a question first." He took her silence as acceptance. "I heard Mittelwin address you as Mastress. Why? I have never heard that term used before."

"That is because it is rarely used." She crossed one leg over the other and, with a sibilant shiver, her robe parted slightly. "I am Great Caste. I am attached to a very special V'ornn. Hence my title."

"What kind of V'ornn is your mate?"

"One question, Pack-Commander." She smiled sweetly. "Now please tell me what you are doing in the Northern Quarter of Axis Tyr."

"I came to get what I deserved."

She eyed him curiously. "And did you?"

"I don't know. I am still alive."

Her smile widened as she downed half of the canister's contents, offered him what remained. "Well, then, it is safe to say that you do not know if your journey is yet at an end."

He hesitated for but a moment. It had crossed his mind that this might be a setup engineered by either Olnnn Rydddlin or Kinnnus Morcha to inject the last bolt in his coffin. Then the image of Giyan rose up like a daemon in the night, and he grabbed the salamuuun and inhaled it wholesale.

Mastress Kannna's eyes glittered. "Lie back, Pack-Commander. Let the salamuuun take you where it may."

He liked the sound of her voice. It was comforting, like his mother's had been. He hadn't thought of his mother in many years. He realized that he did not know where she was or even if she was alive. He closed his eyes and saw her standing before him. She smiled and spoke to him, and at once he felt how much he had missed her.

I wanted to find you, but I never had the time.

I know. Don't blame yourself, Rekkk.

But I do.

You had your life to live. That was more important.

It shouldn't have been.

It's the way of life.

He cried as she enfolded him within her arms.

Do not grieve for yourself, Rekkk. Live your life as you always have.

I cannot. I love a Kundalan, but she will never return that love.

How can you be so sure?

I have injured her grievously, permanently.

Nothing is permanent, Rekkk. Not even death . . .

He floated for a long time on the sea of his own tears. This sea rocked him, cradled him, spoke to him in the soft susurrus peculiar to oceans. Deep below him, in those unfathomable depths, he felt life moving, creatures larger, more alien than he could imagine, though already in his lifetime he had seen his share of alien life. He did not fear them. Listening to their distant songs, understanding their meanings without knowing their words, he drifted on currents unknown . . .

When, at length, he opened his eyes, he saw that Mastress Kannna was gone. In her place sat someone wonderfully, heartbreakingly familiar.

"Giyan," he breathed. "How did you find me?"

"On the contrary," she said. "You found me."

"I love you," he told her.

She smiled. "I know."

"And yet you are so sad, so very sad."

"In my life I have lost things, Rekkk, precious beyond

your imaginings. My heart is ash. I cannot fathom why it
continues to beat."

"You will never lose me. I swear this to you, Giyan."

"And now," Nith Sahor said, as he morphed once again
out of one body and into another, "we come to the finale of
our little drama."

Rekkk felt the psychogenic effects of the salamuuun dis-
sipating like fine strands of silk, draining from every synapse
in his brain, leaving him to feel as if he was nothing but a
long, lonely shadow.

"Where is Giyan?" he asked thickly.

"She has gone the way of Mastress Kannna."

His eyes cleared. "You mean she never existed."

"Not in the way you had imagined. But both of them exist
just the same. For now I am Nith Sahor."

The Gyrgon arranged his hands atop his crossed knees.
Rekkk watched those hands, cloaked in alloy mesh, as if they
were the jaws of a razor-raptor. To his horror, he found that
he was trembling uncontrollably. He had been trained almost
from birth to be fearless, but to be this close to a Gyrgon
was something entirely out of his ken. With an enormous
effort, he pulled himself together.

"Well, Rekkk," the Gyrgon said, "are we feeling any better
after our salamuuun flight?"

"I have heard of the Gyrgon affinity for cruel jests," he
said. "But I never thought I would be made the butt of one."

Nith Sahor leaned forward. "You misunderstand me. Nothing here was done in jest. It was all in the service of discovering the—how shall I put it?—the inner nature of
things." Rekkk regarded the Gyrgon with alarm. "Ask yourself this, then: now that you have taken a peek at the map
of your own universe do you know more about yourself than
you did when you were getting the N'Luuura beaten out of
you?"

Rekkk was wary. "Not that I could tell."

"No?" Nith Sahor cocked his long, elegant head. "Perhaps,
then, I should tell you about my flight. In it, I was on a ship,
and that ship was sailing across a sea of turquoise blood.

Like most V'ornn, I hate the ocean. In any event, Eleusis Ashera is on the ship with me. He is headless. His bloody body is fountaining the blood that has made the sea we are sailing on. And then I realize what I have done, the mistake I made with Eleusis. Gyrgon, you see, have limited experience in dealing with the outside world. It is why we delegate all the mundane jobs to others.

"I loved Eleusis Ashera—as I know you did, Rekkk. He had a special affinity for the unseen forces all around us. He was drawn to the Kundalan as I am. Without knowing why. This feeling frightened me. I tried to get him to explain it to me. He could not, of course. Who can explain love, desire? They are inexplicable. But I did not yet understand, so I grew wrathful. I treated him shamefully. I did not protect him when, perhaps, I could have. Now he is dead, and that weight lies heavily upon me."

Stunned by this unprecedented confession, Rekkk Hacilar said nothing.

"It's true, I am afraid, the vaunted Gyrgon are fallible." Nith Sahor's eyes sparked in the oil-fired lamplight as he briefly put a forefinger across his lips. "You see, Rekkk, your circumstances are not entirely unknown to me. In that light, I have a proposal to make you."

A moment ago, Rekkk would have laughed at the absurdity of the comment. Now he could only make a small sound in his throat. His entire world had been turned upside down, and he was still trying to make some kind of sense of it.

"I have trusted you with many secrets, Rekkk. Do you think you can trust me now?"

Rekkk Hacilar stared at the Gyrgon, his hearts beating heavily in his chest. "If you are aware of my circumstances, you know I no longer have a reason to live."

"Is that what your salamuuun flight revealed?"

Rekkk's voice was so clotted with emotion for a moment he could not answer. "No," he said at length.

"But you still feel suicidal? You wish to die?"

He stared down at the floor and thought of Giyan's anguished face. "Yes."

"What if I could change that?"

Rekkk put his forearms on his thighs, licked his lips. His mind seemed on fire. He wanted to scream out his rage and frustration at the circumstance that led him to love an alien female who despised him.

"What do you say, Rekkk?"

"How could you possibly bring back my desire for life?"

"On, I can't do that, Rekkk. No one but you can do that."

Just as his mother had told him in the salamuuun flight.

"But I can deliver what you want most."

The air shimmered and, for a tantalizing moment, Giyan lay before him. Then, the Gyrgon returned.

"You will not coerce her in any way."

"Absolutely not."

"She will love me of her own free will."

"Yes, but beware of what it is you desire most, Rekkk. This is my best advice to you."

Rekkk took a deep breath. He was filled with thoughts of Giyan; his hearts were pounding fiercely in his chest. *In for a blood-weight, in for a body-weight*, he thought. "Apart from your promise, there must be another payment for services rendered."

Nith Sahor nodded.

"Anything I want."

"If I can provide it, it will be yours."

"You must need me very much."

"Better by far not to know the answer to that question, Rekkk."

Rekkk remembered to let his breath out. This was Gyrgon he was dealing with, after all. He put his hands together. A distant memory surfaced. As a small child, he could remember his mother putting her hands together in prayer to the war god Enlil. In those days, religion was still embraced by some members of the Khaggun Caste. "Agreed," he said.

Nith Sahor sat back, his eyes hooded, his expression a mask. "Are you aware that the Kundalan Ring of Five Dragons has been found?"

"No." Rekkk Hacilar frowned. "Who has it?"

"Wennn Stogggul had it. He gave it as a gift to the Comradeship."

"Surely not as a gift. What did he want in return?"

Nith Sahor smiled. "He wanted to be named regent; he wanted the salamuuun trade stripped from the Ashera Consortium and given to him."

"Did the Comradeship agree?"

"He is regent, that much they have granted. But as for the salamuuun trade . . . Well, let us just say that I was able to table that decision for the moment."

"What would you have me do? Find The Pearl?"

Nith Sahor raised a gloved hand. "Why do you say that, Rekkk?" The Gyrgon seemed pleased by the intelligence of the question.

"You Gyrgon have been trying to find The Pearl for some time, else why all the interrogation of the Ramahan?"

"Ah, the interviews." Nith Sahor steepled his fingers. "It seems the majority of the Comradeship is obsessed with finding out what lies in the Unknown Territories on the other side of the Djenn Marre. As you do doubt know, the perpetual ice storms render the area unmappable. None of our systems can penetrate the theta radiation flux in the dense cloud layer. I, alone, have been pursuing my studies of Kundala lore and myth. In this interest, I have met with ferocious resistance from others of my kind who did not believe in the existence of The Pearl, who felt I was wasting both time and resources that were better put to use in a more . . . acceptable manner. So I needed to continue in secrecy, in my spare time."

It seemed to Rekkk that every moment he was in Nith Sahor's presence required him to reevaluate the Gyrgon. "In any event, now you must take another path, is that it?"

Nith Sahor's eyes glittered. "The Balance has changed. It is an evil, dangerous change—but one that, regrettably, is necessary."

"You are speaking now of Morcha and Stogggul," Rekkk said bitterly.

"They are, of course, part of the equation."

"Would you mind being a tad more specific?"

"I have discovered an alarming and thoroughly disturbing secret: Kundala appears to be a nexus point in our history."

"Future or past?"

"I do not know. Perhaps both." Nith Sahor appeared deathly serious. "A clock is ticking, Rekkk, and believe me when I tell you this ticking is most ominous."

After a hearts-pounding moment, Rekkk nodded. "I suppose you leave me no choice."

"Oh, there is always choice, Rekkk." Gyrgon sat forward again. "What else is life but a dance of choices?"

"What is it you want me to do, exactly?" He shifted uneasily. "You know I was joking when I mentioned The Pearl."

"It is no joke, Rekkk. The Pearl must be found if all of us are to survive. The Ring has been used by my colleagues in a most injudicious manner. Against all my protests, they tried to use it to open the Door to the Storehouse."

"I do not see the problem. That is what it is meant for, isn't it?"

"Among other things, yes. But according to Kundalan legend, the Door can be opened only by the hereditary leader of the Ramahan, or the Anointed One."

"The Dar Sala-at?"

"Yes." Nith Sahor's star-sapphire eyes were glittering.

"But the Dar Sala-at is part of a folktale. He doesn't really exist."

"He exists, Rekkk. Of that I have no doubt. The Ring of Five Dragons has already killed three Gyrgon. It remains affixed to the Storehouse Door, a kind of time bomb whose mechanism we cannot even guess. Only the Dar Sala-at can stop the process the Gyrgon foolishly set in motion. You must find him and bring him safely back to the Storehouse by the ides of Lonon—less than four weeks from now. Otherwise, everyone on Kundala will be destroyed in a series of cataclysmic seismic quakes."

Rekkk felt a shiver of terror go through him. "You could leave the planet, return to your explorations of the universe."

"I could, but I will not."

"Every V'ornn on Kundala could be evacuated."

"But not the Kundalan."

Rekkk stared at the Gyrgon. "I would expect the Comradeship, at least, to be clamoring to leave."

"True enough." Nith Sahor inclined his head. "If any of my colleagues knew, I am certain they would take the first transport off-world."

"They do not know?"

"There were four Gyrgon outside the Storehouse Door the morning they tried to use the Ring. I am the only one left alive. The Comradeship knows only the Ring is lethal to us, nothing more."

Rekkk let out a long-held breath. "You are playing a deadly game."

"Both of us, Rekkk." Nith Sahor spread his hands. "We have been given no choice. It is, it seems, our fate."

"You are giving me an impossible task." Rekkk was shaking his head. "In the matter of finding the Dar Sala-at, I wouldn't even know where to start."

Nith Sahor appeared prepared for that question. "As it happens, in that regard you have the best resource close at hand."

"I do not understand."

"Ah, but you will, Rekkk. This I guarantee."

"I hate it when you talk in riddles."

"I know." Nith Sahor smiled. "Now say whatever it is you need to say."

"All right. If I am going to do this I want my payment now."

"That is highly irregular."

"It's a deal-breaker, believe me. Take it or leave it."

"I will take it. Name your price."

Rekkk stood. "I want Giyan to be able to see Annon again."

"Impossible. He is dead."

"Yes, but his birth-caul still exists. Wennn Stogggul has it."

Nith Sahor leapt up. Green ion-driven fire leapt from his

gloves, arced about the chamber. "What you ask is . . . impertinent."

"But it *is* possible, isn't it?" He had heard rumors of Gyrgon raising the dead for short periods to commune with them.

"It is, but it has never been attempted with any other than Gyrgon."

"Nevertheless, this is my price."

The cold fire abruptly died in Nith Sahor's hands. "All right," the Gyrgon said.

Rekkk was listening very carefully. Was it his imagination, or had Nith Sahor given in too quickly. Rekkk could not shake the uneasy sensation that the Gyrgon had somehow expected this very price.

"Rekkk," Nith Sahor was saying now, "know this is not a matter to be undertaken lightly. There is great risk involved—to you and to the Kundalan female, as well as to myself. To do what you ask I must conjure antienergy. It does not belong in our universe and is, therefore, a deadly menace. It must be closely confined. Come too near, even for a split instant, and you will be obliterated. Do I make myself clear?"

"Perfectly."

"All right, then. There are preparations to be made. In three days' time, at the hour of midnight, return here with Giyan. The Visitation will be enacted."

Rekkk nodded, turned to leave.

"Rekkk—"

He turned back, waiting.

"No illusions, please. Annon will not be reborn; he will not live or even be alive as we understand the term. The Visitation will last a very short time. Giyan must be fully cognizant of this."

"I understand, Nith Sahor."

The Gyrgon shimmered, morphed back into Mastress Kannna. Despite his training, Rekkk shivered. Being witness to the manipulation of the stuff of life was profoundly unsettling.

Mastress Kannna regarded him levelly. "You must consider the consequences of our pact one last time. Once we leave this chamber it is irrevocable."

Rekkk felt his stomachs plummet. "I understand."

Mastress Kanna smiled her strange smile. "I chose well, Rekkk. You ask for payment—anything that is within my power—and what do you choose? Reinstatement for yourself? Death for those who have wronged you? Wealth beyond measure? No. Your wish it to ease the anguish of a Kundalan female."

"My life is an open data-sheet to you, isn't it?"

"Not quite," Mastress Kannna said. "I am not God."

"It is common knowledge that Gyrgon do not believe in a god."

Mastress Kannna smiled more broadly, more enigmatically as she ushered him out into the hushed corridor, where the new world awaited.

13

Heavenly Rushing

As every acolyte at the abbey knew, the most onerous duty was to take the monthly rations upland to the Ice Caves. These rations were for a good purpose: to help feed the Kundalan castoffs, undesirables, and petty criminals excised from society. These unfortunates lived high in the Djenn Marre, under the crushing physical conditions of constant cold, wind, snow, frost, and thinned oxygen. The trek up from the abbey was a difficult one under the best of conditions. But when the sudden and unpredictable weather kicked up ice storms or cyclone-force winds it was nothing short of perilous. Nevertheless, acolytes made the monthly trips without fail. Not that any of them had ever seen the misfits—nor did they want to. They simply emptied their full packs inside the Ice Caves and retreated as quickly as was practicable. That was not as easy as it sounded, for the descent was invariably made during the darkening of the late afternoon, the acolytes were tired from the trip up and from taking in less oxygen. Almost invariably, the weather worsened as the day wore on. Certainly the biting winds picked up.

All of these factors were on Riane's mind as she shifted her heavy pack, making her way through the dense kuello-fir forest, up the steep, rocky path that led toward the Ice Caves. The path was quite narrow, twisting this way and that through the boulders and kuello-firs that marched up the mountainside toward the tree line. She moved carefully; there was little margin for error, for the mountain face dropped away on each side with dizzying suddenness. The air was thin; the sun, blazing whitely out of a cloudless sky, burned her skin. Despite being up so high, it was brutally hot.

From time to time, she stopped, breathing deeply. She used those moments to drink water, bite off a chunk of food concentrate, and wonder why she didn't go through with her plan to make her way back to Axis Tyr so that she could kill Kinnnus Morcha and Wennn Stogggul for the murderous crimes they had committed. But when she thought about the reality of her revenge, she was plunged into complete despair. She was without status, coins, or allies. She had thought briefly of trying to get in touch with Kurgan, but Kurgan would never believe that Riane was Annon. N'Luuura, half the time Riane did not believe it herself!

She had had a good plan, she knew that much. She had stayed up three nights straight reading *Utmost Source*. In that time, she had read and memorized the entire *Five Sacred Books of Miina*. How she was able to do this she had not the slightest idea. Annon had been bright and quick, but it had taken him months to master modern-day Kundalan. This abrupt disconnect and all the others she had been experiencing kept her off-balance, oddly unsure of who she was. There were times when Annon's masculine warrior personality felt as if he were drowning in a sea of confused alien emotions he found repellent. However, this same part of Riane had to admit these female feelings often came in handy when dealing with those around her.

In any event, as a consequence of her all-night vigils, she had missed morning devotions. Bartta was quick to punish her, as Riane knew she would be. The worst detail Bartta could give her was the Ice Cave run. Just what Riane had wanted. But now, freed from the walls of the abbey, she decided not to run for her freedom. Freedom? That was a laugh.

Kundalan—especially the females who Annon knew only too well were often prey to V'ornn males—had no freedom. And, of course, Bartta knew that, which was why she obviously had had no compunction about allowing Riane to walk out the abbey gate. No, when Riane thought about it rationally, the only recourse was to stay the course, gain power—learning Kyofu would surely help!—and wait for the proper time to take her revenge.

Revenge.

She started; it sounded like an echo in her mind. She quickly swallowed the mix of dried nuts, cured herbs, and honey, put her water bottle away, began again to climb. Out here, in the mountains, she felt extraordinarily good, as if she were coming home. She thought again of her alien memories of rough escarpments, glittering ice fields, sheer cliffs, of her sudden knowledge of breathing in thinned air, of her memorization skills, of being able to read Old Tongue Kundalan. And, that night, the voice that seemed to emanate from deep inside her. *Open the book*, it had said as if it already knew that the book was *Utmost Source*.

Had she encountered Riane—the real Riane, Annon had pushed aside while her body had been on the cusp of death? Had Riane, in truth, not died? Was part of her still present, emerging and receding like a tide? That would explain everything: her new abilities, the alien memories of places Annon had never been to, the mercurial changes of temperament and emotions.

"Riane?" Riane whispered to herself. "Are you there? Are

you hiding from me? I won't hurt you, you know."

A bird cawed, startling her, and she looked around, laughing at the way she was talking to herself as if she were a mad V'ornn. What did the Kundalan call their insane?

Tchakira.

Riane froze. It was the same voice that had echoed in her just before. Once, she had asked Bartta to tell her about Riane. Bartta had said testily: *Forget her. She had no memory of home, parents, who she was. She was Riane, but her given name was the beginning and the end of it. She was a meaningless rune.*

Maybe Bartta was wrong.

"Are you there?" she whispered to herself, but there was no reply. She supposed she could hardly blame Riane for hiding. When you stopped to consider, this present Riane was a living metaphor. Annon, the V'ornn, had invaded her body, and now here a V'ornn sat, lording it over a Kundalan yet again.

"I'm not lording it over anyone," she said.

Inside her, silence. But she sensed something listening, waiting.

With that in mind, Riane redoubled her pace.

Already, the path had steepened considerably, but she kept up her pace, testing her body's endurance. The wind howled around the craggy rock cornices. Gradually, the kuello-firs had given way to stunted, weather-twisted briar firs and scrub-wood. At this altitude, the sun burned in a sky that was green around the horizon, an eerie purple overhead. After her time inside the abbey, her skin felt as if it was on fire. The heat was a palpable presence. Clouds appeared as they might to a bird, revealing more of their tops, scudding by at a quicker pace, shredded by winds and the bony fingers of dark basalt and glittering schist. There were no gimnopedes or other small birds up this high. This was the exclusive territory of the large predator birds—stone-falcons, muer-hawks, and the like. They used the altitude to drift on the thermal currents, scanning the countryside below, diving down quickly, silently, surely to snatch an ice-hare or baby snow-fox in talon or beak and swoop back up to their eyries.

Bartta had given her a map—a crude thing of tanned cor
hide—much scarred and stained. In fact, she harbored the
suspicion that several of the stains were dried blood. She had
still made no friends among the acolytes, and what attention
accrued her came in the form of derision. This was never
more apparent than when she had been setting out for the
Ice Caves. Her punishment had spread through the abbey like
wildfire. Acolytes jeered, and not a few of them gleefully
reminded her of the handful of doomed acolytes who had
never returned from the journey on which she was about to
embark.

Annon had never been jeered at or been made fun of, but
Giyan had, many times. Annon had seen how Kundalan
shopkeepers spat on the ground when she walked away from
their establishments; he had seen the smirks on male V'ornn
faces as she passed them, heard the muttered invectives, "the
regent's skcettta." Now Riane found herself wondering
whether Giyan had been aware of those slurs. If she had,
Annon was certain she had never let them affect her. If Giyan
could be that strong of spirit, so could Riane.

There was an ache inside Riane when she thought of Giyan. It astonished her how much she missed Giyan. She
thought of how often Annon had taken Giyan for granted,
the times he had been angry at her, had taunted her, been
cold to her. She thought of how often Giyan had tended
Annon when he had been ill or frightened or had been disappointed when Eleusis had canceled a visit. How she had
joked with him, made him laugh, told him incredible tales
of Kundala, of Miina, of Seelin, Eshir, Gom, Paow, and
Yig—the Five Sacred Dragons. Riane knew them all: their
colors, their personalities, their traits. From an early age they
had fascinated Annon. She remembered how Annon used to
play with the carvings on the wall of his father's antechamber, even though at first he had had to stand on a chair to
touch them. Seelin, green Dragon of water, of Transformation; Eshir, blue Dragon of the air, of Forgiveness; Gom,
yellow Dragon of the earth, of Renewal; Paow, black Dragon

of wood, of Vision; Yig, red Dragon of fire, of Power. Seelin was mercurial, Eshir was swift and sure, Gom was slow and steady, Paow was the mediator, Yig was hot-tempered and impatient. Giyan had told him elaborate tales of the Dragon courtships: Eshir and Gom had fallen in love in a shower of racing meteors, Paow and Yig had joined in the gigantic crater of Shallmha, the largest volcano of a chain on the southern continent, their lovemaking causing the largest eruption in Kundala's history. Annon had found these stories—touching, funny, scary—endlessly fascinating, and now Riane recalled them with a certain pleasure. Silently, she thanked Giyan for this legacy, even while her heart ached in its loneliness. When she thought about it, she had a great deal to thank Giyan for.

She came around a switchback turn in the path. Jagged, blue-grey boulders rose up on each side, creating a difficult, narrow defile. Threading her way through, she heard something scream. Lifting her head, she saw a gigantic gyreagle. She watched with eyes shaded by her hand as it glided through the sunlight, its shadow splashing across the rough rock faces. The gyreagle was almost directly overhead. It circled the defile three times before dropping below the tops of the boulders. In a way, Riane thought, Annon's strange journey began with a gyreagle. If the gyreagle hadn't attacked him, leaving its talon buried in his side, he never would have felt the throbbing, never would have left Giyan's chambers. He would have been caught up in the coup, murdered like his father. Instead, he had found the hidden passageway down to the Kundalan Storehouse, and there had encountered the Dragon, Seelin, who had healed him. In a way, Riane thought now, it was the gyreagle talon that had led him to the Dragon. As if it had all been meant to be.

Riane felt a little tremor run through her as she kept moving cautiously through the defile. To do so she was obliged to swing her pack off her back, hold it at her side so she could slip through the narrowest places. The V'ornn inside her was instinctively uneasy as this was a perfect spot for an attack. Of course she told herself over and over there was no one to attack her. Nevertheless, she did not take a full breath until she had passed through the defile.

The path on the north side was a bit wider, though steeper still, and more difficult to climb since moss and lichen were embedded in the moist ground. She was about to check her map, but found that she did not need to. Just as she knew the moss and lichen underfoot came from constant runoff, she knew what she would see within the next half kilometer. Again, she felt a wave of uncertainty, a loss of a sense of self. But, now, mingled with that was a glimmer of light, and of hope.

"Riane, unless I am completely mistaken, this is your territory," she whispered. "I am going to rely on you to guide me."

Hurrying on, she cocked an ear, heard the dim roar of falling water.

Heavenly Rushing, she heard in her mind.

The path pitched downward a little, and she began to run, her heart pounding fast with elation. Water ran off to either side, dribbling in small rivulets that darkened the rocks. Now the ground rose, winding through a graveyard of boulders that looked to be the result of an ancient rockslide. Scrambling over them, she heard the roaring increase. Then she was over the summit, looking down at a sight that took her breath away.

Heavenly Rushing, Miina's sacred waterfall, rose up for hundreds of meters, towering into the purple sky. Curtains of water cascaded down, lifting veils of mist into the air, creating sparks of light and minirainbows that flashed in and out of existence as she ran, laughing, toward its base. It was an odd feeling, this shock of first sight underlain by a sense of familiarity. Just as odd, it seemed, was that she was getting used to the duality, even to enjoy it.

Annon had heard Giyan speak of Heavenly Rushing many times, for it held a particular place in the myths of the Kundalan. It was there that Miina directed the Five Sacred Dragons to dip their tails, for it was said that the pool of water at the bottom of Heavenly Rushing went down to the center of Kundala. Other myths told of Kundalan Queens—when there were Queens in the time before the Long Becoming—doing battle there, vying for territorial control of Kundala in defiance of the basic precepts of the Great Goddess. Deaf to Her voice, they continued decimating each other's armies until Miina caused the cascading waters of Heavenly Rushing to become blood, sweeping away the warring Queens and their minions. *"Bloodthirsty you are,"* She had cried in Her wrath. *"Blood you shall drink until you drown and are no more."*

Thus were born the modern-day Kundalan, from the headwaters that fed Heavenly Rushing. Above those headwaters lay Riane's destination, the Ice Caves.

It was the hour before noon, Riane having made excellent time. She was hot and sticky with the sweat and grime of hard travel. At the spume-hidden edge of the pool, she threw down her pack and bathed in the spray of the sacred waters. She threw her head back, stared up at the huge sheets of water, so brilliantly white they might have been cascades of fine, granulated sugar. Taking in the grandeur of the falls, she felt almost happy, in that special way one feels on coming home. She unlaced her boots, tied up her acolyte's robes around her hips, and dangled her bare feet in the icy water. So close to the falls, she was completely immersed in the mist. The roaring was a physical sensation, vibrating through her like the heart of a machine. The icy sensation crawled up her legs, numbing their ache. She bowed her head and, without conscious thought, began to recite the devotions.

Up until now, they had seemed a meaningless jumble of phrases and stupid pieties. But here at the fountainhead of the Great Goddess she began to discern a thread. She slipped into the pool, walking out until she was waist deep. Again, that peculiar sensation of newness and familiarity. She was certain that Riane had bathed here many times. Her robes pooled around her like the wings of Miina's butterfly, fluttering in the wavelets. As she continued her devotions she seemed able to stand apart, to hear the words and make sense of them as if she were observing herself. Odd for a V'ornn to have this thought, but she was certain this place was holy. Inexplicably, she began to cry, tears rolling freely down her cheeks. She felt filled up with the enchanted beauty of this spot, that seemed to have appeared from out of a dream.

She launched herself into the deep water. She turned over, floated on her back. The lowering mist was the most beautiful translucent white. Within its constantly changing heart colors were born and died like tiny flames. As the sunlight struck them, the billowing clouds of mist took on shapes, as if she were dreaming with her eyes open. She saw tantalizing snippets of Riane's life before she had contracted duur fever: faces she did not recognize, hulking shapes like monsters, vast icescapes, blood flying and a thin screaming as death came.

The water grew even colder as she floated out toward the center of the pool. There, the water was almost black, and she could well believe that it was virtually bottomless. A small breeze stirred the mist, sending long tendrils down to scud across the turbulent water. She was still a good distance from the base of Heavenly Rushing, but she could feel its immense power. For some reason, it had a special meaning for her. She strained to bring into focus emotions, thoughts, experiences that remained hazy and unreadable in an alien memory that had lost its focus. "Why blood, who was screaming?" she cried, enraged again at the deaths of Annon's family, of the injustice of it all.

High above her head, above the mist, on the cliff face where the falls spilled down, a snow-lynx that had come to drink from the headwaters skittered away as two large shapes loomed out of the forest of Marre pines. As they stood in the deep shadows at the lip of the cliff staring down, the huge gyreagle descended from the bowl of the sky. It alighted on the shoulder of one of the shapes, began fastidiously cleaning itself of the droplets of ice-hare blood.

Can she see us? thought the first creature.

Not through the mist, the other replied. *But if I do this . . .*

An appendage moved out past the rim. *It will seem as if a breeze has stirred the water vapor.*

Many tangled threads come together here.

She is the fulcrum and the lever.

Will she find it? one thought.

She must, the other replied. *If not . . .*

What if she is not the One? If she is not the One, she will fail and we are lost.

She is the One. Miina has told us in so many ways—Her messengers, the gyreagle and the owl, marked them; they were both injured before they were brought together in the annealing fire and storm of the Nanthera.

That is what frightens me. The holy circle of the Nanthera was violated, if only for a moment. Even we do not know the ultimate consequences of that.

All the more reason to believe in the Prophesy. It is this very imperfection, which binds two incomplete souls, that has forged the One.

The first creature peered down through the veils of billowing mist. *Already she has powerful enemies.*

The imperfection that created her also binds her to her enemies. There is no other possible path.

If they find her before she is ready, they will crush her like a marc-beetle. She must choose her allies carefully.

Indeed. One will love her, one will betray her, one will try to destroy her.

The gyreagle's feathers rustled as she lifted her great wings, disturbed perhaps by the grave nature of the conversation.

The first creature resumed, *I am filled with foreboding. It was prophesied that the Dar Sala-at's coming would coincide with the possibility of Miina's death. Miina may die, and we cannot save her.*

That is true enough. Only the Dar Sala-at holds that chance. The only chance.

The first creature shuddered. *If the Great Goddess dies, we die, even us Immortals.*

The second creature nodded. *Yes. Kundalan, V'ornn, Us. It will be Anamordor, the End of All Things.*

Our enemies have begun recruiting allies—many against the few of us who are left.

We have the Dar Sala-at.

Perhaps we should provide . . .

No, no. We are forbidden to interfere.

Simply by being here we have interfered. Surely we can take one step further. The first creature extended both upper appendages, and it was as if a shadow passed across the sun. The gyreagle spread its wings, launching itself into the air. *There. Thigpen will know about the Dar Sala-at as we now know.*

The second creature followed the huge bird's flight. *Ah, no! If Thigpen is forewarned, who else will be alerted?*

With the stirring of the mist came strange voices in Riane's head. Not Riane's voice, and not Annon's, either. It was as if she sat at one end of a shell-like theater, listening to a conversation being held on the other side. The strange acoustics picked up the sounds—an eerie susurrus as of wind echoing through an old, abandoned house. These voices stirred up odd ideas and emotions inside her, so that she grew by turns elated and terrified, as if she were a baby who could not yet understand the language of her parents. She stopped her floating and, treading water, strained to make comprehensible what was not. In a moment, the mist darkened as if with the fall of night. When the brightness returned, the conversation had ceased.

Riane looked around as if ghosts or spirits or even daemons might be observing her, but past a few meters the billowing mist hid everything from view. Weighed down by her sopping robes, she climbed back onto shore. Her pack and boots were where she had left them; nothing had been disturbed. She walked away from the spray, into a patch of intense sunlight, stripped off her clothes. She had a small but nutritious lunch while her robes dried. As she ate, she strolled around the base of the immense waterfall. She drank in the beauty as before, but now she had another agenda. What language had the unknown being been speaking? It seemed vaguely familiar, but . . .

Old Tongue, the voice in her head said.

"How is it you know the Kundalan Old Tongue? Were you Ramahan from some other abbey?" Riane asked, but there was no reply.

By the time she returned to her robes, they were dry enough for her to put on. She tugged on her boots, shouldered her pack and set off toward the east side of the falls, where a kind of crude staircase had been hewn into the cliff face, presumably by the Ramahan, or perhaps it was Riane's tribe, whoever they might be.

As she renewed her assault on the cliff face, she recalled the story Astar had told her of how The Pearl came to be lost. How, she wondered, could Ramahan turn on one another, murder their own, use the Kundalan's most sacred object for their own ends? What kind of creatures were the Ramahan instructors turning out, what kind of society existed within the abbeys that could breed such evil?

Once upon a time, Astar had said, the abbeys of the Ramahan were impervious to evil. How had that changed, and why? At the center of all these questions stood Bartta, like a spider in her web. Everyone inside the abbey was afraid of her, even the other konara. *Utmost Source* taught that Ramahan did not amass power, they distributed it evenly among the Kundalan. And yet, it seemed clear that Bartta was doing just the opposite.

Riane clutched her head. These days when she thought about Bartta's evil her head began to throb with intense pain.

Relax and breathe.

Closing her eyes for a moment, she rested her sweat-streaked forehead against the naked rock. This high up, she could feel the changes the altitude wrought in the weather. Though the sun still burned in the purple sky, the temperature had dropped considerably, and the biting wind had picked up. She shivered. It was High Summer. What would this trek be like in winter? Instantly, a memory surfaced of howling winds, white-out blizzards, temperatures that sucked the warmth out of flesh and bone.

She licked her lips, thirsty. But she did not have the leverage to reach behind her for her water bottle. She knew she had to distract herself so she could keep going, mechanically climbing until she reached the top. She resisted the urge to look down. Annon, like his father, had a kind of vertigo. But when she did look down she felt no vertigo at all. Instead, she had the unmistakable sensation that she belonged on this cliff face, that high altitudes were something exhilarating and energizing.

She continued her ascent with renewed confidence, grateful for Riane's innate abilities. It was odd how things had changed so rapidly. She no longer felt invaded when Riane's memories or abilities bubbled up. Her emotions were a bit more difficult to deal with, however. As she went, she turned her mind to the section of *Utmost Source* on the Spirit House.

Accessing the Spirit House is not to be undertaken lightly, for the risks when the two planes of existence intersect are legion. First and foremost, the planes are essentially incompatible. The corporeal and the noncorporeal may stand side by side; they may, in a few highly specific instances which will be enumerated later, exist one within the other. But under no circumstances are they interchangeable. If the noncorporeal should be allowed to cross into the corporeal without the proper safeguards and supervision, the resultant derangement would be terrible to witness, unimaginable to experience.

Riane had read in the first chapter of the book that there were three hundred ninety-seven known planes of existence; an infinite number lay unknown and unexplored. According to Scripture, these realms of reality overlay one another like an unimaginably immense multitiered sphere. Each one had what Astar had described as an orbit (though the *Utmost Source* text referred to it as an energy harmonic) so that at any given time they were nearer or farther from one another. Riane had tried to imagine an infinite number of layers all moving in different rhythms peculiar to their own harmonics, but failed. In the time when *Utmost Source* was written the Ramahan's chief purpose was apparently discovering and exploring new planes of existence, though now, it seemed, the priestesses were caught up in far more mundane matters. This ability to move between planes was called Thripping.

> *The second risk to Thripping involves energy flow—or behavior. Everything in the known and unknown universe conforms to principles of energy. These energy behaviors are not always known to us. They are surely not the same for the many different planes of existence, but they are unwaveringly consistent within their own set of principles. Therefore, it is essential for High Ramahan to be conversant with as many sets of principles of energy behavior as is practicable.*

The book went on to enumerate the ways in which the energy behavior of the Spirit House differed from those of the Kundalan corporeal universe. This was the key to understanding how to access the energy from that ethereal place. No mention was made of qi. It dawned on Riane, as she chewed over the densely worded paragraphs, that the book was discussing Thripping without the use of the sacred needles—just as Astar had told her Mother used to do in the time before she was murdered by her own shima.

"*There are always alternative paths,*" Astar had said. Riane wondered now whether the Nanthera was one of those alternatives. Surely during the rite Annon had walked upon ground that was not firm. He had peered into the heart of the Abyss, had seen the five-headed daemon grinning at him . . .

Enough! Riane shivered. She was frightening herself. And yet her thoughts kept returning to the poisoned well for that horrible moment, when Annon spanned two worlds, two planes of existence, was affected by two separate energy flows. What had really happened to him there? What had happened to Riane—the Riane who had died from duur fever?

It does not matter. Go on.

What else *could* she do?

She commenced once more to climb, her fierce V'ornn determination meshing with the Kundalan expert knowledge of this cliff face, and this time she did not stop until she reached the top. Hauling herself over the lip of the cliff, she emerged onto the upper plateau not very far from where the creatures had hours before discussed her fate. Almost all the slopes above her were crusted in snow, which the wind whipped downward, lacing the thin air with showers of sparkles. She sat in the shade of a Marre pine while she drank and ate a little. At this elevation the air was noticeably thinner, her lungs had to work harder to get the same amount of oxygen into her system, and yet, as had happened when Konara Laudenum had made her enter the Cube of Tutelage, she found that she had no trouble breathing. Nor did the growing cold disturb her. She was beginning to feel a power long hidden, a sense of self-reliance returning that Annon had once had, that Riane, too, had had, before the terrible events that had overtaken them both. For it seemed clear to Riane that the girl she had once been had tragically lost her parents, just as Annon had lost his.

Soul mates.

She smiled to herself as she spread out her map on the soft bed of Marre pine needles and took a look at where she was. *I'm almost to the Ice Caves,* she thought even before she was fully oriented. She knew that she had only to negotiate the icefall at the northern end of the narrow plateau, and she would have reached her goal.

As it was growing late, she gathered her belongings and began the short trek to the base of the icefall. Within several hundred meters the stands of Marre pines disappeared, to be replaced for a time by low, twisted brush that by its pale grayish color looked more dead than alive. Finally, those too petered out, and all that remained was bleak tundra—bare rock and permanently frozen subsoil that supported grey-green lichen and not much more.

By a mountaineer's standards the icefall wasn't large, but from its base it looked intimidating enough. Annon had never encountered this kind of terrain. No matter. Without a moment's hesitation, Riane unhooked the narrow-bladed ice ax from her pack and began her ascent. The part of her that was still Annon was astonished at the ease and facility with which this body transported itself over the jumbled, glossy surfaces. For once, the female's lighter weight and less dense bones were a distinct advantage. Riane had no difficulty leaping over seemingly bottomless chasms, hauling herself up virtually vertical expanses via the hand- and boot-holds she hacked into the ice with the ax. Moreover, she instinctively knew the best and fastest path up. It felt good to be stretching her muscles, to be doing instead of thinking.

Inside of two hours, she had reached the Ice Caves. They were gargantuan holes in the upper face of the mountain. At the mouth she felt as dwarfed as if she were on a raft in the middle of the Sea of Blood. She walked inside. Her legs ached, but in a good way. She slid off her pack, stacked the contents just inside the mouth. The floor was almost unnaturally smooth and, owing to the immense size of the caves, even the tiniest sounds were magnified and iterated.

While it felt good to put down her burden she found that she was restless. There was something about the caves, something familiar—the light, perhaps or a smell—that reminded her of home. She was at once gripped by an intense desire to find out what it was. She could see numerous signs of habitation, not the least of which were several fire pits. Stacked along one wall were cords of well-seasoned firewood. She brought several pieces of firewood to the nearest pit and, with emergency material from her pack, got a fire going. She picked out a thinnish length of wood and shoved one end into the flames. In a moment, she had a kind of makeshift torch.

Taking her water bottle with her, she began to explore the caves. Unlike the other acolytes, she felt no fear of the outcasts who lived up here, despite the many stories she had heard of their fierce, bloodthirsty existence, their unwavering enmity toward the Kundalan who enforced their exile. On the other hand, she was constantly on the lookout for perwillon scat. Having come upon one once, she had no desire to repeat the encounter.

She fancied she could feel the lure of the Unknown Territories, which lay beyond the impenetrable barrier of ferocious ice storms that constantly scoured the land beyond the immense jagged pinnacles of the Djenn Marre. In Axis Tyr, Annon had often stared out at the misty mountain range, wondering what lay on the other side, although everyone knew perfectly well: a dread wilderness rendered uninhabitable by a climate so harsh even the Khagggun in their off-world armor couldn't survive. So why give a clemett about it? Riane did not know. Each day of her new life it seemed more questions arose than she could possibly answer.

When she had mentioned this gush of unanswerable questions to Astar, the leyna was not perplexed. On the contrary, she had laughed, and said: *My dear Riane, how wonderful! In a trice you have identified the very nature of life.*

Now she had a sense of what Astar meant. She felt drawn forward as she followed a thread of questions. Every time she came upon an answer, that answer opened up another question along the thread.

She paused for a moment, listening. With every step she took the floor made an eerie crackling sound. She swept the torch in an arc in front of her, saw that the cavern floor was strewn with thin, shalelike shards of rock. She picked one up and crushed it easily in her hand. *Odd*, she thought. *This rock ought to be igneous, not sedimentary.* All at once, she was swept by a feeling of danger. The next moment, her boot crunched through the floor of the cavern. She tried desperately to right herself, but in so doing her other boot went through. Her weight opened up a hole in the floor, and she plummeted down perhaps four or five meters. She landed hard, grunting as the air went out of her. Her torch went rolling, and she scrambled after it. Her robe was wet, and she moved the torch over. Her water bottle had broken. She looked above her head, saw that she had fallen between what appeared to be two beams or bars of solid rock. They were seamed and cracked, weakened by a series of seismic shocks. She did not see any way she could climb back up.

Don't panic.

She didn't. Instead, she decided to have a careful look around. This lower cave seemed to be a roughly circular chamber not more than fifteen meters in diameter. There was no exit that she could see. The chamber was sealed save for the hole she had made when she had fallen through. The floor was a thick bed of the brittle slatelike shards, the walls smooth as V'ornn viewing crystal, except where a huge rockfall had piled the slate shards all the way up to the ceiling. Riane paused, holding her torch higher. The walls were covered with paintings—ancient by the look of them. They reminded her of the murals in the garden at the regent's palace in Axis Tyr, except there were more. Some walls depicted strange, menacing beasts, golden with black spots, great snapping jaws filled with razor-sharp teeth, and even stranger Kundalan with towering bodies and five faces—

Her finger traced the lines of the ferocious spotted beasts. Something about these beasts struck a chord deep inside her; they should have terrified her, but somehow they didn't. What were they? She wished with all her heart that she could ask Giyan.

Abruptly, she took a sudden step back, her breath coming in quick, hot gasps. Her gaze, roving still over the paintings, had come upon the vivid depictions of the creation myths of the Kundalan race. Arrayed before her in all their splendor were the major participants: the five Sacred Dragons, the great Goddess Miina, and Pyphoros, the personification of evil. The sight of him caressing the back of one of the spotted beasts made her flesh crawl; it brought back in a rush Annon's moment in the Abyss, where the terrifying presence had turned its five faces in his direction and grinned.

He knows who I am, Riane thought now, *and where I am.* Sweat poured off her and her pulse pounded. *Why does he care about me? Who am I to be of interest to Pyphoros?*

She continued to circle the cavern, studying the paintings, as if they might provide an answer. She saw unfolding the panoply of Kundalan lore, and with each step she took she began almost unconsciously to match up the scenes with sections of *Utmost Source.*

The light flickered and she saw that the torch had burned down faster than she had anticipated or perhaps she had been absorbed by the mystical paintings longer than she had imagined. A quick stab of panic pierced her as darkness lapped at the periphery of the chamber. All too soon she would be plunged into an endless night. How was she ever going to find her way out?

14

Thripping

When Rekkk Hacilar returned to his residence, he told Giyan that he was taking her out. Then he stripped, showered, and put on his finest clothes. She was ready, waiting wordlessly for him as he emerged from his quarters.

"Where are we going?" she said at last.

Her neutral words were a small triumph compared to her stony silence.

"To dinner," he said.

He, himself, rarely had the time or the inclination to dine out, but these were strange days; they called for different actions. Water Spring was a Kundalan-run cafe on the eastern edge of the market district. Few V'ornn went there, which was one of the reasons he chose it. The other was that he hoped Giyan would like it, or at least feel comfortable there.

For the hundredth time, he touched the small leather box

in his pocket. Inside was the present he had bought for her at the shop Nith Sahor had recommended. As the green-robed female ushered them to a table in back, he decided that he had never been this nervous, not even before his first kill.

Water Spring was built in the shape of a triangle, an ancient and sacred Kundalan shape. It had lacquered-bamboo walls and a beautifully scrolled bleached ammonwood bar along one side. A skylight let in the deep cerulean of the evening sky, bathing the candlelit diners. He had deliberately not worn his uniform, but there was no mistaking that he was a V'ornn, and their entrance caused something of a stir. A sinuous melody began, played by a trio of reed-thin Kundalan musicians; eventually everyone went back to their food.

"Have you eaten here?" Rekkk asked.

Giyan glared at him. Her hands were carefully folded in her lap.

Rekkk ordered them cloudy rakkis. When they were alone, he produced the small square leather box, placed it on the table, and pushed it toward her.

"What is that?"

Giyan was eyeing it with such suspicion that he almost swept it back into his pocket. Ever the good warrior, he bit his lip and pressed on. "It is a gift."

"You wasted your coins. I do not want it."

"Take a look at it, at least."

When she made no move, he opened the box. Despite herself, her eyes were drawn to the contents. He heard her tiny gasp of breath.

"Nephilia seeds!" She took the box in her hand. "Where did you find them?"

"I called upon an apothecary friend. He does a trade in esoteric Kundalan herbs."

"But Nephilia. I have never seen them before."

"They are sorcerous in origin, I understand. Among other things, they are said to heal a broken heart."

"It is true," she said quietly.

There was a pause while their drinks were set upon the table. Rekkk waved the waiter away.

Carefully, almost reverently, Giyan closed the box. "I cannot accept the Nephilia."

His hearts sank. "Why not?"

She looked up at him, her gaze piercing right through him. "Because it comes from you."

And that seemed to be that. But Rekkk was not used to being defeated, and he also had Nith Sahor's word that she *would* love him, of her own free will. He poured the cloudy rakkis, but she refused to drink. When he asked her what she would like to eat, she replied, "Nothing."

He leaned forward. "Giyan, I struck you. I promised I wouldn't touch you, but I did. I am sorry. But you must see, you drove me—"

"Now this is *my* fault?" Her face was full of fury.

"No, of course not. I did not mean—"

"It's what you said."

"Words," he said, and smiled at her through all his pain. It was one of the most difficult things he had ever done. He leaned even closer. "Giyan, I swear to you this is true. The way you are acting now is killing me just as surely as if you did run me through with my own shock-sword."

"Pack-Commander—"

"Call me Rekkk, I beg you."

"Calling you Rekkk would presuppose a certain . . . intimacy that does not exist."

"I know your heart cannot be this hard."

"Once it wasn't," she said. "Your kind have made it so."

"That is your truth," he said. "What about mine?"

She shrugged. "What about it? You are V'ornn. Why should I care?"

"You cared about Eleusis Ashera's truth."

"Do not speak his name to me," she hissed.

He held up his hands. "I meant no disrespect. Just the opposite, in fact."

"If you were a friend of Eleusis's, prove it. What did he love most?"

"Besides you? He loved the Djenn Marre. He told me many times that he longed to hike along the snow-packed ridges of their spine, to learn all the mysteries they hold."

"That was Eleusis." She sat back, contemplating him. The quiet din of the cafe enfolded them, protecting them from the outside world. "So what is the truth?" she said softly. "The *real* truth."

"The truth is that Kinnnus Morcha never trusted me."

"Do you really expect me to believe that?"

"I am the son of a Rhynnnon. I have been suspect ever since my Channeling into manhood. I was forced to prove myself every step of the way."

"Yet Morcha made you his adjutant."

"That is finished. After Olnnn Rydddlin reported the incident in Stone Border I am in limbo, awaiting my punishment."

She frowned. "Why should you be punished? Morcha loves you."

"Then why did I know nothing of the coup against Eleusis Ashera?"

She appeared stunned and, for the first time, flustered. "You . . . were not part of the conspiracy? I assumed—"

"Because I followed you and Annon." Rekkk nodded. "Another part of the hidden truth: I think the Star-Admiral was testing my loyalty. What better way to see if I was allied with the former regent than to assign me to bring back his son and heir."

"What if you failed in your duty?"

"He had Olnnn Rydddlin to take care of me—and of Annon."

"Your First-Captain?"

"You see, when Kinnnus Morcha commands an off-world cadre his first order of business is setting up a series of observation posts, even if that entails extreme danger to those manning the posts. To be sure, Khaggggun die carrying out this order, but their deaths serve a larger purpose. He subscribes to the philosophy of keeping his enemies close to him, the better to monitor their activities."

She tapped a finger against her full lips. "Are you speaking of a spy?"

He nodded. "First-Captain Olnnn Rydddlin."

She seemed lost in thought for some time. At length, she said, "Why didn't Eleusis ever mention you to me?"

"I am quite certain that was deliberate," he said. "He was protecting you."

"He was good at that," she said. "We had—" Her eyes brimmed with tears. "At least if I had Annon. If I could see him one more time." She broke down, sobbing, and buried her face in her hands.

Rekkk's hearts broke to see her in such agony. "Ah, Giyan, if only you would let me help you."

She lifted her head. Her cheeks were tear-streaked. "Pack-Commander, believe me when I tell you that you are the last person who could possibly help me."

"Here's a bit of hard-won advice," he said gently. "The last person you want to help you is sometimes the only one who can."

As night cloaked the city Rekkk led Giyan to the entrance to Nimbus.

"Are you ready?" he asked.

She looked at him with her whistleflower-blue eyes, and his knees went weak. "Why are you doing this?"

"Is it important?"

"To me it is," she said, and he was grateful for the victory no matter how small. He waited. "This confuses me," she said at last.

The night was dark—moonless, starless—filled with forbidding clouds, restless on a warm, rising wind. Often, this was a sign of the morena—short, often brutal southern-latitude storms that drove across the Sea of Blood in High Summer, hammering Axis Tyr with their wrath.

"Confuses you how?"

She drew her sifeyn more tightly over her head as it was tugged by a gust of wind. She wore a thick robe with sleeves so long no one could see the thick bandages on her hands and forearms.

"I heard all the tales of your ruthlessness and brutality. You have found countless ways to murder my kind."

"I was a Khaggun," he said softly. "I followed orders."

"Yes, of course, but that is no defense," she said quickly.

"Then I will tell you that the moment I met Eleusis Ashera I began to question not only my orders, but who I was."

"You have killed."

He nodded. "Many times. As Eleusis Ashera did. You know what good lay within him, but on the day he captured you in Stone Border you knew only that he was V'ornn. He was the victor and you the vanquished."

"How that changed, in time."

They walked slowly to the door of Nimbus. The kashiggen appeared closed.

He stood soberly in front of her. He found that he had no measure for the pain in her eyes. "I know what you have lost, Giyan. Those things can never return. But I can give you back yourself."

"How so?" She cocked her head. "Did you not tell me that I was yours, whether or not it suited me? That my life is at your side?"

"I . . . misspoke. After tonight, you are free to go where you will, to do whatever you want without interference from me."

"Surely you cannot mean that."

"But I do. I would scale the obsidian fortress of N'Luuura if you asked me to."

"I would never ask that of you." The mocking tone had left her voice, another small victory.

He hesitated a moment. "Where would you choose to go?"

"I . . . do not know. I am cut adrift. Eleusis is gone and with him my life here. But I find that my time among the V'ornn has changed me. I fear I am no longer suited to my previous life."

"Then something new, something different awaits you."

Her beautiful face held a curious expression. "It has been some time since someone said that to me."

He knew she meant Eleusis Ashera. His hearts felt suddenly lighter. "Come," he said as he pulled the door open. "It is time for the Visitation."

Inside, darkness flushed ruddy by candles. She stood just inside the door, hesitating.

"What is it?"

"I find that I am afraid."

"Shall I cancel the Visitation? There is still time."

"No, I . . . I ache to see Annon again. But I . . . I must confess that the strange technomancy of the Gyrgon terrifies me. The Gyrgon are, after all, the holy engine that imbues the V'ornn with their power. The Gyrgon identified Kundala and directed the Khaggun to occupy the planet to strip it of its natural resources."

"This particular Gyrgon is different, Giyan. Trust me when I tell you this."

"The Gyrgon are notorious for their lies and ruses."

"Yes, but this one has an agenda he is keeping secret from everyone, including the rest of the Comradeship."

Giyan's eyes opened wide. "If this is true, he is playing a dangerous game."

Rekkk nodded. "One in which I have agreed to become a player."

"Do you think that wise?"

"Someone else will have to make that determination. I am no longer Khaggun. Like my father before me, I am Rhynn-non. I have become the Gyrgon's disciple."

He ushered her into the hushed interior. Unlike the last time he had been there, the place was deserted. No one greeted them at the door; only a lone oil lamp flickered on the old seer's table. Giyan went to it, picked up several small animal bones, and roiled them onto the tabletop.

She gasped, backing away.

"What is it, Giyan?"

Her face was white and she was trembling. "I saw our

deaths," she moaned. "Dear Miina, we must leave—now!"

"Good evening."

Giyan started, and they turned to face the Gyrgon emerging from the shadows.

"You have brought her, ahhh!" Much to Rekkk's astonishment, the Gyrgon bowed a little to Giyan. "Lady, I am Nith Sahor."

Giyan stiffened. Rekkk saw fear in her eyes. "Why do you call me Lady?"

"Surely you know why."

"V'ornn know nothing of Kundalan affairs. You could not know."

There was a small sparkle in Nith Sahor's star-sapphire eyes. "And yet it seems I do."

Rekkk looked from one to the other without understanding what had passed between them. He was about to ask when the Gyrgon continued.

"I have waited long to meet you, Lady."

"I wonder why," Giyan said. "I was under your nose for fifteen years. You had but to instruct Eleusis to bring me to a Summoning." Rekkk saw that she had regained a semblance of her composure.

"The reasons were legion, Lady," Nith Sahor said. "The time was not yet ripe. Your presence at the Temple of Mnemonics would have alerted and alarmed my brethren. Besides, Ashera Eleusis would have resisted such a request."

"I was not aware that Eleusis resisted you in any way."

"Ah, Lady, he often found the ways to do so," Nith Sahor said. "It is this annoying and admirable quality I believe I will miss most."

"I miss everything about him," she said.

Nith Sahor lifted an arm, indicating an open doorway they had not noticed before. "The time for the Visitation grows nigh. We must prepare ourselves."

Giyan did not move. Rekkk stayed by her side.

"Have you changed your mind, Lady?" Nith Sahor inquired.

"I have rolled the seer's bones, Nith Sahor. I have seen

my death and the death of the Pack-Commander."

The Gyrgon directed his gaze toward the tabletop. "It is true, Lady. Death stalks every chamber of this establishment tonight. For the Visitation to occur, it cannot be otherwise. My technomancy draws two worlds nigh—two worlds inimical to each other. The bones could do ought but echo this anomaly. They have lost their usual reliability."

She said nothing; she had begun trembling again. "You will find him with your technomancy?"

"Yes."

"Will you be able to tell where he is?"

"That is a question not to be asked," Nith Sahor said. "Ashera Annon will appear; whence he comes even I cannot know. It would violate too many laws of the known universe."

Giyan nodded. "Miina help me, I want to see him again."

"Let it be so," Nith Sahor said as he ushered them down the long corridor that ended in the small conical chamber Rekkk had been in before.

"Giyan," Rekkk said, "how is it that a Gyrgon calls you Lady? It is not an honorific I have ever heard any Kundalan use."

"No Kundalan does," Giyan said.

Nith Sahor had that strange smile firmly affixed to his face as they entered the chamber. What is so N'Luuura amusing? Rekkk wanted to ask him, but did not.

In almost all ways the chamber looked different. It had been lacquered black. The comfortable furniture had been replaced by three concentric circles of braided germanium-alloy wire in the center of the floor within which rose a narrow three-sided scaffolding of dull grey tantalum incised with scientific runes. Affixed to this scaffolding was a series of faceted crystals embedded with networks of biochips. On the floor within the scaffolding was Annon Ashera's birth-caul. When Giyan saw it, she gave a little cry. Tears stood out at the corners of her eyes.

"Do you wish to continue, Lady?" Nith Sahor asked.

She nodded, averting her eyes from the caul.

Nith Sahor directed Rekkk to stand against the curving wall, then led Giyan to a spot just inside the innermost germanium circle. When he was satisfied, he took up his place directly across the circle from her.

"You need do nothing more than listen—and watch," he told her. "Heed my words, however. Under no circumstances should you try to touch Ashera Annon when he appears, or move at all. To do so will bring disaster upon us all. Is this clear?"

"Yes," Giyan said.

"One more thing," he said. "As I invoke the antienergy from the other world you will find it difficult to breathe. Do not struggle against this feeling. I will protect you."

Giyan inclined her head. "I understand."

"So," Nith Sahor intoned, "we begin." The Gyrgon raised his hands. Blue fire leapt from his mesh gloves, arcing to the talantum scaffolding. Instantly, it glowed with a golden hue. Even from this distance, Rekkk could feel the heat emanating from the center of the chamber. It felt as if they were inside a kiln. Already his lung was gasping for oxygen. The chamber drained of light, color, substance. Everything seemed transformed into translucent crystal. All at once, his lung stopped functioning. Antienergy ringed the room, throbbing with a lambent brilliance that made his eyes ache. Tears came to his eyes, seemed to freeze up on the surface of his lenses. The air—what remained of it—shimmered.

"He comes," Nith Sahor intoned. "Beware now. We are immersed in a poisoned singularity. One imprudent motion and we perish."

As his words died out, an image began to appear in the space between the network of crystals. It gained definition as it turned three-dimensional.

Giyan breathed Annon's name.

A *nnon."*
      Lost in the blackness of the cave, Riane's head came up. She heard Giyan calling as if from a vast distance. Like sand from an hourglass, she felt something being drained out

of Riane's body. This was followed by an agonizing sensation, as if the fabric of Riane's essence was being torn asunder. She had the eerie, breathless sensation of being in two places at once.

He was Annon again. His surroundings shimmered and morphed. He saw Giyan standing in front of him, and he called to her to help him. Then he became aware of the others: Pack-Commander Rekkk Hacilar and a Gyrgon. What was going on? He tried to ask her, but as in a dream he could not speak. He was rooted to the spot, able only to observe. He wondered at Giyan's tears, wanted to reach out for her, but he couldn't.

Like a ripple on a pond at night he became aware of something alien, malign. He looked beyond the three figures, saw a cyclopean shadow. It was striding across the vast, black ether that surrounded them all. The shadow emerged into the light. Annon wanted to scream. The five faces of Pyphoros turned in his direction and the daemon of daemons grinned.

"*I have marked you,*" Pyphoros said. "*You have become mine.*"

"No!" Annon screamed.

"*You were foretold. It is my due.*"

Annon squirmed, trying with all his might to move. But he was caught as securely as a marc-beetle in amber. The daemon's jaws hinged open. He had to do something.

Think, Riane's voice said in his mind, *of what is written.*

Desperately, he tried to think of passages in *Utmost Source* but nothing came to him. The more he tried, the further the sacred text seemed to slip from the grasp of his memory. It was as if he had never memorized it.

Pyphoros' jaws opened to an impossible angle. His five faces merged into one and grew so large it seemed to be the size of Kundala. At this rate, his mouth would engulf everything. *I am doomed,* Annon thought.

Look, Riane's voice said, *at what he carries.*

Annon saw something in Pyphoros' hand. It was a birthcaul—Annon's birth-caul. How had he gotten it? But such questions did not matter now. This was how Pyphoros had tracked him down, even here in this unknown and terrifying place.

For the first time in his life, Annon felt at a disadvantage by being V'ornn. Somehow he knew that Pyphoros, powerful as he was, had no inkling of the Riane personality. The daemon of daemons was fixated only on Annon Ashera. For an instant, Annon glimpsed something—a concept so vast, so unthinkable that he could not get his mind fully around it. Compared to Pyphoros, the V'ornn seemed weak, inconsequential, and Annon was shaken to his very core.

The space around them was beginning to roil with evil emanations. There was no more time to think. Only to act.

Annon let himself go—rushing backward into the shell of Riane. The moment he returned inside her, the agony he had felt lifted. The entire *Five Sacred Books of Miina* was hers again, and she knew what to do.

Something is wrong," Nith Sahor said.

The lambent antienergy was increasing in intensity instead of holding steady. It had stripped the walls bare, it was encircling them with a rapaciousness that was almost sentient. Three crystals exploded as their circuits overloaded. Nith Sahor redirected the ion flow from his cortical net to compensate. The blue emanations from his glove-grids pulsed at a higher rate, but it seemed to do no good. Something unknown and immensely powerful had thrown off the Master Equation. He recalculated on the fly, but the components were changing too rapidly for him to keep up. The barrier he had erected to protect them was beginning to collapse and there was nothing he could do about it.

In the midst of this chilling thought, he saw Ashera Annon move. This was impossible, and yet his eyes were showing him another truth, one so profound it shook him to his core. The image began to spin. Faster and faster it went until it was merely a blur.

Six more crystals blew, and the containment field collapsed. The lambent antienergy dived into the center of the chamber. If it touched any of them . . .

As if having a will of its own, it coalesced into a single
ball, so bright even Nith Sahor was forced to turn aside his
gaze. It dived toward the spot where Giyan stood. There was
no time to save her or even to warn her. A flash erupted so
intense it blotted out everything and everyone in the chamber.

The solution was at once supremely simple and immensely
complex. On top of that, it was impossible. And yet it
appeared to Riane as That Which Must Be.

That Which Must Be was written about often in *Utmost
Source*. It was the least likely solution, the one that could
not possibly be accomplished, the path to success that required of the one who would take it every ounce of faith
she had. You *thought* it would work and it *did* work. It was
the Way of instinct, of illogic, the Way rejected by everyone
else.

Riane conjured the required passages and did That Which
Must Be.

She sent herself Thripping.

She knew that she should not have been able to accomplish this feat. It was Mother's ability, lost to the Ramahan
for over a hundred years. Members of the current Dea Cretan,
including Bartta, had tried to Thrip and failed. The ability,
it seemed, had been lost along with *Utmost Source* and The
Pearl.

And yet, Riane sent herself Thripping.

Inhaling the instructions from the book she began to spin,
and in spinning loosed herself from the amber in which she
had been trapped. The cavern in which she sat, the chamber
in which Annon's image whirled, now fell away, flat as scen-
ery in a stage set. Beyond beckoned the true reality—an infinity of realms beyond Time or Space, beyond even Order
and Chaos, Life and Death. Here everything simply *was*.
Planets did not spin; they did not revolve around suns. There
was no gravity, no laws of astrophysics. Nothing aged, was
born or died.

Riane watched the energy fluxes with confusion. She was

instantly disoriented. The fluxes were neither lines nor circles nor any other geometrical analog. Instead, like everything else in this reality, they simply existed. Where was she? Where was she going and how was she going to get there? She couldn't walk, run, sprint, swim, crawl, or use any other imaginable means of locomotion.

And then, looming on what her mind could only conceive of as the far horizon (though it was farther or nearer than anything else around her) she saw Pyphoros. His faces swiveled this way and that, searching. She wanted desperately to hide but, disoriented, she did not know how to move, and in any event where in this infinite, open expanse was there a place to hide?

The chamber inside Nimbus smelled of incinerated material and burnt flesh.

Nith Sahor's scaffolding had been reduced to a lump of metal, the germanium-alloy wires had been crisped, their remains black smoking lines branded into the floor. All the crystals had been fused, down to the shattered shards.

Giyan stood within the circle. Her robe and sifeyn had been burned off her.

Rekkk leapt to her side, wrapping her in his long, dark cloak. "What the N'Luuura happened?"

"Are you well, Lady?" Nith Sahor asked.

"I do not know," she said, and lifted her arms for them to see.

Her unhealed wounds had been transformed. Now the skin from the tips of her fingers to her elbows was black as pitch.

"Nith Sahor, what has happened?" she asked with a catch in her voice.

"I do not know, Lady." He came across the circle and tentatively touched her fingertips. "Hard as stone." Blue energy patterns gathered and ebbed as he manipulated ions. He gave her a quick glance. "Can you still move your fingers?"

She nodded. "Yes."

"Then do so."

"I am."

"Now?"

"Yes."

Her fingers were still as death.

"What is it?" Rekkk demanded. "Tell us, Nith Sahor."

"It looks organic, like a shell of some sort." The Gyrgon was probing gently all over from fingertips to wrists. "Chrysalides of some sort."

"Miina protect me," Giyan whispered. *The Nanthera was interrupted,* Bartta had said. Giyan closed her eyes. She had put her hands into the sorcerous circle to try to save Annon. *No one can say what the outcome will be.*

"Is there any pain?" Rekkk asked.

"Not now, no." She licked her lips. "My fingers have very limited movement. I can feel the inside of the chrysalides."

"I'm going to get them off you."

"That would be exceedingly unwise, Rekkk."

Rekkk paused. "What do you mean?"

"Nith Sahor is right." Giyan took a breath. "I can feel a forest of fibers growing." Her eyes flicked from his to those of the Gyrgon. "I . . . I think they are attaching themselves to me."

Rekkk grew angry. "Nith Sahor, I demand an explanation."

"At the moment I have none, save to say that I warned you about the dangerous properties of the antienergy. Something went wrong during the course of the Visitation. I cannot say what. Somehow, the antienergy broke free of the containment field."

"But there must be some way to free her," Rekkk cried.

"She will be freed when the chrysalides have completed their task."

"But we don't know what that is!"

"Transformation is the task of every chrysalis."

"You are a technomage!" Rekkk thundered. "Make this go away."

"Preliminary findings show that if I try to pry the chrysalides off, I will put Lady Giyan's life in grave jeopardy."

"I don't believe you!"

Nith Sahor inclined his head a little. "Forgive me, Lady." So saying, he fabricated out of blue ion fire a wicked-looking surgical instrument. Applying the wire-thin blade to the chrysalis on her right hand, he began to make an incision.

Immediately, Giyan cried out in agony. Her eyes rolled up on her head, and she collapsed into Rekkk's arms.

Nith Sahor caused the implement to disintegrate into its subatomic component parts. "You see Rekkk," the Gyrgon said sadly, "I do not lie to you."

Rekkk saw Giyan's eyes fluttering open. "Are you all right?" he asked.

She nodded and, with his help, regained her feet.

"Lady, again I apologize." Nith Sahor handed her a silver chalice. "Please drink this. It will speed your recovery."

While Giyan did as he asked, Rekkk turned on the Gyrgon. "Don't tell me there is nothing you can do."

"I fear there are still some things outside the control of the Gyrgon."

"That would come as a surprise to many Kundalan as well as V'ornn," Giyan said, handing him the empty cup.

Nith Sahor went and found a robe and sifeyn for her to put on. "Lady, I would very much desire the opportunity to research these chrysalides."

"No," she said immediately. "I do not wish to seem ungrateful, Nith Sahor. Thank you for letting me see Annon one more time. However, I will be no one's laboratory subject."

Again, Rekkk was astonished to see the Gyrgon bow.

"As you wish, Lady. I will not intrude on your privacy."

"It grows late, and we are both weary," Rekkk said curtly.

"Rekkk," Nith Sahor said as he escorted them back down the corridor, "in your anger you have blamed me. I cannot deny that you have every right to be angry, but these circumstances could not have been foreseen even by the most gifted Kundalan seer."

"I will not allow anything to happen to her," Rekkk growled.

He did not see Giyan's glance, but Nith Sahor marked the

expression in her eyes. "Lady, it seems you have quite the formidable champion by your side."

Giyan said nothing as she went out, Rekkk just behind her.

When they were gone, Nith Sahor returned to the conical chamber. He scoured every square centimeter searching for the origin of the energy intrusion. Of course he had given no hint of it to the others, but the surge had unsettled him. He had never experienced the level of energy flow he had witnessed tonight. Whatever—or whoever—had caused it was clearly a threat to him and to the Gyrgon Modality. It disturbed him profoundly to think that it might be the Centophennni. If that were the case all was lost.

No residue of the intrusive force remained—at least none that his extensive battery of tests revealed. Ashera Annon's birth-caul was gone as well, incinerated, he guessed, when the energy fused the dynamic bionetwork. That loss was a great tragedy.

He turned his mind in another direction. This Visitation was unique in more ways than one. Something quite remarkable had occurred even before he detected the anomalous energy intrusion. The image of Ashera Annon appeared to him differently than it had to Lady Giyan and the Pack-Commander. To Nith Sahor it was composed of an incredibly complex equation. There was about all the Visitation equations a common component. This was logical because the subjects were all dead, and this state of being was represented by an embedded energy signature. Except in this instance there was no signature, though Nith Sahor had spent precious seconds searching for it. Then the image of Ashera Annon had begun to spin. This, too, was absolutely remarkable. Unheard of, in fact. Nith Sahor had been so taken aback that the energy intrusion had been able to gain hold very quickly.

Nith Sahor stood in the center of the burnt chamber and contemplated the curious and unexpected twists and turns life took. The Visitation image was able to move of its own accord. Further, it did not contain the Death Signature. The logical conclusion was that despite all the hard evidence to the contrary Ashera Annon was, in fact, alive.

That revelation changed everything.

15

Thigpen

Riane's dilemma was this: having Thripped into Miina only knew where, she was ignorant of the principles of energy at work here. She could see the strands of energy pulsing like a web in every direction, but they did not lead anywhere. It wasn't as if she could climb upon a strand and Thrip herself away from here. As far as she could tell there *was* no away from here.

She watched in terror as Pyphoros morphed from place to place, looking for her. She thought if she observed him long enough, she might be able to fathom his means of locomotion, but no matter how carefully she scrutinized him, she could not even imagine by what method he disappeared from one place, only to appear in another.

Though he had not yet seen her he was coming ever closer. It was just a matter of time—though Time as the V'ornn and Kundalan measured it did not seem to exist here—before he saw her. What was she to do?

A silvery flicker, like that of a reflection on a lake, caused her to turn her head. She saw to her astonishment the gyreagle that had circled over her head on her climb up to the Ice Caves. It winked in and out of existence, coming head-on, its wings spread wide, its talons raised, his beak open. It was not flying, not even moving. It was simply there, then gone. It reappeared and stayed, still as if it were a statue of carved tiger eye. And as Riane watched, stupefied, the gyreagle mor-

phed into a magnificent green Dragon, its great sealed wings
arched, its golden eyes holding her gaze.

"Seelin," Riane breathed, though sound could not travel in
this realm.

The Dragon was not moving, but either it was larger than
the gyreagle or it was closer to Riane. It vanished, reappeared, vanished again. When it reappeared, it was so close
to Riane she would have backed away if she had been able.

Come now, Seelin said in Riane's mind. *It is unsafe to
remain here.*

Was this an illusion? An hallucination? Was she dreaming?

Seelin's image winked out. Riane continued to stare at the
place where the Dragon had been.

In a moment, Seelin reappeared. *Come now. Pyphoros has
sensed me and is coming.*

Tell me how.

How? The same way you came here.

But I do not know the laws here.

Use the energy webs you see all around you.

But how?

Like this. The Dragon dissolved herself into the web and
immediately reappeared. She smiled. *We travel by transforming from one energy state to another. Everything is transient
here. Your thoughts are still static, moving within the artificial constraints of Time and Space. Banish your old way of
thinking. Move Outside and you will see.*

Riane reached out. Her fingers grabbed at a strand of the
web, passed right through it. She glanced over her shoulder.
Pyphoros was almost upon her. Seelin had vanished. She
grabbed again for the energy web, and it vanished.

She thought of what the Dragon had said. This time she
kept her hand inside the strand. A sense of melting tugged
at her. She began to resist, when she heard the singing of
the power bourns. The melody coursed through her, and now
she could hear all the nuances, harmonies, grace notes *because she was entering the song itself.* The energy web was

composed of the power bourns she had felt at Bartta's house and in the abbey.

Deliquescing, she slipped all the way into the bourn just as Pyphoros appeared in her quadrant. Inside the web, transforming from one energy state to another, she felt the presence of the Dragon. It was as if just ahead of her she could feel the personification of Change. Seelin tugged at her, drawing her on. One with the energy web, she saw constant movement all around her as ions, electrons, photons, and other subatomic particles she could not identify streamed around her, over her, under her, through her, changing from positive to negative and back again in the never-ending dance of life.

Thripping deliriously, she returned to her underground prison. Now she felt the constraints of Time and Space as others would feel an excess of gravity. Boundlessness gave way to the finite world into which she had been born. The color spectrum seemed painfully truncated without the infrared, ultraviolet, radiation bands spiraling outward to infinity.

Riane doubled over and began to retch. She dropped to her knees as waves of vertigo hit her. She grabbed for the wall; she felt as if she were falling down a well with no bottom.

She lay on the rubble-strewn floor of the circular cavern, panting, her eyes tearing up. Her breathing was labored, and she was covered in clammy sweat. She felt as if she had been poisoned. She closed her eyes, but that just made everything worse. Through the gathering gloom, she stared up at the hole through which she had fallen. She knew her makeshift torch was almost guttered, knew that she needed to find another piece of wood, but she felt death moving through her like a cork-worm.

She tried to vomit, but nothing would come up. Groaning, she turned on her side, curling her legs up, and came face-to-face with something staring at her.

She went into an offensive crouch, her hands balled into fists. "Stay back!" she warned. Her hand scrabbled for the fallen torch, picked it up, and waved it in front of her. The creature sat still, waiting, unperturbed.

It was about twice as large as an ice-hare, with six legs, a long, expressive tail, and a thick coat of striped fur. It had a tapering black muzzle, green eyes, and flat, triangular ears.

"What the N'Luuura are you?" Riane said.

"I am Thigpen," the creature said, cocking its head. "What is a N'Luuura?"

The wind howled through the streets of Axis Tyr. Here, in the northern part of the city, the spacious Kundalan boulevards were in short supply. When the Mesagggun had been assigned to this quadrant, they had found the housing inadequate to their number. As a consequence, they had halved the width of the streets in order to make room for more residences, which now tumbled upon one another like a litter of unruly kittens at their mother's teats.

It depressed Giyan to be here, to see how nonchalantly these aliens could transform beauty into ugliness. It was one thing having one's cities occupied, quite another to have them turned into squalid garbage heaps.

"Giyan, I know—"

"When it comes to me, you know nothing," she snapped.

Confounded once again by this infuriating, inflaming female Kundalan, Rekkk kept his own counsel as they made their way toward his residence in the heart of the city. Mesagggun hurried past them without giving them a second glance. Rekkk was not wearing his Khagggun uniform, would never again put it on. As he had told Giyan, he was Nith Sahor's disciple now, a warrior who had turned his back on his command. Ironic. He had become his father.

In truth, he had only a vague idea what it meant to be Rhynnnon. For better or for worse, this was what he was now, and, as he was about to discover, he would have to bear the consequences his changed status had not only on himself but on those in his company.

From somewhere up ahead he heard shouting and the unmistakable sizzle of ion weapons' fire. They turned a corner, saw that the southernmost edge of the Mesagggun section of the city was awash in flames. The fires were so hot that the rain and howling wind did little to gutter them.

"What is going on?" Giyan asked.

Rekkk took in the well-disciplined pack of Khagggun methodically gutting residence blocks. "It looks like a raid of some sort."

"But why?"

Abruptly tense, he ignored her question. He took her arm, and they began to back away. "I think we'd better find another way—"

But it was already too late. A heavily armored Khagggun stepped out of the shadows.

"Halt and state your business," he said in clipped tones. "As of midnight this has been designated a restricted area."

"Do you not recognize me?" Rekkk said. "Pack-Commander Rekkk Hacilar."

"Yes? You are not in uniform. This is strange."

"I am off duty, escorting this female—"

"A Kundalan!" the Khagggun spat. "And now that I see her more closely, the former regent's Looorm. What are you doing with this skcettta?"

"What I am doing here, who I am with, are none of your business, First-Major." He took Giyan firmly by her elbow, began to walk past the Khagggun.

"Just a moment, Pack-Commander." The First-Major leveled a short-barreled ion cannon at him. "I have standing orders to bring all nonauthorized personnel to my commander for questioning."

Rekkk felt anger rising in him. "This is ridiculous. As soon as your commander sees who it is you've detained, it will go hard with you."

"Believe me, I will suffer far more if I disobey him. I have personally seen the unpleasant fruits of his discipline. I have no desire to have my tender parts tested that way."

Using the ion cannon, the Khagggun began to herd them toward the periphery of the firefight. Changing tactics, Rekkk decided to ask him about the raid.

"Oh, that," the First-Major said, laughing. "Well, our new regent has gotten it into his head that the last traces of religion need to be eradicated from the Mesagggun. He says worship of the war god, Enlil—the worship of any deity, for that matter—runs counter to Gyrgon edicts, so we are rooting out all the temples and their priests, shabby though these remnants are."

"You mean the Gyrgon have given the new regent this mandate?"

The First-Major shrugged. "That would be my guess. As far as I know, the order originated with regent Wennn Stogggul and was relayed to Star-Admiral Kinnnus Morcha. Frankly, that suits me. Lately, I haven't seen nearly enough action. I've grown restless and lazy. Nothing better to cure that malaise than spilling the enemies' blood, eh, Pack-Commander?"

Rekkk shot Giyan a glance, but she was staring straight ahead, acting as if neither of them existed. The First-Major led them past a block of smoking, half-razed Mesagggun buildings. An image of Enlil lay broken in the gutter running with the turquoise blood of fallen priests and their Traditionalist followers.

Taking in the carnage, Rekkk was reminded of something Nith Sahor had said to him at their first meeting: *The Balance is subtly changing. It is an evil, dangerous change—but one that, regrettably, is necessary.*

As they entered the periphery of the fighting, he could see the commander, whose back was turned to them. He was dressed in an officer's full battle armor—articulated plates of chronosteel brazed dark by the intense heat of their manufacture. His helm was pushed back as he barked orders. Various members of his pack ran off to carry out his wishes.

"Sir! First-Major Tud Jusssar reporting from north perimeter with two nonauthorized persons," their escort shouted. "One of them is Pack-Commander Rekkk Hacilar."

"Is that so?" The commander issued a final order to bring out alive the last of Enlil's priests, and turned to face them. Rekkk tensed as he recognized Olnnn Rydddlin. Sensing his alarm, Giyan pulled her sifeyn partially over her face.

Olnnn Rydddlin grinned. "Well, well, Rekkk Hacilar, the hero of a thousand wars. I haven't seen you since . . . well, since I've been made Pack-Commander. We have been looking for you."

Rekkk could not believe that he was staring at his former second-in-command.

"Let me see." Rydddlin tapped a forefinger against his lips. "You entered your first off-world campaign when you were fifteen—lied about your age, didn't you? Yes, and by the time that campaign had ended, you had killed half a dozen—let me see, it was so long ago I had yet to come of age." He snapped his fingers several times. "Who was the enemy then?"

"The Krael," Rekkk said. He did not like where this conversation was headed.

"Ah, yes. Mysterious creatures the Krael, but dull, weren't they? We slaughtered them like cor. Thousands, hundreds of thousands, millions, all the same to us. We laid waste to their world, but not before we plundered it of everything of value."

Rydddlin, in his darkly gleaming armor, took a step toward them and plucked the sifeyn off Giyan's face.

"Ah, the dead regent's mistress, I thought I recognized you. Can't keep away from V'ornn males, can you, skcettta?" He clucked his tongue. "Too bad for you you don't pick the right ones." He turned to Rekkk. "Stand away from her. She aided the escape of Annon Ashera and is an enemy of the V'ornn Modality. She will be detained to await public execution."

"We are of equal rank. You cannot order me," Rekkk protested. "She is under my—"

"Oh dear, it seems that you are woefully out of touch. By the order of Kinnnus Morcha, you have been relieved of your command."

"What? Impossible!"

"And yet, it is reality. As of seven this evening." Rydddlin thrust a data-decagon into the port on his portable holoscreen, held it out for Rekkk to view. "Here it is. It bears the Star-Admiral's signature and seal."

As Rekkk read the order in disbelief, two Khagggun dragged a priest of Enlil down the flaming street, dropping him at Rydddlin's feet. The priest was quivering and moaning, clasping his hands in front of him. His robes smelled of burnt fabric and flesh.

"Pray all you want," Rydddlin said, "for all the good it will do you." He unsnapped the armor plate from his left forearm, revealing an odd-looking okummmon. His dark eyes sparkled as he observed the look on his former commanding officer's face. "I am among the very first Khagggun to be implanted. This is one of the more tangible benefits of the alliance forged between Star-Admiral Kinnnus Morcha and the regent Stogggul. The Gyrgon specially designed these okummmon. We cannot be Summoned, but we can do other things more pertinent to our interests."

He drew out a small, odd-looking item no longer than a Kundalan stylus and fitted it into his okummmon. Six tiny spiderlike legs clicked open and arched up. "Why don't we see how well your god, Enlil, will protect you from *this*." He put his hand on the crown of the priest's head. Thin tongues of cold blue flame spurted from the ends of each of the legs. When they met at a nexus point, the fire flashed through the priest's body. He jerked and spasmed and fell over before he could utter a sound.

"I needn't have killed him right away," Rydddlin said in a conversational tone of voice. He whirled and placed his hand on Giyan's shoulder. Once again, the blue fire spurted, and Giyan cried out in agony.

Rekkk lunged toward him, but the two armored Khagggun intercepted him, pinning his arms to his side.

Ignoring Rekkk for the moment, Rydddlin whispered to her, "I have a message for you from Kurgan Stogggul. He hasn't forgotten how you humiliated him with your accursed sorcery." He watched with avid eyes as her shoulders slumped and tears came to her eyes. Addressing Rekkk, he said with the brisk voice of a commander outlining a campaign, "As you see, I can turn up the volume to a roar or turn it down to a whimper. Quite a formidable weapon, this spider-mite, is it not? And I have hardly begun to explore its uses." He grinned. "You see? You are nothing now, hero of a thousand wars." He kicked the corpse at his feet. "Nothing more, at any rate, than this insignificant priest."

Rekkk dropped the holoscreen and with the heel of his boot ground it into the bloody street. "Magic tricks are for children," he said. "Real warriors do not wear the okummmon."

"That's right. We are soto, those who cannot be Summoned. But you, you are to be pitied because now you are not even that." Rydddlin removed the implement from his okummmon, replaced it with a wicked-looking bolt. "But as for who is the real warrior and who is not . . ."

His hand was a blur as he aimed and loosed the bolt in virtually the same instant. Rekkk grunted as the bolt embedded itself in the flesh of his left thigh.

". . . well, we'will just have to see about that."

Rekkk's legs began to buckle, and, at Rydddlin's silent command, his guards let go his arms so he knelt on the ground between them.

"I don't know about you, Giyan," Rydddlin said, laughing, "but I rather like our former Pack-Commander on his knees."

Closing his mind against the pain, Rekkk pulled the bolt free of his flesh and jammed it into the interstice between two panels of armor worn by the guard on his left. As the Khagggun howled in pain, he took a jagged shard of the broken holoscreen and, rising to his feet, neatly slit the cables at the rear of the helm worn by the guard on his right. When the Khagggun put his hands up to try to wrench off his helm, Rekkk snatched his ion cannon. As the wounded guard turned, leveling his own weapon, Rekkk discharged his. The Khagggun was thrown three meters back, into the flaming wall of a building. First-Major Jusssar, engaging his ion cannon, was sent flying by Rekkk's next discharge.

Rekkk turned, searching for Olnnn Rydddlin, but the coward had vanished into the gutted interior of a nearby building.

Rekkk was about to go after him, when Giyan's cry brought him up short. He whirled, heard what she had heard: the tramp of booted feet. More Khagggun, reinforcements contacted, no doubt, by Olnnn Rydddlin.

He nodded at Giyan, and they melted into the shadows, hurrying south, away from the conflagration.

The first thing you'll be wanting is some more light."
    Riane watched Thigpen as she—it was quite clear that the creature was female—scurried around the chamber gathering small chips of black, friable rock.

"Just what kind of creature are you?" she asked.

"Hurry hurry hurry," Thigpen said, taking a quick glance at the guttering torch. When she had enough rock chips she began to crush them in her paws. Riane could see that these paws were more like fingers. And they had opposable thumbs. "I could have asked you the same thing, couldn't I? But I haven't, have I? Do you know why, little dumpling? Because, unlike you, I was brought up to have proper manners."

"I . . . I'm sorry," Riane stammered. "I didn't mean—Hey, wait a moment, you're a Rappa, aren't you?" Riane cocked her head. "I thought the Rappa had been wiped out after you killed Mother."

"Heard that in the abbey, didn't you?" Thigpen did not look up from her work. Crush, crush, crush, like a furry ion-charged machine. "As you can plainly see, the reports of our demise are highly exaggerated. And, for your information, we didn't kill Mother. Didn't harm a hair on her head. Know who did, though, yes indeed."

Riane took a step forward. She remembered Giyan telling Annon that she did not believe the Rappa were evil. "What do you mean?"

"Mean what you mean and say what you say."

"Don't you mean 'Say what you mean and mean what you say'?"

Thigpen looked up sharply. "Did you mean that, what you just said?"

Riane was suddenly dizzy all over again. "I'm sure I did."

"All right, then my job is half-done." Finished with her crushing, Thigpen beckoned Riane over. "Put the end of the torch just there, in the center of the pile of powder I've made."

Shaking her head, Riane did as the strange creature asked. Immediately, the powder flared up, providing instant illumination, not to mention heat. It had grown cold, exacerbating the inherent underground dampness. Riane warmed herself by the fire as she took a good, long look at Thigpen. The creature sat beside her, methodically grooming her shining pelt.

"Can I ask a question?"

"You can ask," Thigpen said. "After that, no guarantees."

This response made Riane laugh, despite the straits in which she found herself. "About that question. If Rappa weren't responsible for killing Mother, why do the Ramahan believe it?"

"Because we make convenient scapegoats, don't we? Aren't around to refute the lie."

"So who did kill Mother? The male Ramahan, I bet, who tried to read The Pearl."

"Now we're getting into dangerous territory."

"You are a curious little thing."

Thigpen ceased her grooming. "Not half as curious as you, little dumpling. You're in quite a fix, aren't you?"

"As you ask, yes. I crashed through the floor of the tunnel above us and landed here, and there's no way out."

"No, no, not *that*," Thigpen said with no little impatience. "I mean the Thripping."

"What?" Riane was quite rightly taken aback. "What do you know about Thripping?"

"Now you *really* insult me. What do you have to feel superior about when I have six legs and you only have two?"

"But you're an *animal*," Riane said reasonably. "It's a well-established fact that animals are inferior to V'ornn. Or Kundalan, for that matter."

"Am I an animal simply because you say so, little dumpling?"

"I have eyes," Riane said as she turned her back to the fire. "I know what you are."

"Mmm, just as you knew the boundaries of the Cosmos before you went Thripping."

This comment made Riane stop and reconsider. She found that she was beginning to feel foolish. "Well, you certainly *look* like an animal."

"Safe to say you won't make a successful xenobiologist," Thigpen sniffed. "Well, we can't have everything we wish for, now can we? Ha! At least, not right away."

Riane decided to crouch so that her head was on the same level as the creature's. "Will you tell me what you know about Thripping? I know next to nothing."

Thigpen snorted. "That first Thrip just about did you in, didn't it? Or were you simply coughing up a lung for sport?"

"Is that why I felt so bad? From the Thripping?"

Thigpen edged closer. Apparently, she liked Riane's reduced height. "Well, not from the Thripping exactly. The rapid redeployment of differentiated energies one picks up as one Thrips can be toxic. These energies are potent, and quite often, little dumpling, they do not like one another. In other words, Thripping can be poisonous to one's health."

Riane was about to remark on how oddly Thigpen talked, then thought better of it. Taking a metaphorical step back, perhaps she, Riane, was the one who talked oddly. "Is there something I can do so I don't feel like this?" she said.

"Oh, yes," Thigpen replied. "The first is: don't Thrip."

"Well, that's obvious. But what if I want to Thrip—or need to?"

"Then you require a filter, something that gobbles up the energies before they interact and poison you."

"Do you have something like that?"

"I do." Thigpen looked her up and down. "But by the looks of you you won't like it. No, you won't like it one little bit."

"Try me," Riane said. "I might surprise you."

Thigpen's long striped whiskers lay back against the black fur of her face. "Well, now, little dumpling, as I positively *live* for surprises, I imagine it's worth a shot." One paw came up. "A word of warning, however. There will be no second chance. The filter is irreplaceable. You must accept it or it will die."

"You mean the filter is alive?"

"Indubitably. Large or small, we're all creatures in the Cosmos." Thigpen opened her mouth wide, stuck a paw inside. In a moment, her forefinger and thumb extracted a long, wriggling thing. She held it up. "The Thripping creature catches the mononculus, as the saying goes." She grinned, showing three sets of wicked-looking pale blue triangular teeth. "Now open wide, little dumpling."

Riane drew back her head. "You mean you want me to *eat* that thing?"

"Eat a mononculus? My goodness, no! It's too precious to eat. No, you will open wide, in it will go. It will become part of you. It will protect you, consuming in a trice all the foul energies as you Thrip."

Riane could not take her eyes off the long, wriggling mononculus. It was red and shiny with a million tiny cilia all over it. "No, I can't."

"See, I knew it. But you promised me a surprise; now I must have it." Thigpen brought the mononculus closer. "Quickly quickly quickly. It will die without a new host."

"Put it back inside you," Riane said, disgusted.

"I cannot. Did I not tell you? There is only this one chance. Once the mononculus vacates its host it must find another. It cannot go back."

"But what about you? How will you protect yourself when you Thrip?"

"Ah-ha, don't you worry about me, little dumpling. I'm loaded with tricks you couldn't even imagine." Thigpen dangled the mononculus over Riane's head. "Now come on. Is this any way to treat such a lovely protector?"

Riane quite literally had her back to the wall; there was

nowhere else to go. Her mind and her instincts pulled her in
two opposite directions. What to do?

Open wide and say ahhhh.

Listening to the Riane part of her, she shut down the primal yabbering in her head and, arching her neck back,
opened her mouth wide and squeezed her eyes shut.

She almost gagged when the head of the mononculus
grazed the inside of her mouth. She tried to relax, to think
of a place far away, Middle Palace in Axis Tyr, the stream
where Annon and Kurgan had stumbled upon Eleana. When
she felt something in her throat, sliding downward, she almost jumped out of her skin. Her eyes popped open, and she
saw Thigpen sitting calmly in her lap.

"Look at me," the creature said.

Riane struggled to breathe, fought the gag reflex that
would make her vomit the thing up and, according to Thigpen, doom it.

"Little dumpling, please look at me." Thigpen was smiling, and what a smile it was! No V'ornn or Kundalan could
smile like that. It arced from one side of her furry face to
the other. The sight made Riane laugh and, laughing, she
relaxed. The mononculus slid the rest of the way down.

"There will be a little pain now," Thigpen said. "Not
much, nothing more than a pinch. Yes, little dumpling, just
like that. Now that wasn't so bad, was it?"

Riane shook her head. Her eyes were watering.

"Tell me, what color do you see?"

"What?"

"Everything is haloed in a color, isn't it?"

Riane nodded. She saw haloes everywhere she looked.
"Green," she said. "All the auras are green."

"Ah, the mononculus has taken up residence around your
heart shaatra."

"What does that mean?"

"It is a good omen." Thigpen smiled. "Do you feel any
pain now?"

"No."

"There. It's done." Thigpen extended her neck and, with

a rough blue tongue, licked away Riane's tears. "How interesting!" she cried. "They're salty. Mine are sweet."

Riane laughed again and, without thinking, reached out to stroke Thigpen's fur. The creature stiffened.

"What are you doing?" Thigpen asked suspiciously.

"I was going to pet you," Riane said.

"Why would you do that?"

"It's a form of affection, like you licking off my tears."

"Oh, I see." Thigpen relaxed. "Well, go ahead then, if you must."

Riane stroked her fur, which was extraordinarily soft, thick, and silken. Thigpen began to purr, her eyes closed, and she put her head down. "Now that's what I call pleasure," she whispered. "Where did you learn your technique?"

Riane was laughing again. "Just doing what comes naturally, I guess."

"Well, don't stop, little dumpling, this 'petting' is making me one happy—" She broke off as her head came up.

"What is it?" Riane asked.

"Hush!" the creature hissed. "Whatever happens next, don't move. Got it?"

"Yes, but—"

"Keep *still*, would you!" Thigpen's whiskers were twitching like mad.

Riane did as she was told. She could feel the slightest vibration and wondered whether an earth tremor was forming. A moment later, a shower of rock burst toward them, revealing a connection to another chamber that had been concealed by the rockfall.

"Uh-oh." Thigpen leapt off Riane's lap as something very big and foul-smelling charged through. It was a perwillon—one far larger than the beast Annon had encountered when he was with Eleana and Giyan. It towered over Thigpen; she wouldn't have a chance against it. Despite Thigpen's warning, Riane scrambled to her feet. Drawing out her ice ax, she ran at the beast and, when she was within a meter of it, slung it into the perwillon's face. It struck the huge snout head-on, sending the perwillon into such a rage it swatted out blindly with one forepaw, knocking the breath from Riane as she was spun away.

She hit the cavern floor hard, spraying rock this way and that She turned, saw Thigpen launch her furry body at the perwillon. Her jaws locked on to the perwillon's throat and blood fountained outward in such a rush the perwillon's attack faltered. Thigpen bit again, deeper this time, her mouth with its triple set of teeth coming away with flesh, fur and cartilage.

The perwillon bellowed in terror of its imminent death even as it collapsed onto its side. There was no strength left in the huge beast. The ferocity of Thigpen's attack astonished Riane, who could do nothing but watch the last of the perwillon's death throes.

At last, Thigpen was finished. Dwarfed by the black-furred carcass of the perwillon, she crouched by its side and feasted. With her long, clicking claws and pointed muzzle, she presented an oddly elegant sight as she ripped thin strips of bloody flesh from the brute. When she was done she rolled in the beast's fur, wiping the blood off herself. Then she trotted back to where Riane sat in a kind of stupefied daze.

"I told you to stay put. Didn't I tell you that? Are you injured?"

Riane shook her head. "I was afraid for you. I wasn't going to let the perwillon eat you."

"Fat chance of that!"

"You're telling me!" Riane exclaimed. "But how was I to know?"

"There you have a point." Thigpen licked the last drop of blood from her whiskers, smoothed them back. "I imagine you think it admirable that you had no thought for your own safety, only mine."

"Well, I—"

"You could have been killed by the perwillon, and for what? Remember, little dumpling, you must gather adequate knowledge of a situation before you act. That way no one can accuse you of being either smug or stupid." She glanced back over her shoulder at the fallen beast. "You must be hungry. Shall I tear you off some meat?"

"I'm not . . . I don't think I can get anything down right now."

Thigpen frowned. "The perwillon is a sacred beast, a relic of the old days. It can resist Osoru spells, though its heart may be pierced with a simple weapon like any other beast's. However that may be, eating its flesh gives you strength."

"I have already tasted perwillon flesh, thank you very much, and it was none too palatable."

"Now that is interesting," Thigpen said. "You must tell me of this sometime. However, now I suggest you eat your fill. Without a full belly you won't have enough strength for the trek back home."

Riane's eyes opened wide. "You mean you know a way out of here?"

"I know ten thousand ways," Thigpen said with a certain amount of pride. "The only decision comes in which one to take."

Does the wound pain you?" Giyan asked through the downpour.

"Not at all," Rekkk replied, just as his punctured leg gave out, and he fell into a gutter overflowing with rainwater.

Giyan knelt next to him and examined the wound. "You have lost a lot of blood."

"I hadn't noticed."

"Yes, Khagggun that you are." She tore off her sifeyn, wrapped it around his thigh above the wound.

"Khagggun no longer," he said. "I am Rhynnnon."

"You are still V'ornn," she said now as she put his arm across her shoulders. "Come on. We dare not stay here long."

"I will not lean on you."

"Do you think me too weak?"

"You are a female."

"A *Kundalan* female," she said as she wrapped her arm around him. "I have the determination of ten of your V'ornn Tuskugggun." She hauled him to his feet.

Together, they stumbled through the rain- and windswept night until, at length, they came to Rekkk's front door. Inside, everything was as they had left it.

"It is not safe for us to stay here long," Rekkk said as he limped to his weapons room. "Olnnn Rydddlin is sure to send Khagggun for us, and the first place they will look is here." While he leaned against her, he took down an ion cannon and his shock-sword before they returned to the living room where she dumped him into a hard, chronosteel chair. He groaned, wishing for the comfort of Kundalan furniture.

Giyan went and dried herself off, then got a bowl of hot water and cloths. "I have no herbs," she said as he tore open the bloody fabric of his trousers leg. "And no access to any."

He used the cloth she handed him, drying himself as best he could. He found himself quite dizzy. She was right; he *had* lost a lot of blood. He should have tied a tourniquet right away, but pride had forced him to walk away from Rydddlin and his pack without a sign that he had been injured. Now he was paying the price.

He winced but did not cry out as she began to clean the wound. The pain was like a brush scouring away the last vestiges of his old life. If he had harbored any doubts about the path he was on, Rydddlin's order had put them to rest. In the eyes of those he had once called comrades he was already dead. But the death they thought they saw was in fact his new life as Rhynnnon, free of V'ornn stifling strictures, one they could neither live nor understand.

A sudden warmth suffused him so that he relaxed totally. Drifting on the shoals of sleep, he saw his mother again. She was standing knee deep in the Sea of Blood, calling to him, beckoning. And when he spoke her name, she smiled, and he felt at peace . . .

He awoke with a start. His leg felt stiff and sore, but all the pain had washed out of him. Looking down, he saw a livid scar where the wound had been.

"What?" he said. "What?"

Just then, Giyan emerged with a platter of hot food and

drink. "Eat," she told him as she set the platter down on a table in front of him. "You need to build up your strength."

He looked from his healed leg to the food she had prepared. "I cannot eat alone. It is an old habit, one I could not shake even in the field." He glanced up at her. "You have made more than enough for two people."

She handed him some meat. He tore off half and offered it to her. She hesitated a moment, then took it from him. She watched him as he ate, nibbling tiny bites herself.

"My wound is healed. Did you use your sorcery on me?"

"Yes."

"Can you tell me something about it? Do all Kundalan have this power?"

She hesitated a moment before answering. "It is called Osoru. Nowadays, very few Kundalan possess the Gift. In fact, with each generation there are fewer who possess it."

"Then you are born with it?"

"The Gift itself is inherited. But controlling it is another matter. A hundred years ago, Osoru's guiding principles were taught as part of the religious curriculum at the abbeys. Now that teaching has been banned."

A thought occurred to him. "Is that why Nith Sahor calls you Lady?"

She hesitated again. "I imagine so."

"But how would he know?"

"Yes, how *would* he know? I have been asking myself that same question." She put down the piece of meat he had given her. "It chills me to think Gyrgon could target the few of us who remain."

"I told you Nith Sahor was different, and this should prove it to you," Rekkk said. "If he were like all the other Gyrgon, don't you think he would have rounded all you up and interrogated you? Instead, he did nothing, and you were right under his tender parts."

Giyan frowned. "Your thesis has merit."

"Of course it does." Rekkk rubbed his hands together. Each moment he was feeling better and better.

"Giyan—"

Her head came up, and those whistleflower-blue eyes connected with him.

"I am not very good at this, but thank you for healing me. I know it can't have been easy to—"

"Healing you was easy," she said in her straightforward manner. "Deciding whether or not to do it was the difficult part."

"I am heartened by your decision," he said almost formally.

She looked up at him. "Tell me something. How did you coerce Nith Sahor into performing the Visitation?"

"One does not coerce Gyrgon," he said. "But you already knew that." He hesitated a moment, thinking of lying to her. But he was certain she would see through it. "Nith Sahor wants something from me. I made the Visitation a condition of my acceptance."

"Why?"

"Because . . ." He felt defeated by emotion. "Just because."

At that moment, there came an almost explosive pounding on the door.

Giyan leapt to her feet. "Rydddlin!" she cried. "He's found us!"

Rekkk had the ion cannon in one hand, his shock-sword in the other. "Let Olnnn Rydddlin bring his command. I am ready!"

With a deafening crack, the thick chronosteel door blew inward.

16

Technomancy

Ready?"

Riane looked dubiously at the expanse they had to leap. "So you *do* live down here."

"A troglodyte, me?" Thigpen cried. "I don't think so!"

Having seen her step daintily over the perwillon's great outstretched paw it was difficult to imagine her as the ferocious engine of destruction that had brought the huge beast down.

"No I live . . . elsewhere."

"Why won't you tell me where you're from?" Riane asked.

"Because, little dumpling, you're not ready."

"But how can you say that?" she protested. "You don't even know me."

"Did I say that?" Thigpen turned. "Did you hear me say that?"

Riane stifled the urge to blurt out the forbidden knowledge of who she was. No one must know that inside this Kundalan female lived the soul of Annon Ashera, especially not a creature she had just met and knew nothing about.

They had been walking for nearly three hours, as best as she could determine, and she still had no clear idea of where they were or whether they were even any closer to emerging from the bowels of the Djenn Marre. About a half hour ago they had come upon a cavern so gigantic Riane had not been able to see the far side. Light, sufficient but eerie, radiated from a series of phosphorescent striations that ran like veins through the rock. As far as Riane could tell, the only way across the cavern was by traversing a narrow ledge, which was more or less a natural outcropping of the wall. As such, it was often difficult to negotiate, as when it narrowed down to almost nothing or when a bulge in the cavern wall caused it to disappear entirely. Still, Thigpen never paused or seemed uncertain; her six legs—not to mention her tail— gave her an unparalleled security when climbing even virtually sheer rock faces. Now they had halted at a gap in the ledge of nearly three meters. Thigpen had calmly told her they needed to jump. Examining the width of the gap, Riane wasn't so sure.

"So you know something about the Kundalan," she said in hopes of drawing information out of Thigpen, not to mention trying to prolong the decision she had to make.

"I know *everything* about the Kundalan," Thigpen said. "Well *nearly* everything, anyway."

"Like what? Tell me something."

Thigpen's eyes glittered. "I know, for instance, that you can make this jump. Now stop procrastinating." So saying, she set her four hind legs and sprang forward. Her small furry body arced through the air, and she landed gracefully on the other side. She turned, waiting expectantly.

"I can't," Riane said. Unaccountably, Annon's old innate fear of heights had resurfaced. She felt pinned to the rock wall, unable to move either forward or back.

Thigpen sat down and began to groom herself. She paid no attention at all to Riane.

"What are you doing?" Riane shouted. "Give me some help!"

"Why should I?" Thigpen did not look up. "Clearly, you are not up to the challenge."

This got Riane angry. So angry, in fact, that she squashed Annon's old fear like a bug and without another thought took a three-pace running start, leaping off the edge of the ledge. As if knowing what to do on its own, her upper body leaned forward, her legs windmilled, her arms stretched straight out in front of her.

"Incoming!" Thigpen called, and got out of the way just as Riane hit the far side of the ledge with her boot soles.

Tumbling head over heels, Riane tucked herself into a ball, rolling on the hard rock-strewn face of the ledge. She got up and dusted herself off.

"How do you feel?" Thigpen asked innocently.

Looking back at the gap she had just traversed, Riane said. "To be honest, my breath is coming fast, my heart is thumping in my chest, my pulses are pounding in my ears."

Thigpen was grinning from ear to ear. "Most exhilarating, isn't it!"

And it was. The only thing stopping Riane from doing it again was that she was suddenly exhausted. "Could we rest here for a while? I haven't slept in over a day."

"Sleep! Ah, that's right. You creatures have a daily restoration cycle. But of course! How thoughtless of me!"

Riane sat gratefully down with her back against the wall. The ledge was a bit wider there, allowing her to stretch out her legs without her feet dangling over the side. She closed her eyes, heard Thigpen pad quietly toward her, felt her curl up in her lap.

"There now, that's ever so nice, isn't it?"

"Umm-hmm," Riane murmured. "Tell me about the Ramahan."

If Thigpen found this an odd request, it was impossible to tell. "Since the V'ornn's arrival, many beliefs have been inverted. Did you know that the Ramahan used to believe that the perwillon was Miina's steed? It was so sacred an animal, in fact, that no paintings or writings of it were allowed outside the abbeys. And then there are the Ja-Gaar, great spotted beasties they were, ferocious-looking but ever so intelligent." Riane thought immediately of the eerie creatures she had seen painted on the cave wall. "Telepathic, some said. And, of course, the unihorned narbuck, who faded away when the lightning ceased to play in Kundala's skies." Her whiskers twitched. "Nowadays, everything's different, of course. The narbuck, like many other of Miina's animals, have retreated into the dimness of the past, waiting patiently for the time of their return."

"You mean they all still exist?"

"Well, you've seen a perwillon yourself, haven't you?" Thigpen snorted. "Of course they still exist."

Riane, already on the colorless cusp of sleep, conjured in her mind a mailed warrior-goddess riding a ferocious beast, sheathed in speckled, glowing armor. Where this vision came from she could not say.

"Tell me what happened on your first Thrip," Thigpen urged. "Where did you go?"

"I haven't the faintest idea. But I saw Pyphoros."

"Oh dear." Thigpen stirred. "That's not good."

"And Seelin, the Sacred Dragon of Transformation."

Thigpen's eyes opened wide. "Well, now. This is a narbuck of quite a different hue, isn't it?"

"It is?"

"Well, of course it is, little dumpling." Thigpen padded around and around on Riane's lap. "I mean to say, Seelin does not show herself to just any Thripper."

"What does this mean?" Riane asked.

"It means, little dumpling, that my information was right on target. You are Miina's Chosen One," Thigpen purred. "We have been waiting for you."

"What do you mean?"

"Your existence has been writ in Prophecy." Thigpen seemed to be examining every square centimeter of Riane's face. "The realms have been waiting a long time for you to be born."

Riane shook her head. "Why has Pyphoros marked me if I am Miina's Chosen One?"

"He has marked you *because* you are the One. You are a threat to him."

"How can I be a threat to anyone? I'm nothing more than a prisoner."

"It will become clearer now you're here, and make no mistake." Thigpen rubbed herself against Riane's chest in a most delicious and hypnotic way. "Sleep now. Go on, close your eyes. You've earned your rest."

Rest, thought Riane, and fell promptly into a deep and dreamless slumber.

*   *   *

The strong scent of clove oil and musk was all that lay between Rekkk Hacilar standing his ground and emptying his ion cannon into the figure who stood in the doorway.

"I understand there has been an incident," Mastress Kannna said as she came into the residence. She was surrounded by a sparkling blue-green aura.

"N'Luuura, I could have killed you," Rekkk breathed, lowering his weapons.

"Not likely. My ion exomatrix was engaged."

"This is no ordinary-issue ion cannon." Rekkk hefted the weapon. "I modified it myself. Instead of splitting the ions, it rips them to shreds."

Mastress Kannna regarded him with lustrous, sultry eyes. "You are in possession of illicit intellectual property, Rekkk. Inventing science is Gyrgon domain. Very naughty of you." She smiled her strange, compelling smile.

"Or perhaps it is simply that you chose wisely."

Mastress Kannna inclined her head. "Perhaps. You do not look the worse for your violent encounter."

"That's entirely Giyan's doing. She used her—"

"Who is this female?" Giyan demanded.

"Mastress Kannna," he said. "She—"

But the female form was already morphing into that of Nith Sahor, clad in a purple alloy exosuit that looked very much like armor. "We must leave at once," the Gyrgon said. "There is an elite pack of Khagggun on its way, answerable only to Kinnnus Morcha."

Nith Sahor ushered them outside. "Now face one another. No, closer." The Gyrgon stood between them and at once everything in the immediate vicinity was drained of color. Rekkk felt an odd, sinking sensation in the pit of his lowermost stomach, then the giddiness he associated with drinking too much fire-grade numaaadis. The world faded and vanished altogether.

"We have arrived," Nith Sahor announced in a voice oddly muffled.

Rekkk shook his head. His ears popped, and sound levels returned to normal. They were in a turretlike eyrie high above the city, in the uppermost reaches of the Temple of Mnemonics. This impression was fortified by a golden-eyed teyj—a large and rather formidable specimen of the four-winged birds the Gyrgon kept—which sat on its perch, staring at them with preternatural inquisitiveness. Nith Sahor's ion exomatrix had vanished. He was covered from shoulders to ankles with a tasseled greatcoat, black with crimson trim. His pale amber head was bare, his star-sapphire eyes calm as still water. It was virtually unheard of to see a Gyrgon with his head uncovered. To Giyan, the filigreed lat-ticework of tertium and germanium circuits implanted in his skull lent him the wild and barbaric aspect of a member of the Sarakkon, the tattooed race she had heard of who lived on the southern continent, across the Sea of Blood.

The circular walls, which dropped below them thirty diz-zying meters, contained a helter-skelter warren of niches within which were jammed a bewildering array of scientific equipment, some engaged in ongoing experiments, others awaiting their turn. A series of metal walkways encircled the eyrie like a giant spiderweb, but since they were not linked in any visible way, it was difficult to understand how one reached them. Until, that is, the floor on which they stood began to descend.

When they reached the third level from the top the floor glided to a stop; they followed Nith Sahor's lead and stepped off onto the metallic ring. The Gyrgon directed Rekkk to sit in an odd-looking and faintly menacing chair.

"Events are accelerating at an alarming rate," he said as he busied himself with opening shining black canisters, tantalum-freezer drawers, and masses of linked biocircuits. "Now that you have become Rhynnnon, I want you armed."

"I *am* armed," Rekkk pointed out, as he hefted his ion cannon and shock-sword.

"Insufficient. Your encounter with Pack-Commander Ry-dddlin proved that." Nith Sahor turned back to him. "Expose your left arm, please."

Rekkk, with a glance at Giyan, did as the Gyrgon asked.

"This will not be a pleasant experience," Nith Sahor said as he bent over Rekkk. "But it will not last long." He strapped Rekkk's arm to the chair. As he did so, Giyan came and stood behind Rekkk, put her hands on his shoulders. The Gyrgon towered over the two of them like some terrifying basalt idol they had come upon amid the sand dunes of the Great Voorg.

"Let's get on with it," Rekkk said.

"As you wish." Nith Sahor's right glove glowed and sparked. The ion-energy stream circled Rekkk's forearm, split off, weaving threads until the arm was completely enclosed. Rekkk felt his arm go numb as the anesthetic took hold. Four gleaming implements appeared in the Gyrgon's other hand. Without hesitation, he made a long vertical incision down the center of Rekkk's forearm. Turquoise blood overran the skin. Quickly, Nith Sahor, made short horizontal cuts at each end of the first incision, used the second implement to peel back the seven layers of dermis, all the while using the third implement to syphon off the welling blood. He laid the biomatrix into the incision, positioning the thing with the fourth implement.

"The anesthetic will wear off momentarily. The nerves need to be free of outside chemicals for the okummmon to align itself with them." He stood up and went out of the laboratory, for the moment finished.

The numbness vanished all at once, and Rekkk gasped. His arm felt as if it had been dipped in fire. The nerve endings on that side of his body vibrated with agony, and he had to fight to continue breathing normally. If this was a Gyrgon's idea of an unpleasant experience, he had no wish to sample their idea of real pain.

Gradually his eyelids closed, and he passed into that state of dreamless sleep where even such agony as he endured could not reach.

Nith Sahor reappeared in time to syphon off the excess blood, although now there was far less, as if the okummmon itself was absorbing the bulk of it.

"I can feel it sinking into me, attaching itself."

"That is normal," the Gyrgon assured him.

As the filaments of the biomatrix attached themselves, knowledge flowed through him. He became aware that this was a living thing, a neural network of biochips that grew and adjusted to the host around it. He also saw Nith Sahor's gloves—the black greatcoat he wore—for what they were: a network of thousands of minute, incredibly complex biomachines that made up another kind of living thing, a neural matrix.

The biomatrix was overrunning the incision, and Nith Sahor released the skin, which was immediately annealed by the okummmon. "Almost complete." He applied his blue ion fire to the okummmon. "I am now Summoning it into semisentience, so it will be forever a part of you."

The muscles in Rekkk's arm jumped and spasmed with each application of the energy. He was drenched in sweat, his contracted pupils the only other outward manifestation of what was being done to him. To keep his mind occupied, he looked around the Gyrgon's laboratory. With eyes somehow enhanced by the semiorganic okummmon, he could see that the arrays of paraphernalia, which had previously seemed chaotic, had, in fact, a highly sophisticated pattern—that of a series of helices. Fascinated as he was, his racking pain receded into the background.

Nith Sahor switched from working on the okummmon's center to its edges. "Now you will have a veritable arsenal at your disposal."

"Like Olnnn Rydddlin," Rekkk said.

"Oh, no. It will be much more, Rekkk. You will be able to fashion weapons from your okummmon out of the five elements you find around you. Earth, air, fire, water, wood will do your bidding." The Gyrgon pointed. "Place it here, in this slot, slide it in so. Then fix an image in your mind of what you need. Keep the image clear and bright, Rekkk, see it, feel it, own it, and it will be made manifest." Nith Sahor raised a finger. "But remember, whatever element you use cannot be converted twice in a row."

Rekkk was awed. "Only Gyrgon are able to transmute the elements," he whispered.

"Correct," Nith Sahor said, finished, at last. "You are Transcended. The first of your kind who is truly beyond caste." Nith Sahor stood back, regarding his handiwork. "I have waited decades for this moment. I have remade you, Rekkk. You are more now than even the Bashkir. You are part Gyrgon."

How did you decide on which route to take?" Riane asked, as they moved downward through a snaking tunnel. "You said you knew thousands."

"Ten thousand, actually," Thigpen said. "I am just following my nose." Her tail was arched up over her back, the end of it curled around a small glowing sphere. Before they left the cyclopean cavern, she had dug out this gemlike object and, holding it in her forepaws, had licked it all over until its glow lit up the space around them.

Riane felt a painful lurch in her chest. "Even if I am this Dar Sala-at, what of it? I haven't a clue what to do next."

"Have a little faith."

"Faith is just another in a long list of things I don't have." Riane put her fists on her hips, thinking, *V'ornn put no store in faith of any kind.* "Anyway, that's no answer."

Turning, Thigpen gave her that huge ear-to-ear grin. "Contrary to the impression I give, I don't know everything." Riane found it impossible to stay annoyed with her. "Wouldn't want to, really. What would be the point?"

"The point of what?"

"Of *life,* little dumpling. Why, if there were no more questions to be answered, what in the world would we do with ourselves? Nothing pretty, I can tell you. You only have to observe Pyphoros or one of the lesser daemons to know that."

Riane paused. "What do you mean?"

"Well, the thing about daemons—the truly *horrible,* terrifying thing about them—is that they have lost the ability to find answers. Instead, they simply ask the same questions over and over."

"You mean they're stupid?"

"Now that depends upon your definition of stupid, little dumpling." Thigpen continued them on their downward trek. "On one level, yes, they are exceedingly stupid—as evil always is. But on another level, well, goodness there are scarcely any creatures more clever than they. They want what they want, you see, and they spend *all* their time scheming to get it."

"What do they want, Thigpen?"

The creature snorted. "I would have thought you had had enough experience with Pyphoros to know. They want *everything*—dominion over our world and all the other realms through which we Thrip. They scheme and they keep on scheming until either they get what they want or are destroyed."

"But they'll never succeed."

"Don't be smug, little dumpling. The daemons were powerful before Miina threw Pyphoros down into the Abyss with them. But now—well, he has a grudge to settle and all eternity to settle it in."

Riane thought about this for some time. "But if Pyphoros increased the daemons' power, why did Miina send him there?"

"What else was She to do? He was far too dangerous to leave bound in this realm."

"If he is so dangerous, She should have killed him."

"Perhaps she tried." Thigpen shook her head. "Anyway, it is not our place to question the decisions of the Great Goddess. We have neither Her knowledge nor Her wisdom."

At length, the tunnel straightened out, then gradually leveled off. Riane guessed that they were deep in the heart of the Djenn Marre. How she was ever going to see sunlight again she could not guess, but for better or for worse she had put herself in the paws of this strange, remarkable creature.

The tunnel forked, and Thigpen led them to the left. A

short way on, the fork debouched upon an enormous, low-ceilinged cavern. Grey-green stalactites and stalagmites grew like the teeth of a huge unseen beast, contriving to make the space unpleasantly claustrophobic. In fact, there was something about the cavern that sent a shiver of apprehension through Riane. As she pulled back into the mouth of the tunnel, Thigpen said, "What is it, little dumpling?"

"I don't know," Riane whispered. Some sixth sense caused her to keep her voice down. "I don't like this place. I'd rather not go in."

"Nonsense." Thigpen took her hand. "I was born and raised near here. I assure you there is no cause for alarm. This is a peaceful place, where a body can think undisturbed."

Reluctantly, Riane allowed the creature to lead her back into the cavern. As Thigpen wended them through the eerie forest, Riane tried to ignore her rising anxiety. Instead, she directed her attention to the floor of the cavern, which was growing damp. Soon puddles sloshed as they made their way forward.

Gradually, the stalagmites grew more stunted, then petered out altogether. Riane could see why. Thigpen had led them to a vast underground lake. The waters, utterly still, were black as pitch, so unlike water kissed by sunlight and moonslight as to be unrecognizable as the same substance.

"What is this place, Thigpen?" she whispered.

"Most sacred ground, little dumpling. It is called First Cenote."

"Why have you brought me here?"

"Because you are the Dar Sala-at."

Riane glanced at the creature. "What am I supposed to do here?"

Thigpen met her gaze. "Tell me what it is."

"Me? You must be joking!"

"I assure you I am not. I know that First Cenote has existed here since the beginning of Time. I know that it is the origin of Heavenly Rushing. I know that it is supposed to be depthless, though myself I rather doubt this last."

"You also said that it was sacred."

Thigpen nodded.

"So this is Miina's lake."

Thigpen blinked. "I have every confidence that you will tell me if that is so."

Riane laughed at the absurdity of the notion. "Your confidence is misplaced. How would I possibly know such a thing?"

"There is a Prophecy among my race. It is said that the Dar Sala-at will gaze into First Cenote and see the power of the Cosmos made manifest. That is why for centuries my ancestors have lived in its shadow." She nodded. "Now the moment has come. The Prophecy is upon us."

"You can't actually expect me to—"

"Please, little dumpling. It is your destiny."

Riane sighed. She did not for an instant believe the creature's mumbo jumbo. On the other hand, she did not have the heart to disappoint Thigpen. So she nodded and, as solemnly as she knew how, she walked to the very edge of the lake. It was eerie, seeing so much water still as death. Not a breeze stirred, not a ripple appeared. Staring into the water was like looking into a black mirror.

In the dim light, she saw the ghostly image of her own face, but, curiously, after a few minutes that slowly evaporated. In its place, nothing. The enigmatic blackness of an utterly starless night. She was no longer aware of her body. Instead, she seemed to be floating above the still, black lake. Then, she was entering it, being pulled down into its depthless center.

And there she saw the grinning face of Pyphoros rising up toward her like a bubble of noxious air seeking the surface. A terror she could not control gripped her and, in a panic, she retreated, rushing backward, upward, until she was returned inside her body, staring at the surface of the still, black water, now not nearly so enigmatic, but altogether hateful.

All at once, she was aware that she was gasping for air. Thigpen was holding her shaking body.

"What is it, little dumpling?" the creature asked. "What did you see?"

For a long time, Riane was silent. Then she whispered, "I saw Pyphoros."

"Are you certain?" Thigpen frowned as she backed up.

Riane nodded.

"This is an unexpected outcome," Thigpen said. "There is something evil at work here."

They retraced their steps. Back in the tunnel, they took the right-hand fork, continuing on in silence for a while. Now and again, Riane could hear soft echoes ricocheting off the walls of the tunnel, and the doleful dripping of lime-hard water was a constant companion. She tried to determine where the echoes were coming from, but they seemed all around.

At last, she said, "Are we ever going back to the surface?"

"How impatient you are!" The long tail swished back and forth, and the light with it. "Well, we are almost at our destination."

"You mean we'll soon be out of this underground labyrinth?"

"Not quite yet. There is one last thing you must see."

A short time afterward, the tunnel grew narrower so that they were obliged to walk single file.

"Mind me, little dumpling," Thigpen warned. "And don't wander away."

Riane wondered what she was talking about, but very soon afterward, she saw the first of what would be many branchings on either side of the tunnel. They were so small she would have had to crawl with her head tucked down in order to enter them; others were smaller still. Looking closely at one, she determined that they were not natural. Someone or something had made this warren. She sniffed the dank air, using, she supposed, Annon's old hunting instincts, but there was no telltale animal spoor, such as one would find near a mammal's den.

"Now," Thigpen said, stopping and holding the light high over them, "be a good little dumpling and don't move."

Riane watched as Thigpen gave a low whistle. Small rustlings started up, as of a wind through the willows, and small heads began to show themselves at the openings. They were flat, ugly heads. The black beady eyes stared out at her without discernible expression.

"Lorgs!" Riane cried. "This is a lorg hatchery!"

The heads snapped back into the darkness of the warren holes.

"Come," Thigpen said. "I want to show you something."

Just past the warren, the tunnel opened out into a medium-sized cavern. Thigpen's tail swept along the ground, and the gemlike light source rolled into a corner. It was no longer needed because this cavern was illuminated by daylight. Riane craned her neck and looked at the chimney cut vertically into the ceiling. Though the chimney seemed a long way off, the sight set off an almost painful longing in her heart for sunshine, clouds, and a distant horizon.

Riane heard rustlings and redirected her attention to the grid of stripped saplings that stretched from one side of the cavern to another. She saw lorgs there. Some were sleeping, curled into balls. Others were partially covered by a webbing of fine, white filaments, while others were completely encased.

A shiver raced through her. "Is this where lorgs go to die?"

"In a sense." Thigpen pointed. "Look!"

On another section of the grid, almost directly over their heads, one of the white filament casings was cracking open. A lorg is about to be born, Riane thought. But then she gasped, for what emerged from the casing was not a lorg at all, but a tiny version of Thigpen.

"I don't understand," she said.

"Of course you do." Thigpen stood very close beside her. "Lift up your arm."

As soon as Riane complied, the baby creature crawled onto her hand and down her arm. Curling up in the hollow at the side of her neck, it went to sleep.

"Lorgs are the larvae," Riane said, "and you are the adult being."

"Our secret, little dumpling, kept even from the Ramahan. And a good thing, too. It was the reason we weren't wiped out when they turned on us." Thigpen nodded as she gestured. "Look, Riane, and remember. The true meaning of Change is right here in front of you. You—the Dar Sala-at— are the agent of Change. You are the only one to know the secret of how we Rappa have survived."

17

Flute

The night is at an end," Rekkk said to Giyan. "You are free to go wherever you choose."

She looked at him with her whistleflower-blue eyes, and said, "I have not yet made up my mind. I will stay with you a while longer."

He was so overwhelmed he simply stood, mute, in the center of Nith Sahor's tower laboratory. They were back on the upper tier, and he could look north out the window to the jagged ice- and snow-laden peaks of the great Djenn Marre. In a few days time, he would get his wish—he would be quits with this occupied city; he would be in the heart of the mountains, beginning his quest for the Gyrgon. But now he knew that it was a quest just as much for himself. His future, he knew, lay waiting for him there on those forbidding slopes. He could sense it, breathing, waiting, living. . . . What might come, he could not say. But he knew that he was going—going with the female he loved beyond all others—and his hearts were light with joy.

"Are you quite recovered, Rekkk?" Nith Sahor asked. He had been on the other side of the eyrie, consulting one data-decagon after another. Now, apparently, he was finished.

"I feel like a newly born V'ornn," Hacilar said truthfully.

Nith Sahor uttered his peculiar and unsettling laugh, which set the teyj to trilling a complex melody in its gorgeous flutelike tones. "Quite rightly so. I could not have said it better myself." He rose. "That being the case, you should be off. Our enemies must not get wind of your whereabouts, or those of the Lady."

"Wait a minute," Rekkk said. "I am still no closer to knowing how to find the Dar Sala-at."

Beside him, Giyan stiffened. "What is this?" she said in low voice. "What are you talking about?"

"Nith Sahor has charged me with—" Rekkk stopped at Nith Sahor's signal.

The Gyrgon looked at Giyan, and said politely, "You wish to know our hearts, Lady?"

Giyan stared from one V'ornn to the other. "Yes," she said in a strangled voice.

"Are you one of us, Lady? Shall we confide in you all our darkest secrets?"

"For the love of Miina, tell me!" she fairly shouted.

With a low trill, the startled teyj spread its wings and rose into the air. It was astonishing to see the pale fluff of its underwings compared to the sleek night-blue sheen of its powerful upper pair. It settled a moment later upon Nith Sahor's shoulder. With a gentle rustling, it folded its primary wings, keeping the others spread for balance. Above the curved green beak, its golden eyes observed, it seemed, everything at once.

"I understand your agitation, Lady Giyan," Nith Sahor said softly. "You have a keen interest in the Dar Sala-at, isn't that so?"

"All Kundalan have a keen interest in the Dar Sala-at," she said. "He is our savior. The One destined to free us from your tyranny."

"Yes, but, Lady, *your* interest in him is special, is it not?"

Rekkk turned to Giyan. "What does he mean?"

Giyan kept her gaze on Nith Sahor. "How much longer do you plan to terrify me?" Her voice contained the slightest tremor.

"Dear Lady, do not think so ill of me." The Gyrgon moved slightly, his tertium circuits flashing. "Terror may be used in many ways. In this case, I needed you to understand the crucial nature of the nexus point at which you now find yourself."

"What do you mean?"

Nith Sahor continued. "One thing you should keep in the forefront of your mind, Rekkk. On this planet, legend and fact are often one and the same. Is that not so, Lady?"

Giyan started again, "I . . . I wouldn't know."

"Oh, but of course you would. I believe it is time for you to tell Rekkk the true meaning of your honorific."

"But she told me—" Rekkk looked over at her. "Did you lie to me?"

"No, I . . ."

She met the Gyrgon's gaze head-on, without intimidation or fear, and Rekkk found that he loved her all the more for her bravery. "I withheld an element of the truth," she said. "In truth, I am stunned that you know, Nith Sahor." Her eyes clouded over. "Or do you?"

"I assure you, Lady, that I—"

"Then *you* tell him," she said simply.

"Testing the tester?" Another sort of smile spread over the Gyrgon's face. He nodded. "Very well. Rekkk, she is called 'Lady' because it is written in Prophesy. It is she who is destined to guide the Dar Sala-at. This, too, is fact as well as legend."

"Are you saying the Prophesy has been fulfilled? That the Dar Sala-at exists?"

"That is precisely what I mean," Nith Sahor said. "Lady Giyan is the living proof of the Dar Sala-at's existence. The two go together; they are linked by a bond that transcends Time and Space. So it is written in Prophesy, is that not correct, Lady?"

"It is," Giyan said in a very small voice. "But how do you know of the Prophesy?"

"It and the Dar Sala-at have been my field of study for

many years, Lady." He now switched to a language with which Rekkk was entirely unfamiliar.

On the other hand, Giyan blanched. After a moment of stunned silence, she replied in the same incomprehensible language.

"What are you two speaking?" Rekkk said shortly.

"The Gyrgon is fluent in the Old Tongue," Giyan said somewhat breathlessly. "It is shocking to me."

Nith Sahor switched back to V'ornn. "Lady, believe me, there are others—enemies of the Dar Sala-at, enemies of ours—who also know of his existence."

Giyan's heart constricted. She regarded him for some time. Nith Sahor said 'he,' which meant he did not know who the Dar Sala-at actually was. Which meant the enemies to which he had referred also did not know. That, at least, was a relief. "Are you ready to tell me all of it?"

Nith Sahor lifted one hand. "Listen well. The unimaginable wrath of the Comradeship had been aroused." He lifted the other hand. "They are like water following the path of least resistance, which means that they have allowed the regent Stogggul to give vent to his cruelty and hatred for all things Kundalan. The evenhandedness of Ashera Eleusis is at an end. The pain and suffering your people have endured for a century is nothing compared to what is about to be unleashed on them. They will sorely need a leader—the Dar Sala-at."

Giyan turned to Rekkk. "Is that what this is all about? You want me to help you find the Dar Sala-at? So you can do what—destroy him? You must be insane, both of you. You must know that I would die before I—"

"Please, Lady." Nith Sahor's expression was pained. "If you do not allow me to finish, I fear we will all die."

She folded her arms across her chest, her expression a set mask.

"Here is the origin of the Comradeship's wrath: Three Gyrgon tried to use the Ring of Five Dragons to open the Storehouse Door. Three Gyrgon are dead."

Giyan looked deathly pale. "The Ring is in the Storehouse Door?"

"Squarely in the mouth of the carving of Seelin."

"I do not believe you. The Ring of Five Dragons has been lost for more than a century."

Nith Sahor held forth the palm of his hand. A swarm of excited ions rose, swirling, coalescing into an image of the caverns below the regent's palace. There was the Storehouse Door and, as the image grew larger, the Ring of Five Dragons could be seen clamped between the carved dragon's jaws.

Shock had rooted Giyan to the spot. "Tymnos!" She barely breathed the word. "The Ring has activated a mechanism of destruction. It is older than Time itself. It is said that it was created by the Great Goddess to ensure the contents of the Storehouse would never fall into profane hands. In the days when Mother ruled the Ramahan there was a Keeper, trained by Mother, who, like Mother herself, possessed the ability to enter the Storehouse. The last of the Keepers is long dead, murdered during the Ramahan uprising. Now only the Dar Sala-at can open the Door."

She nodded numbly. "I understand. We have until the ides of Lonon to find the Dar Sala-at. The Dar Sala-at is the only one who can take the Ring from Seelin's mouth, the only one who can stop the mechanism from cleansing the planet."

"Why was this mechanism put into place?" Rekkk asked.

"It was assumed," Giyan said, "that if Miina's Sacred Ring fell into evil hands, and if the Dar Sala-at was dead and therefore unable to wrest the Ring from the Dragon's mouth, then all was lost. A cataclysm of such dimension that we cannot even imagine it will shake Kundala, destroying us all, paving the way for a new beginning so Miina can start all over again shaping Life as She sees fit."

Nith Sahor clasped his hands together. "Lady, it is my fervent wish to keep Kundala safe because, as Ashera Eleusis never failed to remind me, there is something about you Kundalan that is special, an ineffable quality that speaks to the V'ornn psyche in a way that frightens most Gyrgon. And also because my studies show it to be a crucial nexus point in both our histories. Your people and mine share a prophesy about the City of One Million Jewels."

"Za Hara-at," she whispered. "Eleusis' dream."

Nith Sahor nodded. "Lady, Rekkk cannot find the Dar Sala-at on his own. Will you help him in his quest?"

Giyan stood white and shaking. "So it is true." Her voice was a reedy whisper. A new path was opening up before her, and like all new paths it had a fork. She remembered with astonishing clarity her vision of standing on the wishbone, seeing the Ramahan konara at the end of one fork, and at the end of the other fork, the armor-clad V'ornn holding her child, shining like a star, in the neural net of his gloved hands. Like all her visions, this one was coming true. With every fiber of her being she knew that the next step she took would be down one fork or the other. "I foresaw this moment, in a moment of madness, I thought. Ever afterward I have been trying to deny its validity."

"And yet the moment has come, Lady."

"The moment to trust a Gyrgon and a former Pack-Commander with the fate of the savior of my people." Tears streamed down her face. She knew which fork she would take, which fork she was *destined* to take. There was no turning back. Of course. The path had been there all along. Waiting. She would be reunited with her child far sooner than she had anticipated. She felt exhilarated and terrified at the same time. What changes had been wrought in the Nanthera, and afterward?

"Nith Sahor," she said in a thin voice, "how came the Ring into the possession of the Gyrgon?"

"It was a gift given none too freely by the new regent."

"Wennn Stogggul! But how—?"

"That I do not know, Lady." Nith Sahor spread his hands. "And I am not now in a position to Summon him." Nith Sahor's head turned, the tertium circuits in his skull flashing in the light. "The moment I watched the Ring of Five Dragons kill my brethren, I broke with the will of the Comradeship. I suspect my movements are being monitored. I have taken the necessary precautions here in my laboratory, but to Summon the regent now would be unwise. These recent decisions have been . . . difficult. But I find that I have no choice."

"Neither do I," Giyan whispered. "My people must be saved, no matter the cost."

Nith Sahor nodded. "It is settled then." He turned to Rekkk. "Despite your heightened powers, I must urge you to exercise extreme caution. Our enemies are legion. Worse, they are often masters of disguise. Try to trust no one, but if you must, offer your trust wisely."

"I understand."

"I know you do." Nith Sahor put his ion-gloved hand on Rekkk's shoulder. "You are my eyes and ears. My disciple. I have shown you how to use your advanced okummmon, both as a weapon and as a communicator, but because it is still a work in progress, you will have need to improvise as you go. Though I assure you it is as flexible as it is powerful, there will be limitations, ones that, inevitably, I have not foreseen."

He returned his gaze to Giyan. "Lady, you better than any other know the dire consequences should you fail in your quest."

"We will not fail," she said.

"May whatever gods or goddesses you believe in go with you and protect you."

Climbing up the rock chimney proved quite a bit less daunting than it had looked, due in part to a good, hot dinner, some more sleep, and, most of all, Thigpen's guidance. Riane was relieved to find that they emerged much farther down the mountainside than where the Ice Caves were—on a heavily wooded promontory more or less level with the middle of Heavenly Rushing.

"This is as far as I go, little dumpling," Thigpen said.

Riane knelt down. "Why don't you come with me?"

"Too much to do, too much too much too much." Thigpen began to lick herself. "You go on now."

"I can help you."

"No, you cannot. Something odd happened at First Cenote; something that should not have happened. I smell a scheme of Pyphoros' making. Trust me. You are not prepared for him yet."

Thinking of Pyphoros, Riane shivered. "If, as you say, things are worse, all the more reason for me to stay here with you."

Thigpen looked at her as if she were the stupidest female on Kundala. "You know you must go back."

"I am tired of being told what I must and must not do." Riane looked south where, in the far distance, Axis Tyr lay and, within its walls, Kinnnus Morcha and Wennn Stogggul. "If I am the Dar Sala-at, then I have power; if I have power I can exact my revenge—"

"Now you sound just like a daemon."

"My parents were murdered by two V'ornn!" Riane cried.

Thigpen was looking at her with sad eyes. "You remember what happens when you forsake searching for answers. Evil comes. You are not evil, Riane, but I daresay you are being tempted by evil."

"They must pay for what they did!"

"And they will. But it is not the Dar Sala-at's destiny to have her hands covered with their blood."

"What *is* my destiny, then?" Riane said bleakly.

"Your destiny right now is to return to the abbey. And it is your obligation to fulfill it."

"All right," Riane said. "I will do what you ask."

"It is not what I ask, little dumpling. It is what is written; it is what must be."

Riane looked at her a long time. "What if I say 'No'? What if I simply walk away?"

"You won't." Thigpen's intelligent eyes held hers fixedly.

"Will I see you again?"

Thigpen smiled. "Miina willing."

Riane looked down at the path that led back to the Abbey of Floating White. She knew that she had gotten all the answers she could from the creature. "I'll be off then."

She had turned to go when Thigpen said, "Wait." Thigpen trotted over to her and stood on her four hind legs. "You may pet me, if you wish."

Riane bent over, stroked Thigpen's lush silky fur. The long tail swished back and forth in pleasure.

Thigpen rubbed her head against Riane's hip. "Miina's blessings be with you, little dumpling."

Riane held everything in, and it was only when she was out of sight of the creature that she allowed herself to feel the sadness of their parting. She missed Thigpen already, but on the other hand she cheered herself with the knowledge that she would be seeing Leyna Astar soon. What luck that Konara Laudenum and Bartta had had a falling-out. The only saving grace of life inside the abbey was her growing friendship with Astar.

Five hours later, she arrived at the rear entrance to the abbey. Apparently, she had been spotted coming down the path to the Ice Caves because the huge iron-banded doors were swinging open. A large group of acolytes—many of whom had so derisively seen her off—as well as a goodly number of novices crowded the courtyard, staring. She craned her neck, searching for Astar.

"Riane, we thought you were dead!" called one.

"Where have you been?" called another.

"Are you injured?" asked a third.

"I am fine," she said, slightly bewildered as they crowded around her. "I was delayed by a mountain squall." This was the story she had decided to use to explain her absence.

"Riane!" a commanding voice cried. All of them—acolytes and novices alike—fell silent and bowed as they parted to make way for Konara Urdma. Her persimmon-colored robes roiled around her, mirroring her vexation. She was a slight female with an elongated face that made her look like an ice-hare. "You are long overdue. Do you have any idea the fretting your absence has caused?"

"I am sorry, but I had to wait out the squall," Riane said, her stomach clenching in anger. After her days of freedom, coming back here seemed like a terrible prison sentence. She had to steel herself not to run back up the path into the mountains.

"If there ever was a squall; which I very much doubt," Konara Urdma snapped. "Let me tell you, Riane, that insolent tone of voice will be your downfall." She took Riane by the ear and twisted. This caused a titter to run through the assembled throng, and very soon that titter had gathered force, becoming first a ripple of giggles, and then a tidal wave of laughter.

Riane gritted her teeth. She was obliged to run to keep up with Konara Urdma's long strides, but at least it got her away from the jeering crowd.

"I have heard overly much of your rebellious spirit." Konara Urdma kept up the pressure on Riane's ear even though there no longer seemed to be a need. She exuded an unpleasant smell, as if she had been rooting around in damp earth. "You were given a specific assignment and were expected to carry it out to the letter. The Calling is sacred. The rules must be obeyed."

Riane opened her mouth to protest, but shut it again without making a sound. She knew there was nothing she could possibly say that would change Konara Urdma's mind.

She hurried them along until they arrived at the chamber where Bartta sat hunched over a thick manuscript. As they came closer, Riane could see that she was translating the thick cor-hide sheets from the Old Tongue into modern-day Kundalan.

Bartta looked up when Konara Urdma half flung Riane into the side of the old wooden desk at which she sat.

"Konara, this acolyte of yours—" Urdma began, but stopped abruptly at a curt signal from Bartta.

"Riane, are you injured?" Bartta asked as she rose.

"No, Konara," Riane said.

"Or ill?"

"No, Konara."

"She is willful and disobedient," Konara Urdma said with some distaste.

"Do you not recall your own difficult beginnings, Konara

Urdma?" Bartta put her arm around Riane's shoulders. "Do not judge others so harshly lest you forget your own prior sins."

"Yes, Konara," Konara Urdma said, genuflecting.

Bartta smiled. "You have my gratitude for bringing Riane safely back to me. You are dismissed."

"Yes, Konara," Urdma whispered. "Thank you, Konara." She bowed her way out.

When they were alone, Bartta turned Riane to face her. "Now let me have a look at you. None the worse for wear, I warrant." She sighed. "But when you did not return last night, you gave me quite a turn. In another few hours, I was going to organize a search party."

"I am sorry for frightening you, Bartta," Riane said.

Bartta nodded. "Well said, my dear." She guided Riane out of the chamber. "No one knows better than I how difficult the Order can sometimes be. But, trust me, it is simply a matter of adapting to our insular way of life. All that is required is patience and obedience to Miina. Soon you will be the most accomplished of acolytes. I myself will see to it." They were walking down corridors, moving deeper into the heart of the abbey. As they progressed, however, the corridors become darker, less ornamented, and gradually colorless.

"As part of your homecoming, I have a surprise for you," Bartta said.

They had arrived at a small, dark, cramped, passageway in a section of the abbey wholly unfamiliar to Riane. There was something about this area that reeked of extreme age, of power long forgotten, and lost magics most ancient.

Bartta stopped in front of an old scarred heartwood door. When she unlocked it using a key on a long chain attached to her robes it creaked on massive unoiled iron hinges.

Riane's heart was beating fast. She liked nothing about this, but now, upon walking down this dingy passageway, upon seeing this door, a wave of foreboding swept through her.

Don't go in there!

"Why are you hesitating, dear?" So saying, Bartta shoved her roughly through the doorway, then turned and locked the door behind them. Flames from old-fashioned reed torches illuminated the high-ceilinged, windowless chamber in a fitful orange glow. Riane gasped.

The chamber was pyramidal in shape, without ornament or furniture, save for a large glennan chair, exquisitely carved and turned. The same peculiar quality about both chamber and chair was intimidating in its primitive power. The beautiful chair sat on a raised plinth in the center of the room. Old runes were carved into the plinth, and these same runes, Riane noticed, were also incised into the four legs of the chair.

Astar sat in the chair. Metal mesh straps held her tightly at wrists, ankles, and forehead. Her head was tilted far back so that her mouth was pointed at the ceiling. She looked as if she were about to swallow a long, slender crystal rod which hung rigid and unmoving from a device at the back of the chair.

"What . . ." Riane had to swallow before she could go on. "What are you doing to her?"

"Now what do you suppose I am doing?"

Riane saw Astar's terrified eyes, and ran toward her.

"I thought as much," Bartta muttered, and swinging her arms wide, spoke three words. Immediately, Riane was frozen in place. Though she struggled, mightily, she was paralyzed completely. She could see and hear, but the more she struggled the tighter the grip on her until it became laborious for her even to breathe.

"Try to relax, Riane," Bartta said. "There is nothing you can do."

Bartta went across the chamber until she was standing directly behind Astar. Lovingly, she stroked the crystal length above Astar's head. "From time immemorial it has been known as the *had-atta*. Do you know that word, Astar? In the Old Tongue, it means 'flute.' It is an ancient method at divining true intent." Bartta stroked the crystal tube again. "You see, my dear, I have had my eye on you. Having come by rumors of your disrespectful tongue, I have for some time suspected this beautiful exterior harbored a rebellious, even a deceitful spirit. Therefore, I assigned you to be Riane's instructor."

She whirled on Riane. "You formed a bond with her. In your company, I knew she would relax her guard. If the rumors about her *were* true, I needed to know. And if not, well, no harm would be done." She turned back to Astar. "I spied on you. I saw what you did to her, how you used the qi, the sacred needles on her." She leaned in. "How, Astar? How did you, a mere leyna, a novice, gain knowledge available to just a few konara?"

Astar squirmed, her eyes open unnaturally wide. Her beautiful lips were grotesquely distorted in order to accommodate the flute.

"And the ideas you put in her head about Kyofu! What would a novice know about Kyofu, Astar, hmmm?"

Bartta began to lower the crystal tube down Astar's throat. The flesh bulged out, Astar began to gag. Riane tried to shout "No!" but only the tiniest whimper emerged. Tears of anguish and frustration rimmed her eyes, held in place by whatever sorcerous stasis she was in.

Bartta lowered the flute again, and Astar began to scream. But it was not like any scream Riane had ever heard. The sorcerous flute absorbed the vibrations of the vocal cords, channeling them through its matrix, amplifying them, spewing them out as an eerie keening. Bartta held the *had-atta* steady. "Of course, there is the chance that even the guilty may be redeemed."

She turned to Riane, and said matter-of-factly, "I imagine you would like to know what will happen. Unless she relents, I will lower the flute into Leyna Astar's esophagus. The deeper the flute goes, the louder she will scream, the more the flute will amplify those screams. If the flute shatters, it will be proof that she is unrepentant. If it does not, then she can be rehabilitated."

Astar's beautiful face was ashen. Sweat stained her robes, ran off her skin in rivulets. Tiny tremors commenced to in-form her body with a life all its own until she looked like a marionette dancing at the ends of invisible strings. Her nostrils flared as she frantically sucked air into her lungs, and she wept openly.

Bartta smiled at Riane. "Oh, do not cry. Custom dictates that she who has been wronged has the right to administer the sentence." Riane saw the flute tremble slightly; she was terrified Bartta would let it go all the way down. "Say the word now, Riane, so Astar will be punished to the full extent of the law."

Riane opened her mouth and, to her astonishment, her vocal cords at least were freed from the spell. "I will not," she croaked. "Nothing Leyna Astar has done merits punishment."

"Is that so?" Bartta cocked her head. "Then you vote for life."

"Yes," Riane whispered through dry lips. "Grant her life, I beg you."

"Yes, beg me."

"Please, Bartta, let her live," Riane said again.

" 'Please, Bartta, let her live,' " Bartta mimicked, her face distorted. "Well, yes, I suppose that can be arranged. But it is entirely up to you, Riane. Astar's one chance at life is for you to do as I say, now and forever. To become obedient as a lamb. Will you do that?"

"Yes," she said in a parched voice. "If you will save her, I will do whatever—"

A scream emanated from Astar.

Riane, sickened and horrified, sensed what was to come. She struggled with all her might against the paralyzing spell. "No, don't, please," she cried. "I can save you. I will do—"

The scream came again, louder, harsher this time, ringing around the walls.

"No, you don't! You'll give me all your secrets! I swear!" Bartta lunged for the flute's thong, but it was too late. Astar had already begun her death scream.

It billowed up from the very core of her, passed through every cell in her body, gaining strength as it went, and when she released it, the flute shattered into ten thousand jagged fragments that embedded themselves in her.

"No, no, you cannot die!" Bartta unstrapped Astar even as she was drowning in the powerful surf of her own blood. "You must tell me what you know!"

Astar vomited blood all over Bartta's magnificent persimmon-colored robes.

Book Three

WHITE BONE GATE

"The ascendancy of evil is as inevitable as the rising of the sun or the shifting of the tides. The face of evil may alter, but its underlying nature remains constant. Evil enters us through a rupture in White Bone Gate. The precise site is often difficult to locate and even more difficult to repair. Given the nature of this Gate, restoration of the individual is exceedingly dangerous, and often impossible. . . ."

—Utmost Source,
the Five Sacred Books of Miina

18

Malistra

Long shadows enrobed the regent's palace. Here and there, red highlights—the last traces of the setting sun—sparked and died on V'ornn heavy cut-crystal glassware, plates and cutlery arrayed on the long, ornate state dining table. Kundalan servants, overseen by members of the Haaar-kyut, the regent's personal guard, saw to the last-minute preparations for the banquet that was about to begin.

The regent Wennn Stogggul, dressed in wine-red robes, a ceremonial dagger sheathed at his left hip, surveyed this area of his domain with a highly critical eye. This was his first formal banquet since he had assumed the regency and he was determined that it would be a memorable one. He went around the table, checking the holoIDs, memorizing where each invited dignitary would sit. This was especially critical, since for the first time in V'ornn memory members of the Lesser Caste Khagggun had been invited to sit alongside Great Caste Bashkir and Genomatekks. Assuring himself that all was in order, he passed through the high window-doors, strolling along the terrace. Twilight had overtaken Axis Tyr. Beneath the deepening blue of the sky he could hear the sounds of the city—the singsong calls of the street-sellers, the clip-clop of cthauros' hooves, the laughter of children, the orations of oracles—and he was reminded all over again that he was on a backward world.

Not that his Gyrgon masters would ever let him forget it. Nightmares had followed him to bed after his last Summoning. The Gyrgon with the ruby-red pupils still filled him with dread, and the depths of the dread that racked him made him sick to his stomachs. They knew him, these Gyrgon. They knew his darkest fears; they knew what kind of leash to put him on, what kind of punishment he would respond to. He ran a trembling hand across his forehead, wiping away the dampness. He would have to tread carefully with them. *Very* carefully. The less contact he had with them the better.

And yet, there was an aspect of the Summoning that most mystified him: the rage, and their anger toward him. What had he done, except provide them with what they had wanted, the Ring of Five Dragons? But, ah, what if it had gone badly? What if they could not break the Ring's secret, or it had turned out to be useless—as he had suspected all along?

Glancing down, he saw Star-Admiral Kinnnus Morcha appear in the courtyard, on his way to the banquet. Stogggul made a face. He had thought long and hard before seeking to enlist Morcha's assistance. An alliance with the Khaggun was a perilous endeavor; it had the potential to be disastrous. Who knew how these Lesser Castes would act when given nominal Great Caste status? The accursed Ashera Consortium—*N'Luuura take them all!*—had forced his hand. He knew better than anyone the extreme danger in moving against the Ashera. And although his plan had met with success on Kundala, he was painfully aware that his victory would not be complete until he had brought down the Ashera Consortium. Unlike his peremptory strike here, the next phase of his plan would take some time, it would have to be finessed. No V'ornn family—especially one such as the Ashera, which enjoyed enormous prestige, wealth, and goodwill—could be laid low quickly. Three Bashkir handlers were in charge of the Ashera Consortium. Normally, Eleusis' brothers would have run it, but he had had no brothers. Instead, he had handpicked a trio of V'ornn, swearing them in seigggon—blood oath—to his family. Wennn Stogggul knew he would have to either co-opt them or kill them, one by one. But not until he discovered the great Ashera secret: the origin of salamuuun, the drug whose sale was the central pillar of their wealth. Gaining control of salamuuun, the regent knew, was the key to breaking the Ashera Consortium completely, absolutely, and irrevocably. He clenched his hands into fists. He would not rest until he had achieved the utter destruction of the Ashera, body and soul.

Through the gathering gloom of evening he saw that the Star-Admiral was no longer alone in the courtyard. Dalma was talking to him. She was dressed in a robe that clung most provocatively to her, and it did not escape him that the Star-Admiral's gaze never left her curvaceous form. As he watched, she threw her head back and laughed. Then the Star-Admiral escorted her across the courtyard. As they approached the doorway to the first floor, Dalma glided ahead. Stogggul saw the Star-Admiral drink in her supple body before he, too, disappeared from sight.

The regent stood thoughtfully for a moment. A small smile informed his face as he turned and went back inside. He circled the banquet table once more. Finding Dalma's holoID he switched it with another at the opposite end of the table.

A half hour later, the fusion lamps had been powered on, spherical hoods directing the illumination at the holoimage of Kundala, spinning slowly on its axis. The holoimage, hanging above the center of the table, reflected and refracted the excited-ion light, bathing the vast room in a multicolored glow. It was an impressive display, one that was not lost on the guests. Equally impressive was the list of Bashkir and Khagggun luminaries sitting around the table drinking the regent's finest fire-grade numaaadis.

Looking down the table, Stogggul was gratified to see that the Star-Admiral, cheeks flushed purple, was talking animatedly with Dalma, who sat at his right hand. She was the only female in the room and as such was inevitably the topic of many conversations buzzing around the table. Whenever there was a natural break in the conversation flow, he caught her glancing at him with a look of intense curiosity. Of course she was used to sitting at *his* right hand; she must be wondering if she had angered him in some way. He smiled at her and quickly shifted his eyes to the Star-Admiral, who was at that moment answering a question from Kurgan. Dalma, attuned to the hidden intimations of command, understood his glance and returned his smile. She put a hand on the Star-Admiral's shoulder, causing him to turn back to her.

Satisfied for the moment, the regent, without appearing to, listened in on a conversation Kefffir Gutttin, a leading Bashkir, was having with Bach Ourrros. The contrast between the two V'ornn was striking. Bach Ourrros was tall, thin as a cadaver, with a long, tapering skull and a gaudy string of tertium rings through his left ear. Kefffir Gutttin, on the other hand, was as brawny and muscular as any Khaggun. Rumor had it that, as a lad, he had fought in the Kalllistotos, the game ring, officially outlawed, but unofficially sanctioned. It was the one place where all castes—save the Gyrgon, of course—came together and, for the moments of the ferocious no-holds-barred Kalllistotos, were one. Whether or not Kefffir Gutttin had, in fact, fought in the Kalllistotos, he was a brute of a man, and one not to be trifled with. The two Bashkir were talking of a business deal—three thousand metric tons of raw tertium ore and how much it would fetch after it was shipped from the refinery.

To their immediate left, Sornnn SaTrryn, the new Prime Factor, weighed in with his opinion. Tall, lean, with a vaguely dangerous air Stogggul rather liked, he had been making his charismatic presence felt from the moment he had arrived. It was interesting to see these two older Bashkir deferring to him. Of course, his father, the recently deceased Hadinnn SaTrryn, had been an old friend of Eleusis Ashera, and it was the SaTrryn Consortium that had first aligned itself with the Ashera in planning to build Za Hara-at in the wastes of the Korrush, before either Bach Ourrros or Kefffir Gutttin had come on board. Now that Eleusis was dead, the construction of Za Hara-at had come to a screeching halt.

Stogggul had given Sornnn SaTrryn the Prime Factor's position purely as repayment for the Ring of Five Dragons. But in the short time he had been in the position, Stogggul had been made aware that he had made the most of the position. He had realigned the territories of squabbling Consortia, and had successfully presided over a tricky dispute concerning the discovery of a highly lucrative deposit of raw tertium in the hills outside Silk Bamboo Spring to the west of the Borobodur forest.

All this time, Stogggul had been furtively watching Kurgan out of the corner of his eye. He could not get used to seeing a Bashkir in a Khagggun uniform, much less his own son! But then Kurgan had always been a strange child. At age eight he had begun to hunt with a precision and a passion that bordered on obsession. Stogggul's sons were his burden. Terrettt, Kurgan's younger brother, had been born mentally impaired, and was housed in a section of Receiving Spirit, the vast hospice complex the Kundalan had built at Harborside, overlooking the docks and the Sea of Blood. Stogggul never went to see him, but rather relied on periodic reports from Marethyn, the younger of his two daughters, who visited Terrettt often. Not that these reports were needed, really; there was never any improvement.

Marethyn took the female trait of empathy to extremes. It was she who cared for her brother when no one else could be bothered. This was something of an annoyance to Stogggul, who believed that she was possessed of a great artistic talent that was lying dormant while she went on her foolish missions of mercy.

Kurgan was a problem—but then he had always been a problem. First, periodically disappearing from his hingatta, then befriending Annon Ashera, and now worming his way into the Star-Admiral's good graces. Morcha might be too thickheaded to see it, but Stogggul knew his son well enough to know that he had some dangerous and illicit angle in mind. There was something wrong with that boy. From the earliest age, he had ignored rules and regulations. As a result Stogggul was always disciplining him. Not that it seemed to matter overmuch. Kurgan had no sense of history or tradition. It had gotten so bad he had even heard that Bach Ourrros had been making jokes about it. Well, now Kurgan was the Star-Admiral's problem, and as far as Stogggul was concerned the Star-Admiral was welcome to him.

And speaking of Bach Ourrros, Stogggul had invited him

specifically to pour silicon into the wound. It had nearly killed Bach Ourrros when Stogggul had stolen Dalma away from him. From that incident, a bitter and protracted mercantile war had started between the two Consortia. No matter. Everyone would interpret his inviting Bach Ourrros and Kefffir Gutttin to this first banquet as a sign of his benevolence and magnanimity.

Stogggul, laughing inside, smiled deeply as he rose from the head of the table. As he did so, the participants fell silent.

"I trust you all have been enjoying yourselves," he said. "I would like to formally introduce a V'ornn many of you already know, our new Prime Factor, Sornnn SaTrryn." He raised his hand, and the young V'ornn stood up, bowed to the applause, then sat. "In between business trips to the Korrush our new Prime Factor has been very busy reforming our caste, ensuring higher profits for every Bashkir Consortium." His gaze moved from the Star-Admiral to Olnnn Rydddlin to Kurgan, and thence to everyone in between, finally settling on the long, pale faces of Bach Ourrros and Kefffir Gutttin. *Two praen in a podlet,* he thought. *One thinks the treasonous thought, the other carries it out. But then Kefffir Gutttin, with his hair-trigger temper and frightening physical prowess, is well suited to be Bach Ourrros' huntsman. Well, we shall see how long that lasts.*

"My next announcement concerns the proposed construction of Za Hara-at. I am afraid my office has discovered a number of irregularities in the permits and covenants that have been filed with the regent's office."

"What? What is the meaning of this," Kefffir Gutttin blustered right on cue. "We were assured by the regent Eleusis Ashera himself—"

"I am the regent now!" The hackles rose at the back of Stogggul's neck. He bared his teeth. "Perhaps these irregularities would not have arisen had the former regent not also been involved in this . . . business arrangement. A conflict of interest, don't you know."

Bach Ourrros stirred. "And when, pray tell, will these irregularities be dealt with?"

Stogggul turned his bared teeth on the other Bashkir. "My dear Bach Ourrros, believe me when I tell you there were far more urgent matters requiring this office's attention."

"What is your opinion on this delay?" Bach Ourrros said to Sornnn SaTrryn.

The young Prime Factor shrugged. "It is as Wennn Stogggul says. It is a matter for the regent's office to unravel. That is the law."

"Oh, yes, I know what urgent matter takes up the regent these dark days," Kefffir Gutttin cut in, growling. "Decimating the Mesagggun population."

"Only the priests of Enlil and their most virulent supporters were rounded up," Stogggul said evenly.

"Rounded up, tortured, and killed." Kefffir Gutttin was getting himself worked up. "You would do us a kindness not to *edit* your report."

"Report? Since when does the regent *report* on his affairs?"

"Eleusis Ashera did. He solicited our input in each step of the design and construction plans for Za Hara-at. There are those of us who have a stake in its completion. Such an important cross-cultural experiment—"

" 'Cross-cultural experiment!' " Stogggul's contempt was obvious to all. "How dare you use a euphemism to describe a city of *alien*-lovers."

"That was Eleusis Ashera's phrase."

Ourrros could have curbed his huntsman with a single word or gesture. Instead, his stony silence, giving tacit sanction to this outrage, goaded Stogggul on.

"Do not speak to me of the former regent. For years loyal V'ornn have stood on the sidelines watching while he sanctioned this misguided mingling of races. It disgusts us, and well it should. We are V'ornn! We are the masters of the universe! We do not wallow in the muck of the gutters. Za Hara-at was the former regent's folly. As far as I am concerned, it died with him."

"Eleusis Ashera!" Gutttin thundered. "The former regent

had a name. An illustrious name. You dishonor him and all of us when you do not use it."

"I am the regent now," Stogggul repeated with every iota of menace at his disposal. He was sick to death of Eleusis Ashera. Even death could not kill his memory. "And you are in the regent's palace at my invitation. You dishonor yourself and those who stand with you when you speak to your regent in this treasonous manner."

"Since when is it treason to speak one's mind? Are you so afraid of opinions contrary to yours? You are not *my* regent; you are not the regent of anyone sitting here listening to your farcical lies. If you are regent at all, it is of and for the Stogggul Consortium and only the Stogggul Consortium."

Stogggul wondered how long the Star-Admiral would allow this blowhard to spew his heretical invective. "I knew you were a fool, Kefffir Gutttin. But this evening you have proved yourself to be a dangerous fool."

Kefffir Gutttin leapt up. "Is that a threat, *regent*? Will you murder me in my private chambers in the same cowardly manner you murdered Eleusis Ashera? Will you murder each and every one of us who does not conform to your way of thinking?"

"There you have it, my friends and colleagues!" Stogggul cried. "He is condemned by his own words!"

"Regent, you have no idea of the consequences of your actions. Mark my words. As surely as I stand here—" Gutttin's face abruptly changed expression. A harsh gurgle escaped his lips, along with a thin trickle of turquoise blood. Then he fell over, a bolt buried in his back.

Behind him, Kurgan was standing, his left arm outstretched, pointed directly at where Gutttin had stood. It was he who had shot the bolt.

"Be warned," Kurgan said. "This is how the Khagggun deal with traitors."

Stogggul stared at Gutttin's corpse. This had been a complete surprise. And not a pleasant one. It was the Star-Admiral's duty to spring into action. That he had allowed

Kurgan to do his wet work bore further study. On the other hand, Kurgan had performed the task most efficiently. Perhaps the decision to allow him to become the Star-Admiral's adjutant had indeed been a good one. Once again, Dalma had given him sound advice.

As Kinnnus Morcha gave the order for Gutttin's corpse to be taken away, Stogggul said, "My friends and colleagues, no one regrets this unfortunate incident more than I." His gaze swept over the assembled V'ornn, trying to read their expressions. He wondered how many of the Bashkir here secretly sympathized with Ourrros and Gutttin. This was something he meant to discover, though he knew it would prove to be a lengthy and painful process. At last, his eyes fixed upon his sworn enemy. "My dear Bach Ourrros," he said in a light, sweet voice, "do you wish to finish what Kefffir Gutttin began?"

"Kefffir Gutttin's opinions were his own," Ourrros said stiffly. "He is dead. Allow him to rest in peace."

Stogggul bowed his head. He could see Bach Ourrros struggling with the death of his friend and fellow collaborator. He reveled in Bach Ourrros shock and grief. Sornnn SaTrryn, on the other hand, was evincing no such trauma. He sat placidly, watching Stogggul from beneath hooded eyes. Was there the ghost of a smile on his face?

Stogggul called for more fire-grade numaaadis, and, shortly after the wine was poured, platters of steaming food began appearing and the banquet was begun in earnest. In true V'ornn fashion, the sudden death the participants had just witnessed was forgotten, and when the empty chair and place setting had been removed from the room, the last vestige of Kefffir Gutttin vanished with them.

It was during dessert that a member of the Haaar-kyut approached the Star-Admiral and whispered in his ear. At once, Kinnnus Morcha's eyes found Stogggul's and he gave an imperceptible nod. He rose from the table, followed the Khagg,gun out of the room. A moment later, Stogggul also rose, told the guests to continue enjoying themselves, and excused himself. Sornnn SaTrryn's eyes caught his on his way out.

Wennn Stogggul found the Star-Admiral and a heavily armed Haaar-kyut escort waiting for him. "There has been an incident," the Star-Admiral said. "A crude bomb has gone off in the main Haaar-kyut barracks."

The regent Stogggul shook and angry fist. "I told you Eleusis Ashera was too lenient with the Kundalan. Well, what have you done about this incident?"

"Two resistance members have been executed. Unfortunately. They did not give us an opportunity to interrogate them. A third is still at large."

"How bad was the damage?"

"Bad enough. Fifteen dead, a score more wounded."

"Find the third resistance member and make an example of him."

"Yes, regent."

Together, they went down the central staircase, descending past the ground floor, into the subterranean caverns upon which the palace had been built.

"On a matter closer to home," the Star-Admiral said, "Kefffir Gutttin is not alone in his opinions."

The regent grunted. "Have the traitor's head spitted on a pike and display it outside the main entrance to the palace until it turns black. That should make those sympathetic to his cause retreat to their dens."

The Star-Admiral called for one of his Khagggun to carry out the order.

Stogggul whispered to him. "I want the beheading done in plain sight of the populace. Make a ceremony of it." He waved his hand. "You Khagggun know more about ceremonies and rituals than we Bashkir do." He did not notice the expression that flickered across Kinnnus Morcha's face. "I want those who witness it to remember, and everyone else to hear about it from those who saw."

"As you wish, regent," the Star-Admiral said in a clipped tone.

They had arrived at the caverns. As they hurried past the

cyclopean Storehouse Door, Stogggul gestured. "There it is, Star-Admiral, the Gyrgon apparently think this is greatest prize and the greatest mystery on Kundala."

"Let them have it, then."

"But it is odd that there are none of them around. I gave them the key to this Door, the Ring of Five Dragons. I see it there in the center medallion, yet the Door remains locked. Odd, don't you think?"

Kinnnus Morcha shrugged. He had no more use for Kundalan legends than the regent did. Quickly, he led the way down the passageway to the series of cells. All had been empty when Annon and Giyan had passed through here on their flight from the palace, Now, the farthest one was guarded by a pair of burly Haaar-kyut, who came to attention at the arrival of the group.

"This is the priest, Pa'an," the Star-Admiral said. "He is the last of his kind."

Stogggul, peering into the gloom of the cell, saw an emaciated male V'ornn, naked save for a few pathetic tatters of clothes. The smell of fresh blood and waste matter made a miasma that was almost palpable.

"As you can see, regent, we have been doing our best to keep the priest entertained."

"And has he returned your favor in kind?"

"Oh, yes, indeed, regent. Shall I demonstrate?"

Stogggul lifted an arm. "By all means."

The Star-Admiral deactivated the security grid, and the two V'ornn entered the stinking cell. The priest, hanging from a ring in the ceiling, looked at them from bloodshot eyes that barely focused. He blinked and moaned as the fusion lamps came on.

Kinnnus Morcha stood in front of the unfortunate with his feet firmly planted and wide apart. "Where is your god now, priest, eh?" he said, prodding him in the ribs. "Where is Enlil, whom you have sworn to follow, whose gospel you preach to the ignorant and the gullible?"

"Enlil is here," the priest rasped through lips swollen and

black with dried blood. "He is all around, in the very air we breathe."

"Really?" The Star-Admiral's voice was mocking. "Then he must be as sick to his stomachs as we are." He grunted. "You really have made a mess of yourself, haven't you?"

" 'Enlil is my sword, my guide, my righteous wrath—' "

The priest's recitation was abruptly terminated as the Star-Admiral struck him a wicked blow just above a kidney. He moaned and sagged; fresh blood drooled from his mouth.

"Do not jabber in the regent's face, priest."

"That is enough, Star-Admiral." Stogggul grabbed hold of the priest to take the pressure off him and unhooked him from the chains binding him.

"Regent, what are you doing?"

Ignoring him, Stogggul laid the priest down on the bench set into the stone wall. "Listen to me, Brother Pa'an," he whispered. "I want to know everything you know. You are the spiritual keeper of the Mesagggun. Though vast in numbers, this caste is utterly unknown to me, as it was to the previous regent. He was content to leave them alone with their vestigial religion that preaches heresy against the Gyrgon will. That changes now. But before I bring them to heel, I must first know their fervent hopes, their dearest dreams . . . and their darkest fears. All this you will reveal to me."

"I will die first," the priest said. "Enlil will take me in his arms and keep my spirit safe."

"Is that what you think, Brother Pa'an?" Stogggul took his own cloak and laid it over the priest. "That I will torture you until you die? That you will heroically hold out because of your piety to a god long forgotten? Enlil is dead, my friend, if, indeed, he ever existed. The only living gods in the universe are the Gyrgon."

"You mistake me for someone else," the priest croaked. "I am not your friend; I am your enemy."

"Who would have guessed? A priest with a sense of humor." The Star-Admiral grunted. "Now what will you do, regent? The only thing these vermin understand is pain and more pain."

"Brother Pa'an has suffered enough." Stogggul looked down at the haggard face. "Haven't you, my friend?" He gently fed him some water, then keyed in a code on his okummmon. A tertium wire snaked out, inserting itself in the left side of the priest's neck in the center of a small pale scar. "Now," he whispered to the priest, "if memory serves you were bonded to your god with a piece of his war shield, isn't that right?" The priest's eyes stared up at him blankly. "This fragment of Enlil's shield is what allows you to be his emissary in this world. It allows you to bond with him, it allows him to hear your prayers and to answer them. Without it, you are cut off from your god. Have I got it right so far?"

Understanding bloomed on the priest's face as he felt a short, sharp stab of pain. "What are you going to do?" he whispered through his cracked, bloated lips. A thin trickle of blood began to pool in the sunken hollow of his shoulder.

"Why, I have already done it," Stogggul said, showing him the small fragment the tertium wire had extracted from his neck.

The priest closed his eyes and moaned. Tears leaked from his eyes.

"Now you are nothing, Pa'an. You are bereft of Enlil. If I choose to kill you—which I very well may—he will not be there to receive you. Instead, your soul will sink into the Abyss, there to share all eternity with the unbelievers, the blasphemers, the defilers. That is what is in store for you. Unless . . ."

The priest's eyes flew open. "Unless what?"

"Unless you tell me what I want to know about your flock."

For a long time there was silence in the cell. Then, slowly, haltingly, the priest began to speak. "Give me back that which is ordained for me."

Stogggul placed the fragment on the tip of the wire and again it snaked into the side of the priest's neck. "There, Brother. Your link to the god Enlil has been restored."

Tears flowed again down the priest's cheeks. "There is great unrest among the Mesagggun. Their enmity toward the

Khagggun is at a boiling point. So much so that the Traditionalists and the Forwards have forged a pact of unity."

"Now there's as useless a piece of disinformation as I have
ever heard," the Star-Admiral said. "The skcettta is making
fools of us."

Waving him to silence, Wennn Stogggul whispered, "If
what you say is true, it would be unprecedented. The enmity
between the Traditionalists and the Forwards goes back
many generations. How did this alleged pact come about?"

"It was brokered," the priest said.

"By whom?"

"I do not know."

"Oh, kill this lying piece of excrement now!" Kinnnus
Morcha thundered.

Stogggul pressed on. "Brother Pa'an, I warn you. If you
lie, if you withhold information, I will remove your ordina-
tion piece, and no amount of supplication on your part will
make me give it back.

"It is not a lie," the priest said firmly. "I only know they
are not V'ornn."

"So this priest would have us believe that aliens have not
only made contact with the Mesagggun but are conspiring
with them against us?"

"On the face of it, it sounds absurd," the regent agreed.
"And yet I cannot afford to ignore him, Star-Admiral. If there
is any truth to what he says, we must know about it, do I
make myself clear?"

"Yes, regent."

Stogggul turned back to the priest. "One last question, my
friend, and then you may rest. What is it your caste wants
so badly that they have put aside generations of hate and
mistrust?"

"The building of Za Hara-at. The City of One Million
Jewels is important to us. We are uniting to continue its
construction."

"This is all very amusing, but hardly alarming." Stogggul
leaned over the priest. "We have ways of dealing with your
kind."

"You will not be able to split the Mesagggun," the priest said dully.

Stogggul paused, looking at the priest who had averted his face. "What is it, Brother Pa'an? What are you not telling me?"

The priest's eyes were finally dry. "Trust me, regent, you do not want to hear this."

Stogggul put a hand tenderly on the priest's brow and brought his head around. "Be that as it may, I *will* hear it."

"As you desire, regent." The priest licked his lips. "At the core, it is fear that binds the Mesagggun factions."

"Fear? What could they fear save the regent's retribution?"

"They fear the Centophennni."

The Star-Admiral's face went white. He looked stricken. With a curt gesture, he sent the Haaar-kyut outside of hearing range.

"What about the Centophennni?" Stogggul asked in a voice a shade less commanding than before.

"It involves the most ancient of prophecies. You who have cut yourself off from the god Enlil are ignorant of it," the priest said. " 'In the center of a million jewels/At the nexus of the universe/When worlds collide/When the Usurper arises/The Centophennni slaughter in his wake.' "

"This is nonsense!" the Star-Admiral cried. "Why would the Forwards care about a Prophesy from a dead god in whom they do not believe?"

Stogggul held up his hand. "That is the wrong question to ask. Brother Pa'an, what now has given this *ancient* Prophesy its urgency?"

"We have heard that it parallels a Kundalan Prophesy."

"He is lying," the Star-Admiral growled. "In all their debriefings I have never heard this spoken of by any Ramahan."

"That is because it is not a Ramahan Prophesy," the priest replied. "It is Druuge."

"Druuge?" Wennn Stogggul said. "What care I for these desert nomads?"

"The City of One Million Jewels appears in their cosmology. It is known as Earth Five Meetings. Earth Five Meetings is the nexus of the universe, a holy city built upon the ruins of an ancient fortress, the place where the Kundalan will make their last stand against Eternal Night. The Druuge believe Za Hara-at is that city."

"What care I for primitives who stupidly choose to live their lives in the middle of three thousand square kilometers of nothing?"

"Perhaps you should, regent. You see, their prophecies also tell of the Usurper. The coming of the Usurper heralds the beginning of Anamordor, the End of All Things."

Stogggul sat back on his heels. "And who is this Usurper who is to bring the Centophennni down upon us, who is to cause the end of the universe?"

"Why, regent, I would think by now it would be clear," the priest said. "The Usurper is you."

"Me?" Wennn Stogggul leapt up. "Now you go too far!"

"On the contrary," the priest said. "I have not gone far enough." So saying, he snatched at the dagger at the regent's left hip, slashed the curving blade across his own throat.

"No!" Stogggul cried, whipping the dagger out of his spasming hand. But it was too late, the priest lay dead in a pool of his own blood. "N'Luuura take him!"

"Or Enlil," the Star-Admiral said. "It matters not."

The regent turned. "Let us swiftly away from this noxious place. Make arrangements for the priest to be burned as befits his beliefs, but do it quickly."

"Yes, regent."

The two V'ornn walked hurriedly back to the Door to the Storehouse. For the moment, they were alone. The Star-Admiral stood engrossed by the new okummmon embedded in his forearm with a mixture of elation and distrust. "Will I ever get used to this thing?"

"It *is* what you have desired, isn't it?" the regent Stogggul said. He was staring fixedly at the pale, blood-streaked corpse of the priest as members of the Haaar-kyut carried it out of the cell.

"Oh, of course." Kinnnus Morcha prodded the flesh surrounding the new implant to see if it was still sore. As a

Khagggun he had been trained to trust only those who had fought beside him in battle, those who had proved their mettle in the terrifying cauldron of interspecies conflagration. "One merely needs to change one's thinking." Though this was the crowning moment of his life, a moment he had dreamed of ever since he was young, he frowned. "Thinking which has sidereal centuries of tradition behind it."

"It is precisely this tradition from which you have been longing to break free. Or so you claimed when we made seigggon."

"Regent, the seigggon is a sacred blood oath. Those who renege on it are butchered like cattle."

Stogggul nodded. "Then neither of us have anything to fear."

Morcha bristled, his back ramrod-straight. "The Khagggun fear nothing."

Now the regent looked at him. "You fear the Gyrgon, Star-Admiral."

"And the Gyrgon fear the Centophennni."

"As do we all," the regent replied. "Listen to me, Star-Admiral, what transpired back there is for our ears and our ears alone, do I make myself perfectly clear?"

Kinnnus Morcha nodded. "No one knows this better than I, regent. I was at Hellespennn, remember? I have fought the Centophennni. The Prophesy of Enlil we have just heard cannot possibly be true. It is too terrible to contemplate."

"A Prophesy of a dead god? I think we need not worry. But there is something in what the priest said that disturbs me. He would have us believe by inference that it was this Druuge tribe who brokered the alliance between Mesagggun factions. No, it is more likely a ruse the clever priest used to distract us from discovering the true identity of the alliance brokers. Tell me, Star-Admiral, who has the most to gain by a Mesagggun uprising?"

"The Kundalan resistance, regent."

"Exactly! The Ashera regime taught them to be bold. They attack the Haaar-kyüt barracks, they are meddling in V'ornn affairs. I like it not. The resistance needs to be taught a final lesson."

"I will have Olnnn Rydddlin see to it immediately."

"No, Star-Admiral." Stogggul lifted a finger. "I have something else in mind for Olnnn Rydddlin. Have you another who can fit the bill?"

An oblique admonition, but one that rankled all the same. "Most assuredly, regent," Kinnnus Morcha said crisply. "It shall be done."

Stogggul nodded. "Gird your packs for immediate battle," he said. "We have the full backing of the Comradeship."

"Speaking of Gyrgon, regent. My new okummmon has begun to pain me overmuch."

"The implant takes time—"

"No. It just started. Here. When we came abreast of the Kundalan Storehouse Door." The Star-Admiral looked around, then went down on one knee. "What have we here?"

"What?" Wennn Stogggul said. "What have you found?"

The Star-Admiral had unhooked a Tracker from the belt he wore beneath his robe. He ran the device across the floor directly in front of the Door. He grunted, then looked up at the regent. "It is blood, spilled quite recently." He stood. "The truly odd thing is that it is Gyrgon blood."

"Are you certain?"

"The genomics analyzer on the Tracker is faultless. More than one Gyrgon died here, regent. Of that you can be certain. What do you think it means?"

"I have no idea," Stogggul lied. Because now he understood everything: why the Door remained locked, why no Gyrgon was there though the Ring remained, and why they were so full of rage at the last Summoning. *This infernal Kundalan Door has killed a Gyrgon, he thought, and I gave them the key! Imagine if I had kept the Ring of Five Dragons and tried to unlock the Door myself.* He stared at the Ring, embedded in the stone Dragon's mouth. What sorcerous power did it hold, a power beyond even Gyrgon ken? Blood pulsed in his skull. This was power beyond V'ornn imagining. Had he been wrong to discount everything Kundalan?

There was a secret here worth exploring. But how to go about it? That would require considerable thought.

Everything has changed," the Old V'ornn said, taking the sixth position, "since last I saw you, Stogggul Kurgan."

For as long as Kurgan could remember, the Old V'ornn had always called him by the formal appellation. He liked that. It showed respect.

"The House of Ashera has been destroyed." Kurgan assumed the mounted-star defense. "My father is the new regent of Kundala. I am adjutant to Star-Admiral Morcha."

During the next fifty minutes, he and the Old V'ornn fought hand to hand in the Ka Form, a fluid and complex method of fighting that had long ago been forgotten by others. They were in the Old V'ornn's vaulted gymnasium. Padded walls held three tiers of increasingly narrow ledges on which lessons were taught.

When they were finished, Kurgan watched the Old V'ornn with an emotion bordering on affection. The dark, gleaming skull, the wrinkled face, the strong, capable hands, these were all as familiar to him as the scent of his own body. The Old V'ornn had taught him everything of importance. But he also listened to what Kurgan had to say. And he was patient. Patient as a stone, patient as the ocean lapping at that stone.

"I made proper use of your lessons this evening," Kurgan said with no little pride. "Kefffir Gutttin died like the traitorous marsh-lizard he was."

"You shot him in the back, did you not?"

Kurgan stood very still, watching and waiting with apprehension. He had known the Old V'ornn since he had been seven years of age—a lifetime, it seemed. They had met quite by chance at a street stall where Kurgan liked to go to look at the long-bladed knives for sale. While his mother was buying leeesta from a baker across the street, the Old V'ornn had approached him and asked him which knife was his favorite. Kurgan had immediately pointed to one with a long, thin, triangular blade. The Old V'ornn had bought it on the spot and had told Kurgan that he would teach him to use it to hunt, that when he became sufficiently proficient with it, it would become his to keep. A week later, Kurgan slipped away from hingatta liiina do mori for the first of what would be many difficult and exhilarating lessons at the Old V'ornn's gymnasium.

Now, he watched warily as the Old V'ornn walked away. "Tell me, Stogggul Kurgan, why do you puff out your chest like a rainbow-cock when your best friend has died?"

Kurgan was so taken aback that he could not find his tongue.

The Old V'ornn paused and turned to face him. "Ashera Annon was brought back here to Axis Tyr and his head was delivered to the Gyrgon. Is this not correct?"

Kurgan nodded mutely.

"And in the glare of your recent triumphs are you to tell me that you have not spent even a moment contemplating his demise?"

"I was the agent of his death. I gave Morcha what he wanted, and in return . . ." He spread his hands wide. "He gave me what I wanted."

The Old V'ornn pursed his lips. "I trust when you speak of *me*, Stogggul Kurgan, you do so with the proper respect."

"I never speak of you."

The Old V'ornn smiled a secretive smile. "Ah, yes, part of our rules, isn't it?" The skin on his skull was almost copper-colored, and so thin Kurgan could see the network of purple veins pulsing with the rush of blood. Eyes pale from extreme age met his and held them. "But to return to our topic, you should not underestimate the price you will pay for your newfound stature."

"Price? What price?"

The Old V'ornn walked to the far end of the gymnasium. A wall panel swiveled open at his touch. He looked out upon a courtyard he had built himself. It was filled with rocks, stones, boulders of every conceivable size and shape. Somewhere within water gurgled but, Kurgan knew, unless one stood in the exact center of the courtyard one could not see the small pool. That, too, was a lesson he had learned from the Old V'ornn when the two of them had built the pool around the small spring on the property: to stand at the center is to see everything.

"You had a friend, once. Now he is ash. Because of you, Stogggul Kurgan. Because of you."

Something had caught the Old V'ornn's attention. Kurgan followed him out into the courtyard. The Old V'ornn carefully picked his way toward the center. In the many times Kurgan had seen him do this he had never once taken the same path.

"That was three months ago," Kurgan said. "Ancient history. If I shed a tear I would be a hypocrite."

"Of course. Remorse is but an aspect of conscience, and you have none." There was a look of contentment on the Old V'ornn's face, as if he was at last seeing the color and shape of a long-awaited horizon. "Nevertheless, be aware that there *is* a price to pay. Now or later, it matters not. This is the Way of the Universe. The Law of Balance."

"You have taught me that the path to power is never straight. I am not frightened, if that is your concern."

The Old V'ornn's smile was like the wrinkles in ancient leather. "In your case, my concern is that you are *never* frightened."

"Again, you taught me that."

At last, they had reached the center. The small but deep pool bubbled up from its hidden source. The water was black as pitch, even in the brightest sunlight. Kurgan still remembered how cold it felt when his hands and forearms were immersed in it. At the edge, stood a small chased-silver chalice, more delicate than anything a V'ornn Tuskugggun could fashion. He imagined the Old V'ornn coming out here, dipping it into the icy water, slaking his thirst.

"If that is your belief, then you have learned improperly. I have taught you not to be frightened. But there are times when fear is the only thing that will save your life. A healthy fear hones the senses, attunes the mind. In this way, opportunities appear. To be ruled by fear is weakness; to be utterly fearless breeds arrogance." He looked into the heart of the pond. "Your arrogance gives me pause."

"Why? You have taught me that arrogance is strength."

"The sun is your emblem—your talisman as well as your symbolic goal; it fairly pulses with limitless power. But if you stare at it too long, you will go blind."

"Not if every so often you focus on the dark spot."

The Old V'ornn thought of Kundala's sun with its mysterious purple spot and laughed delightedly. "Ah, me, one is never too old to learn; that makes life good again." He put his arm around Kurgan, and the boy could immediately feel again the strength that lay hidden inside the ancient, bony frame. That was the way of him: Kurgan was convinced that he was composed entirely of secrets.

"Nevertheless, arrogance misused becomes a weakness," the Old V'ornn continued. "You have crawled out from under the shadow of your father. This is no mean accomplishment."

Kurgan felt warmed as if by the noonday sun. "Thank you."

The Old V'ornn's long, spidery forefinger waggled. "Do not forget, however, that it is but a *momentary* triumph."

"I will not underestimate him."

"Oh, but in your arrogance I believe you already have." He tapped his thin, almost black lips with his long, translucent fingernail. "You hold your father in the greatest contempt."

"He earned that contempt."

The Old V'ornn's face darkened. "Listen to yourself. Emotion has gained the upper hand. This contempt you feel for your father rules you. He has seen it, felt it, and acts accordingly. Therefore, it has the potential to be your ruin." He smiled his enigmatic smile. "If Wennn Stogggul is contemptible, that is one thing. It is a fact—certainly a useful one, in the right context. But it is nothing more than a fact. It is your *emotion* that is dangerous because it will blind you to his power and his cunning. In this state, you *will* underestimate him."

For a long time, Kurgan said nothing. Processing the Old V'ornn's words was never easy; sometimes it seemed impossible. "You are right, of course," he said at length. "Who is Wennn Stogggul? From this moment on, he ceases to be my father. He is simply another player in the game."

"If you mean that—if you can truly *feel* it, Stogggul Kurgan—then we are finished for tonight."

The regent Stogggul was in the now empty banquet hall, staring intently at the holoimage of Kundala when Dalma came through the open doorway.

"My love."

He turned to her and scowled. "I observed you this afternoon. How many times have I warned you about showing yourself around the public rooms? They are reserved for state business."

"Growling at me so quickly?" She approached him in a swirl of brocaded silk. Lately, she had taken to purchasing lushly embroidered Kundalan fabrics and having them made into robes. "Why, I cannot recall you *ever* warning me about anything." She insinuated her leg between his.

He ignored her ministrations. It would not do to let her see how much he had come to depend on her avaricious mind and her contacts. As a Looorm with many clients, she had intimate access to levels of society—both V'ornn and Kundalan—he could never penetrate no matter how great his power grew. Pillow talk was a powerful tool given the proper direction. "I have told you that you may have the run of my private quarters. Evidently that is not enough for you."

She smiled ever so sweetly while she pressed against him with the heat of a sun going nova.

"You know you should be grateful that I let you live inside the palace walls," he continued. "What other Looorm could make that claim?"

"That is because I am like no other Looorm, my love." When she licked the side of his neck, he grabbed hold of her wrist and jerked her away. She made a little cry of pain, which pleased him.

Now she was pouting. "I came here to present you with a wonderful surprise, and now you have hurt me."

He pulled her to him in gentler fashion. "I am lately put in a foul mood. Forgive me."

"Always, my love. But what base work transpired in the caverns below to cause you such anguish?"

He turned away, collapsing the holoimage.

"No matter. I guarantee your mood will lift when you see my surprise." So saying, she led him out of the room, down the hallway, past the grand staircase, along passageways that became increasingly disorienting to him. There was no doubt that she had a far better grip on the palace's labyrinthine structure than he did.

At last, they came out on the balcony he knew overlooked Giyan's herb garden. He had had all the plants ripped out and was going to have the ground cobbled over until Dalma begged him not to. He liked it when she begged, and so he had acquiesced. Now she led him to the filigreed balustrade, and said, "There. What do you think?"

Looking down, he saw in the moonslight a young Kundalan female with thick platinum-colored hair kneeling in the midst of what looked like neatly planted rows of weeds. A freshening wind swirled in the interior garden, bringing to his nose a succession of pungent odors that made him sneeze.

"What is this?" he shouted. "Not only are these weeds ugly, but they stink to low N'Luuura!"

At the sound of his voice, the young female stood and turned her face up to him. She was very tall, willowy, fine-featured. Her thick hair was pulled back off her face, plaited into a wide plait that hung like a shock-sword to the gentle flair of her buttocks. At that precise moment, Wennn Sto-gggul was certain that his hearts had ceased to beat. He grabbed the top of the balustrade with whitened knuckles to keep his knees from buckling. To say that he had never been susceptible to the charms of the Kundalan female would be something of an understatement. In fact, truth be known, he found their aspect as abhorrent as the fire-beetles of Phare-seius Prime, and he considered them to be just as low on the food chain. But as her large, exceedingly pale eyes studied him gravely some sensation previously unknown to him pierced his flesh, spread a curious fever throughout his system that left him weak.

It was as if her robes had melted away. He imagined he could see her body, the cool curves, the secret dells, and every alien place on her became a source of intense curiosity and profound eroticism. He could feel the heat rising from her even from this distance; he could smell her curious scent. Every aroma in the garden smelled delicious every plant dripped moisture he longed to hold on the tip of his tongue.

"It is difficult, I know, to believe that such 'stinking weeds' could have a salubrious effect on V'ornn and Kundalan alike."

The female Kundalan's smile played over him like delicate fingers, and he felt a shiver run through him. He tried to respond, swallowed his jumbled thoughts instead.

Intuiting, perhaps, doubt from his silence, she continued, "I assure you, Lord, I speak the truth." She offered up a black-basalt mortar and a white-agate pestle. "I can give concrete example to my words, if the Lord will permit me."

Stogggul gathered himself sufficiently to say, "Tell me your name, female."

"Malistra, Lord."

He liked that she called him Lord. He nodded and beckoned to her. "Come up here, Malistra, and I shall divine the truth of your words for myself."

As soon as Malistra had disappeared, Dalma said, "This is the Kundalan sorceress I told you about. I have had her plant her herbs here so that she can tend them and harvest them just for your use."

The regent frowned. "The accursed Ashera skcettta Giyan has used her sorcery to put herself under the protection of Rekkk Hacilar. Doubtless, it was her sorcery that got them past Pack-Commander Rydddlin and his Khaggun four nights ago. Since then, we have been unable to trace them."

"You see what Kundalan sorcery can accomplish?" she

said. "Now you will have your own sorceress to fight Giyan on her own terms."

He looked deep into her eyes while a slow smile crept across her face, and allowed a sigh to escape his lips. "Perhaps you are right."

She laughed deep in her throat. "You know I am."

"Do you think she can find the fugitives for me?"

"You must ask her that yourself, my love." Her hands kept moving beneath his robes. "Now tell me why you have me playing up to that smelly bannntor?"

He made a disgusted sound. "The Star-Admiral is living down to my initial assessment of him—of all Khagggun." He shook his craggy head. "There is good reason why they are Lesser Caste. His elevation to power will make him dangerous unless he is put on a leash."

At that moment, Malistra appeared on the balcony. Standing there, silent and respectful, holding the mortar full of ground herbs, she exuded the gravely erotic aspect of a priestess. Seeing her now, his mind clicked into gear and his plan—his delightfully malicious plan—moved to its next phase. Two teyj with one call, wasn't that the Gyrgon saying? To possess Malistra, to get her to use her sorcery to unlock the Storehouse Door would prove a double coup. He would assuage the fire inside him and get the Gyrgon to wrest control of salamuuun trade from the Ashera Consortium and give it to him. Finally. Just revenge. But first this Malistra had to prove herself to him. He had to move with caution. More than one Gyrgon dead. The Ring of Five Dragons had already proved itself far too dangerous for any further precipitous action.

He turned Dalma around. "While I try out this Kundalan nonsense, you are to go to the Star-Admiral."

"Toward what end?"

"A liaison."

Dalma's eyes opened wide. "Are you mad?"

"Mad as a Kraelian sundog." He was so delighted with himself that he decided not to punish her for her disrespect. Besides, her abhorrence at leaving him sent a pleasurable jolt through his tender parts. "I want you to give Morcha the opening he hungers for."

"Opening?"

He led her to the far end of the balcony, where there was no chance of them being overheard. "All Khagggun are trained to find their opponent's weakness. Why have him search too hard to find mine? Morcha secretly lusts after you. I know it. Make him believe that you have grown tired of me and my corish ways." He chuckled. "Of a certain, that will appeal to him. I want him to think that through you he has a direct source to what I am thinking and planning. That way, he will relax his guard. I will have him right where I want him." He chuckled. "In the palm of your hand."

Dalma, who liked intrigue better than the next Looorm, laughed mightily as she kissed him. "How utterly delicious, my love! It will be a pleasure to deliver him to you just as you ask." She pouted. "My only regret is that I will be spending less time with you."

"We all need to make sacrifices, don't we?" Stogggul looked past her to where Malistra stood at the other end of the balcony, the moonslight caught in her platinum hair. Dalma kissed him hard on the lips. She squeezed Malistra's shoulder briefly as she passed by her.

When he was alone with the Kundalan female, Wennn Stogggul gestured for her to approach. Close-up, her appearance was even more striking. The platinum hair, flat to her skull, and her strange, pale eyes contrived to make her not only alien but exotic as well. She wore a simple dark cloak meant for traveling. Her well-formed arms were bare. A bronze band, cleverly worked into the aspect of a fierce serpent, wound around her right arm from just above her elbow to just below her shoulder. The flat, wedge-shaped head seemed to stare at him without emotion of any kind.

"I understand you have a facility with this," he said, gesturing at the herbal mixture.

"It is a gift, Lord, though modest."

"Sorcery." He shook his head. "It is nothing but corwash."

She let him see the ghost of a smile. "Is your Gyrgon's

technomancy so different, Lord? Both seek to make explainable what is beyond our ken."

The regent grunted. "You can be sure Gyrgon are not interested in ground herbs and roots."

"But you appear to be, Lord."

He scowled menacingly. "You are an impudent thing. Shall I punish you?"

"I meant no disrespect—none at all, Lord. On the contrary. You are benevolent and progressive for a V'ornn. For allowing me to plant and harvest my crops inside your palace grounds I am grateful."

Wennn Stogggul kept his scowl firmly in place. That way she would never detect how fast his hearts were beating. "How grateful, I wonder?"

Malistra slipped to her knees. Setting down the mortar and pestle, she scooped a handful of freshly ground powder and spat into it until she had made a thick paste. Deftly, she snaked her hand through the parting of his robes, probed deeper, smeared the paste onto his tender parts.

Her magnificently strange face raised to him like a flower to sunlight. "Shall I show you, Lord, the length and breadth of my gratitude?"

She was gripping him, or perhaps the paste she had concocted was starting to work. Be that as it might, he had no choice but to nod dumbly as her face followed her hand between the thick folds of his magisterial regent's robes.

Afterward, he lay staring up at the glittering stars, their light hard as crystal. Malistra rose up on her elbow beside him and said, "Have I pleased you, Lord?"

"You have."

"Though I am an alien?"

The regent Stogggul reached for the thick plait of her hair. Malistra smiled, drew his hand away, placed hers on his hairless chest, and he felt his tender parts stir again. The bronze serpent gleamed and glistened, its incised scales seeming to undulate with her movements.

"You are Kundalan. What we have done is transient." He lifted a hand, let it fall. "You see? It is already gone."

"But I wish for something more permanent, Lord."

"You are Kundalan," he repeated. To him, this said it all.

She rose up to a sitting position and folded her legs beneath her. He could not take his eyes off the thick plait of hair that draped over her shoulder and hung between her breasts. "As a token of my sincerity, will you allow me to show you another use for my powder?"

"I liked greatly the first use." He nodded. "By all means."

Quickly, she mixed a pinch of the herb mixture in a dram of clear liquid and told him to drink it down.

"What effect will this have?"

"It is best for you to experience it for yourself, Lord."

Since it had had only the most salubrious effect on his tender parts, he did not hesitate, swallowing it down in one gulp. Almost immediately, he felt sick to his stomachs. Sweat broke out all over him and he grew so dizzy that when he tried to swipe at her he managed only to crack his head on the finely fluted uprights of the balustrade. Hanging his head miserably over the side, he vomited into the garden below. He rolled over, groaning. He felt as weak as a starving blood-flea.

"You . . ." he stammered. "You . . ."

She held his head up with one hand and proffered a small cor-hide flask. "Here, Lord, drink this."

The warm liquid dribbled down his throat. He had barely enough energy to swallow. But once he did, he began to feel his strength flow back into him like a stream cresting in springtime.

"What . . . what did you do to me?"

"I could have killed you, Lord," she said with a curious tenderness. "And it would have been so easy. All it would have taken was to double the dose. Your Haaar-kyut are nowhere around, no one knows I am here, and an autopsy would have revealed nothing. The herb mixture breaks down into its biochemical parts within minutes of ingestion."

He stared at her, wide-eyed. "I will have you beheaded."

"Certainly, Lord, if that is your wish." She pushed over the mortar full of ground herbs. "But first, accept this gift, to use against your enemies, if you wish. Having ingested the half dose, you yourself are now immune."

He was silent for some time. She could tell he was weighing matters in his mind. At last, he came to a decision. "Dalma informs me that this garden was once used by the former regent's skcettta, Giyan."

"Ah, yes."

"You know her?" He was at once suspicious.

"Only by reputation, Lord."

"By all reports, she is a clever one." The regent rose. He leaned his elbows on the balustrade and, for a long time, stared down into the garden filled now with sorcerous herbs, roots, and mushrooms. "Tell me, who harvested these druggish herbs for the skcettta?"

Malistra laughed, a soft tinkling sound like water falling against crystal. "It surely wasn't me, Lord. A sorceress cannot receive her herbs from another; the oils of that individual would contaminate them, rendering them inert or worse—reversing their effect. They cannot be harvested by machine because they are too delicate, and even if you used gloves, your aura would infect them. Like all sorceresses, Giyan grew or picked the herbs herself, just as I am doing."

At length, Malistra came and stood beside him, her arm loosely around his waist. "What are you pondering so deeply, Lord?" she asked in a gentle voice. "If I can help, you have only to ask."

Stogggul's mind was on fire. His desire for her had, if anything, multiplied beyond his comprehension. He looked down at the herbal mixture. What other fruits of her sorcerous powers could she provide? He wanted her so badly he could feel his tender parts throb. "There are fugitives I seek," he said thickly. "One of them is the skcettta, Giyan. She has used her sorcery to disappear. You will find her for me. Your sorcery can do that, yes?"

"Most assuredly, Lord."

"If you can find her and her companion, then I will know the truth to your words and you can have your more permanent relationship with me." *But not before you use your*

Kundalan sorcery to get me the Ring of Five Dragons, he thought.

S tar-Admiral Kinnnus Morcha was stretched out naked on the veranda of his pavilion, bathing in pale moonlight. He lay in an openwork cradle-chair; another identical cradle-chair was next to him. Neat rows of sheared, densely limbed ammonwood trees ringed the circumference of the veranda, shielding it from curious eyes. The flooring was constructed of a synthetic stone material, white as snow, which reflected and magnified the moonlight. He heard soft footfalls and knew who it was approaching because he had given orders that only his young adjutant be allowed into the pavilion. He said, "Do you know, Kurgan, that the night is a time for intrigue."

"I do now, sir."

"Where have you been?" the Star-Admiral snapped in an altogether different tone of voice. "Your absence since the end of the banquet has been noted."

"There is a female, sir." Kurgan stood stiffly at attention.

"A female? At your age?"

"She is a Looorm, sir." The lie came easily, almost gleefully to his lips. "She is teaching me."

"It is good to have such teachers in life, adjutant. We are taught to feel only contempt for Tuskugggun, especially Looorm. But there comes a time in life when one creeps under your skin, when you find yourself feeling something for her you did not think it was possible to feel. Then, and only then, do you know what you are missing by being Khagggun."

"I hope to find such a Tuskugggun one day." Kurgan, who held no such hope, wondered who this Looorm of the Star-Admiral's might be.

"If you do, I promise you will wonder whether she is a blessing or a curse." Kinnnus Morcha lifted a thick, powerful arm. "But enough of sentiment. Come, then, adjutant. Shed your uniform again and join me." Sensing the boy's hesitation, he rose up on one elbow. "This is part of my nightly regimen. In my travels I have been exposed to any manner of atmospheric radiation, and I say unequivocally that Kundala's is by far the sweetest. I had these stone blocks made for me; they amplify the radiation, the sense of well-being." He winked. "Between you and me, I have found that it rejuvenates the tenderest of tender parts."

As Kurgan began to shed his uniform, the Star-Admiral lay back down with a long sigh. In a moment, he heard his young adjutant settle into the cradle-chair beside him. "And it is a certainty that we both need a little rejuvenation after that nasty banquet your father served up."

"I thought it all went rather well," Kurgan said.

"Did you now? I suppose you marked the surprise on your father's face when you loosed your bolt into Kefffir Gutttin's back."

"I did not."

"That diatribe of his was fully planned. He meant to call out one of them—Bach Ourrros or Kefffir Gutttin. Bach Ourrros is too clever to allow himself to be drawn into a public shouting match with the regent. Kefffir Gutttin, however, was not so circumspect."

"I know that my father wants Bach Ourrros dead."

"They want each other dead," Kinnnus Morcha grunted. "But the regent also had something else in mind. He devised a clever test for me—a test to prove my loyalty."

"Haven't you already proved your loyalty to him?"

"Your father is, I think, testing the practical feasibility, shall we say, of the new intercaste society he and I are creating. It is an entirely new world; I don't blame him." He held up his left arm. "I have barely begun to understand the workings of my new okummmon; how can he possibly understand me?" He rolled over heavily. "What he did not expect was for you to kill his enemy."

"He said nothing to me."

"Would you expect him to?"

"I would expect him to acknowledge my first kill."

The Star-Admiral sighed. "Then, adjutant, you are doomed to disappointment. I can tell you how proud you made me because you knew what was required even before I could signal you. I was impressed. But your father? No, never. He is not that sort of V'ornn."

Even as a wave of satisfaction coursed through him, Kurgan knew that Kinnnus Morcha was right. Without realizing it, he had reverted back to his old way of thinking of the regent as his father. The Old V'ornn would be displeased at how poorly he had learned his latest lesson. He must concentrate harder than he had before; he must make certain that he never again mistook Wennn Stogggul for his father.

"I am grateful that I have pleased you, Star-Admiral. I was wondering if I could join one of the packs in the attacks against the Kundalan resistance."

"Ah, but you are a bloodthirsty young thing, aren't you?" The Star-Admiral smiled up at the open sky. "That campaign is going well enough without my needing to risk you there. Imagine your father's wrath, adjutant, if I let anything happen to you."

"What purpose do I serve if I cannot participate in campaigns?" Kurgan said. "Does the Star-Admiral doubt my prowess?"

"I do not, adjutant. On that score, you have proved your worth. But I have many superior Khaggun at my disposal to do my wet work. There are other campaigns, on other fronts for which you are far better suited." The Star-Admiral moved his palm, and a holographic image of Kundala slowly spun. "Tell me, adjutant, why have we no presence here, on the southern continent?"

Kurgan shrugged as he stared at the holoimage. "An early foray determined there wasn't enough profit to merit occupation. The climate is inhospitable, a breeding ground for a number of opportunistic viruses. The people native to the continent, the Sarakkon, are a xenophobic, primitive lot."

Kinnnus Morcha grunted. "Yet we trade with them, do we not?"

"As do the Kundalan, Star-Admiral. The Sarakkon are clever and devious. They mine a number of highly radioactive substances the Gyrgon are studying as a stable power source."

"Tell me, do you know what happened to that first Khaggun expedition? No? Fully a third of the personnel died of acute radiation poisoning before the rest could retreat. It penetrated right through their off-world biosuits. Those that did return were held in quarantine for months while the Gyrgon worked on detoxifying them. Their biosuits and personal effects were vaporized; their shuttle was deemed unfit for V'ornn life and sent to the bottom of the Sea of Blood."

"A dangerous lot, Star-Admiral."

"That is the avowed consensus among my colleagues." Kurgan thought he caught the hint of a smirk on Kinnnus Morcha's face. "The Sarakkon colony is in Harborside, is it not?"

"It is, Star-Admiral."

"And you are at least somewhat familiar with that area, are you not?"

"Sir?"

"Well, I mean to say your brother is, um, living in that section of the city." Kinnnus Morcha pursed his lips. "And, if memory serves, it plays host to the Kalllistotos."

Kurgan held his breath and tried to gather his thoughts. He wondered how much the Star-Admiral knew. He admonished himself not to underestimate either Morcha's guile or his network of informants. He would do well to find out whether Morcha had unearthed elements of his private life or whether he was trolling for information. "It is true that I have been known to visit the Kalllistotos now and again."

"And from time to time participate in it."

"I require diversion from the ordinary," Kurgan said carefully.

"*Diversions* is more like it," the Star-Admiral said dryly.

So he knew it all. Kurgan bit his lip. He shouldn't be so surprised. Well, he could not do anything about it now, but he certainly could ensure the flow of information would cease.

Kinnnus Morcha closed his eyes and breathed deeply. "I

want you to go to Harborside and insinuate yourself into the Sarakkon enclave."

"That will not be easy, sir. As you know, they are somewhat hostile to outsiders. They do not even fully trust the Kundalan."

"Adjutant to the Khagggun Star-Admiral, and one that participates in the Kalllistotos, at that. Xenophobia or no xenophobia, it seems to me that from their point of view you would make a formidable friend."

Kurgan turned onto his side. "And should I find them amenable. Star-Admiral, what are your orders?"

"Gather information. Anything and everything. I want to get their perspective on the Kundalan."

"The resistance, sir?"

"Naturally." The Star-Admiral stretched. "Also, see what they can tell you about the Druuge."

"The Druuge, sir?"

"A minor curiosity, that is all."

Kurgan's lips curled into a smile of admiration. "I am overwhelmed by your trust in me, Star-Admiral."

Kinnnus Morcha heaved his bulk again so that he was looking out at the distant peaks of the Djenn Marre. "My father passed on to me one valuable piece of advice, adjutant, and it is this: 'Trust is only as long as the blade of a shock-sword.'"

"I will remember that, sir."

The Star-Admiral closed his eyes again. "Many have tried; few have succeeded."

19

Avatar

W hy?"

"I have already told you why," Rekkk Hacilar said. "You know, but you do not yet believe me."

Giyan and Rekkk, riding cthauros the Gyrgon Nith Sahor had provided for them, were making their way through the high-elevation forest where Rekkk, as Pack-Commander, had once pursued her and Annon as they had fled toward Stone Border.

"You have forsaken everything—your caste, your status, your power—everything that makes you V'ornn," Giyan said. "For what? Please do not tell me it is to be with me."

Rekkk ducked his head out of the way of a trailing branch. "How can I talk to you when you still distrust and hate me so?"

"You are a V'ornn. You are used to difficult situations. Try," she said, dryly.

He nodded. "Like Eleusis, like Nith Sahor, I feel as if I am in service to a higher calling. To be honest, my life never made much sense to me. Like my mother, I was pulled in a direction I could never understand, I only knew it was away from other V'ornn. In the closest-knit caste in V'ornn society, I felt like an outsider. And now . . . now I have a chance to help my people and yours." He spurred his cthauros up beside her. "I see the expression on your face. No matter what you may think, I hate Wennn Stogggul and Kinnnus Morcha more than you do."

"Impossible."

"Ah, yes, let us now argue degrees of hatred. We are such experts."

She turned to him after a moment, nodded. "I take your point."

"Let us agree on this, at least. Let us leave the arguments concerning hate to the regent and the Star-Admiral, shall we?"

She spurred her cthauros forward, and he went silently after her. The day was warm and still. Insects swarmed and, overhead, birds flitted from branch to branch. Swaddled in green shade, they made their way northward, always ascending the outriding slopes of the mountain range.

"I trust you know what you are doing," he said. "This girl Eleana. Tell me how she will help us find the Dar Sala-at."

"I already know where the Dar Sala-at is," Giyan said shortly. "Eleana knows the terrain from here to the higher elevations better than I do. Plus, she has many friends who can help us along the way, feed us, shelter us from prying eyes."

"In other words, she is resistance."

When Giyan did not reply, he said, "Are you worried I will run her through with my shock-sword?"

"No," she said. "I am worried she will run *you* through."

He leaned over his saddle toward her. "I should be offended, but as you can plainly see, I'm not. In fact, I am pleased you are concerned for my well-being."

"I promise I won't make a habit of it."

"Don't make promises you can't keep."

She gave him a sharp look, then reined in her cthauros and dismounted. "Stay here," she cautioned him. "It will be more trouble than we need if Eleana sees you before I have a chance to explain your presence."

"What can you possibly say to her that would stop her from wanting to spit me on the spot?"

"I am still working on that."

"Why don't you use your sorcery on her?"

"Osoru cannot work like that on someone who is not your enemy," Giyan said shortly. "You would need Kyofu, the Dark Sorcery, for that. I have little knowledge of Kyofu, and even less desire to use it."

He swung off his mount. "In that event, I think I'd better go with you."

"I told you to stay here."

For a moment, they stood deadlocked, not more than a meter apart.

At length, he nodded. "Forgive me. I am unused to taking orders from a female."

"It was not an order. I . . ." A sudden gust of wind rose against Giyan's face. She brushed hair out of her eyes. "I thought . . . I think my making contact with Eleana alone makes the most sense."

"Go on, then."

She blinked. Her eyes searched the rough contours of his face, seeing for the first time softer edges. "I will be back with her as quickly as I can. In the meantime . . ."

"I know how to occupy myself," he said.

"It wasn't an order. Really."

"I believe you," he said pointedly.

Giyan nodded, lifted a hand halfway, a kind of awkward farewell, then she turned and vanished into the forest.

Eleana crouched behind a huge heartwood tree, watching the slow play of sunlight as it filtered through the forest. The birds sang, the insects droned just as they had ten minutes ago. But now there was a difference. Something had entered the forest that had no business being here. She could feel it, like a ripple of cool air on a hot summer's day. The fine hairs at the back of her neck stirred, causing a premonitory shiver to run through her. Ever since the V'ornn had abruptly stepped up their attacks on the resistance, she and everyone in her cell had been on edge as they heard that one cell after another was being systematically rooted out and annihilated. She had stopped counting the number of friends who had died in just the past week.

She drew the V'ornn shock-sword that hung at her left hip. She had spent weeks training herself to manipulate the heavy weapon. Though she was far from deciphering its idiosyncrasies, she felt proficient enough to draw it with an eye to using it. She moved a little into deeper shade, both to protect herself further and to gain a wider view into the forest glade just to her south. Her scalp began to tingle. Something was coming. She gripped the shock-sword with both hands, her muscles knotted with tension.

No doubt Dammi would laugh to see her now, as he had laughed watching her try to swing the unwieldy V'ornn weapon. Of course, with his size and bulk it was far easier for him to train on the shock-sword. These days it seemed she and Dammi constantly butted heads.

Poor Dammi, he loved her so. The frustration he felt at her lack of response often bubbled over into their professional relationship. Perhaps, after all, he would be happier giving her orders, though he denied it vociferously every time she brought it up.

And so the pointless squabbles continued. Pointless, because in reality they were not arguing about power so much as unrequited love. Pointless, too, for her to explain his sub rosa hostility because the one time she tried he stalked out and would not speak to her for a week. Maybe this had something to do with their youth. Who would have expected Kundalan of their age to be leading their own cell of the resistance? Sometimes, she found herself wondering if she and Dammi were up to the responsibility. But who else was there? In this area, the V'ornn had long ago killed most of the adult males, murdering them in their periodic hunts. Of course, she harbored another theory concerning their escalating disputes, or perhaps it had to do with Kara. He could not understand her refusal to reject Miina and join him in Kara's wholesale embrace of the "here and now." No more wondering why Miina had turned her back on them. No more waiting for a sign of the Great Goddess's return. No more bitter and divisive arguing over the Prophesies of the Dar Sala-at, The Pearl, and Anamordor. No more wondering where they had come from and where they were destined to go. Simply the promise of a better life today.

On the other hand, she wondered how much his current reaction had to do with the appearance of Annon Ashera.

The day Annon and Kurgan had come upon her swimming she had been inside Axis Tyr, stowing away in the bottom of a Kundalan dray carrying fertilizer to spread over V'ornn gardens. There, she had reconnoitered, looking for weak spots in V'ornn defenses and, with the help of resistance members in the city, had located a back passage into the Haaar-kyut main barracks. Weeks later, Dammi had returned to plant the bomb he had made from cor manure bolstered by a stick of tertium-gelignite he had bartered for. The resulting blast had been devastating for the V'ornn. But two of her contacts in the city had been killed; only her skill and daring had prevented Dammi himself from being captured.

She stiffened as a shadow stole through the thick foliage of the heartwood trees on the south side of the glade. Coming, yes. Something was coming. Her heart constricted at the thought of another Khagggun hunting pack.

Annon. His appearance had, as the saying goes, upset her carefully stacked muodd cart. Her opinion of the V'ornn had been set in stone. They had killed her parents, her aunts and uncles, her friends and compatriots. But that was before Annon had saved her, before she had fallen madly in love with him. It was that mad love that had so enraged Dammi, that had shattered their relationship, her own insular world. Hatred of the V'ornn was what had dominated so much of her life. Her love for Annon—so unexpected, so startling, so thrilling—made her bones ache with longing, made her blood sing, made colors electric. Returned to her were the sweetness of birdsong, the beauty of a sunrise, the fastness of the mountains. He had made her live again.

At a soft whinnying, she looked to her left without moving her head. Through a mass of leaves, she saw someone cautiously leading a cthauros into the dappled sunlight of the glade. Her heart leapt. What if it was Annon?

The figure emerged from the leafy forest. Eleana, her shock-sword at the ready, drew in a quick breath.

"Giyan!"

"Eleana, it gives me great pleasure to see you again," Giyan said as she walked toward the girl.

"I did not know whether I would ever see you again. How is Annon?"

Before Giyan had a chance to reply, Rekkk stepped out into the leafy glade.

As soon as Eleana saw his face she cursed under her breath and drew her shock-sword, thumbing on its ion flow.

"Behind me, quickly!" she cried. "It is a trap!"

"Eleana, no!" Giyan whirled on Rekkk. "What do you think you're doing?"

But Eleana was already rushing headlong toward him, brandishing the weapon. Rekkk did not touch the shock-sword hanging at his waist. Neither did his hands move toward any of the other weapons he carried. She was already halfway across the glade when she felt another bout of the odd dizziness that had come over her during the last few weeks. She recovered, came on toward him, but, oddly, he had not armed himself.

Abruptly, she came up short, her heart in her throat. "What is your game, Khagggun?" she spat. "Are your pack members all around me? Is this the nature of your trap?"

"Only the two of us are here," Giyan said desperately. "This is no trap, Eleana."

"I am no longer Khagggun," Rekkk said, careful to keep his hands away from his weapons. "I have declared myself Rhynnnon."

Giyan had walked between them. With a brief basilisk glare at Rekkk, she turned to Eleana, her palms upraised. "Please believe me when I tell you that neither Rekkk Hacilar nor I mean you harm." She smiled as she put a black, stiff-fingered hand on the girl's arm.

Eleana looked from Rekkk Hacilar to Giyan. "He is still V'ornn."

"Oh yes." Giyan's whistleflower-blue eyes held Eleana's. "But he is with me, and we are on a mission of such vital importance that we must very soon be on our way. Put down your weapon, Eleana, I beg you. We need your help."

Eleana did no such thing. "Are you now reduced to being a defender of the V'ornn?"

"I am no defender of the V'ornn," Giyan said softly. "Just *this* V'ornn." There followed a tense silence in the glade.

Giyan, coming up against another Kundalan's fierce and determined antagonism, realized that a profound shift had occurred deep inside herself. Like a leaf taken downstream by a swiftly flowing river, she had unexpectedly arrived at an unfamiliar part of herself. When had she ceased to think of Rekkk Hacilar as the enemy? When he had arranged the Visitation with Annon for her? When he had become Rhynn-non? When he had tried to protect her against Olnnn Ry-dddlin? When he had dealt with Nith Sahor in such courageous fashion? Again, a new path was opening up before her, and she was at its fork. There was another decision to make, just as there had been back at Nith Sahor's laboratory. Her new path was waiting for her to take the first step. She could use her rage and despair over Annon like a weapon to keep punishing them both, or she could see Rekkk Hacilar for who he really was.

"What mission could you be on that would involved a V'ornn?" Eleana's eyes narrowed. "You aren't under duress, are you?" She reached out suddenly, took hold of one of Giyan's blackened arms. "Did the V'ornn do this to you?"

Giyan shook her head. "There was an accident while I was trying to save Annon. I am now able to move my fingers inside these chrysalides, but I do not know whether that is good or bad. The chrysalides put out thousands of fibers that have seemingly completed their connection to my hands, and now I fear they are a part of me, but as to what is happening I do not know."

"I am so sorry. Truly."

Giyan nodded her head. "As I said, we need your help. We are on a mission—a mission to find the Dar Sala-at."

"What say you? In front of the V'ornn?"

"The V'ornn has a name, Eleana, just like you and me. And, yes, Rekkk Hacilar knows about the Dar Sala-at."

The girl looked at them wide-eyed. "The two of you must be mad."

"Is there somewhere nearby where we can go and talk? Please. Time is of the essence."

Eleana shook her head numbly.

"I know it appears strange that I am in the company of a V'ornn Rhynnnon who is searching for the Dar Sala-at. But perhaps not any more strange than my rearing a V'ornn child."

"You were the V'ornn regent's slave," Eleana pointed out. "In that you had no choice."

"But I had a choice whether or not to love Annon, didn't I?" She gave Eleana a meaningful look. "And you would know something about loving a V'ornn, wouldn't you, my dear?"

Eleana averted her gaze for a moment while her cheeks grew hot. "I did not think my feelings were so transparent."

"Nothing about you is transparent, save your earnestness and honesty." Giyan put an encrusted hand over Eleana's and smiled into her beautiful face. "I knew the moment Annon looked at you that he loved you as much as you love him. So, V'ornn are not all beasts, are they?"

"But Khagggun are bred for battle."

"I cannot help but notice," Rekkk said to Eleana, "that you are armed with a shock-sword. For a Kundalan even to touch a V'ornn weapon is an offense punishable by death. You know this, do you not?"

"Very well," Eleana said through gritted teeth. She tensed, watching him closely.

Rekkk raised his hands. "I applaud your ingenuity, but your technique is sadly lacking. I could teach you—" He started. "Giyan, what is it?"

Giyan's face was drawn and pale. She had begun to shake as with a terrible ague.

"Giyan!" Rekkk gathered her into his arms, while Eleana watched them, dumbfounded. "Is it the chrysalides?"

"No." Her trembling voice was a reedy whisper. "There is sorcery being used against me. Kyofu. There is a beacon. It is trying to find us." Her eyes closed, and her brows knit together. He could see that she was fighting some kind of monumental battle inside herself. Frightened for her, he held her all the tighter, but it was no use. He could feel her slipping away from him. He called out her name, but he was certain that she did not hear him.

All color leached away, leaving in its wake the starkness of shadow and light. She was aware of the concentric circles of her own energy pattern—her aura—as they impacted her immediate environment, an environment where the concepts of up, down, left, right, front, behind did not exist.

It had been many years since Giyan had entered into the Osoru deep trance-state known as Ayame. She had always found the release of her corporeal being disconcerting and somewhat painful. In fact, the pain at the moment of jihe—of disconnect—was akin to that of a limb being severed. Of course, the sheer elation of Ayame almost always blotted out the pain—except now. The Beasts of Kyofu had been unleashed; she could see them rushing toward her across the expanse of shadow and light. Of course, they were not flesh-and-blood creatures, but dynamic Kyofu Avatar spells, cunningly cast, powerfully loosed.

The Beasts were cast in the aspect of the Ja-Gaar—the ferocious, mythical creatures with dark, gleaming coats, huge, snapping jaws, long tails, and golden spots flung across their muscular backs. Their green eyes, lambent with sorcerous spells, cast about them for her presence.

Giyan began to whirl and, as she did so, cast this way and that one concentric circle after another. But the Avatars were only briefly distracted by her hasty ploy. Soon enough, they were back on her scent. These sorcerous Ja-Gaar were exceptionally powerful. She recognized their Caa—their energy auras. The sorceress was so powerful, so arrogant that she had made no attempt to conceal her Caa in her Avatar spells.

It was Malistra, no doubt of it. Malistra was trying to locate her.

The Ja-Gaar Avatars were gaining ground, and she knew that she must act. Distractions had not worked, so she tried retreating, backing up into inky pools of shadow she cast out around her, willing herself into shadow-substance so that she could melt in. Still, the Avatars advanced on her, and now the question that had plagued her since she had become aware of her Gift arose again, more urgently. She had been taught that Osoru was the sacred sorcery of Miina, but her Gift had shown her another side. She had glimpsed the Darkness that was Kyofu, and she had wondered at its origins. If Osoru was Miina's sorcery, what, then, was Kyofu?

The Avatars entered her world of inky shadows, and Giyan, breathing in through one nostril, out through the other, morphed into her own Avatar—Ras Shamra, a bird of enormous wingspan, of great scaled talons, and a long, wickedly curved beak. As Malistra's Avatars came at her, she spread her powerful wings, launching herself at them talons first.

They wheeled as she bowled them over. Ignoring their swipes at her, she went straight for their eyes—the repository of the cast spell—blinding one on her initial attack. The other Ja-Gaar leapt on her back, raking its claws down first one wing, then another. She dropped out of the air and as it pounced upon her, she punctured one eye with a curved talon. Spell to spell they attacked and counterattacked, until Giyan was thrown onto her back. At once, the one-eyed Ja-Gaar was at her throat. Its power grew exponentially. In that instant, she looked into its good eye and saw all that lay in wait for her.

Her essence blew apart, opening to the very depths of her spirit, to the prison in which she had kept her Osoru chained and bound. Rage gave wings to her Gift, unleashing it fully. Part of her with a kind of transfixed awe as her counterspell dismantled Malistra's Ja-Gaar, strand by strand, unweaving the spell that had been so cleverly and painstakingly cast.

Giyan had but a moment to celebrate. A livid scar, like the opening of a Cyclopean iris, was already forming, transmuting the shadow and light. The forming Eye possessed an ultraviolet hue, violating the lack of color of Otherwhere. The power of it wrinkled and strained the very fabric of the

Osoru Otherwhere. Giyan had just enough time to cast White Well, a gathering spell, claiming the information she needed, before she broke away. Already she felt the fearsome tidal pull of the great Eye. It took all her desperate strength to evade the spell.

At once terrified and horrified, she fled.

Giyan's whistleflower-blue eyes flew open, and she gave Hacilar a stricken look. "They are coming for us!"

"Who? Who is coming for us?"

"I recognized her. They are using a powerful Black Dreaming sorceress to guide their hounds of war." All at once, she gasped, and spasmed in his arms. "Olnnn Rydddlin. He is leading your old pack against us!"

20

Kells

Astar's severed head rolled along the blood-streaked floor, coming to an uneasy rest between Riane's legs. It grinned ghoulishly, smacked its blackened lips, and said, "*There is a shadow about you, young sir. Beware. You have been marked by the Ancient One. The scar runs right through you. I see death and more death! Only the equilateral of truth can save you!*"

Then, it mouthed a name she could not hear no matter how much she tried. . . .

Riane awoke, drenched in sweat, her heart pounding painfully beneath her budding breasts. The words of the old Kundalan seer in Axis Tyr haunted her. What had he meant? What was the equilateral of truth? She rubbed her bleary eyes with the heels of her hands.

Ever since Bartta had forced her to witness the execution

of Leyna Astar, the rage she had first felt upon finding herself in Riane's body had begun to reassert itself. She felt helpless and terribly guilty. The very sight of Bartta sickened her. That a Kundalan—especially a Ramahan konara!—could destroy an innocent life, destroy it in the sadistic way Bartta had, only proved Astar's theory that a terrible evil had invaded the abbey. She could sense the evil, poison under Bartta's skin, making her darting eyes sink into the hollows of her skull, turning her skin coarse and ashen, making her hair lank and lifeless. Bartta rarely slept, drank instead her dreadful potions in the dead of night when she was certain Riane was asleep. She exuded a smell not unlike that of the grave. And Riane was bound to her, dependent on her to remain safe. Safe in the arms of a fiend! The irony of her situation was not lost on her. She put on a neutral face, knowing the importance of being able to keep her true feelings from Bartta, but she could feel her aggression rising to the surface, bubbling and frothing. Unless she was able to tame it, she knew it was going to land her in very serious trouble.

As a consequence, she threw herself into her studies with a renewed vigor. All her teachers, from Oracular History to Comparative Phytochemistry, noticed and commented to Bartta, who was thus gulled. From dawn until dark, she was busy at her morning lessons, her evening devotions. In between, during the long, hot summer afternoons, she worked on a detail that was enlarging the subterranean refectory where the acolytes took their abstemious meals. It was in the most ancient section of the Abbey of Floating White and was, therefore, in serious need of renovation. Who knew how many centuries ago it had been built?

She did not complain when Bartta informed her that she would be working in what the acolytes only half-jokingly called "the Underworld." When Riane informed her of the acolytes' chatter, Bartta had laughed.

"These acolytes are spoiled. Unlike you, Riane, they have no idea what it means to work, or that physical labor can be an act of purification in its own right. I must say that I am pleased with your progress. I don't mind admitting that I had my doubts when you returned from the Ice Caves. You appeared to have no conception of what is and is not permissible here."

A week after the recurring dream of Astar had first awoken her, Bartta was standing behind her, brushing her long, lustrous hair with a vigor and a pleasure Riane rarely saw in her during the day. This had become a nightly ritual, as sacred as any of the daily devotions.

"Perhaps that was partly my doing. I let you fall under the influence of Leyna Astar. If only I had been a better judge of character. Never mind . . ." She fanned the air with her fingers, as if cleansing it of noxious words. "Here in Floating White we are at the very center of our spiritual and moral universe. Without rigorous discipline, spirituality and morality would fly right out the window. Sloppy habits lead to disorderly thinking." She put her hand on Riane's shoulder and squeezed. "It is gratifying to see you apply yourself to our discipline. You will soon see how these rigors bear fruit in your deepening connection to Miina and everything holy."

Bartta recommenced the brushing, which often lasted a very long time. Riane should have been repelled, but she wasn't. Afterward, she would wonder why, but the question always faded from her mind. There was something soothing about the rhythmic stroking, as well as the sound of Bartta's voice, which was also different than the tone she used during her long hours of duty.

"Because you are my disciple, sooner than you might imagine you will be rising up through the ranks from acolyte to leyna and eventually to shima." She put her hand against Riane's cheek. "Continue applying yourself with the same devotion, and I will see to it. No other konara can make that claim, you know."

Riane turned her head. "We are taught that all Ramahan within their level are equal. But that's not true, is it?"

"Of course not!" Bartta gently turned her head back and continued her brushing. "Official doctrine reads well on parchment, but reality dictates that within each level there is an unspoken order."

"Based on what?" Riane said thoughtfully. "It ought to be seniority, but it's not."

Bartta laughed. "No, it isn't. In fact, I am the *youngest* konara at Floating White." She was always in a good mood when talking about herself. "Let me tell you something. Leaders are made, not born. This is a touchstone of my life, one you would do well to adopt." She lowered her voice. "How do we become leaders, Riane? By being ever so much more clever than those around us. And how do we *promote* this cleverness? There are methods of dealing with our fellow Ramahan—secrets I will teach you over time—that when properly applied make a far more dramatic difference in the order than mere seniority. This is why I am supreme among all the konara; it is why they defer to me on matters of both secular policy and sacred dogmata. I have made myself indispensable. They *rely* on me, *depend* on my will."

She put aside the cor-hair brush, admiring her handiwork as if it were calligraphy. "And now because you have pleased me, I will tell you your first secret. The more you make others depend on your will, the less they think for themselves. Soon, your opinions are adopted unopposed. They are *embraced* as the new dogmata."

"But I do not yet know enough—"

"Of course you don't, not yet, anyway. That is where I come in," Bartta said in Riane's ear. "I will prepare you, guide you down the path you need to take. Do not worry; I will be at your side every step of the way."

The work project to which Riane had been assigned was headed by Vedda, a rosy-cheeked, rotund shima, whose specialty was archaeology. Riane liked her far more than the shima who ran the first detail Bartta had put her into, which did the daily washing for the abbey. Shima Wirdd had fallen suddenly ill, and the work detail had been reorganized, something that had needed to be done, according to the ubiquitous acolyte grapevine.

One morning, Shima Vedda had appeared in the drear,

windowless, subterranean laundry, choosing three acolytes, Riane among them. Riane was overjoyed to escape from the boring wash detail. Shima Vedda was very strict about discipline and procedure; but she was cheerful and, more importantly, a veritable font of history, especially concerning this section of the Djenn Marre. She absorbed every word Shima Vedda taught her about the history of the region. It was as if her fascination knew no bounds, as if something unknown at the very core of her was at last being fed.

Often, she stayed later than the other acolytes on the detail, helping Shima Vedda, who seemed as reluctant as she was to leave her beloved work. By flickering lantern and torchlight they did their careful renovation, referring constantly to the architectural plans Shima Vedda had resurrected from the Ramahan vaults, and then had painstakingly restored over a period of months.

Each day before their work began, they donned special robes cinched by wide cor-hide belts from which hung the implements of archaeological exploration—small knives, pry bars, files, whisks, hammers, and the like. Always, Shima Vedda addressed them solemnly while they changed. "It is imperative that the new refectory look exactly like the old one," she reiterated over and over, "so that when the konara see it they will not know where the old walls end and the new ones begin."

Save for Riane, the detail of twelve acolytes needed this quotidian reminder, since they exhibited little interest in the archaeological aspects of their work that so fascinated Riane and Shima Vedda, and actively disliked the physical labor, which they considered both beneath them and a kind of punishment. They were bitter, these acolytes, Riane soon discovered. They resented being trapped down here and were constantly dreaming up schemes for, as they put it, their "reinstatement to life."

It happened one still, oppressive evening when Riane and Shima Vedda were working late. Alone at the far end of the excavations, they were engulfed by the stern silence of the speckled granite which their pickaxes were slowly consum-

ing. Coated in fine dust, white as glennan flour, acolyte and
shima continued their work. On hands and knees, they used
their curved implements to carefully pry up the cracked mosaic tiles, trying to preserve them as best they could. They
felt the seismic tremor and kept still, their eyes locked together. Riane could hear the thunder of her heart, the sound
of Shima Vedda breathing. When the tremor had passed, they
resumed their work. It was then that Riane noticed the anomaly in the ancient underfloor.

She called Shima Vedda's name as she pointed to what
looked like a low spot that had cause two stone tiles to cant
inward. Together, they pulled up the tiles and discovered that
the underfloor was rent with seams and tiny veinlike fissures.
Shima Vedda used her hammer to tap lightly on the stone.
Immediately, it collapsed in a shower of friable shards. The
miniquake had opened a fault-seam in the bedrock.

"Stand back," she told Riane as she used the hammer to
widen the hole. After another shower of rock shards fell inward, she said, "I think perhaps we have been excavating on
a fault line."

"I don't think the abbey would have been built on a fault
line."

"True enough," Shima Vedda said. "But the recent seismic
activity all through the Djenn Marre has created thousands
of these fault lines. Some, like the one we see here, are so
small they cannot be detected. I suspect our excavations en-
larged this one."

Without being asked, Riane went and got a couple of
torches, handed one to Shima Vedda as she peered into the
hole. Excitement caught in the shima's throat. "Riane, there
is something down there!"

Riane brought a rope ladder to the edge of the hole and
deployed it. She anchored the top rung and looked at Shima
Vedda.

The shima's eyes were alight. "Why stop now, eh, Riane?
Let's both have a look."

Riane hesitated. "Really?"

"Of course! You are the one who discovered the fault. It

is your duty as a student archaeologist to follow through on your find." So saying, she lifted the torch high over her head and stepped down onto a rung of the rope ladder.

Riane watched her slowly descend.

"Come on!" Shima Vedda called. "You are not going to believe this!"

Reluctantly, Riane descended into the flickering gloom. Jumping from the last rung of the ladder, she found herself in a chamber wholly unlike the refectory above. For one thing, it was triangular, the walls pitched at an angle so that they reached a point—or they had before the cave-in.

"Where are we?" she asked.

"I am not altogether certain." Shima Vedda, her voice trembling with elation, was slowly walking around the room, lighting the walls and corners with her torch. "But if I were to make a guess, I would say that we have stumbled upon the Kells."

"What are they, tombs?"

"A splendid guess!" Shima Vedda's eyes were alight. "Kell is a word from the Old Tongue. It means 'sanctuary.' It also means 'tomb' or 'concealed place.' " She continued her exploration of the chamber. "Legend has it that when Miina created the abbey, She placed within the bedrock at its very heart the Kells—a series of three sanctum observatories from which She could monitor unseen the holy work of Her disciples."

"If you are right," Riane said, "then Miina has not been here in many centuries."

Shima Vedda nodded distractedly. She was running a hand along a stone bench carved out of a shell-like niche. There was one of these niches in each of the three walls, scalloped and sparkling as if with polished jewels. "Each Kell was said to be in a different geometric shape sacred to Miina: a cube, a sphere, and a triangle."

"Why are those shapes sacred to Miina?"

"I am surprised your lessons have not covered this. The cube is the symbol for the female; the sphere is the symbol for the male. And the triangle—Miina's most sacred symbol—represents the three medial points." She touched Riane's heart. "The Seat of Dreams." The top of her head. "The Seat of Truth." And a spot in the center of her forehead. "The Seat of Deepest Knowledge."

Directly above each niche was a medallion carved from black basalt not unlike the one set into the center of the circular Storehouse Door in the caverns below the regent's palace. Each contained a carved figure. Shima Vedda lifted the torch even higher. "Look here! More evidence that this was the Great Goddess's sanctum observatory. Here is Her sacred butterfly." She stopped beneath the medallion on the second wall. "And here is Her sacred double-bladed hoeing ax." At the foot of the third wall, however, her brow furrowed. "Now this is odd. See, this medallion holds an intricately worked carving of a citrine serpent." She stood upon the bench so that she could run her hand over the stone. "Unlike the other images which are carved into their medallions, this serpent stands out as if it was alive. But, well . . ." She beckoned. "Come have a look for yourself." She made room for Riane to stand beside her. "Observe this serpent, Riane, and tell me what you see."

Riane spent rapt minutes staring at the exquisite image. For her, there was a vivid sense about it of the living, a quality of breath, of a peculiar light, unseen, but nevertheless felt, that emerged to grip her. This light—this force—she imagined, was what gave the archaeologist sleepless nights. The voices of ancestors seemed to speak in her mind, a chorus of ancients chanting in the Old Tongue, giving up secrets in the slow, methodical cadence of the pickax exposing the crumbling layers of history. Reaching up on tiptoes, she traced with her fingertips the line between the citrine and the basalt medallion. "I think the serpent is a full carving set into the basalt," she said.

"That was my conclusion as well!" Shima Vedda's excitement continued unabated. She climbed down from her perch, and Riane followed suit. "Tell me, Riane, have you ever seen the citrine serpent—a serpent of any kind—associated with Miina?"

"No. We are taught that the serpent is a symbol of evil—of lies, deception, and the Underworld. It is the Avatar of Pyphoros, is it not?"

"Yes." Shima Vedda raised a finger long ago discolored by stone dust. "At least, that is the Scripture currently being taught. But I have for some time been aware that the dogmata we learn are at times at odds with the past I unearth. Take, for example, this citrine serpent. We have never encountered its like in any temple, abbey, or shrine. And yet we know that the mineral citrine is sacred to Miina. Now we encounter a serpent carved out of that very stone. Here it lies in a place of honor in the Kells, Miina's own sanctum."

"What makes you say it has a place of honor?" Riane asked.

"You yourself told me."

"Me?"

"Yes. Did you not say that you believed that the serpent was carved whole and set into the basalt?"

"I did."

"Were the butterfly and the double-bladed ax—the other images sacred to Miina—the subject of such loving attention?"

Riane looked around the triangular chamber. "No. Their images are merely etched into their medallions."

"Precisely!" Shima Vedda smiled. "And what is the first law of archaeology?"

" 'The more time put into a structure, an artifact, a carving, the more important it was to our ancestors.' "

"And that would make this citrine serpent important, indeed, would it not?"

Riane cocked an eye in its direction. "*Very* important," she said.

"I agree. There is an anomaly here. The archaeology is directly contradicting what both you and I have been taught. That the serpent is so prominently displayed indicates that it was once not only one of Miina's Avatars, but also one of Her most important ones."

"How could such a monumental mistake in doctrine be made?"

"If it is a mistake at all." Shima Vedda walked all around the room. The ancient stone gave off its own powerful scent. "Here is another question for you, Riane. How does one get in and out of this chamber?"

Riane thought for a moment. There was no door in any of the three walls. "If this chamber was meant for Miina, no door would be needed."

Shima Vedda smiled. "True enough. But let us imagine for a moment that every once in a while a konara was required to perform sacred tasks for the Great Goddess—preparing the space, for instance. How would she get in and out?" She waited a moment. "I want you to pay particular attention to the second rule of archaeology. Do you remember it?"

Riane nodded. " 'The more intricate an artifact, the greater its purpose.' "

"Quite right." Shima Vedda spread her arms to take in the whole of the Kell.

Riane turned slowly, trying to absorb everything. What struck her was the organic nature of the space, as if she were inside the belly of a beast whose shape defied mortal understanding. She looked but could find no obvious evidence that the Kell had been *built* as structures inevitably are. Rather, her impression was that it had been formed much as her own body had been formed, by a primal act, by a natural but mysterious manipulation of elements, by growth. After a moment, she climbed back onto the bench. Stretching herself to her limit, she pressed the flat of her hand against the convex surface of the citrine serpent. She started a little when it gave. Pushing it in farther, she heard a gnashing of stone against stone, and turned in time to see a two-square-meter section in the center of the floor begin to descend slowly. Shima Vedda was already standing on the square. She held out one arm toward Riane.

"Hurry, now! Hurry!"

Jumping down, Riane ran to where Shima Vedda's strong arm whisked her aboard.

"You knew the true meaning of the serpent, didn't you?" Riane said breathlessly.

Shima Vedda smiled. "We shall say that assiduous study has its rewards and leave it at that."

Down they went, deeper into the bedrock upon which Miina had constructed the Abbey of Floating White. When the odd lift ground to a halt, they found themselves in another chamber, perhaps three times the size of the Kell above. This one was enameled a glistening black; it was a perfect cube. The mechanism for the lift itself was ingenious, appearing to be a corkscrew fashioned out of heartwood. Because heartwood exuded oil constantly, the corkscrew mechanism worked as well now as it had when it had first been built many centuries ago.

Again, that sense of breath, of *aliveness* informed the air Riane inhaled, so intense this time she felt a sadness welling in her breast. A sense of loss, this sadness, for what had passed, for what had been leaching away for centuries. The coming of the V'ornn had merely hastened the decay.

"Miina protect us, look at this!" Shima Vedda was kneeling beside the wall. From its flat surface projected three high-relief carvings of huge and terrifying animals, golden and glossy as the wall itself save for the black spots on their backs. They had sleek, catlike heads and powerful-looking jaws bristling with sharp teeth. Long, slender tails curved over their backs. Their mouths gaped open, deep slots carved into the wall, as if these beasts were alive and could devour their prey.

As Riane stared at the beasts peculiar pricklings ran up the back of her neck, making her scalp contract. They were the same beasts she had seen painted onto the cave walls above Heavenly Rushing. She tried to look away, but could not. She felt like a fly caught in a spider's sticky web. "Shima, what are these beasts called?"

Shima Vedda's voice was filled with awe. "They are Ja-Gaar."

"Tell me about them."

Shima Vedda shook her head. "I fear I have told you too much already. Konara Bartta has removed Ja-Gaar from the teaching in the abbey."

"This is an important archaeological find. You must tell me," Riane said. "Besides, no one will hear us."

Shima Vedda hesitated for a moment before replying. "The Ja-Gaar are the night slayers, the white-bone daemons, the guardians of the Abyss, the beasts of Pyphoros."

Riane had been to the Abyss. Annon had seen no Ja-Gaar there, but of course she could not tell Shima Vedda that.

"I wish Leyna Astar were here to see this," Riane said.

"Ah, yes. She was your teacher for a time." Shima Vedda made a concerned face. "I did not know her at all. Still, one must deplore her bad luck. That fatal fall down the cistern shaft was an accident of tragic proportions."

Startled, Riane said, "Where did you hear about Leyna Astar's death?"

"Why, I was there when Konara Bartta and Konara Urdma were pulling her corpse out of the shaft." She shuddered. "It was an ugly sight—her body so bruised and broken. That was quite a fall!"

Riane made no reply. She knew that Leyna Astar had not died from falling down the cistern, but, again, this was something she dared not tell Shima Vedda, who, doubtless, would run to Bartta with the story and possibly end up as Astar had. Turning her mind in another direction, she followed the play of torchlight over the black floor, which was set in a pattern of large basalt squares and small obsidian circles. She crawled on hands and knees across the gleaming black floor. At the very center, she stopped. "Shima, what is this thing?"

Shima Vedda knelt, bringing the torch closer. "It appears to be a circular plate of some sort." Her fingers traced around the raised circumference. She estimated that the plate had a diameter of three meters.

"Another medallion?"

"I don't think so." She put her torch into an iron wall

bracket so that she could use both her hands. "I believe it is a cover."

"To what?"

She looked at Riane. "Perhaps, after all, your first assessment was correct."

Riane stared down at the cover. "A tomb?"

"We'll soon find out." Shima Vedda unhooked a short iron pry bar from her belt, wedged the curved end into the narrow groove between the thick floor tiles and the basalt cover. "Now, if you are up to it, give me a hand, child."

The two pushed down on the opposite end of the pry bar, leaning all their weight on it. Slowly, the cover began to lift. They worked the pry bar into the widening gap to get greater purchase and leaned down again. The cover moved. By turning the pry bar, they managed to lever it all the way off.

Together, they stared into a pitch-black well. As Shima Vedda retrieved the torch and played it over the well, they saw their reflections.

"How could a tomb be filled with water?" Riane asked. Perhaps Shima Vedda answered her, but if so, she did not hear her. Her own reflection grew until it filled her entire field of vision, and as it grew it began to spin. Or perhaps it was she who was spinning. As she spun, the walls of the cubic Kell dimmed, became translucent, transparent, vanished altogether. In their place, she saw the molecules, atoms, protons, neutrons, electrons, and gravitons that, massed together, made up the known universe. Everything was in motion at once. Chaos ruled! And yet, nothing was random. She could sense an order, an immensely complex pattern emerging from every direction at once. It was enthralling, disconcerting, utterly overwhelming . . .

Riane, bound in pure energy, was gripped by the sensation of falling—falling through the subatomic realm. "I am Thripping," she said to herself in wonder and awe.

The pure energy that she had become burned like a redhot coal, and then, all at once, she was herself again—corporeal, flesh and blood—standing in a solid world. Staggering with vertigo, she looked around her. She found

herself in a small, dimly lighted, spherical chamber that
smelled as musty as a long-disused cupboard. Leather-bound
books lined the curved filigreed silver shelves of this curious
chamber from floor to ceiling, and more were piled in unruly
stacks upon the stone floor. The sole piece of furniture was
an enormous, intricately scrollworked heartwood chair on
which sat an equally enormous female clad in billowing turquoise robes edged with gold tassels.

"Welcome, Riane," she said in a deceptively light, musical
voice. "I have been waiting centuries to meet you."

21

Eye

"I care not who these outsiders are," Dammi said in his
most belligerent tone. "They cannot stay."

He was a strong, agile male of sixteen years who, like
Eleana and all Kundalan since the V'ornn occupation, had
been forced to grow up too quickly. Both orphaned when
their parents were killed in the V'ornn hunts, it was perhaps
preordained that they become freedom fighters. What else in
the world had they but each other and their hatred of the
V'ornn? They had grown up together, and it had been
Dammi's dream that they share the rest of their lives together. He had always assumed that they would. She was
sure that her growth into a thinking, independent-minded
huntress had dumbfounded—and, in an odd way, saddened—
him. Which was why he fought so hard against her periodic
forays into Axis Tyr to meet with the contact who provided
them with intelligence, coins, and weapons. She had been
one of the two things he could count on, and now he had
lost her to the world. She supposed that her understanding
of this dynamic had come the moment she had made her

emotional break with him. She knew she had undone his notion of their little hermetically sealed world, but it disturbed her that he could not see that she was suffocating inside it. Annon's coming had been tangible proof that she no longer had any future staying here. Now she had fallen madly, deeply, irrevocably in love with Annon. Now too much damage had been done. There was no going back, even if she had wished it. She knew it, and so did Dammi. Still, she had to try to get along with him.

"How can I make you see?" she asked.

They were in the underground center of the resistance cell, below a structure adjacent to the one to which she had led Giyan and Hacilar. It was even more heavily camouflaged than the nearby house. The building above them was nothing more than an old barn, well used and filled with stalls holding cor on one side and cthauros on the other. A hidden trapdoor beneath the dried wrygrass strewn over the packed-earth floor led, via a rustic heartwood ladder, to the nerve center of their operations. The rooms which were stark, covered with topo maps, defined what they were without revealing a trace of who they were.

"It is you who does not see. If you had embraced Kara as I and the other members of the cell have, we would not be having this stupid argument. This new religion makes us stronger, bonds us to no Goddess, no ancient ritual. If you came to even one service, you would understand. These outsiders threaten us—all of us."

"Now you are being melodramatic," she said.

"I am thinking of the cell, Eleana. Who are you thinking of? Yourself? You call these outsiders friends, but one of them is V'ornn—a Khaggun, to boot! And as if that were not in itself an inexcusable breach of security, he is also the Pack-Commander who led the last attack on us not more than three months ago."

"I explained all that, Dammi."

"Yes, you did, and to be honest I think you have gone mad! Harboring a Kundalan sorceress and a V'ornn Khagggun, both of whom are wanted by the new regent of Axis

Tyr!" He shook his head. "Had I not seen them with my own eyes, I would not have believed it!"

"Their enemies are our enemies, surely that must count for something. From a tactical point of view, they could be so help—"

"No, Eleana, this decision is nonnegotiable."

She wanted to stamp her feet with anger. "You are so thickheaded! Don't you see that you're cutting off your nose to spite your face?"

He folded his burly arms over his chest. "With these intensified attacks, the V'ornn have made their intentions crystal clear; they mean to annihilate us. The majority of the cell has spoken."

"I do not believe they have turned against me."

"They believe that circumstance has turned against you, that you are under the sorceress's spell."

"Do you believe that, Dammi?"

"I know you are not the female I used to know. I have told them as much. It would been remiss on my part not to."

"So you have turned against me. You think I have changed, but it is you who are different. Kara has made you hard and rigid."

"It has opened my eyes to new threats."

"I am under no spell, but maybe you are. The threats I see come from within the resistance as well as from the V'ornn. Remember how it was five years ago when we were being trained? Where is the communication, the co-ordination between cells? Nowadays, cells disagree in methods, principles, goals. The cell leaders have turned away from the teachings of the Great Goddess, they have embraced this new synthetic religion. They have become tyrants."

"I was right. You have become a liability—worse, a threat to morale."

She laughed in his face. "Morale? There is no morale. Morale can't exist without idealism. And where is our idealism? It's been ground out of us by attrition, the deaths of our families, our elders for whom idealism burned like the sun. We have become no better than the V'ornn we fight.

Our shared belief had been replaced by an ugly, mean thing, a different thing altogether—the mindless spasm of bloodletting."

"Enough!" It was clear that he had ceased to listen to her. "The outsiders must be out of our territory by nightfall, and that is the end of it."

He turned to leave the room, but paused when she called his name.

"You are making a mistake, Dammi."

"It is you who called me a tyrant." He came back, stood face-to-face with her. "It is you who almost brought wholesale disaster on us the last time you gave succor to this sorceress and her accursed V'ornn charge. How you could have spent time in the same room with him, let alone have helped him is beyond me. But I do know that it was foolish and wrongheaded."

Her heart was beating fast as her determination drove her to the brink—a brink she realized now she had been heading toward almost all her life.

"They need my help. You cannot stop me from doing what I want."

Dammi's eyes blazed with righteous anger. She felt sick to see the look of loathing on his face. "Careful what you wish for, Eleana."

"What I cannot understand," Rekkk said, "is how a Kundalan sorceress is in the employ of Wennn Stogggul."

"I do not know Malistra well enough to say for certain," Giyan replied. "But what I *can* tell you is that unless we stop her, it will go evil with us."

"Pardon me for saying so," Eleana broke in, "but it seems to me that the first order of business must be to stop Olnnn Rydddlin."

They were sitting around a rickety wooden table in the cottage where Eleana and Dammi lived. Eleana had no little trepidation about bringing the V'ornn here, but the sorcerous incident had frightened her sufficiently to make her at least listen to their proposal. Upon entering, she saw them look around and, as often happens, saw it herself through their eyes. The small cottage was furnished poorly, with what she and Dammi had salvaged of their parents' lives—old, beat-up furniture, souvenirs that suddenly seemed meaningless, nothing more than junk. It suddenly occurred to her that there was nothing of their own—unless you counted the maps, charts, and topos of the area that covered most of the walls. But that was resistance property. The entirety of their lives encompassed fighting the V'ornn, which they had been doing since they were ten, when their parents had been hunted down and killed by Khagggun.

Giyan had turned to Eleana. "Does that mean you will help us?"

"I don't know." Eleana was eyeing Rekkk nervously as he continued to take in the place. "I haven't yet decided."

Rekkk's head swung about, his wide intelligent eyes catching her staring at him. "Topo maps, shock-swords, detailed intelligence on Khagggun movement. You are an exceptionally well provisioned cell." His smile caused her to shiver. "In any event, I agree completely with your assessment. Olnnn Rydddlin is the immediate threat. Knowing him as I do, it will not take him long to get here."

Giyan was frowning. "Of course, both of you are right. But Malistra's part in this troubles me deeply. If she is now doing the regent's bidding, there will be dire consequences far beyond Olnnn Rydddlin and his Khagggun pack."

Eleana stood up abruptly. "He makes me uneasy," she said to Giyan.

"That was not my intent," Rekkk said.

"Then why make that crack about how well provisioned we are? Are you looking for me to reveal my supplier? I would die first."

"I believe you absolutely." He spread his hands. "I suppose I was intrigued. It was a simple observation, nothing more."

Giyan gestured. "Please sit down, Eleana. I know how easy it is to read into innocent comments. We can only be undone by fear."

Eleana took a breath, calming herself. Then she sat across from Giyan so she could look into her eyes. "Tell me what you want me to do," she said.

"The Dar Sala-at is in the Abbey of Floating White in Stone Border," Giyan said. "We want you to help us get there undetected."

"You said your mission was urgent."

"It is," Giyan said, and she proceeded to tell Eleana about how the Gyrgon had tried to use the Ring of Five Dragons to open the Storehouse Door beneath the regent's palace in Axis Tyr, how the Ring killed three of them, how it was now lodged in the Door, turned into the detonator of a doomsday device that would cause a series of immense seismic shocks. "All life on Kundala will be destroyed," she concluded, "unless we can get the Dar Sala-at to the Door by the ides of Lonon, when the shocks will begin."

"This is truth, Giyan?"

"I am very much afraid it is, my dear."

Eleana said nothing for a moment, but a line of sweat had popped out at her hairline. She rose, poured mead into three tankards, came back to where the two sat.

"I know a good path north," she said, handing them the tankards and ripping a map from the wall. She spread it open on the table. "Here, I can show you." She pointed with a forefinger. "It is a ridge crossing, dangerous, but the higher the elevation, the better chance you have of losing the pack."

Giyan nodded. "This is good, Rekkk."

"It's not good enough," Rekkk said shortly. "As you said, we need Eleana's contacts to keep us in hiding all the way to Stone Border."

Giyan looked at the girl. "What do you say?" She put her hand over Eleana's. "We need you with us."

"If Eleana agrees, she will take you north along this ridge path," Rekkk said before Eleana had a chance to reply. "I am going south."

"What?" Giyan said.

"Listen, I know Olnnn Rydddlin. He will not stop until he has found me. Either I face him now or later. If I do it now, it will be at the time and place of my choosing."

"You must be crazy. This is hardly the ideal—"

"In battle, Giyan, nothing is ideal. You must fashion your victories out of courage and ingenuity. In the end, there is nothing else."

Eleana, who had been looking from one to the other, suddenly said, "Spoken like a true V'ornn, and just like a stupid Khagggun."

Rekkk sat very still, watching her from beneath hooded eyes. Giyan felt the tension in him like a coiled spring. "This is a difficult situation for everyone," she said. "I am sure Eleana didn't mean—"

"I mean every word of it." Eleana stood over them, fists on her hips. "I know this region better than you—better than Olnnn Rydddlin and his pack of murderers." She glared at Rekkk. "You do it this way, and the pack will eat you alive."

He gave her a tight smile. "What alternative do you propose?" he said, slowly and carefully.

"You are right about one thing. Turning tail is not the answer," Eleana said. "We head toward the enemy because that is precisely the opposite of what he expects us to do. All three of us will go south. All three of us will prepare to fight Olnnn Rydddlin and his pack."

"Out of the mouth of babes—"

"I am not a baby!" Eleana shouted. "I have been fighting your kind since I was ten." She leaned on her arms, bending over the table. "Do you have any idea what that means, V'ornn?"

Rekkk looked up at her calmly. "As a Khagggun, I began training when I was six months old. I killed my first enemy when I was eight." He picked up his tankard, drained it, wiped his lips with the back of his hand. "I had nightmares about that kill for a year afterward. I could hear his voice begging me for mercy. But Khagggun do not dispense mercy, do they?"

An awkward silence ensued, after which, Eleana said, "I need to tell Dammi, to collect some things." She looked pointedly at Rekkk. "But I want to make two things perfectly clear. I do not trust you, V'ornn."

"I can accept that," Rekkk said. "We V'ornn have a saying: 'Trust does not come in a lifetime.' " He stood up. "However, I myself find that notion completely alien."

"What is the other thing?" Giyan asked tensely.

Eleana was still looking at Rekkk. "If you have lied to us, if your purpose is false, if you try to betray us, V'ornn, I *will* kill you."

"Your commendable zeal is duly noted," Rekkk said without animus.

Giyan stood as well. "It is true. The world is suddenly a different place for all of us. We must learn to settle into our new roles in our own time."

Rekkk Hacilar nodded solemnly. "So be it, then."

"May Fate treat us mercifully," Giyan whispered.

"Death to our enemies!" Eleana cried, in a very Khaggaun-like manner.

The underbrush was dense, its bright green turning to indigo as the sun sank into the west. Gimnopedes, still in sunlight, flitted about the higher tree branches, and golden-eyed lemurs stared down at the trio as they made their stealthy way south. Eleana was in the lead, with Rekkk next and Giyan bringing up the rear.

The day had grown hotter and more humid. Somewhere in the distance, there was the rumble of thunder. Biting insects, massing in the still, heavy air, were becoming more than a nuisance. The sky was white with heat, opaque as a sheet of silver. They had spoken not a word since they had set out from Eleana's cottage.

Rekkk glanced back at Giyan. "Let's take a breather. We've been at it for five hours straight."

They settled in a glade carpeted with high wrygrass, Rekkk and Giyan together, Eleana a small distance away. Whistleflowers bloomed where during the day patches of sunlight broke through the forest canopy, and woody vines with tiny orange flowers fearlessly climbed the trunks of the heartwood trees. Now all was carpeted in the white heat-haze.

Eleana broke out water and dried fruit. They sat with their backs against the tree boles, eating slowly and methodically.

"Giyan," he said at last, "thank you for believing me."

She said nothing, stared straight ahead at a copse of trees.

"I know you hold me responsible for Annon's death."

"No, I don't," she said abruptly, and rose, walking a little way into the trees on the other side of the clearing.

Rekkk, stunned, saw Eleana looking at him. She bared her teeth. He bared his own back at her, then got up and made to follow Giyan.

"I would not do that if I were you," Eleana said softly.

"Then thank N'Luuura I am a V'ornn," he said as he walked away from her.

Giyan heard him approach, but she did not move away.

"Have you felt any more stirring of Osoru?" Rekkk asked.

She shook her head. "I think Malistra will in future be more circumspect in her attacks."

"You are expecting more?"

"Do not look so concerned. I will fight Malistra." It was a shame she did not feel half as confident as she sounded. The Kyofu attack had shaken her badly, especially what she had felt at the end. It was clear that Malistra possessed a power unheard of in sorcery for many centuries. During her own studies, Giyan had come across only one mention of the Eye of Ajbal, the Eye of Darkness. It had been in an ancient tome, *The Book of Recantation*, one of many she had been sent to clean in a remote and infrequently used section of the vast Library in the Abbey of Floating White. The words had filled her with such dread that she had snapped the book closed, returned it to its shelf without finishing the section. For weeks afterward she was pursued in her dreams by this spectral horror.

Now she knew that it existed she wished that she had read the entire book. If she had, she would have had a better chance of knowing how to combat it—or even what, in fact, it was.

She closed her eyes, put her head back against a nearby tree trunk, and willed her racing pulse to slow. Panic would only make things worse, she knew. Panic stopped reason dead in its tracks. She would simply have to be on her guard until she found some explanation for the dark sorcery being used against her. She knew of Malistra only dimly, and then only because as Eleusis Ashera's mistress she had had her ear to the ground. She had heard that Malistra was an orphan. No one knew where she had come by her training. One day, so the story went, she had simply appeared in Axis Tyr and had begun her work, using Osoru in matters of love and revenge in exchange for money, food, clothes, shelter. In due course, she gathered a reputation, but never an okuuut, the V'ornn implant worn by all the other Kundalan who resided or did business inside the city's walls. How she managed to escape the V'ornn security net was, doubtless, another casting of Osoru, but a fiendishly subtle one, since even Giyan had had to be fitted with one. Which meant that Malistra had had to keep to the shadows, had had to keep moving to different quarters of the city. This, too, was in keeping with her reputation. But now she had come out into the light. For some reason, at this particular time, she had made herself known to Wennn Stogggul. Curious. Disturbing. Terrifying. To think that the new regent could command the Eye of Ajbal—if Malistra had told him of it.

"We should be going."

Giyan opened her eyes to see Eleana standing, flexing her legs.

"I will reconnoiter first," Rekkk said, heading south into the forest.

Giyan returned her attention to Eleana. It was difficult to believe that this proud, accomplished female was but sixteen. Giyan thought back to how she had been at that age. How she had been taken by a pack of V'ornn Khagggun. It had been her fortune that they had been hunting with Eleusis Ashera; otherwise, she would have been raped and killed like so many others. She remembered vividly those first moments among the alien V'ornn. Her terror oddly mixed with a curious kind of fascination. Eleusis had spoken Kundalan to her, had not been laughed at by the Khagggun because he was the regent. But they were filled with rage, those Khagggun, at being denied their fun. Their eyes smoldered with they looked at her, and their smiles were as brittle as a dead leaf. But they did not touch her; they did not murmur angrily among themselves. This was her first glimpse of the strict caste culture of the V'ornn. All that vast power kept in check by their rigid societal structure. What would happen, she found herself wondering, if that power broke free of its constraints?

Living all her short life at the Abbey, being in Axis Tyr was bewildering. And so terribly sad. The wall, the other V'ornn modifications, the desecration of Middle Palace, the regent's residence, and the Abbey of Listening Bone, now home of the Gyrgon. For months on end, she had been inconsolable; and then one night as she had been staring out at her beloved Djenn Marre, Eleusis had come to her, and she had seen beneath the fierce, stern V'ornn exterior into his yearning hearts.

"Giyan." Eleana had paused in her stretching. "Are you all right?"

Giyan wiped away a tear "Just an old memory, nothing more."

"If I can help you in any way. I would gladly do so."

Giyan could see the goodness in her, as well as the desire to be appreciated. "Just being here is help enough. I know you must have made quite a sacrifice to leave your family."

"I have no family, save for Dammi and the rest of my cell. But it seems they have all turned their backs on me."

"What you did took extraordinary courage," Giyan said from the bottom of her heart.

Eleana flushed. "Thank you. I . . . well, it may sound foolish, but I feel closer to Annon when I am with you."

Giyan put her arm around Eleana, her heart hammering in her chest. "You do not sound foolish at all . . . But I—" At the last moment, her determination faltered.

Eleana was looking at her expectantly.

Giyan steeled herself to lie in order to protect her son. "It is about Annon."

Eleana's face was suddenly white. "What about him?"

"He is dead, Eleana. He did not survive the perwillon attack."

Eleana's heart seemed to collapse inside her. "But that cannot be! There must be some mistake!"

Giyan squeezed her hand, shook her head. Eleana let out such a heartfelt sob that Giyan was moved to take her in her arms and rock her gently.

"I am so sorry to be the bearer of such terrible news."

"Oh, do not tell me this!" Eleana was sobbing openly. "I can bear anything but this."

"I wish I could say otherwise, my dear." And she did, with all her heart. She wished she could tell Eleana the truth—that Annon was only dead in one sense, in the sense that his body had died. But she could not risk telling anyone, not even this girl who obviously loved him so. And, even if she violated her own ironclad law, what would be the point? Annon was Riane now, a Kundalan female, unrecognizable to this girl. Next to this half lie, the truth would be unendurable.

"He cannot be gone," Eleana moaned. "Not after he and I ate the flesh of the perwillon."

Giyan smoothed back Eleana's hair. "Your meaning eludes me."

"It is an ancient custom here in the highlands," she said. "The raw flesh of the perwillon, when eaten by two lovers, is said to bind them together for all time."

"Ah, my dear." Giyan stroked her as she had Annon when as a child he had been frightened by a nightmare. "I am so sorry to have caused you this pain."

Eleana turned to gaze deep into Giyan's whistleflower-blue eyes. "I *still* love him. I can feel it here, in my heart." Her expression was so intense she stopped Giyan's reply. "I told you, we are bonded, he and I, bonded for all eternity."

Giyan felt a ripple run through her as, again, she felt the urge to tell this girl the truth. But she could put no one—

especially not Rekkk or Eleana in that kind of jeopardy. The Ashera had too many powerful enemies. Riane's secret must stay with her and her alone.

"The heart is a powerful beacon," she said. "I know. I have lost one love. But another will come. For you, as well, Eleana. Be patient. Give your wound time to heal."

Eleana wept as she had not allowed herself to do while she was with those who knew her best. Sobbing, she clung to Giyan like the lost girl that she was beneath the impressive facade of her bravado.

Rekkk returned then. Giyan saw the look on his face and was instantly alerted. Eleana heard him, as well, and quickly dried her eyes, regaining her composure.

"There is a ridge several hundred meters to the south," he said as he came up. "It is well forested. From it, you can see many kilometers. We need to get there as quickly as we can. The sooner we spot the pack, the better prepared we'll be to stop them."

Without another word passing between them, they headed out of the glade, into even denser heartwood forests. The underbrush, however, had changed. It was now filled with green ferns and blue lichen, indicating that they were near either a stream or an underground water source. When Rekkk asked her, Eleana confirmed that a shallow river snaked its way several hundred meters to the east. Rekkk, now in the lead, took them southeast, in a diagonal line that would intersect with the river. They heard it before they saw it, which was the point. The burbling of the water would safely mask their sounds so that the Khagggun's sophisticated equipment would not be able to pick them up.

They followed the river as it broke out onto the plateau, keeping to its west bank until they reached the edge of a clearing. Twilight was fast fading. Already the eastern sky was dark enough for the first-magnitude stars to stud the velvet backdrop. Rekkk hunkered down onto his haunches, and the females followed suit. They scanned the terrain to the south, where the forest petered out at the northerly end of a series of terraced orchards, searching for movement.

"I know Olnnn Rydddlin," Rekkk said. "He will not use any of my own strategies. He is too much the egotist. For him, a victory over me using my own strategies would be no victory at all."

"Have you any idea what he will do?" Eleana asked.

"A few. When I see the pack scouts I will have my first clues."

Giyan looked at him. "I am worried. Try as I might, I do not see a way that the three of us can defeat an entire Khagggun pack."

"Olnnn Rydddlin won't, either." He smiled. "And therein lies our edge."

The water whirled and eddied against smooth, shiny rocks as it made its way to the end of the plateau, spilling over the side in a sudden cascade. Iridescent-winged saw-needles scooted low over the river's surface. A green-and-red speckle-backed wer-frog raised its head out of the water, took one look at them and vanished. Tiny grey-shelled freshwater muodds lined the bank at the purling waterline.

Rekkk became aware that Eleana was staring at his okummmon; he contrived to ignore her scrutiny.

"How steep is the southerly approach to this plateau?" he asked her.

"Steep enough for us to have to rappel down." She shrugged. "But then we don't have hovercraft."

"What about to the east?"

"We usually return that way. Though it's longer, the terrain is less forbidding, steep enough for a strenuous hike, but not so sheer that we have to use ropes and pitons." She made a movement with her head. "Are you going to tell me how you came by that? It is not like any okummmon I have ever seen."

For a moment, he considered ignoring her question. But then he got to thinking. Despite her comparative youth, she was an exceedingly clever female. Evasion would not sit very much better with her than prevarication. In any event, neither would engender her trust, and without her trust he might never complete his mission. "It's not an okummmon," he said. "At least, not by the standard definition."

"But it was implanted by the Gyrgon."

"I am an experiment," he said. "I cannot be Summoned. How could I? I am Lesser Caste. Why would the Gyrgon care about my opinions? But this okummmon can do what the ones the Bashkir have cannot. It can transform the five elements—earth, air, fire, water, wood—into whatever I want them to be." He extruded a thin, articulated wire from the okummmon.

Eleana watched it with a kind of fascinated horror. "But you can't . . . I mean, that is the technomancy of the Gyrgon."

"It is as I told you," he said, digging idly in the damp earth with the wire. "I am an experiment. I am part Gyrgon now."

"As far as I'm concerned," she said, "this makes you even less trustworthy."

He nodded. "You are right to be suspicious. Believe it or not, I, too, had my suspicions about the Gyrgon—their obscure motives, their apparent disregard for other life-forms. These are part of V'ornn culture from time immemorial. But of late, I have come to see the Gyrgon in an altogether different light. For one thing, they are not the united caste they appear to be. Basic philosophical differences have fractured the fabled Comradeship. Then, too, there is something about Kundala."

"Something about Kundala?" Eleana frowned. "What do you mean?"

"Nith Sahor—this particular Gyrgon—is not like the rest," Rekkk said. "He is a champion of change, whereas the rest of the Comradeship stands steadfastly as they always have, for uniformity, the status quo. The truth he has seen, that I am beginning to understand, is that we V'ornn have stagnated. The eternal search of the Gyrgon for knowledge has been for nought. We are at a dead end. Now, of all the planets in all the galaxies, we end up here, at this time. The Gyrgon wants to save Kundala, as did Eleusis Ashera, as do I."

Eleana scooped one of the shiny purple-black beetles out of the air. "This marc-beetle is utterly harmless." She watched as it scuttled back and forth between the bars she had made of her fingers. "But its first cousin, horned, slightly smaller, contains a deadly poison." She looked up at Rekkk. "It is difficult to tell them apart, often impossible in the shadows or at night." She opened her hand and the marc-beetle flew off to help repair its nest. "At those times it's a matter of sheer instinct whether or not you will survive."

"And what does your instinct tell you?" Giyan asked.

Eleana looked at Giyan. "After one hundred and one years of ruinous V'ornn occupation, give me one concrete reason why I should believe anything he says." She brushed dirt off her hands. "We should camp here for the night. That way, at first light we will be able to see them coming. But no fire. We cannot afford to give away our position."

Rekkk and Giyan set about making themselves comfortable. By the light of four moons they ate a cold dinner. None of them had much appetite, and the conversation was as spare as their meal. Rekkk seemed lost in thought. Giyan stared with a curious sense of foreboding at the chrysalides. She did this periodically, when she was alone or when Rekkk wasn't looking. She did not want him so see how terrified she was. She had lied to him about the true origins of the chrysalides; he had no inkling that they were sorcerous in nature. What laws had she violated when she had invaded the sorcerous circle of the Nanthera? She did not know and, therefore, had no clear idea of the consequences. What were the chrysalides doing to her hands? Already she could feel a peculiar strength flowing through them, making them feel like spring-loaded iron bars flexing back and forth. Often, she felt odd pulses of heat running through her fingers, as if the rootlike connections the chrysalides had made with her flesh were pumping an elixir into her veins. Other times, her hands felt cold as ice, almost deadweights at the ends of her wrists, and she would grow frantic, trying to move her fingers, terrified that they had become paralyzed.

As for Eleana, she sat with her arms wrapped around her

drawn-up legs. She could not yet think about Annon, and she was trying not to think about Giyan and Rekkk. She had spent many years convincing herself that she was better off without parents, that they were nothing but an annoyance and an encumbrance. So successful had she been at this that she and Dammi had spent many nights making fun of the teenagers who did have parents to boss them around and control their lives. It was only now, in hindsight, that she could taste the bitterness of that derisive laughter, recognize the envy that had given rise to it. She thought of their home, the walls covered in maps and charts, the precise annotation of their surroundings giving them the illusion they knew where they were headed. It occurred to her now that those maps had transformed the old house into a temporary dwelling, a war camp fashioned quickly and cheaply, which could be dismantled in the blink of an eye. They had not only forgotten who their parents were, but had turned their backs on their parents' way of life. In their fervor to destroy the V'ornn they lost not only themselves but their connection to their culture.

Tears rolled silently down, burning her eyes and cheeks. She averted her face; these thoughts were making her crazy. Standing up, pretending to stretch, she announced that she would take the first watch.

Rekkk watched her vanish into the darkness as he sat beside Giyan. "It would be best if you got some sleep."

"I'm not very tired." She was acutely, almost painfully, aware of him next to her. After a long time, she worked up the courage to identify the agony of longing inside her.

"That was an inspiring speech you made to Eleana," she whispered. "I wonder how much of it is true."

"If I lied to her, then I am lying to you."

"I am thinking about Nith Sahor. Does anyone ever know what is in a Gyrgon's mind?"

His eyes glittered as he turned his head toward her. "I know that he is sincere in his desire to save us from destruction."

"Oh, I don't doubt that. He told us about the activation of

the Tymnos device, didn't he, and in so doing admitted that
the Comradeship is fallible—and vulnerable. No, I do not
question his sincerity in helping us find the Dar Sala-at. But
I strongly suspect there is more. What does the Gyrgon really
want?"

"I do not know," Rekkk admitted. "Perhaps he does have
a longer-range plan in mind."

"He knows the Old Tongue, he knew who I was. He mentioned the City of One Million Jewels, a holy place we call
Earth Five Meetings. The city existed once in the Time before the Imagining, but it was obliterated in a terrible conflagration. Legend has it that he who finds Earth Five
Meetings and drinks of its Heavenly Well will become immortal."

"The Gyrgon holiest of holies!"

"Yes, Eleusis told me this. But, you see, Heavenly Well
cannot be opened without The Pearl and The Pearl cannot
be found without the Dar Sala-at. You see why I do not trust
him?"

Rekkk nodded. "And Eleana does not trust me. A fine
bunch we are!"

She looked at his silhouette in the darkness. "Right now
we have no other choice, do we?"

"Of course, we do," Rekkk said sardonically. "The alternative will be crossing those orchards at first light."

A brief wind stirred the tops of the heartwood trees. An
owl hooted. The wisp of a cloud passed before one of the
moons, making the light seem like gossamer strands. Gradually, the sky darkened further and they felt the pressure of
lowering clouds. The rumble of thunder crossing the plateau
sounded like a charging hindemuth. The patter of rain came
to them briefly, and the leaves all around them dipped and
danced.

"I arrived on Kundala during the first wave," he said
softly. "Why is it that in all that time I have never seen
lightning?"

Giyan did not answer at once. "I will answer your question
if you first answer one of mine."

He nodded his assent.

"There has been much speculation about this among my people, much debate. How long-lived are you V'ornn?"

Rekkk smiled. "I am almost two hundred years old, Giyan. I daresay Nith Sahor could be six hundred. And yet a life span of close to a thousand years is not enough for the Gyrgon. Their search for immortality has taken us across uncounted galaxies, cost other races millions of lives." He turned to her. "Now, what about the lightning?"

She moistened her lips. "For more than a century there has been no lightning," she whispered. "And for all that time no one has known why. Perhaps it is because lightning is sacred to Miina, or perhaps it is just another of those ancient things that have passed beyond the pale in this new time."

"The time of the occupation, you mean."

"But now that Nith Sahor has spoken to me, I believe I understand these disappearances. It is the time before Kundala's death."

"Do not think such dark thoughts," he said. "If we are successful, Kundala will abide; it will live to see the dawn of a new era."

"But, honestly, what odds do you give us? Now that Wennn Stogggul is using Malistra, I think they cannot be good at all!"

"Rhynnnon are used to overwhelming odds, Giyan. Any odds, no matter how slim, are enough to keep hope burning."

She sighed heavily. "Why is life such a struggle? It is so full of sorrows, disappointment, and fear."

He stirred beside her. "What would it take, I wonder, to return the lightning to Kundala?"

She knew what he was asking. He had loved her through her hatred, her contempt, her fear. Nothing she had said or done had made a whiff of difference. His love for her was like a rock, like the sea, like the stars that shone down on them even through the lowering clouds. The clouds would pass; the stars remained.

She turned to him and, at last, said his name, just his name, "Rekkk," and nothing more.

He did not move; he scarcely seemed to breathe beside her.

"Giyan," he said quietly, "this is a moment I have been dreaming of for a long time. In Stone Border—"

"Rekkk, no. You don't have to."

"But I want to." He took a shuddering breath. "Giyan, I have loved you from the moment I first saw you, moving through the regent's quarters. And then when you walked into the plaza my very soul melted. I wished at the moment that I could have taken away all your pain and suffering, but I could do nothing."

"Not nothing," she whispered.

"I did what I could," he said, "but the tragedy was there at my feet. Poor Annon, caught up in a bloody power struggle."

"Yes, poor Annon."

Tears slid silently down Giyan's cheeks.

She could hear the comforting rhythm of the rain as it pattered against the wide leaves of the heartwood tree against which they sat, just as she could feel the primeval drumbeat of the forest so like the thrum of her own pulse. Moment by moment she could feel her new life forming around her.

She said his name once more, and he sighed, put his head back against the rough bark and closed his eyes.

Eleana crouched alone in the forest. That was all right with her. She was used to being alone and, besides, ever since she could remember the forest had been her friend. The rich, loamy scents, the small, stealthy sounds of the nocturnal predators, the darkness leavened with the gentle patter of the rain never failed to make her feel safe and comforted. There was not a creature that lived in these forests, even the largest predators, that she did not love. She respected them rather than feared them, and that was an important distinction for survival out here. Most city folk had no business being in the wilds. Like as not, they ended up with bruises, a broken bone or two from a fall, or wounds from being mauled by a snow-lynx or any number of other predators they stumbled over.

She moved on, soundlessly making her way along the perimeter of the camp. Without moonlight it was treacherous work. Often, it was impossible to tell where the slippery, weather-eroded edge of the plateau lay. One false step could send her hurtling down the three-hundred-meter drop. Inside the tree line, she paused, listened to a far-off qwawd, then she went down to the river, drank water from her cupped hand, felt the rain on her shoulders and hair.

She was thinking of Annon. She could not believe he was dead. It just didn't seem possible. She had set her mind toward the day when they would meet again, when she would tell him how she felt, when they would fall into each other's arms and be one.

Gone now, leaving a hole in her heart.

Tears ran down her face as she wiped her lips with the back of her hand. The heavy blow on the back of her head came without warning, pitching her, insensate, into the cold water.

22

Mother

The huge female stirred her voluminous turquoise robes around her like a sorceress tending a pot of fulminating herbs. The folds of her skin hung off the shrunken flesh like a second robe. Her skin was white as cor milk. Her hair, bound by black muodd-shell pins, was platinum. She had a high, wide forehead, the powerful, commanding, Goddess-like face that primitive races would trace in pigments on the walls of their caves, carve into stone monuments, bow down to in awe and wonder. Compassion and strength swirled around her in equal strength.

Riane shook her head. "You say I know you, but really I don't."

Grey-green eyes, enigmatic, guileless, regarded her intently. "Astar told you about me."

"Astar is dead," Riane whispered.

"I know."

The turquoise robes shimmered like quicksilver, the folds rolling into darkness and out again like combers along a beach. There was a fleeting sense that the robes were not made of cloth at all.

"Bartta held me in a spell. She made me watch while she put the *had-atta* down Astar's throat." Tears slid down Riane's cheek. "I could not help her."

Mother took her hand, squeezing it in sympathy. "Neither could anyone else."

The Kell was mainly dark. Light came from an unexpected source: sorcerous flowers with bright cores, the surrounding petals reflecting and magnifying the light. The walls appeared metallic, curved panels joined together by huge rivets. They amplified the smallest sounds, so that the two females spoke in hushed tones that rushed back at them in murmurous response. A ghostly chorus.

"You are the someone else involved, the secret she could not tell me because of all the evil—"

"I am a prisoner, Riane. Just like you."

"Who are you?" Riane was wide-eyed. Her heart hammered in her chest.

"Thigpen told you about me." She offered a smile. "But you know who I am, don't you, Riane?"

"Mother?" Riane wiped her eyes.

The enormous female nodded, moved slightly so that the ornate gold tassels stitched to the hem of her robes swayed like handbells.

"We are taught that Mother was killed by the Rappa more than a century ago."

"You were also told that the Rappa were destroyed. Is that the truth?"

Riane shook her head. "No."

"Having met Thigpen, do you think her kind could have murdered me?"

"No, of course not. It's an absurd notion."

"So is my death, Riane. As you can plainly see, I was not murdered." The intonation of her voice abruptly changed. Riane knew she was about to hear a long-held, closely guarded secret. "One hundred and one years ago. It was the dawning of the seventh day of the High Harvest Festival, which began on the ides of Lonon, the Fifth Season. For six days and six nights the Kundalan had been celebrating the bountiful harvest. They had sung and danced; they had given thanks to the Great Goddess Miina and had mated like gimnopedes; they had eaten and drunk their fill, only to dance and sing again, give thanks again, and mate again. It was the day the V'ornn landed, the day The Pearl was misused, and vanished. The day I was taken prisoner by Nedhu, the leader of the dissident male Ramahan.

"I knew that the V'ornn were coming. It had been prophesied; it was why The Pearl had been created. I ordered the Keeper to open the Storehouse Door. Seizing this opportunity, Nedhu waited until the Keeper had opened the Door, then he had her murdered. He forced me to go with him into the Storehouse. We went across a bridge so narrow that two people could not walk side-by-side. There were no handrails, nothing whatsoever to guard against a false step that would send an unwary or clumsy traveler over the edge. It was an unimaginably long way down.

"On the far side, Nedhu confronted the young girl I had sent to fetch me The Pearl. There came a rustling, not from her, but from the deep gloom immediately behind her. The sudden pungent odor of bitterroot, so familiar to me, made Nedhu gag. Something huge was emerging out of the darkness at the far end of the cavern. The Hagoshrin, the guardian of the Storehouse.

"Nedhu did not wait to get a closer look, but darted forward. As he jerked the girl toward him, slapping her hard across the face, I uttered an cry in the Old Tongue. The

Hagoshrin answered my call. It advanced on Nedhu.

"Bellowing with rage and fear, Nedhu tore the decahedron from the girl's desperate grasp and shoved her with all his might. She toppled head over heels over the side of the span, vanishing into the blackness without even giving him the satisfaction of a scream. Nedhu turned, moaning, and ran. As he passed me, he flung me backward into the Hagoshrin's embrace."

Mother appeared abruptly exhausted, not by talking but by the terrible memories stirred up like embers that still contained enough heat to burn. "For my stupidity and my sin the Hagoshrin should have killed me as Nedhu imagined, as he informed everyone at Middle Palace. But it did not. Because it was Miina's will, the Hagoshrin took me, cared for me, sustained me until I was ready to return to the abbey."

"You are a great sorceress. How could you allow Nedhu to take The Pearl?"

Mother sighed. "That day one hundred and one years ago, without my knowing it, I was severely . . . damaged."

"By Nedhu?"

"No." Mother shook her head sadly. "By The Pearl."

"But The Pearl is the most holy object. It was made by Miina Herself. How could it possibly cause you harm?"

"I was foolish. I trusted Nedhu. He preyed upon that trust. I was the guardian of The Pearl, and I failed in my duty. I allowed those who should not see it, those who should not touch it to do so." Mother's hands lifted, only to fall back into her ample lap. "I was punished, Riane. The Pearl made me weak when I most needed to be strong. Much of my sorcerous power was stripped from me. Afterward, I was delirious with a sorcerous fever for five years. When I returned from my convalescence in the caverns, I found that Middle Palace had been desecrated by the V'ornn. Miina's holy temple was no longer Ramahan; Kundala was no longer ours.

"Eventually, I discovered that the Dea Cretan had been formed here at the Abbey of Floating White. But when I arrived, I posed a threat to those konara who had wrested control from the male cabal. They had reformed the Ramahan entirely. Male priests had been banished; the Rappa had been slaughtered; the very teachings of Miina had begun to be altered. When I argued that these changes were unholy, sacrilegious, the konara turned on me. That was when I found out that they were using Kyofu only, that those with the Gift were being culled out."

She lifted a finger, a hand, an arm. The robes shimmered, the tassels jostled one another. Her eyes had grown dark with memory. "Fifty years went by, and then . . . Feeble though my powers were, I was finally able to make contact with a shima with the Gift. Wisely, she had kept her Gift a secret and had not been culled with the others. I told her to find those novices with the Gift and to instruct them to keep their talent hidden. To instruct them secretly, if she was able. This was how Giyan learned Osoru. But these incidents were few and far between with precious little gain seen, just a holding action, you see. We were waiting, Riane. For you."

Her hands, small and delicate for such a huge female, were eloquent as a dancer's. They were very pale, veined like marble, translucent as alabaster, the fingers flowing like silk in the wind. The nails were long, curved like the runes of the Old Tongue. "Kyofu has bound me here in sorcerous chains through the regimes of three powerful konara. Each one was worse than the one before, until now we have Bartta, the worst of all."

She paused a moment, listening to the chorus of echoes, grown unused to the sound of voices, of even her own voice.

"I can cast a minor spell here or there, nothing much, but more than Bartta suspects. Astar did my bidding, but it was a difficult and extremely dangerous business. When Bartta guessed that Giyan was being taught in the ways of Osoru, she went straight to Konara Mossa, who immediately began a clandestine investigation. I was forced to retreat, to keep silent, motionless as a lorg, patient as a kris-spider in its web. I learned to do nothing—nothing but think. Years passed. The investigation tapered off, and I began again. It took time and stealth. I trained Astar myself. But the effort drained me, and I have no more reservoirs of power. Still, I persevered. Astar was my eyes and my ears. To the abbey at large she was a simple leyna, but she was more knowledgeable than half the konara here."

"Bartta used me to set a trap for her. Astar is dead because of me."

"Not so." Mother's nails clicked together, the quick beat of gimnopede wings. "She is dead because Bartta murdered her. I set Astar on her path. She begged me to do so because if you were the Dar Sala-at, she wanted a hand in your training. She died because that was her fate." Mother's eyes held Riane's. "You must believe this because it is the truth, and the truth is your path."

"I understand." Riane nodded, struggling with her emotions. "The evil inside the abbey has spread, Mother. It has gained much power."

"More than you know."

Here, in this holy place that had become a prison, the shadows had significance. There was the sense of the hours, days, nights never having left the Kell at all, but rather accumulating in the recesses, documents, diaries, maps, sketches, paintings recounting the frustration, patience, failure, sorrow of Mother's incarceration. There existed a grave weight, as if every moment Mother had spent here remained, tumbled as the books all around her, squeezing the air out of the chamber.

"Mother, what did Bartta do to you?"

Mother smiled sadly, drew another memory out of the shadows. "She set the Sphere of Binding upon me. It is an extraordinarily potent spell. How she learned it I have no idea. It was never taught here at the abbey. Once, I would have beaten it back, but now I have no remedy for it, and no memory of one."

Riane stared at her. Both halves of her seemed to be aligned for a moment, fused by the injustice of Mother's plight. Each day, it seemed Riane was more astonished at the pain and misery the Kundalan had inflicted on themselves. Was the suffering the V'ornn had inflicted on them any worse? If she was, indeed, the Dar Sala-at, how could she possibly end this cycle of misery? Which brought up another question.

"How did you know I am the Dar Sala-at?" she asked.

"The result of the Ya-unn, the test Astar administered to you with the qi, proved your true identity beyond a shadow of a doubt. You spoke the word."

"Djenn."

"Djenn, who lights the way for the Dar Sala-at," Mother said. The Kell was suddenly filled with her words, their echoes, the syllables of power. "You are the Dar Sala-at, the sign from the Great Goddess Miina, the One we have all been waiting for, the One who will lead all of Kundala back to goodness and glory."

Mother's hands opened, the white palms unlined by time. "Once Astar brought me the confirmation, I contrived for you to find me. Using the small spells at my disposal, I caused Shima Wirdd to fall ill, then caused Shima Vedda to choose you for her archaeological work detail. I knew she was excavating near the Kells. A third spell widened a fault running through the bedrock. But that was all I could manage."

"I understand," Riane said at once. "You want me to be your eyes and ears like Astar was."

"No, not at all." Mother inclined her head. "Come here, please, Riane. Now give me your hands." She gazed into Riane's eyes, and immediately Riane felt that same sensation of being hooked up to an engine that had overcome her when Astar had put the qi in her.

"Miina tells us that the Dar Sala-at will be born at 'both ends of the Cosmos,' " Mother said softly. "For centuries this phrase has sparked remarkably vitriolic debates among Ramahan. There have been nearly as many interpretations of the phrase at there have been konara in all the abbeys on Kundala." She spread her fingers over the backs of Riane's hands as if they were the petals of a flower. "Now Miina has given us Her answer through you, the living manifestation of Her Prophecy."

Riane felt a sudden clutch in the pit of her stomach. "What

do you . . ." she stammered. "I don't understand."

"Of course you do," Mother said. "I know your secret, Riane. I know you are half V'ornn."

"No, I . . ." Riane was forced to look away from those piercing eyes. "I was sworn not to tell *anyone*," she whispered.

"And you haven't—Look at me, Riane. And you haven't broken that oath, have you?"

Riane shook her head. "I haven't. I wouldn't."

"But you will," Mother said. An odd faraway look in her eyes. "Once and once only. It will bring great joy and great pain." Her eyes came back into focus. "But that is for another day."

Riane was silent for a long time, and Mother was clever and patient enough not to disturb her thoughts.

"It is a terrible struggle," Riane said at length.

Mother said nothing, her serenity creating an atmosphere in which Riane would be able to continue this difficult topic.

"No longer V'ornn, yet not fully Kundalan either, I felt trapped in an alien body, lost in a primitive wilderness, unable to trust or rely on anyone, knowing that there was no one like me, that there never would be."

"This is the fate of the Dar Sala-at, Riane. To be at once one with the Cosmos and yet apart from all who inhabit it. But perhaps what I say next will help you somewhat. In all glory there is a sadness. One must not allow that sadness to gain the upper hand, to become all that you feel, for it will all too soon turn to desolation and despair. In that weakened state, the forces of evil find their opportunity for incursion, stealing the light, running amok, perverting everything."

"How can I prevent that from happening?"

"Learn, my dearest one. Expand your mind. Absorb *everything*. Miina, in Her infinite wisdom, has given you many Gifts. It is up to you to find them and use them."

"You will help me, Mother?"

Mother nodded. "Rest assured I will do everything in my power to do so." She settled herself a little. The tassels at the hem of her robes shivered. "It is not only space that is alive with mysteries beyond our ken," she said. "But Time, as well. This we learn when first we go Thripping." She smiled as she stroked Riane's cheek. "No one else is brave or truthful enough to tell you this, but the true danger in Thripping is in discovering just how little knowledge we have. The very Cosmos throbs with life unknowable! How small and insignificant that makes us! And yet, for we who Thripp, for we who can move at will through this magical macroverse, this glimmering Cosmos, comes a grave responsibility. For it is through this power that we possess the ability to become *more*. More than Kundalan; more than Ramahan. More than we could ever imagine!"

Somewhere in the recesses of the Kell water dripped. There was a brief whiff of something that was not precisely dampness; memories, perhaps, buried so deeply they were no longer accessible.

"This is the risk Miina took when she bestowed upon us the Gift of Thripping. Knowing this, we took every precaution we could think of to ensure that the power at the disposal of the Ramahan would not be abused. But Kundalan being Kundalan, we could not plug every loophole." She lifted a forefinger. "Power pollutes, Riane. And absolute power pollutes absolutely. You must remember this, for it is a truism in every realm of the Cosmos. Inside every conscious soul is a dark place waiting for its chance to eclipse the sunlight. Perhaps this is the price we pay for self-awareness."

" 'Evil enters us through a rupture in White Bone Gate,' " Riane said instantly.

Mother paused, regarding her. "White Bone Gate, yes. Tell me, Riane, how do you know these sacred words?"

"I do not know . . . I just do."

Mother gave her a little smile. "Do you imagine that I do not know the words? They are from *Utmost Source*, Miina's Holiest of Holies, lost now since the Uprising over a century ago. Where would you have learned them, I wonder? This knowledge has long ago slipped beyond the ken of even the eldest of the abbey's konara."

"From the book," Riane said. She had the strongest sense

that Mother was the one person in whom she could confide without fear of anger or retribution.

"The book?" Mother had begun to tremble. "What book?"

"*Utmost Source*," Riane said.

"Praise Miina, the Sacred Text has been found." Mother's eyes closed for a moment.

"I memorized it. The whole thing from first word to last." Riane recounted how Annon had found it lying beside him after the encounter with Seelin, the Dragon lurking behind the Storehouse Door.

"Yes, Giyan was right, of course, you were meant to have it. Seelin gave it to you. But, tell me, Riane, how were you able to read the book?"

"The Kundalan part of me knew it, Mother. Giyan told me the book was written in the Old Tongue. The female who was Riane must have been taught the Old Tongue."

"This is a significant discovery." Mother's eyes were alight. "Giyan was mistaken. It is understandable. She has never seen *Utmost Source*; it was lost before her time. But she has seen the companion volume, *The Book of Recantation,* which is written in the Old Tongue. It would be natural for her to assume that *Utmost Source* was written in the same language." Mother shook her head. "*Utmost Source* is far more ancient, however. It belongs to another time. It is written in Venca, the Root language. Venca has seven hundred and seventy-seven letters in its alphabet, ten times the number of letters in the Old Tongue. It is a language of pure sorcery. Nowadays, it is used only by the Druuge, the nomads of the Great Voorg."

"Then Riane is a Druuge?" Riane shook her head. "How can that be? She is adept at mountain climbing. She is used to thin air and brutally cold weather. When fragments of memories come up, they are always of icescapes and high tors."

Mother sat back. "Well, this is something of a mystery, isn't it?"

"I would very much like to know who she was," Riane said.

"I understand perfectly," Mother nodded. "Isn't that what we all want, to know ourselves completely?"

"For me, it seems an impossible task," Riane said. "It seems I know next to nothing about myself."

"Ah, enlightenment!" Mother smiled. "How far you have come from the impatient, imperious V'ornn! By identifying the problem, you have already taken your first step. In the end, understanding ourselves is all that stands between us and the Dark."

"By the Dark do you mean Kyofu? Astar told me about the Black Dreaming sorcery."

"That is one meaning of the Dark," Mother said. "Those who embrace only Kyofu are destined to be consumed by it."

"Like Bartta."

Mother inclined her head. "But they are to be greatly feared because their fervor for the Dark Dreaming sorcery is a power in its own right. It is what makes the Sphere of Binding such a potent and dangerous spell, one that no Osoru sorceress would dare cast."

"And you are an Osoru sorceress, aren't you, Mother?"

"Not exactly." Mother squeezed Riane's hands. "I am the first and last of my generation to use Eye Window. It is an amalgam of Osoru and Kyofu."

"Leyna Astar explained that to me."

"Indeed. Riane, you are also destined to be an Eye Window sorceress."

Riane was shocked. "But I do not even know Osoru yet."

"It is true that you have much to learn, and the lure of Kyofu is very powerful," Mother said. "But you can Thrip. And Astar told me that you were able to resist the Rings of Concordance. There will be spells that are more dangerous, ones you will not be able to repel without proper training, but for now I think we have a chance."

"A chance for what?"

"To free me." She turned Riane's hands over so that they were palms up. "Tell me, can you feel the power bourns?"

"Yes, Mother."

"Good, for I cannot. You Thripped in here; you can Thrip out."

"But I will not leave you."

Mother shook her head. "Tell me, you know where the Library is, don't you?"

"Of course. I have spent much time there, some of it with Astar."

"As you were meant to do." Mother lifted a forefinger. "Far back in the deepest recesses of the Library there is a small, cramped, virtually lightless chamber. On one of its shelves is *The Book of Recantation*. It is rarely, if ever, read. Most Ramahan have no idea it exists, and the ones who do think it is of little import. They believe it to be an irrelevant relic from an outmoded era. But we know they are wrong.

"*The Book of Recantation* is the primer for Kyofu. I have studied parts of it, but not all. Some sections are protected by a very powerful spell. Somehow, Bartta learned of *The Book of Recantation* and studied it assiduously—all of it. I do not know how she broke the protection spell, but of a certainty she could not have done it on her own."

"The evil inside the abbey," Riane whispered.

"The evil, yes. You see, Bartta doesn't have the Gift, unlike Giyan, who is an exceedingly accomplished sorceress—far more accomplished, I should say, than even she knows. And Bartta was always bitterly envious of Giyan. That made her particularly susceptible to the Dark, creeping in on silent feet.

"In any event, *The Book of Recantation* holds the remedy to the spell holding me prisoner. Astar would never have been able to break the protection spell, but I feel certain that you, Riane, with your extraordinary Gift, will be able to do it.

"But first things first. You will Thrip out of here. When you do, my spirit will be free to come with you, but only for the space of one hour. In that time, you must enter the Library, steal *The Book of Recantation*, and return here to me, where you will attempt to break the protection spell, and I will seek the remedy."

"What happens at the end of the hour?"

"If you are not able to return to here, my spirit will not be able to rejoin my corpus and I will die."

Riane felt a shiver run through her.

"Never mind that now," Mother continued. "I want you to concentrate on what lies ahead. You must do everything I have outlined without being found out. If Bartta discovers what you are doing, she will cast another spell—one neither of us is prepared to repel. That is why we need the book. It will protect us from her Black Dreaming sorcery."

Riane shook her head. "I know how well attended the Library is. I do not think it is possible to do what you ask in an hour."

Mother smiled. "Oh, but I know you can accomplish it, Riane. I will help you." She held Riane's gaze with hers. "Remember, when you arrive in the Library I will be with you."

Her expression grew so grave Riane felt her knees begin to knock together. "Now listen to me carefully, Riane. This is why you must be extra specially careful not to be seen. If Bartta discovers you, she will reinvoke the Sphere of Binding, and I will be trapped inside you. She will have me—and you—for all time, and there will be nothing either of us can do about it. Do you understand me?"

"Yes, Mother." Riane's insides had turned to ice, but still she rose to the challenge. "I am ready for whatever must be done. Time is already running out. We should start at once."

Mother nodded. "We must keep the Thripping to a minimum. The slight disturbance in the realms can be monitored. Too much of it within the precincts of the abbey will bring unwanted attention to you. Now I want you to close your eyes. Touch the spot in the center of your forehead. No, with your mind. There is a well there, the Seat of Deepest Knowledge. It will take you to Ayame."

Already, Riane heard Mother's words as if through the tissue of another realm. Then, with a tendril of her mind, she touched the Seat of Deepest Knowledge. There was an instant of pain and of profound cold, and then as if a veil had been torn she found herself falling, falling perhaps down the well that Mother had described, falling into the absolute darkness of Ayame.

23

Squall Line

I cy water filling up Eleana's nostrils activated her autonomic nervous system, and revived her.

She awoke in a panic, underwater, and tried to scream. Water that had invaded her sinuses rushed into her mouth, threatening to choke her. She tried to get out of the river, but there was a heavy pressure at the back of her head. She fought it to no avail. Thrashing, she had the presence of mind to blow the water out of her mouth rather than swallow it.

Someone was doing his best to drown her. She pushed back. But the harder she tried to lift her head, the more oppressive the pressure became. She felt panic rising in her and fought to dispel it, trying to think. She felt a fire in her lungs, a certain lassitude creeping through her at the lack of air. All her thrashing was doing was using up her precious supply of oxygen.

Instead of fighting futilely, she willed herself to relax, though that was the last thing her body wanted to do. She felt the current against her left side, orienting her. She drew her shock-sword, thumbed on the ion flow, but it got jammed into the silty riverbed. She tried to pull it out, but it struck a rock. Instantly, the energy blew backward like a ricochet. She screamed silently as it drove up her arms and threatened to dislocate her shoulders. She hung on for dear life, and was rewarded when her whole body blasted upward with such force she rose, gasping, out of the water.

She freed the shock-sword and whirled it around her. She felt the edge slice into something hard, the energy flow shifting subtly as the weapon pierced armor plating, then flesh. She exulted in the feel of it as she turned to see a Khagggun stagger backward, a gout of blood pumping from rent shoulder plates in his armor.

Recklessly, she went after him, misjudging both the severity of his wound and his stamina. He parried her awkward follow-up with one mailed fist, struck her square in the chest with the other. Stunned, she sat back down in the muddy bank, still gasping for breath. He regained his feet, drew his own shock-sword.

She scrambled to her feet, holding her weapon in a two-handed grip. He lashed out, giving her barely enough time to parry. As the two ion-charged blades struck, she felt a painful jolt numbing her hands.

The Khagggun advanced, swinging his shock-sword back and forth in short, vicious arcs. Eleana retreated, blocking one, then another thrust. Each time, her hands were numbed all over again. He was playing with her, wearing her down without even launching a serious attack. It was clear that there was a great deal to learn about the V'ornn weapon. Her arms were shaking, and she could no longer feel her fingers.

The Khagggun feinted right, made a swift, powerful lunge to the left, and, with a clear ring of alloy against alloy, sent her weapon spinning out of her hand. Quickly, she drew her knife, but he tromped down on her wrist, pinning it to the muck.

He stood over her for a moment, faceless and terrifying in his battle helm, and it struck her that she would never know the identity of her killer. He raised his shock-sword, preparing to drive it through her heart, but in the instant it began its descent, he arched back, his body vibrating horribly, tearing itself to pieces in front of her eyes.

Behind him, Rekkk stood with his shock-sword, as if the weapon were drinking its enemy's blood, eating the ribboned flesh. He reached down a large hand, hauled her upward.

"Retrieve your shock-sword," he said. "As I said before,

if you are going to rely on it, I had better teach you how to use it properly."

Eleana scooped it out of the water, thumbed off the ion flow. "Thank you for saving my life," she said.

He grunted. "You are surprised."

"Hugely," she admitted. "Wasn't this Khagggun one of your pack?"

"I have no pack," he said without emotion. "I told you. I am Rhynnnon. I am without caste. I am sworn to my mission."

She eyed him. "You V'ornn—"

"Did he come from the south or from the east?" he broke in. "I require your expertise as a practical tactician."

"Wait a minute. Was that a compliment?"

"Just answer the question," he growled.

Eleana licked her lips. "I heard no hovercraft activity. Besides, I had just finished reconnoitering the south perimeter. I would not have missed him."

"He was trained—"

"So am I."

He had to admire her grit. "Still . . ."

He took her on another quick check of the terrain at the very southern lip of the plateau. They found no evidence of ropes, pitons, or other climbing gear.

"From the east, then." Rekkk rubbed his chin. "Intriguing. Olnnn Rydddlin has decided to take the long way around. It is the conservative, careful approach."

"Your Olnnn Rydddlin does not strike me as a conservative, careful Pack-Commander."

"Yes, I agree. What's wrong with this picture?"

"If that was a scout, then there are bound to be more coming from the same direction. I think that is where we ought to go."

Without another word, they followed the shallow river north, heading back to camp. When they passed through the scene of the attack, Eleana swept the Khagggun's gore-spattered shock-sword into her free hand.

"Sixth rule of engagement. Never let anything on the battlefield go to waste."

"I was not aware that the resistance was so well trained."

"Ah, there may be much about the resistance that is beyond your ken."

He paused, turning to her. "If I teach you how to use your shock-sword, will you teach me your rules of engagement?"

"What? You cannot mean now?"

"Most assuredly I do. I want to know that I can rely on you in the battle to come."

She cocked her head. Then she threw him the dead Khagggun's weapon. "The first rule of engagement is bring your enemy to your field of battle."

He lunged at her. "The first lesson of shock-sword combat is to keep hold of it." The instant his blade crossed hers, the jolt numbed her entire right side, and her weapon fell to the ground.

Eleana, looking very angry indeed, rubbed her right hand. She eyed Rekkk warily.

He gestured. "Well, go on. Pick it up. You want to learn how to use it, don't you?"

"You could kill me now," she said. "I could not get to it in time."

"Now why would I want to do that?"

She stared at him a moment more, before stooping to pick up the shock-sword. "That Khagggun disarmed me the same way."

Rekkk nodded. "The trick is in using the ion flow. It should be used for defense as well as offense." He beckoned to her. "Come on. Attack me."

She did. He parried her blow without any apparent ill effect. She came at him again and again, varying her strategies. He handled them all with ease, turning his blade this way and that, until she gave up with a disgusted snort.

"The trouble is you are treating this weapon as if it was a simple sword," he said. "It's not. When you induce the ion flow, it creates an energy arc between the two blades. They begin to vibrate as such a high level it is invisible to the naked eye. If you parry the blow so your blades are at a ninety-degree angle to your attacker's you'll nullify his charge." He lifted his sword. "Got it?"

He charged her again. She felt her nerves tingle as she twisted her shock-sword just off the mark. However, she parried his second blow perfectly and felt nothing. She was still grinning when he locked his twin blades with hers. She cried out as she was blasted back off her feet.

"This time you lost your weapon *and* your balance," he said, laughing.

"I am forced to admit that fighting the V'ornn way is more complicated than it looks." Wiping mud off her hands, Eleana grimly took up her shock-sword again and began to circle him. "The second rule of engagement is always take the high ground and keep it."

Rekkk nodded as he turned with her. "I created an ion-charged feedback loop that took my energy and combined it with yours. It is not an easy maneuver. It is imperative that you engage your opponent's weapon at the tips. If you get it wrong—lower down the blade or near the guard—the feedback loop will shatter your sword, possibly all the bones in your hand as well."

"I will try to remember that," Eleana said as she lunged at him. He twisted away, but on her second attempt, she engaged the tips of his blades with hers. She could almost feel the charge as he grimaced. But he did not drop his weapon as she had expected. Instead, he thumbed off his own ion-charge, disengaged, thumbed it on again, and deftly disarmed her.

"Eleana, you must try to keep hold of your shock-sword."

"Believe me, I am trying." Once more, she picked up the weapon, wiping mud off it.

"Try harder."

"I am trying as hard as I can!" she shouted, just as he lunged at her.

She parried, danced away, struck back, engaged the tips of his shock-sword for just an instant and, as she saw him react, whipped her weapon in toward his neck, where the twin blades hung, just centimeters from his skin.

"Third rule of engagement," she said without a trace of smugness. "Make your enemy see your strength as your weakness, and your weakness as your strength."

He smiled, and she relaxed. "You are a quicker study than I had imagined."

"For a female, you mean?"

He laughed. "I am learning that Kundalan females can be formidable in their own right."

The compliment took her by surprise, as it was meant to do. In the time it took her to blink, he had moved inside her defensive perimeter, jammed the heel of his hand under her chin, and grabbed the guard of her shock-sword. This time, however, though he had taken her somewhat by surprise, she did not let go of her weapon. Instead, she twisted it in his grip and, using his own strength against him, pushed instead of pulled. The hilt of the shock-sword smashed into his chest, knocking him back a pace.

They faced each other, back on equal footing, within the circle of combat.

"That was well done," he whispered. "But don't you think we should concern ourselves with the possibility that more Khagggun scouts might have infiltrated—"

"The fourth rule," she said, never taking her eyes off his, "is to learn your opponent's tactics while never repeating yours."

"I mean it," he whispered. "There are two more Khagggun behind you. They are watching us right now."

"I don't believe—"

But he had already recommenced his circling, deliberately bringing her around so that she could see what he had seen. When he saw the tremor of recognition go through her, he said, "Right now they do not have a clue what is going on. That is the only thing that has saved us."

She looked into his eyes. "The fifth rule of engagement: when outnumbered by your enemy, divide him."

He grinned. "Strike me down."

"What?"

"Do what I tell you!" he hissed furiously. "N'Luuura take it, strike me dead!"

Fire in her eyes, she lunged at him, saw him try and fail to parry her thrust. Her ion-charged blades ripped open his clothes on the left side. She saw turquoise blood spatter, and he went down as if poleaxed. But now she understood his intent. From where the Khagggun crouched, it would look as if she had delivered a mortal blow. Playing the part to the hilt, she straddled his prone form.

"Die, V'ornn scum!" she cried, and drove her shock-sword into the ground not a centimeter from his neck. These two near misses must have hurt Rekkk, she knew. She was stunned by his iron-willed courage.

From their point of view, the Khagggun scouts chose their moment well. Together, they leapt from their hiding places the moment she buried her weapon in the ground. She heard them, tried to turn, but she could not pull her shock-sword free.

"Turn off the ion flow!" Rekkk shouted as he slid out from under her and jammed his weapon into the lower belly of one of the oncoming Khagggun. The force of his momentum carried Rekkk down and onto his back, while the spitted scout, blood streaming from his wound, kicked and flailed frantically.

The other Khagggun had one mailed hand on Eleana by the time she had extracted her shock-sword. He spun her around, driving to lock the tips of his shock-sword with hers. Eleana kept her ion flow off as his weapon touched hers. Then she deftly turned her blades ninety degrees, switched on her ion flow. The resulting jolt sent the Khagggun to his knees, and she stepped inside his defense.

He was bent over so she was taken unawares when he jammed the short-hafted studded globe into her rib cage. She screamed with pain, but did not drop her shock-sword. Her breath whistled through gritted teeth, her knees trembled and her legs turned to jelly. She thought of the pain Rekkk had taken. Could she do any less? Vision blurred as her eyes leaked tears. Dimly, she was aware of the Khagggun grinding the globe into her. She felt as if her body was being ripped apart, the agony exploding every nerve ending in her body.

She narrowed her concentration on the weight of her shock-sword as she swung it in a horizontal arc. It seemed to move in slow motion. She was aware of a screaming coming as if from far away. The blades swept ever closer. The screaming threatened to derail her concentration. She was weeping as she sliced the blades through the Khagggun's armor plating. They stuck at the juncture of his shoulder and neck while his blood spurted through the rent.

The pain overcame her and she slid to her knees, her forehead resting on the bloody V'ornn armor. She could feel him spasming and shaking, and now she left her blades to do their work on his neck while she grabbed his fists, jerked them upward. The studded globe smashed into the underside of his helm and he toppled backward.

She lay athwart him, half-insensate, grateful that the screaming had stopped but curious as to what kind of creature had made it. Her throat was raw. Which was when she realized she was the one who had been screaming.

At length, she felt someone pulling her up and, thinking it was another scout, ripped the studded globe out of the Khagggun's grip. Snarling, she brandished it.

"Easy. That ion mace is a nasty weapon," Rekkk whispered in her ear. "Its ion excitation jumps from spike to spike in an energy web that is tuned not to cut and slice but to overstimulate nerve endings." As she reared back, he opened his arms wide. "Do you want to kill me, too?"

She began to sob, then, clinging to him as he carried her and her weapons back to where Giyan was waiting, white-faced with worry.

"Miina protect us!" she cried when she saw the blood all over them. "Is she hurt?"

"We're good," Rekkk said, unconsciously slipping into Khagggun battlefield terminology.

She pointed to his side. "You're bleeding."

"It's nothing. Look, just a flesh wound."

She directed him to set Eleana down on the riverbank. She

stroked the girl's hair as she began to wash her hands and face.

"Scouts from Olnnn Rydddlin's pack," he said as he hunkered down beside them to wash away the Khaggun's blood and viscera. "Eleana's convinced they came from the easterly passage, and I agree."

She gave him a quick look.

"All dead." He nodded in Eleana's direction, "She was very resourceful, very brave." He put his hand on the girl's shoulder and turned her toward him. "We who have faced death salute your first kill." He set the ion mace in her lap. "Sixth rule of engagement." He saw her smile and put the back of his hand against her cheek. "Or as we V'ornn say: to the victor belong the spoils."

Dew glittered at the ends of spear-shaped leaves. The tips of ladylace ferns unfurled like dark sails. A qwawd lowed, deep in the underbrush. The sky, dense with cloud all night, was clearing and, with it, the scent of bitterroot rose from the damp, springy earth.

"They're coming," Giyan said.

It was still dark. They could see nothing beyond the treetops at the edge of the plateau. The sky was a lambent black, fading now in the east.

Rekkk knew she was using Osoru to "see" their movement in the darkness. Osoru was good for many things, but as Giyan described it, it was Miina's Gift, never meant for battle. There were no means in Osoru to subdue a score of fierce Khaggun. He believed her. Otherwise, the V'ornn would never have been able to subjugate the Kundalan.

"What approach are they taking?" he asked her.

"The east," she said. "The south."

"Which is it?" Eleana asked.

Giyan looked at them. "Both."

It was first light. Crawling to the edge of the plateau, they saw signs of movement far off in the shadowy orchards. Clouds crowded the western sky, but in the east it was clear, and when the sun broke above the horizon its pellucid, piercing light threw every object into stark relief.

"I count a score," Eleana said.

"Another score is coming from the east," Giyan told them.

"What is going on?" Eleana whispered.

"Olnnn Rydddlin has once again moved up in the world," Rekkk said. "He is commanding *two* packs. He has chosen to attack us in Squall Line formation."

"That cannot be good," Giyan said.

"No." Rekkk stared out at the mass of Khagggun swarming past the orchards on their way to scaling the plateau.

Eleana came and stood beside him. "The sixth rule of engagement you already know," she said softly. "The seventh, and last, rule is: always have an exit strategy." She looked at him. "Rekkk, do *we* have an exit strategy?"

24

Ghosts

Star-Admiral Kinnnus Morcha was preparing for sleep when a discreet knock sounded on his bedroom door. For a moment, he stood still, contemplating the anomalous sound in the night. The door was hidden, as were the walls of the bedroom, by the protein-net battle tent he had had erected inside it. Truth to tell, he had spent so many nights on the fields of battle, he felt most at home this way. Inside a battle tent, he always knew where he was and how to act.

"Come," he said, not bothering to cover his near nakedness.

"There is a visitor, sir." Julll, his deputy protocol officer, stood just inside the tent flap.

Kinnnus Morcha studied Julll's face without success. One

of the protocol officer's assets was that he never betrayed his emotion.

"A Looorm, sir," Julll said.

"It is late, First-Captain. I ordered no such entertainment."

"This Looorm is the regent's own, sir."

If the Star-Admiral had had eyebrows, they would have been raised. "At this hour? Tell her to come back in the morning."

"Perhaps that would not be the wisest choice, sir."

Over the years, Kinnnus Morcha had learned to listen to his protocol officers. They never opened their mouths unless they had something cogent to say.

"Continue."

"It has been my experience that Looorm are repositories, sir."

"Of precisely what, besides social diseases?"

To his credit, Julll would not be goaded. "Because they are invisible, sir, they are often witness to bits of intelligence unavailable elsewhere."

The Star-Admiral grunted. "As you can see, First-Captain, I am unprepared for visitors."

"She is a Looorm, sir. No protocol is required."

Kinnnus Morcha sighed and nodded. Julll vanished, reappearing a moment later with Dalma. She stood demurely, hands clasped loosely against the folds of her deep red robes. The regent's color. Kinnnus Morcha was momentarily reminded of the former regent's Kundalan Looorm, whom he hated beyond all reason. Unlike Wennn Stogggul, the Star-Admiral had once admired Eleusis Ashera, believing him to be a good regent who had allowed himself to be compromised by the Kundalan sorceress. He could not in all good conscience stand idly by and allow the regent to be corrupted.

"Thank you for seeing me, Star-Admiral."

"It is very late," he said irritably. "Please state the nature of your business."

When she hesitated, Kinnnus Morcha signed to Julll, who promptly left the room.

Silence enveloped them. Dalma put on her sexiest pout. "Won't you even offer me a drink?"

Kinnnus Morcha grunted. "You are the regent's Looorm. How could I refuse you anything?"

She smiled. "Must you look so cross about it?"

He went to a folding camp table and poured two glasses of fire-grade numaaadis. Handing her one, he lifted his glass in toast. "To the regent," he said.

She touched the rim of her glass to his, the resulting sound like hail upon a metal shell. "It is about the regent that I have come," she said. There was a brief pause while they sipped the strong liquor. "Would you mind if I sat down?"

"As you wish," he said, perching himself on the end of the bed.

"I enjoyed our little conversation at dinner this evening." When she sat in the simple folding chair, her robes parted slightly. It appeared to Kinnnus Morcha that she was naked underneath. Her oiled skin shone in the fusion-lamp light.

"I cannot imagine that the mind of a Khagggun would be of interest to you."

She rose abruptly, tossing off her drink. "I will tell you what is of no interest to me. That cor of a V'ornn!"

Kinnnus Morcha watched her with enigmatic eyes.

Dalma smiled sweetly at him and went to pour herself another drink. As she bent, he received like an unexpected gift a full view of her unbound breasts. "Do you know how badly he treats me? I am a virtual prisoner in the regent's palace. He castigates me if I even leave the private quarters. He treats me like dirt. He has . . . strange habits in the bedroom." She took a sip of the numaaadis. "I have come to despise him."

The Star-Admiral, watching her carefully, shrugged. "Why tell me, my dear? It is the regent you need to communicate with."

She tossed off the second glass of liquor. Then she came and sat on his lap. As she straddled him, her robes fell open, revealing creamy thighs. "He's hurt me." Her hands lay flat on his bare chest. "I want to get back at him." They began to move in slow, deliberate circles. "I want to hurt him as much as he has hurt me." She leaned in, her tongue running around his lower lip. "That is why I have come. Advise me how to do that."

His arms, browned, scarred, muscled, drew her to him. His tender parts rose to meet hers. Their hips locked as their tongues met. For a long time, they rocked together, intermittently shuddering like ice moving in spring. The night air, scented by the ammonwood, gentled them in a caress. The small sounds of their lovemaking filled the tent, quickening, signaling the end was near. It came for her, but he held back, letting her pleasure build again, spill out again until she was like a spring, now taut with quick tension, now released, over and over until at last her wet gasping sent him hurtling over the edge.

Spent, they crawled over each other into the bed and the night closed around them. Sounds of the insects entered the open window, mingling with the soughing of their breath. Her body glimmered with oils and sweat, reminding him like a ghost of stealthy and treacherous campaigns past. None, however, was as treacherous as this one.

"I thought I ordered you never to come here," he said at length.

"I had no choice, darling. It was the regent's idea."

He stirred. "You're joking."

"It's true." She made a sound, muffled by her hand, and he knew she was giggling. "He wants me to gather up all your dirty little secrets and deliver them back to him."

The Star-Admiral sat up. Then, abruptly, he threw back his head and began to laugh. He laughed until his chest hurt and his eyes watered. He laughed, and Dalma joined him. "Oh, this is rich," he finally managed to gasp. "This is too much."

"The Kundalan sorceress works quickly. Already she is leading Stogggul around by his tender parts. She is daily making him weaker and more predictable." Dalma looked up at Kinnnus Morcha, her dark eyes shining. "Please remind me, darling, which one of you I am spying for."

The Star-Admiral reared over her, rampant again. "How is *this* for a reminder?"

"Oh, yes," she moaned, clutching at him. "Oh, yes."

Malistra began to pour the hot wax. Beneath her, Wennn Stogggul shuddered but made no sound. Very quickly she had learned that he needed to endure pain. It was like an addiction to laaga, something you knew was unhealthy yet could not do without. Enduring pain made him feel worthy, better than his father, better than everyone else. Without the secret knowledge of his victory over it he could not face the daylight world and win. All this and more she had gleaned with the first sweep of her fingers over his hairless skin, simply by touching the three medial points—the Seat of Dreams over his hearts, the Seat of Truth at the crown of his head, the Seat of Deepest Knowledge at the center of his forehead.

There was an ecstatic pleasure in this for her, a kind of intimacy denied her in the joining of the flesh. There was a level of cruelty to it she could never find in mundane activities. The stealing of another's secret self had been taught to her many years ago, by direct example, in an act so profound its mark disfigured her soul as a war wound deforms a warrior's face, transforming it into something other, something both unknown and unknowable. What bleak landscape now occupied the core of her only one being could say, and he never delivered up secrets, only gathered more like a miser hoards his wealth.

Malistra's mother never married. She liked to tell stories of Malistra's father's midnight visit—was he a thief, a would-be murderer?—when he appeared as if out of thin air. Of course he must have been a thief of sorts; he had successfully picked the lock of their back door or else had gained entrance by defeating a locked window. Whether Malistra's mother had been afraid of the outside world or been in love with locks was irrelevant. Whatever the truth of it, the house was sealed day and night like a tomb or an armory.

In fact, the house achieved similarities to both. Dark, still, unvisited even on holy days, it yet held secreted within its most closely guarded keep several kinds of weapons Malistra's mother obsessively sharpened, oiled, but never used.

Nine years after Malistra was born she still had no name. Her mother referred to her as "You," or sometimes "Girl." But in her ninth year, all that changed. The house was again invaded. At the twelfth hour of a sleepless, moonless, starless night he came again, this nameless thief, this would-be murderer, but instead of stealing into her mother's room he crept into hers.

She saw him first as a shadow, one among many that moved when the wind lifted the bare tree branches, when the coming winter's chill stirred the snow-lynxes to emerge from their warm, subterranean dens to call to each other in plaintive, melancholy concert. Then, so slowly that at first she was unsure whether she was awake or dreaming, his shadow detached itself from all the others, moving contra, against the capricious lift and fall of the night gusts. Once, when she was six or so, crouched naked over a rushing, rain-swollen stream, she had watched a golden-scaled fish winnowing its way against the flow, shadows and light coursing over its spine, making ripples like a strong wind. She grew dizzy with the illusion of it and toppled into the water. Watching the shadow move in her bedroom, she had this sensation once more of being in the water, of watching the fish circling her, of light dancing hypnotically off its luminous scales.

"Malistra," he whispered, crouched by the side of her bed.

She watched him, unmoving, too fascinated to feel fear.

"That is what I call you," he whispered. "That is how you will be known."

Her lips parted. "Who are you?"

He rose to stand over her. "I am your father, Malistra," he whispered.

Her eyes opened wide. "Where have you been?"

"Far away." He bent over her, one spiky knee on the edge of the bed. He had no scent, none at all. "I have returned to give you your education." And then he had placed the center of his dark palm upon her heart, upon the crown of her head, upon the center of her forehead, taking from her everything that she was. For this violation, she received knowledge. He brought her the gifts of Kyofu, the Black Dreaming sorcery, and its central jewel, the Eye of Ajbal. All night he lay with her, touching her with his mind as well as with his hands, his feet, lips, eyelids, his sexual organ. She was like a cup of steaming water infused with a mixture of exotic spices, herbal tonics, psychoactive roots. She grew and, in growing, became potent. As she suckled at this shadowy font of knowledge she was dimly aware that the room had come alive. No, not the room precisely, but the window that now lay unlocked and open against her mother's strictest warnings. Her eyes were closed, her mind dreaming. Nevertheless, it seemed to her that she "saw" the open window crowded with the curious faces, luminous eyes of strange nocturnal animals, who sighed and growled low in their throats and showed gleaming ivory teeth, who placidly swished long tails and carried the stars on their backs.

This shadow, her father, stayed with her one night. Before dawn he was gone; so too the strange audience. Her window had now mysteriously returned to its usual closed and locked state. Examining it in the cool, watery light of late autumn, she wondered whether it had ever been open. She looked beyond the greenish pane of glass, beyond her tomb to see many-colored leaves skittering along the ground, fleeing.

She waited three long years. Three more years of being dead. Then, on the coldest day of the year, she broke the glass in her window with a fist bound in black muslin and, bundled in a thick traveling cloak, stepped out into winter. Snow swiftly erased her fugitive footprints. She never looked back, one never does when one escapes the place where one has been buried.

In the unsteady lanternlight the wax was clear and hot. She poured it from high above him, a stream thin as a single strand of a spider's web. It turned the purest white as it hardened against Wennn Stogggul's alien skin. White as the snow of that long-ago bitter-cold winter morning. She had moved down from his chest, down to his tender parts. The wax, cooling, must hurt him very much. For his sake, she hoped so. To her, this form of pain meant nothing. Less than the dimly remembered dreams of her childhood.

"I have not cried out," Wennn Stogggul whispered. "I have not uttered a sound."

"No, Lord, you have not." She leaned down so that her bare breasts scraped against his hairless chest. "Truly you are brave, Lord. Braver than all the rest." She licked the hollow of his throat, the slightly bitter taste of the hardened wax on her tongue.

These are our conquerors. She thought this without a trace of bitterness or rancor, merely curiosity. *What does this say about us?*

That first winter should have been difficult for her, but it was not. Along the route she took south to Axis Tyr she invariably found shelter, food, a roaring fire, and company, if she wished it. She was never left to forage at night in the bare-limbed forests or the fallow snow-slicked fields. Most curious of all, not one of her benefactors ever asked what a twelve-year-old girl was doing alone in the dead of winter. It was as if someone or something watched over her, spreading its dark wings in protection. In this manner, she passed through the countryside like a shadow herself, causing barely a ripple in the quotidian lives of those who took her in. Even more curious, they forgot all about her the moment she left their company.

In the afternoons, she roamed through the dense, hard-wood forests, searching for mandragora and, beneath wispy firs and larches, Amanita soma. When she reached the more cultivated lowlands closer to the city itself, she contented herself with plucking the seeds of morning glories, drying them by moonlight as her father had taught her to do. She ate these dried seeds slowly and with a great deal of pleasure as she removed the orange caps of the Amanita from their spongy, cream-colored stems, while the mandragora she had slivered was brewing. Inhaling the rising steam, she sailed far away.

When spring came, she worked in the orchards, plowing and planting, her body growing hard-muscled and sun-kissed. When she grew bored with pure physical labor, she performed small tasks for the orchard owner, providing potent herbal fertilizer, advising him on coming droughts, and how to guard against ravaging stydil infestations and withering blight. She was always right, and the orchard owner was sorry to lose her. With the onset of summer and the passing of her thirteenth birthday, she had grown restless. Imagining the city was no longer enough. She had to see it for herself.

I have received a message from Olnnn Rydddlin," Wennn Stogggul whispered during a brief period of respite. His body was bound in sweat, racked by pain. She knew he would not give in. "Your sorcery has found them for me."

"I am here to serve you, Lord."

"About the Portals . . ."

"The Portals, yes." She was preparing more wax, clear, bitter, pure.

"I want to know more." His skin was a hieroglyph of angry welts. "I want you to take me there."

"I am gratified you trust me, Lord." She watched the wax drool down, the smell of him burning coming to her strongly. "I pray that you are the Chosen One," she said truthfully. "For you are strong, and, come what may, you will survive."

He stirred. "What do you mean 'come what may'?"

"Significant journeys, Lord, always contain elements of peril."

Using the Eye of Ajbal, she passed through the North Gate without the V'ornn guards being aware of her. Using money that had been lavished upon her by the orchard owner, she settled into a small house in the bustling, over-crowded northern district. Her first clients were, naturally enough, Mesagggun looking to settle long-standing grudges.

The first few happy patrons quickly passed the word of her prowess, and she was in business.

What was her business? That depended on your point of view. It might be termed foretelling the future, or rebalancing the scales or, again, killing people who needed to be killed. In truth, it did not matter to her how her calling was defined. She merely did what she had been taught to do. In those early days, she neither liked nor disliked how she made her living. And so, through a kind of reverse alchemy, the most recondite sorcery was reduced in her mind to nothing more than a common job.

That perverse state of affairs did not, however, last long. One evening eighteen months after she had arrived in Axis Tyr, a Mesagggun appeared at her home. It was well after the hours of business, but she let him in anyway. He was very handsome, his face rugged and windburned, free of the smear and smell of lubricants that infested most Mesagggun. He smiled with his mouth as he wormed his way inside, but his eyes told her everything she needed to know. Within moments of allowing him entry, she found herself at the wrong end of a wicked-looking brindle-stick he had modified. While the razor-sharp point pricked her throat he looked deep into her eyes and, in a voice tight and cold with fury, informed her of his intent.

It happened that this Mesagggun, the brother of one of her victims, had just returned home from a long trip to discover that his sister had expired from a rapacious illness no Genomatekk had been able to diagnose, let alone cure. The sister had been cheating on Malistra's most recent client. This client wanted her dead, and, for a fee, Malistra had obliged. In a sense, the mistake was not hers, but the customer's, who bragged of what had happened to the Mesagggun who had cuckolded him before he beat him senseless. Hearing rumors of his sister's affair, the brother went to see his sister's lover and so heard through jaws wired half-open what Malistra had done.

"Your sister died of illness," Malistra said.

"How you murdered her, sorceress, does not matter." A

thread of blood traversed her collarbone. The wet point of the brindle-stick was a millimeter from the pulse at the side of her neck. "How long it takes *you* to die is the only thing of interest to me."

This was the moment when she understood that reputation was a two-edged sword. Cursing herself for her hubris, she opened the Eye of Ajbal and stepped away from herself. The Mesagggun suspected nothing, assumed the almost imperceptible flicker of light was a function of the Kundalan lantern in the living room. The truth was, he held nothing now, nothing but an illusion. The truth was, Malistra stood behind him, that she had him in her power.

What to do with him? This was not an easy question to answer. She had no wish to kill him—she had no wish to kill anyone, ever. Events simply worked out that way. Death is part of life and life is part of death. This was one of Kyofu's main tenets, and she believed it with all her heart and soul. It was Truth; the Universe confirmed it every day in so many ways, large and small. If she harbored no wish to kill him, still she clearly could not simply let him go. He would come after her again, and she could understand why. Anguish had fermented into hate, guilt into a need to make amends. If only I had been there, he must have told himself a thousand times since he had returned home. If only I had been there I could have saved her. In reality, that was a false assumption. All the same, it was true, it was true enough for him.

Kyofu had taught her the way out of this seemingly impossible situation. She lifted her arms, opened her mind, and transformed him. All at once, in the swiftly gathered darkness, the brindle-stick clattered to the floor. There was no longer a hand to hold it. Instead, a copper-and-black serpent writhed upon the floor. Its cool, glossy scales reflected the lamplight which had scattered the sorcerous darkness back into the corners of her house.

Smiling, she had picked up the serpent. She stroked its flat, wedge-shaped head, allowed its forked red tongue to find her and familiarize itself with her contours and her scent.

She felt its weight, shifting like the sands of the Great Voorg, restless, always in the act of moving from one place to the next, the ultimate nomad.

When she had the serpent's full attention, she spoke to it, and it spoke back in the voice of the white-bone daemon before coiling around her right arm, shrinking, morphing into a sinuous band of bronze with incised scales, always admired by her clients but never understood.

25

Why the Ja-Gaar Eat Their Young

Inside the darkness and the light, Riane found the living Cosmos, and confronted the frightening illusion that was the world she—and Annon—had known. She could feel the fear creeping through her with the acceptance of this knowledge. And this profound fear threw into darker relief White Bone Gate. She could see it there, waiting patient as stone, the stoutest bastion of her soul's defense and also its weakest link. It was through White Bone Gate that Mother cautioned she could lose herself. Now she understood that fear, despair, greed, envy—all the emotions of Chaos—could under the right circumstances open White Bone Gate, that if even one was allowed too near it was drawn as if magnetized to the very gate that would, in other instances, repel it. In a moment of profound weakness, the Chaos emotion would act like a key, opening the gate's lock and gaining entry to the soul.

That's right, Riane, Mother whispered from nowhere and everywhere at once. *You have learned in thirty seconds what would take an exceptionally gifted konara years to understand.*

Now you are a part of me, Riane said. *I feel you in every cell of my body. Can you help me protect White Bone Gate?*

Only by telling you this: never leave it unattended, and it will remain your first, best line of defense.

Riane imagined herself atop the gate, and all the fear evaporated like mist in sunlight. *Time*, she said, *to Thrip.*

She began to spin, and the Otherwhere of Ayame spun with her. Light became dark and light again. She felt her essence melting, deliquescing into its component parts, slipping through the realms of Otherwhere, the swirls and eddies of Space and Time coalescing in an endless living tapestry more complex than could be comprehended.

In an instant, she felt herself coalescing through the living tapestry, her component parts rebuilding themselves into the physical realm inhabited by Kundala. She found herself standing in a lofty, shadowy corner of the main room of the Library. She stood very still, only her eyes moving as she took in every square centimeter of the cavernous chamber. Wide shafts of sunlight slanting through the towering, arched, east-facing windows illuminated flotillas of golden dust motes. Riane was astonished to discover that she had been down in the Kell with Mother all night.

Though it was early in the morning, the Library was far from deserted. The triple-tiered polished ammonwood catwalks that ran completely around the book-lined chamber were alive with acolytes, leyna and shima hard at research or course study. Far below her, the highly polished surface of the agate floor glimmered with light and shadow. Behind a long, scrolled heartwood counter set on a raised plinth sat a row of stern shima, the librarians. They were constantly reading. Nevertheless, their trained eyes flicked upward at intervals, following everyone, attentive for any movement or sound out of place. They were living reminders of the strict importance of time here, seconds crucial as minutes in completing assignments. Arrayed before them, Ramahan of all ranks crisscrossed the floor on one errand or another. They walked purposefully, looking neither to the left nor the right. Or they sat at communal lamplit desks, heads buried in open books, styluses poised or writing furiously in tablets. They looked grim, absorbed by their tasks, chained to the unnatural silence.

I trust you are not prone to vertigo, Mother said.

She was on the third and highest catwalk. No one had noticed her sudden appearance in the cool, remote shadows.

Annon was, Riane whispered in her mind. *It was an Ashera family trait. But Riane is not afraid of heights.*

She was about to move, but immediately froze. Down below, Konara Urdma had entered the Library, sweeping in with her rather imperious air. Something unseen brought her up short and, for long, agonizing moments, she gazed around the main floor.

Still your thoughts, Mother cautioned. *She has caught a whiff of your agitation.*

I don't know how. Riane stared down in terror as Konara Urdma continued her psychic scrutiny of those using the Library. *And it will just be a matter of time before she sees me, even here in the shadows.*

Your thoughts are scattered, angry, impatient, therefore detectable. Calm yourself, Mother said. *If you do your part, I will ensure that she does not see you by casting a spell of blindness about you.*

Riane tried to slow her breathing, tried to find a core of serenity. The trouble was, Annon's personality contained very little of it. She was prepared for full battle mode; standing still without a thought in her head seemed next to impossible.

Then, into her head, popped this question, *Utmost Source makes reference to the Ja-Gaar. The sacred text says they are the holy of Miina. But there had been no reference to the Ja-Gaar in any of my studies here.*

The name Ja-Gaar has become anathema among modern-day Ramahan, Mother told her. *But the truth is the Ja-Gaar are serving Miina's will. They are the guardians of the Abyss.*

Riane remembered her conversation with Shima Vedda. *Which accounts for why the Ja-Gaar are nowadays never seen in temples or shrines. Or why we are taught that the translation of Hagoshrin is "that which cannot be named."*

In the original root language of the Old Tongue Hagosh-rin means "beloved of the Goddess."

Which is why I saw them depicted in Miina's sacred Kells. Well, that's one mystery solved. She held herself completely rigid. *But if the Ja-Gaar are sacred to Miina, why did they become anathema to the Ramahan?*

Because there was a time when the Ja-Gaar ate their young, Mother said. *I think now is the perfect moment to tell you how that came to be. In the Time Beyond Imagining, when Kundala was being formed through the Cosmic Dance of the Five Sacred Dragons, when this realm was still alive with the Goddess-like confluence of Time and Space, the Ja-Gaar were already present. They were creatures of Other-where, of Eternal Night, creatures of a terrible and fearsome beauty. In this Time Beyond Imagining, all was composed of Goddess-stuff, everything was Immortal, including the Ja-Gaar.*

But, with the completion of Kundala, everything in this realm changed. The physical form became manifest, domi-nant, immutable, and very quickly the Goddess-stuff vanished into the other realms of the Cosmos. The Ja-Gaar, too, were affected, at least that generation of them. They found a so-lution. By eating their children, they returned them to Eternal Night whence they had all sprung. There, in the center of living Time and Space, the children of the Ja-Gaar found Enlightenment and were reborn, immortal as their forebears had been.

Reborn how? Riane asked. *If they were dead . . .*

They were returned to this realm through the Portals, gateways from this realm to the realm of Eternal Night.

Do the Portals still exist?

Yes. But their location is a closely guarded secret. And well it should be. The Portals have been locked to keep the daemons from emerging from the Abyss.

Throughout this dialogue, Riane had watched Konara Urdma's face as her eyes scanned upward, taking in the cat-walk tiers, one by one. She almost flinched when the konara's gaze passed across the shadowed corner in which she stood. But there came no flicker of recognition or concern. And, at last, done with her psychic sweep, she shook her head and proceeded to the stacks diagonally across from Riane's position to begin her work.

When she was engrossed in the book she had pulled down from the shelves, Mother said, *All right. The chamber we require is on the ground floor. Let us proceed.*

Riane immediately walked to the ladder to her right, went swiftly down it, and across the middle catwalk to another patch of dense shadow. This put her in close proximity with a shima she did not know. This Ramahan had her back to Riane as she paged through a large tome, methodically taking notes on a slate tablet. The problem was that she was between Riane and the closest ladder to the catwalk below. This meant that in order to reach the ladder on the opposite side she would have to walk through three patches of sunlight. If Konara Urdma happened to glance up at the wrong moment . . .

The spell of blindness will protect you as long as you are standing still, Mother said. *You must be very quick, very clever now, because Konara Urdma is a sorceress of the first rank.*

Riane turned, making her way down the catwalk to her left. She walked quickly and silently, with a controlled urgency she could tell Mother appreciated. She passed through the first patch of sunlight without incident. No one looked up; no one noticed her. But just as she was entering the second patch, Konara Urdma snapped shut the book she had been referencing and looked about her. Riane throttled the instinct to run and immediately stopped. A shima glided up to the konara and engaged her in conversation. Riane took advantage of the distraction to traverse the second patch of sunlight. She kept on going. Below her, the shima thanked Konara Urdma for her help and departed for another section of the Library. Riane was passing from dimness into the third and last patch of sunlight when Konara Urdma chanced to look up. Riane froze.

Was it a blur Konara Urdma saw from the corner of her eye? A ghostly vision, perhaps? What did it matter? Riane felt the first tentative probing of Kyofu, like the translucent tendrils of a cuttlefish waving through water. At once, she shut down her mind, thinking of nothing but undisturbed darkness, utter blackness, the emptiness of nullity.

Konara Urdma's concentration did not pass over her as it had before—at least, not exactly. She could feel those translucent tendrils sensing the space around her ever so carefully. For a time, nothing further transpired. Riane became aware that a silent war of subtle sorcerous spells was being enacted between Mother and the high priestess. She wished that she could help, but she did not know how.

Patience, Mother said in her mind. *Patience.*

Riane felt her heart skip a beat. Konara Urdma had returned her book to the shelf and was crossing the sun-splashed agate floor directly toward the ladder beneath Riane. The instant she was out of sight, Riane leapt ahead, passing beyond the opening in the catwalk into which the top of the ladder was set. She stopped dead in her tracks the instant before Konara Urdma's head popped up onto her level. The high priestess turned the other way, her gaze centered on the sunlit spot where Riane had been standing. She emerged onto the catwalk and immediately walked away from where Riane now stood. In the disc of sunlight, she turned in a full circle, her arms halfway raised, her palms upturned and slightly cupped.

She is casting a spell of gathering, Mother said. *She is trying to find what it was she saw.*

Will she find me?

Mother was silent. Konara Urdma was now looking down the catwalk in Riane's direction.

"You! What are you doing there?" the high priestess said sharply.

An uncomfortable prickling broke out on Riane's skin, but she forced herself to think of nothing. Just a vast emptiness devoid of Kundalan life.

"Finishing our morning studies," a soft voice came from

behind Riane. A pair of acolytes had emerged from the stacks, walking together toward the ladder.

"No, you weren't," Konara Urdma said crossly. "You were talking in a most unseemly manner. Perhaps even gossiping."

The acolytes, having been caught out, said nothing.

"Where were you a moment ago?" Konara Urdma snapped. "And do not even *think* about lying to me!"

"No, Konara," said one in a tremulous voice.

"We were studying in the stacks," the other one said. "Back there."

"You weren't here, where I am standing now?"

"No, Konara," they said in unison.

"Did you see anyone here?"

"We were in the stacks, Konara, as we said."

The high priestess flicked a hand in their direction. "Be gone then! You are of no use to me!"

The two shot past Riane as if she did not exist and scuttled down the ladder as fast as their legs could carry them.

"Nitwits!" Konara Urdma said under her breath. "If they are our future, whatever will become of the Order?"

She put her fists on her hips, took one last look around, and shook her head before striding off down the catwalk. Moments later, breathing a long sigh of relief, Riane gained the ladder and scrambled down to the agate floor. Keeping to the deep shadows of the catwalk overhang, she made her way around the circumference of the Library to the far side, where she slipped into a passageway that led to a warren of smaller chambers where books and charts on various specialty subjects were kept. She passed the open doorways, peering into each. Most were unoccupied, save for one, where a pair of shima were bent over a long table lit by small floodlights. She sidestepped the lozenge of light slanting out into the corridor, kept going until she reached the end.

A lantern had guttered here. In the gloom, Riane found her way to the narrow doorway. Lifting the ancient iron latch, she let herself in.

The small chamber was dark and musty, smelling of age

and water seepage. Mold grew in the corners, making her nose itch.

Mother guided her to a shelf filled like all the others with books.

You will find it in the extreme upper left-hand corner, Mother said, guiding Riane at every step now.

Riane brought over a kick stool and stood on it in order to reach the uppermost shelf. In the cool, clammy dimness, she read the spines of each book on the shelf.

It's not here, she whispered, and began a search of the shelf just below. She kept on going until she had read the spine of every book in the entire chamber. *It's not here,* she repeated.

Bartta has taken it, Mother said.

Oh, no! It could be anywhere in her quarters.

It is strictly forbidden to take books out of the Library. I do not think she would have taken such a chance. Look at the shelves. There are many more spaces here than I remember, especially on the lower shelves. A whole group of books has been moved out of here in order to protect them from the dampness and mold. The Book of Recantation must be among them.

Riane remembered the room she had passed. She saw again the shima bent over the brightly lit table. What had they been working on?

I recognize that equipment, Mother said. *Book restoration.*

Riane went back down the corridor. Standing just outside the light spilling onto the stone floor, she took a quick glance inside. Only one of the shima was at work now, thumbing slowly through the pages of a thick tome; the other shima was making notes on a tablet across the room. Riane ducked back into the corridor.

How will I get inside without being seen?

Think of a rat, Mother replied. *Think of a rat being inside that room, at the hem of the shima's robes.*

Riane, thinking the exercise silly, imagined a large, plump rat sitting up on its hind legs, cleaning its whiskers. For good measure—and because it amused her—she imagined this rat leering up at the shima.

A moment later, she heard a muffled shriek, but no one ran out of the chamber.

She had no time to ask Mother what had happened. She raced into the chamber. Sure enough, stacks of moldering books lay open on the table beneath drying lamps that filled the space with heat. The sorcerous rat she had summoned was nowhere in sight, however. Instead, the shima who had been taking notes lay prostrate on the floor. The other shima's hands were clamped tightly around her throat. Her tongue protruded between bloodless lips. Riane pulled the shima apart. The one still alive, snarled at her through a mouth full of foam, then backed up into a corner. Her eyes were wild and staring.

Mother, what has happened here? Riane asked.

I do not know. But there is no time to investigate. You must find The Book of Recantation. *It has a red cor-hide cover with a symbol of a raven stamped in gold leaf on the front.*

Quickly and methodically, Riane went through the volumes, praying to Miina that Mother was right, that she would find *The Book of Recantation*.

The volume, bound in cor hide that had once been stained red, lay open under the drying lamps. Now it was virtually colorless, centuries of grime, oils, and animal matter giving it an unhealthy-looking patina. It had been the one the shima crouched in the corner had been restoring. Riane grabbed it.

Just then, she heard a commotion at the far end of the corridor and beat a hasty retreat back into the chamber. Ramahan were coming in response to the shima's cries.

Time to Thrip, Riane said, feeling much like the illusion of the rat she had created. She had already started to spin, when a silent warning from Mother stopped her.

You dare not Thrip now, Riane, Mother said. *Bartta is in the Library. She will feel the disturbance between realms and follow it back to the Kell.*

How much time is left until you are trapped?

Less than three minutes.

Riane's heart felt like a trip-hammer in her breast. *There is no other way out. What am I to do, Mother?*

The sounds of cor-hide sandals slapping against stone, the swishing of robes as Ramahan ran down the corridor toward the chamber where Riane stood, transfixed.

Mother?

A clamor of voices, approaching very quickly. And then the sound of Bartta's commanding voice saying not to worry, that she would deal with whatever emergency had arisen.

MOTHER . . . ?

26

Bug

They swarmed up the cliff face like bugs, like a pack of particularly nasty, armored insects carrying a host of deadly poisons.

"This is not good," Eleana said. "Not good at all." She watched, dumbfounded, as Rekkk scooped up a couple of golden Marre pinecones, fitted them into his okummmon. He knelt at the edge of the plateau and aimed his left arm straight down.

"Don't!" she cried, running toward him. "Are you crazy?"

Ignoring her, he fired. The missile slammed into the helm of one of the leading Khagggun, twisting him around so that he lost his footing. He fell a meter or two before his guide rope caught him up. There he hung, head down, dripping blood onto his ascending compatriots. Rekkk ducked back as they fired handheld ion cannons at him.

"What are you doing?" Eleana said. "You've given them our exact position."

"Precisely." Rekkk grabbed her by the elbow, hustling her

back to where Giyan waited in a grove of trees. "Now would be a good time," he told her.

Giyan closed her eyes. Her arms rose from her sides and her hands, palms upward, were cupped slightly. Eleana gave a stifled gasp as the air around them began to stir—rippling as with excessive heat, as if it had momentarily become too heavy to support itself. A moment later, she saw three figures crouched near the edge of the plateau. One of them was her. The other two were Rekkk and Giyan.

She looked from Giyan to Rekkk with an incredulous expression.

Rekkk grinned as he herded them quickly northeast, back toward the river. "You were quite right. I have shown them where we are, and there is where they will find us."

"Impressive," Eleana said. "But this sorcerous illusion will delay them only so long."

"Long enough," he said.

They were again in sight of the river when Eleana faltered. Indeed, she would have fallen had Giyan not grabbed her and held her upright.

"What is it?" Rekkk asked. "Are you faint or ill?"

"Neither." Eleana fought the waves of blackness lapping at the corners of her vision. "Just a little dizzy, that's all."

Giyan regarded her with a concerned expression. "Has it happened before?"

"No," Eleana lied. They were counting on her, and she did not want them to worry. "But I have neither eaten well nor slept enough this past week." She grinned at them. "I plan to do a lot of both this night. Do not be alarmed; I will be fine in the morning." She stood up straighter. "In fact, I'm fine right now." She spun around. "See?"

Rekkk grunted his consent, but she could see that Giyan remained unconvinced. Well, there was nothing more she could do about it now. And, in any event, they all had far more pressing matters to attend to, such as how they were going to survive the day.

"Are you certain about the number of Khagggun coming from the east?" Rekkk was asking Giyan.

"I was using a quick surface probe, just as quick in and out. It was an impression." She frowned. "Why?"

"I'm not sure." He shrugged. "Just a hunch, that's all." They had reached the riverbank and were walking northeast along it, their boots making imprints in the marsh soil, disturbing more of the marc-beetle nests. "Is there any way to make certain?"

"They couldn't possibly—" She stopped abruptly, put her hand to her mouth. "Oh, Miina protect us! Malistra!"

"Yes. Malistra. Could she use Dark sorcery to fool you into thinking there were Khaggun coming from the east?"

"No," Giyan said. "But it would be theoretically possible to magnify the number."

He took her farther upriver. "Giyan, I need to know exactly how many Khaggun Olnnn Rydddlin is using to try to flank us."

She nodded. "Give me a moment alone, will you?"

He took her hand briefly, then returned to where Eleana was standing ankle deep in the river. "Do you or do you not have a plan?"

"That depends," he said.

"On what?"

"On whether Olnnn Rydddlin is really leading a double pack in the Squall Line formation or if that is merely what he wants me to believe."

"In either case," she said, "we have to deal with the pack to the south."

"Indeed we do." He knelt down, dug in the spongy soil for a marc-beetle nest. Taking an insect up in his hand, he deposited it into the slot of his okummmon. "I have seen this poisonous marc-beetle you spoke of."

The okummmon emitted a slight hum and spat out the insect. Eleana could see that it was different, horned and slightly smaller.

"How did you do that?" she gasped.

"I wish I knew," Rekkk said, grabbing another marc-beetle. "But for right now what matters is that very soon we will have the army we need to defeat the pack."

"What?"

"It's bug power, Eleana!"

By the time he had transmogrified his sixth marc-beetle, Giyan reappeared. She looked white and drawn, but there was a definite expression of relief on her face. "Three Khaggun are coming from the east," she said. "That is all."

All of a sudden, Rekkk began to laugh. "Oh, this is rich," he said. "This is very, very rich!"

Giyan knelt beside him. "What is it, Rekkk?"

"It's Olnnn Rydddlin. He's trying to finesse me." He curled his hand into a fist. Opening it, another poisonous marc-beetle flew out. "Well, we shall see who is finessing whom."

He continued capturing the marc-beetles, inserting them into his okummmon, transmogrifying them.

"I am going into the forest," Eleana said. "We need an update on the progress of the Khagggun trying to outflank us."

Rekkk looked up at her, was about to caution her, then thought better of it. He nodded. "Try to keep in earshot, all right?"

Eleana grinned, trotting through the river and up onto the far bank. In a moment, the thick stands of lingots and briar firs had swallowed her up.

"What has happened to them?" Giyan said, pointing toward the poisonous marc-beetles. "They are not acting like normal insects."

"They aren't," he said. "From what I have been able to gather, this okummmon Nith Sahor implanted in me vibrates at a specific frequency. That is how he alone can contact me. But this frequency changes the molecular structure of anything fed into it, like the leaves and Marre pinecones I made into missiles." He released another insect from his okummmon, inserted another. "Take these marc-beetles, for instance. They have been slaved to the okummmon. They will follow my directions as accurately as if they were extensions of my hands. They will crawl between the armor plates of the Khagggun and kill them. I suppose you could say they are alive, but in an entirely new way."

She put a hand on his arm. "Like you."

He smiled and kissed her. "Yes. Like me."

Giyan sighed. "She is lying, you know."

"Eleana?" Another marc-beetle out, another in. "About what?"

"Those dizzy spells. She has had them a number of times over the past week. I can tell."

"I'm sure you can," he said. "But what do you make of—?"

He broke off as Eleana reappeared. She was slightly out of breath. "They're right behind me," she gasped. "We have run out of time."

"Rekkk, do you have enough marc-beetles?"

"I certainly hope so." As he rose, the swarm of poisonous insects took to the air. They hovered in a purple-black cloud, absorbing his silent instructions. Then, as one, they flew south, directly toward the oncoming pack.

"Let's go," Rekkk said, fording the river. "This is our forest. Let's keep it that way."

Giyan followed, holding up the hem of her robe to keep it from getting wet.

"Stay behind us," he told her.

"Do you think I cannot defend myself?" She was clearly annoyed.

"That is just what I think," he said. "This is war. Do not argue. Follow orders like a good soldier."

The forest stretched away from them, a mysterious green cathedral of many pillars. Between dead twigs, overhanging branches, the detritus-covered ground, it took a great deal of care and concentration to keep their presence silent. Eleana, leading them, had reverted to hand signals. She pointed in three different spots. Rekkk understood immediately. The Khagggun were in wing formation—the three of them fanned out more or less horizontally, each one twelve paces behind the other. In this way, they could cover the maximum amount of territory while minimizing the danger of an ambush. He was about to give Eleana an order, when she pointed upward with her forefinger.

They chose their spot with care—a particularly dense area of the forest filled with ladylace ferns. He nodded, watching her choose a tree and clamber up. It was astonishing how quickly and completely she vanished into the foliage.

He signed for Giyan to retreat back into the shadows between a pair of huge heartwood trees. When she complied, he redirected his attention ahead of him. He knew how these Khagggun hunted, how they thought. After all, he had taught them tactics and strategy. He projected himself into their methodically advancing wing formation. They would be looking for traps, so he decided to give them one.

Quickly, he scaled a heartwood tree, tied two vines together, then another two, making a rough X-shape. When he returned to the ground, they hung perhaps five meters above his head. Just below, he gathered the dead material of the forest floor, respreading it so that on close inspection you could see subtle differences when you compared it to the ground around it. Then he crouched behind a nearby heartwood and waited.

The small, quotidian sounds of the diurnal life rose and fell around him in a rhythm all its own. Insects droned, birds sang, twittered, and fluttered, small mammals foraged stealthily. A line of migrating butterflies dipped in and out of patches of sunlight, dazzling bits of floating color, zigzagging their way north. An iridescent-blue dragonfly alit on a leaf near his cheek. He wondered what its huge, faceted eyes saw that his did not.

Then he heard them. Not in any definable way, but threaded into the normal hum of the forest. They were very good; he had made them so. As if picking up on the battle vibes, the dragonfly took off. The butterflies were gone; the foraging mammals had moved to another part of the forest.

He saw the first one, a flash of his armor as he passed through a patch of early-morning sunlight, then the edge of his helm. The Khagggun he held his new position as he took a look around. Then he came on. Rekkk could imagine him

updating his two fellow Khagggun over their closed communication line. That would have to end, but not quite yet.
For the moment, everything had to appear normal.

In preparation, Rekkk bent over, blew across his okummmon. The air he forced into it began to solidify. Because
Khagggun often had to communicate in the vacuum of space,
pack transmissions used a null-wave method devised by the
Gyrgon. Nith Sahor had briefly described the technology to
him. The Gyrgon had chosen the spread-spectrum photonic
system because it was the least susceptible to space-particle
clutter and varying off-world atmospheres. It did have a
weak spot, however. The only way to temporarily disrupt the
transmission was to use a simple mirror, which reflected the
photon stream back at its sender.

The mirror was ready. He slipped it out of the okummmon
slot still warm, pulling it like taffy so that it opened up into
a square.

The lead Khagggun, having taken his inventory of the immediate environment, was advancing farther toward Rekkk.
He froze in mid-step. He looked up to the vines Rekkk had
tied together, then scanned the forest floor directly beneath.
Rekkk could see the faint blue glow appear in the area he
had made to look like a camouflaged pit as the Khagggun
scanned it through his helm. Not understanding the readings
his ion beam was giving him, he began a slow circumnavigation of the area.

Rekkk waited until his back was to him before drawing
his shock-sword. He crossed the space between them in a
quick sprint. The Khagggun heard him at the last instant and
began to turn. But Rekkk was already upon him. The edge
of the shock-sword opened a seam in the battle armor, stove
in six ribs on its way to the Khagggun's hearts. He went
down hard, and Rekkk sheathed his shock-sword. Kneeling,
he removed the Khagggun's helm long enough to insert the
mirror between the photonic membranes in the upper left-
hand quadrant. He did not mean to look at the Khagggun's
face, but it registered anyway. Durrr, Third-Marshal. Rekkk
remember when he had joined the pack. He remembered

teaching Durrr hand-to-hand strategy. That was long ago and far away. Solemnly, he replaced the helm on the corpse's head and headed back to his hiding place.

It was not long before the second Khagggun showed himself. Rekkk admired how hard you had to look to find him. He watched Durrr's fallen body for a long time. Rekkk knew he was trying communicate with his comrade without success. He was not able to reach the third member of the pack, either. That would both confuse and alarm him. It would also bring the third Khagggun, which was the point.

Rekkk moved slightly, and the Khagggun's helm swiveled toward him. Thinking of the butterflies, he zigzagged back toward the heartwood where Eleana lay in wait. The Khagggun did not immediately follow, and Rekkk knew why. He was waiting for his communication link to reestablish itself. Khagggun did not like to act independently; the pack almost always moved in concert. This is what interested him most about the strategy Olnnn Rydddlin had chosen; it was thoroughly unorthodox. He would do well, he told himself, to keep this tendency in mind. What was it? Ah yes. The fourth rule of engagement: learn your opponent's tactics while never repeating yours.

He saw the two of them now, conferring with the faceplates of their helms slid up. One of their number had been killed. He had to give them a reason to discard their newfound caution. He stuffed a handful of heartwood bark into his okummmon. With his shock-sword drawn, he emerged in full sight of them, holding it point down.

"I have two females with me," he shouted to them. "I will surrender to you if you promise not to harm them."

They emerged from the underbrush, their weapons at the ready. One aimed an ion cannon at Rekkk. His finger was curled tautly around the trigger.

"This is a dispute not of our making, Pack-Commander," he said.

"We have been told that you are Rhynnnon," the other said. "Is this true, Pack-Commander?"

"It does not matter," Rekkk said. "My concern is for the females."

"We will not harm them, Pack-Commander," the second one said as he advanced a few paces under the cover of the other Khagggun's ion cannon. "You have our word."

Rekkk nodded, dropped his shock-sword.

"We require more of a commitment from you, Pack-Commander," the first Khagggun said.

"I understand." Rekkk unbuckled his weapons' belt and let it drop to the forest floor. "I am unarmed."

They came on, as carefully and warily as he would have done. At that moment, he could not stop his pride in them.

"Ah, Marnnn and Grwaed. How goes it with Olnnn Rydddlin?" he asked, as they approached.

"He is not you, Pack-Commander," Grwaed said. "He lives to torture and kill."

"Once I was like that," Rekkk mused.

"Not this way," Marnnn, the Khagggun with the ion cannon, said. "Not with his single-minded devotion."

"He will see you dead, Pack-Commander," Grwaed said. "We hear that he begged for this mission."

"Disgusting for one of us to beg," Marnnn said.

They were passing beneath the heartwood where Eleana had secreted herself. She let Grwaed pass, timing her leap so that she knocked the ion cannon from Marnnn's grasp. It went off, scorching a tract of the forest floor. As she crashed down on him, Rekkk raised his left arm, releasing the transmogrified bark from his okummmon. The missile could not penetrate the battle armor, but it knocked Grwaed to his knees. Enough time for Rekkk to retrieve his shock-sword.

"Pack-Commander!" Grwaed shouted, and fired off his own ion cannon, but too high.

Rekkk dived beneath the blast, heading straight for the Khagggun. He tucked himself into a ball, landed on the spot between his shoulder blades, rolled and swung his shock-sword all in one movement. The edges of the blades were knocked aside by a downward blast of the ion cannon. Rekkk drove both his powerful legs upward, trapping the weapon between his boots. Grwaed spent precious moments trying to wrest control of it as Rekkk stabbed the tips of his shock-sword into the Khagggun's midsection.

Blood spurted as Grwaed doubled over. But he was far from done. Unhooking his ion mace, he smashed it into Rekkk's face. Blood spurted from Rekkk's nose as pain exploded inside his head. Rekkk felt his grip on consciousness become tenuous. Grwaed ground the ion-ignited spikes into his cheek, and blackness rolled in a tidal wave over him.

He gritted his teeth and with all the force left in him slammed the shock-sword home. The vibrating tips sliced clean through Grwaed's spinal column, and his nerves went dead. The ion mace slid from his ice-cold hands. His body convulsed, as if trying to shake itself apart.

Rekkk tried to suck in as much oxygen as his lung would take. The aftershocks of pain throbbed through him, and he fought against passing out. He rolled away from Grwaed's corpse, kicked at it as if it were a rabid animal. He lay on his back, gasping in a pool of blood, for the moment his mind blank as he struggled to master the agony shooting through his head. He thought he heard screaming, but it seemed to come from an awfully long way off.

Not two meters from him, Eleana was struggling with Marnnn. He had recovered from the shock of her ambush far more quickly than she had anticipated. As a result, she had dropped her shock-sword, useless in close quarters, using her ion mace. But he had countered with his own ion mace and, without real knowledge of how to wield it, she was at an immediate disadvantage. She found herself occupied with fending off his attacks. You could not exactly call it parrying, since it appeared as if the spiked globe was used in directly forward thrusts.

Alloy rang against alloy as he thrust at her over and over without surcease. She was tiring quickly, not so much from the physical exertion of wielding the weapon but from the sheer effort of concentration required to defend herself. At the next attack, she miscalculated a fraction. As a consequence, her ion mace slipped off his and one of the spikes slid along her arm, bringing up a weal of fire that went all the way up into her shoulder.

Marnnn grinned hungrily at her grimace, and pressed his attack, bringing his ion mace within centimeters of her forehead. Instinctively, Eleana cringed backward, and he struck her a powerful blow on her thigh. She screamed as blood spurted, and she collapsed.

As she fell, Marnnn struck the ion mace from her hand. On her belly, she went squirming after it, received for her efforts a blow to the small of her back. Tears came freely as she writhed in a sea of agony. She tried to get away, but he only ground the ion mace more deeply into her. She could not breathe, could not think. But she saw the ion cannon lying where Marnnn had dropped it. She writhed in pain and, in her writhing, contrived to crawl closer to it.

Marnnn, seeing her intent, took his ion mace from the small of her back, jammed it against her outstretched hand. Flames of agony shot up her arm, and she snatched her hand away, holding it close against her chest. She curled up into a ball, her back against the bole of a heartwood tree. Marnnn, grinning, swinging the ion mace around and around his head. Eleana could do nothing but prepare herself to die.

It was then that she saw Giyan running toward her. But what could she do? She had no weapons, and those on the ground were too far away. Eleana, meeting her end, began to cry. It was like a nightmare—a nightmare in which she died. But unlike a nightmare, there was no escape, no hope. . . .

And though there was no hope, Giyan came on. Eleana saw her raise her arms straight out in front of her. Her blackened, crusty palms were facing Marnnn's back. Here came the fatal blow from the ion mace. Eleana, weeping still, anticipated the shredding of skin, the ripping of flesh, the crunching of bone. And the pain, the terrible, lacerating pain . . .

Instead, she saw the eerie glow of an orange light. She blinked away her tears, not believing what her eyes were seeing. The center of each of Giyan's palms had turned a lambent orange and, just as Marnnn began his downward swing, a spear of that lambent light struck him flush in the back.

His eyes opened wide as he arched so far backward his vertebrae snapped. He let out a soundless scream, his eyes bulged out, and blood gouted from his mouth and nose. The air was abruptly, sickeningly filled with the stench of roasted meat as Marnnn's flesh turned black and shiny as if it had been coated with lacquer.

"What—!" Eleana could see that Rekkk had also seen what happened.

He was getting to his feet when a figure emerged from the shadows. With one gloved hand, he seized Giyan by the neck, with the other he jammed the muzzle of an ion cannon against her temple.

"This accursed Kundalan sorcery," Olnnn Rydddlin said. "My entire pack is dead, and I have no idea why." His battle armor had been painted to camouflage him in the forest. He had either lost his helm or discarded it. Rekkk could see his newly implanted okummmon gleaming evilly in the sunlight. "But I *will* have my victory, Rhynnnon, that much is clear."

He plucked from his okummmon an implement in the shape of a stylus. Rekkk stiffened. He had seen Olnnn Rydddlin deploy the spider-mite before, on a priest of Enlil, just before he and Giyan had fled Axis Tyr.

"I urge you not to do this, Pack-Commander," Rekkk said. "Your quarrel is with me, not with the Kundalan female."

"On the contrary, Rhynnnon, my orders are to secure the two of you in any manner I see fit. You are a criminal and a fugitive from the Khagggun tribunal. You and those with you have forfeited all rights." Olnnn Rydddlin placed the stylus-shaped weapon on the crown of Giyan's head and six spiderlike legs splayed out. This was how he had killed the priest.

Olnnn Rydddlin smiled. "You know what happens next, Rhynnnon, don't you? The blue fire comes, fusing every nerve ending in her body. Admittedly, it is a thoroughly unpleasant way to die. Ignominious, as well, I should imagine.

But, in this case, a fitting end for the Ashera skcetta."

Rekkk was monitoring the expression on Giyan's face. She appeared calm, almost resigned to her fate. He knew he could not let her die. "I am begging you, Pack-Commander, spare her life."

"*Begging?*" Olnnn Rydddlin sneered. "How the mighty are brought low." He spat at Rekkk's feet. "You deserve your contemptible status, Rhynnnon. You are no more Khagggun than a Kundalan dray-master."

Tongues of blue fire began to emanate from the ends of the spider-mite's six legs. Rekkk knew when they met in the center Giyan would be dead. He stared deep into Giyan's eyes, but they were blank. It seemed as if she had already said good-bye.

27

Equation

I am going to Thrip, Riane said.

No! You cannot! Mother cried silently. *If you do, Bartta will know you have the Gift. She will imprison you once again, and this time she will make certain you can never escape.*

If I do not Thrip, you will die. I cannot allow that.

I am nothing, Mother said. *You are the Dar Sala-at. Your survival must be ensured at all costs. For the sake of every Kundalan living and dead!*

But the group of Ramahan were just outside the doorway, and Riane had already begun to spin. *I have made up my mind, Mother. I will not allow you to die.*

Riane, listen to me. You are still forming, and your enemies are legion. Right now, your best weapon against them

*is anonymity. You do not understand the danger you will face
if—*

It was too late; they were Thripping. The walls and floor
turned transparent as they dissolved into their component
parts. They slipped into Otherwhere as Bartta led the Ramahan into the chamber.

*If you return to my Kell prison, you will lead Bartta di-
rectly there*, Mother said.

Time.

My corpus will expire in less than sixty seconds.

*You are my spiritual mother. Do you really believe I would
allow you to die? There must be another way.*

An idea came to her. She directed herself to Thrip
obliquely, so that she would pass through the Kell where
Mother's body lay dying without remaining there. In fact,
she did not know whether it could be done, and there was
no time to ask Mother's advice. There was just enough time
to act. And pray to Miina it would work.

The interior of Mother's Kell rose up before her in ghostly
geometry. She slowed her spinning as she approached the
transparent walls, as she slipped through, but she did not
stop. Inside her, Mother understood instantly. Riane felt the
psychic pain of the separation, an instant's gaping hole inside
her spirit before her own soul rushed back in like surf to
cover it over. She saw Mother's corpus stirring. She was
about to release her hold on *The Book of Recantation* when
Mother's voice stopped her.

"I cannot keep it here. Bartta checks on me regularly,"
Mother warned her. "You must hide it from her."

"I will come for you, Mother," Riane said, and she passed
out of the Kell. "This I promise." She Thripped back to the
spherical Kell where, the night before, she had been exploring with Shima Vedda. Of course, the Kell was deserted.
Shima Vedda was long gone, returned to the upper reaches
of the abbey to doubtless receive her punishment for not
taking care of Konara Bartta's disciple.

Materializing fully, Riane lighted one of the torches they
had brought down with them and took a quick look around.

She went immediately to the carved Ja-Gaar. The middle one was slightly larger than the two that flanked it. She put her hand inside its mouth, then quickly slid *The Book of Recantation* in to see if it would fit. It did. She took out the book, wondering how long she had before Bartta found her. Bartta did not have the Gift; therefore, she could not Thrip. That meant that she would have to find her way down here on foot. A half hour, perhaps a few minutes more. That was all the time she had left.

She thought about Mother, imprisoned for nearly a century in that Kell, and shuddered. How could one Kundalan do that to another? And a Ramahan, at that! Mother was right. A profound and insidious evil had penetrated the Abbey of Floating White. Having taken root more than a hundred years go, it had flourished. And it was slowly and methodically rewriting the history, the very Scripture of Miina. It had made scapegoats of the Rappa, had daemonized the Ja-Gaar, and had left Mother for dead. Everything that had been sacred and holy in the abbey had by now been tainted by this evil. No wonder the Great Goddess had turned her back on her chosen ones. The Ramahan were spiritually ill. Touching the Ja-Gaar as reverently as if they were goddesses, she thought again of the vibrancy of the past, compared it with sorrow to the twilight of the present. *Who better than I,* she thought, *part V'ornn, part Kundalan, yet apart from both races to bear witness, to understand the dusk of Kundalan civilization. Is this, then, the task of the Dar Sala-at, to become the great archaeologist, to begin the process of resurrection, to remember the past with such flaming intensity that it rekindles the here and now, gives form and substance to the future? How could any one person alone, even the Dar Sala-at, hope to effect such a Transformation?*

With tears in her eyes, she put her back against the wall and slid down until she was sitting on the cold, black floor. She opened the *Book of Recantation* and stared at the runes. As Mother had told her, this was not written in Venca but in the Old Tongue. She saw similarities, but could make no immediate connections.

"Riane," she whispered. "Help me read this."

Venca is made up of a series of mathematical equations. So is the Old Tongue, Riane said in her mind. *You can build the necessary equations from the letters you see.*

Once she saw that, the entire language fell into place. With a speed almost beyond imagining, Riane began to construct the Old Tongue word, phrases, sentences, paragraphs using Venca equations. Part of her—the Annon part—sat back and watched astonished at what this brain of hers could accomplish. In no time at all she commenced to read.

Page after page floated before her vision. She wanted to read even faster, but feared that her comprehension would falter. Still, she read more swiftly than could be imagined. This, too, was part of her unique Gift. She came to an entire section of blank pages. But she knew they were not blank. They were being protected by a sorcerous spell. Mother said that she was the only one who might break the spell. But how?

It did not matter now because she had run out of time.

She heard Bartta's approach in her mind like the tolling of a far-off bell. She had set up a perimeter of psychic sentries without even knowing it. Quickly, she withdrew them, drew a veil in her mind across her Gift. She rose and slid the book into the mouth of the middle Ja-Gaar. She patted the top of its head, which somehow did not seem nearly as fearsome as it had before. She felt unaccountably protected here, as if she had come home.

A last lingering touch, then she crossed to the well in the center of the floor. Luckily, Shima Vedda had left the lid to the well ajar. She had lacked the strength to close it on her own. Her only hope now was to give Bartta the impression that she had fallen down the well when Shima Vedda had not been looking. Knowing Bartta, this ruse might not work, but she could not think of another alternative. She had to present Bartta with a semblance of doubt about who stole. *The Book of Recantation,* about who left the Thrip trail.

Taking one last look around this Kell, which she had inexplicably come to love, she blew out the torch. Engulfed in absolute darkness, she lowered herself into the well. She almost cried out as the frigid water closed around her, but she forced herself to continue her descent until she was all the way in. The cold sucked the breath from her. She had to force herself to breathe and to remain calm, to inure herself from the thought of the deadly chill. It was darker than night, darker than death in here. How deep did the well go? Where did it end? She had no idea, but something inside her felt that the depth was endless. In those first few moments, she struggled a little, beating back her panic, waiting for exhaustion to set in. The sides of the well were smooth and slippery. There were no hand- or footholds. She simply trod water and allowed her mind to wander.

She was back in her previous life, hunting gimnopedes and ice-hares among stands of sysal trees. . . . Side by side with Kurgan as he pulled one of his clever pranks . . . Hearts beating with Eleana in dappled sunlight, under the heartwood canopy, staring at the mystery of Annon's face . . .

. . . Perhaps she was hallucinating. Then it no longer mattered. The water had risen over her head. It was clear she was drowning.

Bartta was led to the termination of the Thripped emanations like a reader to the period at the end of a sentence. She appeared in the black spherical chamber, and found it deserted. Unlike earlier that morning, she herself had not been here in many years, had supposed that it would never be seen again by Ramahan eyes. Accordingly, when Shima Vedda had reported back to her, she was more disturbed than irate. Not that she let the Shima see that, no, that would not do at all. Let the punishment fit the crime, that was one of her mottos known from one end of the abbey to the other.

Bad enough that this stupid priestess had broken into an area of the abbey she should never have known about, but she had also managed to lose Riane. Her description of how the girl simply disappeared before her eyes had led Bartta to assume that she was either lying or insane. That was until

Bartta had felt the peculiar emanations still ambient in the restoration room of the Library. Impossible as it appeared, someone had Thripped.

Opening the Eye of Ajbal, she had followed the increasingly faint emanations down through the bowels of the abbey until she had arrived here. By the light of her lantern, she now saw what in her haste she must have missed before, that the unholy cenote was open.

Miina protect me, she thought. Her first instinct was to push the lid back into place. Then she had the thought to look inside. To do so, she had to pass the three carved Ja-Gaar. She shuddered as she did so, averting her gaze as best she could. Ever since she had learned Kyofu, they had given her a profound sense of dread.

Setting the lantern down beside the blankets she had brought in case she found Riane, she got down on her hands and knees, peering into the pitch-black water of the cenote. It took all her formidable willpower to do so, and she shuddered profoundly at the thought of what was waiting greedily at the bottom. She lifted her lantern over her head and immediately saw a body floating in the water.

Reaching in, she got a grip under an armpit and hauled upward. Miina, but the water was frigid! Whoever had fallen in would have little chance of being alive. The head emerged from the water.

Riane!

Bartta dropped the lantern and grabbed her with both hands. Miina, the water made her heavy! Bartta spread her legs to get better traction, pulling upward with the muscles of her thighs, shoulders, and back as well as her arms. Slowly, agonizingly, she prised Riane from the watery grave.

Gasping, she lay for a moment on the cold stone floor before rousing herself to pump the water out of Riane's lungs. She jammed the heels of her hands against the girl's diaphragm several times, then slapped her across the face.

Riane coughed and began to choke. Bartta returned to her ministrations and, tense moments later, Riane vomited up all the water she had swallowed. Bartta scrambled over the wet floor and, using every form of power at her disposal, caused the lid to slide with a heavy grating sound back into place, sealing the cenote.

She knelt with the girl's head cradled in her lap, wrapping her stone-cold body in blankets, listening to her breathe while her heart hammered in her chest. She rocked the girl back and forth, murmuring prayers of healing. What would happen to her if the Dar Sala-at died? She shuddered, and wrapped Riane more tightly in the blankets. *How quiet it is here*, she thought, *how utterly still*. Save for the disquieting gaze of the three Ja-Gaar she would not mind it at all, even though she was so far below ground, even though she was within spitting distance of a cenote.

If only she could sleep, as Riane slept now. Instead, she peered into opals she had bought from itinerant traders, looking for her lost youth. But all she ever discovered was the lorg she stoned to death, lying mute and bloody, accusing her of the deaths she had bartered for.

Bartta shook her head. *The Book of Recantation* should never have been marked for restoration. She had not authorized it, and yet the precise annotation on the restorer's tablet indicated that the shima had begun working on it. Whatever had possessed them? Now it was too late, for both of them. She turned her mind away from what had already occurred. What concerned her at present was that the Sacred Book was missing. She herself had only found out about it through sheer happenstance, when years ago Giyan had told her how she had stumbled upon it.

Was it possible that Riane had learned how to Thrip, that she had discovered what *The Book of Recantation* meant and had stolen it? How was it possible, who would have told her? Bartta was quite certain that Astar did not know the real meaning of the book. Neither did she have the facility to teach Riane how to Thrip.

An idea struck her. She pressed her lips to the center of Riane's forehead, feeling the circle of cold, the Sphere of Binding. She opened the Eye of Ajbal and peered into the depths of the spell she had cast on Riane. The Sphere of

Binding linked one person to another. It linked Bartta with Mother. It also linked Riane with Mother. If Mother had somehow managed to make direct contact with Riane, the Sphere of Binding would show it.

Bartta peered into the heart of the spell and cursed softly to herself. The Dar Sala-at had found Mother! At least Mother had not been able to detect the Sphere of Binding Bartta had cast on Riane. Night Blindness, the second Kyofu spell she had woven in, had done its work. That certainly gave her a measure of grim satisfaction.

Bartta stared down at Riane, her thoughts racing. The revelation of Mother's clandestine activities only led to more urgent questions that demanded immediate answers. She could not delay. Unmasking Astar had confirmed her long-held suspicion that a conspiracy against her had arisen inside the abbey. If the conspirators should get wind of who Riane really as, of how much power lay dormant inside her, they could use the girl against her. And Sphere of Binding or no, Mother would recognize Riane as the Dar Sala-at, of that Bartta had no doubt. This was something she could not allow. Riane was hers, and must remain hers, lifting her on the rising tide of power.

Concentrating, she shifted the focus of the Eye of Ajbal. It took great mental effort. She held Riane's fingers, peering at the pads through the lens of the sorcerous Eye. Her heart turned over. There was the unmistakable residue of the sticky spell she had cast on the margins of the book's pages, a sorcerous alarm to warn her if anyone had been reading it. Which was why she would never have authorized the restoration. Here was her proof that Riane had stolen the book, that she had Thripped here. How? Mother! How many other conspirators had she recruited? Casting a remedy, she removed the residue of the sticky spell, so Riane would not go mad like the restorer had who had also touched the book's pages.

Riane moaned in pain, and Bartta cast a Cloud of Slumber to gentle her. Riane quieted. Bartta closed down the Eye.

She rubbed her temples to stop the terrible throbbing.

Every time she used the Eye pain threaded through her sinews like venom. In the universe—any universe—one principle at least was a constant: for every action there is a reaction. So the use of the Black Dreaming sorcery left behind a noxious residue, a sludge distilled from the fibrous rootstock of envy-hate-lust. This substance clung to her with the tenacity of tar. Only drugs gave her a measured amount of surcease. She massaged her temples, moaning a little. The sorcery had entwined itself through the very fibers of her being as dexterously, as insidiously as any jungle creeper. Now she could not survive without it. It was no different than the food she ate, the water she drank, the air she breathed. She was it and it was she. There could be no turning back. It had changed her as surely, as irrevocably as if it had replaced her lungs with gills.

She steeled herself for what she was about to do. It was so dangerous, but she dared not turn back. Her entire life depended on keeping the power, just as Konara Mossa had before her. The Dar Sala-at was already too powerful, and it had happened right under Bartta's nose. It was now clear to her that Riane was uncontrollable. What would happen if she allowed Riane to continue to gain power? It would be the end for her. She would be cast out, disgraced and humiliated. All she had ever wanted was to lead the Ramahan. She had dedicated herself to that goal, had sacrificed everything for it, and now that she had it in her grasp, no one, nothing was going to make her give it up. What was the Dar Sala-at but a myth? Mother had come back from the dead, but did she have the sorcerous powers she was supposed to have? No. Had The Pearl protected Kundala from the V'ornn? No. Did Miina have the power to save her chosen people? No. So who was to say that this girl was what she said she was? Who was to say that she could save the Kundalan? Miina? On all these matters, Miina was silent, as she had been silent for more than a hundred years.

No, if Bartta had learned anything on her way up to leading the Dea Cretan, it was that power was of the moment. She had no choice but to act and act now.

Taking a series of ritual deep breaths, she wove a Skein of Serenity about herself. Her surroundings faded slightly, and with that their effect upon her. She made the most of this respite, carrying Riane out of the monstrous Kells, back to the familiar and comforting abbey—*her* abbey, where the late morning announced itself in thick golden shafts of sunlight within which dust motes danced in silent, twisting counterpoint.

She encountered no one as she strode down the hallway. Iron hinges squealed in protest as the scarred heartwood door opened. Light streamed into the darkness, illuminating the way as she set Riane down in the ammonwood chair covered with runes that sat on the incised plinth in the middle of the room. Months ago, she had scrubbed the last dried patches of Astar's blood off the stone floor.

Having strapped Riane into the chair, she went briskly about the circumference of the chamber firing the reed torches until all was suffused in their hot orange glow. Then she went to the door and closed it quietly, almost reverently, her forehead damp against the ancient wood.

Slowly and deliberately, she set up the *had-atta*, the scaffolding of the ancient implement rising in shadow along the opposite wall like a mythical narbuck. At length, she slid the flutelike crystal column between Riane's slackly opened lips. She used the Eye of Ajbal to keep her from thinking about what she was doing. One of the many benefits of the Black Dreaming sorcery was that it was an insulation against questionable or distasteful acts. She never regretted what had to be done, or second-guessed herself.

All was in readiness.

Lovingly stroking the *had-atta*, she woke Riane.

28

Nemesis

Giyan, discovering that a simple spell of paralysis had no effect on Olnnn Rydddlin, had sunk deep into Ayame. There, she discovered the Avatar circling, guarding his essence, a gigantic brown-black insect with an armored thorax, veined wings, serrated mandibles, and faceted eyes. This was not like casting a spell that embedded itself in the recipient. Malistra had somehow projected this emissary of her power over many kilometers to keep Olnnn Rydddlin safe. Giyan knew of no other sorceress, including herself, who could accomplish this massive feat. The implications terrified her to the core. She did not dare attack the Avatar because she did not recognize it. Without recognition, she had no way of knowing either the nature or the extent of its power. She had read in the section of *The Book of Recantation* of Avatars of the Black Dreaming sorcery that could drain your power, others that could actually take your power if you used it against them. She could not take the chance that this was one of those.

She could feel in the physical realm a pain starting in her head and knew that the spider-mite was beginning to kill her. She was forming a plan, but it was very risky. She did not see a choice. Still in Ayame, she located first Rekkk, then Eleana. The pain was becoming intrusive; time was running out, a matter of seconds at most.

She began.

Eleana, watching Olnnn Rydddlin slowly killing Giyan, was suddenly filled with a toxic rage. With a cry of fury, she rose up, twirling the ion mace. She ignored Rekkk's shout of warning, cocked her arm back to throw the weapon directly at Olnnn Rydddlin's unprotected face. It was their only chance; she knew it as surely as she knew her own name.

She saw Olnnn Rydddlin's right arm directed at her. A heartbeat later, she was knocked off her feet by the ion-cannon blast. Pain filled her to overflowing. She tried to cry out, but failed. She tried to move, but failed at that, too. She lay on her back, the light slowly leaking out of the world. Then, a starless night engulfed her, taking her far, far away.

Y ou've killed her," Rekkk said through gritted teeth.
"First the girl, then the skcettta. One by one they fall." There was a sly smile on Olnnn Rydddlin's face. "Why should you care? They are Kundalan. A true Khagggun would rejoice at their demise." He cocked his head. "But you are no longer Khagggun. Now I wonder whether you ever were."

Giyan uttered a little cry, falling to her knees. Blood drooled from the epicenter of the weapon. Rekkk was shaking with rage.

"Come on, Rhynnnon. Attack me." The muzzle of the ion cannon found him. "I would like nothing better than to kill you the same way I killed that Kundalan girl. She was armed with Khagggun weapons. How did that happen, Rhynnnon? I am sure the Star-Admiral will be pleased to ask you that question himself."

Giyan toppled over, her body in the fetal position. Her eyes were wide-open, staring into a dimension neither of them could see.

"It is almost over, Rhynnnon." Olnnn Rydddlin could not keep the edge of gloating off his voice. "She is dying. Don't you want to help her?" The muzzle of the ion cannon lowered; a short blast caught Rekkk in the meat of his right thigh. Rekkk grunted. He felt nothing for a moment. Then the pain hit him full bore, and he collapsed to his knees.

"There, that's better, isn't it?" Olnnn Rydddlin placed one boot on Rekkk's hip. "On second thought, you're not close enough." He kicked Rekkk on the point of his hip. "Not down far enough yet, Rhynnnon." He kicked again and again until Rekkk lay prone at his feet. He bent over, his face a mask of rage and disgust. "What are you now? Nothing more than the skcettta you're lying next to. She corrupted you, just like she corrupted the regent Ashera. But no more. This is all at an end, Rhynnnon. The Star-Admiral charged me with bringing you back, and that I will do. But not before you have watched your 'friends' die. Not before you have received your first portion of pain."

He raised his leg, brought the heel of his boot hard onto Rekkk's wounded thigh, ground it deeper into the pulpy flesh. Then, using all his strength, he tamped down hard. "What was that sound I just heard, Rhynnnon? That snap? Was it your bone breaking? Oh yes, it must have been. There's the end of it poking through your skin." He crouched beside Rekkk, staring into his red-rimmed eyes. "I must say I am impressed. You haven't made a single sound." He smiled as he put a hand on Rekkk. "Well, we will soon remedy that."

Eleana was aware of someone screaming. Like a thread of air bubbles, she followed it to the surface of consciousness. For a moment, she lay staring up at the patterns on the leaves. Sunlight played through the latticework curtains of the treetops. She saw a pair of gimnopedes flitting through the branches as if playing hide-and-seek. She heard the steady drone of insects, the gurgling of the unseen river.

Then the blood-chilling scream came again, and she started out of her pain-induced daydream. Everything flooded back to her at once. She did not question why she was not dead, paid no attention to the residual pain. She saw Olnnn Rydddlin crouched over Rekkk and Giyan. Were they dead or alive? The killing rage still dwelled within her. Without further thought, she took up her ion mace and, swinging it over her head, let it fly.

It struck Olnnn Rydddlin squarely on his left temple, throwing, him backward. She drew her shock-sword and, on leadlike feet, stumbled toward him. He rose in time to parry her first blow with his own shock-sword, but on his back he had a weak defense, and her next strike swept the weapon out of his hand. She prepared herself for the killing blow, but Giyan's voice stopped her.

"Eleana, no! Do not touch him!"

The shock-sword was bare millimeters from the side of his neck where his pulse throbbed. He smiled wickedly up at her. "Do it! You know you want to kill me!"

Eleana's muscles bunched; the end of the shock-sword quivered.

"Eleana, listen to me! He is protected by sorcery."

Eleana, her chest heaving with rage, exertion, and fear, turned and gasped. "Are you—"

Giyan was on her feet. "I will be fine." Blood matted her hair, coursed down the side of her face, lacquered her neck. It took all of her concentration not to run to where Rekkk lay, bloodied and insensate. She sent a tendril of healing to him as she steeled herself. "You have saved us, Eleana. Now you must help Rekkk."

"Don't listen to the skcettta," Olnnn Rydddlin hissed. "All she knows is lies. Kill me! Kill me now while you have the chance!"

Eleana turned back to him, expecting the killing rage to galvanize her. But it had vanished as quickly and mysteriously as it had come. "No." She licked her lips and backed up until she was standing over Rekkk, but did not take her eyes off of the Pack-Commander. Then she knelt.

"Put the palms of your hands on his thigh," Giyan instructed her, "just above the wound. Feel for the major pulse. When you find it, keep your hands there."

Giyan approached Olnnn Rydddlin. She ignored the bleeding from the wound in her scalp. "Look what I have, Olnnn," she said in a soft, buttery voice. As his defiant gaze dropped to her outstretched hand, she opened it like a flower. Inside, sat the spiderlike weapon he had affixed to her.

She stood over him, spread-legged. Eleana was in awe. Somehow, bloodied and hurt, Giyan seemed even more majestic, even more powerful than she had before.

"Once this thing failed to come off as the other one had, I knew that it had been modified." She spun the weapon in the cup of her palm. "Modified by sorcery. Isn't that right, Olnnn?"

"How is this possible?" Olnnn Rydddlin rasped. "She said no one but me would be able to touch it."

"Malistra was wrong," Giyan said. "I used a spell of my own to break its hold on me." She would not tell him how many spells she had tried, or that she had had to modify on the fly the one that had worked. "It was a mistake to align yourself with a Dark sorceress, Olnnn."

"Do not address me in the barbaric Kundalan manner," he spat.

Without another word, she slammed the sorcerous weapon onto his thigh in the same spot he had so grievously wounded Rekkk.

Olnnn Rydddlin threw his head back, screaming in agony. Writhing, he attempted to crawl away. Giyan went to where Rekkk lay in a pool of blood. Eleana made room for her.

Giyan passed her hands over his wound. "I am sorry. It was the only way." She looked up at the girl. "I used him to distract Olnnn Rydddlin while I protected you from the ion-cannon blast."

"But—"

"Do you remember the rage, Eleana?"

"Yes, of course—"

"I put it there, inside your head. So that you would act."

"Then you saved us. You saved us all."

Giyan cradled Rekkk's head. She had to bite her lip to keep from weeping. I have to keep myself in check, she told herself sternly. If she had any hope of keeping him alive she knew she needed to have her faculties unclouded by emotion.

Eleana's head turned at the scraping noise Olnnn Rydddlin was making as he continued to crawl away. "What will that thing do to him?"

"It employs a sorcery I know only dimly," Giyan said. "It

has already crippled him. It is possible if I leave it in him, it will kill him."

"Good," Eleana said. She watched, stupefied as Giyan rose, strode after Olnnn Rydddlin.

"Just like a worm," Giyan said. Without warning, she stooped, plucking the sorcerous weapon from him.

Eleana cried out: "What are you doing? This daemonic Khagggun must die!"

He gasped out loud, and so did Eleana when she saw the devastation the thing had caused. It left no blood, but something far worse. The flesh of his leg was being eaten away by an unnaturally accelerated necrosis. Olnnn Rydddlin was moaning, grasping his dying leg with both hands. His eyes were open wide, and sweat had broken out all over him. He began to shake, his eyes rolling up in their sockets as he went into shock.

"Take his ion cannon." Giyan turned away from him, watched Eleana as she did what she was told. "This sorcery is more dangerous than you can imagine, more dangerous to us than one lone Khagggun. It is vital we have the weapon to study." She gave one last glance in Olnnn Rydddlin's direction. "In any event, he may die anyway—or wish he had."

Then, filled with terror and anxiety, she rushed back to Rekkk, wondering whether in the next few minutes she would heal him or bury him.

29

Handmaiden

Riane arose from that odd, disorienting coma that is the handmaiden of death into the realization that her ruse had failed.

"This is all very simple," she heard Bartta say.

She tried to move and couldn't. She opened her eyes and knew immediately where she was and what was about to happen to her.

Bartta stepped into her field of vision. "As I say, very simple indeed. You have been witness to this procedure before." The leather thong was wrapped around her hand. "You know the outcomes, both good and bad."

Riane made a sound.

Bartta came closer. "You are the Dar Sala-at. I have no wish to hurt you, but at the same time I know you harbor secrets. I cannot allow that, Riane. These secrets are too important, too dangerous for you to keep to yourself."

"What secrets?" Riane just managed to gasp, though her words were distorted by the crystal flute between her lips.

Bartta's eyes grew hard and dark as basalt. "One: besides Mother, who is helping you? Two: who taught you how to Thrip? Three: why did you steal *The Book of Recantation*?

"I don't know what you are talking about."

"Do not lie to me. I will not hesitate to kill you."

Riane stared at her, unblinking.

"Answer my questions!"

"Why should I? You murdered Leyna Astar, you treat me like a slave. You keep me locked up like a house pet."

"There are two sides to every story." Bartta's tone turned wheedling. "Giyan would want you to tell—"

"That's a lie!" Riane shouted. "She would not have wanted this for me! She does not know you as I do!"

Bartta took a step toward her, and the flute rose so that it hung just above Riane's mouth. Her eyes narrowed, and her tone grew cold. "You stole *The Book of Recantation*. Why? Who did you give it to?"

"No one. I told you, I fell down the well."

"Why do you continue to lie? I myself checked that Kell after Shima Vedda reported you missing."

"But you didn't look into the well, did you?" Riane said.

Bartta said nothing.

"Why are you doing this to me?"

"You conspire against me. I am doing only what has to be done."

"Like you did with Leyna Astar?"

"Yes. She was a traitor! She deserved—"

"You are as crazy as a Kraelian sundog!"

"You dare use a V'ornn phrase?" Bartta slapped her hard. "Answer my questions."

Riane ignored the stinging in her jaw. "I have no answers."

Bartta looked at her for a long time. Riane could see the war going on behind her eyes. Then, abruptly, she grasped either side of Riane's jaws, forced them open. She positioned the flute in her mouth, then stepped back off the incised plinth.

"Now it is too late. Too late for omens, too late for miracles, too late for faith." Her expression was rigid as she unwound the leather thong the space of one loop.

Riane gagged as the flute touched the back of her throat.

"You *will* tell me, Riane. Everything I want to know."

The leather thong was loosed again, and the flute continued its slide down Riane's throat, this time the length of two loops.

Despite her best efforts to control herself, Riane began to scream.

Book Four
ASCENDANCE GATE

"Ascendance Gate is the most diffi-cult Gate to quantify. It is the mys-terious bridge over the dark and turbulent sea of a troubled spirit. It is the great leveler, the equalizer. As-cendance Gate is the most powerful portal to the soul, opening the poten-tial for either great joy or unending misery . . ."

—Utmost Source,
The Five Sacred Books of Miina

30

Of V'ornn and Sarakkon

Y ou aren't actually leaving us now, are you?" Wennn
Stogggul bellowed. "You just got here."

"My apologies." Kurgan stood up from the table. "I
have an appointment."

"At this late hour?" The regent made a face. "Where? With
whom?"

"The Star-Admiral's business."

Wennn Stogggul watched his son for some time. They
were in the regent's private quarters, the low chronosteel
table between them still covered with the repast the three of
them had been served several hours ago. Larded with the
rarest of delicacies, it was the kind of meal available only to
regents bent on flexing their extraordinary power.

"Do you hear that, Malistra? The Star-Admiral's business!
If I did not know my son so well, I would believe that he
had actually found his calling." He grunted. "But perhaps he
has. Doing Kinnnus Morcha's bidding has its advantages, I
would imagine. Perquisites a mere *Bashkir* could only dream
of. Am I right, Kurgan?"

"As you say, Father. You know better than I."

"What's the matter?" Wennn Stogggul leaned forward,
pushing aside a tureen of snow-lynx stew. "All evening you
have been acting the dutiful son."

"Nothing's the matter."

The regent sat back. "Really? Then I must conclude that
you are either ill or deranged."

Kurgan turned to Malistra and smiled. "Do you find your
accommodations at the palace satisfactory, Mastress?"

"What the N'Luuura do you care?" Wennn Stogggul snapped.

Malistra smiled in return. "Quite satisfactory, Kurgan Stogggul, thank you for asking."

"There is no point in being polite to him," the regent said sourly. "He seems eerily compliant now, but there is no telling when he will turn on you."

"That is all in the past, Father." Kurgan stood at the door, perfectly calm. "I was immature. Wild, uncontrollable. I admit that. But I beg you do not continue to punish me for old sins already repented."

"Words." Wennn Stogggul said with a wave of his hand. "They are cheaply bought. Deeds are what matter in this life, my son. If you could only remember that I could turn you into a decent V'ornn yet."

To get the foul stench of his father's power flaunting out of his nostrils, he decided to go to the Kalllistotos. On his way there, he smoked twenty milligrams of laaga. Laaga was illegal. Not that Kurgan cared a clemett. Laaga was far cheaper than salamuuun and, more importantly, readily available in the city's back alleys. Cultivated on the southern continent, laaga was smuggled in by the Sarakkon, along with their legitimate imports.

He smoked rather introspectively as he walked the ink-dark streets of Axis Tyr. He was wondering which of his acquaintances at Harborside had given him up to Kinnnus Morcha. When he thought about it, the list covered just about everyone. He would have to give it some thought, keeping it in the forefront of his mind tonight. Still, he wondered if it should trouble him that Morcha knew he smoked laaga.

Inhaling a lungful of the thick, sweet smoke, he gave a coarse laugh. *To N'Luuura with it.* Another secret he had withheld from Annon. He was quite sure Annon would have been horrified if Kurgan had told him that he smoked. Just as he would have balked at venturing into the rough-and-tumble of nighttime Harborside. More differences appearing like fissures between the former best friends. Differences his father was all too quick to throw in his face.

Taking the Old V'ornn's warning to hearts, he had accepted his father's invitation to dinner in order to mend some of the fences he had broken. Not that his father had made it easy. Belittling him was one of Wennn Stogggul's favorite pastimes; it had been for years. Bitter old V'ornn. His hatred of the Ashera was eating him alive. It informed every decision he made, every risk he took, every aspect of his life.

Kurgan was rather proud of his responses: the warm smiles, the civilized compliments. He had acted like the charming and admiring son, all without expending a milliliter of genuine feeling. Once upon a time such playacting would have been beyond him. That was before he had buried his father, mentally and emotionally cutting himself free of the House of Stogggul and everything it stood for. And, tonight, he had received the added benefit of putting his father off-balance.

He knew the meaning behind the Old V'ornn's words, just as he had known the meaning behind the Star-Admiral's request. To stay in the shadow cast by his father was to be strangled by a tradition that had never held meaning for him. Wennn Stogggul had become just another adversary he was obliged to manipulate or sidestep in order to get what he wanted. And right now he was in a sweet spot: out from under his father's thumb, in a position of potential power if he played his hand cleverly and underestimated neither Star-Admiral Morcha nor Wennn Stogggul.

His way was abruptly blocked by a Kundalan dray, piled high with Borobodur forest heartwood boards from the mills in Exchange Pledges to the west. He shouted at the Kundalan drovers, but the team of water buttren were being balky, and the dray remained squarely in front of him. *Idiots!* he thought as he hauled one Kundalan drover down and began to pummel him into unconsciousness.

"Get down here and drag this sack of excrement away!" he screamed at the top of his lung.

The second Kundalan crept cautiously down, keeping hold

of the reins to the stamping water buttren. As he crept past, Kurgan tripped him, struck him a vicious blow on the back of his neck, and proceeded to kick him repeatedly as he lay on the ground. At length, he stopped, panting, and looked around for someone else to maul. Blood was everywhere. He spotted a young Kundalan at the edge of the crowd that had gathered to gawk and started to go after him. Just then, three Khagggun shouldered their way through the throng. Kurgan handed them the reins to the dray and curtly told them to clean up the mess. Then he continued on his way.

He produced his second laaga stick and, lighting it, took the smoke deep into his lung, holding it there for as long as he could. Yes, indeed, he had no difficulty whatsoever being the model son for his father.

As he headed farther into the southern district, the avenues widened even more. Elaborately decorated residences and shops gave way to enormous triangular warehouses with thickly mortared cornices and sculpted friezes depicting mythical beasts of burden. Crowds that had thinned considerably as he had bisected the industrial heart of the city swelled as he approached the northern fringe of Harborside, home of the Kalllistotos. Kundalan were queued up at the line of Khagggun security checkpoints, through which they had to pass when returning to the city from the Harborside district. He lifted a hand in greeting to the Khagggun he knew as he went through.

He supposed the Khagggun had set the game ring in Harborside primarily because the Sarakkon loved it so much. The Sarakkon were inveterate gamblers, wagering enormous sums of money on the outcome of the ten nightly contests. The Kalllistotos appeared to be the only aspect of V'ornn culture that interested them. They were widely known as freewheeling and somewhat wild. Woe betide the Kundalan or V'ornn foolish enough to cross them in a trade, for the entire colony would mass like points of light come together in a blinding flash of enmity. Perhaps they possessed some low-grade form of telepathy. In any event, they were difficult to approach, almost impossible to get close to. Trust was evidently not a concept they applied to alien races.

How they viewed the occupation of the northern continent was any V'ornn's guess. There existed between them and the V'ornn an uneasy and unspoken arrangement. The V'ornn had seen no reason to squander Khaggun and resources in colonizing the inhospitable southern continent. Besides, the Gyrgon wanted access to the radioactive compounds the Sarakkon manufactured. So the Sarakkon were left on their own, unmonitored and free as long as they agreed to continue trading with the V'ornn. How that affected their relationship with the Kundalan was also a mystery.

Difficult and time-consuming as it had been, he had managed an entry point with a Sarakkon captain named Courion, though admittedly it was a tentative one. If it was a truism that you never knew where you stood with the Sarakkon, then he meant to nullify it.

He passed Receiving Spirit, the monolithic white-stone hospice where the family had stashed his moron brother, Terrettt. At least, he assumed he was still there. Ten years and he hadn't gone once. Why should he? The less he thought about that embarrassment, the better. Only his sister, Marethyn, visited Terrettt. That was about right. That idiot was the only one apt to listen to her stupid ideas about the expanded role of Tuskugggun in V'ornn society.

Chuckling to himself, wrapped in a fragrant cloud of laaga smoke, he came upon the seaport. Beyond, the Sea of Blood reflected the lights of the city like a defective mirror, a vast expanse only the Sarakkon had mastered. He had heard stories of Sarakkon seamen spending years on their ships without ever coming in sight of land. It was beyond him why anyone would want to take to the sea. Doubtless, he would be bored to tears within days.

Nearing the Kalllistotos, he began to see clots of Sarakkon. They were tall, slender folk, with elongated heads, dark glistening skin the color of pomegranates, teeth like ivory tiles. All had facial hair—thick, curling beards in which seadiadems were threaded, long mustaches, twisted and oiled into points, sharp, triangular goatees from which hung tin-

kling lines of tiny shells—spotted, striped, incandescent—
and semiprecious stones. Their shaven skulls as well as most
of their bodies were covered with tattoos of unfathomable
runes. They were all male, these fierce and curious sailors.
Where their females were was anyone's guess.

Though they wore clothing made from the lightest-weight
Kundalan fabrics for which they traded, the style was decidedly different. Because they lived in a warm, tropical climate,
they did not wear robes, but rather favored a kilted skirt that
ran from waist to knee. A kind of wide belt, woven of cured
sea grape, circled the waist and hung down the front of the
skirts in stupefying patterns of knots, each one signifying
something, perhaps status or rank of some kind. Their feet
were clad in high boots of glittering pebbled rayskin, tanned
aboard their ships in vats of sea salt and mercury. Their oiled
torsos were covered only by sleeveless sharkskin vests, tough
as armor plate, painful to brush up against. They wore at
their hips wicked-looking dirks of dark steel and huge gleaming scimitars with engraved blades made from petrified saw-
fish snout, hilts of carved coral or sea-cor bone.

It was not long before Kurgan spotted Courion. Courion
was captain of his own ship, though the Sarakkon had never
invited Kurgan on board. He judged Courion to be no more
than ten years his elder. He was a smart, aggressive, confident trader. Kurgan had failed to find his weak spot, and so
had yet to get the better of him in a deal. Much to his surprise, he found that he admired the Sarakkon. He might be
a primitive in many respects, but he knew more about trading
than just about anyone Kurgan knew, including Wennn Stogggul. There was much to learn from someone with his
skills.

As dictated by Sarakkonian custom, he did not approach
Courion directly, but rather insinuated himself into the
sweaty crowd ringing the Kalllistotos, positioning himself
where Courion was certain to see him. Courion was talking
to two massive Sarakkon seamen—presumably members of
his crew. Palms were slapped as bets were made on the current contestants, then raised and redoubled. Through the

swirling mob, Kurgan caught a glimpse of the contestants inside the ring. A burly Mesagggun with a beetling brow and, it appeared, nothing more on his praen-sized brain than cracking some bones and laying on the hurt was being pitted against a young Bashkir with wide, powerful shoulders, a narrow waist, and muscular legs. Whoever he was, he was new to the Kalllistotos. Kurgan had never seen him before.

"Have you sniffed them out? Do you have a preference?"

Kurgan did not turn. He knew by the sound of the voice who was talking to him, and was pleased that Courion had approached him in the Sarakkonian manner, without mentioning his name or greeting him in any way.

"I just got here." He knew he did not have much time to answer. He was determined to look as confident as any Sarakkon. "But I do not have to think twice. I favor the Mesagggun."

"In that event, we would have presented a wager," Courion said coolly. He had a sleek, compelling face, with dark eyes and a slight curve to his lips that made him appear as if he were constantly amused. In his beard were carved runes made of lapis lazuli and jade, on his fingers were huge rings of star sapphire and ruby and lynx-eye. His rayskin boots were dyed a dusky orange. "But a pip-squeak like you surely lacks sufficient funds to make it worthwhile."

"If I was not prepared to wager, I would not have opened my mouth." It was true. In Sarakkonian circles, wagering was almost a sacred rite. If you had an opinion about anything—anything at all—you had best be prepared to make a wager on it just as the Sarakkon did. Otherwise, you would lose what little respect they had for you. "I will bet twenty."

"We will put up fifty."

Kurgan knew the Sarakkon was studying him. Sometimes, he had the unsettling impression that Courion tolerated his presence simply because the Sarakkon found him amusing in some secret manner.

"Fifty would suit me as well," he said, determined to play this game as a Sarakkon would. You never ended up wagering what you had first offered. That would have been an insult of the first magnitude.

Courion appeared unimpressed. "It is the ninth match." The penultimate fight of the evening. "Is that all you can muster, the bare minimum? All right, then. Fifty it is." When the wager had been sealed, he laughed. "You have not been at Kalllistotos for some time, Stogggul. It will be a pleasure to take your coins. This Bashkir has been the champion for two weeks now. The Mesagggun is overmatched."

Kurgan, feeling trapped in a scheme of Courion's making, was now desperate to keep up his appearance of confidence. He realized that this was Courion's purpose. A test to see if he was worthy of being in the company of these high-spirited aliens. "If that is your opinion, then we should go to one hundred seventy-five."

"Oh-ho!" Courion cried. "Indeed, then! We match you with added pleasure!"

A reckless wager, surely. Kurgan did not have one hundred seventy-five. But it would not matter if he won. He tried to keep the alternative out of his mind.

The two of them, followed by the pair of Sarakkon with whom Courion had first been wagering, made their way toward the boundary of the Kalllistotos. The jostling crowd parted magically for Courion and closed back around the group as soon as they had passed. Soon enough they were in the front row. And just in time. The match was about to commence.

The Kalllistotos was a five-sided ring with precisely three meters between opposing angles. It was a simple affair— three strands of ion-charged wires strung between alloy uprights—as befitted its humble origins as an off-world entertainment among the Khagggun. The idea, too, was simple: force your opponent onto the wires, where the ion charge would knock him senseless. The ion charge affected contestants differently, of course, and it was rumored that there were ways in which one could build up a certain tolerance for the muscle-spasming pain. Kurgan had seen one contestant last twelve seconds before succumbing. In terms of the Kalllistotos, that was a long time.

The two combatants had begun to pummel one another with the kind of gut-grunting, no-holds-barred style dictated by the event. Blood spurted as first the Mesagggun, then the Bashkir landed solid blows. They broke, regrouping, circled around, and both attacked at once. The Kalllistotos was so brutal, so violent, most matches lasted no more than a few minutes.

The Mesagggun landed two bone-crunching blows, arching the Bashkir's sweat-streaked back, backing him up. Taking advantage, he came on with pile-driver force. The Bashkir's knees seemed to buckle beneath the terrible onslaught until he was perilously close to the wires.

Wedged in beside Kurgan, Courion grinned and struck two coins together. Both his arms were tattooed with likenesses of the chief sea goddess, part Sarakkon, part sea serpent. The skin of his head was one dizzying pattern overlain on another. The whole gave him the aspect of a walking work of art.

The harried champion fell to his knees beneath the Mesagggun's furious attack. There was no letup, no surcease.

"I am greatly looking forward to taking your coins," Kurgan said with a smirk.

Courion said nothing. The Mesagggun had his failing opponent at his mercy. He picked him off his knees and sent him hurtling backward into the wires. The Bashkir arched back as the full brunt of the ion charge blasted through him. Not wanting to leave anything to chance, the Mesagggun pressed his opponent more firmly against the wires.

Three, four, five. Kurgan was counting how many seconds the Bashkir had been against the wires. Then he saw something that sent a shock wave through him. The Bashkir took the Mesagggun's head between his hands and slammed it full force into the top wire. The ion charge flayed the skin off his nose and cheeks and, as the Bashkir continued to apply pressure, burned off his eyelids, blinding him.

With the bellow of a hindemuth in heat, the Mesagggun

went down with a resounding crack and lay insensate at the feet of the champion. The Bashkir came off the wires slowly as the roar of the crowd swelled and ululated. He lifted his arms over his head. He was bleeding profusely from his nose, mouth, and back, and one shoulder had been dislocated.

Without a word, Courion held his hand out. "Our winnings, if you please," he said over the roar of the throng.

Kurgan licked his dry lips. "I don't have it."

Courion's face darkened. He was about to reply when one of his crew made his way through the sweating throng and whispered in his ear.

"Is that so?" Courion said. Laughing, he turned to Kurgan. His expression sent a shiver of trepidation through Kurgan. "Listen, pip-squeak. We will forgo the coins you owe us."

"You will?"

"On one condition." The amused smile had returned. "The final challenger has taken suddenly ill and cannot fight. You will take his place."

Kurgan said nothing, though he wanted to shout his fear at the top of his lung. "Surely there must be another way—"

"You have fought before in the Kalllistotos, yes? You have told us as much, yes? Have you lied to us?"

"No, of course not. But I have never—that is, I have only fought in the preliminary rounds. This is—I am unprepared for—"

The huge Sarakkon took him by the front of his robe. "We fear you do not fully appreciate the situation you find yourself in, pip-squeak. We do not tolerate bettors who cannot pay. There is no negotiation. None at all." He swept his arm in the direction of the bloody ring. "We offer you this chance to repay us in recognition of our relationship." He put his face close to Kurgan's. "But that relationship can be terminated at any moment. Do we make ourselves clear?"

Kurgan nodded. He pulled himself together. It would do no good to panic. What would the Old V'ornn think of such weakness?

"I accept your terms."

"Splendid," Courion smiled. "We will escort you into the

Kalllistotos. Your name has already been entered into the bettors' sheets." He clapped Kurgan on the back. "Tell us, pip-squeak, who should we put our coins on, you or the Bashkir?" He threw his head back and laughed long and hard as he pushed Kurgan through the milling throng, past the security guards, up the ramp to the perimeter of the ring.

"Kalllistotos!" he shouted, boosting Kurgan over the highest wire. "Tenth match!"

To Kurgan, everything outside the Kalllistotos ring seemed a blur. He thought he caught a glimpse of Courion's grinning face, but he could not be certain. The Kalllistotos smelled of blood, sweat, the mingled musks of victory and defeat.

Close-up, the Bashkir was even more frightening than he had appeared from the safety of the crowd. Through slitted eyes he watched Kurgan with the naked greed of a gyreagle observing its prey. He came up to Kurgan.

"This is a joke, isn't it?" With a sickening crack of his hand, he reset his dislocated shoulder. "*You* are a joke!"

Kurgan stepped back in the star defense and, laughing, the champion came after him. Using the huge V'ornn's momentum as a lever, Kurgan took hold of his leading arm, jerking him quickly forward. As the Bashkir's heels came up, Kurgan kicked him square on the right shin. He lost his balance, slamming onto the hard microcanvas surface of the Kalllistotos with a sound like the roll of thunder.

He rolled, scissoring his legs, catching Kurgan's ankle between them. He smashed his balled fist into Kurgan's solar plexus the moment Kurgan was down, following that up with powerful blows to Kurgan's skull.

Kurgan, on the verge of passing out, somehow arranged his pain-filled body into seventh position. As the Bashkir lunged for him, he whirled, then tramped his knee into the thick, corded neck. Bellowing in rage, the Bashkir swung him into the wires.

Searing pain spasmed the muscles in his back. Sensing quick victory, the champion pinned him against the wires.

. . . one, two, three . . .

This was how the Bashkir had won his previous match, using the wires to beat the fight out of the big Mesagggun. The Bashkir butted him, filling his nose and mouth with blood. Kurgan's eyes fluttered; black spots danced in his field of vision. The crowd was roaring, a sound like the bellowing of a storm. Consciousness was drifting away on a tide of agony and growing lethargy.

Then he thought of the Old V'ornn. He thought of the hard, painful lessons that had been ingrained into his body. He forced himself back from the brink. He spat a mouthful of blood into the Bashkir's mocking, triumphant face. As the champion put his hand up to clear his vision, Kurgan ducked down, crawling between his legs. Emerging behind him, he struck him a two-fisted blow on the recently dislocated shoulder joint. The bone popped out. As the Bashkir went to his knees, Kurgan vaulted over his shoulders, balancing on the uppermost wire. He kicked hard. The toe of his boot connected with a bone-jarring crunch, sinking into the Bashkir's eye socket.

The champion howled, clutching at his face, and Kurgan kicked again, striking his adversary's exposed throat. He went down, choking and gagging. Kurgan jumped off the high wire, right into a double-fisted smash to his belly. He went down in a heap, gasping. He felt himself being dragged toward the wires. He tried to fight back and, for his effort, got a balled fist in his face. Then the full brunt of the ion charge struck him and his eyes fluttered up.

There was a buzzing in his ears. Then, as if from a very great distance, he heard Courion's voice.

"Enough," the Sarakkon said, presumably to the champion. "It is over."

It is over between you and Kurgan Stogggul."

Wennn Stogggul, lying naked in bed, looked over at his companion. "Is that supposed to mean something to me?"

"It should." Malistra stretched.

How magnificent her body looked, he thought. She had made him replace the fusion lamps in his bedroom with her own copper-and-bronze filigreed Kundalan lanterns, from which she burned incense-infused candles she had made herself. It was no secret that he had no love for Kundalan design, but in this case he had made an exception. In fact, she had been right. The low-flickering perfumed light kept his sexual appetite well honed. These days, he was possessed of a stamina unknown even in his youth. He had only to catch sight of her hair in the lanternlight! He could never have conceived that he could find patches of hair erotic.

He yawned. "Why should it?"

"Because it concerns your son."

"If you are referring to Kurgan's bizarre behavior this evening, I would not let it trouble you. The boy is unfathomable."

"All to the good. I sensed great strength in him, great purpose."

"If only it could be harnessed."

"He seemed sincere enough."

The regent was possessed of a harsh and grating laugh. "You may be a sorceress but, after all, you are only a Kundalan. You do not know Kurgan as I do. He is mercurial— charming and cunning all at once."

"He may mean what he says this time."

"Indeed he might. But, as I said to him, I need proof of the change in him. Tangible proof." He shrugged. "Until then he is Kinnnus Morcha's responsibility."

"Listen to me—"

He struck her without warning, snapping her head back. "Enough! You presume too much. You have an annoying habit of forgetting who and where you are. I will not warn you again. You serve at my pleasure. If you think otherwise, you are sorely mistaken."

"I am most apologetic." Malistra's lowered face was hidden by shadow and the sheaf of her platinum hair. "I assure you, Lord, it is only my zeal to assist you in all ways that makes me—"

"And therein lies the problem. Pray enlighten me as to

how a Kundalan female is equipped to, as you so naively say, 'assist me in all ways'?"

"Perhaps I used the wrong—"

"First Kurgan, then Dalma, and now you." He sat up, his face suddenly flushed with blood. "N'Luuura, will no one give me the respect I deserve? Must I always live in the shadow of the accursed Eleusis Ashera? Even from the grave he haunts me!"

"Ten thousand pardons, Lord," she whispered. "I did not mean to offend."

His continued wrath was stayed at the last moment by a pounding on the door.

"What is it!" he shouted. "Who dares disturb the regent's rest?"

"Sir! The Star-Admiral is here! And he is not alone!"

Stogggul recognized the voice of Wing-General Nefff, one of the two commandants of his Haaar-kyut. One or the other was always nearby. Wrapping himself in a black-and-brown robe, he said, "Enter."

Wing-General Nefff strode into the room. As usual, his gyreagle eyes instantly took in everything before focusing on his regent. "The Star-Admiral apologizes for the lateness of the hour, but he felt his news was most urgent."

"Indeed." Stogggul's blood was up, and he was in no mood for intrusions. "You said he is not alone. Who is with him?"

"Pack-Commander Olnnn Rydddlin, sir."

At Rydddlin's name, Malistra's head turned like an animal scenting her young.

"Already?" The regent rubbed his hands together. "Then they bring news of our enemies' demise!"

"I am afraid not, sir."

"What do you mean?"

Wing-Commander Nefff's expression was pained. "I think you should see for yourself, sir."

Despite Stogggul's orders, Malistra rose. She appeared unconcerned by her nudity. "Olnnn Rydddlin is protected," she said. "No evil can befall him."

Wing-General Nefff's gaze remained squarely on his regent. For him, she did not exist. "They are in the regent's salon, sir."

Stogggul sighed and nodded. "Tell the Star-Admiral I will be with him in a moment."

"Very good, sir." There was absolutely no inflection in Wing-General Nefff's voice.

When he had withdrawn, Stogggul said curtly to her, "Put on something appropriate."

She had sense enough to keep two paces behind him as they went down the darkened hallway and into the regent's private salon. It was here that he had brandished the severed heads of all the Ashera, here that he had drunk himself into oblivion on the night of his coup, his greatest triumph. Now the room was dominated by the portable litter borne by four of the Star-Admiral's own Khagggun wing. On it lay Olnnn Rydddlin—or, more accurately, what used to be Olnnn Rydddlin.

"Where are the members of his pack?" Stogggul barked. "They are duty-bound to carry their commander."

"None are left," Kinnnus Morcha said.

"What?" The regent blinked. "What did you say?"

"Dead. To a Khagggun. And, as you can see, Olnnn Rydddlin is in a coma." Kinnnus Morcha looked from the regent to Malistra. "You swore this would work, but it has ended in complete disaster. Twenty of my elite pack gone, their lives winked out as if they had never existed."

"Calm yourself, Star-Admiral. Casualties are bound to occur when one engages the enemy."

Kinnnus Morcha was livid. Imagine a Bashkir telling a Khagggun about the consequences of war! With an effort, he controlled his rage. "Unlike you, regent, I take the deaths of my own seriously. I knew them all personally. One hundred percent casualty rate is utterly unacceptable."

"Olnnn Rydddlin still lives," Stogggul observed.

"Is that a joke? It is not a life you or I could tolerate." Kinnnus Morcha watched the Kundalan sorceress stalk the litter as if she were some rough predator.

"This is impossible," she murmured. "Impossible!"

For the first time, Stogggul took a close look at the damage that had been inflicted on Olnnn Rydddlin.

"I warned you," the Star-Admiral said. "This is what comes of putting your faith in alien sorcery."

Since he had no immediate rebuttal, Stogggul ignored him. "N'Luuura, what has happened to his leg? There is nothing but bone. No skin, no flesh, muscle, tendon, vein, or artery."

"I do not know," Malistra said. She was standing over Rydddlin, making peculiar motions with her hands.

"By the looks of him he ought to be dead," Stogggul said.

Kinnnus Morcha glared at him. "He lives, though by what strange grace I cannot say. Even our Genomatekks are mystified."

"Rekkk Hacilar did this," the regent growled.

"No." Malistra was bending over the body. "This is sorcerous work."

Kinnnus Morcha stirred. "Sorcery breeds sorcery! I tell you no good can come of this, regent."

Oh, shut up, you old fool, Stogggul thought. "Can you undo it?" he asked Malistra.

"You misunderstand sorcery, Lord. It can undo nothing." She was sniffing the air around Rydddlin. "But I believe I can heal him." She turned to look at Stogggul. "After a fashion."

He waved a hand. "By all means."

"What do you mean, 'after a fashion'?" Kinnnus Morcha said uneasily.

By way of a warning, Malistra produced a frosty smile. The witch actually seemed to be savoring this, he thought. He despised himself for fearing her.

"The sorcerous necrosis is self-limiting. That is why he still lives. But it is irreversible. I can heal the rest of his body which has undergone first-degree trauma and shock. But I cannot return flesh and blood to the area."

The Star-Admiral felt his flesh crawling. "Meaning?"

"I can ensure he does not die, though I very much doubt

he will be grateful. He will walk again, if you give me permission to do what may be done."

"The outcome!" Kinnnus Morcha shouted, thoroughly agitated.

"Though I can strengthen and protect it, his leg will look precisely as it does now."

"You're not serious." Kinnnus Morcha stared at her. "This leg will be . . . entirely skeletal?"

"It will be as you see it now."

"Absolutely not! I forbid it!"

"On the contrary," Stogggul said. "I order you to proceed."

"What?"

"You heard me, Star-Admiral."

"Regent, lest you forget, Pack-Commander Rydddlin is one of my Khagggun. He is *my* responsibility."

Wennn Stogggul smiled sweetly. "This situation comes under the heading of V'ornn security. He may possess vital information about our enemies."

The Star-Admiral's face darkened in fury. "Clearly, it was a mistake to allow him to be tainted by Kundalan sorcery. If you think I will let him become some kind of freak—"

"If, as you say, he is a loyal Khagggun, then he will do his duty. I say he will be restored, and he will be." Stogggul nodded to Malistra. "Proceed."

Proceed, almost-champion!" Courion cried.

There were twelve large beakers of mead lined up on the scarred wooden table at which they sat.

"You must drink all within five minutes, or I will lose even more coins on you than I already have."

Their table was in a corner in the smoke-and alcohol-laden confines of Blood Tide, a raucous and roguish tavern on the Harborside Promenade favored by the Sarakkon. The low-ceilinged tavern was filled to overflowing with the spectators and participants of the Kalllistotos. Many of them had already approached, clapping Kurgan on the back, offering their congratulations even though he had lost. A fifteen-year-old boy taking on the champion! It did not seem to matter to them that he had lost. Kurgan was dizzy with confusion and pain, but he would not give up playing Courion's curious game. He only wished the Old V'ornn had been here tonight to see him in the finals of the Kalllistotos.

His aching, swollen hand curled around the first beaker, brought it to his lips. He began to drink, downing the contents of each beaker in one long swallow. It was not until he had drained the seventh that he vomited. The thick, sweet mead exploded out of his mouth, then out of his stomachs. As if anticipating this display, Courion had inched backward. Now he laughed uproariously as Kurgan doubled over, puking his guts up.

"Seven!" he cried with the same enthusiasm with which he had heralded Kurgan's entrance into the Kalllistotos. The patrons of Blood Tide burst into a round of applause.

"N'Luuura!" Kurgan wiped his lips. "N'Luuura take it!"

Courion was laughing so hard he shook all over. The applause continued.

"What is happening?" Kurgan asked.

"You made us back all the coins we had lost, and more! You did well, Stogggul! Very well! The current record is nine! Most did not believe you would manage even four!"

Courion clapped him on the back, then hauled him to his feet. "Time for some fresh air, eh?" He laughed again, presenting Kurgan for another round of applause and obscene catcalls as he collected his winnings.

The night was thick with salt and phosphorous. The restless sea, all but invisible in the starless darkness, broke and sucked at the pilings. Courion arched his back and breathed deeply.

"You are a good fighter, Stogggul, brave and clever. You are also a good sport."

Kurgan held his throbbing head as he leaned against the Promenade's railing. He felt like vomiting all over again, but he hurt too much. The endorphins that had protected him were fading along with the adrenaline, leaving him feeling spent as a rotting piece of flotsam.

"Here," Courion said, handing him a lighted laaga stick. "This one is on us."

Nodding his thanks, Kurgan drew the smoke deep into his lung, absorbing it all. The throbbing in his head receded, and the pains in his body became vaguely tolerable. A fist of youths passed, talking animatedly of the blood and violence of the Kalllistotos. A couple, not much older, followed arm in arm, laughing at something so intimate no one else would understand. The vendors were packing up for the night. Not an elderly soul around.

"We thought you were going to cost us a great deal of coinage tonight, Stogggul."

"Sorry about that. I should not have bet what I couldn't afford to lose. I must have been crazy."

"But you have courage to spare, eh?" Courion, standing beside him, was staring out over the Sea of Blood. Pelagic birds with soot-black wings and yellow beaks dipped and swooped, sweeping low across the waves, then rising, looping around as they called into the darkness. "To us it is not surprising, this madness. Cities makes us a little crazy. We feel hemmed in by streets, buildings, crowds. We prefer desolate wastes, clean air, hot sun, and a following wind. We have always equated the trappings of civilization with weakness, illness, decay."

Kurgan was high on leeesta and the knowledge that Courion was speaking to him as an equal.

"I am curious. What is it you love about the Sea of Blood?"

"Oh, it is not just the Sea of Blood, Stogggul. It is all oceans. And not only oceans. The deserts, as well."

"These are dangerous places, so I have heard."

Courion chuckled. "As is the Kalllistotos!"

"At least the Kalllistotos isn't boring."

"Is that your opinion? That the oceans and the deserts of this world are boring?"

"It is."

Courion frowned. "But you have never been to either. From what knowledge have you formed this opinion?"

Kurgan bit his lip. How was it this primitive could make him feel the fool? "Of course you are correct. I have been relying on the opinions of others."

"No, Stogggul. Not opinion. Bias. This is an important distinction. Your race sees no intrinsic value in deep water or shifting dunes, so they disdain both." Courion put his hands together, lacing the tattooed fingers as he leaned easily against the railing. The swell beat against the pilings in hypnotic fashion, as if directed to do so by a great ocean beast. "It is V'ornn hubris. A serious flaw in your makeup that happily works to our advantage."

Kurgan shrugged. "If the Sarakkon want the Sea of Blood and the Great Voorg, I could not care less."

Courion gave him an enormous leer.

"What?" Kurgan said, immediately alert. "What am I missing?"

What am I missing?"

W   Dalma watched Kinnnus Morcha as he paced back and forth inside the tented bedroom, not liking what she saw. She willed herself to be patient, knowing that he would tell her everything in his own time and in his own way.

"This accursed Kundalan sorcery has been wedded to the V'ornn power nexus." He was still in the full battle armor he had donned for his late-night meeting with the regent. "Wennn Stogggul is clearly under the spell of this sorceress. He is relying more and more on her evil spells." His face was white and strained. "N'Luuura, you should have seen Olnnn Rydddlin. You would not believe that anyone could live with . . ." He shook his head. "His leg is bone—bare bone! N'Luuura take it, how does one live with such a horror?" He licked his lips. "Malistra did something to those bones. They can flex but cannot be shattered. They glisten, oiled by her sorcery. They bow and bend as Olnnn Rydddlin walks."

"What of Olnnn Rydddlin?" she asked softly.

"I do not know."

She recognized the sorrow in his expression and felt compassion for him. Of all the lovers she had had, all the masters she had served, only he had wormed his way into her hearts. Some years ago, she had awakened early one morning with his powerful arm draped across her and, unaccountably, had started to shed silent tears. It had taken her some time to discover what his close presence evoked in her. She had felt both safe and content. Without waking him, she had put her hand on his forearm, had twisted her torso enough to kiss him on each eyelid. Then she had closed her eyes, falling almost immediately into a deep sleep.

Her love for him she hoarded, keeping it deep within her core. She knew better than to allow anyone—especially him—access to this potential power over her. Better by far for him to be drawn to the musk of her tender parts, and leave it at that. Wasn't it enough that he owned her with coins? The rest of her needed to remain free of entanglements.

"I do not know," he repeated.

Seeing the sorrow on his face was like looking in a mirror.

"But when I looked into his eyes, Dalma, I saw nothing. Nothing at all."

"You mean he did not know you?"

"Not at all. He knew me; he knew the regent. He was perfectly cogent as he recounted the unutterable tragedy of what had befallen him and his pack. Perhaps too cogent. I cannot help but think that some essential part of him was consumed along with the flesh and sinew of his leg."

"But he, at least, has survived. He must be thankful for that."

I should be thankful I am alive, but I am not. Olnnn Rydddlin sat in the inky darkness of his quarters.

Nothing looked the same; nothing felt the same. Food sickened him; water bloated him. A fierce fire had burned inside him, bright as a nova. Now, all the quarks had been drained from him, leaving nothing but dense black matter.

The Genomatekks had prescribed medicines which he had thrown away, knowing they would be useless. They had counseled him to sleep, but he was no longer able to rest. So he sat in the darkness, alone with his thoughts.

On Corpius Tertius, he had heard a legend of the living dead, explorers unlucky enough to have been caught in the periodic radiation storms that raged across the planet. The radiation did not kill you, so the legend went. Rather, it transformed you into another form of creature—devoid of feeling or emotion. It was as if the radiation destroyed everything that had been of importance inside you, leaving a hulk powered by a radiation-hyped central nervous system. This eerie army of the living dead could not be killed, though Olnnn Rydddlin had often hypothesized that they must want to be.

He had slept only fitfully the night he had been told the legend. Corpius Tertius was infamous for its nights, fifty hours long, colder than N'Luuura. What the V'ornn had been doing there in the first place had never been properly explained to them. They only knew that the Gyrgon were searching for someone or something, and the Khagggun were the grunts doing the heavy spadework. Afterward, a trio of Gyrgon spent less than an hour at the site they had been for months excavating before departing as mysteriously as they had arrived. Soon afterward, the off-world pack was told to gather its gear and strike camp. He had not once seen a member of the living dead, but he had witnessed any number of the radiation storms, spinning through the jagged mountains on the far horizon. He could not help wondering what would have happened if he had been caught in one. Ever since leaving Corpius Tertius, he had an unreasoning dread of those creatures.

Now he had become one.

He forced himself to keep his hands away from the bare bones of his leg. When he had first caught sight of them he had gagged. A terror such as he had never known before had imprisoned him in its icy grip.

Now he had become one.

The living dead. He ought to catch an off-world graveship back to Corpius Tertius so that he could be with his own kind. He started to laugh, but it quickly dissolved into a sob.

Many times that night he considered ending his life—what was left of it. Once, he came very close, the muzzle of the ion cannon a sour taste in his mouth. He had failed the Khagggun under his command—his first and now surely his only pack command. They had trusted him, followed his orders to the letter, and now they were dead. All of them. He could hear them clamoring, the chorus of their voices raised across the gulf between them. Trapped in N'Luuura, they were calling to him to free them. The revenge they craved, the revenge they deserved was in his hands. He knew as long as Rekkk Hacilar and his Kundalan skcettta remained alive he could not take his own life. Making his decision to go on living, he vowed the remainder of his life would have one focus, one purpose: tracking down his mortal enemies and making them pay for what they had done to him.

31

Cusp

A fearful beauty had invaded Rekkk Hacilar. It danced through him like thunder out of bruised cloud, like the thin air at the top of the world, like a snowslide in the dead of winter, like blood tide overrunning Harborside's Promenade, like a school of fish fluttering through skeletal coral.

He felt opened up, sawed in half, his softly pulsing insides exposed to the cosmos. Blood flowed all around him—his blood and her blood. He was as aware of Giyan as he was of the triple beats of his own hearts. It was as if she had entered him on a cellular level. He felt like a mummified artifact, having been held lightless, airless for centuries, suddenly invaded by an army of busy insects pouring over his ruined, pain-racked frame.

Part of him would have given up, preferring the lightless, airless vacuum that sucked even his pain away. But for her. Even at the brink of eternity his love for her survived, swinging through the lightless expanse like the beacon from a lighthouse, illuminating her ministrations, the joyous recognition of a language he could not read yet understood perfectly. The pall of death had been upon him, the chill gossamer membrane that stands between life and death already touching his face, acquainting itself with him, like an old friend, blind now, yet terrifying in its prescience. Not that Rekkk was frightened of death. Far from it. But in the instant he hung, suspended, part of both worlds, part of neither, when the *possibility* of death was made manifest, she had come, illuminated in his mind, and the scent of her would not allow him to cross that membrane.

Cell by cell, he was restored to life, to the world he had known. To the only thing that mattered to him. To her . . .

R ekkk."
      He opened his eyes into a soft dappling of sunlight and shadow. An orange-and-black butterfly flickered across his field of vision. He saw Giyan leaning over him.

"Giyan . . . What happened . . . ? The rest of the pack?"

"Eleana found them on her reconnoiter. They are all dead from multiple stings. Your genetically engineered marcbeetle crawled between the crevices of their battle armor just as you instructed."

"Good." He gave a sigh. "But time is short. It is almost the ides. We must find the Dar Sala-at." But when he tried to move his head he found that he could not.

"You are trussed like a qwawd for the spit." She looked down at him, trying to stifle the awful fear that had blossomed at the moment Nith Sahor had told her that the Tymnos device had been activated. She forced a smile to her face. "You must rest now, or you will be of no use to me or to the Dar Sala-at." He began to protest, but she bent down, putting her moist lips over his. He felt her mouth open, her tongue pushing a soft, wet ball into his mouth. He screwed up his face at the intensely sour taste. "I know, but you must chew it slowly and swallow every bit. It is a combination of Pandanus and mandragora." When he made another face, she laughed. "I spent hours scouring the forest. Now you must do your part to heal yourself."

He tried to answer her, but he lacked the strength. Instead, he slowly began to chew. Soon enough, he drifted off into the sleep Giyan had prescribed for him.

The mandragora wasn't only for Rekkk. Both Giyan and Eleana sipped tea made from boiling the cut-up root. They sat around a fire Eleana had made while gimnopedes, usually diurnal creatures, chased each other through the treetops. Rekkk lay to one side, insensate. Though the night was mild, he was covered with several layers of Khagggun uniforms stripped from the corpses of their enemies. It seemed ironic that a Khagggun helm was serving both as the pot that had brewed the potent medicinal tea and as the vessel from which they drank it. In other circumstances it might even have amused them, but not now, not tonight. It was almost Lonon, the Fifth Season. The Season of Change. When Miina's Five Sacred Dragons returned again through the Cosmos, when the V'ornn had first come.

Neither of them spoke of the dread danger hanging over them like the five gibbous moons; neither of them could. The end of the world was not an easy topic to discuss. Even thinking about it raised their flesh, gave them thrashing nightmares, sent shivers of terror down their spines. And when their eyes met, as they inevitably did, they could see their own fear mirrored in the face of the other.

The fire cracked and sparked, smelling strongly of Marre pine resin. Giyan sat with her blackened arms wrapped tightly around her drawn-up legs, her cheek on her knees. She was staring at Rekkk. An owl hooted in the distance; the river frogs gave voice to their nightly chorus.

Eleana, looking at Rekkk's sleeping form, said, "He loves you very much."

Giyan stirred. "Yes. I know."

"You are right to trust him; he is not like other V'ornn."

"You never knew Eleusis Ashera."

"Perhaps in a way I did. I knew Annon."

Giyan turned her head. "In time, you will forget him."

Tears sprang into the girl's eyes. "In this I know you are wrong."

Giyan picked her head up, suddenly angry. "For your sake, for everyone's, you must forget him."

Giyan got up and, walking to the periphery of the firelight, stared out into the night. Eleana watched her for some time before she followed her. The two females stood side by side. At length, Eleana put her arm around Giyan's waist. They stayed like that for a very long time, listening to the forest breathe around them.

"What happened to your parents?" Giyan said.

"The V'ornn hunted down my mother when I was nine. My father went after them and never returned."

Giyan's arm fell lightly upon her shoulders. "It must have been a terrible loss—your family, your home."

"In truth, I find that I cannot recall their faces. That is the worst part, I think. I dream of them sometimes. Always, they are standing in the distance, at the top of a rise. They wave to me. I strain to see them, but the sun is in my eyes."

Rekkk stirred, moaning a little in his sleep, and both females ran to him. Eleana watched as Giyan passed her hands over his head and chest. She could feel the heat emanating as if from a white-hot coal. Moments later, he drifted off again.

They both gazed up at the night sky as, doubtless, they had done when they were children, filled with awe at the mystery of those stars. Now that mystery had descended from the heavens, had made its home on Kundala, had changed the world, so that tonight, looking up at those same stars, they felt only the drawing near of death, the dreadful chain-rattle of death's appallingly swift approach. But this was another kind of death than the death that comes in the last exhausted exhalation at the end of days or fiercely on the field of battle. It was senseless, this death. The mass obliteration that comes when, unthinkably, an entire world perishes. The idea was too terrible to focus on for long.

"Giyan, would you tell me something about yourself?"

Giyan was relieved to think of other, less consequential matters. For the moment, at least, she had had enough of mystery, the acute peril of walking the world with a pock-etful of secrets. "To begin with, my sister and I are twins."

"I have heard that among your people twins are banished or killed."

Giyan's eyes were made dark by some trick of the fire-light. "The story goes that my mother tried to strangle my sister and me with our own umbilical cords. We were saved by my father's intervention." She circled her hands over Rekkk's wounds. "However, this version was told to us by my father, who by that time had every reason to despise my mother. He left us for Kara, for the new religion. It seemed inconceivable to me, but perhaps he had other reasons to want to get away. Shortly after he left, I heard another version. In it, he was having an affair with the midwife. She made the mistake of threatening him with exposure, and he killed her before she had a chance to tell my mother."

"How awful!" Eleana cried. "But which version is the truth?"

"I have no idea."

"Couldn't you use your sorcery to find out?"

"No," Giyan said abruptly, turning away.

"My apologies. I did not mean to cause you pain."

She looked across the fire at the girl. "Stirring ashes can be a dangerous business. You know that, don't you?"

"Yes. We are taught that at a very early age."

"Why is it dangerous, Eleana?"

"Often, a live coal is hidden at the bottom of the heap. If it is disturbed, it can roll into Marre pine straw or a dried-out log and start a forest fire."

"I have seen the results of forest fires. Devastation," Giyan said. "So, too, with the past."

Later, as they lay down for the night, Eleana said softly, "I am no sorceress, but I know what I know. It matters not what anyone says. Annon will not leave my heart alone."

Giyan turned on her side, away from the girl, and wept for the child she had lost, for the son she knew she would never see again.

Riane, held rigid by the *had-atta*, would not recant the lies she had told Bartta, and for that the *had-atta* would punish her. Instinctively, she tried to Thrip, but nothing happened. The sorcery of the ancient flute must somehow be blocking the power bourns; she could not sense them at all even though she knew they must be there. She raced through *Utmost Source*, desperately searching for a remedy, counterspell, anything that would free her. There was no mention of the *had-atta* in the Sacred Scripture, and now, as the pain hit new peaks, she thought she knew why. The flute was Kyofu, Dark sorcery, about which she did not know enough. She had run out of options.

Bartta lowered the *had-atta* all the way. She had fought to keep silent, but now the agony was too much, and she screamed and kept on screaming. Bartta stood in front of her, tears streaming down her face.

"Please, Riane, tell me the truth," she pleaded. "That is all it will take to end this. The *had-atta* will be removed, and I will love you again. You will have everything I can give you, everything you desire. I promise."

She moved closer. "Confession is good for the soul. Once you start, you will see. And I will prove it to you. I will begin the confession. I will tell you something no one else knows. It would cause the most widespread panic if it became common knowledge."

She whispered into Riane's ear. "Miina is gone, Riane. She has passed from our realm to some other, distant place for which we have no name. Her time has come and gone. We disappointed Her once too often, and She is no more." Bartta was shaking with rage and despair. "How could She do that? What kind of deity abandons Her children? She is no Goddess; She is a monster, unfeeling, uncaring." She stood up, her face shiny with tears. "How was I to carry on in the face of that certain knowledge? How was I to govern the Ramahan, the spiritual leaders of our race? Where were we to go? What were we to do? We had to survive the occupation. No matter the price, we have survived!"

You have survived the Kalllistotos," Courion said, as they walked down the Promenade in Harborside. "Now we will take a boat ride."

"Now? At night?"

Courion ducked under the sea rail. "We are on the cusp of dawn, Stogggul. The time when all fishers set sail."

The Promenade was at last virtually deserted. Here and there, the lights of an all-night tavern like Blood Tide could be seen like an oasis in the desert. The youths were smoking laaga behind a tavern, the lovers had retired to their beds. The drunken Sarakkon slept in stupor.

On the sea side of the rail, Courion turned back to Kurgan. "The time is now, Stogggul. It will not come again."

"I have no love for the sea."

"You V'ornn are deaf, dumb, and blind. What we love about the oceans—why we are drawn to it, feel at home on it—is that sailing we are not allowed to make a single mistake—not one. A mistake, even a small one like misjudging the wind or the tide, could cause a boat to capsize and all aboard to drown. On the oceans there is no place to hide from others or oneself. We have no other choice but to come face-to-face with ourselves. It is the confrontation, you see, Stogggul, more difficult by far than being a cog in a phalanx, doing battle with an alien race. In cities, among teeming millions, it is all too easy to lose one's self, to hide one's true nature in cacophony. So we love the starkness of the seas—and the deserts—which offer us limitless possibilities. But not you, Stogggul. In this you are sadly like the rest of your kind."

Kurgan, stung to action, ducked down, joining the Sarakkon just as he stepped out into the darkness. Kurgan watched him disappear, heard the thud of him landing on what he surmised was the deck of a boat. *In this you are like all V'ornn.* He took the leap himself.

His knees flexed as his boot soles struck the wooden deck. It was a longer drop than he had imagined. He felt the shock all the way up his spine. The deck swayed back and forth, creating an unsettling rhythm inside him. He stumbled a little as the boat pitched, and Courion steadied him with an iron grip.

"You will come upon your sea legs soon enough," Courion said as he cast off lines. The boat began to move, by what means of locomotion Kurgan could not determine. At midships, he held the top rail in a deathlike grip. As the swells struck the boat's hull, he felt his stomachs lurch. He looked back longingly at the Promenade, whose sturdy bulk moved farther away with each triple beat of his hearts.

He turned to the loud crack and ripple of monofilament canvas; the triangular persimmon-colored sail had been deployed, and a second one was on its way. The canvas filled, and the boat shot ahead. They were on the Sea of Blood.

He saw Courion laughing at him as the Sarakkon took the wheel. Gritting his teeth, he made his laborious way toward him, hand over hand like a rock climber negotiating a sheer cliff.

"Courion, why do you mock me?"

"Better to mock you than to ignore you, eh, pip-squeak?"

Courion clapped him on the back, a gesture that sent splinters of pain through him.

"You mock me because your knowledge is superior to mine."

"I have had more years amassing that knowledge. How far have you ever traveled from Axis Tyr, eh? I have been to many places on Kundala, made many friends."

"Resistance friends?"

"Eh? What interest would I have in the Kundalan resistance?"

"It seems to me that they would pay top coin for some of your black-market goods."

"Now you impugn my good name. I do not deal in black-market goods." Courion offered a sly smile. "But were I of such a black heart, I would have more than enough business without getting involved with the resistance. In any case, their cause is futile, isn't it? Your kind is seeing to that. My clients stay around to pay for their orders. They do not wind up spitted by a shock-sword."

"And what of the Druuge?"

Courion cocked his head. "Are you pumping us for information, Stogggul? What is your angle?"

"I gather information wherever I can. That is my stock-in-trade. My coinage."

"I understand."

"And the Druuge?"

The Sarakkon stared at him for some time. "We could make inquiries if the price was right."

"I will keep your offer in mind." There was something the Sarakkon was not telling him, he could feel it. For the moment, though, he sensed it would be unwise to press him.

A swell washed over the port bow, flooding the deck. Kurgan tried to move out of the way.

"There is no escaping it," Courion said. "Do not waste your time trying."

Kurgan stood his ground, his eyes locked with the big Sarakkon's, as the seawater inundated his boots. They were, by this time, quite a distance from shore. It had become a clear night. Far off to starboard, he could see the light that marked the southerly edge of the promontory known to the Kundalan as Suspended Skull. Beyond, was the Illuminated Sea. The stars shone down through the ether with a diamondlike ferocity, bathing them in cool blue light.

Looking forward, he could see movement in the open hatchway midships. Someone else was on board. Courion, cocking an ear to a familiar sound, smiled. "Our people have an ancient saying, Stogggul. 'When your fate approaches, walk swiftly toward it.' " He nodded as the figure emerged from belowdecks into the starlight.

It was the Bashkir, the champion of the Kalllistotos who had beaten Kurgan senseless, except he had no bruises on his face, no swelling or cuts—no marks at all. "What is this, Courion?" Kurgan said, suddenly tense and wary. "Do you imagine I will take part in a private match for your amusement?"

Courion watched him carefully out of enigmatic eyes. "He fears you," he said to the huge Bashkir who now stood beside him.

"Excellent," the Bashkir said. "He *should* fear me."

He was right. Kurgan watched in utter disbelief as the Bashkir began to morph, and morphing, grew even taller. The exoskeleton of his black-alloy suit refracted the starlight like a prism. His pale amber skull and neck were studded with tertium and germanium circuitry. In this light, they could have passed for some of Courion's tattoos. His black eyes had pupils the color of rubies. At the point of each cheekbone was implanted a tertium neural-net stud.

"What the N'Luuura is this?" Kurgan, alarmed, backed up a pace.

"I am Nith Batoxxx," the Gyrgon said. "You gave me a good fight, a nasty fight, an insightful fight. In return, I gave you an invaluable lesson, did I not?"

"I don't . . ." Kurgan tried to swallow but his mouth seemed to have gone dry.

"He is slow?" Nith Batoxxx said. "You neglected to report this."

"Not slow," Courion said, coming to Kurgan's defense, and possibly his own. "Simply stunned by your appearance."

"Ah, yes." Nith Batoxxx nodded. "I was wise to have elicited your expertise. I find the outside world"—his head turned from side to side—"psychically toxic."

His far-reaching gaze returned to Kurgan. Those ruby-colored pupils were unsettling, to say the least. Kurgan decided his best course of action was to ignore them; he was determined that intimidation was one weapon the Gyrgon would find useless on him.

"What is it you want from me?" he shouted into the gusting wind.

"Your fealty," Nith Batoxxx said without preamble.

Kurgan glanced over at Courion. "Is this some kind of Sarakkonian joke?"

"Your fealty." The Gyrgon took a step toward him. He seemed entirely oblivious to the rolling deck.

"No one owns me," Kurgan declared. "Not you; not any-one."

The Gyrgon stopped in his tracks. "What does one make of such ignorance?"

"Arrogance, Nith Batoxxx." Courion shrugged. "We told you."

"Yes, you did." Oddly, the Gyrgon appeared pleased. He addressed Kurgan. "Sooner or later, everyone is *owned*. By someone or something, it matters not. You are no exception. You are owned by your ambition."

Kurgan said nothing. He ground his teeth and glared at Courion, hating him for entrapping him. "You are Gyrgon," he said. "What need have you for me?"

"That is none of your concern."

"On the contrary," Kurgan said. "If you mean to take away my freedom, I would know the reason why."

"You who have been Summoned do not dictate the terms of the Summoning." Nith Batoxxx's arms unfolded like sails. The ion grids in his gloves began to spark and snap. "If you do not swear fealty to me, I will kill you here, now, without a moment's hesitation, and Courion will find me another more compliant than you."

Kurgan knew enough about Gyrgon to believe him.

"Courion will provide support," Nith Batoxxx continued. "Should you have need of other requirements, you will con-tact me. I will set your okummmon to a frequency only I can hear."

The Gyrgon loomed before him. "Now choose."

Imprisonment or death, Kurgan thought. There *must* be another way. One of the first lessons the Old V'ornn had taught him was to think your way out of—

"Enough! Your time is at an end!" The Gyrgon raised his ion-bound fist.

Kurgan bowed his head. "I swear fealty to you, Nith Batoxxx."

"Let me see your eyes." The Gyrgon looked down at him with an incomprehensible expression. "You will repeat this oath, Stogggul Kurgan: 'In blood, I swear my life to you.' " He waited while Kurgan repeated the first part of the oath. " 'In blood, I swear your goals are my goals.' " Kurgan repeated it. " 'In blood, I swear to carry out that which you may command of me.' " Kurgan repeated it. " 'In blood, I swear that if I fail this oath, my life will be your property to do with as you will.' " Kurgan hesitated only an instant before repeating the end of the oath.

While Nith Batoxxx used a surgically precise ion beam to slice through the skin of his palm, Courion broke out a syrupy liquor Kurgan had never seen before. It smelled of clove oil and burnt musk. Taking his hand, the Gyrgon let his blood run into the crystal cups. Then they drank. It was as black as coal tar and nearly as unpalatable. It had a fiery kick, though. They raised their empty cups and threw them into the deep water, sealing their pact.

Nith Batoxxx began the alteration on Kurgan's okommmon.

"Will you tell me now why you have recruited me?"

Nith Batoxxx shrugged. "I have an enemy—Nith Sahor. I have suspected for some time that he is a renegade, a dangerous dissident following his own mysterious agenda. He has lately gathered to his bosom a small group of followers. You know Rekkk Hacilar?"

There was some pain in his arm, deep, swift, dark. "Of course. He is allied with this other Gyrgon?"

Nith Batoxxx inclined his head. "Along with two Kundalan females, one of whom is purportedly a sorceress."

Giyan, Kurgan thought.

"As I say, I am unused to life outside of the Temple of Mnemonics. I require the eyes and ears and hands of a clever V'ornn, an ambitious V'ornn, an unscrupulous V'ornn."

"Courion told you I am all these things?"

"Never mind what Courion told me," Nith Batoxxx said

shortly. "All you need to know is that you will benefit greatly from this alliance."

If it got him closer to the Gyrgon, he would willingly do Nith Batoxxx's bidding, Kurgan thought. But only so long as it also served his own purposes. Right now he was determined to get his first kilo of flesh from the new alliance. "There is someone in Star-Admiral Morcha's employ who has informed on me," he said. "I would know the identity of this skcettta."

"You need to consult a seer."

"I am asking you. It is a simple request."

"I care not for your tone—or the implications of your words."

"I assure you I had no hidden meaning in mind. We have just consummated an alliance, after all." He touched the still-painful okummmon on his arm. "I think I have shown my good faith. As a gesture on your part, I would have thought—"

Nith Batoxxx stood up, his task completed. "Ask the owner of Blood Tide. I believe she can provide the answer you seek."

"Thank you, Nith Batoxxx." Kurgan nodded, flexing the stiff muscles of his forearm as the Gyrgon disappeared below. Courion was leaning against the aft rail, smoking laaga, that enigmatic smile pasted on his face. His tattooed fingers turned the wheel.

The sea had quieted. The boat was swiftly tacking to take advantage of the change in the wind. Kurgan, drawing a deep breath, saw in the slender pink arm thrown across the eastern horizon the cusp of dawn.

The flute was about to come apart. Riane could sense the fractures beginning to form inside the *had-atta*, could actually see them in some part of her mind she never knew existed. It was like looking into a storeroom full of mirrors all reflecting back the same image from different angles. Another part of her mind held the terrifying memory of Astar's insides blown apart as the *had-atta* shattered into ten thousand shards.

She ceased to scream. She shut off the terrors that scattered her thoughts. The V'ornn in her redoubled its will, finding a calm center in the swirl of horror forming all around her. *Think, Riane. Think.*

Mother trusted that we would know how to remove the spell of protection from The Book of Recantation. *We have the knowledge.*

Think, Riane. Think.

The *had-atta* was not mentioned in *Utmost Source.* Where had it come from, then?

The Book of Recantation.

It had not been mentioned in the sections of the book she had managed to memorize before Bartta approached. It must be in one of the protected sections! Riane formed a mental picture of those blank pages.

The first crack appeared, spearing outward from the flute's core, weakening its glassy surface.

Her heart beating fast, Riane concentrated on the image of those blank pages. She considered the Old Tongue passages visible before and after the blank pages. Nothing there. A wave of despair gripped her. She was going in circles.

Another crack formed, this time on the opposite side. Not much time left before the *had-atta* split asunder.

But the V'ornn inside of her would not let her give up. And all at once a thought popped into her head. Mother had told her that *Utmost Source* was far older than this book, that Venca was the Root language of the Old Tongue. *It is a language of pure sorcery*, Mother had said.

Pure sorcery.

It was becoming increasingly difficult to wall her mind off from the terrible pain the flute was inflicting on her. The first shard dug into her throat, making her gag. She tasted her own blood.

She made herself look at the images of those blank pages as she recited the Venca alphabet, and she saw it forming very faintly—the word-web of the protective spell. There were spaces in between the web of words. Intuitively, she chose the letters, formed the words that would fit into those spaces, chanted the words in her mind, saw the spaces filled in, the whole appear, moving off the pages, forming a star-shaped sphere that rotated and pulsed with sorcerous energy.

The Star of Evermore.

It was an Eye Window spell, she knew it as certainly as she knew anything. It was the spell that could free Mother.

She took the Star of Evermore and sent it into Ayame, into Otherwhere, toward Mother. Would it work? There were only seconds left for her to find out.

And then time ran out.

With a terrible roar, the *had-atta* shattered inside her.

She felt ten thousand shards begin to rip her to shreds. And then nothing. Nothing at all. She could not move, could not even blink. Her heart had ceased to beat, her blood lay stagnant in her veins. The shards of the flute, pulling apart from the whole, were stopped. Her mind, at least, remained working. She saw Bartta frozen in the act of reaching for her, her face a mask of anguish. Who knew what had been going through her mind at the moment Time ceased to flow? Did she feel pain, remorse, loss? Was she capable of feeling love or even compassion? How could she be if she had been willing to subject Riane to the *had-atta*?

As these thoughts ran through her head, Mother materialized in the chamber. She had Thripped out of her prison! She was free!

She smiled at Riane, put a forefinger across her lips as if Riane could make a sound. She passed Bartta like a moon-shadow stealing across a forest glade. Mounting the plinth, she whispered in Riane's ear, "I bow to the Dar Sala-at. Only she could have broken the spell that had bound me for more than a century. I told you you were an Eye Window sorcer-ess. Thank you."

As she grasped the fracturing flute, her expression changed. "Courage, now. You must relax your inner mus-cles." She placed her hand lightly on Riane's shoulder. "I know you think you cannot move, but I assure you that you can. I have made it so. So relax now, my warrior. Relax."

Slowly, she began to pull the *had-atta* out of Riane's esophagus. Because it was now barbed with the shards in the process of exploding outward, it was as if Riane had swallowed a porcupine. Pain exploded from the inside out. Her diaphragm contracted, and she made a mewling sound. Her eyes grew big, and sweat broke out all over her face and body. Mother stopped, repeating her direction for Riane to relax. She resumed withdrawing the *had-atta*.

Riane felt the excoriating scraping, the quick, hot flow of blood inside her, tasting its sweetish tang. Thinking of it, she began to tremble, and Mother stopped once more, waiting. Riane steeled herself, willing her muscles to relax. She closed her eyes, but tears leaked out anyway. The pain just built and built until she let it all go with a sigh. The partially exploded *had-atta*, glistening with her blood, emerged still in its sorcerous stasis.

Mother had unstrapped her. Now she caught her as she toppled out of the chair, gathering her into her massive arms. As she crossed the cubicle, she lifted one torch out of its holder and threw it onto the ancient device. In a moment, flames began to lick upward, beginning to devour the chair and its plinth. The flute itself hung suspended, dripping blood onto Bartta's frozen feet. Even through her pain, Riane could feel the stasis of Time, as if she and Mother were wading through a viscous fluid that pulled and sucked at their limbs like quicksand. Every time she breathed in it felt as if she had inhaled a fistful of ice. Everything moved in such slow motion she could no longer be certain of where she was or what was happening. It was like living in dreamtime, where nothing followed the logical laws of the known universe.

Gradually, she became aware that the walls, floor, ceiling of the room were expanding, breaking up into their subatomic parts. Just before everything deliquesced into the Great River of Space-Time, she twisted her head, looking back at her prison. She saw Time resuming its flow, the shards of the *had-atta* exploding. She saw Bartta with her arms crossed over her face. She saw tongues of flames bright-hot and sin-

THE RING OF FIVE DRAGONS   531

uous, voraciously consuming the device of torture.

And then they were gone.

E leana woke up screaming. Instantly, Giyan was crouched
   at her side, holding her.

"What is it?" She drew Eleana's sweat-slick hair back
from her damp face. "A nightmare?"

"I dreamed of death. Bloody death."

Annihilation dreams, Giyan thought. *We can no longer
escape our terror of the death that rides herd on us.*

She put her hand against the girl's cheek. "Get some rest."
She sniffed the cool mountain air, settled her thick robes
more closely around herself. "By tomorrow Rekkk will be
able to travel. We will find the Dar Sala-at. You must believe
that."

Eleana nodded.

Giyan smiled down at her and rose. She was halfway back
to her pallet next to Rekkk's when she heard the girl's voice
and turned back.

"Giyan, I am frightened."

Kneeling again beside her, Giyan took her hand. "We are
all frightened, my dear. But it was just a nightmare, nothing
more."

"You don't understand."

"Ah, my dear, you have so much courage—"

"Not for this." Eleana's eyes flicked away and then returned to Giyan's beautiful face. "I fear that I am with child."

"Those sudden dizzy spells. I knew something was amiss."
Giyan moved closer. "Who is the father?"

"I am thinking it must have happened that day when I was
bathing in the river, when I first met Annon." She waited for
a moment, searching Giyan's eyes. "He did not tell you."

Giyan shook her head.

"He was hunting with his friend—the one with the colorless eyes and the cruel mouth."

"Kurgan."

Eleana repeated the name as if it was food she had never
tasted before. "I was foolish, bathing in the river so close to

V'ornn habitation. But my mission was complete; I had made sure there were no Khagggun packs about. I let down my guard, but only for a moment. Hidden in the copse of sysal trees, they must have been watching me. Annon's friend leaped on me. Annon tried to stop him, and he would have, but then the oddest thing happened. The largest gyreagle I have ever seen appeared from nowhere and attacked Annon.

"While he lay unconscious his friend . . . raped me." She stared up at Giyan. "Several weeks ago I started getting the dizzy spells. At first, I thought nothing of it, a slight inner ear infection—I have had them before. But when they started to come more frequently I began to consider other causes. Still, it was confusing. I had shared Dammi's bed a number of times. But if I was pregnant with his child, I would already be showing a bulge. But, look. My belly is as flat as ever. I know I am not ill. I can feel the baby stirring like a thought or the memory of a dream."

Giyan put her hand on Eleana's belly. "Your intuition is correct." She fought back her dismay. "A fetus that is half-V'ornn will not show for many more weeks, but when it does you will be near to giving birth."

Eleana was wide-eyed. "How do you know this?"

"Many of the females in my village were raped by Khagggun. Some were impregnated. As you know, Ramahan are healers. The young ones were enlisted to help with the pregnancies." This was the truth as far as it went. It was not, of course, the whole truth. No one must ever know that she herself had been pregnant with a V'ornn's child just as Eleana was now. The poignancy of the situation did not escape her.

"It will come out before a Kundalan baby would," she continued, "but its growth in the first days, weeks, months, the first year is astronomical by our standards." She covered the girl's nakedness. "My dear, why didn't you tell us before?"

"You and Rekkk were counting on me. I did not want to give you any cause for concern. I did not want you looking out for me while we were fighting for our lives."

THE RING OF FIVE DRAGONS

"Admirable, but foolish."

"Also"—she looked away for a moment—"I did not know whether I could trust Rekkk with this information. I have seen the V'ornn with their collection bins, combing the countryside for what they mockingly call the 'spoilage of war.' "

"The V'ornn will never take your baby," Giyan said fiercely. "This I promise you."

"Your offer of protection moves me greatly, but . . ." Eleana put her head in her hands, raking her fingers through her hair. "I have been thinking. This nightmare—I had tonight. . . . I am afraid I know its meaning." She looked up suddenly. "The V'ornn—Kurgan—who raped me was hateful. It will be his offspring. I do not want this baby."

"But it is also yours." She put her hands on Eleana's shoulders. "Eleana, I beg you not to punish this unborn child for the sin his father committed. This is an innocent we speak of. It has no advocate to protect it but you. Its life is in your hands."

Eleana's eyes were beseeching. "I am afraid that every time I look at it I will see the father. I want my revenge for what he did to me."

"Your anger is understandable, but let me ask you a question. What if, when it is born, you see yourself. Don't you have faith that will happen? Don't you have confidence that you will teach this child to be better than his father is? Isn't *that* the best revenge you could take against Kurgan?"

Eleana was shivering, and Giyan held her to her breast and rocked her.

"I am afraid. I am so very afraid. This is not what I want, not what I had dreamed about. It was Annon's child I wanted."

"Fate often takes us down strange paths, Eleana. Our task is to be prepared, so that we may better understand who we are and where we are going."

Eleana began to weep.

"Ah, my dear."

"Giyan," Eleana whispered, "am I foolish to fret over my own life when the fate of all of Kundala lies in the balance?"

"With each breath we take," Giyan said softly, "life goes on. It is our nature, a survival instinct. It cannot be otherwise."

Eleana considered this for a moment. "What if I am headed down the wrong path?"

"Ah, my dear, who among us is wise enough to make that determination? It seems that just when we near the end of our journey another path appears and takes us in a different and unexpected direction. At the beginning of each journey there is a fork in the path. Which fork to take? Often, your heart says one thing and your mind says another." She was thinking of her own life, now, as well as of Eleana's. Were they so very different? She thought not. In this teenage girl, she saw stirring echoes of herself. "Tell me, Eleana, at this moment, what does your heart tell you?"

Eleana turned her head away and made no sound. Giyan released her into the night, and she rose, walking a little away from the crack and spark of the firelight. She stood for some time, looking out at the blesson firs. Four moons rode in the sky, the thinnest sliver of the fifth just visible above the ice-clad peaks of the Djenn Marre. Midnight had marked the beginning of Lonon, the Season of Change.

"Giyan?" The girl's voice seemed lonely as an owl's call.

She gathered her legs under her and went to where Eleana stood. She said nothing. She felt the other trembling slightly and fought the urge to put her arm around her. She had spoken her piece; she knew better than to force the issue.

"If I decide to abort the baby, will you try to stop me?"

Giyan cursed the evil circumstances that forced children to become adults before their time. Her heart went out to Eleana. She had been robbed of something so precious and unique it could never be ransomed or retrieved. But, on the other hand, she saw the possibilities that Eleana could not. Having given birth to a son who was half-Kundalan and half-V'ornn, she already had a sense of the future. In her mind, Annon had exhibited the best traits of both races. He had been growing into a warrior who questioned everything, who looked at the Djenn Marre with longing, who could put an

arrow through an ice-hare at twenty meters, but could feel
the pain of the Kundalan. She bit her tongue. She could say
nothing of this. But, on the other hand, her Gift revealed to
her all the words, emotions, thoughts in the night air, a depth,
perhaps, that other might call the future—or, at the very
least, *a* future that carried with it what resided in the sanctuary of her heart: love, trust, hope. Important ideals, profound ones, she knew she had passed on to her son. Would
Eleana do less? She did not think so.

"If you decide to abort the baby," she said, choosing each
word carefully, "my energies will go toward keeping you
safe."

Eleana said nothing. She remained as she had been, trembling a little, staring at the fork in the path that lay before
her.

"You are a warrior, Eleana."

"Come to that, so are we both." She turned to Giyan. "This
battle has delayed us long enough. We must make all haste
to Stone Border." She pointed off to the northwest. "Just over
the next ridge is the village of Joining The Valleys. We can
purchase cthauros there from a blacksmith I know."

Giyan recognized the longing and the sorrow in her eyes,
and kissed her gently on each cheek.

32

Four and Twenty Gimnopedes

Have you come to arrest me?" Bach Ourrros said
when Wing-General Nefff appeared on his doorstep.
He was wearing a blue-and-yellow swirl-patterned
robe Wing-General Nefff found more than a trifle effete.

"Not a bit of it," Wing-General Nefff said politely. "May
I come in?"

It was twilight. Lights were coming on all over Axis Tyr. The city was astir as the end of one tour of duty overlapped with another. Bach Ourrros, looking over the Wing-General's broad shoulder, saw plenty of Khagggun marching in twos and threes, but none of them appeared in the least bit interested in him.

"You are alone, Wing-General?"

Nefff raised his arms and let them drop. "Entirely."

Taking one last visual reconnoiter of the wide, well-traveled street, Bach Ourrros nodded and stepped aside. They entered a large room that looked out over an interior courtyard recently planted with ammonwood saplings, fairylace ferns, and flowers. A clemett tree, its fruit just beginning to ripen, had been given center stage. All the window-doors had been thrown open, and the room was redolent with the smell of the thickly clustered fruit.

"You will forgive my distrust," Bach Ourrros said, "but when one sees the head of one's best friend on a pike in front of the regent's palace day after day, it is natural to have qualms about any Khagggun."

"Perfectly understandable." Nefff nodded his thanks as Ourrros handed him a drink, and took the opportunity to look around. The Ourrros Consortium was in the first rank of the wealthy Bashkir, and the residence reflected it. Expensive furniture on fine V'ornn rugs was interspersed with even more expensive artwork, some of it off-world and imported at great expense. Antique vases appeared to be Ourrros' passion. A squad of them resided in a large scrollworked ammonwood cabinet fitted with V'ornn crystal doors. In all, it was a peaceful space; one perhaps more suited to an artist than a high-powered Bashkir bent on landing the next deal. "Quite a residence you have here."

Bach Ourrros said nothing. He was watching Nefff with hooded eyes.

Having made his circumnavigation of the living room the Wing-General turned back to Ourrros and smiled. "I imagine you are anxious to know what brings me here."

"That would be an understatement," Ourrros said dryly.

"Quite." Nefff radiated a regulation smile, which merely tugged at the corners of his mouth. "This is rather awkward." Ourrros made no comment. Nefff cleared his throat. "To be frank, the regent sent me. He felt if he came himself—or if he summoned you—you might naturally jump to the wrong conclusion."

"Naturally."

The tight smile tightened further. "The regent regrets the . . . incident over dinner."

"Is that what he calls it? My friend was shot to death by his son."

"That was regrettable. Kurgan Stogggul is hotheaded, unpredictable, which is why he was transferred to the Star-Admiral's command in the first place."

"Forgive my bluntness, Wing-General, but it appears that Kinnnus Morcha has his work cut out for him."

That brought a more natural smile to Nefff's face. "It does seem as if he has his hands full." He set his empty glass down on a side table. "In any event, considering Kefffir Gutttin's hotheaded nature, the regent feels that in the long run you might be better off severed from the relationship."

"Severed? Is that some form of sick jest?"

For the first time, Nefff seemed on the defensive. "Forgive me, my choice of words was unfortunate. I assure you that it is the regent's wish to make up for the unpleasantness."

"If the regent is truly sincere, he can prove it by allowing the construction of Za Hara-at to continue."

"As it happens, that is just the topic he wishes to talk to you about. Shall we say at the twentieth hour? You will be escorted to the regent's private quarters."

Bach Ourrros nodded. "Considering the tenor of the times, I trust the regent will not take it amiss if my bodyguard accompanies me."

"This is a full-scale truce," Nefff said. "However, if you feel the need to exercise a measured amount of caution, by all means feel free to do so."

*   *   *

Just after the twentieth hour, Bach Ourrros and a forbidding-looking bodyguard presented themselves at the front gates of the regent's palace. Ourrros noted with curiosity and interest that his friend's black and withered head was gone and with it the Khagggun pike upon which it had been displayed. Wing-General Nefff himself appeared shortly after he had given his name to the Haaar-kyut on duty.

"I am gratified you have come," he said conversationally as he guided them through the labyrinthine depths of the palace's first floor. "Being aware of the long-standing enmity between your Consortium and the regent's made my visit earlier somewhat awkward. Nevertheless, when a time for change comes one must be ready, eh?" He led the two V'ornn past three more sets of Haaar-kyut guards, then up the massive and ornate Central Staircase to the second floor and down the corridor. At a set of carved heartwood doors, he stopped and rapped with his knuckles, then opened the doors inward and stepped aside. "I wish you good fortune," he said, and disappeared around a corner.

For a moment, Bach Ourrros stood still in front of the open doorway. All at once, as if a cold wind had passed over him, he felt exposed and vulnerable.

"I do not expect trouble," he muttered over his shoulder to his bodyguard, "but you must be prepared for anything."

The regent Stogggul was in a jovial mood when Bach Ourrros and his bodyguard entered the residential suite. In truth, this was the first time Ourrros had ever seen the regent's private quarters, and he could not fail to be impressed. The lavish artwork, which Stogggul for the most part ignored, was what interested him most.

"Ah, Bach Ourrros," Stogggul cried, leaping to his feet, "I thought you would appreciate viewing the treasure trove here in the residence ring!" He ignored the bodyguard, who shadowed Ourrros two paces behind.

"I deem it a great honor, regent." As Ourrros made his rounds, pausing to admire statuary here, a magnificent textile there, he became aware that Dalma was nowhere in evidence.

Neither was any member of the regent's personal guard, though their shadows could be seen now and again as they patrolled the corridor. Only a young servant boy stood stiffly by a low carved heartwood table, laden with platters of fragrant foodstuffs, carafes of wine and fire-grade numaaadis. Ourrros found Dalma's absence mystifying. Ever since Wennn Stogggul had seduced her away from him, the regent had used her constant presence as silicon to rub into the wound he had inflicted on Ourrros' pride.

Stogggul stood in the center of the room, waiting patiently for Ourrros to complete his examination. A gentle wind entered the suite through the open window-doors, where the stones of the balcony glowed in the dusky, flickering light of filigreed Kundalan lanterns. The room was filled with the sweet tremolo of the gimnopedes' mating song.

"A marvelous collection withal!" Ourrros declared. "I commend you, regent. Your rooms are a veritable museum of priceless artwork."

Stogggul spread wide his arms. "Is there a piece that moves you above the others?"

"Well . . ."

"Come, come. You must have a favorite."

"Well, as a matter of fact I do." Bach Ourrros pointed to an alabaster vase so thin it seemed spun out of membrane. "That VII Dynasty Nieobian prayer vase is utterly magnificent."

Stogggul cocked his head to one side. "Do you really think so?"

"Oh, yes. Quite remarkable. I would give anything to own such a specimen of—"

"Take it, then. It is yours."

"What?"

Stogggul snapped his fingers, and the servant boy sprang to life. Taking the precious vase off its lighted stand, he held it out to the stunned Bashkir.

"Oh, no, regent. I couldn't."

"Why not? You want it; I want to give it to you. What could be simpler?"

Still Ourrros made no move. Stogggul signed to the boy, who set the vase down on the floor at one corner of the table.

"Please sit," Stogggul said. "The vase will be at your left hand during supper. You must get used to having it close to you."

The three V'ornn sat on the oversized jewel-tone cushions piled around the low table, Ourrros beside the Nieobian vase, his bodyguard at his right hand, the regent opposite.

"I have taken the liberty of setting the meal as the northern Kundalan tribes of the Korrush would eat," the regent said, as the boy poured wine and liquor into matching crystal goblets. "My kitchen staff has prepared an authentic meal. I hope you like slingbok stew."

Bach Ourrros looked over the field of unfamiliar dishes. "I must admit I have never had it."

"Neither have I," the regent confided as he gestured at the platters. "But were we camped outside of the Za Hara-at construction site, I am assured by reliable sources that we would be eating slingbok stew and gimnopede pie."

At the mention of Za Hara-at, Bach Ourrros stiffened. He held the goblet of fire-grade numaaadis the boy had put into his hand, but made no attempt to drink.

"Come, come," the regent said again, "we must endeavor to put the unpleasantness of the past behind us." He hoisted his own goblet. "This is a new day, Bach Ourrros. A new era. Let us toast Za Hara-at."

Ourrros was still far from comfortable with the regent's newfound bonhomie. "I notice Dalma is not at your side tonight."

"Nor will she be tomorrow or the night after." Stogggul bent forward, lowering his voice in a conspiratorial whisper. "I will tell you a secret. She is with Star-Admiral Kinnnus Morcha. The rogue has seduced her away."

Bach Ourrros' mouth twitched. "I would offer my condolences, regent, but I cannot bring myself to it."

"No. I suppose not." Stogggul sat back. "Well, we are in the same hoverpod now, aren't we, whether we like it or not."

Ourrros grunted, mollified to some degree that the regent had gotten what he deserved, at least as far as Dalma was concerned. "So tell me, why should we be toasting Za Hara-at? The last I heard, you had forbidden the construction to go forward."

"That is all in the past." The regent lifted his goblet again. "As I said, this is a new day, a new era. My wish is for Za Hara-at to be completed."

Bach Ourrros grunted. His expression made it clear he did not believe what he was hearing.

"You see, I have been thinking long and hard on the merits of such a city, and it occurs to me that there is a fortune waiting to be made there."

"So you see the value in such a trading city," Bach Ourrros said tentatively. "That was why Kefffir Gutttin, Hadinnn SaTrryn, and I asked Eleusis Ashera if we could help finance it in the first place. Even using Kundalan slave labor, we knew the city was too expensive for one Consortium—even the Ashera—to fund on its own. As first partners, we stand to reap the highest percentage of reward in negotiating fees, rents, services, and so on."

"Now, regrettably, Kefffir Gutttin is no longer with us."

"His Consortium survives, regent."

"Not for long. His disgrace has destroyed his business."

"Then I will offer aid."

"Do you really think that is wise?"

Ourrros looked from the regent's face to the magnificent Nieobian vase at his left elbow.

"He was my friend, regent. What else can I do?"

"Move on." Stogggul put his elbows on the table. "Use your resources to help build Za Hara-at. With me as your new partner."

"You?"

"Together, as partners, our Consortia make a formidable trading bloc. Formidable enough so that the Ashera Consortium will not fight our involvement in Za Hara-at no matter how distasteful my presence may be to them." The regent clinked the rim of his goblet against Ourrros'. "So. Let us start afresh. What do you say?"

"I cannot forget what you did to Kefffir Gutttin."

"Another lifetime. But still. What can I do to prove my intent? Shall I punish the perpetrator?"

"Kurgan Stogggul is your son."

"Sons can be punished, just like all the rest of us." He pursed his lips. "Tell me, Bach Ourrros, is that your wish? If so, it shall be carried out at once."

"I am not like the Gyrgon. I do not mete out revenge by proxy."

"Then let us this night forget all about revenge. Let us eat our slingbok stew and our gimnopede pie while we imagine ourselves on the Korrush. Let us talk of the future and of Za Hara-at."

Grudgingly, Bach Ourrros brought the goblet to his lips, but he did not drink until the regent had swallowed his first sip. "Excellent numaaadis," he said, his eyes watering with the trail of fire down his throat.

The regent nodded, gestured to the boy, who had been standing silently by, to begin serving. The boy spooned out the spicy slingbok stew into copper bowls, cut the huge gimnopede pie into thick wedges, serving them first to Ourrros, then Stogggul. When he brought food to the bodyguard, however, he refused.

"Do not take offense, regent," Ourrros said. "He does not eat or drink on the job."

"It is his loss," Stogggul said, glancing at the servant. The boy took away the food, setting it down on a side table behind the bodyguard. He remained there, motionless, silent as the statues that ringed the room.

"How do you like the Korrush food?" the regent asked as he spooned up some stew, then ate a large triangle of the pie.

"Both dishes are delicious," Ourrros said. "I do not think I have ever tasted anything like them. The gimnopede pie is especially savory."

"I imagine we would do well to get used to this food. What do you say?"

Bach Ourrros knew what Stogggul really meant. He considered a moment before speaking. He could, of course, say nothing or turn the conversation to another topic, but his desire to see the regent's reaction was overpowering.

"Even though you have shut down construction as I ordered." Wennn Stogggul said, "there is the huge Mesagggun work detail to consider, along with the materials that have already been bought on credit. The Gutttin Consortium currently stands in default of their payments." He wiped his lips. "As I understand it, under the terms of the agreement, they must now bow out of the project. The SaTrryn Consortium has the leverage to come up with the additional capital, but you, I fear, do not." He smiled. "Sornnn SaTrryn has informed me that he is unwilling to commit more capital at this time. That is where the Stogggul Consortium comes in. We are ready, willing, and able to provide the sum needed in exchange for first-partner status."

"I, too, have been informed of Sornnn SaTrryn's unfortunate decision," Bach Ourrros said. "I have made arrangements with my bank for a loan that will cover the required sum." He smiled. "I am sorry to disappoint you, regent. It's only business."

"I see you have finished your gimnopede pie." Stogggul signed to the boy. "Will you take another slice?"

"As a matter of fact, I think I wi—"

Bach Ourrros' face was suddenly drained of blood. He tried to retch, but could not. As his bodyguard lunged toward him, the boy, who was just behind him, slashed down with a carving knife. The point went clear through the back of the bodyguard's hand, pinning it to the table. The boy left him to struggle with removing the blade, gripped his head on either side, and, with a quick, efficient movement, broke his neck. He stepped back, then, and the bodyguard toppled over. Meanwhile, Bach Ourrros, clawing at his throat, was dying of the poison Stogggul himself had sprinkled onto the gimnopede pie after it had been baked. This was the sorcer ous herb mixture Malistra had tricked him into sampling on their first meeting, making him immune.

As Stogggul watched Bach Ourrros' death throes with curiosity and pleasure, he said, "Your problem was that you always considered yourself more clever than I."

Bach Ourrros, his eyes almost popped out of his head, was making gasping sounds like a dying lorg when Wing-General Nefff entered from the corridor.

"Everything in order, regent?" he said as he surveyed the room.

"Quite," Stogggul said. "It seems as if Bach Ourrros is having something of an allergic reaction."

Nefff came over to the table. "V'ornn with allergies should be more careful of what they eat." He stepped back as Ourrros' mouth opened wide and blood spilled all over the gimnopede pie. "We will just have to incinerate that now, won't we?" He signed to the boy, one of his handpicked Haaarkyut assassins, who quickly took up the platter of gimnopede pie and disappeared with it.

"Now comes the fun part," Nefff said, hoisting Bach Ourrros over his shoulder.

"Pity," Stogggul said as he dabbed grease off his chin. "In other circumstances he might have made an excellent partner. He was an honest Bashkir, to that I can attest. Hardworking, as well. But as I hurt him deeply, I knew him all the better; he would have murdered me at the first opportunity."

The next day, when the regent Stogggul had returned from his meeting with Sornnn SaTrryn cementing Stogggul's control of the Za Hara-at construction project, the magnificent Neiobian prayer vase had been returned to its lighted stand. This time, however, there was a ten-centimeter layer of fine pale grey ash in the bottom, giving it, in the regent Stogggul's estimation, at least, an added beauty all its own.

Now, nightly, Kurgan and Courion made wagers on the Kalllistotos and, afterward, haunted Blood Tide. The was rife with Sarakkon to whom he was introduced. being on the fringes of Sarakkonian affairs was a thrilling accomplishment. *Truly,* he thought, *I have done something no other V'ornn has been able to do.* He got drunk with the raucous alien sailors, heard their tales of the sea, learned their ribald songs, and was heartily applauded for trying his best to sing along with them in their own tongue. They liked best that he had had the courage to step into the Kalllistotos for the tenth match with the reigning champion. They seemed to like even more that he had been beaten to a pulp. One night he asked Courion about this oddity.

"It is simple," the Sarakkon said. "My race admires courage in the face of great adversity. None of our mythic heroes survived their ordeals. It does not matter. They were pure. Their idealism remained untainted by temptation or corruption. What makes them dear in our hearts is the way their unwavering courage illuminates the way for us. We follow the path they have set for us because we can do no less."

Kurgan, for whom emerging triumphant was everything, was astonished that he was considered by the Sarakkon a hero simply because he had defied the very great odds in surviving the Kalllistotos. Whether he had won or lost was irrelevant. He might have been quick to dismiss this philosophy had he not felt that in his own way the Old V'ornn had been trying to make him understand the very same thing.

So he drank and sang and listened with an increasing amount of enjoyment. He also smoked laaga, which was freely given among his new Sarakkon friends. And all the while he watched the owner of Blood Tide, a slim, buxom Tuskugggun with a no-nonsense air about her. He noted with interest that even the rowdiest Sarakkon never gave her trouble, that she seemed to know personally every V'ornn who frequented her establishment. As far as that went, there was another anomaly here. Blood Tide was a casteless tavern, unusual among V'ornn businesses. It would have been easy to attribute that to the proximity to the Kalllistotos or to the presence of the Sarakkon, who were, in any case, contemptuous of caste societies. But by the end of the week, Kurgan was fairly certain that the open atmosphere of Blood Tide stemmed from the owner herself. Her name, Courion h informed him, was Rada. Inside her establishment, believe it or not she was regent. Though she was a Tuskugggun, and a young one to boot, she stood up to everyone and prevailed. No wonder the caste system had broken down here. He found her heretical behavior both curious and perverse. He told himself that he had not approached her right away because of his concern that Nith Batoxxx had played him for a fool when he had told Kurgan that this Tuskugggun would know who had betrayed his vices to the Star-Admiral. But the truth was he found himself fascinated by her despite his instinctive revulsion.

By the end of the week, he knew he could procrastinate no longer. He had been drinking and singing with the Sarakkon for hours. He had smoked three laaga sticks. Lurching up from the table, he wended his way through the shouting, swaying mob to where she stood at the far end of the bar, surveying her domain. She was dressed in a night-blue robe with blood-turquoise trim. In defiance of custom, she wore her sifeyn around her shoulders. Her long, tapering skull gleamed with spiced oil and an artful diadem of tertium-bronze alloy.

"Rada," he said without preamble. "I am Kurgan Stogggul."

She replied first with a cool, appraising gaze. "You are not unknown to me."

"I shall take that as a good sign."

"You may take it any way you wish."

Her hardness amused him. "I was told you had some information I might find useful."

"I have all kinds of information."

She looked past him for a moment, signaling the bartender to bring up more kegs of mead from behind the bar. Kurgan saw Courion get up from the table, cross the packed room, and disappear down the rear corridor, where the toilets were.

"Nith Batoxxx said you could tell me who has betrayed me to the Khagggun."

"You *are* Khagggun, dear. Or at least you are now. What 's your problem?"

"My problem is that I do not like V'ornn going behind my back. I would very much like to put an end to that situation."

"I could tell you, but then I suspect you would kill the informer."

"Yes, I would."

She smiled indulgently. "You have a lot to learn, dear. You are drunk or stoned, probably both. Go off and play with your Sarakkon buddies."

"I am as sober as you are."

She half turned away from him.

He had tried to intimidate her and failed. He rubbed the side of his head, as if he could apply a balm to his fearsome anger. It would serve no good purpose, he knew, to attack her. Not everyone deserved his rage. "Why did you say that?"

"What?" She turned back to him, but seemed barely to be listening.

"What would *you* do—in regard to the informer."

She folded her arms across her breasts, studying him. In that brief moment she seemed to inhale him like smoke deep into her lung. "The Sarakkon have a saying: 'The enemy you know is better than the unknown.' " She shrugged. "Why kill an informer when you can feed her information that will benefit you?"

"Her? Are you telling me that the informant is a *Tuskugggun*?"

"Her name is Dalma."

Kurgan laughed out loud. "But she is the regent's Looorm."

"She is a spy."

"Even if I believe that, which I do not, pray tell me how the Star-Admiral would come by her information?"

"That is simple. She is Kinnnus Morcha's spy." She smiled. "Surprised, adjutant? I thought so. Excuse me, won't you? I am needed elsewhere." She hurried off to hurl herself between two drunken Sarakkon about to damage one another.

After a moment, Kurgan realized that he was still massaging the side of his skull. He struggled to digest the information she had given him. Dalma was Kinnnus Morcha's spy? Now *that* was a kick. He smiled, knowing that he had found Morcha's weakness. Dalma was the Looorm Kinnnus Morcha longed for and loved. Such information, he was quite certain, was going to prove extremely valuable.

He looked around. Courion had not yet returned from the toilets. That was odd. He hoped the Sarakkon had not been taken ill. His own bladder being in need of relief, he beat his way toward the back of the tavern. Thankfully, the unholy din was somewhat muffled here. He could use a little quiet right about now to figure out his next step. As he emerged from the noisome toilet, he heard Courion in conversation. The other voice he found maddeningly familiar.

Continuing down the narrow corridor, he turned to his left, found himself in a small hallway that led to the kitchens. The layers of grease stains were like archaeological strata, marking the age of the place. Midway down on the right was an open doorway. It was from there the voices emanated. Pressing himself against the wall, he inched closer until he had a clear view of a wedge of the interior.

He saw a small room, most likely Rada's office. He could see Courion but not the other individual.

"It has been a week," the voice said. "Why has it taken so long?"

"I do not know," Courion replied, "but I have been loath to prompt him."

"Why is that?"

"He is more clever than you think."

"Ah, so you know him that well."

"Well enough to understand that he is a man in a boy's body."

"I had no idea Sarakkon were themselves so insightful." The voice held a sarcastic edge that stifled Courion's reply. Courion backed up, and Nith Batoxxx came into view.

"Do not concern yourself," Courion said a bit breathlessly. "He is talking to Rada now."

Nith Batoxxx's gloved fingers curled into a fist. "He had better be. It is imperative that he have the information. Once he knows the Looorm is Kinnnus Morcha's spy he will know what to do."

"How can you be so certain?"

Kurgan, watching in astonishment, felt his stomachs cave in on themselves as Nith Batoxxx's form wavered, dissolved, only to reestablish itself as that of the Old V'ornn. As if it were a crystal ball, Kurgan felt his perception of reality shaken up, turned upside down. Had he, in truth, no allies?

"I have very little time left," the Old V'ornn was saying. "I have been priming him, shaping him for this moment ever since he was a small child. But now everything is in its proper place. The trap has been set. It is time that *he,* my unwitting hunter, be sent on his fated path to bind the enemy in chains of ions."

33

Lorgs Don't Cry

Mist rose from the apex of Heavenly Rushing, thick as the outer walls of the abbey. Within it, only the turbulent spill of the waterfall existed. Until two shapes appeared, shifting their centers with the ebb and flow of the mist. These were the same creatures who, weeks ago, had watched Riane bathing in the pool at the foot of the waterfall.

The inflection point has arrived, the first creature thought. *Now the Transformation prophesied with the coming of the V'ornn has begun in earnest.*

The Prophecy is unclear as to the outcome, thought the other. *Good and Evil hold equal chances for victory.*

We could sway the Balance, the first one thought. *We could help the Dar Sala-at.*

Impossible! Miina's life would be forfeit. This we know for a certainty.

Though the Dar Sala-at wields mighty power, she is untrained. She is the first since Mother to be able to combine the two sorceries—Five Moon and Black Dreaming—to create out of the sundered halves the ancient sorcery, Eye Window, as it was first created, as it was meant to be. The danger she is in—

No! We will hear no more!

The danger she is in if she be discovered by her enemies before she is fully trained, before she can adequately defend herself, is horrifying. What they could do to her—

Would you have us sacrifice the Great Goddess at the altar of your fears?

The Dar Sala-at's enemies have already bound one of our kin. Shall we allow them free reign?

The Dar Sala-at will defeat them. Or she will be defeated by them. It is her Battle. This is foretold.

I grow weary of our roles as observers. It has been eons . . .

Our Sister has acted. This is all that is allowed.

And yet, I long for revenge. The taste of blood is in my mouth!

You know the way that can happen. We must wait for the call to be unleashed. It is the only way. Be patient.

Fire has no patience! It is my nature.

Of course it is. Which is why we are mated. I am the calm one, the voice of reason and control. It is the Way of Balance.

The first creature shook its head in extreme vexation. *The lack of lightning makes an old, useless one of me. When will it return?*

Come now, Dear One. Let us withdraw to the promontory so that we may observe without ourselves being observed.

I will comply. But I will also weep for our kin, who has

been so unjustly imprisoned. Miina would not have allowed—

Unutterable sadness.

I cannot act; I am enjoined from speaking my heart, so I will weep.

Would that You were a lorg, then. Lorgs don't cry.

We are what we are. In the Old Days I would have plucked the eyeballs from our kin's tormentors and licked my lips while chewing them up.

The Old Days are gone.

Not for me. I must do something.

Have a care, Dear One!

One small thing, so tiny it will not be noticed except by us. I will choose the time and the place when I will act.

Let us pray now for the Dar Sala-at's success.

I do not know how to pray.

Then I will teach you, Dear One. . . .

The smokelike smudges of their existence soon departed, leaving the mist to continue its serpentine coiling. Birds cawed, slicing their way through the thick, moisture-laden air. The thunder of the falls echoed down the sheer basalt-and-schist mountainside. Butterflies danced and six-winged saw-needles hovered, feasting on tiny, milling things. Sunlight cast thousands of miniature rainbows, twinkling like stars in the mist's constant ebb and flow. Animals came and went in the safety of the mist. They ventured close to the water to drink their fill, their triangular ears swiveled back, alert for anomalous noises. They stared at one another, their muzzles dripping, their nostrils flared as they scented, so still they might have been carved statues. Then, in the blink of an eye, they had darted away to forage and hunt in the fastness of their domain.

Into this tranquil scene Thripped Mother. She was holding Riane in her arms. Riane, in turn, was holding tight to the two volumes, *Utmost Source* and *The Book of Recantation*. It had been centuries since the Sacred Books had been together. Even Mother could not remember that time.

"I feel like I am on fire," Riane said, as Mother set her down. Her mouth was still full of blood.

Mother laid the back of her hand along Riane's cheek. "You have been severely traumatized. You need time to heal."

Riane lay back. "I am so tired." She closed her eyes.

"You are in need of sustenance and rest." Mother's hands moved over Riane's throat and chest. "I can only do so much with sorcery. You have lost a lot of blood, but with your insides torn up, you will not be able to eat. Rest here while I forage for the herbs and mushrooms I need to make a healing tea."

Riane would have replied, but she was already somewhere between consciousness and dreaming. She was aware of the grass on which she lay, the spray of water on her skin, the somnolent drone of insects, the twittering songs of birds. All of this was filtered through the pain scouring her insides, an inelastic shroud in which she was wrapped, so that the grass felt like nails, the water like icicles, the sounds like screaming in her ears. She shivered and trembled and moaned a little. For a time, she drifted on this unhappy raft of semiconsciousness, shouldered this way and that by dim and gauzy sensations. She wished only to be plunged once more into the cenote's depthless darkness, the icy water numbing her against all pain and travail.

Dimly, she became aware of Mother returning, of the smell of a fire, and then another, more complex odor. Mother's hand behind her neck, lifting her head. She was being asked to drink. Her lips parted, and she drank down all the healing tea. Her eyes closed as Mother set her back down on the ground, whispered that she was going to get more mushrooms.

Riane was too tired to respond. She had sunk into the memory of recent events, revived in the vivid detail of a fever dream. She saw again through the omnipresent lens of the dreamer how the Abbey of Floating White had been thrown into a panic by the explosion in the pyramidal chamber that had housed the *had-atta*. She had directed Mother to Thrip them into the cubicle Kell, where she had with trembling bloody hands withdrawn *The Book of Recantation* from the shadowed Ja-Gaar's mouth. The tolling of bells reverberated like small seismic shocks into the foundation. Smelling smoke and alarms along the ancient stone corridors, they had Thripped back to her cell, where she had recovered *Utmost Source* and the knife Eleana had given Annon. Young Ramahan, wide-eyed and panting, raced down fire-filled corridors, carrying buckets of water, while the canny konara of the Dea Cretan met to speak of lobbying, vote-gathering, the politics of religion. Alliances formed like eddies in a tide pool, only to break apart, sundered by distrust. It was difficult for her to imagine Bartta dead. Was Konara Urdma on the ascendancy? She could not even guess as to how the new hierarchy of konara would establish itself.

Had it really happened, or was it just another unsettling part of this strange dream from which Annon would at dawn awake, safe in his bed in Axis Tyr, calling for Giyan and Kurgan?

All at once, a thought struck her like the boom of thunder, and her eyes flew open. The Sacred Books! She rolled over onto her side, groaning with the pain it caused her, and got up on her hands and knees. Her head hung down as waves of dizziness assaulted her. When she was able, she looked around. The books were not where she had left them. She got up slowly and went looking for them. Beetles crawled over the ground, digging, industrious, and colonies of midges hovered, waiting to be sucked up by darting saw-needles. Hart-bees droned from flower cup to flower cup, their legs swollen with bright orange pollen. But no books. She searched the near flank of the river, thinking perhaps that they had tumbled down the embankment. On hands and knees, she hunted through forests of fern and deltas of mud, through rough, brushy swales and rocky, wind-scrubbed ridges, microclimates in which she discovered a wealth of flora and fauna, but no books.

On the edge of the Marre pine forest she stopped. What could have happened to them—unless Mother had taken them? But why would she do that? Riane held her head and tried to think. She was feeling distinctly unwell. She put two fingers in her mouth, removed them to find fresh blood.

All at once, an odd thought struck her. What if Mother wasn't Mother, after all? What if she was really Bartta? What if the *had-atta* had broken her? She could have told Bartta everything—bringing *Utmost Source* into the abbey; learning to Thrip; finding Mother; dismantling the Sphere of Binding; stealing *The Book of Recantation*. Dear Miina, what if Mother was still in her prison, dead? What if this had all been a sorcerous ruse to get her to lead Bartta to both the Sacred Books?

The more she thought about it, the more it made terrifying sense. Stirring herself to action, she reconnoitered along the edge of the conifer forest until she discovered recent footprints. They headed north, directly into the forest. She followed them.

Though they were soon lost amid the cushiony Marre pine needles, to her trained eyes the thick underbrush provided signposts of recent passage. Each moment made her more confident of her reasoning. Her mind seemed clearer than it had ever been since this nightmare had begun. In fact, she wondered now why it had taken her so long to stumble upon the reality of the situation. No matter. She had it figured out now.

The route she was following took her more than half a kilometer into the dense forest. The circuitous nature of it only confirmed her suspicions. If this were really Mother she was following, there would be no reason for her to try to cover her tracks.

She saw someone up ahead, and crouched, watching. Her heart hammered in her chest. Her teeth had begun to chatter in terror. There were the two books by the figure's side. Whoever she had come upon was wearing the robes of the Ramahan, all right, but they were Bartta's persimmon-colored robes, not Mother's turquoise ones. So she had been right! Her fingers curled into fists. She could not allow Bartta to possess the Sacred Books. Mother had warned her against that.

Pulling a low-hanging branch back out of the way, she made her way toward Bartta. She had crossed perhaps a-third of the distance between them when she heard a snap! She froze, glancing down. Miina! She had stepped on a dry twig. The figure whirled—it was not Bartta at all!—and a roaring like an avalanche echoed through the forest.

She felt a wave of fetid air wafting toward her, like cor meat stinking in High Summer. The creature's black twelve-legged body was segmented like a gigantic insect's, its ballooning thorax protected by a hard carapace. Its long flat head, brown-black, shiny as obsidian, was guarded by wicked-looking mandibles. It swiveled and she saw twelve ruby flashes, a terrifying impression of faceted insect eyes. With another roar, the hideous beast stood up on two sets of appendages.

Riane reacted on pure instinct. Snatching up a Marre pine branch that lay on the ground, she rushed the thing, smashed the branch into its horrifying face. The branch broke in two, the soft wood splintering. By that time, she had drawn the knife Eleana had given Annon, slashed once, twice as the thing tried to grab her wrist. Maddening. Why didn't it attack? Instead, it kept retreating. And roaring. What was it trying to do? Then she understood. It was trying to lure her deeper into the forest. Perhaps it had reinforcements there. Perhaps these things wanted her alive. The thought of being imprisoned once more—and by these hideous beasts—was too much for her. She ducked under a clicking mandible and buried the blade to the hilt in the thing's thorax. Cloudy yellow ichor gouted out, cool on her clenched fist. In a frenzy she struck again and again, while the creature bellowed and moaned. She was panting and weeping, ignoring for the moment how easily the blade entered soft flesh where it should have met resistance from hard carapace.

She stood over it, bloody and victorious. She went to where the books lay and gathered them up. As she bent down, she experienced a wave of dizziness. She sat down heavily, her head in her hands. When her vision cleared, she saw the blade lying across her thigh like a wound. But it was covered in blood, not ichor. Her blood?

The world snapped back into focus. She felt as if she had just awakened from a serious illness in which her fever had been abnormally high. She turned, then, looking back at the creature, which was no creature. She saw voluminous turquoise robes, running now with Mother's blood. With a sobbing moan, she pushed herself up, staggering over to where Mother lay. Where was the hideous creature she had been fighting? It had attacked Mother. Then, with a wail of horror, she saw the stab wounds in Mother's belly. She fell to her knees, weeping.

"Ah, Mother, how has this happened?" she cried. "What have I done?"

Mother's eyes opened. There was no fear in them, no hatred. Riane felt her heart bursting. "You have done nothing, Riane, but fulfill the Prophesy of the Dar Sala-at. I knew the moment Astar told me that you were the Dar Sala-at that you would be my savior and my end. It was foretold that you would be the cause of my death."

"No, Mother. No!"

"It is the wheel of life turning. Riane. In my youth, I would never have allowed someone like Bartta to get the better of me. But my power has wasted away. I am old, Riane. Ancient, even. It is time to die."

Riane began to conjure healing spells as she gathered Mother into her arms as best she could. "Quiet now," she said through her sobbing. "I will use Osoru and Kyofu to heal you."

"I am beyond healing."

"No, no, don't say that!" Part of Riane's attention was directed at summoning Osoru and the limited knowledge she had of Kyofu, as she desperately tried one spell after another, failing to find one that would counteract the damage she had done.

"Listen to me now," Mother said, ignoring her. "You must not go on blaming yourself. Bartta used the same fearsome spell, the Sphere of Binding, on you that she used on me. But she must have added Kyofu spells that hid its presence from me. Do not blame yourself, Riane. I did not know. You could not know." Her mouth worked silently for a moment. "The Sphere of Binding—You did not attack *me*, did you, Riane?" She was making soft wheezing sounds. "It was not me you saw, was it?"

"No. I was sure you were Bartta. Then you were this huge insect with twelve eyes."

"The Tzelos is a daemon from the Abyss. Miina forever exiled it from this realm. You see how impossible that is?"

"But I tell you I fought one just now."

"The Sphere of Binding caused you to imagine the things you are most afraid of. This is what the Sphere of Binding does. It unlocks that part of your mind where your worst fears lurk and drags them into the light. What I cannot understand is how you saw a daemon from the Abyss. Did you see a Tzelos during the Nanthera?"

"No, but something happened while Riane and I were in the Abyss. At the last moment, Giyan tried to pull me back. She put her hands into the sorcerous circle."

"Ah, it is far worse than I feared," Mother said. She was clearly struggling to stay conscious. "The Portal has been breached. There is a danger that it has been weakened, that the daemons may find a way into this realm. And as for Giyan, Miina protect her from the forces she momentarily interrupted."

"What do you mean?" Riane whispered. "Will something happen to her?"

"There will be consequences, yes." Mother's head was nodding. "But since no one has ever dared try to break the Nanthera circle, it is impossible to know the result or even to speculate."

Riane felt an icy flash of fear pierce her. She had gone through every spell she knew without it having the slightest effect on Mother's mortal wounds. Why wouldn't they heal? How could she fail at this? She was the Dar Sala-at. If she could not even save Mother, how was she expected to save all of Kundala?

Mother's eyes began to roll up in her head. With a supreme effort, she refocused. "I took the Sacred Books, Riane. They would have been ruined by the spray from Heavenly Rushing if I had left them where you dropped them. Like me, they are delicate with age. They cannot be subjected to sunlight or to dampness. You are their guardian now. You must care for them. They are like living things. Memorize what you do not already know, then keep them protected in a safe place." Blood was leaking from the corner of Mother's mouth. When Riane wiped it away, more welled up. Like a storm on the horizon, it seemed to be gathering momentum.

Riane held her closer. "Mother, I've done everything I know how. There must be something I can do!"

"You have already saved me once, little dumpling, at considerable risk to yourself. It is not for you—or anyone—to save me again." The rattling made her shudder and shake. "I have become weak. I am vulnerable to Dark sorceresses like Bartta. It is time." Her head lolled.

"Mother?"

Mother blinked several time. "Riane, you must find the Ring of Five Dragons. The Dar Sala-at's first duty is to open the Storehouse Door, to unlock the secrets inside, the secrets that have been waiting for you. The Ring is the key. Only the Dar Sala-at may use the Ring. All others who try will die."

"What is in the Storehouse, Mother?"

"Even I do not know. The Pearl was always kept there before it was lost. To find The Pearl you must first enter the Storehouse. Only The Pearl can stop the daemons of the Abyss if they are set free, and only the Dar Sala-at may look into The Pearl. This is your path, your fate. It is a dangerous one, for there are always those avaricious, scheming, greedy souls who covet The Pearl for their own. You must safeguard it against them at all costs. In this I was unsuccessful, and disaster has befallen us."

"But Mother. I know nothing about this Ring or where I can find it."

"Miina has hidden the Sacred Ring. To find it, you must cast a spell. The Spell of Forever. It will tell you where it is." Mother licked her lips. "Now listen carefully to me. Half of the spell is in *Utmost Source*, the other half in *The Book of Recantation*. Separately, the spells are minor things; they were designed that way so that no one would know their true nature. I will tell you where in the Sacred Books to find them."

"But I am a novice at casting spells," Riane said. "I will bring you the Sacred Books and—"

"I cannot cast the Spell of Forever," Mother said. "No one can, save for the Dar Sala-at. It is an Eye Window spell that is beyond even me." She lay panting like an animal in acute distress. Then she coughed thickly, turned her head so that she would not choke on the blood.

"Mother, don't die. Don't . . ."

"Thigpen will know what to do. Summon her. She will help you."

"I want *you,* Mother."

"Find the Ring, Riane. The Ring . . ."

Something was coming, just over the near ridge. So close Riane could feel its chill aura. She whirled, at the ready to defend Mother, even now. Too late. Like sand in the Great Voorg, that life had already slipped through her fingers, was passing into the ghostly mist, guided by Riane knew not what.

A certain darkness lay upon the noonday landscape. Riane threw her head back, screamed at the cruel world into which she had been born. She wished only to die, to follow in Mother's ghostly footsteps through the darkling mist, to a land unknown, unsought, unfurrowed, there to atone in any way she could for the murder she had committed.

Love. What was that to her? She had loved Giyan and Eleana, both lost to her. She had loved Mother and had killed her. Most monstrous fate that had tainted her, turned her poisonous as an adder.

She broke, at last. Her throat raw and aching from her screaming and her recent wounds, she doubled over, trying to smother herself in Mother's cool bulk. She gritted her teeth, grabbed handfuls of Mother's turquoise robes, beat herself about the head.

At last, spent, a curious calmness stole over her. Her mind, taken outside her grieving self by the last effervescence of Mother's aura, became a pellucid lake without even the breath of emotion to ruffle its skin. Onto this clear surface rose the image of beloved Thigpen. Weeping as if she would never stop, Riane summoned the creature to her side.

Giyan watched the rain gather in the distance behind Rekkk's back. His broken bones had knit, but he was not yet altogether healed. He walked in a different manner than he had before his encounter with Olnnn Rydddlin. His stride was shorter, and because it was more difficult to heal muscles and tendons with sorcery than it was to knit bones, his right shoulder dipped slightly every time he used his right leg. Giyan found it extraordinary how these little things seemed to change him. He seemed to her more overtly dangerous now, like an animal with one limb caught in a trap.

There were other changes, not so easy to quantify. He seemed not only quieter but also more reticent to show emotion, as if he had beat a hasty retreat into the guarded core of himself, leaving the prickly shell of his Khagggun training to protect him. For him the world had become a darker place, laughter fleeing to another, unseen realm. He trembled with the effort of concentration. His dark expressive eyes were fixed on the horizon, as if by his will alone he could extract Olnnn Rydddlin from wherever he lay, bring him hence like flame from two fiercely rubbed sticks.

Nights were the worst. He grew feverish from his wounds and began to dehydrate from an excess of sweat. He drank greedily the water Eleana fetched from the river, but almost immediately vomited it back up. Nor could he tolerate the herbal remedies Giyan prepared for him. She held him, telling him stories of Kundala in its infancy, of Miina and the

Five Sacred Dragons, of Pyphoros, the daemon of daemons, and the white-bone daemon. These stories continued even after he had fallen into an exhausted, fitful sleep, because once begun they would not be stopped. When she herself dropped off during a story, it continued in her dreams, and she would awake at pearly dawn more fatigued than before.

Having purchased three sturdy cthauros from Eleana's friend, the blacksmith at Joining The Valleys, they were making good time as they headed northeast through ascending tiers of heavily forested valleys toward the Abbey of Floating White. But near the end of the second day, foul weather moved in, forcing them to find shelter.

Having passed a series of caves less than a kilometer back, they retraced their route back down the ridge path they had been following just past the edge of the blesson-fir forest. Giyan and Eleana lighted a fire well inside the mouth just as the rain swept down upon them. Giyan called to Rekkk, who stood, unmoving, close by the blesson firs, but not among them, inundated by the downpour.

"What is the matter with him?" Eleana asked.

"I don't know."

The girl sat with her back against the rock wall. She wrapped her arms around herself and glanced into the cave's lightless interior. Giyan knew that she was thinking about Annon and the perwillon. She sighed inwardly. It had hurt her to see the continuing pain her quasi lie had caused the girl. But she knew that she must keep her child's secret from everyone, even those who had once loved him. There would be too much risk to Riane and to Eleana to allow personal feelings to take precedence over guarding the Dar Sala-at's safety.

They were on the last of the basalt plateaus that led to the higher reaches of the Djenn Marre, where the abbey waited for them. Even in Lonon, the nights at this elevation were cold enough. The windswept rain simply made it worse.

She went out of the cave and stood close beside Rekkk. Within seconds, she was soaked clear through her robes. It was raining so hard it hurt.

"Rekkk, come with me," she said. "You will find no answer out here."

He said nothing, did not move.

She heard a deep roll of thunder traversing the ridges below like an itinerant warrior. It filled the valley between like food waters. The earth beneath their feet briefly shuddered. The blesson firs bowed down before the wind, black with rain, blurred as smoke.

He took a breath, let it slowly out. "Though I may have forsaken the Khaggun Caste, I am still a warrior. That was what I was bred for, that is what I will always be. It is in my blood." He walked into the closest line of blesson firs, stood under the dripping arbor until Giyan joined him. Then he pointed down toward the spines of the ridges below, to the armies of blesson firs marching over them. "You see how fierce this storm is? It matters not to the firs. They bend, but they do not break. Olnnn Rydddlin broke me, Giyan. That is a humiliation I cannot bear."

Giyan pointed to the same ridges he had picked out. "Do you see those bare spots, Rekkk? They were made in the depths of winter, when the severe slopes of the ridges could no longer hold the snow and ice. They began to slide, and in sliding they took the trees with them." The downpour filled her cupped palm until she turned it over. "Every living thing has its breaking point, Rekkk. Even the bravest, the truest, the most flexible. Even those blesson firs."

"Trees cannot be humiliated," he said shortly.

"We Kundalan believe that there resides in every living thing the spark of the spirit. The blesson fir is no less noble for having been broken. If anything, its nobility has been validated."

"I feel like a hollowed-out log." He stared out into the hazy distance, and at last he said what was on his mind. "The death of this world, this magnificent place . . . Giyan, if it happens it will be because of us, because of the V'ornn. I am being driven mad by the thought."

"If you concentrate on the possibility of death, it might come, Rekkk." He turned to look at her.

"Concentrate on the inevitability of life, on your role in saving Kundala." She slipped her fingers through his, tugging gently at him. But instead of returning to the cave, she led him into the tree line. Her shoulder brushed against his with an electric kind of thrill.

The rain seemed farther away now, part of another universe. Here, beneath the giant blesson firs, dewdrops glittered like stars. The air was rich with resin, the mossy ground was soft and springy beneath their feet. All was still; even the nocturnal creatures had retired to their deep burrows and hidden boughs to wait out the weather.

She turned her face up to his, and they kissed. Passion rose like steam between them. Her mouth opened under his, and she shivered, feeling his desire mingle with hers.

They dropped to the moss. Their intense desire transformed the forest into a bower of new and trembling life. Her excitement grew as he undid her robe. Unaccountably, she felt as shy as a young girl. She released a tiny moan as his hands moved over her. She closed her eyes, firmly put aside her memories of her life with Eleusis, the aftermath of Annon's death. Her life was here, now, and she would do what was required to keep her ghosts at bay.

"Rekkk . . ."

She bit into his shoulder as he pulled her atop him. His impossibly smooth, muscular body was sheened with the rain that filtered through the branches and leaves. It was so beautiful. She was determined to grasp the moment, hold it tight, and never let it go.

"Rekkk . . . Ohhh!"

Night had fallen by the time Rekkk and Giyan returned to the cave. To her credit, Eleana did not ask where they had been. Anyway, Giyan was sure she knew. The rain had abated. Giyan sent them out to hunt down dinner. They might have made do with the smoked meat and dried tubers they carried with them, but she needed the skull of a small mammal. Besides, it was good for them to be in each other's company. Giyan was aware, even if they were not, of the synergy between them, a kind of energy field that arced and fed upon itself like the V'ornn ion-based power source. It was a magic all its own, more powerful than any sorcery, for it possessed the ability to open the heart.

When had they become a unit? she wondered. But she knew. She knew very well. Not that she could tell Rekkk, but Olnnn Rydddlin had done the three of them a great service, after all.

While she mulled over these thoughts, she laid out the dried herbs and powders she had gathered during their trek from Joining The Valleys. First, she drew a circle in the dirt floor of the cave. Next, she drew a line through the circumference at the four cardinal points. Into each of the indentations, she poured an herb or powder.

She had just finished the fourth line when she sensed a shift in the darkness at the interior of the cave. She raised her head. She was squatting on her haunches, bare elbows on her thighs. The fire cracked and sparked, warming her back. There was no sound, no movement at all, save for the stark shadows cast by the flames. Knowing it would be useless to peer into the lightless space, she relaxed, allowing her eyes to go out of focus. She breathed easily and deeply, drawing into her belly all the minuscule scents of the cave and the stormy night. Slowly, she damped her heartbeat, the noise of the blood pulsing in her veins. Now there was nothing but the flickering in the darkness. With patience, she discovered its rhythmic nature, darkness being inhaled and exhaled like breath, and something inside her quailed in recognition.

Tzelos!

She could see the six pairs of eyes, could sense the coldness emanating from it. She had never actually seen a Tzelos before, nor any daemon for that matter. How could she? Miina had imprisoned them all in the Abyss eons ago. Nothing could unseal the sorcerous Portal the Great Goddess had Herself locked. How could . . . ?

The Nanthera!

The Nanthera momentarily opened the Portal to the Abyss.

It was the only way to transfer a living spirit into a dying body. But she knew that the Nanthera rite was designed with safeguards to ensure that nothing on the other side could use it to return to this realm. And yet, a Tzelos watched her from the darkness of the cave's interior. She would have staked her very life on it.

And then it hit her. She was the one who had let the daemon out of the Abyss when she violated the circle of the Nanthera in a last desperate attempt to save her son. No one knew the consequences of that violation, but she had suspected from the very first that the chrysalides on her hands and arms were a direct result. So was the Tzelos. It was the only explanation.

A more agitated disturbance in the darkness broke into her thoughts. The shadows seemed to have taken on an added dimension, as if they had turned aqueous. The disturbance rippled and purled, bulging outward, then ebbing back. All at once, it drew itself inward, and the stench of rotting flesh almost made her gag.

It appeared, drawing the darkness to it like water rushing toward a drain. Twelve red eyes regarded her. Its hideous insectoid face was unreadable. Its curved mandibles opened like the gates of the Abyss itself.

A ferocious clicking emanated from its mouth. "*I have come for you.*"

"Stay away. I want no part of you."

"*You have no choice. You have been marked.*" It advanced farther. "*I will take you.*"

Without taking her eyes off it, Giyan stooped, took a sliver of burning wood from the fire.

"*Do you imagine fire will deter me because I am a creature of Darkness?*" The way it clicked it almost seemed to be chuckling. "*I will devour your fire.*"

Giyan placed her bare right foot inside the circle she had drawn in the dirt.

"*What are you doing?*"

"You know," she whispered. "If you truly are Tzelos, you know."

"Malistra informed me of your sorcerous ways."

"Malistra!"

"She sent me. She is much vexed with you. What you did to her plaything, to Olnnn Rydddlin. Oh, yes, much vexed."

Giyan lit the west line of herbs. West, the direction the dying walk in the last moments before their breath gives out. The pungent mixture slowly smoldered and burned.

The Tzelos paused, its mandibles clicking away. *"Desist. You cannot change what is."* It unfolded one of its upper appendages. Coarse, hairlike filaments hung from the bony arm.

Giyan's eyes fluttered as she recited incantations in the Old Tongue. Nothing seemed to make a difference. All at once, she remembered the spider-mite she had confiscated from Olnnn Rydddlin, the one that had been impregnated with Malistra's Kyofu spell. She drew it out. Though nightly she had been examining it, experimenting with extreme caution, she had yet to fathom how it worked. She held it out in her cupped palm, and the Tzelos began to chuckle—at least its clicking sounded like a chuckle.

"She promised you would have it. She promised you would," it hissed.

She thumbed it on. The spiderlike legs opened, and she threw it at the Tzelos.

It began to deliquesce. *"Now or later,"* it clicked just before it vanished, *"it matters not to me."*

With trembling hands she knelt to gather up the hateful spider-mite.

"Giyan, what are you doing?" Rekkk said from the mouth of the cave. "I thought we had agreed to work on that thing together." He and Eleana had returned from their hunting foray. Two good-sized ice-hares hung from a cord in his left hand.

"The Tzelos—"

"Tzelos?" he said. "What is a Tzelos."

"A daemon from the Abyss. It was here."

"I don't see anything."

Giyan, feeling abruptly faint, put a hand across her eyes.

Rekkk dropped the dead animals, water flying off him as he ran to her. "Giyan, what is it?" He put an arm around her waist.

"I don't know. I—" She took a deep breath, trying to regain her equilibrium. There was a ringing in her ears, and colors seemed abruptly sharper. That was when she knew what had happened.

"Rekkk, I've had a vision," she said. "A most terrible premonition."

"This Tzelos you saw," he said. "It wasn't real?"

"No. The Tzelos—the daemon—is not of this realm. Miina consigned it and all other daemons to the Abyss—a kind of sorcerous prison—ages ago. They cannot get out." She shuddered, thinking of it saying, *I have come for you.* She would not tell them this.

He drew her to the fire, where the three of them sat. While Eleana skinned and dressed the ice-hares, she told them what she had seen. "The Tzelos are what you might call the scouts in the army of daemons. They are the seekers of soft spots, weaknesses, the terrorists that worm through defenses, the harbingers of what is to follow."

"But why did you see it now?" Eleana held the knife just above the head of one of the ice-hares.

"I don't know." She shook her head, trying to clear it. "I know this much: my visions are warnings—a sign that my subconscious has identified a danger that my conscious mind has missed. They always come true."

"Your mind is giving you clues, like symbols in a dream." Eleana neatly severed the head and began to strip it of skin and flesh. She had not forgotten that Giyan had need of the skull.

"Perhaps. In the vision, the Tzelos said that Malistra had told it where to find me. But that is impossible. I have set spells to keep us hidden."

"What about this Eye of Ajbal you said Malistra commands?" asked Rekkk, ever the practical warrior. "The Eye found us once before."

Giyan accepted the yellow-white skull from Eleana with

a nod of thanks. "The Eye of Ajbal is frightfully powerful, it is true," she said. "But I have found a remedy, albeit temporary, for that particular spell." She smiled. "I have spent years turning away from my Gift, minimizing it. Now that this path is no longer feasible or even wise, I have to admit that I am surprised at the power I am discovering inside myself."

Eleana was up on her haunches, her body tense. "What do you propose we do?"

Giyan had laid the skull in the center of the circle she had drawn in the dirt of the cave floor. She hinged the jaws open, then refilled the four lines with her herbs and powders. Before she put fire to them, she produced a small, perfect opal. It gleamed fire-red, yellow-green with astonishing brilliance. Placing it in the ice-hare's jaws, she began to chant in the Old Tongue. She lit the lines.

"I must contact the Dar Sala-at with all due haste," she said, as pungent smoke rose from the circle. "I will find her in the depths of this opal."

A h, little dumpling, the world has changed mightily since we last saw one another."

Thigpen crouched at the mound of earth beneath which she and Riane had buried Mother. Thunder rumbled and rolled through the mountains below, but the rain had yet to gather overhead. Light from the five moons drenched them in monochrome. Wind soughed fitfully through the treetops. Branches swayed as if in a sadness.

Riane felt all cried out. And yet, the world did not seem big enough to contain her grief. "Thigpen, I will do whatever you say. I must atone for what I have done."

Thigpen's huge eyes regarded her with immense compassion. "It is no sin to be held sway by another's sorcerous spell, else Mother herself would be as guilty as you believe yourself to be." She held Riane's eyes with her own. "Do you hear me? Do you understand what I am saying?"

"Yes, Thigpen."

"Do not speak to me as if I am about to mete out punishment to you. Now you are making me cross!"

"But I—"

"You are the Dar-Sala-at! It is past time you started acting like the One."

"But that's the trouble!" Riane was suddenly angry. "I am a male V'ornn trapped inside a female Kundalan body. I have powers I have scarcely explored. My mind is a tumult of conflicting emotions. The fact is, I don't know how to act, and now there is no one but you to tell me."

"It is not my job to tell another being how to live!"

"Then I am lost!" Riane shouted, running to the edge of the ridge.

Twitching her whiskers in consternation, Thigpen padded over to where Riane stood, looking down into the valley full of dark rumbling clouds. "Look here, Mother is dead. Nothing either you or I can do about that. It was her fate; it was written in Prophesy."

"I know. She told me."

Thigpen regarded her solemnly. "You say you know, but I see that you do not believe."

Riane felt her heart welling. "I think she was just trying to make me feel better."

"No, little dumpling," Thigpen said. "Only you can do that."

"So it's true." Riane knelt down to be at Thigpen's level. "It was prophesied that I would kill Mother."

"Yes. The Prophecies have enormous force, a life of their own. As you know, Miina bade the Five Sacred Dragons to create Kundala. As powerful as they are, they could never have done so without The Pearl. The Prophecies emanated from The Pearl. They are the residue, the lees of the Creation. It is said that the Prophecies are burned into a series of ascending rock ledges inside the Storehouse. The Pearl is said to be buried in the topmost ledge. I myself have never seen the Prophecies, but I know they are there. I feel it. And so will you, given time and training." The creature blinked. "If we cannot bring Mother back from the dead, then let her death have meaning. Let it reveal to you this truth: having killed once, tragically, you will need a compelling reason for doing so again."

"But Mother—"

"Mother would not have told you how to act any more than I will. She would not have known the answer to your question, and neither do I. How could we? *You* are the Dar Sala-at. Only you know the answer." She put her head next to Riane's. "No one can live your life for you, nor tell you the right path to take."

"Will you teach me the construction of the spells as Mother would have?"

"I do not have that Gift."

"Thigpen, I don't have the strength for this—or the courage."

"Oh, but you do."

"How do you know?"

"You are the Dar Sala-at."

"That is no answer!"

"It is the only answer. But if you require another, then I will offer this: you have already demonstrated your courage a dozen times over."

Riane wiped away the last of her tears. "Mother said I have to get to the Ring of Five Dragons. She told me to cast the Spell of Forever so I can find out where the Ring is." Riane closed her eyes, imagined reading *Utmost Source*. Mentally thumbing through the pages, she came upon the spell Mother had described. Then she went through *The Book of Recantation* until she found the second spell. At once, she understood how to combine them. It was like seeing two halves of a mathematical equation and understanding instantly that they belonged together.

She began to chant in the Old Tongue, the words, as always, seeming hauntingly, tantalizingly familiar and comforting. A field of dancing lights appeared before her, revolving, resolving themselves into the shape of a small sphere. Slowly, the center of the sphere changed, the color deepening until it was deepest purple. All at once, into this darkness a scene appeared. Riane recognized the Door to the

Storehouse in the caverns below the regent's palace—Middle Palace, using the Kundalan name. The Ring of Five Dragons was in the medallion in the center of the Door, in the Sacred Dragon's mouth, where it belonged if the Door was to be opened. The Door, however, was locked as tight as it had ever been save for that one hallucinatory moment when Annon had seen . . . What? A Sacred Dragon? Impossible! All at once, she saw something that made her gasp. The deepest purple returned to the center of the spangle of lights.

"What is it, little dumpling?"

"You've been right next to me. Didn't you see?"

"None can peer into the Spell of Forever save the one who cast it."

"The Ring of Five Dragons is in the Storehouse Door. It killed three Gyrgon who tried to use it to raid the Storehouse."

Thigpen frowned. "Now this is bad. Very bad."

"What do you mean?"

"The Ring is now Transformed by Seelin, one of the Sacred Dragons of Miina. It has become the detonator, activating the Tymnos device that will shatter the entire planet. Our only hope is to get you to it before the ides of Lonon. Only you have the power to take the Ring from Seelin's mouth and stop the device."

"But it is already Lonon."

"Yes, we have only three days left." Thigpen considered for a moment. "A vexing and most disturbing question has occurred to me: How did the V'ornn gain possession of the Ring?"

"I have no idea."

"The Spell of Forever will tell you. You have only to ask."

Returning her attention to the sparkling sphere, she peered into its depths, asking for the Ring's most recent chain of custody. The lights revolved, the center cleared, revealing the answer. She blinked, then lifted her hand. The Spell of Forever vanished with the tiny pop of a burst bubble. She sat for a long time, sunk deep in thought.

"Well," Thigpen said, "are you ever going to tell me?"

She turned to the creature. "The last person to have it before the Gyrgon was the V'ornn regent Wennn Stogggul. He received it from Sornnn SaTrryn, the new Prime Factor, who got it from a tribal digger in an archaeological site north of Okkamchire in the Korrush."

"The Ring was buried centuries ago in the Korrush. Well, there's a huge mystery solved." Thigpen's whiskers twitched. "What is it? What is troubling you?"

"The Spell of Forever has revealed something interesting about the SaTrryn." Riane's fingers began to fidget in her lap. "Sornnn SaTrryn's father, Hadinnn, was a secret Kundalan sympathizer. Like Eleusis Ashera, he felt guilty at the way the Kundalan were being treated. Through a Kundalan intermediary, he established a pipeline with a female from the highlands. He provided her with support—intelligence, ordnance—for her resistance cell, all without her having the slightest idea it was coming from a V'ornn. This female—I know her. She would not recognize me now, of course."

"She knew you as Annon."

Riane nodded. "Her name is Eleana."

"My best advice, little dumpling, is to forget all about her."

"I can't," Riane said miserably. "I love her."

"Oh, Miina preserve us!" Thigpen rolled her eyes. "Well, you can just forget about that. You are not Annon anymore. You are the Dar Sala-at. Your fate is to remain apart from all mortal concerns."

"Says who?"

"So it is written; so it will be."

"You mean I cannot love?"

"Your love is for all the races of Kundala, little dumpling, not for one solitary individual."

"To be solitary. That is the Dar Sala-at's fate?"

Thigpen made a disapproving sound low in her throat.

"Thigpen, please tell me, how does a female love another female?"

"Why am I always asked impossible questions? I am a Rappa. What do you want from me?" she said with uncharacteristic asperity. "Let us please return to the Ring. How long ago, pray tell, was it buried, and by whom?"

With difficulty, Riane turned her mind away from her confused thoughts of Eleana. "A female planted it there."

Thigpen's whiskers were twitching more than ever. "What do you mean, 'planted.' "

"Just that. A Kundalan sorceress was at the dig not more than a day before Sornnn SaTrryn was taken there. I can still feel the slight emanations of Kyofu trailing from her."

"Oh dear, that cannot be good," Thigpen said. "How came the Dark sorceress by the Ring?"

"The Spell of Forever did not reveal that—after the sorceress the images dissolved into a kind of milky fog."

"Even worse," Thigpen said fretfully. "Someone has blocked the spell. Someone very powerful, indeed."

"The sorceress?"

"No, else you would not have been able to detect her."

"Who, then?"

"I do not engage in speculation. In any event, the sole possibility that springs to mind is unthinkable, not to mention impossible." She shook herself. "Never mind. Let us return to our most pressing problem. You must reach the Ring within the next three days."

"But it's simple now," Riane said. "We will Thrip into the caverns below Middle Palace and—"

"It is anything but simple," Thigpen said. "You cannot Thrip into Middle Palace. Like the device that the V'ornn stupidly activated, sorcerous safeguards were established long ago to make sure no one could Thrip into the Storehouse or anywhere in Middle Palace."

"Then we will Thrip into Axis Tyr and from there go by foot to—"

"Try to Thrip, little dumpling. Go on. Try."

With a dark foreboding, Riane settled herself and tried to spin. Nothing. She tried again, and again failed. She licked her lips nervously. "What is happening?"

"The Tymnos device is at its last stage. It has closed the Portals to all realms."

"But without being able to Thrip, how will I be able to get to Axis Tyr in time?"

"You have friends," Thigpen said, "and along the way we shall encounter others."

"Friends? What friends do I have besides you?"

"The Druuge, for one, the nomads of the Great Voorg."

"Mother told me of them. I can speak Venca, their language."

"Well, now, that *is* interesting." Thigpen's whiskers twitched. "Did you know that their technology is language? They manipulate words the way the V'ornn manipulate ions and gravitons."

Riane nodded. "Like mathematics."

"*Just* like mathematics." Thigpen appeared very pleased. "The Gyrgon manipulate charged ions in ten million different ways, right? The Druuge do the same with the seven hundred and seventy-seven letters of their alphabet. They like to explain it this way: One letter, alone, is as meaningless as a single grain of sand. It is in *combining* the letters that the technology manifests itself, becoming like the living ecosystem of the desert, a system that is ever-changing, always in flux."

Riane nodded. "All right. But, still, why would the Druuge even be aware of me?"

"Because, little dumpling, you are the Dar Sala-at. You are in Prophesy. They have been waiting for your coming for a thousand years."

Riane stopped abruptly. Her nostrils flared as with a significant change of the wind.

"What is it?" Thigpen whispered. "What have you sensed?"

"An opal. A sorcerous opal."

"Yes." Thigpen kissed Riane on the cheeks. "Come, little dumpling. She is ready to find you, at last."

"Who?"

"The Lady. The one who is destined to stand forever by your side."

34

Desire

D
alma sat alone in a park in central Axis Tyr. Double
rows of sheared ammonwood trees surrounded her in
a graceful oval. Crushed marble pathways, neatly
raked, radiated out from the center where two opposing cres-
cents of fluted heartwood benches were set. The serenity of
the formal geometry appealed to her. It provided a measure
of order and balance in her otherwise tumultuous life.

The rainstorm that now rumbled in the north had swept
through the city hours ago, leaving the streets freshly washed
and glittering in the Lonon moonlight. She had a particular
fondness for this park. It was here she had first plied her
trade, partnered in sweaty assignations beneath the dense
nighttime shadows of the ammonwood. Ever since she could
remember, she had had a taste for the daring. Stripping naked
for bouts of strenuous sex with a necklace of powerful clients
gave her pleasure over and above the act itself. No beds for
her! Splinters in her buttocks were proof of the audacity of
her intimate encounters.

It was in this very park that she had first met Bach Ourrros,
recognizing in his reckless desire for her an opportunity to
ascend from simple street Looorm to something better. If she
had a keen taste for sex, it was matched by her own desire
for power. Not that she had any illusions about her role in
society. She was Tuskugggun, and a Looorm at that! She
would never be accepted in a visible position of power; but
if she was clever and lucky enough, she knew that she could
remain near those who did hold power, whispering from time
to time in their ear, snatching the crumbs from their tables.
Thus she had risen from Bach Ourrros' side to the regent

Stogggul's palace. Not that it had been a pleasant climb. She
regretted hurting Bach Ourrros, of whom she had grown
fond, and being with Stogggul was unsatisfying in almost
every way. She contented herself with each secret betrayal
of him to Kinnnus Morcha.

She had met Morcha at almost the same time that she and
Bach Ourrros had been introduced. Kinnnus Morcha was
clearly superior in both intelligence and sexual prowess. The
problem was that though he was a high-ranking Khagggun
with plenty of influence, he was Lesser Caste. He simply
would not do as a rung in her private power ladder. But she
knew he could be a useful liaison, and so she used him as
assiduously as he used her. The fact is, she liked spying for
him. When, at his connivance, she had allowed Wennn Stogggul to seduce her away from Bach Ourrros, she liked it
even more.

She rose now, slowly wending her way through the ammonwood grove until she found the very tree against which
she and Bach Ourrros had first made love. She knew each
tree in this grove individually. All of them had stories to tell
her, lessons to teach her, memory as history of the V'ornn
Empire on Kundala. She was blessed with the kind of memory that never forgot a single client. She could see them now,
ghostly forms, the residue of their power still inhabiting the
grove. This was as close as she would ever come to wielding
real power. If it had been her misfortune to be born a Tuskugggun, then she had done everything she could to control
her own destiny. But now, at this moment, wandering
through the safety of her trees, she wondered whether it was
all an illusion. After all, she was still alone. She would always be that way. She was denied the friendship of other
Tuskugggun, which she might have had if she had chosen
another profession, if she had entered the communal world
of hingatta, where Tuskugggun raised children and practiced
their arts. There was no room for her in such quarters. Neither did she have the protection of a V'ornn mate. Kinnnus
Morcha would never marry her, and as for Wennn Stogggul . . .

"Dalma."

Ah, she heard his unlovely growl now. Slipping from the shadows of the ammonwood grove, she walked over the crushed white marble to where he stood in the center of the garden. It was late. There was no one else about, which was why they had agreed upon this assignation point.

She felt his coolness as she threw herself into his arms. Now they were both playing roles, which was fine with her. If she never again had to fondle his tender parts, she would count herself lucky.

"What news do you bring me?" he asked, pushing off, maintaining a discreet distance.

She told him what Kinnnus Morcha had instructed her to say. "The Star-Admiral is besotted with me, but it is taking time for him to trust me. He is somewhat paranoid."

"Tell me something I don't know," Stogggul muttered. "I thought he was going to take Malistra's head off when he saw Olnnn Rydddlin. Does he harbor any ill will toward me?"

"I think he did in the beginning. But since he has debriefed Rydddlin his demeanor has changed. He is grateful Malistra was able to save Rydddlin's life." This was, of course, an outright lie. The fact was, Kinnnus Morcha seethed with rage at what he considered the mutilation—both physical and emotional—of one of his top officers. Privately, he told her that he was quite concerned about Olnnn Rydddlin's frame of mind. He was growing convinced that Rydddlin was quite mad.

"Excellent," the regent said. He passed her a small box, which she opened with a little gasp.

"The bracelet to match the ring you gave me!"

"And you will get the necklace that completes the set if you keep up your good work. Remember, Dalma. You are in the Star-Admiral's bed for one reason: to alert me should he contemplate moving against me."

And that was the lesson the assignations within the ammonwood had long ago taught her. Power bred paranoia. The loneliness of her life was nothing as compared to the isola-

tion of these males. Poor Morcha! He was like all the rest,
made half-dead by the fierce struggle for power. She felt a
brief moment of self-pity and bit her lip in order not to cry.

Instead, she smiled into the regent's face, and he kissed
her briefly, coldly, his thoughts already elsewhere even before he turned and left the park. Alone again, she took herself
to a bench, where she sat, breathing in the perfume of her
trees. Their leaves rustled, speaking to her in tongues, and
she sighed, closing her eyes.

Kurgan drew his knife, the knife given to him as a prize
by the Old V'ornn, Nith Batoxxx. I will kill her now,
he thought as he watched Dalma on the bench. His father
had just departed, having received the disinformation Kinnnus Morcha had doubtless concocted to stir his ear and his
ego. Kurgan laughed silently. In a way, it would be a pity
to end her life, for it would surely shorten his father's even-
tual agony when he discovered how his ally had led him
astray. But just as the Star-Admiral had plans for the regent
Stogggul, Kurgan had plans for the two of them. Because of
Kinnnus Morcha's fondness for Dalma, her death would
serve as a flash point for his simmering wrath.

He wondered now how he should do the deed. Should it
be a quick slice across her throat, a neat and bloody death?
Or should it be slow, filled with terror as a stream is stocked
with fish? Should she know the identity of her killer, the
reason for her death? Did he want to hear her plead for her
life, in the middle of that plea, end it? So many choices, so
little time!

He fantasized about killing her quickly, with one gout of
blood, her eyes rolling up as he cupped her chin, offering up
her neck to his knife blade. Perhaps the act of recognizing
him would be her last. But the thought of raping her, here,
in this serene, secluded spot where she was most vulnerable,
where his father had so recently been with her, was so appealing that, like a lover in the act, he felt impelled toward
its delicious promise.

As he moved through the shadows in which he had been

hiding, he became aware that he and Dalma were not alone in the park. Another watched and waited.

Despite his growing sexual excitement, his curiosity was piqued. He wondered whether the watcher might be a security guard the Star-Admiral had attached to his precious skcettta of a spy. That possibility presented an inconvenience but nothing more. He switched direction, moving silently within the perimeter of the grove of ammonwood, one eye on Dalma while the other searched ahead for the watcher.

The ammonwood trees rustled all around him. He felt like an actor upon the stage, an understudy perhaps who had been unexpectedly thrust into the piercing light of prominence. There was about this place, on this night, at this lonely hour the unmistakable tang of history in the making. Kurgan loved nothing so much as subversion. He was interested in the machinations of power simply because he was out to undermine them. Someone who knew him incompletely might mistake him for a nihilist, for he possessed the nihilist's obsession with tearing down authority in any form. The crucial difference was that, even at the age of fifteen, he had a clear idea of the new order with which he would replace the old. He was, at core, a student of K'yonnno, the Gyrgon Theory of Chaos and Order.

Kurgan saw himself as a Lord of Chaos.

His thoughts were abruptly cut short by the sight of the watcher breaking from his cover. Sure enough, he was a Khaggun, but Kurgan noticed that he moved with a curious gait, an awkward lope. A little shiver ran up his spine as he saw that one leg was nothing more than fleshless bone. Moonslight flashed on the Khaggun's face, and Kurgan recognized him as Olnnn Rydddlin. *Hadn't he and his pack been dispatched to bring back the Ashera skcettta and the traitorous Rhynnnon, Rekkk Hacilar? What the N'Luuura happened to him?*

Dalma had seen Rydddlin. She jumped up, backing away from the bench, pushing away from him. Clearly, he was not her bodyguard. Then why was he here? What did he want from her?

A shock-sword flashed in Olnnn Rydddlin's hand, and Dalma turned and fled, right into Kurgan's arms.

"Kurgan Stogggul," she cried, startled. "Please help me. I am being attacked by—"

"Step away from her." Olnnn Rydddlin waggled the point of his shock-sword at Kurgan. "Step away, I say, or you risk being killed along with her."

"No!" Dalma cried. "What do you want from me?"

"You are the Star-Admiral's spy," Rydddlin said.

"You have mistaken me for someone else. I am a simple Looorm." Dalma was squirming in Kurgan's grip, frightened not only for her own life but that he would reveal the depths of her treachery.

"I know what you are. Through you I will get to him. If I cannot kill him outright, then I will diminish his power, I will make him suffer."

Now she was truly terrified. "You are mistaken, I tell you."

Clearly, Olnnn Rydddlin wasn't listening. "He is about to take my life away from me. He has ordered me to report to Receiving Spirit tomorrow morning to undergo psychological tests. He says this is the only way I will regain my command. But I know better. Having gotten what he wants from me, he will throw me away. I will check into the hospice, but I won't check out. I will be held there against my will. No one wants to see me like this, let alone the Star-Admiral."

Her voice turned liquid, pleading. "I will go to the regent, now, this moment. He is your ally; he fought to have Malistra heal you over the Star-Admiral's objections." She turned her head. "Kurgan Stogggul, quickly, take me to your father."

"If you try to take her anywhere," Olnnn Rydddlin warned, "I swear to N'Luuura I will run you through along with her."

"Relax, Pack-Commander." Kurgan swung Dalma around to face him. "I have no intention of letting her leave this park alive."

The blood drained from Dalma's face. "Kurgan Stogggul, what are you saying?"

He hit her then, a powerful blow to the face that felled

her. As she lay prone and stunned, he kicked aside her robe. "But first youth must have its pleasures, eh, Looorm?"

He fell upon her, already rampant. " 'Informers must be rooted out and interdicted in the harshest manner possible as a visible means of deterrence,' " he quoted as he slapped down her feeble attempts at defense.

"The Khagggun counterinsurgency manual," Olnnn Rydddlin said. He appeared impressed.

"She spied on me—reported back to the Star-Admiral on my personal life."

"No one can be trusted," Olnnn Rydddlin said with a peculiar kind of sadness. "Least of all the Looorm of powerful V'ornn."

Dalma was weeping. She pleaded with him to no avail. Finally, she said, "I have something you will find of value. If I tell you, will you let me go?"

Kurgan paused. "That depends," he said, "on how valuable I find the information."

"There is much I know about your father—"

He laughed in her face. "What could you possibly tell me? I know all there is to know about Wennn Stogggul."

"You know he's controlled by Malistra?"

"I have heard that, yes."

Dalma licked her lips. "I have information that concerns Malistra."

He nodded. "That might fit the bill."

She shook her head. "How do I know I can trust you?"

He seized her by the throat and squeezed until her face was blue with blood. "Tell me now!"

Dalma, gasping and choking, nodded. He let go. She took several jagged breaths. "Malistra lives on mesembrythem."

"What the N'Luuura is that?"

"It's some kind of sorcerous root."

"So she's got a strange diet. She's a sorceress, isn't she?" His fingers curled around her throat again.

"Wait! Wait! You don't understand. She *needs* this root. Without it she cannot live."

"Thank you," Kurgan said, and parted his robes.

"What are you doing? We had a deal!"

"I never agreed to anything," he said. "And if I did, I don't care. You're a Tuskugggun, a Looorm, a spy."

With a moan of despair, Dalma raked her nails down his chest, drawing blood. He hit her hard enough to stun her, but not hard enough to knock her out. He wanted her to be very much aware of what he was doing to her. He used his rampant member like a shock-sword, and she cried out. He wiped the smear of blood that had appeared under her nose and tasted it. He grunted heavily. His grunting became rhythmic, picking up speed and intensity.

When he was finished, he stood up. She was weeping. She tried to close her legs, but he kicked the insides of her thighs until she relented.

He backed away, his heaving chest sweat- and blood-streaked. "Your turn," he said.

The two V'ornn looked at one another for a moment. There occurred an unexpected electric contact that encompassed, if not trust precisely, then the acknowledgment of shared intent. Rydddlin jammed the point of his shock-sword into the crushed marble. He knelt awkwardly. Clearly, he was not yet used to the working of his bare bones. Perhaps he never would be. He loosened his robes and fell upon Dalma as if he had come upon an oasis in the Great Voorg. The sound of animal grunting arose from the odd beast squirming and thrusting upon the sharp white moonlit gravel.

Then, with the abruptness of a furious storm passing, it was over. Olnnn Rydddlin lay panting atop her, dizzy with the aftermath of lust, his mind for the moment blank and uncaring. He sensed a stirring beside him, like the motion of a bee or a butterfly and he twisted his head to see Kurgan holding the shock-sword he had thrust into the ground. With the Khaggun's quick practiced motion, his dagger was out and at the ready, an undeniable fury in his eyes.

"You are the Star-Admiral's adjutant. He wants to put me away. Where do you stand?"

Grinning, Kurgan crouched, presenting the shock-sword to

him hilt first. Olnnn Rydddlin stifled his surprise as he saw Kurgan's hand grasping the twin blades. He knew just how much pain that caused him. Again that electric moment arced between them. Something unspoken yet as alive as their breath. Sheathing his dagger, Olnnn Rydddlin quickly took his shock-sword and buried it between Dalma's breasts. Her eyes opened wide, she gave a tiny yelp, and her torso arched up as it had when she was trying to throw him off her. She began to thrash, disturbing the studied harmony of the garden. Kurgan, reaching over, placed his hands over Olnnn Rydddlin's on the shock-sword hilt, keeping it in place. Slowly, her thrashing subsided. Her mouth opened, and a sound like the ticking of a clock issued forth. Blood welled up around the wound, overrunning her robe, staining the crushed marble black in the Lonon night. Clumps of gravel filled her knotted fists.

Momentarily sated, the two V'ornn lounged on a bench in the center of the park. The night was once more serene. The leaves of the ammonwood rustled, but they no longer spoke in tongues to Dalma, whose corpse lay in front of them like an offering to some dark god. Her body seemed in repose, belying the violence of her death. Except for the blood, she might have been sleeping. The bruises on her thighs continued to darken.

"She *was* beautiful, wasn't she?" Olnnn Rydddlin said. "And clever."

Kurgan sat forward, his elbows on his knees. "Not clever enough, it would seem."

"Well, she was only a Tuskugggun, after all. What are Tuskugggun, anyway, of what use are they, beyond the temporary? No high-ranking Khagggun to my knowledge has ever married one, except to procreate, to give him a son, an heir, to carry on the line. They never see them, the wives, but the mistresses come and go as they please through front door and back."

"You envy them, your superiors."

"Once, perhaps." Olnnn Rydddlin wiped blood off the toe of his boot. "I hate them all now."

"The heart of the beast rages inside you."

Olnnn Rydddlin stared hard at Dalma, at nothing.

"I suppose it isn't difficult to recognize in others what is also inside yourself."

Olnnn Rydddlin grunted. "I will say this for you, you are not like any Bashkir I have ever encountered."

"I am not Bashkir, though I was born into that caste."

Olnnn Rydddlin smirked. "You think yourself Khagggun simply because your father forced the Star-Admiral to make you his adjutant. It is an illusion, nothing more. You were born Bashkir, and that is what you will always be."

"The Sarakkon would take issue with that."

Olnnn Rydddlin laughed. "You are something. Sixteen years old, and you are telling me about the Sarakkon."

"Are you familiar with them?"

"Why would I be? No V'ornn is."

"I need a drink," Kurgan said abruptly. "What do you say?" He felt the need to assert himself. He was tired of being dismissed because of his age.

Olnnn Rydddlin's hands were clenching and unclenching. "I have not been in a tavern in some time. I have not been in society since—" He flexed his skeletal leg.

"Neither have I. At least, not in the way you mean." Kurgan stood. "All the more reason to prove to ourselves that we can still fit in."

Olnnn Rydddlin's head swiveled like an owl's. He was young, though not nearly so young as Kurgan. "Do we want to fit in?"

Kurgan was pleased. Now they were on his home ground. "Not exactly. But we want to give that impression so that we can move within society without suspicion."

Olnnn Rydddlin nodded, and on his bony leg rose. "This I understand."

Outside the ovoid ring of ammonwood trees, the city glowed, still but for infrequent Khagggun patrols, the odd hoverpod crossing just above the low rooftops. An inconsequential conversation came to them from far away, borne by the wind and the emptiness of the hour. The sharp angles of buildings lay in the streets, offering up the secrets of the day, but the city itself seemed blinded by the night. Behind them, the park continued to pulse with the act they had committed, as if the taking of that life had caused an awful weight to form, a black hole, a gravity well so that Kurgan had the momentarily disorienting feeling that the wide boulevard on which they set out was tilting backward toward the corpse which lay in its own blood, a question mark, a promise, all the future ever was or could be.

He laughed, then, the sound ringing down the boulevard, preceding them onto the Promenade. He had not meant to walk so far—he had no idea of Olnnn Rydddlin's capacity for exercise—but when at length they turned into the bright doorway of Blood Tide, part of him understood that he needed to be on his own turf in a tangible way. The Old V'ornn had taught him that much: he would not cede control again. Not for anyone, not for any reason. Not ever.

The two V'ornn sat amid the detritus of the long night— snoring Sarakkon, drunken Khagggun telling the same jokes for the fifth time that evening, big Mesagggun nursing angry bruises from the Kalllistotos. Of Rada there was no sign. No surprise there; it was late enough for her to have retired to her bed.

They drank fire-grade numaaadis from a bottle Kurgan bade the bartender leave on the table. The tavern smelled of blood and sweat and sweet fermented mead.

Olnnn Rydddlin examined Kurgan with a critical eye. "You are the Star-Admiral's adjutant yet you take a hand in the murder of his premier spy." He grinned. "I understand you now. You are an agent yourself. You violated her on orders from your father."

"You are wrong about that just like you were wrong before. Becoming adjutant was my own idea; knowing my father, he was probably against it. On the night of the coup, I went to Kinnnus Morcha and made him a deal."

"What kind of deal could you have made the Star-Admiral?" Olnnn Rydddlin scoffed.

"I gave him Annon Ashera."

"Is that right?"

"I had spied on Annon and his skcettta, Giyan. I watched them escape the palace. I saw them steal a pair of cthauros. I knew where they were going."

As Olnnn Rydddlin looked at him with curiosity, Kurgan got up from the table. He suddenly realized how hungry he was. He went down the rear corridor to the kitchens, where he discovered Courion taking a predawn meal. Nith Batoxxx was not around.

"Eat with us," Courion said without preamble. "This chowder is memorable. The cook uses only deep-water snapper. Do you have any idea how difficult it is to net those big fish? They fight like daemons."

"I am with a new friend." Kurgan pulled up a stool beside the Sarakkon. "A special Khagggun."

Courion grunted. "What an oxymoron! All Khagggun are good for is to die on command."

"You should come meet him."

"As you can see, we are eating. Go back to your drone-ish friend."

"I am reluctant to leave you," Kurgan said. "Anyway, there's a question I've been meaning to ask. The other day, someone offered me some mesembrythem. Have you heard of it?"

"Of course. I sell laaga, why wouldn't I sell mesembry-them?"

"It's a drug?"

Courion shrugged. "It's weird stuff. More like a root with psychotropic properties."

"Really? Perhaps I ought to try some."

"Only if you have a death wish. It's very strong, very potent. If you're not careful, it can rearrange your brain for you. You won't like the results, trust me. You will grow to enjoy inflicting pain."

Kurgan held up his hands. "Consider me warned." He

rose, but when he was at the doorway Courion said, "Just out of curiosity, what makes this drone-ish friend of yours so special?"

"Sorcery," Kurgan said with a grin.

"We will wager twenty you are blowing hot air."

"Forty would be the least I would consider taking from you."

Courion put down his spoon and wiped his lips. "Do you have seventy-five, or will we have to take it out of your hide?"

Kurgan went back, put the requisite amount beside the Sarakkon's bowl.

Courion scooped up the coins, nodded, and rose. "Now that our stomach is full we will see this 'sorcerous' figment of yours."

Returning to the table with the Sarakkon, Kurgan saw that in the short time he had been absent the level of numaaadis had decreased considerably. As they approached, Olnnn Rydddlin looked up. He seemed startled when Kurgan introduced them, even more so when Courion sat down at their table.

"Stogggul tells us that you are a sorcerous thing," Courion said in his blunt Sarakkonian manner.

Olnnn Rydddlin glared at him.

Courion laughed. "Ready to run us through with your shock-sword, Pack-Commander?"

"I will, if you give me any more cause."

Courion put his forearms on the table, lacing his fingers. "We have heard that you Khagggun are a hot-blooded lot."

Olnnn Rydddlin tossed his head. "Ask Kurgan here. He fancies himself Khagggun."

"Stogggul has proved his mettle in the Kalllistotos. Can you say the same?" Taking a quick sidelong glance at Olnnn Rydddlin's skeletal leg, Courion put a pile of coins in Kurgan's waiting palm. "Meeting your friend has proved instructive," he said to Kurgan before walking out of the tavern.

"Did you make a bet with him?" Olnnn Rydddlin asked.

"It is useless to have a conversation with a Sarakkon without wagering. It is the only way to gain their respect."

"A Sarakkon friendly with a V'ornn. If I had not seen it myself, I would not have believed it."

Kurgan placed some coins on the table.

"What is that?"

"Your half of the winnings. After all, it was your leg we were betting on."

Olnnn Rydddlin poured himself more numaaadis. "Give it to the bartender," he said after he knocked off the liquor. When Kurgan had returned with another bottle, he said, "So. Your father did not order you to follow Dalma and do away with her duplicitous self?"

"That would have been awfully clever of him." Kurgan seated himself close to Olnnn Rydddlin so they could speak in hushed voices that would not carry. "Except for two things. He never suspected her, and he and I do not have that kind of relationship."

Olnnn Rydddlin frowned. "Too bad. You could have asked him to intercede on my behalf. I will not obey the Star-Admiral's order that would have me incarcerated in Receiving Spirit. I swear I will kill him first."

Kurgan seized this opening in his predatory jaws. "Why attempt such a risky endeavor when someone else can do it for you?"

Olnnn Rydddlin, who had just poured them both more fire-grade numaaadis, lowered his glass. His dark, haunted eyes seemed to dart this way and that as if of their own volition. Kurgan wondered whether Kinnnus Morcha's assessment of him might be correct. Maybe he was mad. Did it matter? Sooner or later, he believed, everyone was driven mad by the chaos of life.

Olnnn Rydddlin pursed his wet lips. "I assume you have something to say, so say it."

"What do you think the Star-Admiral would do if he was convinced the regent, discovering that Dalma was a spy, had killed her?"

Olnnn Rydddlin paused before answering. It was clear he was taking this discussion more seriously than he would have

an hour ago. "Kinnnus Morcha is Khagggun. He would re-
taliate in kind. But he would have to have evidence."

"Then we will give him evidence." Kurgan produced a
blood-spattered box from beneath his robes. In it was a piece
of V'ornn jewelry.

"Is this supposed to mean something to me?" Olnnn Rydddlin said when he saw it.

"Dalma was in the park to meet with the regent."

"I know. I saw them together."

"Did you see him give this to her?"

"No."

"Well, he did." Kurgan put his hand over the bracelet.
"Did you see him murder her?"

Olnnn Rydddlin gave him a querulous look.

"Well, he did. At least, that is what I will tell the Star-
Admiral. And this bit of jewelry will be all the proof he
needs."

Olnnn Rydddlin shook his head. "The bracelet is nothing.
They are allies."

"It is everything to a Khagggun who hates, mistrusts and,
most importantly, fears his 'ally.' It is everything to a Khagggun who is so paranoid that he will want to believe the
first shred of evidence."

"You are not Khagggun. You underestimate the Star-
Admiral's intelligence."

"Intelligence does not enter into this equation. Kinnnus
Morcha loved Dalma; he told me as much himself. He will
be quick to condemn my father because it will confirm his
own suspicions about him. It is true I am not Khagggun.
Nevertheless, I have come to know a great deal about them.
Khagggun fancy themselves strategists. They love nothing
better than to be proved right, isn't that so?"

"Yes," Olnnn Rydddlin said after a very great time.

"So, you see, the *quality* of the evidence, or even the *quan-
tity* is of no consequence. Providing the *perception* of guilt
is all that is required of us. The Star-Admiral will believe
what he wants to believe—that the regent is his enemy."

Olnnn Rydddlin drank his numaaadis in a kind of brooding

silence. It was impossible to read his expression. "You are serious."

"Deadly serious. You want the Star-Admiral dead, and I want the same for my father. I shall pit them, one against the other. Let those who lust after power most deeply fall upon their prey like carrion-creatures and rend each other limb from limb. The beauty of the plan moves me. With my father dead I assume the regency. Then I appoint you to the rank of Star-Admiral. You see? It's simple. I take my father's place, and you take Kinnnus Morcha's."

Olnnn Rydddlin sat back as if stung. His eyes narrowed. "You're mad. We would never succeed."

"Who will stop us?"

"The Gyrgon, for one. They make the rules we live by."

"First, the rules say that I must succeed my father upon his death."

"The Gyrgon would surely balk—"

"The Comradeship is fracturing from within."

Olnnn Rydddlin's eyes widened. "How can you know such a thing?"

"Listen." Kurgan leaned forward, lowering his voice even more. "I am allied with a Gyrgon by the name of Nith Batoxxx. He needs me because he has an enemy within the Comradeship who has also allied himself with others."

"This is astounding, unprecedented."

"My point precisely," Kurgan said. "Now is the time. We use the Gyrgon power struggle to our own advantage. If we do it now, do it right, we will be installed before anyone knows it. And once there, we move to squelch any form of resistance. What do you say?"

Olnnn Rydddlin stirred, reaching down to rub his skeletal leg. There was a sound that came from this, like locusts screaming. "When I was little," he said in a strange tone of voice, "I wanted to be my father. He was a great V'ornn. He achieved great status; he was a venerated Wing-General in his day. I became instead a Pack-Commander. I settled, and now I am nothing."

Kurgan was not a V'ornn to tell truths. But he recognized

this night, this moment, this Khagggun as singular, and he made an exception. "What I want more than anything," he said, "is to bring down the Gyrgon." Now that he had discovered the Old V'ornn's real identity, he had been seething with rage. The Old V'ornn had been his mentor, his spiritual guide, the one V'ornn he had come to trust and rely on. And it had all been a lie. Nith Batoxxx had targeted him as a child, had seduced him, using him for his own mysterious purposes. Now Kurgan had nothing but hatred in his heart for Gyrgon. Nith Batoxxx had done to him what Gyrgon did to all V'ornn: controlled him as if he were a marionette, pulling strings whenever it suited him, using him to do his incomprehensible bidding.

"That's all?" Olnnn Rydddlin laughed. "And how do you propose to do that?"

"First, as I already told you, the Comradeship is splintering. For the first time in V'ornn memory, the Gyrgon are vulnerable. How to attack them? The Gyrgon use fear to impose their will on us. What could be more effective than turning their own technique against them? As I see it, my task is straightforward enough, though not, I admit, without considerable risk: first, discover what the Gyrgon fear; second, gain control of it; third, use it against them."

"You will die in the attempt."

Despite his words, Kurgan could see that the Khagggun was impressed.

"It cannot happen overnight. Like all subversion, it takes clever undermining. Nothing will show on the surface for a long time, and then, of a sudden, the undermining will deliver the desired results—a landslide, taking all with it!"

Olnnn Rydddlin laughed again. "Well, they can only kill us once, eh?"

"You're with me, then?"

"You will have to save me from getting thrown into Receiving Spirit."

"Done!" Kurgan cried.

"How will you do it?" Olnnn Rydddlin asked.

A sly smile broke across Kurgan's face. "You leave that

to me. Now we shall swear seigggon to seal our pact!"

When the blood oath had been sworn, Olnnn Rydddlin inverted the empty bottle and called for another. When it was set down on the table, he quickly filled their glasses. "Better to be dead than to be marginalized, I always say." They raised their glasses, clinking rims.

"Death to everything," Olnnn Rydddlin said.

"Everything except power," Kurgan said.

They drank to that, deep and long, and then to further slake their thirst, put their heads together and talked of many things. Outside, the sky lightened, birds skimmed across the water, fishing boats ran from their slips into a following wind, sails full out, nets stretched across their decks, prows directed toward clouds of seabirds circling above unsuspecting schools of fish. Through the hours of daybreak, they spoke in hushed tones, knocking off another bottle of numaaadis, eating their meal in fitful bursts like machines of destruction fueling themselves before the call to battle.

35

Perfume

I like you in this guise," Malistra said. "You have the appearance of an old, worn boot, something no one would look at twice."

The Old V'ornn produced the special smile reserved only for her. "When you reach my age you develop a reverence for ancient surfaces. They remind you of the impetuousness, the fallibility of youth."

"I am hardly old!" she cried in mock alarm.

The Old V'ornn laughed and, taking her by the arm, led her out into his garden, where they could be enchanted by the purling of the pool, the songs of the birds, smell the perfume of the flowers. Light fell from the white sky, glaring off the walkways. But once they passed beneath the trees overhanging the pool, the dark water predominated.

"Not all youth is flatulent with ego, my dear."

His weathered arm snaked around her slender waist. She kissed him with great tenderness on his leathery cheek. They sat side by side on a bench with thick basalt legs and a carved onyx seat. The black water of the pool was at their feet. In the deep shade beneath the trees, Malistra's face seemed suddenly pale and timeworn. Spry as a youngster, the Old V'ornn stooped, picking up the chased-silver chalice that sat by the edge of the pool, filled it with water. He offered it to her. Her hand shook a little as she brought it to her mouth.

The Old V'ornn frowned. "You are waiting too long." He watched her greedily gulping the water. "I have warned you against that."

"There is too much to do." She wiped her lips with the back of her hand. "There has been unexpectedly vigorous opposition."

"From Giyan, yes." His black lips curled into a smile. "That will be seen to."

"In the meantime she has sufficient power and skill to make a great deal of mischief. She has blocked all my prying spells. Luckily, I did not underestimate her. I am tracking her through another means."

"Excellent."

"Still, I cannot 'see' who the Dar Sala-at is or where he is."

He waved a hand through the perfumed air. "It is of no lasting import. We know where the Dar Sala-at *will* be."

"The Ring of Five Dragons."

"Yes. The Dar Sala-at is drawn to it like a compass to true north."

Malistra was watching her hand tremble. "I need more."

"You cannot have more. An overdose will kill you. As I have explained often, there is a thin line between maintenance and disintegration."

"But it is no longer maintaining me!" she cried. "Look!"

She held her trembling hand in front of his face.

The Old V'ornn took her hand between his, stroking, soothing her. "You are overusing the Kyofu I taught you, that's all."

"I don't know, I don't know." She laid her head against his shoulder.

"Calm yourself, my dear. I am distressed to see you so agitated."

"I will be better in a moment." She produced a drawstring bag spun of finest gold thread. From it, she pulled a white root veined as the inside of her arm or his temple. She put it into her mouth and bit down, grimacing at the bitter taste.

"How much of the mesembrythem are you taking now?" he asked quietly.

She shook her head, shuddering a little.

"My dear, you must be ever so careful. Mesembrythem has the potential to permanently disrupt the synaptic activity of your brain."

She swallowed, pulling into herself, gathering her energies so that the root could restore her. "I am well aware of what it can do. I have seen the effects with my own eyes, remember?"

The Old V'ornn did remember, though he did not care to. "That will not happen to you, my dear. I promise to keep you safe."

"You have watched over me. You have provided for me. I have done everything you have asked of me."

"Everything and more," the Old V'ornn said. "You have made me proud."

"Our most difficult work is still ahead of us." She was regaining a good measure of her enormous inner strength. "The events set in motion when you gave me the Ring of Five Dragons is about to reach its climactic moment."

"Yes," the Old V'ornn said. "We have used it as bait to lure the Dar Sala-at out of hiding. The Ring will draw the Dar Sala-at to it, and when his identity is revealed to us, the trap will be sprung. We will have him; we will lock him away in the sorcerous prison of the Abyss." He rubbed his veiny hands together. "With the Dar Sala-at out of the way we can proceed unimpeded with the rest of our plan."

A silence ensued in which the birds and insects interjected the geometry of their daily lives. It was difficult to believe that beyond the high garden walls, draped with flowering vines, sprawled the cacophony of the city, gigantic engine of a million parts, humming and wheezing, shouting and gesticulating, singing, laughing, bargaining, cajoling, imploring, ordering—the dominant and the submissive, the polyglot marketplace. Here, there was the space of ancient life, a demarcation, clear as a line of latitude on a map, between this garden and the outer world.

Malistra rearranged her robe. "There is Wennn Stogggul to consider."

The Old V'ornn yawned deeply. "What about him?"

"He is counting on my sorcery to retrieve the Ring of Five Dragons."

"Well, of course it cannot."

"That is just the problem. If I fail, I will lose power in his eyes."

The Old V'ornn smiled. The trickster in him was tickled. "Then we shall give him a ring to fit precisely his ambition." He held out his palm, cupping it. The long-nailed fingers waved in the air like sea anemones, closing together until they touched. As they did so, the air just above their tips shimmered, grew dense and dark. A ring of carved red jade appeared. It looked just like the Ring of Five Dragons, except for the tiny thorn protruding from the inside circumference.

"He will try to use it," Malistra said as she plucked it from its perch.

"Of course he will." The Old V'ornn's smile deepened. It was an awesome thing, this smile, like the growl of a perwillon. It would have frightened even Kurgan. "He will want to use it against his enemies. We will be prepared for him to do precisely that. This ring is hollow. When he puts it on, the thorn will prick him and his blood will fill the ring. Then he will have sorcery enough." He began to chuckle.

"He is a cor-headed V'ornn. The potions you mixed into

the candles burning in his suite must have a potent perfume."

"Perfume is what he responds to," she said. "I knew it from the moment he first met me. He scented the musk I gave off, and he was mine."

"It must be interesting to have such sexual imperatives."

"It makes you weak," she observed with some contempt.

The Old V'ornn seemed lost in thought. He rose without a word and stood, staring down into the utter lightlessness of the pool. Midges danced just above its glassy surface. She had become used to his strange mood shifts, deep silences, sudden pronouncements. All at once, he passed a hand across the water. The rippling ceased for an instant, then started up again. He inclined his copper-colored head. "Remember, Malistra: we are all actors upon a stage. The trick is in knowing when to enter and when to exit."

Who is this female who is looking for me with an opal?" Riane asked.

"All in good time," Thigpen said. "First, I must tell you about the opals."

They rode swift cthauros Riane had procured for them in the mountain hamlet of Outer Market. The Rappa were still in hiding, so Riane had to go into Outer Market alone. Walking the packed-dirt streets, she had felt self-conscious and terribly guilty. Thigpen had fashioned for her an exquisite robe out of the turquoise material of Mother's clothes. At first, she had refused to put it on, but at Thigpen's insistence, had finally relented. "The Dar Sala-at must wear Mother's mantle," Thigpen said in that tone of voice that brooked no argument.

Through dense Marre pine forests and towering ammonwood copses, across the ripening fields of Lonon, along rocky wind-scoured ridges, down grassy dells they sped. Riane had taken the lead.

Guided by the emanations of the opal, they were heading almost due south, more or less on a direct line to Axis Tyr. The opal directed Riane to come to Middle Seat, a small backwater of a village fifty-five kilometers northwest of the city.

"Firstly, opals are exceedingly rare," Thigpen said, settling into her expository mode. "They are older than Time. Some believe that they are actually small shards of The Pearl, the lees, if you will, left over from the moment of The Pearl's creation."

"Do you believe that?" Riane asked.

"As proof, they point out that all opals contain inclusions, imperfections that caused them to be discarded at the moment of the Creation."

"Yes, but what do *you* believe?"

Thigpen frowned. She was an odd sight, anyway, her small furry rotund body lying athwart the cthauros' muscular back. The cthauros did not appear to mind. In fact, with Thigpen's face alongside his, he seemed to listen to her as intently as Riane did. "I believe in the possibility of all things," Thigpen said in a definitive tone. "I also believe that you—Kundalan, V'ornn, whatever—have a fundamental need to have the Cosmos explained."

"Don't you?"

"I am curious about other, smaller matters—how fragile trust is, forming like a pearl in a muodd shell; how enmity brews over time, strengthening like tea steeping; how love overtakes you, dissolving the callus from a guarded heart. I am content to let the Cosmos confound other minds."

"What are the opals used for?"

"In the right hands, they find things. Important things. Like you, for instance."

"But why would I need an opal? I can use the Spell of Forever."

"That particular spell allows you to 'see,' not to find. The two are separate and distinct."

"So if I had an opal, I could look into it and find things."

"Lost things, yes."

"Like Giyan. Or Eleana."

The cthauros began another steep descent down a shale-strewn switchback. They were still within the heart of the

Djenn Marre, but the highest peaks shouldered aside the sky along the northern horizon at their backs. The sun was very strong, but a cooling wind wicked the sweat off them, and in the shade there was a distinct chill, pockets of air, denser than the rest, left over from the night. High overhead, a brace of brown-and-white stone-falcons circled lazily, using the thermals as springboards to begin swooping dives. Bees hummed merrily in the hottest patches of sunlight, dancing from flower to flower. Gimnopedes flickered through shadow and sunlight, darting behind trees as if pursued by predators.

"It would not be such a good thing, I think, for you to find Eleana."

"It does not matter what you or anyone else says, I will never stop loving her."

"She loved Annon," Thigpen pointed out. "You are Riane now. You are the Dar Sala-at."

"What I am," Riane said, "survives." She shook her head. "Annon is still inside me, as is Riane. We both exist, one inside the other, like a set of nesting boxes. It is often exceedingly confusing, I admit. Sometimes I still do not know whether I am Kundalan or V'ornn, whether I am male or female."

"You are both; you are neither," Thigpen said. "You are Other, something new that is still evolving."

The switchback ended abruptly. At its terminus, they splashed through a shallow stream, the cthauros' hooves shattering the flaked shale of the bed. On the other side, a cleared, flattish expanse, dense and hot with glittering sunlight. Boulders throbbed with radiant heat.

Within an hour, they came to the end of the flatlands, entering another fallaway, this one even steeper than the last. Riane sat back on the cthauros as they descended single file. Beside them was a small cascade, tinkling and twinkling over moss-covered rocks, sending bursts of fine spray onto lady-lace fern.

"I have been thinking about what you said regarding love," Riane called back to Thigpen. "Time cannot change love, neither can a different body. I am who I am, Thigpen. In this life or any other. What robe I am forced to wear is irrelevant."

"And what of Eleana? She knew you as a V'ornn male. Assuming you see her again, what do you imagine her reaction will be when she sees a Kundalan female? Do you think she will recognize you? Do you think she will even believe you when you tell her the truth?"

"Eleana is someone who recognizes the truth when she hears it," Riane said. "I cannot say what she will think when we meet again—as I am sure we will! But I can tell you this. What we are comes from inside us. If she had somehow been changed into a V'ornn, I would recognize her. I would still see what I first saw in her. I would still love her."

"But are we not inextricably bound up in what we look like? Did you not mistake me for an animal because of my paws and tail?"

"I made a snap judgment without thinking. It was a knee-jerk response."

"A typically V'ornn response."

"I will never make that mistake again."

"So you admit it. You are not the same male V'ornn who—"

"Now you put words in my mouth, Thigpen! I have changed. All thinking self-aware creatures change, it seems to me. It is part of our genetic makeup, what sets us apart from the beasts. A cor is born a cor and dies a cor. That is *their* nature. It is not ours."

"I can see that philosophy is one of your strong suits," Thigpen called back happily. "All the better for me. It has been centuries since I have been treated to such a debate!"

Gradually, their shadows lengthened as the afternoon burned itself out. Colors that had flared midday now descended into deeper, more subdued hues as the heated glaze of the afternoon gave way to the cooler tones of twilight. Above their heads, clouds were still incandescent, but toward the horizon the day was already muffled in the hem of night's cloak.

The cthauros needed their rest, their food and water, so

the pair looked for a protected glade at which to make camp. They found one within the hour, at the northern fringes of an Atlas cedar forest. The stream fed by the cascade that had been their afternoon companion meandered nearby through the woods. While the mounts lowered their heads, drinking and cropping wrygrass, Thigpen and Riane brushed them down, then foraged for wood and edible roots, mushrooms, and ferns.

Though Thigpen cooked a delicious stew, Riane had no appetite. Her heart ached for Mother. She wished only to turn back time, to have another chance, to change the path fate had dictated for her. As if sensing her distress, Thigpen put aside the food and crept closer to her.

"Black thoughts unspoken have a nasty habit of multiplying," she said softly.

"I don't want to talk about it."

"All right."

Riane turned on her, flaring. "How can you be so calm?"

"Little dumpling—"

"What's the matter with you? Don't you ever get angry?"

"What would be the point?"

"The point?!" Riane shouted. "How can I even talk to you when you say something so stupid!"

Thigpen put her paw on Riane's shoulder. "Listen to me, you must find a way to forgive yourself."

Riane stood, walking a little bit away, staring into her V'ornn heart, seeing a bloody vengeance she could not have.

Later, in the stillness of early evening, they sat around the fire. Riane had been silent a long time. Thigpen tended the fire with a long stick, giving Riane the occasional sidelong glance.

"It's odd," Riane said at length, "but in this the Kundalan part of me agrees with the V'ornn. I want my kilo of flesh."

Thigpen put the stick down, came and sat by her side. "I absolutely understand the pain you feel now, but know that it has its good side, too."

"How can you say that?"

"Because I have a little more experience than you do, little dumpling." She put her paw up to her mouth. "I suppose that, warrior that you are, I should not call you that anymore."

Riane smiled a little. "Tell me how anything I am feeling now can be good."

"This pain will make you steadfast," Thigpen said. "You will know the difference between Good and Evil even when those around you may be fooled, because Good and Evil come in many guises, and at the beginning are often difficult to tell apart."

Riane's hands curled into fists. "I want my revenge for what was done to her—and to me."

"That is the V'ornn side of you speaking."

Riane stared thoughtfully into the flickering firelight.

Thigpen settled herself more comfortably. "As a Kundalan, consider what the V'ornn have done to your people. It is simple. Vastly cruel, in fact, in its simplicity. They have replaced your faith with hardship, knowing full well that with hardship comes a narrower focus. The world is reduced to the need to survive. And what is undermined then is your belief in Miina, the faith that nourished and sustained you and all who came before you. This the V'ornn have taken from you, it is gone, and you are changed, diminished, sundered, directionless.

"But the V'ornn have stripped you of something even more vital. In the old days, before the coming of the V'ornn, when you spilled blood it was to make sacrifice to Miina. It was a clean death, a purposeful death, a necessary death that you invoked, and therefore innocent.

"Why do you think the Old Tongue was abandoned by the Kundalan at large? Even the Ramahan use it only sparingly, in ritual and in prayer, never for idle conversation. It is too powerful. When everything is in equilibrium the language is, by default, direct. Those who would seek to alter the past in order to control the future must do so in another tongue, one that is ambiguous, malleable, open to interpretation. Deceit is ever so difficult when using the Old Tongue."

Riane looked away for some time, watching night steal over the mountains, smother the valleys, make mysterious the fragrant forest. At last, she nodded. "I will try to forgive myself, Thigpen. I will try my best."

The creature squeezed her knee briefly.

Riane's gaze returned to the encampment. There was a nest of gimnopedes high up in the cedars. The birds' soft cooing made of the place a tiny village in the wilderness. The fire snapped and sparked, the cedarwood logs releasing their rich perfume. The horizon lay quietly sleeping against the stars. "Will you tell me who we are going to meet at Middle Seat?"

"It is the female sorceress who will protect you, who will steadfastly stand by your side. This is her calling. It is bred in the bone."

"Can she help me get to the Ring of Five Dragons in time?"

"Like me, she will get you there or die trying."

"Will she help me find The Pearl?"

"This, too, is her calling."

"Tell me about The Pearl, Thigpen. Why is it so important?"

The creature was curled into a ball, eyes reflecting the flames. "There are many reasons, depending on whom you ask. The origin of the Kundalan is lost in the mists of Time. I do not think this is a good thing. I have found that if you do not know where you came from, you cannot determine where you are going."

"Are you saying The Pearl contains the origins of the Kundalan?"

"I do not know. But I surmise this is so. As I told you, the Kundalan are a lost race—they have been lost for a long time."

Riane thought of Bartta and the other Ramahan. The torture and murder of Leyna Astar; her own torture. She thought of the arrogant konara, the spoiled acolytes, how poorly they were being taught. She thought of the rewriting of Sacred Scripture, the distortions of Miina's holy words, the outright lies being promulgated in Her name, not the least of which was Bartta's contention that the Great Goddess had passed beyond to another realm, abandoning Her children without hope. She knew everything Thigpen said was true.

She stared into the fire, her gaze going out of focus. "This is the Dar Sala-at's true purpose, isn't it? To return to the Kundalan their spiritual birthright."

"*Your* true purpose."

They met at K., an old Kundalan cafe on the Boulevard of Crooked Dreams. It had painted plaster walls and a marble floor and small round porphyry tables protected from sun, rain, and wind by a bright crimson awning. The polished heartwood chairs were dark with oil, the scars down their legs proof of long and dedicated service. White-robed waiters wended their way through the thick field of patrons, trademark oval copper trays held high over their heads. In the market directly across the boulevard were arrayed bins of red, orange, yellow, and black spices. The air was perfumed with their sharp scents and the hard bargaining between patrons and clerks.

Kurgan found Olnnn Rydddlin already ensconced at a sidewalk table, sipping thick, honeyed tea. He did not smile when he spotted Kurgan or when he sat down opposite him.

"It is early in the day for you to be so fully armed," Kurgan observed.

"I imagine the Star-Admiral's Khagggun will be out looking for me any moment now."

"So. You do not trust me. We swore the seigggon."

Olnnn Rydddlin pursed his lips. The early-morning light, flaming through the woven crimson fabric overhead, struck his face at an oblique angle, making it appear as if he was wearing a battle helm. "I have yet to find the full measure of you."

Kurgan smiled as he ordered breakfast from a passing waiter. "You are still alive and free, aren't you?"

"For the time being. I like the way you talk. I have yet to see you act."

"Spoken like a true paranoid Khagggun!"

The street sweepers had hosed down the wide boulevard, choked now with traffic of every manner and description. An itinerant musician unwound an ancient Kundalan melody from the brass bell of his horn, counterpoint to the clip-clop of the black water buttren harnessed in tandem to passing drays. Spice dust hung in the air like early-morning mist. A brief argument erupted from the depths of the spice market.

Kurgan's breakfast came—braided wrybread, golden cor cheese, and fragrant hot chocolate. He busied himself with the food.

Olnnn Rydddlin was fidgeting. "This waiting is killing me."

"Relax. This wrybread is particularly delicious, don't you think?"

"Who knows? These days I have no appetite."

Out of the corner of his eye he saw a knot of Khagggun— members of the Star-Admiral's own wing judging by the crimson-and-gold braid on their uniforms—roughly shoulder their way through the milling throng in the market. He smiled at Olnnn Rydddlin and put a piece of cheese between his teeth. "On the other hand, perhaps you were right to be anxious."

Olnnn Rydddlin sprang up as the Star-Admiral's Khagggun spotted him. His chair fell over with a bang, he drew his shock-sword.

"You were supposed to help me," he growled. "N'Luuura take it, that's what I get for putting my trust in a Bashkir—a fifteen-year-old at that."

The Khagggun were at the edge of the spice market, trying to make their way across the packed boulevard. Olnnn Rydddlin thumbed on his shock-sword. He glanced at Kurgan, who continued to calmly eat his breakfast. "I ought to kill you first, before I wade into them."

He turned at a sudden commotion. The boulevard was being quickly and efficiently cleared, but it wasn't by the Star-Admiral's Khagggun. Olnnn Rydddlin's jaw dropped open. Wing-General Nefff, leading an entire pack of the regent's

Haaar-kyut, strode down the deserted center of the boulevard. He was dressed in full battle armor, as was the pack he commanded. Four of his Haaar-kyut took up station on either side of the cafe where Olnnn Rydddlin stood, while others formed a line in front of it.

"We have orders from Star-Admiral Kinnnus Morcha himself to detain Olnnn Rydddlin and bring him to the hospice Receiving Spirit," the First-Captain of the Star-Admiral's Khagggun barked. "What is the meaning of this unauthorized interference?"

"Olnnn Rydddlin is under the personal protection of Regent Wennn Stogggul," Wing-General Nefff said formally.

"I have heard of no such occurrence."

"You have now." Nefff presented the First-Captain with a data-decagon within which floated the hologram of the official seal of the regent of Kundala.

"I will have to have this authenticated," the First-Captain said in a waspish voice.

"You do that," Nefff said. "In the meantime, kindly clear out of here."

Watching the Star-Admiral's Khagggun depart, Olnnn Rydddlin threw his head back and laughed, clapping Kurgan on the back.

"It is good to know who your friends are." His eyes were bright and febrile. "Almost as good as having the power of command, eh?"

"That was a quick turnaround," Kurgan said calmly.

Olnnn Rydddlin did not seem to be paying attention. "I should go after that First-Captain, stick my shock-sword between his ribs, and twist until the blood flies!"

Wing-General Nefff entered the cafe. He addressed Olnnn Rydddlin briefly. "You are safe now, Pack-Commander. Rest easy." Then he turned to Kurgan. "Your father sends his compliments, young sir. As you predicted, he is enjoying immensely exerting his power over the Star-Admiral. You have the regent's thanks for the timely information that made his pleasure possible. Mine as well." He hesitated for a moment, regarding Olnnn Rydddlin again. "I just want you to know, Pack-Commander, that all of us in the regent's wing appreciate the sacrifice you've made." He saluted.

Stunned and gratified to his very soul, Olnnn Rydddlin returned the gesture. As Nefff did a smart military about-face, he sheathed his shock-sword and sat back down at the table. "I swear I will never doubt you again, Kurgan." He shook his head, stretched expansively, and grinned. "You know, all of a sudden, I'm famished."

The traffic on the Boulevard of Dreams had recommenced in full force. The voices of the spice-masters rose and fell, the itinerant musician's melody spiraled outward from his horn. V'ornn children, laughing, ran in and out of the crowds, hiding behind robes and carts, playing with toy swords.

36

Once I Was

The Lady Giyan waited for her child—the Dar Sala-at—in Middle Seat. It was a brutally hot day, not a cloud in the whitish sky, Kundala's five moons a pale and ghostly presence across the firmament. They were, in this time approaching the ides, in various phases from crescent to full, reminding all who glanced at them of the ages of life, from birth to death. This was the message of Lonon, the lesson of humility, lost now, as so many other holy messages had been lost in the skirmishes for power, control, the ultimate destiny of the Kundalan.

For once, Giyan's traveling cloak was a nuisance, thick as it was to keep out the dust and wind and chill of long journeys. She was sweating inside it, but whether from the heat of the day or from raw nerves she could not tell.

Middle Seat was a small village, dry dusty and dull, sitting atop a flat-topped knoll, commanding stellar views into the valleys on either side. To the west was the verdant geometry of clemett orchards, the pink fruit just beginning to ripen. To the east ran the gorge through which the Chuun River flowed south past Axis Tyr, spilling eventually into the Sea of Blood. In the old days, before the coming of the V'ornn, before even the eldest of the present generation of Kundalan had been born, the village had been larger, and important. It was here that a secular government had been formed, if only briefly. It ruled the northern continent for close to fifty years before the Ramahan, reinvigorated by Miina, asserted itself, regaining control of the hearts and minds of the populace.

How times had changed, Giyan thought as she strolled the narrow cobbled streets around the central plaza. From the days of its brief blaze of glory, Middle Seat had fallen into gloom and disrepair, forgotten by all but a nominal outpost of Khagggun who, bored by their lowly tour of duty, had similarly fallen into state of manic-depression. In between erratic bouts of terrorizing the citizenry they passed into drunken stupors. At neither end of the pendulum swing did they appear in the least interested in anyone or anything. That, of course, made them far more dangerous than their more disciplined and predictable brethren elsewhere.

Giyan, made aware of these Khagggun even before she and her party had set foot in the village, took great pains to avoid them when she saw them. She had left Rekkk and Eleana at a ramshackle travelers roadhouse on the outskirts of the village, whose loose-tongued proprietor had been only too happy to provide her with bits of local gossip. She told them that her initial contact with the Dar Sala-at needed to be private, which was true as far as it went. She had no intention of telling them of her personal reasons for wanting to meet with Riane alone.

Their trek had been dispiriting and terrifying. They had come upon a dozen open mass graves in which Eleana had recognized many of her resistance comrades, brutally slaughtered. What they could not voice to one another they nevertheless all wondered: was anyone left to defy the V'ornn?

Giyan shook off these dire thoughts. Osoru told her that her child was close. She had deployed psychic markers, much as Riane had done by pure instinct in the spherical Kell while she had quickly read as much of *The Book of Recantation* as she could before Bartta tracked her down. Giyan's markers were, of course, more complex and subtle. She could tell, for instance, precisely how far Riane was from where she watched and waited in the shadows of a dusty sysal tree. Not a breath of air stirred the leaf-laden branches overhead. The green onyx fountain in the center of the plaza glittered, wavering like a mirage in the heat haze. Water leaked from a crack down one side.

Her gaze took in everything at once—the sun-baked facade surrounding the plaza, the sleepy-eyed vendors indifferently hawking day-old prepared food, the children playing where the water dribbled out of the crack in the fountain, the old and infirm seer on his plinth, intoning his singsong come-on in a rheumy voice, Druuge from the Great Voorg, their striped beaded robes swaying hypnotically, the bottom halves of their faces covered in script-drenched white muslin, crossing diagonally in their slow methodical rhythmic pace. It was a highly unusual occurrence to see these nomads. Even in the Great Voorg they were rarely seen, preferring to keep to themselves, trading sporadically with the Sarakkon who made the long pilgrimage from Harborside in Axis Tyr to the enormous desert in the far eastern quadrant of the continent. Stories made the rounds of a sighting in this small hamlet or that, but as to the veracity of these tales no one could attest. Certainly, their presence had never been recorded in Axis Tyr or any other large city. Giyan had heard of them in her later studies at the abbey, where a heretical but persistent theory venerated them as a long-lost faction of Ramahan.

At any other time, this sighting would have excited Giyan; now she paid them no mind. She was busy wondering how she should prepare herself, then quickly decided that there was simply no way to prepare herself to see her child in the form he was now in. It was not seeing Annon in a Kundalan body that concerned her—after all, he had already been half-Kundalan, though of course no one knew that save Eleusis and herself. The question that haunted and terrified her was how would he react? Would he understand what she had done to save him from Wennn Stogggul? What if he felt that she had abandoned him?

She knew she was getting herself worked up, frightening herself as a kind of protection against the worst-case scenario. But in truth she did not know what she dreaded most from Riane—being forgotten or being hated.

Her child—the Dar Sala-at—was close now, just streets away. All at once, her knees grew weak and sweat rolled into her eyes. She felt a sudden burst of panic, like a gimnopede fluttering in her heart. Tears clouded her eyes, stung her cheeks. *Miina protect him always,* she thought.

And then, emerging from the shadows across the sun-drenched plaza, she saw Riane. The girl was dressed in dusty turquoise robes—the color only Mother or the Dar Sala-at could wear. She held the reins to a pair of cthauros in one hand. In the crook of the other arm she cradled something small and furry. Giyan recognized her instantly, although as the girl began to make her way into the plaza, she observed many differences. For one thing, Riane had grown. For another, her skin was sun- and wind-burned, rich color replacing the waxen pallor that had gripped her back at Bartta's house in Stone Border. She had been gravely ill, then, just before the Nanthera. Now as she strode through the sunlight, Giyan could see how strong and muscular her legs had become. And that gait—yes, it definitely had Annon's confident swagger. On the other hand, she seemed thin, almost painfully so, and there were bruises about her, not so much the kind you could see with your eyes, but the kind Giyan could feel with her Gift, deep places, skinned raw, bleeding pain and guilt and remorse. Too much for someone so young!

Whispering a silent prayer to Miina, Giyan went to meet her, but just then she saw three of the local Khagggun burst into the plaza from a side street. They took one look at Riane—young female Kundalan, a beautiful stranger—and made an immediate beeline toward her. Giyan froze.

The children, catching sight of the advancing Khagggun, ceased their playing and ran, as it happened, right into the nomads. The Khagggun surrounded Riane. The nomads continued bisecting the plaza at their glacial pace, their ropey sun-baked hands turning the children like wet clay on a wheel, deflecting them in another direction. Giyan, like a tortoise, pulled her head deeper into the hood of her cloak and moved toward the group, walking at a natural gait so as not to catch their attention.

They were drunk, these stupid sloe-eyed Khagggun. Horny and drunk and deadly. They wanted what they wanted and, being V'ornn, they were going to get it. They touched Riane, laughing as they poked at the creature curled in the crook of her arm. They began to make lewd gestures. They grabbed at the edge of her traveling cloak, drawing it back, baring her long powerful sun-browned legs.

Giyan, walking toward them, prepared to cast a spell. It was not something she cared to do, not here in such a public place, not at the moment the Dar Sala-at was in plain view. What choice did she have? She would do whatever she could to protect Riane. But as she summoned Osoru, her hands commenced to burn. This had happened twice before, most recently last night when she had been dragged out of sleep. The pain had been so severe that she had had to bite her lip in order to keep from screaming. She had lain awake until dawn, terrified that the unbearable pain would return. Then, as now, her hands throbbed, felt swollen to three times their size, as if they had been turned inside out, as if every nerve was raw, exposed. But now the agony flared up her forearms into her shoulders. When it converged in her chest, she sank to her knees, her legs no longer able to support her. Her head lolled, her face was sweat-streaked. She gasped for air, sobbing and rocking, praying for a cessation of the agony that racked her entire body. She felt as though every molecule was being ripped apart, put back together in an alien configuration. The shiny black chrysalides on her hands and forearms seemed to have grown thicker, rougher, scaly. They pulsed as if with nascent veins. *Miina protect me*, she thought. *What is happening?*

Through this scrim of pain, she became aware that the three nomads had stopped. She looked up, glad for the distraction. Pitch-black hair, light eyes, skin beaten to bronze by the desert sun. They were no more than a stone's throw from where Riane was being accosted by the Khaggun. She felt the slightest ripple at the edge of her vision. Without a word passing between them, the nomads fanned out until they had formed the points of an equilateral triangle.

Giyan, crouched and in pain, nevertheless felt a prickling run along her spine, as if she had just stepped in a nest of spiders. She had seen this configuration before: the mammoth equilateral triangle of heartwood posts set mysteriously into the center of the Great Listening Hall in the regent's palace. Was it a coincidence that the nomads had assumed the same configuration? Sunlight spun off the building facades, giving the scene a glaze of unreality.

Thigpen had made Riane aware of the Khaggun the moment they entered the plaza. "Be careful," she whispered, "you are back among V'ornn now."

"I know what males think of females," Riane said. "I used to be one."

"But you are a Kundalan female now," Thigpen warned. "This will be more difficult than you imagine."

"What pretty young skcettta have we here?" the first Khaggun, said as the three of them surrounded her.

"New blood, new meat," laughed the second as he ran a callused hand down Riane's cheek.

The third one belched loudly, releasing a sour waft of cheap numaaadis. "We will have our way with you, slave-thing." He poked Thigpen. "And then we will skin this disgusting *creature* you coddle and have it for afternoon tea!"

The three of them bellowed in drunken laughter.

"The Druuge are here," Thigpen whispered to Riane. "Just as they promised."

"What?" the third Khagggun said.

"Did that creature speak?" the first Khagggun asked.

"Back away," Riane said to them, but they either did not hear her or were ignoring her.

"You're drunk," the second Khagggun said as he pulled back the flap of Riane's traveling cloak. "Mmm, imagine those legs wrapped around you!"

"Why imagine," the third Khagggun cackled, "when we can have it?"

Riane could see that the three Druuge had arranged themselves in the shape of the Sacred Triangle. She had seen it pictured in *The Book of Recantation*. She had spent the last two days committing the book to memory as she had done with *Utmost Source*. One day until the ides began; one day until the destruction of all life on Kundala. The Druuge were forming a power conduit, a Channel from this realm into a whole succession of others.

"I can't wait any longer," the second Khagggun was saying. "Let's drag her into the alley."

"This is your last warning," Riane said. "Back away."

They heard her now, and laughed, reaching for her.

Riane opened her Third Eye, felt herself becoming the focal point of the Druuge's attention. She was the lens through which the energies of the Channel would be magnified. Their heads tilted forward and all at once Riane felt the Channel open. Beneath her, the power bourns began to sing. Chanting like a rainstorm, like silk floating on the wind, thunder hidden in dark hills, owls' wild cries across verdant treetops, snow spiraling off the frigid tops of the Djenn Marre, sails like cities on the edge of the horizon, the beaten brass of sunset laid like a bridge across the ocean, the molten heat of midday, the muodd-shell pink of sunrise, mist in the arms of maidens, the fall of night. With their strange and wondrous words they constructed an entire world. And the world of their creation fountained outward. A sudden percussion, soundless, deafening, profound, filled the plaza. Water from the fountain sprayed in every direction. The vendors' carts rocked on their wheels, the closest one to the center of the triangle crashed over onto its side. Food rolled across the cobbles.

Giyan, still in pain, gathered her legs under her and rose. Panting and dizzy, she made her way to where Riane stood. Of the nomads or the Khagggun nothing remained. They had vanished into the thickening heat-haze as if blending into a sand dune. The cthauros stood oblivious, tails flicking flies from their gleaming flanks. The vendor righted his cart, kicked his spoiled food. The old seer was silent as the grave, head cupped in his hands. He appeared to be weeping. All the others had fled in terror.

Riane's head turned as Giyan approached. She could not see the older woman's face.

"Your opal spoke to me," she said in a voice so rich and melodious it took Giyan's breath away, for she heard in it hints of her son's tenor. "You bade me come to Middle Seat and here I am. My name is Riane, and this is Thigpen." She stroked the creature's fur.

"Good afternoon, Lady," Thigpen said.

So close to her child, Giyan's nerves were stretched to their limits. But to see a Rappa, alive and well, and in the arms of her child! She was so shocked that, for a moment, she could not find her tongue. No time for second thoughts, for the terror that Riane might hate her or not know her at all.

"I imagine you are surprised to see one of my kind, Lady."

"That would be an understatement, Thigpen." Giyan was grateful for this colloquy as she found herself quite unable to deal with this reunion. "But I am very happy to see you. I have never believed the lies perpetrated against the Rappa."

"Thank you, Lady."

"If I might ask, who were the nomads who so fortuitously interceded with the Khagggun?"

"The Druuge. That is their tribal designation, anyway."

"I know them not, Thigpen."

"Like you, they are Ramahan. At least, their ancestors once were."

"So the rumors are true. The Druuge are a rogue offshoot of my people."

"That is one theory. On the other hand, they could be the direct descendants of the Great Goddess, the true lineage of the Ramahan."

Giyan cocked her head. "You are a wondrous little thing, aren't you?"

Thigpen laughed. "The Dar Sala-at said something similar when we first met."

Riane, smiling, said, "How shall we call you?"

Giyan looked deep into Riane's eyes. At that moment, her Gift provided her with a brief and awful glimpse into Riane's life since she had been forced to leave her with Bartta in Stone Border. She saw exactly what her twin had become, as twisted on the inside as she was on the outside. She saw the gaping hole Miina's long absence had caused in the sorcerous defenses of the abbey, felt with a rush of terror the Dark evil that had infiltrated the remnants of the Ramahan. A shiver ran down her spine. *Merciful Goddess*, she thought, *how much pain has my child endured? I could not be there to protect her from the evils of the world.* Bitterness was in her mouth like ashes. She longed to take her child in her arms, hold her close, croon to her. But she could not. Not here, perhaps not ever. Riane was no longer her child—she was the Dar Sala-at.

Giyan pushed back the deep hood of her cloak until it had settled around her shoulders. The girl's eyes opened wide. Eyes wise beyond her years, Giyan could see, eyes that had witnessed much since she had gone through the Nanthera.

"Giyan . . . ah!"

Eyes that were suddenly full of tears.

"Ah, my Teyjattt," Giyan whispered. "I feared that I would never see you again. To be taken from you at the moment you needed me most."

For a long excruciating moment, Riane could not speak. She was, to put it bluntly, an orphan twice over. To see Giyan now, the female who had raised Annon, cared for him, taught him, loved him, to hear again the nickname she had given him as a child filled Riane with an inexpressible joy. She was astonished at the depths of her feelings. All the terrible events Riane had suffered since awakening to her new life in Stone Border and the abbey fell away like so much dead skin. Having Giyan here beside her was like regaining the most important part of Annon's former life.

"You are well," Riane said. "I am happy for that." The formal response was painful but necessary if she was to maintain her composure. She was acutely aware of being in a public place, one in which more Khagggun could show up at any moment. "By what clever means did you escape the V'ornn?"

Giyan smiled at him. "I was no more prisoner of Rekkk Hacilar's than I was of your father's."

Riane cocked her head. "You must tell me more."

"I will tell you everything, dear one. But in a place that is more private and secure."

Unlike most abbeys, this one was built into a sheer limestone defile. It had about it more of the air of a fortress than a place of religious worship and learning. It was constructed, not from the usual milk-white granite, but from mammoth chunks quarried from the surrounding limestone out of which it seemed to spring in an organic pattern, an anomaly created, perhaps, by the ferocious shifting of tectonic plates far beneath the surface.

Like most abbeys, it had served Middle Seat well in its day. But, by the looks of it, that day had long since passed. It was abandoned now, the thick stone walls gone green with lichen, guarding a windblown emptiness, a sighing of sagging trees in the courtyards, tufted growth of yellow weeds pushing aside the stones of the symmetrical walkways, soft cooing of doves and gimmopedes nesting in the right angles of broken-down eaves. Smell of sun-baked stone, and in the shadows decay, dust, mildew, the ammoniac scent of bird droppings. Drone of insects. The scurrying of small mammals.

It was to this lonely and desolate place, once known as

Warm Current, that Giyan brought the Dar Sala-at. In the absence of priests and acolytes, the architecture was now the focus. There was a fierce beauty in the purity of angles, arches, and curves, a design emerging from its rough cocoon, so elemental, so powerful it was like the last cry of Miina Herself. And so, along with a stark majesty, there was a certain sadness, the lees of a vibrant dye that had once, long ago, saturated this place with purpose. Shadows, thick as midnight, fell exhausted upon walls, gates, doorways, moved reluctantly and painfully, ghosts of arthritic Ramahan goaded by the sun making its slow arc across the sky.

Mother and child stood facing each other in the center of a sun-bleached garden gone to seed. They were only a meter apart, but in every other respect there lay between them a gulf of unknown depth. So much had happened since they had last seen one another. They were both changed—in some ways radically so—and yet were they not still at core the same as they had been in Axis Tyr? Over everything loomed the terrible danger they were facing.

While Thigpen stood guard just outside the front gates, Giyan tried to speak. There was an awkwardness, a halting quality brought about by Riane's formal replies that pulled at her heartstrings, that set up a keening inside her, a kind of mourning, for she knew now that she had missed out on a crucial part of her child's development. They were all at once strangers to each other, and something inside her shriveled, quailed from this knowledge, when her child said, "The V'ornn have activated the Tymnos device. If I do not get to the Storehouse Door in the regent's palace before dawn, Kundala will be destroyed."

Whose eyes were those that gazed upon her, whose voice? The taste of ashes in her mouth, a silent scream at a fate that would rob her of her only offspring. She nodded, numb with despair and the agony of longing for what could now never be. She gathered herself, struggling to be the Lady she was meant to be. "This is why I have been sent to find you."

"We are still a full day's ride from Axis Tyr. How will we ever make it?"

"We are in contact with a Gyrgon. He will get us there in time."

"A Gyrgon? What madness is this?"

"It is Lonon, the mad time, Riane. It is also the time of change. This particular Gyrgon brought us together once through his technomancy."

"I remember," Riane said, shivering a little, despite the heat.

"He feels about the Kundalan the way your father did— the way Rekkk Hacilar does."

Riane listened intently. As a V'ornn, Annon, too, had felt the ineluctable pull toward the Kundalan. Annon had assumed it had something to do with being raised by Giyan. Then, as Riane, she felt certain it had something to do with her being the Dar Sala-at. Now, knowing that other V'ornn— Eleusis, Rekkk, the Gyrgon—also felt it, she suspected they were all part of some greater plan. "Can you trust them, Giyan? Trust them with our lives?"

"Do you remember how your father loved me?" Giyan said softly.

Riane nodded.

"That is how Rekkk loves me." She told Riane how Rekkk made a deal with Nith Sahor to allow her to see Annon once again, how courageous he had been in defending her, in killing the Khagg28un of his own pack sent to stop them. "And as for the Gyrgon," she continued, "he has risked his standing within the Comradeship to help us find you. He wishes the holy city of Za Hara-at to be born; he wants your father's dream to come true. He is the one who told us that the Tymnos device had been activated. I fear he is hunted by his enemies within the Comradeship as Rekkk and I are hunted by Wennn Stogggul and his Dark sorceress, Malistra."

"After Bartta, I have had my fill of Dark sorceresses," Riane said bitterly.

Tears came to Giyan's eyes. Her brief glimpse inside Riane made her fully aware of the undercurrents of pain and guilt and remorse in her child. How she had been tortured, humiliated, tested on Miina's holy anvil. "Ah, Riane, what have I done to you? My heart aches. If only I had been there, if only I had been able to stay. . . ." Her words seemed faded by the sun, dying in the heat. What was she to say? How could she ever explain what she had done? To leave her with the monster her twin had become . . . Merciful Miina, what had she done?

"To stay or leave," Riane said, "it was not your choice, but my fate."

Giyan's heart constricted. She swallowed, nodded. As a mother she had already failed. As a sister too, it appeared. She should have found some way to help Bartta; but they had been riven by tragedy, twins who became strangers to one another. Disaster. She wished she were dead. And then, into the morass of self-loathing into which she had sunk, came a lifeline, tossed by her cherished one.

Riane took a deep breath. "I have thought about you so much and so often," she said.

"You have ever been at the forefront of my thoughts." Giyan, her heartbeat fluttering like a gimnopede's wings, took a hesitant step toward her. More than anything, she wanted to put her arms around her child and hold her, feel her warmth, give her hope that she could accomplish her monumental task. Terrified, she did not move. She opened her mouth to speak, knowing she had been given the opportunity to atone for abandoning her child. "I am so sorry for what I did to you. I have no excuse, only circumstance to offer as explanation: I needed to convince Wennn Stogggul and Kinnnus Morcha that Annon was dead. It was the only way to save you."

"And save me you did. I am grateful for that," Riane said. "What happened to my body?"

She tried to read Riane's expression, to figure out where she stood in her child's eyes. She had already withstood so much pain, why bring her more? "Perhaps it would be better if you didn't know."

"Yes. I understand your concern. Nevertheless, I have to know."

Giyan's heart broke all over again. The intensity of Riane's gaze startled her, impelled her to speak when her intention was otherwise. "I took Annon out to where the V'ornn were killing the citizens of Stone Border." Abruptly, she turned away. Her mouth felt full of blood—Annon's blood.

"You must tell me all of it," Riane said.

Giyan nodded, but she bit her lip all the same. "I laid the body at Rekkk's feet. He ordered his Khagggun to stand down. The killing stopped."

"Thank Miina."

Hearing that phrase uttered by her child startled Giyan. Not her child, she reminded herself again, the Dar Sala-at. "As is the Khagggun custom, First-Captain Olnnn Rydddlin wanted your body dragged around the town plaza behind his horse until all the skin was flayed off, but Rekkk would not let him. When they returned to Axis Tyr, Rydddlin reported him. This simple act of kindness brought him disgrace among his own caste." Her gaze faltered for a moment. "The body was brought back to Wennn Stogggul. The head was severed. The new regime's fear was put to rest. As I had hoped, it is assured of its legitimacy, it has forgotten all about Annon Ashera."

"How strange is hearing the fate of your own body," Riane said slowly. She looked into Giyan's eyes. "It must have hurt you terribly seeing what they did."

"Yes, but all the while I was thinking, He's alive! He's alive!"

"Yes, I am alive," Riane said. "Changed, altered, seeing events through Kundalan eyes, remembering fragments of Riane's past. I can read Venca, you know."

Giyan stared at her, and Riane smiled. "Yes, so many things to tell you—good and bad."

Giyan reached out, smoothed a lock of hair back from Riane's face. "Once I taught you. Now perhaps you will teach me."

Riane took Giyan's hand in her own. "Sometimes I dream I am back in Axis Tyr, back in Annon's body. I have returned to my old life, everything is as it was."

"Oh, but my dear one, it can never be!"

"Yes, I know. And now I would not wish it so." Riane smiled. "And do you know I have your Gyrgon to thank for that—at least partially. You see, when his technomancy brought Annon back I was pulled out of this body, I was Annon again. But that was not what I wanted. I learned that you cannot go back, and you mustn't wish it. The path is ahead, Giyan, isn't it, always ahead."

"Yes," Giyan whispered. Her eyes were flooded with tears. What a difficult, painful lesson, she thought, for one so young to learn.

"But my memories of that previous life . . ." Riane hesitated for just an instant. "Giyan, there were times when I treated you—"

"No, please—"

"Let me finish." Riane moved closer. They were but several handspans apart. "I must say it because it eats at me, because I feel shame and remorse for the times I treated you like a slave, like an animal. I ignored your love for me."

"How could you have acted otherwise? You were of the master race."

"Don't say that. Don't even think it."

Giyan smiled through her tears. Her heart was beating fast with her love for her child. "Yes, there was always another part of you, wasn't there? The part that reacted to and remembered my love, the part that could not stand idly by while Kurgan Stogggul raped Eleana."

"Eleana! You have seen her?"

"There is much to tell you, so many changes. She is waiting for us not six kilometers away."

"She is well?"

"Quite well. She—"

"I want to see her."

"And you will, Teyjattt. But, no, I must not call you that. Your identity must remain an absolute secret between the two of us. It is far too dangerous for anyone else to know."

"Surely you cannot mean Eleana."

"But I do."

Anger flared. "I don't care. Don't you understand? I love her. I have to tell her who I really am. I do not think I could see her again without telling her. It would be sheer agony."

"You are not thinking clearly. You are not Annon, any more than you are Riane. You are the Dar Sala-at."

"I know who I am inside! You cannot order me to do something I don't want to do."

"True enough," Giyan said softly. "But hear me well before you decide. It is written in Prophesy that of the Dar Sala-at's allies one will love her, one will betray her, one will try to destroy her."

"There, you see! Eleana loves me, I know she does."

"So do I."

Riane shook her head. "I don't give a clemett for Prophesy!"

"Stubborn as ever." Giyan could not help a small smile. "Now you sound just like Annon."

"Let us not quarrel." Riane reached out to take Giyan's hand, her eyes opening wide when she saw the chrysalides. "What is this? What has happened to you?"

"They are organic. They seem to have a life of their own."

Riane held both of Giyan's hands in her own. "Do they cause you pain?"

"From time to time. More frequently now. Soon, I think, they will break open."

"This happened when you broke the circle of the Nanthera, didn't it?"

Giyan bit her lip. "I had promised myself not to tell you. I did not want you to feel in any way responsible."

"They are sorcerous," Riane said. "Together we shall work on returning your hands to normal."

"I would like that," Giyan whispered, her voice at the point of breaking. Their eyes locked, and between them passed a current stronger than any other in the Cosmos.

"It always struck me as so strange," Riane said at length, "that I felt closer to you than I did to my own mother. I used to fight off sleep wondering how that could be. I was V'ornn and you were Kundalan, and yet there was something between us, an umbilicus that was almost like a shared purpose. I guess I absorbed more from you than your stories, myths, and songs of Kundala. I came to care for its people, began, oddly, to feel that I was almost one of them." She cocked her head. "Can you make sense of that?"

"Yes," Giyan said as she fought back tears. "I can."

"That afternoon when Kurgan and I went hunting, when we came upon Eleana, everything I had learned from you was crystallized by the violence of the moment. I could have killed Kurgan—would have, I think, had it not been for the gyreagle that appeared out of nowhere and wounded me."

"Miina's messenger."

"More Prophesy. Yes, the talon that pulsed in my chest, that guided me to the Storehouse Door, to Seelin the Dragon."

While they had been talking, the bloody sun had slipped westward, impaling itself on the icy horns of the Djenn Marre. Swiftly now, as time began to run out, twilight stole over them.

"We had better go," Giyan said. "Rekkk, Nith Sahor, Eleana are waiting for us. Friends who will help you get to the Ring of Five Dragons."

As they turned to make for the gate, Giyan hesitated. "Riane, please, you must understand. I am the only one who knows your secret, who knows that inside Riane Annon Ashera still lives. No one else must know this. The regent's spies are everywhere. The Gyrgon himself told us to trust no one. And now that Stogggul has somehow acquired the talents of a Dark sorceress we must be doubly vigilant. She found me once, perhaps she can again." She took her child by the shoulders, her heart breaking. "When we leave here, when we meet our friends—even our friends, Riane—you are the Dar Sala-at and I am Lady Giyan. Understood?"

There was a terrible pain in Riane's eyes. "But here," she whispered, "in our private sanctuary, where we love and are loved, you will still call me Teyjattt, won't you?"

Giyan was weeping as she pulled her child into a fierce embrace that shattered all her emotions and, in a magical instant, healed her heart.

The Daemon Is in the Details

Of course I recognize it." Star-Admiral Kinnnus Morcha gripped the bracelet in one fist. "Do you not think I know the regent's handiwork when I see it?"

"Perhaps I should not have pried it out of her fingers." Kurgan's head was bent, his expression downcast. "Perhaps I should have left it for you—"

"No." The Star-Admiral's hand made a cutting gesture. "You did the right thing, adjutant. I would not see her now— this last time—clutching Stogggul's bribe."

It was not lost on Kurgan that the Star-Admiral did not use the regent's full name, that he spoke of him now with contempt as well as hatred.

Kinnnus Morcha willed Dalma to look at him, but her sightless eyes remained staring fixedly at the sky. Overhead, the clouds moved, but she did not. His boots crunched over white-marble gravel dark with her blood. It appeared as if her body was already sinking into the ground, becoming part of the neat path the violence of her last moments of life had disturbed. The entire park was surrounded by members of his personal wing. To a Khaggun, they faced outward, ion cannons at the ready, their backs to the tragedy. "What evil fate has overtaken me that I should have cared for such a one?" He took a deep, ragged breath. "I blame Stogggul for this. Not simply for her death, but for her corruption as well."

"I am your right arm. I could do nothing while the regent's troops defied your order to put Olnnn Rydddlin away. I am humiliated by my inaction. What would you have me do, Star-Admiral?"

"Do?" Kinnnus Morcha looked at Kurgan out of reddened

eyes. He was dressed in full battle armor, as were all of his Khaggun. "You will do nothing. You will make no sound, take no action whatsoever. It seems the regent's stupidity has surfaced sooner rather than later. He rapes and murders Dalma. He countermands my orders to have Olnnn Rydddlin locked away. Rydddlin is mad, of that you can be certain. But he is exceedingly clever, as mad V'ornn often are, to have persuaded Stogggul to give him succor. I see now that I have underestimated him." His eyes sparked with rage. "Either that, or the cursed sorceress who stands ever by the regent's side has taken him under her foul wing." His fingers curled into a fist. "I would not put such a poisonous deed past that accursed skcettta! Poison seems to be her stock-in-trade. She has poisoned Wennn Stogggul's mind, sure enough."

Kinnnus Morcha knelt, cupped the bloody crown of Dalma's skull. "You never knew how much I cared for you. I never told you; I never showed you. How could I? I am Khaggun. But I did care for you. You touched a part of me and made it live. Now it is as cold and dead as your poor self." His fingertips moved over her brow, down her cheek. "Sleep now, and do not trouble yourself. Your pain is ended, but I swear to you on my own life that your murderer's is just beginning."

He rose then and turned away from her. Signaling for First-Captain Julll to approach, he gave orders for Dalma's interment. First-Captain Julll nodded, turned, and marched quickly away. It was a quiet time, a time of reflection. Kurgan observed everything with the detachment he had learned at the Old V'ornn's knee. He felt nothing for these two allies turned antagonists—not compassion, not loyalty, not even the sweet taste of irony at his own role in the escalation of their enmity. If you were not detached you could not be objective, the Old V'ornn had said. And if you could not be objective, you could not see the big picture. If you were as ambitious as Kurgan was, seeing the big picture was everything.

When, at length, the Star-Admiral looked at Kurgan, he

seemed his old self again. "No, we will let the regent and the traitorous Wing-General Nefff make their rash and ill-considered public moves, while in the privacy of our caste we will consolidate our power, prepare for battle. If it is a war the regent wants, then by putrid N'Luuura it is a war he shall get!"

"Forgive me, Father," Nith Sahor said, "for I have sinned."
"It is no sin to follow your convictions," the brilliantly plumaged teyj answered. "It is the way I taught you to live your life."

"For good or ill." Nith Sahor smiled and held out his wrist. The bird flew from its perch, its agile talons gripping the thick glove-grids. Immediately, its translucent yellow talons extruded, forging the link, making contact.

"This cortical net you made for me is extraordinary," the teyj said, preening its feathers. "I revel in all these colors!"

Nith Sahor smiled. "You were quite an artist in your day, Father. You always had an extraordinary sense of color."

"And I gave birth to a scientist! Who would have thought!"

"Once there were many artists among the Comradeship, but no more. You were the last of your kind, Father. Now we Gyrgon are of a piece, technomages all."

"No, my son, you are not like the rest."

"Too much like them, I sometimes fear. I wish I were more like you."

"Well, perhaps it's better that you haven't followed in my footsteps. Children should have their own lives, not be saddled with living their father's all over again."

"Assuming there will be any life left to live," Nith Sahor said.

The teyj looked around. "We are not in your tower."

"Not in the Temple of Mnemonics at all. I had to put you to sleep for a time."

"I hate when you do that," the teyj said.

"Couldn't be helped. My laboratory came under siege."

"Nith Batoxxx?"

Nith Sahor nodded. "He is incensed that I have left the Comradeship. Others are falling in line."

The teyj lifted its four wings and settled back. "How bad?"

"Bad enough," Nith Sahor admitted. "The Comradeship is in disarray. Thanks to Nith Batoxxx their focus has shifted from pure science to political maneuvering. Nith Batoxxx has been the most vociferous voice raised in fury against the three who were killed by the Kundalan sorcery."

"The Ring of Five Dragons! I wish I could write about it! What tales I could compose!"

"If you feel the urge to write, expose Nith Batoxxx and his poisonous tongue."

"I told you he was a bad seed several hundred years ago."

"I'm afraid I was too busy with my experiments to listen to you, Father. My fault entirely." Nith Sahor made his way over the bare floor to a dusty window. "But my real mistake may be in breaking with the Comradeship."

"Not if it is half as corrupt as you say." The teyj swiveled its head, its golden eyes quick and darting. "Colorless, drab sort of place you've picked. Not a stick of furniture to be seen in this wasteland."

"This warehouse is not pretty, but it suits my purposes. Look!" Nith Sahor activated his glove-net. Blue fire sparked around the bare room so that it shimmered, wavered. When it restabilized every nook and cranny was crammed with arrays of equipment neatly arranged on shelves.

"It's a duplicate of your tower laboratory!" the teyj exclaimed.

"One of several."

"You keep altogether too many secrets from me, my son!"

"I need to find ways to keep you amused, Father." He stroked the teyj's feathers. "Creating this bio cortical net to house your electromagnetic force was difficult enough—I could not give you the means to express your artistic side."

"Do not fret, my son. Think of what you have accomplished! I am alive again, and for that alone I am grateful. You have become a great scientist—a technomage for the ages!" The teyj peered out the window. "I see troops, many Khagggun in battle armor."

"The regent and the Star-Admiral are having a bit of a disagreement. I believe they mean to kill each other."

"I am not surprised," the teyj said with asperity. "I have always held the firm belief that you cannot mix Great and Lesser Castes. There is an innate distrust among unequals. Why shouldn't there be? Distrust is bred in their bones."

"This goes deeper than a simple blood feud." Nith Sahor took the teyj away from the window. "I feel certain that another force, powerful, subtle, something we have never before encountered is at work here. It has something to do with Kundala itself."

"I know you have believed from the moment we made planetfall that this planet was special."

"I persuaded none, I angered many. Now I am convinced I was right, Father. Kundala will either be our crowning glory or our doom."

"Doom? Why do you say doom?"

Nith Sahor sat on a stool before one of his mysterious consoles. Banks of holographic runes—red, blue, yellow—spilled across the cortical interface like rain, disappearing and reappearing in a pattern so complex it gave the teyj a headache.

"Sometimes our mission seems endless, Father. We search for the Single Great Equation, the Unifying Theory that will explain the Cosmos. But the Cosmos is in eternal flux. It is Chaos. How can you make sense of Chaos?"

"That is what art attempts to do, my son. That is the purity of its purpose. It was the founding principle of the Comradeship. Now look what has happened. They have descended into the cauldron of politics. Now all they can do is make chaos out of order."

"You are one of the few, Father. You are an artist. You understand uncertainty. But the Comradeship, as a whole, abhors uncertainty. It terrifies them. That is why they are so uneasy here in Kundala, why they have destabilized. There are too many mysteries they cannot solve. The harder they try, it seems, the further away the answers seem."

"Perhaps, in this case, there are no answers."

"That is the romantic in you speaking," Nith Sahor said. "No, for every enigma posed by Kundala there is an answer, I know it."

"What if the answer is not to your liking?"

"Still, we will have a better idea of our place in the Cosmos, won't we?"

"You have my disposition as well as my blood, my son. You do not fear uncertainty."

"On the contrary, I am drawn to it."

"Then your break with the Comradeship was inevitable."

"They will try to destroy me."

"You will not let them."

"Nith Batoxxx is clever, and gaining power inside the Comradeship. They have never had need of leaders. It seems he is a born leader."

"So are you, my son. But you have yet to recognize that quality in yourself." The teyj sighed, much as Nith Sahor's father had sighed when he was alive. "Once we were all One. That was the nature of the Comradeship, after all. The reason it was formed."

"What we have come to is a tragedy."

"I know when it began," the teyj said. "The moment we first engaged the Centophennni. From that point onward, nothing inside the Comradeship has been the same. That one act tainted us, what the doctrine of Enlil spoke of as the Original Sin. This, too, we have rejected as apocryphal."

"You may be right." Nith Sahor was staring at the hailstorm of runes on the interface. "But at the moment, we have a more immediate problem. Nith Batoxxx and his cabal have found me."

He leapt up, his floor-length greatcoat swirling around him. One wall of the warehouse was beginning to balloon outward.

"I don't like the look of this," the teyj said.

Nith Sahor passed a hand over its head and the teyj collapsed into a stream of iconic positrons that flowed, merging into the holographic hailstorm of runes on the console interface.

"Sleep well, Father," Nith Sahor said as he turned, engaging his ion exomatrix.

The walls of the warehouse paled, grew translucent, then transparent as the technomancy wielded by Nith's Sahor enemies was brought to bear on the safeguards he had erected. Green ion fire leapt out from his fingers, shoring up the walls, but he knew it was a holding action at best. He could feel them, feel their enmity, their power, grown exponentially. There were too many of them for him to fight at this time, in this place. He would have to—

Something screamed in his mind as a ruby-red ion-particle beam lanced through the wall and struck him on the side of the skull. He staggered, gritting his teeth. He struck back, but it was no use, more and more of the ruby-red beams were slicing through the last of his defenses. He prepared himself, was almost done when he saw Nith Batoxxx, floating in the air just outside the warehouse. Nith Batoxxx bared his yellow teeth, his arm swept out, and another ion-particle beam sliced through the wall. The wall, stretched beyond its tolerance, shattered, and the beam caught Nith Sahor full on. He went to his knees, half-stunned, and Nith Batoxxx came swooping in for the kill.

There's something wrong." Rekkk grabbed at the okummmon Nith Sahor had implanted in his left forearm.

"What is it?" Eleana asked.

"It's throbbing." He gritted his teeth. "The pain!" He fell to his knees in the second-floor room they had rented in the shabby roadhouse just outside Middle Seat. Eleana held him as he groaned, brushed the sweat off his face with her sleeve. The ceiling was low, smoke-stained. The windows were small as eyes. The furniture was barely usable. Outside, dusk was crawling toward them like a beggar on his knees. The litter-strewn courtyard was deserted except for a wagon pulled by two sorry-looking cthauros. A traveling knife-sharpener had set up shop during the late afternoon and was now plying his trade. Cicadas screamed in the ammonwood trees.

"My arm," Rekkk whispered. "It feels like my arm's on fire."

"Just hold on," she said. "Hold on, Rekkk."

Noises arose like smoke from the public rooms downstairs. A single lamp was lit against the darkness, all the mean room had by way of illumination. Its flame flittered and danced, sending hunchbacked shadows up the wall.

His fingers were twitching, curling and spasming as if they had a will of their own. "Something's . . . something's happened to Nith Sahor."

Eleana bent over him. "What do you mean?" She wished Giyan were here. What was taking her so long? She should have found the Dar Sala-at long before now. What if she had run into trouble—the crazy Khaggun in Middle Seat the roadhouse proprietor had warned them about. She bit her lip, in a knot of worry. She regretted now not insisting that she and Rekkk accompany her. But she had been adamant on going alone. Even Rekkk knew there were times you could not argue with her.

"He is under attack!" Rekkk managed to get out before another wave of fiery pain hit him. "Ah, N'Luuura take it!"

She could feel him trembling all over. He had gone cold as ice.

"He's injured," Rekkk panted. "Badly injured."

He was almost doubled over in pain. All at once, the okummmon emitted an ear-piercing sound. Eleana's teeth began to chatter. Rekkk was on the verge of passing out. The okummmon bulged outward. There was a flash of brilliant blue light, followed immediately by what sounded like a clap of thunder.

Out of the slot in the okummmon appeared a brilliantly plumaged bird.

"N'Luuura, a teyj," Rekkk said hoarsely, as the four-winged bird swooped back and forth near the ceiling.

The colors of the teyj's plumage began to run, dripped through the air, separating, coming apart, disassociating. And just as quickly re-formed into another figure entirely.

"Nith Sahor!" Rekkk pulled himself together, shaking off the pain like an animal shakes off rain.

The Gyrgon, having morphed into his true shape, fell to one knee. As Eleana ran toward him, he held up a gloved hand. Sparks fountained through the air, and the acrid smell of burning components filled the room. His ion exomatrix appeared cracked in several places. Some of his tertium and germanium circuits glowed eerily, while others seemed blackened, fused.

Eleana turned back to Rekkk. "He's bleeding!" she said.

Staggering to his feet, Rekkk approached the figure.

"I am sorry I caused you so much pain, Rekkk," Nith Sahor said. His voice sounded odd, muffled, as if emanating from another dimension. "At such short notice, however, it could not be helped."

"Do not concern yourself," Rekkk said, kneeling in front of the Gyrgon. "What has happened?"

Nith Sahor's head lifted, and he looked Rekkk in the eye. The amber-colored skin of his head was unhealthily mottled. His hollow cheeks were speckled with blood. "I was required to defend myself against enemies most zealous." A small rueful smile played across his lips. "It has been some time since I needed to do that. I fear I was a trifle rusty. I was obliged to beat a strategic retreat."

"How badly are you injured?"

"Whole inside and out, I assure you."

But some dark undertow in his tone, a certain pallor in his startling star-sapphire eyes told Rekkk he was lying.

The Gyrgon turned his attention to Eleana, his body unfolding like that of a golden mantis until he was standing. "So this is the young Kundalan resistance leader."

"You know about me?" the girl said uncertainly.

"Assuredly. Rekkk has been sending me periodic reports of your progress."

"Then you'll know I abandoned the resistance to join Gi-yan and Rekkk in the quest to find the Dar Sala-at. Your

Khagggun have done too good a job at decimating our ranks and killing our idealism."

"A necessary though regrettable turn of the wheel. You have my sympathies."

"What shall I do with them?"

"Pardon me." The Gyrgon blinked. "Is that a joke?"

"I don't know," she said. "I suppose in a macabre way it is. This is my first encounter with a Gyrgon, though I have lost count of the times I have dreamed of this moment. I have dreamed many times of killing such as you, with my bare hands if necessary. Your kind have killed so many of my people, so cruelly, wantonly, with a detached pleasure." Tears trembled in the corners of her eyes. "So many gone, like a river of flesh and bones emptying out into the Sea of Blood, earning it its name all over again."

"What fire!" Nith Sahor said approvingly. "I can appreciate your passion. Believe me, it will prove invaluable in the days and months to come."

Eleana clutched her rage in tightly balled fists. "I would kill you now if I could, if Rekkk would let me."

"I understand. There is nothing I can say that could make up for the blood that has been spilled, the pain and suffering we have caused. A single thought to carry with you through the dark time ahead. One day, it is my hope and expectation that you will see me for what I truly am."

Eleana turned her back, would not respond even to Rekkk's gentle touch.

Nith Sahor looked around the room. "Speaking of Lady Giyan, where is she?"

"She went to fetch the Dar Sala-at," Rekkk said.

Nith Sahor's face darkened momentarily. "On her own? Rekkk, I thought I made myself clear."

"You did. It's just that Giyan has a will of her own."

"She also has a way of making that will manifest." Nith Sahor nodded grudgingly. "I understand." He went slowly and, Rekkk suspected, painfully, to the window overlooking part of the courtyard and the road leading to Middle Seat. "How long has that knife-sharpener been here?"

Rekkk shrugged. "I do not know exactly. He came sometime in the afternoon."

"He may be a knife-sharpener," Nith Sahor observed, "but if so he is honing his own shock-sword."

"What?" Rekkk leapt to the window to have a look himself. "He is Khagggun?"

"Yes, Rekkk." Nith Sahor passed a gloved hand across the window. Blue ions arced briefly, and the Gyrgon's eyes closed, moving rapidly back and forth beneath the lids as if he were dreaming. "He is from Axis Tyr. He bears the mark of the regent's Haaar-kyut. He has been keeping tabs on you. It would be an excellent wager to assume he is waiting for reinforcements."

"How did he know we were here?"

"A good question, Rekkk. It goes without saying that he lacks the intelligence to have found out on his own. He must have been directed here."

Rekkk snapped his fingers. "Malistra! She found us once through a sorcerous beacon. But Giyan swore to me she had blocked it."

"I would not bet against Lady Giyan's sorcery." Nith Sahor turned back into the room. "Therefore, Malistra must have found an alternative means to track you." He began to search their meager belongings. "Tell me, Rekkk, is there anything in your possession she could have tainted? Anything that was lost and now found, something out of your sight for even a few moments?"

"No, I can't think of anything."

"I can." Eleana turned around. In her palm lay the V'ornn weapon.

"A spider-mite," Nith Sahor said.

"Malistra cast a spell on it to protect Olnnn Rydddlin from Giyan's sorcery."

"Put it down," Nith Sahor said. "At once."

Eleana did as he bade, then stepped back, moving to Rekkk's side. Rekkk put a protective arm around her.

"Now we are faced with a fascinating conundrum." Hands clasped at the small of his back, Nith Sahor walked slowly and meditatively around the weapon. From time to time, he paused and, again, Rekkk found himself wondering how badly the Gyrgon had been injured. "What did Malistra do to it?"

"Giyan has been trying to determine that," Rekkk said.

Nith Sahor paused. "She handled it?"

"A number of times."

"It is simplicity itself. One sorceress casts a spell to absorb the aura of another sorceress." Nith Sahor nodded. "All right. We have identified our tracker." He squatted down, hands steepled in front of his face. "Now what shall we do with it? Shall we destroy it and be done with it?" He cocked his head up, looked at Eleana. "What do you say, Resistance?"

Eleana thought a moment. "If it were up to me, I would leave it alone. When we leave here, the knife-sharpener won't come with us. He'll stay right here where the tracker is."

"Better yet, we could send the tracker somewhere else." Nith Sahor rose in a shower of blue sparks. Hyperexcited ions surrounded the tracker, whisked it away at the movement of his hand. "I believe we can now work unobserved." But the smile that tinged his face was already turning into a grimace of pain.

38

Blood-Letting

The Ring of Five Dragons!" With avid fingers Wennn Stogggul plucked the ring from Malistra's open palm. "Allow me, Lord." She smiled as she slid it onto his index finger.

He grimaced. "Tight fit."

"It was meant for Kundalan fingers, Lord." Watching him

from beneath hooded lids. The tip of her tongue flicked out as she saw the single bead of blood leaking from the spot where the thorn had pricked him. She grasped his hand, wiping it away before he could see it.

"Now what do I do?" he asked her. "How do I summon the sorcery of the Kundalan?"

"In time, Lord," she said, wrapping her arms around him. They were walking in her herb-and-mushroom garden in the regent's palace. The sky was a canopy of cerulean blue. Butterflies danced beside Haaar-kyut in full battle armor patrolling the shanstone ramparts. A blood-fig tree she had lately planted bloomed in sorcerous abandon, releasing a scent that appealed to Stogggul particularly. She made certain to bring him here at least once a day so that his system would be infused with the perfume that made him adore her above all others. "The ring needs to become accustomed to its new master. Even as we speak it is attuning itself to you and you alone. Within twenty-four hours the sorcery will be yours to command."

"That long?" He frowned. "I wanted to use it now against Kinnnus Morcha." He lifted his ringed fist over his head. "I want to stamp him out like a dung beetle!"

"And you will, Lord." Malistra licked his ear. "If you grow impatient, why not lay the plans now for his demise?"

"And how would you advise I do that?"

"Enlist your son and Olnnn Rydddlin. Kurgan has the Star-Admiral's ear, yet he has lately proved by deed the sincerity of his pledge to you. He has helped you humiliate Morcha. And Olnnn Rydddlin owes you an enormous debt of gratitude."

Stogggul's eyes gleamed darkly. "Your idea has merit." He inhaled deeply the perfume of the sorcerous blood-fig tree. "I could use Kurgan to lure Morcha into a trap. That will certainly please me. But as for Olnnn Rydddlin, of what use is he to me?"

"He despises Morcha now. He will be only too eager to do what you ask of him."

"And what would that be?"

"He is a masterful warrior. He would be honored to act as your assassin."

"What are you talking about? He is a cripple."

"It only appears that way," Malistra whispered so there was no chance of being overheard. "And therein lies his advantage. He gives the appearance of a grievously wounded veteran, sadly and prematurely retired. But I have made his skeletal leg stronger than it was before. Believe me when I tell you he will be even more formidable as the regent's assassin than ever he was as a Pack-Commander."

As usual, she was telling him as much of the truth as served her purpose. In fact, she had imbued Olnnn Rydddlin with something of herself. No one—not the least Olnnn Rydddlin himself—could possibly guess what she had done to him; it was too soon for such gifts to come to light. First, he had to struggle. He had to overcome his own revulsion of the unknowable, of the chaos that was life. He had, in essence, to transcend his limitations as a V'ornn if he was ever to come into full possession of the gifts she had given him. She had made this decision while she was healing him. He had been unconscious, hanging between life and death. She made a perilous deal with fate. If his will to live was strong enough, this would be her price, and a steep one it was.

They had come to the end of their stroll around the garden. Stogggul turned to her, bruised her lips with his. "Tell me, Malistra," he whispered, "what need is there for me to be regent when you are doing such a neat job of it?"

"I only suggest, Lord. It is you who schemes and makes decisions."

"Foolish female, that was a joke." He laughed, parted her robes, exposed her firm, glowing flesh. He shivered with anticipation as she knelt in front of him. "A very funny joke, oh yes!"

When Riane thought of seeing Eleana she simply could not imagine it. As she approached the roadhouse outside Middle Seat she found herself becoming more and more apprehensive. The simple fact was, she was confused. Deep inside her core, the personality of Annon quailed, his "male-ness" already anticipating the sexual charge Eleana gave "him." But Annon was no longer Annon. Riane had no idea how her body would respond. Why should she? She had limited experience being female. Since becoming Riane, the symptoms of the hormonal changes raging through her system had been suppressed by her terror, isolation, and despair. It was anyone's guess what would happen when she was standing next to Eleana. She was terrified of a cataclysm.

Giyan, seeing the tremors run through her, stopped them in the courtyard. Save for the group's cthauros, it was deserted, unkempt, thoroughly unpleasant. Putting a hand on Riane's arm, she said: "Try to relax."

"Easy for you to say."

Giyan smiled. "As a matter of fact, it's not. I am every bit as apprehensive as you are." She did not have to give voice to her apprehension: Eleana posed the biggest potential threat to them, because she would prove the greatest temptation to Riane to reveal who she really was. Thigpen, lying across Riane's shoulders, placidly observed this exchange between them. Riane was grateful that she had never asked what the two of them had talked about inside the Abbey of Warm Current. The creature seemed to accept with preternatural equanimity these brief enigmatic conversations that pointedly excluded her. "We all harbor secrets, Riane," was all she had said. "This is how the Cosmos continues to manufacture Chaos."

Rekkk was waiting anxiously for them in the courtyard of the roadhouse.

"So this is the Dar Sala-at," he said.

Riane stared at him. Tall and rangy, with a handsome lined face, he seemed not at all the fierce Pack-Commander Annon had seen that day in the forest. His eyes were alive and curious, with none of the cruel remoteness typical of Khaggun. What would he think if he knew Annon Ashera still lived, existing inside this female Kundalan body?

"Rekkk Hacilar," Giyan said, firmly putting a hand on each of Riane's shoulders, "this is Riane."

Rekkk smiled. "We have spent many days trying to find you."

On the other hand, the irony of the situation—being allied with the former Pack-Commander who had chased Annon and Giyan from Axis Tyr to Stone Border—was not lost on her. It was decidedly eerie to have this knowledge—to have known Rekkk without him being aware of it. She remembered Thigpen telling her that it was the Dar Sala-at's fate to be apart from all others. This, her first taste of the enormity of the isolation, made her feel empty inside, a hollow bowl waiting to be filled by rainwater in a place of eternal drought.

"I have never met a Rhynnnon before," she said, "though I have heard much about them."

"You have?" Rekkk frowned. "How would a Kundalan girl—?"

"Rekkk, what has happened?" Giyan said hastily as she gave Riane a warning look. "Why have you risked showing yourself instead of waiting for us upstairs?"

"Nith Sahor is here," he said quickly. "He denies it, but I am certain he has been in a major battle of some sort, doubtless involving Gyrgon technomancy. He is wounded, Giyan, grievously, I believe. Can you help him?"

"I do not know," she said, leading them across the roadhouse's scarred and battered front door. "But I will try."

"Lady," Nith Sahor said the moment they entered the room, "I am gratified that you and Rekkk have fulfilled the commission I asked of you. This, I take it, is the Dar Sala-at. It is an honor to meet a legend in the flesh." His star-sapphire eyes swung from Riane back to Giyan.

"I can feel what you are doing, but you waste your time," he told her flatly. "What has been done to me cannot be undone by your sorcery." His gloved forefinger pointed at his skull. "The circuits are damaged. Since they are a part of me . . ." He shrugged. "But we must not talk about this. There are far more pressing matters to attend to."

"But—"

"The Gyrgon is right," Riane said. "The ides of Lonon begin tomorrow. We must direct all our energies and resources on the survival of Kundala." She turned to Nith Sahor. "Giyan tells me you can transport us to Axis Tyr."

"In the blink of an eye," Nith Sahor said. "The rest will be up to you. Once you are in the city I can no longer help you. I am anathema there. Hunted just as you will be if your identity is discovered."

"And once there, how will we enter the regent's palace?"

"Eleana and I have taken care of that matter," Rekkk said.

And now, at last, the moment that Riane had been anticipating and dreading had come. Eleana had been hanging back in the corner of the room, but now she stepped forward. "I never imagined I would ever see the Dar Sala-at, let alone meet her."

Riane wanted to say something, anything. Out of the corner of her eye, she saw Giyan watching her intently. Eleana had not changed much from the image Annon had kept with him from their first meeting. It was curious. Riane still saw her through "male" eyes. She took in the curve of her breast, the narrowness of her waist, the length and strength of her legs. And her face—well, her face seemed, if possible, even more beautiful than it had been in Annon's memory, as if suffused with an inner glow. She exuded a warrior's aplomb, a female's sensuality. It was a potent mix. The attraction had not ebbed one iota. Riane's knees felt weak, and she could not quite catch her breath. She was overrun with an emotion that had nowhere to go.

In truth, Riane did not know what she would have done next had Nith Sahor not begun to change color. An odd unhealthy pallor had commenced to drain him of his normal amber color. For a moment, he staggered and, out of control, hyperexcited ions rimmed the room in an eerie greenish glow. His eyes had gone all weird. They had lost much of their glitter.

As if responding to an unspoken request, Thigpen leapt up into the Gyrgon's arms. Nith Sahor turned and went to the door.

"Finalize your plans," he said. "I would speak with the Rappa alone."

*   *   *

"You were right to suspect the Sarakkon," Kurgan said. "They know something about the Druuge."

Star-Admiral Kinnnus Morcha, in his battle pavilion within Axis Tyr, looked up from his camp table. Before him, plans of war: formations, strategies, alliances among Khaggun clans, lists drawn up for him by First-Captain Julll of his most trusted Wing-Generals. Lists of those who would die for him, lists of those would might at the last moment falter, lists of those staunchly loyal and those vulnerable to bribe.

"Strengths and weaknesses, adjutant," he said wearily. "Victory in battle comes from assessing and reassessing these polar opposites."

"The Sarakkon are clever deal-makers," Kurgan went on in an even tone.

The Star-Admiral's lips pursed. "Are you proposing an alliance?"

"Actually, it was the Sarakkon's idea. I think they want more freedom of movement on the northern continent."

"What for?" said Kinnnus Morcha, ever suspicious.

"For reasons I find incomprehensible, they find the oceans fascinating. Also, deserts. They want an overland route to the Great Voorg."

"That's it? They want access to three thousand square kilometers of sand?"

"Yes, sir. I believe it is."

The Star-Admiral's interest quickened. "Do you think they will fight for me?"

"If you give them what they want, yes, sir, I do. I have found them strange but honorable. Their word is law, that much I know."

Kinnnus Morcha nodded. "Then by all means, set it up at once."

"This is something I cannot do alone, sir." Kurgan watched the Star-Admiral's face as he proceeded over this exceedingly treacherous minefield. "They insist on meeting you face-to-face."

"Impossible. Especially at this moment in time."

Kurgan pitched his voice lower. "I know them, sir. You are the leader. If you do not consummate the deal yourself, they will feel we have something to hide. They will not trust us no matter what I say."

Kinnnus Morcha stood with his hands on his hips, ruminating. Kurgan imagined that he and Morcha were balanced on the razor's edge of a shock-sword blade. Everything depended on what Morcha said next. "Why should I trust them? They may have made a deal with the regent."

Kurgan, breathing a sigh or relief, said, "I know my father. He is barely aware of their presence. But, even so, it pays to be vigilant. At my insistence, the Sarakkon captain—Courion—has agreed to come alone and unarmed. I have cordoned off the area with our own men."

The Star-Admiral's head snapped up, "Area? What area?"

"Harborside. We will meet on Courion's ship."

Kinnnus Morcha's eyes narrowed. "Whose idea was that?"

"Mine, sir. I have been on the ship before. It is safe. Besides, Harborside is known to me; it is totally unknown to the regent and his people."

Kinnnus Morcha smiled at last. "I see I have taught you well, adjutant. You serve me with admirable devotion. When this campaign is over you will be promoted in rank."

Kurgan bowed his head. "Thank you, sir. If I may say, you have been like a second father to me."

This way," Rekkk whispered, as he and Riane turned down the jam-packed Boulevard of Crooked Dreams. It was night, but fusion lamps burned brightly along the street, the warrens of the spice market as busy as they were at noon. As far as Riane knew, the market never closed. "Eleana said the entrance to the tunnel was at the back."

Wrapped in the preternatural darkness of Nith Sahor's voluminous greatcoat, they had been transported to a copse of sysal trees less than a kilometer from the Northern Gate. This prodigious feat appeared to have taken almost all of the Gyrgon's remaining strength. Eleana had volunteered to stay with him while the others made their way into the city. Before she left them Giyan had conjured a trine of sorcerous markers, glowing green like fireflies. "If anyone approaches with hostile intent, sorcerous or otherwise," she had told Eleana out of Nith Sahor's hearing, "the green will turn to red. You must prepare yourself."

"I am already prepared," she had said as she fingered the V'ornn weapons at her waist.

"No one knows we are here, no one will come." Giyan had kissed her on the forehead. "But just in case."

The rest of them—Riane and Thigpen, Giyan, Rekkk—had set off for Axis Tyr. As she had before, Giyan used Flowering Wand, Osoru's spell of cloaking, to make them appear as V'ornn Khaggun to the guards at the gate checkpoint. It was a short-term spell that could not be cast again for some time.

Inside the gates, they had melded into the bustle of the city. They had not stayed together for long. Thigpen had jumped from her place around Riane's neck. When Riane had asked where she was going, she had said, "The Gyrgon spoke to me. He is gravely wounded and requires my help."

"But I am going to need your help," Riane had protested.

"It is forbidden," the creature had said. "Now is the time of First Testing. The Dar Sala-at must succeed or fail on her own."

"Hold on!" Rekkk said now, as he pushed Riane back into the shadows of a crowded pavilion reeking of cinnamon and clove. "Haaar-kyut!"

Squeezed into a small space with Rekkk, a fat V'ornn, and three sad-eyed Kundalan servant females, Riane watched a half dozen of the regent's handpicked guard marching through the market. They wore purple battle armor, their faces were set in grim resolve. She wondered where Giyan was. She had left them in the swirl of the city in order to prepare in private her sorcerous defenses against Malistra.

Riane and Rekkk waited in the throng, shoulder to shoulder. At length, the Haaar-kyut were out of sight. Rekkk signed to Riane and they made their way to the rear of the market. Eleana had given them detailed directions. She had discovered a back passage into the main Haaar-kyut barracks on a reconnaissance mission before the recent explosion.

When they moved aside sacks of coriander seed piled behind a stall, it was there just as she said it would.

"Maybe I should go with you," Riane said, as they crouched just outside the tunnel entrance. "Who knows what you might find there?"

"Absolutely not," Rekkk said. "We all have our orders, our parts to play. For the moment, yours is to stand lookout." His voice softened as he put a hand on Riane's shoulder. "Forgive an ex-Khaggun's gruff manner. We cannot chance exposing you to more danger than is necessary. All right?"

Riane nodded and, without another word, Rekkk disappeared. Riane moved a couple of the pungent sacks back into place, sat with her back against the space between them. She could feel a cool draft of air issuing from the tunnel. Giyan had thought it too dangerous to get into the palace the same way she and Annon had escaped it. "Someone recognized us the night of the coup," she had told Riane privately before they had left the roadhouse. "Whoever it was may have seen us come out the underground exit."

A grey-faced shopkeeper with spice-stained hands haggled with an irate customer over a bag of twigged myrtle. A line of drays laden with spices, one kind to a dray, were backed up at the side of the market, muscular Kundalan off-loading sacks and barrels, overseen by a covey of lock-faced Bashkir, all with one beady eye on their competitors' wares. Tusku-gggun, their daily work done, their children put to bed, sat at K., the cafe across the boulevard, or strolled through the market, chatting and making purchases. Movement everywhere, in shadows and light, in the heavily trafficked street, in front of the most popular of the stalls, selling bright yellow turmeric, gunmetal poppy seeds, crimson chilies, blue gardenia-root, purple saar, in the choked alleyways, the bustling aisles. Scents drifting like flakes of pepper, like the dust off the top of granth bins, like the dark and mysteriously veined husks of wer-mace. Hooves thudded against cobbles,

voices raised in shouts, arguments, laughter bursting forth
and just as quickly stifled by the heightened air of tension,
short tempers spreading like water overflowing a riverbank.
The heavy press of civilization like a vise around her temples. After so much time in the Djenn Marre, returning to
Axis Tyr, even without the changes she had undergone, was
disorienting.

She saw, in the short time she sat vigil, another cluster of
Khaggun, from Star-Admiral Morcha's wing judging by
their shimmering blue-green armor and the double mailed-
fist insignia on their shoulders. She held her breath as she
watched them make their way through the throng, felt the
sadness welling in her breast to see the Kundalan quail, fall
back from the tramp of marching feet, avert their gaze, as if
even making eye contact was a punishable offense.

While they were still in sight, she felt a pressure at her
back, and whispered, "Stay where you are. Khagggun are
about."

A moment after the Khagggun had gone, she turned and
pushed the sacks of coriander seed aside. Rekkk emerged,
dressed in full Haaar-kyut armor he had purloined from the
barracks. He pushed up his visor, winked at her. Again,
she had a moment of disconcerting disorientation, knowing
the world as she saw it was different than the world of those
around her. They scrambled to their feet. Rekkk nodded and
Riane put her hands behind her back. The eerie feeling of
dislocation intensified as Rekkk snapped wrist-guards on her.

"You are now officially my prisoner," he said, and slapped
her hard on the back of her head as he propelled her, stumbling, into the market.

Slap of water against seaweed-wrapped pilings, ships dark
and low, rocking on the tide, spindrift making tiny phosphorescent whorls like shooting stars. All these elements
were known to Kurgan, but utterly alien to Kinnnus Morcha.
He was, like all V'ornn, uncomfortable near vast areas of
emptiness, where nothing could be built, excavated, or plundered. Especially the kind of emptiness that shifted con-

stantly, that could not be quantified, would not remain stable. He was heartened, however, by the certain knowledge that Harborside would be as inimical to Wennn Stogggul. Still, he stared down at the ocean as if it were the open jaws of a Corpius Segundian razor-raptor.

Above them, as they lowered themselves via a rope ladder onto the aft deck of Courion's ship, Olnnn Rydddlin crouched on the Promenade in deepest shadow. His eyes fairly glowed with the mad light of revenge. His fingers fidgeted at the hilt of his shock-sword. So fixated was he on the figure of his rage that he failed to hear the movement just behind him.

The edge of a dagger was at his throat. "We have been looking for you, former Pack-Commander." Olnnn Rydddlin knew the voice of First-Captain Julll when he heard it.

He did not move. He willed his muscles to relax. "Aren't you a little out of your area, First-Captain? It seems to me you retired from slitting throats when you became the Star-Admiral's deputy protocol officer."

"That is a matter of perception, Olnnn Rydddlin." The blade bit into his skin, drawing forth a turquoise bead of blood. "Protocol is such an ambiguous word. At least, as used by the Star-Admiral. I put administrative matters in the hands of my staff." The bead collapsed, slid down the length of the blade. "As for me, I have my plate full being Kinnnus Morcha's bodyguard."

"Does he not trust Kurgan Stogggul?"

"Only as far as the length of a shock-sword blade."

Even as First-Captain Julll was answering, Olnnn Rydddlin's arms whipped up behind his head, slammed Julll's nose into the back of his own skull. He ignored the bite of the dagger edge, his own blood running hot from his throat, kept his hold on Julll's skull and twisted so violently he heard the stomach-churning triple crack of the First-Captain's neck vertebrae shattering.

The dagger fell to the Promenade, its blade dark with blood. Olnnn Rydddlin threw aside the corpse, ripped a piece of Julll's robes, wrapped it around his neck to stanch the

bleeding. Then he ran full tilt across the width of the Promenade. As he did so, he drew his shock-sword, thumbed on
the ion flow. At the edge of the Promenade, he leapt off into
the night, landed on the pitching deck. The Star-Admiral was
asking Kurgan in a none-too-friendly voice where the
N'Luuura the Sarakkon captain was. Paranoid that he was,
he was already smelling a trap. Cursing, he withdrew an ion
dagger he had secreted beneath the tunic of his uniform.

"Where the N'Luuura have you been!" Kurgan shouted.

As Star-Admiral Kinnnus Morcha whirled around, weapon
in hand, Olnnn Rydddlin drove the singing blades through
his chest, piercing both his hearts in one expert strike.

Swinging in an uncontrolled arc, Kinnnus Morcha saw
both his executioners at once. His last thoughts ran through
his head like faded ribbons. To have it end so ignominiously,
brought to ruin by a mad-V'ornn and a teenage boy instead
of honorably on the field of battle. What have we come to,
we V'ornn, to rend ourselves so? he asked of no one and
everyone.

The faded ribbons broke apart, taken by a swift chill wind,
scattered into the dark, glimmering infinity of the Cosmos.

They did not care for the fact that he had no orders, these
Haaar-kyut. *They are well trained, give them that,* Rekkk
thought. But, on the other hand, he was one of them.

He stood with his prisoner at the gates of the regent's
palace, waiting for them to make up their minds. With every
second that passed, he liked their chances less and less.
V'ornn disliked uncertainty, Khaggggun more than other
castes, Haaar-kyut least of all. He should have foreseen that.
Well, at the spur of the moment, with the end of the world
staring you in the face, you couldn't think of everything. But
you had to. Even one mistake could be fatal.

"N'Luuura take it, contact the regent himself if you want
to," he said through his lowered visor. "I have his verbal
orders to bring this resistance leader to the cells. She may
have information about the Ring of Five Dragons."

"That sounds like old news," Second-Marshal Tynnn said

sullenly. "The regent has been given the Kundalan Ring by Malistra."

Rekkk, his mind working feverishly to keep up with the constantly changing scenario, said, "I know that, dolt! Why do you think I was sent to fetch this one? Now that the regent has the Ring, he needs to learn how to use it."

Second-Marshal Tynnn's brow furrowed. "I didn't think of that."

Rekkk shrugged. "Can't think of everything. Not to worry. Resistance here will soon prove her worth to the regent."

Second-Marshal Tynnn nodded. As they passed through the gates, he put a huge hand on Rekkk's arm. Rekkk stiffened, his fingers closing around the hilt of his shock-sword. He stared hard into the Haaar-kyut's face.

"Let's have a piece of her now." Second-Marshal Tynnn licked his thick lips. "Just a quick one, who's to know, lift her filthy robes over her head, get a look at how much hair is under there, what d'you say?"

"Sure," Rekkk said, "as long as you answer to the regent about the delay. Or would you want me to do it, tell him his education was held up to make way for your pleasure?"

Second-Marshal Tynnn scowled. "Go on then, I know what the regent's like when his ire's up. But, afterward, when you get to the stage when she's all soft and bloody-like, give me a buzz. I want in on the end."

"With pleasure," Rekkk said with well-manufactured zeal.

He frog-marched Riane down the corridor, cuffed her about the head for the amused guards' benefit. When they had turned a corner, he said, "Sorry about that."

Riane was startled to hear a former Khaggun, and a Pack-Commander at that, apologize to a Kundalan girl. "No need," she said. "You did what had to be done."

"How much time?"

"I don't know," she said, but she could feel vibrations deep in the core of her, could sense the shifting of the layers of realms. Just how much damage was this Kundalan device going to do if she failed to stop it? What if it sliced a hole right through into other realms? "Less than an hour, maybe," she added. "But that's simply a rough guess."

"You had better contact Giyan, then."

She nodded, and opened her Third Eye. Like a stone dropped into a still lake, concentric circles of light spiraled outward into the vastness of Otherwhere, until they encountered the first sorcerous beacon Giyan had activated, which guided her to the next, and then the next. To the light that was Giyan.

We are inside the palace, she said in her mind. *On the ground level.* She gave a detailed description of their position.

Very well, Giyan answered. *This is what you must do . . .*

Star-Admiral Kinnnus Morcha, crumpled on the salt-slick deck of a ship hateful to him, stared into the nothingness of death with a rueful expression on his face. The night was still and starless. From a place far away, deep rumblings could be heard, but no storm seemed imminent. The sea had grown agitated by the sound.

"Your father is pleased with what you have accomplished here." Malistra, in green and cloth of gold, stood with her legs spread, as a seasoned Sarakkon would, to minimize the pitching of the deck. "*Extremely* pleased."

"He knows already?" Kurgan said.

"Of course." She regarded the corpse with a kind of detached interest, as if it were an expected entry in a ledger. "I informed him as it was occurring." Her eyebrow arched. "Surprised?"

"I try never to be surprised."

She laughed, but unkindly, like a mistress confronting a willful and potentially disobedient pupil.

Like Wennn Stogggul, she feasted on making her power manifest, on collecting fear like coins coughed out of the mouths of her victims. Kurgan made this mental observation with an assessor's keen eye. Just because he had engineered Kinnnus Morcha's death did not mean he hadn't learned from him. He was an exceptionally quick study, this dangerous lad, a sponge that soaked up experience every waking moment. And in his sleep schemes of power hatching like gimnopedes at Lonon's end.

"Your father requests the pleasure of your company in the regent's palace."

Kurgan gestured. "Olnnn Rydddlin—"

"Olnnn Rydddlin will stay here, to protect the body until the regent can spare Haaar-kyut to prepare it for public viewing." The toe of her boot pressed against Kinnnus Morcha's hollow temple. "Look at those features! For a certain, his head will have impact atop the regent's pike!"

Kurgan, who had failed to find her appealing at their first encounter, was even less enamored with her now. She possessed an utter contemptuousness for life he found distasteful, doubtless because it mirrored his own.

"The regent should know Olnnn Rydddlin's part in the Star-Admiral's demise."

Malistra turned, her voice cold, cruel, vibrant with power. "Don't trouble yourself, dear. The regent knows everything." She tossed her head. "Now, quickly! Come with me. Your father awaits."

She smiled then, an odd, narrow-lipped smile that made his tender parts contract. *Do not underestimate her,* he thought. *She is a sorceress, and she has Wennn Stogggul's ear.* He smiled back, followed her meek as a cor. But in his mind she had crossed the line of no return. A dark nimbus now occluded his image of her as he consigned her to the same noisome pit into which he had dropped his father.

Up on the Promenade, as they hurried through darkness thick as a forest, Kurgan could see the lights of the city, but they seemed oddly dim, smeared as if they were paint on chrono-canvas.

"Where did you get that platinum hair?" he asked her.

Malistra kept walking, an amused smile on her face. She had quicksilver features, one moment stern and unforgiving, the next moment soft and fragrant as a clemett.

"It was a gift," she said. "When I came of age."

"Came of age for what?"

She turned now, her left hand describing patterns in the

air. In its wake, a kind of pale orange fire bloomed and died as symbols overlay each other. All at once, Kurgan felt a weight on his chest, a pain so searing he could not catch his breath. Then, as quickly, it was gone, leaving behind a hollow-bone ache, like an echo of an ion-cannon blast.

"For that," she said brightly, and continued striding along the Promenade.

"This is what you do for my father?"

She smirked, stopped again. "There's a message." She pointed to his okummmon. "It's for you."

Even as she spoke he felt the vibrations running up and down his arm. The okummmon glowed bone-white and from it emanated a wisp of mist. Quite soon, this mist coalesced, forming itself into the holographic image of Nith Batoxxx.

"Time to work, young Stogggul," the image said. The voice sounded thin, far away, as if it was being compressed in some way.

"Make this quick," he said. "My father wants to see me."

"Not really," Malistra said. "I told you that because I did not want Olnnn Rydddlin to know about your connection with Nith Batoxxx."

"Your expertise is required in the regent's palace," the image of Nith Batoxxx said. "A Kundalan will be coming there, perhaps is there already. No one knows of the Kundalan but the three of us."

"Then how could he get through security?"

"The Kundalan is clever, and I believe he has help."

"What does he want?"

"To get to the Storehouse Door in the caverns below the palace."

"Alert the regent. He'll send his Haaar-kyut—"

"Shut your mouth when I am talking," Nith Batoxxx snapped. "And stop jumping to conclusions." The Gyrgon rearranged his arms. "The Haaar-kyut are useless in this circumstance. The Kundalan will elude all of them. Still, I want you to take a handful of them with you."

"And you want me to stop him, is that it?"

"No." Nith Batoxxx was the patient schoolmaster now. "I

want you to use the Haaar-kyut to separate the Kundalan from whoever may be with him. Then, station yourself in sight of the Storehouse Door. When the Kundalan appears—as he inevitably will—you will contact Malistra via the okummmon."

Kurgan, his mind racing furiously, wondered why he was needed at all. Why couldn't Nith Batoxxx do this himself? As a Gyrgon he had access to every nook and cranny in Axis Tyr. Also, if he was so powerful, why did he need someone else to tell him when the Kundalan showed up at the appointed spot? And, speaking of which, the appointed spot for what?

Kurgan touched his okummmon. "I thought you engineered this so that only you and I could communicate."

"This is correct."

"But you just said I should contact Malistra."

"Isn't it obvious?" Malistra said. "Nith Batoxxx and I are linked."

"Silence!" the Gyrgon thundered. "There is no time for idle banter. Make all haste to the palace, and there do as I have ordered!"

They hurried on, swinging off the Promenade, passing the dark and deserted Kalllistotos ring, the clear white-stone facade of Receiving Spirit, shining like a beacon in the night.

"He's not telling me everything," Kurgan said.

"You know what you need to know," she said.

And just like that, with the slam of an imaginary door, Kurgan was put in his place, kept out of the affairs of the important players in this game. The problem was, it was not a place in which he cared to be, nor was prepared to stay for long. He watched the liquid movement of Malistra's hips, the stride of her legs, the unnatural spark in her eyes, *Nith Batoxxx and I are linked.* A Kundalan sorceress linked with a Gyrgon? Everything was wrong with this picture. He knew the answer was right in front of him, he simply couldn't see it. Then they had arrived at the palace, and he began to think of what Nith Batoxxx wanted of him.

* * *

Giyan had guided them to the back stairs—the selfsame back stairs down which Annon had climbed on his first foray into the caverns, the night of Wennn Stogggul's palace coup. A hidden panel on a wall in one of the pantries off the kitchens revealed, as Giyan said it would, the access to the stairs.

Riane, who was leading the way, paused in the darkness. Rekkk had taken off the cuffs the moment they were out of sight of the last set of guards. She found herself on the triangular landing from which three branches of the staircase descended. From the right, she could feel a pulsing, more distinctly than Annon ever had. In her mind, she heard a liquid sound, as if someone were stirring an enormous pot. Blackness, deeper than midnight, denser than the deepest sleep rose to twine around her core, to bring up memories like perfume of First Cenote, deep in the caverns of the Djenn Marre where Thigpen and her kind were born, waiting, like so many others, for the coming of the Dar Sala-at.

There arose like a whirlwind a force now—an awful force that impelled her to the right, even though her skin puckered, her flesh crawled. She could see the reflection in the black water of First Cenote of the five-headed daemon Pyphoros, who had claimed her for his own, who had pursued Annon through the realm of Otherwhere.

Riane. Giyan's voice in her head. *Step back.*

A wave of dizziness washed over her. She felt herself beginning to tumble down the stairs. Then Rekkk had her in his powerful arms.

Go to your left, Riane. Stay to your left.

"Left," she said thickly to Rekkk, and he dragged her back from the edge of the emptiness that rose up like a tomb, a great belching pit, stinking of bitterroot. Then they had stumbled into the spiral chute, were plunging down into the bowels of the Kundalan caverns beneath the palace.

The moment they tumbled out, Rekkk held his hand over Riane's mouth. Riane looked up, expecting to find the oculus, to have to tell Rekkk to move away from it lest they be seen from above, but she saw only rock. She looked around.

Directly across from them was solid rock. It should have been the Storehouse Door. When Annon had tumbled down the chute, he had ended up beneath the oculus. Was there more than one chute? Had they taken the wrong one? Where were they?

A rumbling began under their feet, rolling on and on, echoing through the caverns. A sudden crash made them jump, as a huge chunk of rock was dislodged. The tremor ceased, but the air felt charged with peril and death.

She looked at Rekkk. Haaar-kyut, he mouthed silently, and she nodded, hearing their soft stealthy footfalls. He dropped a fistful of rock dust into his okummmon, drew out of it a boulllas—a double strand of wire, the ends of which were attached to alloy grips into which he slipped his fingers. He thumbed a button to turn on the ion flow. He motioned Riane to move back into the shadows with him, and suddenly she knew exactly where they were—in the interrogation cell where Annon had removed Giyan's okuuut. So long ago. Just yesterday. Remembered in the minutest detail.

Four Haaar-kyut in purple battle armor appeared from around a corner, marching right by them. As the last one came abreast of the cell, Rekkk stepped forward, dropped the wires across his throat, lashed it tight. The ion-charged wires cut through flesh and bone. The Haaar-kyut's thrashing was over almost before it began.

"Stay here," Rekkk said in Riane's ear. "I'm going to take care of the other three."

Before she could stop him, he was gone, slipping silent as a wraith into the cavern. She clung to the shadows, aware of how much each member of the group Giyan had assembled was doing for her, acutely aware that she herself had done nothing to warrant their heroism. The smell of death was overpowering, magnified by the closeness of the space. She stepped over the Haaar-kyut's decapitated body, clung to the shadows at the edge of the cell. Where was Rekkk? Had he killed the three remaining Haaar-kyut or had he himself been killed? Were they at this moment dragging him back here to be interrogated?

Another tremor shuddered through the cavern, chunks of rock flew through the air. The Tymnos device was about to be activated.

She could stay inactive no longer. She had to get to the Ring of Five Dragons. But just as she was about to step out into the cavern, she heard a familiar voice say, "I would not do that if I were you. Too many Haaar-kyut about."

She stood stock-still, scarcely daring to breath. Then she saw him emerge from the shadows across the cavern. Kurgan! The shock that went through her fairly rooted her to the spot.

He was smiling at her, just the way he had smiled at Eleana that afternoon by the pool, an animal's smile, so full of guile and cunning there was no room for anything else. "How did you manage to worm your way into the palace?" He took her chin in his strong hand, turned her face this way and that. "Was it by good looks alone, I wonder?"

With a fierce shove, he pushed her back into the darkness of the cell. Immediately, he fell upon her. They lay beside the bloody Khagggun corpse. "Why are you struggling?" His head whipped back and forth, avoiding her blows. "I am the master, you are the slave. Understand?" He jammed an elbow against her windpipe. "Victor, vanquished," he chanted. His knee spread her thighs, but he was unprepared for the blow he received to his tender parts.

All the breath went out of him. Panting, Riane pushed him roughly aside. On the floor, he caught her leg between his ankles, twisted, bringing her down against him again. But this time Riane had her knife out, the point at his throat.

His eyes opened wide, eyes Annon had known well, eyes of a V'ornn she had loved as brothers love one another.

"Why do you hesitate?" Kurgan rasped. "I am V'ornn. You are Kundalan. We are enemies."

The heat boiled up inside her, the V'ornn-born heat of vengeance. Kurgan's father had murdered the entire Ashera family. He had asked for and had gotten Annon's head on a spike. Why shouldn't Annon take his revenge? It was right; it was just. She thought of Mother, and remembered what

Thigpen had said. *Let Mother's death have meaning. Having killed once, tragically, you will need a compelling reason for doing so again.* She stood up abruptly. "I have no time for you," she said.

Kurgan sneered. "It matters not what you do now. There is a Dark sorceress after your skin."

"I will handle her, come what may."

"Think so? This one is a mesembrythem addict. Do you know what that means? She lives to inflict pain! You will take a long time dying, she will see to that!"

Rekkk had dispatched two of the three Haaar-kyut he had been shadowing, and was grappling with the last of them, when she appeared as if out of nowhere. He had heard enough about her from Giyan to recognize her instantly.

Malistra.

She watched him, gimlet-eyed, while he slit the Haaar-kyut's neck.

"If you were a true warrior, as warriors were meant to be," she said, "you would daub his blood across your forehead and cheeks, down the bridge of your nose. You would anoint your lips with it while you held his still-beating hearts in the palm of your hand." Her lips curved into the smile of a graven image. "But times have changed. The warrior soul grows soft with civilization."

"Get out of my way," he said. "I have a job to do."

"Ah, yes." She inhaled deeply, her breasts rising as if on the crest of a tide. "Protector of Lady Giyan."

Rekkk, in a semicrouch, waited for an opening.

"You love the wrong sorceress, would-be warrior. I am a sorceress worthy of a killing machine. I will teach you the six thousand, six hundred and sixty-six ways to kill. I will show you how to increase your power every time you slay an enemy, how to take energy from the dead and make it your own. I will turn you into the warrior of warriors!"

Rekkk, about to lash out at her, checked himself. A scent was coming from her, a curious perfume that made him weak in the knees, that turned her words into soft raindrops that fell upon his skin like dew. She was so beautiful! Why hadn't he realized that before?

"Warrior of warriors," she whispered, each word now something he strained forward to catch and to hold close to him. "Sit," she said, and he did. Her outstretched hand moved in a slow arc. "Sleep," she said, and he did.

At last, the Storehouse Door was in sight. There, in its center, was the circular medallion with a wave motif into which was carved the powerful figure of Seelin, Sacred Dragon of Transformation.

The red-jade Ring was held fast in the Dragon's open mouth.

As Riane approached the Door, she happened to glance up. The oculus was shrouded, milky, opaque as a blind eye. Beneath her feet, the earth trembled, more violently this time. Far off, chunks of rock crashed to the cavern floor. The acrid stench of sulphur was in the air. Where was Rekkk? Where was Giyan? There was no time to lose.

She ran for the Door, but before she reached it a subtle change in the light made her turn. Above her head, the milky light of the oculus was congealing, crawling toward the center, running ruddy as it did. It became aqueous, dripping down in a crimson stalactite, leaving in its wake only blackness. The oculus had been sealed over.

The crimson column came to rest on the floor of the cavern, rippling with life, reassembling itself into a striking Kundalan female. She was clad in cured-leather armor of red and black. Her long platinum hair was pulled back tightly from her white face. Plaited like a noose, it lay against her spine like the bronze serpent that curled around her right arm from elbow to shoulder.

"Malistra," Riane breathed.

"A female; how surprising." Malistra smiled. "Well, go ahead, what are you waiting for? Time enough to save the world."

"You will not try to stop me?"

"I? I have no dominion over the Dar Sala-at. Not yet, anyway."

Riane reached out, touched the incised medallion on the Storehouse Door. It had been such a long, strange journey since the first time Annon had touched it. Her fingertips slid across the head of the Sacred Dragon. A millimeter from the red-jade Ring.

Malistra moved, and in moving set off a dry rustling like that of a snake shedding its skin. When she spoke again, it was in a deeper, echoing voice that sent chills straight through to Riane's bones. "Remember the five-headed daemon, Dar Sala-at? The five-headed daemon who pursued you through the gulfs of Otherwhere. That daemon lost Annon Ashera, lost him in the interstices between realms. That daemon has pursued him ever since. To no avail. But now the trap has been laid, set, tripped. We know who you are, Dar Sala-at. We have lured you out of hiding with the Ring of Five Dragons we bartered to the SaTrryn spice-master, knowing that Sornnn SaTrryn, having spent much time with the tribes of the Korrush, would recognize it and, with his overweening ambition, know what to do with it. So it is written, so it was done, the Ring placed in Wennn Stogggul's greedy hands in exchange for the SaTrryn becoming Prime Factor. Wennn Stogggul, hubris-riddled dupe, delivered it as we knew he would to the Comradeship, who would try in their curiosity and their ignorance to use it, so they would trigger the Tymnos device, so that you would be brought to us, drawn by your destiny."

Though she still smiled, Malistra's eyes emptied like water draining from a well. "A long and complex path, you might think, but logical enough, yes. And, here you are, on the cusp of your decision. As we said, we have no dominion over you, not until you grasp the Ring. Then you are ours."

A ferocious tremor struck the cavern. Nearby rocks cracked open with a thunderous roar.

"Decide now!" Malistra cried in the eerie voice that seemed to emanate from her empty eyes. "The world is about to end!"

Riane slipped her middle finger through the Ring. She twisted, pulled, and the Ring came free. The tremors stopped. The device had been deactivated. But the Door to the Storehouse remained steadfastly locked. How could that be? She was the Dar Sala-at. She had proved that by taking control of the Ring of Five Dragons, the key to the Storehouse. And yet, it had not worked. She inserted the Ring back between Seelin's open jaws. But still the Door would not open.

"Nothing ever ends the way we expect it to, does it?" Malistra, growing in size, began to laugh. "Now you have made your decision, Dar Sala-at. You belong to us now."

A ring of sysal trees to hide them, to keep them safe from prying eyes. Wind rustling through the branches set the gimnopedes to singing. Nith Sahor lay on the ground, his breathing labored.

His head turned to look at Eleana where she knelt beside him. "Thigpen has not yet returned?"

She shook her head.

"Then let us speak of other matters." The Gyrgon moved a gloved hand in the air. Bright blue sparks cracked and sparked in its wake, but with not nearly the vigor they had an hour ago. Night was waning, and with it, Nith Sahor's life. "You are with child, Eleana."

"Yes."

"But this does not bring you joy."

"It is not a child I wished for," she said in a voice barely above a whisper.

"All children are wished for. It is simply a matter of identifying that wish."

"You don't understand. I was raped. If I allow this baby to come to term, it will be the product of that violation."

"Nevertheless, Eleana, you wished for this baby."

"How can you say that!" She turned her head away. "What do you know, anyway, you're a Gyrgon. You know nothing of life."

"Being male and female," Nith Sahor said, "I know more than most."

Slowly, her head swung back. "Still, you have no right to say that I wanted to be raped."

"That is not what I said." He took her hand in his, felt her fright of him, and was infinitely saddened. "For a long time, you were unhappy with your life. Perhaps you did not know it, not consciously, anyway. But your heart longed for more than bloodletting, didn't it?"

Eleana bit her lip. "Yes."

"You had seen more than your share of death. You had dealt death, had seen it come for you, watched while it annihilated those you loved most until there was nothing left, nothing but an empty pit inside you. And now you have given yourself the means to fill that empty pit. With life, Eleana! With this new precious life!"

She was weeping now, but all at once her head whipped around and her face grew pale.

"What is it?" he asked, being unable to move.

"The markers!" she cried. "The sorcerous markers that Giyan left as warning! They have turned red! Someone or something has found us!"

Riane, recalling the catalog of spells from both Sacred Books, tried one after another, projecting them toward Malistra. None worked. Though she had the raw knowledge, she lacked the expertise. Casting spells was akin to cooking: even the best raw ingredients remained just that unless you knew how to peel them, dice them, blanch them, combine them, and serve them.

Malistra was laughing as Riane grew frantic. She felt like a chii-fox chasing its own tail. And, then, in the catalog her extraordinary memory had compiled in her head, she came across the Kyofu spell, Fly's-Eye, and knew that the cacophony of jumbled thoughts in her head was the mental chaos invoked by the spell. As she watched, dumbfounded, Malistra extended her arm. The bronze serpent uncoiled itself, slithered in a blur along the floor, began to wind itself around Riane's right ankle.

In her mind, she called out to Giyan, but there was no

response. She ran down the cavern, away from Malistra, away the Storehouse, away from the sealed Door, away from Seelin, Sacred Dragon, its jaws open wide, waiting.

She tried to reach down, to tear the serpent off her, but she could not grab it and run at the same time. Behind her, the chilling breeze of Malistra's pursuit. Her skin began to crawl. Jumping over a newly fallen pile of rubble, she made for the opening of the spiral chute, ducked down, crawled inside.

Using elbows and knees, she began a breathless climb. And all the while, the serpent was coiling itself around her leg. She could feel Malistra's presence below her, and she redoubled her effort, climbing faster, though the pitch of the chute had become more extreme, almost vertical. She grew dizzy with the climb, with terror, with the chaos the Fly's-Eye spell was inducing. As fast as she went, Malistra was faster. She felt clumsy, stupid, unable to put two thoughts together. Though part of her was aware that this, too, was an effect of the spell, this knowledge seemed to feed the terror building inside her. She could not stop it, just as she could not stop Malistra from gaining on her.

With a gasp, she gained the triangular landing. Above her lay the regent's private quarters, rooms that had once belonged to Annon's father, and to Giyan. She was about to go on, when something made her pause. A whisper in her ear, in her mind, nothing more than pure instinct, or then again perhaps a timely intervention.

In any event, she turned and, without giving it another thought, backed down the right-hand staircase. Immediately, she was engulfed in the eerie darkness that seemed to pulse with unknown life. She could hear echoes, as of voices thrown across a large body of water, could feel the darkness in the air. Oddly, the sharp tang of bitterroot seemed to calm her thoughts, as if it were a mild antidote to the Fly's-Eye spell.

She braced arms and legs against the side of the stairwell, against the siren call of whatever waited below. She hung there, the serpent frozen on her leg. Her breathing slowed until it was barely perceptible, the blood slowed in her arteries and veins, time seemed to stand still. She waited, sweat dripping off her, each drop plunging into the vast emptiness below her, the silence of the fall ended by a tiny ping, as of water hitting water.

Hanging there, suspended, breathing in the bitterroot, she felt Malistra approaching. Up the spiral chute she rushed, on the landing, and then upward. Riane heard the voices singing from below, but in her head, silence. She moved cautiously upward, back onto the triangular landing. She had one leg into the chute to take her back down to the cavern, when a fist like iron gripped her arm, pulling her upward.

She turned to see Malistra, grinning like a death's-head. Then the Fly's-Eye came back full force, and she was dragged upward. The bronze serpent's forked tongue flicked out, tasting with pleasure the skin of her thigh.

Nith Sahor was dying.

Eleana never saw whatever sorcerous thing had turned the markers red, but Nith Sahor had. Green ion charges had circled the copse of trees, echoing like thunder, burning the blackened, starless sky. The air itself commenced to burn, shimmering and cracking. Eleana wanted to help the Gyrgon, but he waved her away when she tried to approach him, and when a percussion wave threw her off her feet, she took cover behind the thick bole of a tree.

In the stinging white-noise silence of the aftermath, she had rushed to where he lay, battered, blasted. One bloodshot star-sapphire eye watched her bend over him. The other was gone.

Thigpen returned moments afterward. The sorcerous beacons glowed green again. The danger was gone. Nith Sahor had driven it away.

"Am I too late?" Thigpen whispered to the Gyrgon.

Nith Sahor made no sound and yet the little creature appeared to understand. She carried in one of her six paws a small black rectangular object.

"What is that?" Eleana whispered.

"Something from one of his laboratories in Axis Tyr," Thigpen replied.

Whatever it was was something very special, because when Thigpen dropped it into Nith Sahor's hand, he turned to Eleana and bade her go to the edge of the circle of trees. She was loath to leave him, but the look on his face convinced her to do as he asked.

From her position at the edge of the trees, she saw Nith Sahor nod to Thigpen, saw Thigpen's paw touch the center of the small black rectangle, saw it give like a membrane, then expand outward until it filled the center of the glade in which Nith Sahor lay, hiding him and Thigpen from her.

No more than a moment later, the membrane vanished. Slowly, Eleana went back to where Thigpen sat. There was no light left in Nith Sahor's remaining eye.

"Gone," the creature said.

They buried him in the middle of the copse. They wrapped his neural-nets tightly around him like a shroud. His face had about it the unmistakable color of death. Eleana wept. Thigpen sat beneath a sysal tree full of brightly plumaged birds, cleaning her claws. Gimnopedes sang a sad chorus in a dark nimbus above the treetops, serenading the lone four-winged bird among the flock.

Giyan, deep in Ayame, the Osoru Otherwhere, had taken the form of her Avatar, Ras Shamra, the giant bird of prey. She had been fighting Malistra for some time now, and was steadily losing ground. She could not understand it. Each time she felt she had gotten the best of her, Malistra gained in power. It was as if she were an engine of endless power, wearing Giyan down. As Giyan cast spell after spell, Malistra cast counterspell after counterspell. Each time the Ras Shamra ripped a Ja-Gaar to shreds another two took its place. How Malistra could renew her Avatars at will was a mystery to Giyan.

From time to time, she heard Riane calling to her, but only rarely could she respond. It took too much energy, energy she needed to fight Malistra. And yet, she knew she was losing. She could find no solution to the sorcerous conundrum. She knew that unless she could find the source of Malistra's boundless energy, they were doomed.

And now, on the colorless horizon of Otherwhere, she saw a shadow forming out of smoke and darkness. At first, she thought it was yet another Avatar, but then as it leaped toward her, she recognized it for what it was: Tzelos! The daemon from her vision had arrived.

Malistra, gripping Riane by the scruff of her neck, hauled her through the regent's private quarters, past astonished guards, openmouthed servants, stunned advisors, until she came upon the regent himself.

Wennn Stogggul, dressed in bright new Khagggun battle armor he had had constructed to his own specifications, turned.

"And what have we here?" he asked, as Malistra threw Riane at his feet.

"Here is the Dar-Sala-at, Lord," she said with a laugh. "Behold! The savior of the Kundalan!"

Wennn Stogggul, looking down at the Kundalan girl in her filthy robe, put his shiny boot on the small of her back. "What a pathetic sight!"

"I agree, Lord. Pathetic."

He leaned over. "It appears she is in extreme pain." His eyes flicked up toward Malistra. "I should be merciful. I should put her out of her misery." He took a second-century Phareseian ceremonial dagger from its jeweled scabbard on the wall. He eyed the three-edged blade, preparing to plunge it into Riane's side.

"Would it not be better, Lord," Malistra said in honeyed tones, "would it not be more fitting if you used a sacred Kundalan artifact to kill their savior?"

Wennn Stogggul looked at the ring—the ring he believed to be the Ring of Five Dragons—on his index finger. "The twenty-four hours are up?"

"Yes, Lord." Malistra's obsequious tones wound like a

skein through his very soul. "The moment has come to use it."

Wennn Stoggul's eyes were alight with power lust. "What do I do?"

"Hold out your hand," she said. "Point the ring at the Dar Sala-at."

He did as she said. "And then?" He was fairly trembling with anticipation.

"Think death and it will come."

The false ring, filled with his blood and the Old V'ornn's sorcery, flared, turned into a ring of fire. The regent opened his mouth to scream but no sound issued forth. He fell to his knees, his hands palsied, his face ashen.

"There, Lord," Malistra said softly, almost gently. "At last you have reaped the harvest of your desire."

Seeing the Tzelos, Giyan understood what was happening. Malistra was not alone. There was a power behind her, feeding her, keeping her going. Malistra was a shell, a hollow warrior. That was the meaning of the Tzelos—the hint of the true power behind her, within her.

Giyan knew now that she had been wrong. She had been making inroads, sapping Malistra's power. But every time she did so, the being whose Avatar she saw now—the daemon Tzelos—stoked in more energy. Now the Tzelos itself had appeared. Why?

She had been lured into a sorcerous battle she could not win. Why?

Riane!

They were after Riane all the time. This battle was a ruse, a diversion to keep her occupied while they . . .

Girding herself, she ignored the Tzelos, turned the beacon of her power through Otherwhere, through Time and Space, until she found her child, curled on the floor of the regent's private quarters, in terrible pain.

Rage such as she had never known coursed through her body. So great was it that it burst asunder the energy strands of her own Avatar. The Ras Shamra exploded in a rainbow shower. In its stead, she stood, her legs spread, her arms upraised, fisted hands drawing down the lightning from the core of her being . . .

*R*un, Riane! Run!

Giyan's voice in her head freed her for an instant, sent her flying from the room.

"It's no good running away," Malistra said from behind her. "You cannot hide from me. Not while my serpent guides me to you."

Riane reached down, tried to rip the bronze serpent off her. It tried to bite her, copper fangs gleaming, and she grabbed it behind the head, snapping its jaws shut. Hobbled as she was, she slammed into a servant boy, sent him sprawling. With her balled fist, she knocked aside a startled Haaar-kyut, burst out of the private wing, into the short corridor that led to the Great Listening Hall. There were no other doors in the corridor, she couldn't turn back. Forward, then, into the hall.

The asymmetrical space loomed before her. It was in a state of flux. The gallery that ran around the perimeter a level up had been redone. The beautiful Kundalan-painted plaster ceiling had been replaced by V'ornn chronosteel from which hung four winking holographic images of Kundala. The alabaster columns set on black-granite plinths were in the process of being replaced by translucent Gyrgon cortical nets. The three heartwood posts set in a perfect equilateral triangle in the open-air center of the hall remained untouched, however.

Riane took all this in in the split second before Malistra appeared behind her.

"You cannot fight me, Dar Sala-at. You know that now."

Malistra extended her arm toward Riane. Her fist unfolded like a flower, and from the tips of her fingers leapt a bolt of sorcerous red flame that struck Riane in the small of her back, threw her forward, into the center of the hall. Riane picked herself up, ran.

"Why do you continue in the foolish flight? Why try to resist the inevitable?"

Another bolt of red flame struck Riane in the shoulder, spinning her around, pitching her to her knees. Malistra came toward her, as Riane staggered to her feet.

"It is over, Dar Sala-at. What is written cannot be undone."

A third bolt caught her full in the chest, slammed her back against one of the huge heartwood posts with such force that the wood splintered.

Malistra, not more than a handbreadth away, made a sign, and the bronze serpent unwound itself from Riane's leg. Riane let go of it and it slithered back to its master, coiling itself around her right arm.

"You are bleeding." Malistra gripped Riane's head in her hand. "Let me stop the pain now, Dar Sala-at. It is time."

Riane stared into Malistra's face and saw nothing, a mask only, a device of complex evil, a skein that needed unraveling. How? She had tried everything and failed. *No,* she thought. *Not everything.* She invoked the Star of Evermore, the potent spell she had cast to break Mother free of her sorcerous prison. In the single beat of a heart, the Fly's-Eye was gone.

Malistra sniffed the air, frowned. "What are you doing?" Her grip on Riane's jaw tightened.

Riane steeped her mind in the resulting lake of calmness. What did she know about the sorceress? Only what Giyan had told her. And then into her mind floated the brief conversation she had had with Kurgan. She cast her mind back further, into another lifetime.

"Tell me!" Malistra cried. "What are you doing?" She ramped up power, began to reassert her control.

Riane could feel the sorcerous jaws of Kyofu descending on her again, but her hand was already behind her, scrabbling at the shattered heartwood post. With strength born of desperation, she ripped off a jagged shard of heartwood. She felt the oil coat her hand. Gripping the makeshift stake in her fist, she plunged it into Malistra's chest.

Malistra gasped and drew back. Blood gouted out of her,

inundating Riane. "What?" she stammered. "What . . . ?"

She is a mesembrythem addict, Kurgan had said.

Mesembrythem is one of the most powerful herbs in the pantheon of sorcerous remedies, Giyan had told Annon when she was healing his leg wound. *Its regenerative powers can instantly morph into the deadliest poison, either through overdose or the introduction of oil of heartwood.*

Malistra's eyes opened wide. Clawed hands swiped at the air. "I'm dying! Dying!" she screamed. She fell to the floor, arms and legs flailing, body spasming as blood continued to pour out of her, more blood than any one body could possibly contain, streams of blood, rivers of blood, until all that was left of her was a pool of blood. Her empty armor steeping in it.

What was it the old Kundalan seer had shouted to Annon? *I see death, death and more death! Only the equilateral of truth can save you!*

Riane, her heart pounding, stared up at the great equilateral triangle made by the heartwood posts. Then, growing dizzy, she hung her head in exhaustion. Bent over, forearms on her thighs, head aching fiercely, she failed to notice the bronze serpent, its skin shiny with blood, slither away into the shadows.

39

Dawn

Wake up! Wake up, Rekkk!"

Rekkk opened his eyes, shook his head. "You are covered in blood."

Riane pulled him to his feet. "No time now," she said urgently. "The palace is crawling with Haaar-kyut. We've got to get out of here!"

It was true. On her way out of the Great Listening Hall and back down to the caverns, she had had to bypass at least a dozen of the regent's guard. Wennn Stogggul was dead. Deep inside her, she exulted at the revenge unexpectedly exacted on the V'ornn who had slaughtered Annon's entire family.

"Quickly, now," Riane said. "I know a way out of here! Giyan and Annon used it to escape from here the night of the coup." On their way, she recounted as best she could what had happened. How she had found her way to the Storehouse Door, how she had been overpowered by Malistra, brought before the gloating Wennn Stogggul, how the regent had been unexpectedly poisoned when he had tried to use a red-jade ring he wore that was the twin of the Ring of Five Dragons, how she had managed to kill Malistra by using a shard of heartwood. "The heartwood resin is instantly lethal to a mesembrythem addict," she concluded.

"But how did you know that the sorceress used mesembrythem?" Rekkk asked.

"That is the curious part." And she told him about her brief and violent encounter with Kurgan.

"You should have killed him when you had the chance," Rekkk said. "That boy is pure evil."

Riane did not, of course, see it that way. Annon and Kurgan had been best friends. How does one kill a best friend?

"Never mind," Rekkk said. "Kundala is safe. That is what's most important."

She nodded. "But that is more than I can say for us."

Up ahead, a pack of Haaar-kyut in full battle armor were being deployed by Wing-General Nefff.

"Leave this to me," Rekkk said, slamming down his visor. He pushed Riane into an interrogation cell, jogged to where Wing-General Nefff was giving the last of his orders. His Khagggun had fanned out, moving smartly in double time.

"Two resistance intruders," Rekkk shouted at Nefff in a breathless voice. "Pursued them from the regent's private quarters down here. One is in custody, in this interrogation cell, the other is still at large."

Wing-General Nefff barked out orders, and his Khaggun disappeared. "Now let's take a look at the would-be assassin," he said.

Rekkk led him into the darkened cell. "Why haven't you activated the security grid?" Nefff turned abruptly. "Who the N'Luuura are you, Third-Marshal?"

"Rekkk Hacilar," Rekkk said as he buried his shock-sword in Nefff's midsection. The surprised expression froze on the Wing-General's face. Rekkk was already stripping off his armor before he hit the ground. Moments later, wearing the insignia of rank, he let Riane lead him out of the caverns and up into a vertical tunnel. Metal rungs had been hammered into the smooth sides.

They emerged from the cistern head in the narrow alley off Blank Lane behind the row of Tuskugggun ateliers. Riane kept Rekkk hidden for some time, mindful of Giyan's warning that whoever had betrayed them might know of this exit from the palace. Dawn was breaking. The monochrome blue of night was fast draining away. The sky was streaked with pink and mauve. Birds called, longing for food. A Tuskugggun opened the back door to her atelier, took out the trash. A wholesaler drew up with deliveries. Voices were raised. A brief argument. A hoverpod passed over. The slow clip-clop of water-buttren hooves echoed on the cobbles, over-ridden by the thrum of building traffic. The torrent of the city's activity was just beginning. When Riane was certain no one was watching them, she nodded to Rekkk.

They rose and Rekkk began to walk south.

"Where are you going?" Riane said, grabbing hold of him. "We need the North Gate."

"No, we don't," Rekkk said, landing a perfectly timed punch to the point of Riane's cheek.

He caught her as she collapsed and, lofting her over his shoulder, headed toward the center of the city, where an unknown presence stood waiting, drawing him onward.

Dawn came late inside the ring of sysal trees just north of Axis Tyr. They had been spared, Eleana knew, and so, it appeared, had Kundala. Relief and despair warred inside her. The ominous seismic tremors had ceased. The Dar Sala-at must have been successful.

She watched Thigpen crouched beside Nith Sahor's grave and prayed to Miina. She closed her eyes. Birds chirping, small mammals foraging, insects humming, the wind skittering through the branches that curved over her head like a mantle. The first fragile shaft of sunlight brushed her cheek. The world was being born around her. At some point she became aware that she was praying for herself, for the life of her unborn baby. Her hands, fingers laced like a cradle, touched her belly, which was just beginning to swell. She threw her head back at the pellucid sky and, in the pure silence of her open heart, cried, *My* baby! *My* Baby!

Riane awoke with a pain in her jaw pushing aside even her massive headache.

"Rekkk! Rekkk, put me down! What are you doing?"

No reply. Riane traveled inward, opening her Third Eye, piercing the veil between realms, entering Otherwhere. Saw the Cosmos as it really was, with all her senses, not just the five of her corporeal body. She saw Rekkk, a husk, hollow as Malistra had been. She saw the Tzelos crouched upon his shoulders, directing him like a marionette.

The spell was woven around him in a complex pattern, runes of fire and blood intermingling, creating waves of energy that kept him in thrall. Riane knew that no simple Osoru spell could free him; this web was different, chimerical, dark, and light. Something more potent was required. She cast the Spell of Forever, searching for him beneath the potent layers of fire and blood. She found him with the Spell of Forever, at the bottom of a lightless well. Now how to free him?

Becoming aware of a light at the extreme edge of Otherwhere, she turned her full concentration on it. It was a beacon made of priceless jade, intricately carved with the images of five dragons—Miina's Five Sacred Dragons.

The Ring!

She turned it on her finger, saw the Dragons come alive.

Pulsing in the sorcerous center of each one a color: blue, yellow, red, green, black. Their faces turned to her, they spoke their names: Eshir, the Dragon of air and Forgiveness; Gom, the Dragon of earth and Renewal; Yig, the Dragon of fire and Power; Seelin, the Dragon of water and Transformation; Paow, the Dragon of wood and Vision. Instantly, she understood the differences between them, knew which was needed. She turned the Ring so that Gom was facing up. Then she pressed the carving of the Dragon of Renewal into the back of Rekkk's neck.

A shock wave went through Otherwhere. The Tzelos reared back, the strings by which it held Rekkk snapping like ion-cannon shots. Its essence sizzled and began to come apart. It turned its twelve-faceted eyes on her as it vanished, leaving for a heart-stopping instant only an eerie disembodied grimace.

As quickly as she could, Riane Thripped them all to the abbey, which had become their de facto sanctuary. The regent had been killed in his own chambers. The Haaar-kyut were out for blood; the Khagggun had been mobilized. Already hoverpods bristling with the latest weaponry crisscrossed the terrain, and ion-cannon fire was a sporadic background booming. There was little time to mourn the death of Nith Sahor, though Rekkk and Giyan had lingered at the gravesite, holding hands, speaking softly to one another.

Later, while preparations for making the abbey habitable again were in progress, Riane and Eleana found themselves standing together in a corner of the plaza. Riane felt as if she had been run through by a shock-sword. She felt tongue-tied, inept.

Eleana sighed, turned to Riane, and Riane's insides melted. "I hope you don't mind me saying this," Eleana began hesitantly, "but ever since I can remember I have thought of you—of the Dar Sala-at, I mean—as a male. Does that sound foolish?"

"Not at all." Riane was aware of the exquisite irony of

this exchange. By the light of Lonon's five moons Eleana looked more beautiful than ever.

Eleana cleared her throat. "I have to admit, I don't know what to say. I'm a little bit in awe of the Dar Sala-at."

"Don't be," Riane said. Her tongue seemed stuck to the roof of her mouth. Male or female, it did not matter. She loved this girl with every fiber of her being.

Eleana, smiling, touched Riane's swollen cheek. "Does it pain you overmuch?"

"Only when I think about it." Merciful Goddess, this is too much for me, Riane thought. I think I shall go stark raving mad if I'm around her much longer. The longing was a taste in her mouth. She was filled up with it, mad with it, her soul shredded by it.

Eleana came closer, lowered her voice. "Can I confide in you, Dar-Sala-at?"

Riane swallowed hard. "Of course."

She touched her lower belly. "I am with child."

"You're ... what?" Riane thought she was going to pass out. "How can you be—?" She bit off words that would betray her. "How did it happen?"

"By accident. I was caught at a swimming hole by two V'ornn, young, our age. One attacked me. The other—well, believe it or not he tried to save me. He—it seems so odd—he was attacked by a gyreagle, can you believe it?"

Riane said nothing.

"The one named Kurgan raped me. This is his child."

Riane's mouth was full of cotton, her mind was afire. Eleana was carrying Kurgan's baby? She wanted to scream. Every time she cursed the cruel fate that bound her, something worse happened. But now this was it. She had hit rock bottom. Nothing worse could possibly happen.

"I was going to abort it," Eleana was saying. "But I just told Giyan I am going to keep it. She and Nith Sahor convinced me that was the right thing to do, to love it, to teach it right from wrong, to ensure that it will be better than its father ever was or could be." She looked at him. "That's a kind of revenge, don't you think, for what he did to me?"

Riane was mute. It seemed that where Eleana was concerned she could never have the right words.

In sleep, Eshir, Dragon of air, came to Riane. Its color was purest lapis lazuli, its wings ethereal and ever-changing as clouds. Eshir, the Dragon of Forgiveness, summoned by an unconscious mind determined to heal the conscious part. Eshir, who wrapped her cloudlike wings around Riane's sleeping form, bore her aloft into the singing firmament, there to look down upon her deeds from the distance of objectivity. Eshir, of the sorrowful countenance, with horns of rainstorms, hooves of blizzards, scales of thermal currents, and an infinite capacity to love.

Wennn Stogggul was dead, and so was Kinnnus Morcha. Eleusis Ashera had been avenged. The Ring of Five Dragons had been returned to the Dar Sala-at. Somewhere, in the center of the Korrush, at the edge of Forever, Za Hara-at, was about to be born. There was hope now, for Kundalan and V'ornn both.

It was the dawn of a new day.

APPENDIX I

Major Characters

KUNDALAN
Giyan—Bartta's twin sister; Ramahan mistress of Eleusis
Ashera
Bartta—Giyan's twin sister; Ramahan konara, head of the
Dea Cretan
Riane—female orphan
Eleana—female from upcountry

Ramahan at the Abbey of Floating White:
Leyna Astar—Riane's friend and teacher
Konara Laudenum—another of Riane's teachers
Konara Urdma—member of the Dea Cretan
Shima Vedda—archaeologist priestess

Malistra—Kyofu sorceress
Dammi—coleader of resistance cell
Thigpen—one of Miina's sorcerous creatures
Mother—high priestess of Miina
Courion—Sarakkon captain

V'ORNN
Annon Ashera—eldest son of Eleusis Ashera
Kurgan Stogggul—eldest son of Wennn Stogggul
Eleusis Ashera—regent of Kundala
Kinnnus Morcha—Line-General, commander of the Haaar-
kyut
Nith Sahor—a Gyrgon
Rekkk Hacilar—Pack-Commander

Olnnn Rydddlin—Rekkk Hacilar's First-Captain

Dalma—Wennn Stogggul's Looorm

Wennn Stogggul—Prime Factor of Axis Tyr; father of Kurgan

The Old V'ornn—Kurgan's mentor and teacher

Mittelwin—dzuoko of Nimbus, a salamuuun kashiggen

Bach Ourrros—Bashkir rival of Wennn Stogggul

Kefffir Gutttin—Bashkir ally of Bach Ourrros

First-Captain Julll—Kinnnus Morcha's deputy protocol officer

Wing-General Nefff—a Haaar-kyut commandant

Rada—Tuskugggun owner of Blood Tide tavern

APPENDIX II

Pronunciation Guide

In the V'ornn language, triple consonants have a distinct sound. With the exceptions noted below, the first two letters are always pronounced as a *w*, thus:

Khagggun—Kow-gun
Tuskugggun—Tus-kew-gun
Mesagggun—Mes-ow-gun
Rekkk—Rawk
Wennn Stogggul—Woon Stow-gul
Kinnnus—Kew-nus
okummmon—ah-kow-mon
okuuut—ah-kowt
K'yonnno—Ka-yo-no
salamuuun—sala-moown
Olnnn—Owl-lin
Sornnn—Sore-win
Hadinnn—Had-ewn
Bronnn Pallln—Brown Pawln
Teyjattt—Tay-jawt
seigggon—sew-gon
skcettta—shew-tah
Looorm—Loo-orm
bannntor—bown-tor
Kannna—Kaw-na
Kefffir Gutttin—Kew-fear Gew-tin
Ourrros—Ow-roos
Jusssar—Jew-sar
Julll—Jew-el
Nefff—Newf

Batoxxx—Bat-owx
Boulllas—Bow-las (as in, to tie a bow)
Hellespennn—Helle-spawn
Argggedus—Ar-weeg-us

When a y directly precedes the triple consonant, it is pro-
nounced *ew*, as in *shrewd*, thus:
Rydddlin—Rewd-lin
Rhynnnon—Rew-non
Tynnn—Tewn
but:
K'yonnno—Ka-yow-no

Because the following word is not of the V'ornn language,
the triple consonant does not follow the above rules, thus:
Centophennni—Chento-fenny

Triple vowels are pronounced twice, creating another syllable, thus:
Haaar-kyut—Ha-ar-key-ut
leeesta—lay-aysta
mumaaadis—mu-ma-ah-dis
liiina—lee-eena
N'Luuura—Nu-Loo-oora

Normally in V'ornn, the y is pronounced *ea*, as in *tear*, thus:

Gyrgon—Gear-gon

Sa is pronounced *Say*, thus:
Sa Trryn—Say-Trean

Kha is pronounced *Ko*, while *Ka*, is pronounced *Ka*, thus:
Khagggun—Kow-gun
Kannna—Kaw-na

Ch is always hard, thus:
   Morcha—More-ka
   Bach—Bahk

Skc is always soft, thus:
   skcettta—shew-tah

Look for

THE
VEIL OF A
THOUSAND TEARS

by

ERIC VAN LUSTBADER

*Now available in Hardcover
from Tor Books*